The Shadows of Fate

THE CONVERGENCE SERIES

DANIELLE D'ARRIGO

Book Cover by Books and Moods
Interior Design and Formatting by Books and Moods
Editing by Emma Jane of EJL Editing
1st edition 2023
Library of Congress Control Number: 2023913224

*To all of the women who poured their hearts out
with paper and ink before me and paved the way
for my dreams to come true; this is for you.*

Hi readers!

Before you dive into the world of The Convergence, you should know there are mentions of situations surrounding mental health—more specifically anxiety, depression, grief, and PTSD. As well as brief instances of sexual pressure and assaults. There are also some light graphic displays of violence. As well as some "spice".

If any of this is triggering for you or undesired, please read with your own caution.

I have done a lot of work to ensure everything listed above has been written with care and is not ill-natured in any way. It is my job as a writer to provide an escape for the reader and I have made sure that even with these trigger warnings, you are able to enjoy your time within the world of The Convergence.

Happy Reading!
Danielle

Chapter One

"Eight more minutes!" Chloe screamed across the otherwise quiet bookstore. Her delicate yet robust voice carried through the red-ish wood-paneled hall of the shop like a crow's caw in an abandoned forest. The few remaining patrons looked up at her with perplexed and annoyed looks that only a New Yorker could pull off. Yet, those looks didn't stop Chloe. With her pink and purple curls, she shimmied up to Evangaline, who was *actually* doing the job she was hired to do, stocking the box of contemporary romance novels—grossly titled *The Temptation of Mr. Brooks*. Chloe bore a grin to end all grins. It swept up the apples of her cheeks and twinkled with nothing but mischief.

"Oh, what's this one about? Looks spicy …" Chloe chided, snatching a copy out of Evangaline's hands, the light brown skin around her cunning eyes crinkling with a scandalous resolve.

With a smirk and roll of her eyes, Evangaline grabbed another copy of the book with a half-undressed man on the cover from the box by her feet and continued stocking the shelf. "She fucks her boss, falls in love with him … blah blah blah … You know how this kind of smut goes," she muttered, unamused.

"Oh. Tis' spicy then! We have eight minutes till we can go find *you* a Mr. Brooks of your own!" Chloe's tone was a mix of lust and ridicule as she shimmied her shoulders seductively.

Swatting off Chloe's sexual gestures, Evangaline gathered her box and headed to the register to check out the remaining few customers. Only a few more gathered in the old store before she could close the shop and head out for the night. However, the last thing she wanted was a "Mr. Brooks" of her own. Sure, some mindless copulation didn't sound awful, but the last relationship she was in brought her right back here to New York, living with her parents. Just the life every post-college grad wanted. If she could avoid any more unnecessary heartbreak, that was exactly what she was going to do.

Evangaline always felt incredibly shy and quiet—even prudish—when comparing herself to Chloe. Her muted light brown hair fell just above her backside and in the right light had a sparkle of gold and red to it, especially when she curled it as it was. Her admiration of her *suburban mom* hair color, as Chloe so lovingly referred to it, was one of her favorite attributes. Though compared to Chloe's bright pink mane, it *was* a bit lackluster.

Evangaline tended to blend into the background, which, for the most part, was exactly how she preferred to live her life. She wasn't short by any means. Coming in at a proud five foot six—okay five foot five and a quarter, but who was paying that close attention? She was just tall enough and just short enough to blend into society without drawing attention.

She wasn't waif thin like all the models and magazines claimed were the unrealistic standard of beauty. Instead, she thought she was perfectly average. She worked out every day, so she was toned enough and had muscle, to an extent … her love for good food, mostly unhealthy food, won out more times than not directly contrasting the way she enjoyed her fitness therapy. What all that meant was that if she craved a cheeseburger, cheese fries, and a shake … she got it. And she ate it and enjoyed every goddamn minute of it and didn't punish herself for enjoying something she craved with a hard workout on the treadmill the next day.

She was proud and loved her appearance through and through, yet when it came to comparing her personality to Chloe's and the way her mind occasionally worked against her, Evangaline was entirely screwed on many fronts. She was quiet, took care of herself and those she loved. And more importantly, she did not step outside her comfortable little bubble, rather than be a lively, effervescent almost twenty-five-year-old woman—like Chloe.

However, she tried not to dwell on her shortcomings for very long and, in turn, focused on the things that made her forget the jumbled mess that was her inner psyche. Her appetite for good food wasn't all she loved. A good book, Netflix, and her sweatpants all made the shortlist of what she considered elements of a good day. All of which made her a perfect candidate for Chloe's idea of boring. Her friend enjoyed going out and meeting new people, exploring the hidden underground of the city Evangaline grew up in—and never knew existed. Which was fun and exciting, but the hard truth for Chloe to swallow was that Evangaline was just an introverted and—at times—an anxious girl, and if that made her boring, so be it.

The two women met nearly a year ago when Evangaline returned home to New York from the coast of California. Evangaline started a month before her friend came on board at the quaint little bookshop by the park and was entirely too overwhelmed with essentially operating the shop all on her own. Stocking shelves, doing inventory, taking care of customers, setting up signings, running promotions, and so many more tasks that her boss should have taken care of but "just didn't feel like it"—his words, not hers—left her feeling exhausted and frustrated beyond measure. *There was a reason the last guy quit!* she practically yelled to her parents after coming home late and overworked and frustrated. So, the next day, she begged her boss to hire someone else, and that was how Chloe stepped into her life.

Evangaline took the job originally because she could earn money by not overexerting her inane introvert abilities. The thought of being surrounded by books all day instead of people made her more excited than it should have. Or in the words of her sister, she "gave up searching for a job that fulfilled her journalism degree" because at the ripe age of twenty-four—almost twenty-five—Evangaline had already had enough rejection to last a lifetime. Cue the lonesome job as a book retailer.

On Chloe's first day at work, Evangaline was greeted, not in a formal

"Hi, I'm your new colleague" handshake kind of way. No, that would simply not be Chloe enough. Instead, the little she-devil hid under the check-out counter and waited patiently for Evangaline to come over and set her things down. That was when the pink-haired gremlin grabbed both her ankles and screamed "Give me your money!" As any normal and sane person would, Evangaline screamed and kicked Chloe right in the mouth and, well, they've been inseparable ever since.

Chloe and her extroverted, wild, and sometimes neurotic nature were the perfect balance for Evangaline. The yin to her yang. The peanut butter to her jelly. The light to her dark. The tequila in her margarita. And tonight, Evangaline made a promise to try to let loose and enjoy every single second of the night Chloe had planned. Pushing her shy tendencies into the closet, locking the door, and taking the plunge into the mindset of her best friend's carefree lifestyle.

"You only turn twenty-five once!" Chloe celebrated when she finally coaxed Evangaline into going out for a birthday celebration a couple of days ago. Then they got tipsy at a tiki bar in the Upper West Side.

It was late when they finally made it to the last of the *many* quirky places Chloe wanted to take Evangaline to.

Shortly after they locked up the store, they went back to Chloe's studio apartment uptown, crammed themselves into the four-by-four bathroom, blasted some music, and got ready for the night ahead. That took a few hours, especially factoring in the impromptu karaoke sessions, dance breaks, and cans of seltzer they pre-gamed as though the world was ending tomorrow. But, once they felt their buzz and were dressed scandalously enough to *tempt their Mr. Brooks*, they set out onto the bustling streets of New York City.

As they walked into the last of the techno clubs Chloe found by pulling fliers off streetlights, the music suddenly overpowered every rational thought swirling around in Evangeline's vaguely drunk brain. A mix of disco and techno sprinkled in with a little pop, guided the girls to the dance floor, bewitching them in the kaleidoscope of colors that sizzled around them within a fever dream of vivid pigments. A disco ball twirled overhead, shimmering the dance floor in sparkles and fractals of light, just like snowflakes in the wintertime. The smell of alcohol, sweat, and bad choices clouded their judgment and frankly, Evangaline was so transfixed by the cacophony of sounds and light she could not care less that it smelled eerily like the locker room of a YMCA. There was only one thing her highly intoxicated brain wanted to do … dance.

"I'll be right back. I want some water. You?" Chloe yelled over the thunderous beat, seeming not drunk at all.

Evangaline shook her head and continued her dancing—if one could call it that.

As Evangaline danced and sang along to the music, her sweat started to drain out the toxins in her bloodstream, making her slowly sober up—to an extent. Her eyes speared around the closely packed dance floor, searching for her friend. *How many songs have passed?* She thought. Panic set in at the lack of Chloe by her side, and her brain started whirling with anxious thoughts of being left alone.

Teetering on her black rhinestone heeled booties, she scoured the crowd for Chloe's cotton candy hair. She should have been easy to find, wearing a dress that dipped low into a cleverly draped swoosh just in front of her décolletage. The silver sequined dress left little to the imagination, but her friend pulled it off with ease. Amidst a sea of writhing bodies, Chloe with her pink hair and flashy dress should have stuck out, but as Evangaline searched, she was nowhere to be found.

With no sign of pink hair or a shining silver dress, Evangaline approached the bar, hoping someone there might have seen her friend.

A group of women crowded around as she struggled to gain the bartender's attention. All wearing sashes and plastic tiaras reading *"bridesmaid"*, the bar quickly became a cyclone of perfume and high-pitched shouting that set Evangaline's anxiety soaring. With all the women shouting around her, it was impossible to rip the bartender away from the cyclone to ask if he had seen Chloe. Tired, anxious, and a bit annoyed, she turned to the raucous group of women behind her, hoping they would help a fellow woman out.

"I'm so sorry to bother you but have you seen a young woman, about yay high, pink hair, silver dress, you couldn't miss her if you tried!" Evangaline motioned with her hands shouting over the thunderous beat of the bass drums.

"Apparently you did!" The drunkest of the bunch slurred.

Evangaline squinted, unamused at the drunken stupidity of the bridesmaid before her.

"Not helpful, you twit! No, sorry, maybe she's in the bathroom. There were some seriously occupied stalls, if you get what I mean." A woman wearing a rhinestone *"bride"* tiara shouted, pushing the drunken party of bridesmaids away from the bar.

"Thank you!" Evangaline yelled, making her way around the women, "And congrats!"

Sweat dripped down her back as she pushed through the packed club, her curls clung to the exposed glistening skin around her neck and draped like vines of ivy across the expanse of her back.

Stumbling her way through the chaos of the dancefloor, she eventually made her way into a side hallway with rooms splitting off for private karaoke parties. Despite the atrocious attempts at what she could only assume was singing, Evangaline's hearing tunneled out, and the feeling of dread crept into her bones, spiking her anxiety. She knew Chloe was a free spirit, but her friend had never just left her before. Guilt began to creep in. She should have gone with her; Evangaline broke the girl code and allowed Chloe to go by herself in a place they did not know. She knew better as a woman. Men could be creeps! Maybe she seriously miscalculated how much she had to drink while getting ready. Was she really too drunk to not notice her friend disappearing into the night?

She turned the corner, silently berating herself for her recklessness, following the fluorescent sign for the bathrooms, and ran face-first into a solid wall of incredibly toned flesh. Her mind was entirely too preoccupied with dark thoughts of Chloe's fate, that she barely registered the stranger grab onto her arms and step away from her, as though to check if she was all right. Evangaline never looked up. She simply apologized and stepped to the side to continue her search.

The whole encounter lasted mere seconds, but the smell of the stranger's cologne seemed to linger with her—bergamot and rose. *An odd scent for a man*, she thought. She didn't look at him but knew by the feeling of his chest on her forehead he was large, exceedingly large. She *was* able to make out the fact that he was wearing a white button-down shirt rolled at the forearms, a fact her brain registered as she walked away. A man, well, anybody, willing to wear a white anything to a nightclub was a person worthy of a medal. With people so close and drinks sloshing about, she could only admire the mysterious stranger's confidence and faith in not ruining that pristine shirt.

With her mind now distracted from the *Dateline* style montage happening in her mind starring Chloe, she was curious for a glimpse of the toned stranger. One peak wouldn't hurt anybody. But as she turned, hopeful for a glimpse of the man who caught her off guard, she found herself alone in the hall once again. The sound of off-key musical numbers encircled her. She shook her head and reminded herself of her mission, the reason she was in this dank hallway alone in the first place; *find Chloe.*

Pushing open the bathroom door, the sound of a familiar voice drifted from one of the three stalls. Evangaline froze, her nose crinkled in disgust. For one, the bride was entirely right. A lot more was happening in the bathroom than just utilizing the facilities. For two, Chloe left her alone to take care of other needs in the bathroom without a single word. It wasn't Evangaline who betrayed their girl code; it was Chloe.

She didn't know if she should be angry or high-five her friend for her efficiency in procuring a lover in record time. But from the sound of it, all Evangaline had was maybe a few seconds longer before Chloe would saunter out of the stall, sated and dazed. *Bitch*, Evangaline thought jealously. The second Chloe stepped from the stall, Evangaline planned to guilt trip the little pink gremlin for her disregard of the girl code and the way she set Evangaline's heart rate through the roof.

In that time, though, she could decide whether she would high-five Chloe or scold her in a manner befitting her suburban mom title. Slap her across the back of the head or hug her? The decision was tough. Maybe both? A hug, then a slap? A slap, then a hug?

Evangaline stepped out of the doorway around a couple of women taking selfies in a full-length mirror, graffitied with phone numbers and poorly drawn dicks. *Real classy stuff,* she thought to herself as she made her way past the stall Chloe occupied with a cringe. Idly, she leaned against the wall by the paper towel dispenser, patiently examining her nails, waiting for Chloe and her fuck buddy to finish up their hasty club hookup.

With the sound of passionate alcohol-fueled lovemaking echoing through the bathroom, Evangaline knew she had seconds to make up her mind on how to react. Anger or pride?

After a booming finish that somewhat made Evangaline envious, Chloe flitted out of the stall, wiggling her disco ball of a dress further down her thighs. Her rather handsome—though Evangaline didn't want to admit that to Chloe at the present—partner adjusting himself back into his pants followed shortly after. His dark blond was hair messed up—no doubt from Chloe's roving hands.

"I hope you used protection," Evangaline chided, leaning against the wall, startling Chloe half to death as her friend combed her fingers through her pink hair.

The young man glanced down at Chloe, both confused and offended. Chloe just stared at her feet, unable to make eye contact. Frozen, with the smallest hint of a smile, giving away the fact that she wanted to start laughing more than anything.

Evangaline leaned forward, extending a hand to the man Chloe chose to party with over her, but quickly retracted it, remembering what just went down in the stall behind him. "Evangaline Rivers, nice to meet you! I'm Chloe's friend who she abandoned on the dance floor. And you are? He does know your name, right Chlo?" she said, allowing the anger in her voice to come out in a harsh whisper, however, the grin gracing her face gave a mocking smile to balance out the hostility.

Chloe finally looked up, her own eyes giving way to the slightest bit of guilt. She bit her bottom lip and finally opened her mouth to speak, but her partner beat her to the punch.

"Taylor Brooks … my name is Taylor … yes, I know her name is Chloe. I apologize for taking her away from you."

Fuck, he's hot *and* polite. Too bad Evangaline didn't get to mister … wait … mister … Evangeline's smile turned sanguine as she shook her head in disbelief. Chloe's complexion grew redder and redder as the seconds ticked on, speckled with both embarrassment and amusement. Both girls bit down on the laughs bubbling in their throats.

"You little … *Mr. Brooks*, is it?" Evangaline cocked her head and raised her brows at Chloe, then looked back up at the aptly named Mr. Brooks. Fate was a cunning mistress. "Thank you for … uh, satiating her needs. I hope you've exchanged numbers because you have about five seconds before I take her out of here." Evangaline couldn't stop shaking her head in disbelief as she turned back toward the door, motioning Chloe through it with the wave of an arm. Her friend kissed Mr. Taylor Brooks on the cheek and then walked through the door without another word, head hung low. Evangaline gave a nod and wave to Mr. Brooks and then swiftly followed her friend, leaving him alone in the women's restroom to mull over what had just happened.

Linking arms with Chloe, Evangaline felt her laughter bubbling up higher and higher, and finally, once they were clear of the karaoke hallway, let it go. She cackled, smacking Chloe's arm repeatedly as the two made their way through the mass of dancing bodies till they were in the fresh air outside the disco.

"I just can't with you …" Evangaline laughed. "Jesus, let's get some food. I'm starving."

Chapter Two

The lights of the city glistened off the sparkling black water like a mirage as the two girls leaned against the black iron railing. Finishing up their street vendor hot dogs that tasted both heavenly and somehow like plastic, they reveled in the view before them. The addition of food to their stomachs mingled with the crisp, mildly putrid, New York air, completely sobering up Evangaline and Chloe.

Staring out over the expanse of the water and admiring the faint opalescent glow of the Velum, far off in the distance, the two enjoyed their silent companionship with ease.

The Velum, the shimmering dividing wall between the human realm and the fae, was large enough to see from their perch along the shoreline. The faintest glow of the border winked at them but remained far enough away to not know exactly how it appeared up close.

Hundreds of years before Evangaline was born, a cataclysmic event occurred called the Convergence. Enough time passed that the world that Evangaline had grown up in was the new normal. But she had read plenty of books and seen enough photos to know that Vitalis was once a vast and cultured world all on its own. A planet previously called Earth.

The old planet was expansive. Oceans were enormous and people had plenty of land without it feeling crowded or overpopulated. However, on the night of the Convergence, the veil of the realms weakened, thrusting the worlds together through what scientists hypothesize was an anomaly of gravitational pulls. Not a single soul on Earth even knew about the veil that separated the universes. Not a single scientist, past or present, knew what truly happened within the universe those five hundred or so years ago. *"An anomaly of catastrophic proportions"* was the only quotation explaining the event within Evangaline's old high school textbook.

As the history books describe, the night gave way to a copper sky. A sky filled with fire and ash. People cried out and prayed for mercy to their favored gods in their last moments, thinking a meteor was colliding with Earth, *the end of days,* or so they thought. However, in a matter of moments—from both sides of the planet—two other worlds collided, effectively sandwiching Earth between the two mystery worlds, forming a new larger planet; the *New World.* The Convergence was catastrophic, but surprisingly, the Earth, the planet of Celadonia, and the world of Munbra were salvageable. Plenty was obliterated, but instead of total annihilation, the worlds *merged.*

A birth of a new tomorrow through the death of yesterday.

One realm swiftly became three. Mountain ranges formed due to the buckling of the planet. Oceans flooded continents, engulfing them in seconds. Forests were uprooted. Cities and entire populations were completely leveled, all within a matter of minutes. The Americas survived with some flooded coastlines and new mountain ranges here and there. The island of Manhattan went from being an island to a simple metropolitan coastal city. The region known as Texas split in two with a canyon larger than the Grand Canyon, and the panhandle was nearly engulfed in water. The lives of many settlers and natives were lost, but far fewer people perished within the United States compared to other countries. Asia and Europe, for example, were nearly engulfed by water and smoke. To say it was a tragedy would be an understatement. New histories were forged from the days of old and the human race evolved into a people driven by science in an effort to fully understand the parting of the veils that resulted in the Convergence. Earth eventually became one of the three realms and, over time, became known as Vitalis.

The opalescent shield of the Velum that loomed above Evangaline and Chloe in the distance was created by the fae rulers of Celadonia shortly after the Convergence. Evangaline only saw a single image of Celadonia—there are very few photos of the other realms in the New World—but what she saw was beautiful. Rolling hills of bright green grass. Trees with orange and red leaves sprang from the soil where flowers wildly grew. It appeared in her textbook as a true dreamscape out of a fairytale that she would have read as a child. If it were not for her mother's insistence that the photograph in her New World Geography book was real, Evangaline would have assumed it was the product of a skilled artist and Photoshop—that was how out of this world it was to her.

The inhabitants of Celadonia are what the mortals call fae. With their pointed ears and heightened beauty and their immortal lives, they are a far superior race to humans. No illness can take them down, as far as the rumors go. They are blessed with magic. What said magic entailed Evangaline was none the wiser, but the proof of it glittered down over the sea she looked out upon currently.

All of her knowledge of the other realms came from the education she was provided in her studies—so she didn't know much. In truth, there was not much to teach.

The Supreme King and Queen of Celadonia created the shield between their realm and Vitalis shortly after the Convergence once the three realms got back on their feet a bit. The rulers of each realm, for whatever reason, decided to keep separate from one another. The Supreme Leader of Munbra followed suit in creating The Mist to separate his realm from the other two shortly after, taking Celadonia's lead. Thus leaving Vitalis to their own devices, sandwiched within their own little bubble of solitude.

Basically, the rulers chose, for the safety of their given realms, to act as though the others were not just an ocean away but rather to pretend they did not exist at all. A treaty dictating rules and ultimately the boundaries was signed and put into action swiftly after.

Where the Velum appeared glittering and prismatic, the barrier on the Munbra side of the continent was a dark and swirling mist, made of smoke-like tendrils that crawled up the light gray fog. It was ominous and terrifying in every way. Evangaline glimpsed it once when she was on the coast of California and the dread that coiled within the pit of her stomach urged her to not look too deeply into the foggy border, thus turning her attention away from it for good.

In all, the inhabitants of Celadonia and Munbra were not often seen. But the few fae that Evangaline had seen on the news heading into the annual Council meeting—a meeting where the three leaders of the realms converge once a year to discuss the state of the New World—were the most beautifully magnificent beings she had ever witnessed. Tall and graceful. With an ethereal beauty that seemed unrealistic.

Evangaline always pictured Munbra and its residents as the polar opposite of Celadonia just based on the border walls alone. In her mind, the land of the fae was built with color and light, while Munbra was built in the dark and dismal. Truthfully, though, no one truly knows what lies on the opposite side of The Mist. It could be a tropical island full of fruity drinks and turquoise waters and no one would be the wiser.

Over the centuries, many have tried to cross The Mist to see Munbra and glimpse the dwellers that call it home. Whether it be for scientific research or just plain ignorance, people have chartered boats and sailed toward the border, but once The Mist enveloped them, they were never seen or heard from again. Thousands of lives gone over the centuries in just the snap of one's fingers, and still, the curiosity of humans seems to win out. Year after year, people trek into the gray fog like nothing bad was going to happen, like their fate would somehow be different from the people before them. It was foolish and idiotic. Evangaline always wondered if those curious souls felt the same sinister warning that she felt around the Munbra border. And if they did, they were far braver than she was.

Unlike The Mist, the Velum was built by magic and enforced to not allow any humans in or out. Many had tried the same way they sailed to The Mist, but when they pressed into it, the shimmering wall was hard as a brick wall and wouldn't allow anyone through. A few reckless captains sailed their ships straight into the dark depths of the ocean in an attempt to cross into

Celadonia.

The only resident of Munbra ever seen was the Supreme Leader and, even then, *seen* was a relatively generous term. He had represented Munbra within the Council since the Convergence. However, no one truly knows what the Supreme Leader looks like—or if it is the same being for all these years, for that matter of fact. Every year he wore a veil and robes so black the light seemed to be sucked into them and absorbed. His hands were always sheathed under his long bell sleeves, and he had never spoken a word outside of the meetings, making his voice a quandary. He was the truest enigma of the realms. Many artists have guessed as to what the mysterious Supreme Leader looked like, even made creations according to their wildest imaginations. Some ranged from handsome rouges all the way to the most shriveled creatures with fangs and claws. The truth, though, was that no one within Vitalis truly knew anything about Munbra or their elusive leader, which seems only to add to the intrigue.

"What do you think it would be like?" Chloe asked, shaking Evangaline from her trance.

"What?"

Motioning to the Velum, Chloe mused, "Without the borders?"

"I don't know," Evangaline responded. And truly, she didn't. Her ignorance of the other realms sometimes clouded her curiosity of them. The secrets that lie behind those borders are far scarier than the minor inconveniences she deals with on Vitalis day to day. The thought of beings powerful enough to erect such foreboding structures was an awe-inspiring and terrifying notion wrapped up tight in a sparkly bow. And truthfully, it was easy to forget the other realms existed when the towering borders didn't loom in the distance, like they were now.

"My family lost people in the Convergence. I always wonder what it would have been like without the borders. Being able to see across the merged seas." Chloe's eyes were clouded with what Evangaline could only attribute to one thing—longing.

Intrigued, she studied her friend for a moment, the way her eyes glistened with heartbreak and unshed tears. Her body tensely gripped the railing till her knuckles were white, like she was almost holding herself back from jumping into the water and swimming to the very border they discussed. Evangaline followed Chloe's gaze towards the opal glow emitting from the Velum and allowed herself to consider it—a world without boundaries. What would it be like to live side by side with the fae and beings of Munbra?

Thinking about Chloe's comments, the oddest tingle prickled her chest when she faced the fae border and gave it her full attention. It felt as though someone was running their finger sensuously down her sternum. It was a cold pressure that made the hairs raise on the back of her neck in warning despite the toe-curling way it hummed through her body.

Stretching to ease the odd sensation, Evangaline faced back toward Chloe, suddenly longing to change the subject off the fae and borders.

"I'm sorry for scolding you back there. You're a big girl, I know. I just … I don't know. I panicked for a second when I couldn't find you. My anxiety picked up and got the best of me, the alcohol probably didn't help. I was afraid some creep was hurting you or taking advantage of you or something," Evangaline mumbled feebly.

Chloe faced Evangaline, taking her hands in her own. The soft set of her eyes and the smile on her face was one of gratitude and guilt. She shook her head. Then laughed.

"I should be sorry. He hit on me at the bar, and I was all 'chicks before dicks,' ya know?" Evangaline laughed at the single rule of their girl code. The one rule Chloe coined after hearing it from a comedian downtown. "No joke, I ignored him, then he introduced himself, and the minute I heard his name … Evie, my mind exploded, and I just … aside from him being—"

"Hot," Evangaline added, her brows wiggling tauntingly.

Chloe smiled and laughed again. "Extremely. I don't know what happened, but I kissed him. Then I looked at you on the dance floor and for once you looked so … I can't describe it. You looked lost. But in a good way, for once. You were smiling and dancing. The quiet girl stocking shelves at the bookstore was gone and I, aside from really badly wanting to keep 'tempting *my* Mr. Brooks,' I just wanted to let you continue being happy. That's all I want for you, you know? I know how lost you are sometimes."

Evangaline analyzed their entwined hands solemnly, then back at her friend and forced a smile. Chloe was right. She was so incredibly lost more often than not. She took the job at the bookstore because she simply thought it was a means to an end. The simplest route to take after all her dreams crashed and burned. It seemed like the best option to coast along till the darkness claimed her, as morbid as that sounded.

Evangaline had a wonderful family, a stable job, and yet she still felt pathetically alone sometimes, like an entire piece of her was missing. There was a void within her soul that ached with an emptiness that she never could seem to fill. Eventually, the search to fill that void became unfruitful and harrowing and so she just lived with the feeling of being half complete.

Despite moving home with her parents, she seldom felt *at* home. The aching pain of feeling adrift at sea with no shore in sight swallowed her whole more often than not. But she had Chloe, thankfully. Soon after meeting the quirky little pink-haired woman, Chloe became a lifeline, a life preserver as Evangaline liked to think of her. Chloe was cast into the dark to bring Evangaline back to shore. She challenged Evangaline to go on dates and leave the comforts of her gilded cage—to try to experience life—and Evangaline would always be grateful to her for that. But it still didn't erase the numbing pain of feeling like she didn't belong anywhere. She felt homesick, but she was technically home.

She grabbed her phone out of her leather skirt's back pocket and illuminated the screen. *1:04 a.m.* Evangaline smiled and held up the phone to Chloe, the bright harsh light cast over her face, forcing Chloe to squint.

"I'm officially 25 …" she said with a small uptick of her lips, despite a small part of her dying inside. Another year and she still had no idea what she was doing with her life.

"Happy birthday sexy mama," Chloe said with serene ease, chuckling at the way Evangaline squirmed at her compliments.

Evangaline simply wrapped her arms around her friend and brought her in for an embrace. Words could not describe what she was feeling, but a hug could perfectly. In her glittering booties she towered over Chloe easily by four inches, and that *was* including Chloe's platform sandals. They stood there for a good minute before Evangaline pulled away and squinted down at her friend speculatively. The slight breeze of the night ruffled the hair tucked behind Evangaline's ear and made her break out in goosebumps at the sudden bite of chill in the air.

Summer was finally giving way to fall and maybe a sheer black long sleeve shirt, black sports bra, and black leather skirt were not weather appropriate for the change in weather, but she felt strong and sexy and that was exactly what Chloe wanted for her tonight. Her sparkling gold and pink eyeshadow caught the sheen of the streetlights behind her as she peered down at Chloe, crinkling her eyes in thought, bringing out the bright blue and green streaks of her irises.

"How is it my birthday and you're the one getting laid?" she quipped with a teasing grin.

Chloe cocked her head back, howling in laughter, grabbing firmly onto Evangaline's hand and entwining their fingers once more.

"Hey, your birthday technically just started … We've got a few more hours … Anything can happen!" She replied, tugging Evangaline away from the opal sky and sparkling water and straight back into the jostle of the city.

Chapter Three

Approximately four hours, two bars, one bagel, and two purchases of two oversized *I Heart NY* sweatshirts later, Evangaline and Chloe rolled out of a taxi and up the steps to Evangaline's house. Well, her parents' house, technically. Where she was staying for the time being—until she figured out her life.

After her brother, Miles, left for college two years ago, her parents decided it was time for a downsize. After all, her older sister Katherine was newly married and blissfully living her life in the suburbs. Evangaline, at the time, seemed like she had her shit together and was engaged to her college sweetheart and living clear across the country. And Miles, well, Miles was more than happy to be far away from home playing college football and doing whatever it was that Miles did best.

It was the perfect time to downsize from five beds in the suburbs to two beds in the city. Then a year ago, Evangaline lost her job, broke off her engagement, and had to move home and occupy their spare room.

Yay for quarter-life crises!

The townhome her parents owned wasn't overly large but had all the classic charm of the Gilded Age. Carved stone corbels perched upon either side of the elaborately ornate wrought iron door. Small stains peppered the walls where ivy once clung to the façade. The little speckles of where the foliage once resided were her favorite, for some strange reason, the imperfection of the stone made Evangaline feel less out of place and more seen. Not even the dated opulence of her parent's home was immune to imperfections.

Stephen, her step-father, studied architecture in school and became one soon after where he met her mom, Felicity, who worked as an assistant to an interior designer in the city. They were a match made in *HGTV* heaven. At the time, Stephen was a single dad to Katherine, who was four and Felicity had only six months before their meeting given birth to Evangaline.

Felicity never spoke much about why she wasn't with Evangeline's birth father except for an occasional, "I did what I needed to do for my child," and that was it. Evangaline never once held a grudge against the mysterious contributor to her life, nor why her mother needed to be rid of him. Evangaline simply didn't need him. She had Stephen who never once treated her like anything but his own flesh and blood. There was never even a sense of curiosity about the man who sired her. Evangaline had a perfect family that she loved dearly. She felt no need to break that apart for a man who never cared for her existence enough to even send her a birthday card.

Miles came some years after her parents' meeting, and they've been a happy family of five ever since. Well, until Katherine married James and became pregnant with her soon-to-be bundle of joy, so soon to be a happy family of seven!

As Evangaline pushed through the front door and into the foyer, she smelled the decadent aroma of coffee wafting through the air. From the corner of her eye, she could see Chloe perk up at the smell, too. They were two slightly hungover zombies that smelled some nice juicy brains. Chloe shuffled into the kitchen after Evangaline following the life-giving scent, only to run into both her parents standing guard over the decadent liquid fuel they so desperately craved.

Felicity radiated silent anger as she turned around to find her half scantily dressed daughter wandering in at five in the morning with her slightly hungover best friend. The steam practically seeped from Felicity's ears as she took in the two girls in the doorway. Her red hair bobbed with every shake of her disapproving head, her fair complexion grew flushed and her lips slowly pursed behind her half-raised mug of steaming coffee—all of which were not a good sign.

"What do we owe the honor, birthday girl?" Stephen crooned with his back to Evangaline and Chloe, slowly stirring creamer into his coffee.

Evangaline let out a hearty sigh, one her mother did not at all enjoy. She met her mother's gaze unflinchingly, however stubbornly standing her ground. Evangaline barely went out. She and Chloe would get dinner or a couple of drinks sometimes after work and on the off occasion, she would go on a date. That of which she most certainly would not tell her parents about to escape the awkward, embarrassing meddling afterward.

Last night was an anomaly.

The drinking. The staying out till the sun rose. The clubbing. Evangaline simply never did any of it.

It did not help that Felicity's parenting style bordered on the line of overprotective. Even as grown adults, she liked to know where they were and what they were up to. Anything they did was questioned with added lessons on how to be careful, responsible, and polite human beings. Felicity's fears were crammed into all three siblings' skulls, leaving lasting imprints within their lives. She always deemed it was for their own good that she helicoptered over them and that they didn't yet fully realize the way the New World worked. It was a notion Evangaline hated for its condescending tone but understood. Evangaline was a lot of things, but she wasn't stupid, she knew the world didn't always work the way you wanted it to, it certainly never did for her.

Luckily for Felicity, all three of her kids obeyed her rules and lived relatively quiet, unexciting lives. Except for last night, to which Evangaline allowed herself to push her boundaries and live the life of Chloe—carefree and with reckless abandon.

Evangaline turned away from her parents, ignoring the comments and glares to grab two mugs. Reaching in between her parents, who at this point were glaring at her in all the most condescending ways. She grabbed the gaudy silver French press they pretentiously made coffee out of and poured out two hefty servings for her and Chloe. She hated that they couldn't be a normal family and just buy one of the machines with the pods. Why did they have to be the people who French pressed their coffee?

Handing a cup to Chloe, they both turned, heading up the stairs without a single word. She will talk to them when she has had her coffee … and some sleep … and a shower.

She took a sip of her black coffee and hated how good it tasted from that goddam French press. Chloe's moan as she sipped from her cup let Evangaline believe she thought the same thing.

At the top of the stairs, Chloe turned to use the spare bathroom, grumbling something about being right there and not being able to hold it. However, in her sleep deprived state, Evangaline wasn't paying attention in the slightest. She rounded the ornately paneled hallway, giving Chloe a half-assed thumbs up, and made to approach her room. That was when she noticed it. The door to her room was slightly cracked open, allowing the soft white light of day to spill into the dim hallway. Not at all how she left it.

Evangaline slowly approached the unlatched door, her drowsy haze wearing off with every sip she took of coffee and each fear filled step she made to the door. She wasn't sure if she was simply tired and didn't remember leaving her door ajar or if, as every instinct in her body was telling her someone was in her room. Knowing that Chloe was in the bathroom and her parents were in the kitchen downstairs, no one should be in her room and her parents weren't the type to sneak around snooping through her stuff. Her blood writhed through her veins like a warning that something was wrong and yet she was drawn to the door by a phantom thread.

Taking a deep steadying breath, she lowered the coffee cup she unknowingly raised like a weapon above her head and stopped walking. She took a deep breath and tucked her chin to her chest.

"You've officially lost it," she mumbled to herself as thoughts of an intruder waiting to murder her flooded her head. "You listen to too many crime podcasts!" She whispered harshly to herself.

She raised her unoccupied hand to her eyes and rubbed them, shaking her head, and began her weary walk to the door once more. Telling herself nothing was wrong, despite the thudding of her heart in her chest.

Swinging open the door, the light poured in from the opened curtains and was only magnified by the stark white walls of the room. Wincing from the onslaught of light, she began to smell a scent that seemed so familiar she just couldn't place it. As she turned toward the direction of the scent, it hit her—bergamot and rose.

Chapter Four

In a rush of pure adrenaline, Evangaline slung her coffee with the exhilarative force of a professional baseball player. The hot liquid beverage flung in the direction of the scent and the monster of a man it was attached to.

Just as the pit in her stomach told her, the coffee met its mark directly, splashing into the face of an intruder. Her instincts took over from there. Shifting her body into auto pilot and bringing the now empty cup straight into the man's head as he bent over, wincing from the scalding liquid covering his face. The autumn-colored leaf mug broke into jagged pieces in her hand.

She didn't notice until he dropped to the ground that she had cut herself on a ceramic shard in the silent attack. Truthfully, she didn't feel anything because of all the adrenaline coursing through her system, let alone notice the blood now dripping from her hand onto the vintage hardwood floors.

In a fit of panic, she turned around, closing the door behind her, trying her hardest not to alert her parents of the invasion currently underway. The last thing she wanted was to scare them despite the circumstance being terrifying at best. It was always her first instinct to protect the people she loved, and she knew her mom would burst with panic.

Spinning around to Chloe's startled face, Evangáline's wide-set eyes and flushed countenance contorted as she lifted her finger to her lips and made the universal sign for *be quiet*.

"You're bleeding!" Chloe whisper yelled, reaching for Evangaline's hand, completely ignoring the pursed lips and finger raised.

"Shh! I'm fine! There's a man in there!" Evangaline violently whispered.

Chloe slowly blinked at Evangaline, confusion muddling her petite features. "Good for you? Is he cute?" she said, trying as she always did, to bring light to an otherwise terrifying situation.

All Evangaline could do was stare at Chloe, indignant of the comment. Her eyes were wild, her pulse rushing through her veins in hot streams, flushing her in a coat of sweat.

"I didn't get a good look Chlo … I was too busy hitting him in the head with a coffee cup!" Evangaline shouted back in a hushed and panicked tone.

With her bloody hand gripped firmly around the brass door handle, she didn't want to scream or immediately call for her parents. She honestly didn't know why all of a sudden she felt guilty that a man who snuck into *her* room was now lying wounded on her floor. But she did.

Her anxiety pinged a sharp pain in her chest that she tried to ignore. Calling her focus back to the very real situation unfolding.

"Go downstairs and tell my parents to call the police! But be quiet. I don't know how long he will stay knocked out and I don't want to wake him up."

Chloe scoffed, barely lowering her voice, "Hell no! I'm staying with you! You're bleeding! Don't be a hero!"

"I'm fine. I have a first aid kit in my bathroom. I'll get it once we figure this out! Now go!"

Just as Chloe was about to argue back, the door flung open with a force greater than Evangaline had ever felt. The velocity of the tug could only be equated to her arm being stuck in the grasp of a car door speeding off through a green light at one hundred miles per hour. Not like she knew how that felt, but she could imagine it was close to the pain searing up her arm.

The pain that shot through her bloodied hand was insurmountable, enough to make her gasp and back into the wall, all the while reaching for Chloe in a panic as the tiny pink haired woman stood before her, mighty and defensive.

Chloe's small stature came just barely to the intruder's chest. Evangaline couldn't help but notice how Chloe looked so fearsome in her protective stance. Her heeled feet were braced wide and sturdy, her arms were raised in a fighting position with her hands curled into two mighty fists. She wouldn't stand a chance against the monster of a man, but she would get an 'A' for effort.

Suddenly, just as soon as Chloe stood tall and ready to fight, her whole body relaxed. Her hands fell flat against her sides, her shoulders dropped from her ears, and all the tension in her muscles was released with an exhale.

"Bash … you son of a bitch!" Chloe squealed, jumping up to embrace the stranger in Evangaline's room.

What the fuck? Evangaline shouted within the confines of her mind.

With her eyes squinted, jaw agape, all Evangaline could do was stare at Chloe in disbelief. How could she possibly know this man?

For the first time, Evangaline took a *good* look at him. He was tall. Very tall. Evangaline herself came just below his shoulders, even with her heeled boots still on.

His long, dark hair rested just above his collar. The tresses sat messily toward the side of his head, out of the way of the cut that was seeping blood just above his right eyebrow from where her cup made contact. He was scary based on his stature alone. But his jawline was bold and defined.

In every way, the man could be a god of some sort—if such beings existed. Ruggedly handsome, not a conventional type of beauty … he was more harsh and rigid. His muscles were barely contained within the white button-down collared shirt that was quite offensively showing off too much of his sculpted chest. The fact that it was now wet with coffee and clinging to all five thousand muscles on his upper body wasn't helping Evangaline in her effort to stop ogling him. As her eyes traveled back up the length of his torso and meet with his forest green eyes, she relaxed her furrowed brow from its state of shock, only for the muscles along her mouth to bend into a line of flaming rage.

Chloe wedged between Evangaline's simmering blaze and the intruder's bolstering machismo. Between them, she suddenly appeared a lot like prey cowering beneath the claws of two vicious predators.

Slowly, Chloe raised her hands in the air, in a sign of surrender. All she needed was a white flag, and she would be the epitome of a defeated foe. The soft click of her platforms alerted Evangaline to Chloe's slow approach, yet the rage in Evangaline's eyes had one target—the strange man in her doorway.

She knew that smell. That shirt. He was at the club earlier. His presence was too fresh in her head to forget the perplexing smell that filled her nostrils in her attempt to find Chloe. He was the man she ran into, and she knew that for a fact, everything inside of her knew it despite not seeing his face. What she couldn't understand was why his towering frame was in her bedroom. Better yet, how he got there unseen and unheard by her parents. And how he knew her best friend.

"It was you?"

The simple sentence slipped through her clenched jaws, only to be met by a look of conspiratorial awareness from the big bastard. His perfectly pillowed lips tugged into a haughty smile in return. All the proof she needed to confirm her suspicions.

He rubbed at his cut head, smirking. "Glad you remember me. But that wasn't nice … hitting a friend over the head like that, Princess. A simple hello would do just fine next time."

She sneered at his brashness. "There won't be a next time. And I don't warmly greet strange men camping out in my bedroom. Now get out."

With the arrogance that only a man could have, he leaned against the doorjamb, brushing his flowing chestnut hair back with his massive hands, narrowly avoiding the cut on his brow. How he wasn't popping the buttons on his shirt was a miracle in itself. The tightly constricted white linen appeared painted on his sculpted torso by a master artist.

Chloe gently grabbed Evangaline's bloody hand and wrapped her small brown hand around the wound festering bright red blood against Evangaline's porcelain skin. But Evangaline's rage bolstered the adrenaline already coursing through her veins, numbing the prickles of pain radiating up her arm. She could have been hit by a bus and she might not have felt the impact. Her adrenaline made her numb to the pain.

"Evie …"

"I told you, Chlo. I'm fine." Evangaline's voice remained robotic, unamused.

She was certainly not fine.

Never once did she take her eyes away from the arrogant ass standing in her room. Despite his alluring features, something chimed a warning bell in her head. Perhaps it was the unwelcome visitor, the smug smirk on his lips, but something about him scared her.

There would have been a time, possibly hours ago, in her drunken stupor, where she seriously would've hoped a man this ruggedly good looking would be in her bedroom looking as relaxed as he was now, but those would have been much different circumstances. Most likely involving a lot fewer clothes … and definitely a lot less blood.

"Evie, I need you to listen to me. *Look at me.*" Chloe's last words were clipped with authority. The worried cadence in Chloe's voice sent a ping of anxiousness through Evangaline, cutting her with a hot steel blade straight through the rage that was building its insipid inferno. She felt like a volcano preparing to erupt at any moment.

Snapping her gaze to her friend with enough force to give her whiplash, Evangaline bore a hole into Chloe, studying her dainty features.

Chloe's eyes were filled with the same guilt that shadowed them when she got caught with Mr. Brooks, except the amusement behind them was eerily replaced with a pinging sense of dread.

The musty air surrounding them seemed to feel like it was being sucked out of the hallway, particle by particle, bit by bit. The light in Chloe's eyes began to dim, their hazel luster drained of their typical shimmer, and Evangaline saw it then.

Chloe was lying, she was hiding something, and this beast of a man had something to do with it. He scared Chloe, despite her glee at seeing him. He scared Evangaline too, but she wouldn't let him see that.

Evangaline leaned into Chloe, her hair brushing past Chloe's cheek like a curtain of privacy. "Are you in trouble? Who is he, Chlo? What did you do?" Her tone was filled with worry, yet remained harsh and cutting.

Chloe straightened, sucking on her bottom lip in a way she did when she was nervous, once more dropping her gaze from Evangaline. Her tight grip never faltered on Evangaline's wounded hand.

A small shake of her head was barely visible before Chloe glanced over at the man.

Evangaline, with the attentiveness of a hawk at the moment, tracked all of Chloe's movements. Chloe's timid body language gave away the quiet nervousness coursing through her friend's body. Evangaline looked for anything to give her a slight indication of the situation they were now stuck in, but came up empty-handed.

"Talk to him. Please." Chloe's voice was small. Her boldness somehow faded from her very being. It was so unlike her. The sudden loss of bravado in her best friend was almost more alarming than the man watching them behind forest green eyes.

Evangaline stood in a pregnant pause for what felt like an entire lifetime scanning her best friend's face. The instinct in her stomach said to run. Yet seeing Chloe look so small, so guilt-ridden, Evangaline gave in, allowing her rage to dim to glowing embers, allowing her to fight to take a backseat to her curiosity.

With a deep swallow, Evangaline gave a soft nod. Clutching her bloody hand, Chloe turned them and proceeded to Evangaline's room and past the mountain of male arrogance standing in her doorway.

Chapter Five

Chloe softly shut the bedroom door with nothing more than a soft *snickt* and locked it quickly, effectively locking Evangaline, the intruder, and her into the same room. It didn't seem like the smart thing to do, but Evangaline was lacking control over the situation and had no choice but to be a passenger to the conversation.

To distract the growing panic attack surging its way up into her lungs, Evangaline shifted her focus to her hand. Going into her alarmingly white en-suite bathroom, she grabbed a couple of towels and her first aid kit.

The cut on her hand bled enough to create a small trail of red droplets across the floor. It was the most eerie version of Hansel and Gretel's breadcrumb trail she had ever seen. However, this trail led her not to a witch in a candy house, but to a scarily attractive intruder and a guilty friend … and sadly no sweets.

Evangaline's gash was only about an inch long but was bleeding enough for her to know deep down it should take a few stitches, but being that she was exhausted, a bit hungover, and already done with her twenty-fifth birthday, she didn't want to deal with the hassle of going to the hospital. So some antibiotic ointment and a bandage were going to have to do the trick.

"She called you Bash. That's your name?" Evangaline asked, tossing a washcloth to the man leaning against the end of her bed for him to wipe the blood gathering in his unkept eyebrow.

With graceful ease, he caught the rag and began holding it against his head, "Bastian. Only this one calls me Bash." Notching his chin toward Chloe against the door.

"Because it pisses him off. I *really* enjoy pissing him off," Chloe bemused with a quiet smirk.

Evangaline, taking a small uneven breath, didn't acknowledge the comradery between her supposed best friend and *Bash*. Instead, she focused on her breathing. Her whole life, she struggled with bouts of anxiety. *"She's just introverted,"* her mother used to tell teachers when they would poke and prod Evangaline to make more friends and speak up more. Felicity wasn't wrong, but she also missed the part where, under pressure, Evangaline's anxiety peaked to nauseating levels.

Afraid to fail, afraid of being made fun of, afraid to look stupid. She was just afraid. A lot. That was part of the reason Chloe pushed her to party the night prior. The anxiety never reared its ugly head when significant change did not occur. Therefore, she was safe in her secluded monotony. Panic attacks were something that would come and go frequently because of her irrational fears as a kid. Luckily, as she got older, she developed ways to combat the attacks and, truth be told; she hadn't had a bad one since she became friends with Chloe. Something about Chloe calmed her, gave her the confidence she needed to be able to override the fear that tended to sink its nasty claws into her flesh.

All the warning signs of one starting now, however, were present. The one thing she could do was to remind herself that she was safe and to breathe. She took a few deep steadying breaths she learned in a yoga class once and lied to herself that she was safe with this stranger staring down at her.

She sat down on her bed, spreading out the contents of the first aid kit, breathing in through her nose and out through pursed lips.

Both Chloe and Bastian maintained their distance as she silently hissed in a breath, wiping down her hand with an alcohol wipe. It burned like hell, but she just kept breathing. Can't give the monster what it wanted so badly. She couldn't cave to the panic attack and allow it to unhinge its fanged jaws and swallow her whole.

"Okay, Bastian." Evangaline finally peered up at him once the stinging from the alcohol subsided and pushed past the knot of anxiety and fear gathering in her throat. Noticing his cut, now swept clean of blood, she gathered an alcohol wipe and a band-aid and tossed it to him. Once more, he caught it with ease and precision. In every way he could be an athlete, maybe he was? It would explain all the muscles.

He shoot a look at Chloe for what Evangaline only could assume was approval, however, her guilt was completely wringing her through like a wet cloth being emptied of water. She gnawed on the skin around her thumb, flashing Bastian a small nod of approval.

Bastian, with a hint of reproach, turned back to Evangaline. "Ok, Princess. I'm going to say a lot that clearly you have never heard before, so I need you to promise me you won't hit me in the head with anything else."

Evangaline gave the brute an incredulous look and took a deep anger ridden inhale. And on the exhale, she steeled her spine and focused on staying strong throughout whatever bullshit she was about to hear.

Allowing her anger to seep through just a little, Evangaline replied, "First off, *Bash*, don't sneak into someone's room and you won't get hit in the head. Secondly, don't call me *Princess*. I have a name, it's Evangaline. If we're going to pretend to be friends, I suggest you use it instead of using some degrading nickname."

Bastian—a little bemused at her attempt at acting stronger than she so clearly was—strode over to her bed, taking a seat across from her. With an extended hand toward her wounded one, he motioned for her to give it to him.

Hesitant at first, Evangaline eyed him suspiciously, but after he let out a slightly scary sigh, she quickly succumbed, placing her hand palm side up in his, exposing the wound.

Gently, he grabbed the ointment and began to apply it with a feather-light touch. His cold, callused hands were surprisingly gentle in their approach. At this point, she genuinely had no clue how to feel. On one side of the coin, she wanted to hit him with another cup, but on the flip side, she wanted to feel what those large and caressing hands would feel like on other parts of her body.

NO! Evangaline shook the thought out of her head just as quickly as it squeaked its way into her clearly deranged brain. Even though it had been over a year since she'd been touched by a man, that did not mean her brain was allowed to freak out at the first benevolent touch of one. Bastian was attractive and also a stalker, and an intruder, and no matter how gruffly becoming he was, he was a dangerous man … her gut told her so.

She looked away from him toward the windows across the way to gaze at the green leaves of the tree right outside her window, ruffling in the slight breeze of the early morning sun. The sight of the winking leaves for even a few seconds filled her anxious heart with a sense of calm and ease.

"How do you two know each other? Another bathroom stall tryst, Chlo?" Evangaline asked, smirking at Chloe, her tone lacking any semblance of warmth.

"He wishes," Chloe retorted far quicker than Evangaline thought she would. The mischievous light filled Chloe's eyes again. A small smile curved her delicate pink lips as she cut Bastian a mocking glance.

Bastian leered up at both girls, his eyes playing a game of ping-pong, while a wickedly amused smile overcame his roughly hewn features. "I knew you smelled like sex. I just didn't want to believe it. A bathroom stall? Huh? I wondered where you went, little minx. I tried finding you, but you disappeared." He winked. "Don't worry, I won't tell Des."

At the mention of this mysterious Des, Chloe toed her silver platform into the carpet, her face wincing as it filled with the visage of a scorned lover. Her soft black lashes flicked across her blush covered cheeks. The sight of Chloe's flustered and haunted eyes was enough for Evangaline to feel a ping of regret for bringing up her nightly activity. Maybe it was too harsh of a dig too soon.

Changing focus back to Bastian, "You *were* at the club, then?" Evangaline asked, finding his forest green eye line. The smile he harbored began to falter and fade.

"Yes, I was watching you. I came as soon as it hit midnight. I got there just after you both did—right before I ran into you."

He finished up the wrapping of her hand and softly placed his own on top of hers and, for a moment; they sat like that. Evangaline's hand dwarfed between both of his cold, callused ones. Catching her breath before it hitched like an infatuated fool, she quickly pulled her hand away.

No more alcohol and partying all night. It seriously fogs the brain. She thought to herself.

"Thank you," she murmured, then gathered her confidence. "But that is also something a stalker would say so, you have a lot more explaining to do than that." Tucking her hands under her arms, so her arms folded across her chest to create a shield of sorts, she sat up straighter. "Wait, how can you smell like sex? I didn't smell anything. And why did you show up after midnight?" She looked up, perplexed and disgusted at Chloe.

Biting her lip, Chloe shot a look toward Bastian. A threat hidden beneath her fiery gaze. It screamed at him just how much she would like to be the next one hitting him with a mug … and the damage from her would be much worse than a cut to the eyebrow.

Bastian smirked at Evangaline, temptation swirling in his body language like a snake slithering in the garden of Eden. "Oh, I have a lot to teach you, Princess."

"What?" Evangaline's eyes went wide at his comment.

He chuckled. "Not like that. Unless you want me to teach you that way. I enjoy a good hands-on lesson," he quipped, sitting back. This arrogant male would surely be the end of her. She knew it deep within the cloying ache in her stomach. While her brain was malfunctioning with lust, her stomach was screaming, *"Bad news!"*

In that moment Chloe scoffed, tearing Evangaline's gaze from the smug brute before her. Chloe with a grunt rolled her eyes as Evangaline's body flushed with heat under the searing green eyes of the man before her.

Clearing her throat, Evangaline snipped, "Can someone please tell me anything of importance? Why do I need to talk to him Chlo?" She was trying her best to steer the conversation back on track. Anything for her to ignore the blossoming heat in her body.

Standing abruptly, Bastian slapped his hands on his thighs in a jarring clap, "All right, I don't have all the time in the world either, so here it goes. I'm here to take you home to your father and fulfill the bargain. Chloe is a trained guard whose job has been for the past year to follow and protect you, and you, my dear, are a *princess*. Whether or not you want to hear it, it is who you are. You are the only heir to Celadonia and your time here in Vitalis is up. So, time to pack up!"

Evangaline, with a furrowed brow and uncertain smile, leaned back against the pillows on her bed, giving the words that Bastian just spewed enough space to simmer within the already thin air. She had read her fair share of books in her lifetime. Long-lost princesses and dashing princes were a staple of fairytales she would read late at night before bed as a kid, but this ... Bastian's newsflash ... it was entirely absurd. Despite the fae and magic being very real, she certainly had nothing to do with them. She was as boring and normal as a human could be. No magic. Round ears. She was as human as they came.

She tried hard, but the laugh shooting up through her throat was too strong and coming too fast that she could not stop it. It made its way to her mouth, passed her anxious heartbeat and out to the ether of the very awkward room that she sat in. After a solid fifteen seconds of laughter, Evangaline looked around her room, taking into consideration that neither Chloe nor Bastian were laughing.

In fact, instead of amusement, Chloe appeared more likely to jump out the window than be present in the conversation taking place.

Evangaline stood, her hands settling on her cocked hips. "You can't possibly think I am going to believe that bullshit, do you?" With a shake of her head, she began to turn on her heels to make a retreat to the bathroom, "I think it's been a long night for all of us, so if you don't mind, I'm tired and don't have time for this. Chloe can show you out. Thanks for dropping in and nice to meet you. Hope the eyebrow heals," she said briskly, dismissing Bastian with a click of her heels.

With the pressure of two vices, Bastian's hands clamped around her forearms, spinning her to face him. Chest to chest, his heavy breaths rattled through his sternum and into hers, sending chills down her spine. There was nothing gentle about the grip he had on her. It was demanding and angry. It was only when he stole a glance at her lips that his hand loosened slightly.

With the slight release of her arms, she pressed into his chest harder, making her presence and fortitude known. She wouldn't be mistreated by any man. She would stand just as tall and arrogant as him if she needed to get her point across. As she crushed her breasts into his pecs, she felt him tense up and noticed him glance at her lips once more, his breath dipping heavier and heavier. "Get this into your head, Bash. I am not going anywhere with you. I don't care who you are or who sent you here, and I am certainly, absolutely, positively, not your princess."

She yanked her arms from his icy grip and began to back up. Yet just when she thought she was free to turn, his hands curled around her waist. His fingers sank into the muscle just above her backside.

Out of the corner of her eye, she saw Chloe go tense with anger, bawling her fists and growling a warning toward Bastian. She was a small pink-haired feral animal, ready to pounce at any moment. What impact she would have would be questionable, but the thought of her attacking Bastian brought a slight smile of satisfaction to Evangaline's face.

At the sight of her grin, his fingers flexed, loosening and tightening, before falling into fists at his sides. He turned away from Evangaline, a bewildered smile pulling on his own face.

"Maybe you think it's funny, Princess. Maybe you don't believe either of us. And that's just fine …" His voice became deep and rough, matching his wild exterior. With a glance over his shoulder, the air of casual arrogance morphed into a vain sneer as he stalked to the door casually, before slinging it open with a force great enough to throw it off its top two hinges.

"But you will. And I'm not leaving here without you." Bastian boomed from the hall.

Chapter Six

Luckily, Chloe dodged the crashing door just before the sheer force of Bastian's swing flattened her into a tiny pink pancake.

Evangaline herself was frozen in disbelief. Her eyes swung to Chloe for reassurance but unfortunately found nothing but a wide-eyed stare and a rapidly rising chest, no different from her own.

Not thinking things through, Evangaline sprinted through the door—now oddly hanging off one golden bottom hinge—and propelled herself as fast as she could down the hall.

Still in her heeled booties, she ran as fast as she could just as Bastian started his thunderous hot-tempered descent down the stairs. His heavy footfalls made his chocolate-colored hair bounce off the stained fold of his collar. Thanks to his legs, which were the size of a goddam tree trunk, the savage took one step for every three Evangaline needed to take, making it damn near impossible for her to catch up to him.

"Evangaline … sweetheart? Are you okay?" Felicity shouted. Her voice rippled with the essence of fear.

Of course, she heard the door flying off the hinges and the sound of booming footsteps thudding through the hall with the thunder of a stampede of cattle. The house was practically made of paper mâché it was so damn old. One could sneeze on one side of the house and be met with a "Gesundheit" from the other.

Evangaline didn't know this man and had no clue if he would hurt her parents, but she was not willing to test the theory. Her legs rushed along as fast as her heeled boots would allow without breaking her ankle.

She would do anything to make sure he didn't get near Felicity and Stephen. If she needed to, she knew she could grab another mug and lay him out for a few more moments. Yet again, those were in the kitchen. Well, if she went that way, Evangaline thought, she could always see how a good hard whack in the head would lay him out using the whole damn French press! Get rid of two birds with one stone!

Cresting the bottom of the stairs, Bastian turned, a wicked smile on his face and an even wickeder gleam in his eyes. "Hello Felicity! Time's up, darling. Darrin sends his regards." Bastian sneered. Crossing his elephantine arms, his stance wide with feet braced firmly under the weight of his massive trunk like thighs. His stance was graced with how Evangaline imagined a soldier held himself. The firm, unwavering fearlessness that one would stand with when facing an enemy in battle.

Hearing her mom's name leave Bastian's lips slammed Evangaline to a stop mid-step. Just as it did Felicity, stopping dead in her tracks, with Stephen close on her heels.

"Mom? Who's Darrin?" The name sounded familiar, but Evangaline could not place it.

Only a couple more stairs and she would have been able to stop him. She could have leapt and tackled him or kicked him in the back. Something. Anything that could have stopped the fear that now coursed through her heart and perforated it with its thorny vines.

Bastian's pigheadedness wanted Evangaline to believe his outlandish fable of lost princesses, bodyguards, *the fae*; yet all he had given her was even more questions. Ones that now involved her mother, whom of which was frozen, standing in a state of fear and shock, much like Evangaline. Two statues carved from cold, tear-lined marble—frozen in time.

Stephen stood just behind Felicity, until he turned toward Evangaline, carefully watching his wife and the brute before her, ensuring her safety, first and foremost. His cautious yet fearful gaze sent an immediate lightning strike of panic through Evangaline, making her tremble under the weight of it all. Seeing Stephen with a glaze of panic glossing over his wide eyes sent all the hair on Evangaline's neck spiking straight up into the air with a jolt.

She only saw Stephen scared once. It was late winter and the whole family went sledding. It was the greatest day ever—until it wasn't. Evangaline, Katherine, and Miles all got to stay home from school to enjoy the heavy snowfall that coated their sidewalk-lined streets. Filing into the car, wrapped up in easily ten layers of clothes each, they made their way to a desolate area with rolling hills and barren trees and began to take advantage of the fresh glittering powder covering the forest landscape.

Laughing and giggling, the three aimlessly pushed off their ruby-red sled as they already had done dozens of times before, but this onetime Miles's foot fell off the sled, which sent the whole lot careening straight to the side of the hill. Thus throwing Miles off the back like a ragdoll being whipped through the frigid air. He went down rapidly headfirst onto a rock hidden beneath a thin layer of snow, gashing his small forehead. At the end of the day, Miles needed ten stitches, and everyone needed a hot bath and some cocoa. But that was the *only* time she ever saw her dad with this level of fear in his eyes. Blood covering Miles's small face, Stephen's eyes glazed over the same way they were currently witnessing the confrontation before him.

Bastian was a brutish bastard, albeit a good-looking incredibly sexy brutish bastard, but one nonetheless for imposing this level of fear on Evangaline and her family.

Despite his abrasiveness, she could not help but question if the words Bastian spoke to her moments ago in her room were true. Evangaline's gut started writhing, twisting, and turning with the fear coursing through her body. She knew the answer deep down, but wasn't ready to admit it to herself just yet. There was a reason she never felt she belonged, because maybe she didn't belong *here,* in Vitalis?

"Evangaline, go back up to your room," Stephen cautiously said, trying to null his voice of any potential nerves.

"I don't think so, Princess. You want to laugh and call me a liar? Which

I don't appreciate, by the way. You really think I want to waste my time here in this dismal realm? Ask your dear mom. Tell her who she is, Felicity. Who she *really* is." Bastian's harsh tone squashed the smooth tone of Stephen's plea like an ant under a boot.

"Mom? *Please* ..." The nerves in Evangaline's voice reverberated for everyone to hear. *Please tell me he's lying. Please tell me this is all just a big old mix-up.* The words remained unspoken, but the fearful furrow of Evangaline's brows screamed them as Felicity turned to look at her white-knuckling the banister.

A beat of stagnant silence simmered between them. The tension in the air clouded Evangaline in a toxic smoke, wrapping around her throat and constricting like a serpent, killing its prey until her lungs burned with a paralyzing panic. "Mom ..." The whisper slipped past her trembling lips.

With each second that passed, her mom stared down Bastian, but never denied the words existing between them. Instead, Felicity's eyes swelled with tears that crested her lash line.

Evangaline's loitering panic attack was more than eager to make an appearance and prowled toward her, hunting the part of her psyche that was keeping her grounded like a rabid beast looking for dinner. Unable to gulp down a solid breath, Evangaline was practically asking if the beast wanted freshly ground, cracked pepper on its meal.

Slowly her vision clouded with white speckles in the bright light of the townhome. Her breath became heavy and one by one, tears trickled down her cheeks, landing with a hearty plop on the banister without her permission. Her fingernails dug their way into the antique hardwood as her knuckles grew an alarming shade of white, almost yellow, as all the blood leached from her now numb fingers.

With the lack of oxygen making its way into her lungs, her hands went senseless with pins and needles and her legs atrophied with rage. When her body felt like it was beginning to fail her, Evangaline sank to the stairs beneath her feet and forced her head into her hands.

Her tears silently streamed down her cheeks in disbelief.

Her whole life was a lie, and the devil came to collect on her mother's sins personally just to drag Evangaline to her own personal hell in retribution.

She didn't realize at first, but Chloe was talking to her. With her hearing coming in as though she was submerged underwater, she could not determine the words her best friend was speaking. Muffled questions began to seep in one by one in a frantic cadence.

"Are you okay? Evie?" Chloe's hands were braced on both of Evangaline's cheeks, acting like a windshield wiper for her tears. Evangaline simply stared through her friend, mouth agape, like Choe was made of rose-colored glass.

Her mother's silence spoke louder than any words ever could. Bastian wasn't lying to her, not even after she assaulted him with her mug. Evangaline wanted so badly for him to be some coked out hunk that stalked her home from the club. As scary as that would have been, it would have been more believable than all of *this*. Him being a crazy stalker seemed like a better fate than the one now laying before her. Who would have thought?

Her mom, her own flesh and blood, lied. Not for a small while, not a simple white lie. She lied about something as important as her being a fae princess all through omission. She *lied*.

The monster of her panic attack now devoured her in full force. She was drowning in a sea of sorrow, and not even her life preserver in the form of Chloe could get to her. She couldn't go with him, even if what he spoke was the truth. She can't be a princess and there was no way in hell that she was an heir to the throne of a land she had only seen in one or two photographs years ago in school.

This is all a bad dream. She repeatedly thought to herself. *Wake up.*

Her head pounded rhythmically, as though one thousand jackhammers began construction on her aching mind. Closing her eyes, she realized she needed air desperately. The stagnant air within the townhome was musty and stifling. Besides, she was done with the conversation for now. Done with every single person in the room. She needed to simply walk off this entire ordeal, otherwise it would consume her whole with its sharp talons and trenchant teeth. She needed air and space.

Just breathe. Evangaline sat on the stair, struggling to gather anything but the shallow breaths that were seeping past her tear-soaked visage.

One deep breath after the next, she heard Chloe echoing louder and clearer, her pink head nestled in the crook of Evangeline's neck as her arms snaked around her waist. "I'm sorry," Chloe whispered over and over again as hot tears streamed down her cheeks and onto Evangaline's shoulder, soaking into the fabric of her hoodie. Her arms wrapped tighter around Evangaline with each apology.

On any other day, Chloe's embrace would be welcomed. It would feel like the warmest of spring days filled with love and hope. But in this moment, all it felt like was a noose wrapping around her throat and constricting her lungs.

The feeling in her hands came back as she focused on breathing. The pins and needles gave way, allowing her to wiggle the digits in her lap. Flexing her fingers in and out, the pain of her wounded hand seeped back into her conscious thought, reminding her she was awake, and everything happening wasn't some fucked up dream.

She didn't know how long she sat there in the pained silence, but it was long enough for her mother to back away to the couch nestled in the living room to Evangaline's left and weep her tears of anguish. Stephen remained by the banister; his culpability plastered on his color depleted face. As Evangaline took in the room, she shook free of Chloe and made eye contact with Bastian.

He knelt before the first step, his eyes laser focused on her tear-lined ones. She stared into his green eyes, searching for all the answers to the many questions that swirled through her head. She found none. His face was perfectly unreadable.

Slowly, she stood, bringing everyone to attention. Never once did she break eye contact with Bastian, who rose along with her. Chloe tried to hold her hand, but Evangaline shrugged off the advancement before stepping down. One step at a time till she was staring up at Bastian and he was looking down his nose at her. A hair's breadth away, she could smell the coffee drying into his button-down alongside his signature scent.

She knew she should say something, knew in that moment she should confront her mother and father. Knew she should do something other than stand there quietly, but she could not escape the feeling of her whole life collapsing in on itself. She knew the best thing for her then was to leave and not release the tornado of denial swirling inside of her.

So that was what she did.

She walked past all of them and straight out into the fresh air without another word, where she could finally take a deep breath.

Chapter Seven

Her heeled boots blistered her feet with angry red welts, but she didn't care as she burrowed into the oversized sweatshirt that dwarfed her lithe frame.

Central Park was always her favorite place to walk or read. A perfect place to clear her head. The trees lining the bodies of water always made her feel small. Not in a bad way, but in a way that reassured her that there were always bigger problems in the world. There would always be something bigger than any of her small insignificant issues. However, today, not even the grandeur of the trees could dwarf her affairs.

Evangaline made her way to a small green iron gazebo shrouded in trees and shrubs called the Ladies Pavilion. It was her favorite spot in the park, her little oasis in the city. The view of the skyline just beyond the water held a beauty that nowhere else had. With the trees framing the distant towering skyscrapers, she sat on one of the rusted iron benches, tucking her knees into her chest in an effort to make herself as small as she could. Savoring the warmth of her own embrace, she let her mind ease to nothing.

Sad as it was, Evangaline thought when she made her way to leave the house that someone would stop her and beg her to stay, tell her she was being melodramatic, anything other than the silence that filled the repugnant air. She was fully prepared for a fight, and truthfully, she kind of wanted it. Evangaline wanted to scream and cry and smash the damn French press or another mug. But the fact that everyone let her leave annoyed her even more than being smacked in the face with the truth bomb of the century.

She sat in silence, letting her thoughts stew until they were nothing but small murmurs caged within the hollow crevices of her mind.

The breeze tangled in her hair and bees whizzed by on their way to pollinate the small white flowers that surrounded the gazebo. It was so peaceful. She could finally breathe fully, her head didn't feel as fuzzy as it was when she left, and her tears had cascaded their last rivulet down her blush hued cheeks.

Nature and the way the air was crisper, fresher, more alive, always seemed to help clear Evangaline's mind. No matter the time of day, being outside allowed her to fully breathe, to feel whole again. Or as whole as a struggling twenty-five-year-old sudden princess could feel.

Two hours passed in what felt like a matter of seconds. Her mind lost track of time staring at the clouds as they passed over the skyscrapers in a way that bore a resemblance to lovers, embracing one another in a familiar caress. It was a beautiful dance of nature and human ingenuity, and she was transfixed by it.

As she stared at the entwinement of cloud, steel, and glass, she didn't notice someone approach but rather felt the bench behind her groan under the pressure of another person.

The scent of bergamot and rose filled the air. Turning to face forward, swinging her legs off the bench and onto the floor, she faced Bastian with a sigh.

"Here," he said as he handed her a fresh cup of coffee, this time in a non-lethal blue and white to-go cup.

She took it with a grateful smile and leaned forward, bracing her forearms on her knees.

"Who exactly are you?" Her voice was quiet, weak almost. She hated it. Hated showing this man the anxiety and pain she was suffering with.

He paused for a moment, taking in their surroundings. "I did not lie to you, Princess. My name is Bastian. Bash if you want to piss me off like Chloe enjoys doing." He said with a bit of a grin.

She sat back, nodding slowly, biting down on her lip with uncertainty.

A moment passed before she sat up tall, composing herself better. She wasn't a coward. Shy sometimes, yes. Introverted, double yes. But a coward? No! Whatever her mother got her into, she would fix it. She would make things right.

"I gathered that, *Bash*." She grinned back at him, relaxing into the bench. "But who are you? To Celadonia. If I am a *princess*, and they sent *you* to get me, you must be important enough to be trusted and right now you, kind of, are the only one who hasn't lied to me. So, I'll ask again … *who are you?*"

Bastian studied her for a second before standing swiftly, jostling the creaking wood and iron bench.

"I'm Bastian. Hand of the King and General of His Majesties Royal Army…and friend of the princess," he said with a wink and mock bow at the waist.

She couldn't contain her grin, no matter how hard she tried, allowing a breathy giggle to come to the surface.

Matching her smirk, Bastian sat back down, his broad muscular legs stretching out before him, crossing at the ankles. And the casual arrogance that made this male completely frustrating returned with a renewed vigor.

"Bastian, I know we don't know each other, but you hear how crazy all this sounds, right?" Evangaline asked earnestly. No anger or fear, no judgment, just a simple question.

He faced her, nodding, letting the arrogant mask slip, "Being that you hit me with a ceramic mug, I'd say we're well acquainted. Nice hit, by the way … plus I just deemed us friends in my introduction, so no going back now. But I do, Princess. I see how crazy it sounds."

Friends. She made them both bleed. Is that what friends do? If so, he has a twisted friend group.

"How? I can't be a princess. I am not classy and regal. I am not good at public speaking. Hell, I could barely give a presentation on sharks in the fifth grade. I almost threw up right on Victoria Lane in the front row when she laughed at my poor attempt at saying cartilaginous. I can't be a princess to the fae. How could I be a princess?" She shook her head, playing nervously with the lid of the coffee cup.

"Well, your father, my king, King Darrin, met your mother and had one wicked night of passion and love m—"

"God no, Bash, Jesus. I know how I was conceived. Thank you. Holy shit. What I mean is, how did they meet? And why now with all *this*?" She waved a careless hand toward Bastian.

He stared back at her, that wicked smile on his face once more, crinkling the corners of his forest eyes. Softly, he released a chuckle that Evangaline was powerless to not reciprocate, no matter how much she was actively trying to stay stoic and focused on making sense of everything.

"That's not my story to tell, Princess." With a smirk, he snatched the coffee cup out of her hands, taking a big sip of it. *Asshole.*

Without missing a beat, he regained his brooding composure to stare at her. "Go back home, talk to your mom. Then get your things ready. We have till noon, Vitalis time, to be back in Celadonia, and I would greatly enjoy to not be wearing a coffee-stained shirt all day."

She didn't respond. Instead, Evangaline faced him and grabbed the coffee cup, downing a big burning gulp of it before taking a deep breath. Then, daintily like a pretty little princess, placed it back gently in his hands with her pinky raised, wishing with every fiber of her being the coffee was laced with alcohol. One more disappointment for the morning.

She smirked, taking in Bastian in his stained shirt, hair billowing in the soft breeze. "Ah yes, a great fae general, worried about a coffee stain. Trust me, in this city, there are a lot weirder things to see than an attractive man in a stained shirt."

"Attractive, huh?" He chided, raising a bushy brow.

Evangaline scoffed, nudging her shoulder into his rock-hard biceps. "Don't pretend you don't realize you are. Everything you do screams 'Look at me, I'm tall and hot' … You enjoy it. Admit it."

A gruff laugh escaped his pursed lips. "I can't say I *disparage* such attention. But coming from a woman in a skirt so tightly adhering to her curves, I highly doubt you disparage some attention either. Unfortunately for me, you are my princess, and it would be improper to allow you such attentions. But a bit of advice for the future ..." He leaned in close, his breath close enough to softly caress her ear. For a second, all the hairs on her neck stood at his proximity. "Wear something like that again and I might risk everything."

She turned to face him; their faces so close she could feel his breath tangling with hers. The mischievous grin splaying itself across his lips sent a sudden bout of heat straight to the areas she desperately did not want to be feeling anything currently. He stared into her eyes so intensely she wasn't sure in that moment what he was searching for. His bright eyes reminded her of the trees lining the water behind them and she soon got nervous studying them so closely. They carried a glimmer of something that sent a caress of weariness through her bones—one she could not ignore.

For a second, sitting there, she forgot everything that had happened in the past twenty-four hours. All the good, the bad, the ugly ...

"Shall we?" Bastian stood, extending an arm to her, snapping her out of her lustful stupor. Standing, she wrapped her arm around his, placing her hand gently on his forearm.

"Wait! How did you find me?"

He smirked. "Like this."

Without warning, Bastian thrust the coffee cup in the garbage bin to the side and with a flick of his fingers, made a quick circle in the air. It was just the smallest flick of his wrist, something any sane person wouldn't even notice, but something began to take form from his benign gesture.

A portal.

Before her, hues of blue opalescent colors sparkled in circular motions with flicks of holographic starbursts lining the rim. The portal filled the space of the green wrought iron pavilion, simmering its effervescent glow upon Evangaline's perplexed face. As it expanded, she saw a hazy image of her parents pacing studiously around their living room, arms crossed, waiting for her to return.

Evangaline, awestruck, turned to Bastian as the magic of the portal reflected onto her dumbstruck face. "I thought fae magic didn't work in

Vitalis?"

Bastian shrugged nonchalantly. "Perk of being Hand of the King."

And with that, he set her in motion, stepping through the rippling opaline current of the portal.

An effervescent glow of light glittered around her as she stepped into her parent's living room. Her hair fell haphazardly around her as a massive gust of wind echoed through the space as the portal closed behind them in a wink.

Bastian rested his hand on hers, leaning in for a delicate whisper into her ear. "You never forget your first time," he said, closing out the rather crude statement with a sly wink. *Cheeky bastard*, Evangaline thought as she gaped at his smug face.

Removing her hand from his, she fixed herself, suddenly feeling her nerves creep back under her skin. Righting her hair. Tugging her skirt down. Fixing the hood of her sweatshirt. Anything to keep her from being still in the presence of Bastian and her parents as they leered at her back behind glistening eyes.

"Sweetheart?" Felicity mumbled.

Evangaline turned, facing her mom in a slow and tense spin, forcing her eyes to meet her mother's after a beat. Clearly, in the hours she was walking off her troubles, her mom spent crying. Felicity's eyes were red and puffy, and her cheeks flushed a bright pink, nearly covering up the light dusting of freckles across the bridge of her nose. It was selfish of her, but Evangaline couldn't help but feel a tinge of satisfaction seeing her mother just as upset as she was. No doubt her eyes were just as red and just as puffy, a mirror to her mother's torment.

At any point in Evangaline's life, Felicity could have told her who her father was and why she brought Evangaline to Vitalis. Why she felt like this course of action was the best choice for them both, was beyond Evangaline. Perhaps just telling Evangaline that she was a goddamn princess would have saved a whole world of trouble!

Knowing who her biological father was wouldn't have changed anything. The knowledge of being a legitimate princess may have messed with her mind at some point, but at the end of the day Stephen would always be her dad. Right? *Yes. After all,* he was the man who raised her and loved her unconditionally. He was her true dad, and no one could change that, not even a fae king.

Evangaline would never have been angry with her mom, nor would she have cared much about who the man was who gave his seed to her creation. She never cared for what-ifs, preferring to focus on the present and what she had. The dreams that she dreamed at night remained just that, *dreams.* Her vision of the future was always hazy and made her slightly uncomfortable on a good day. So, instead of prophesying where her life could be, she preferred focusing on the now. And in the present Stephen was her father—not *King Darrin*—and the past life her mother lived did not dictate her very hazy, very convoluted future.

Despite it all, she was withheld information that was worth her knowledge, and for that she might never forgive her parents. Any of them, fae and human alike.

Evangaline crossed her arms and stood tall, pushing aside the nerves and fears that pounded against her chest through the steady beats of her heart. "I want the truth. All of it."

It took her mother a moment to work up her courage, but eventually, Felicity relented. Wringing her hands in her tan cashmere sweater, she nodded, "Of course. *Of course.* Yes. Um. I … please sit," her mother stammered. Her voice was soft and yet jagged.

Evangaline lowered herself onto the faded linen sofa nearest the windows. A slight glimpse of the street below offered a welcome and calming distraction with its sudden hum of activity.

Her mother and father took a hesitant seat on the chairs directly across from her. Felicity held Stephen's hands in her own, nervously chewing on the inside of her cheek.

Chloe stumbled her way out of the kitchen. With her hair now pulled up into a messy bun, eyes drooping low with exhaustion, and bags beneath her sinking eyes that deepened to an off shade of purple that rivaled only that of the eggplant-shaded lowlights woven into her hair—she looked thoroughly beat.

Evangaline gave her a small nod of a greeting that perked Chloe up slightly and within a second her petite feet padded over to Evangaline in soft cursory thuds. They embraced for a moment before Evangaline pulled away, eyebrows raised, her face stern and serious. "You are *so* not off the hook yet."

"I know." Chloe breathed out, her smile flipping upside down as she looked away and nodded.

Just breathe, Evangaline, it'll be okay. She took a deep breath as she ripped herself away from her best friend.

Giving a small nod to her mom and a glance upward to Bastian—now resting his hulking frame on the arm of the sofa—whose arms were folded tightly across his chest. A hardened façade of stoicism smeared across his face. Evangaline braced her hand inside Chloe's, shuddering in an eager breath, ready for the truth.

"I was younger than you are now when I met Darrin. At the time, I was working as an assistant for the Supreme President. I was straight out of college and knew someone who knew I needed a job at the time, and they recommended me. I had to get coffee and scan papers, nothing of importance, but it was a job—"

"Okay? How did you meet him if you were just getting coffee and filing papers?" Evangaline interjected anxiously.

"Patience, Princess," Bastian quietly murmured down to her.

Felicity flicked a fiery glare at Bastian, then refocused on the wringing hands in her lap. "I was given the task of setting up the Council meeting that year. As you know, Vitalis always hosts. I was twenty-three and completely out of my league, but I agreed to work it because I got a good bonus, and well, I needed money. When I got there, I met your father—"

"The king. He's not my father," Evangaline angrily interjected.

Stephen straightened. Evangaline could see the grateful smile tug at his lips despite his head being dipped toward Felicity's shoulder. He was Evangaline's father in every way that counted, and he needed to know that from Evangaline before this story dove deeper.

"Yes, the king. I'm sorry … I met him in passing and like any young, naïve, woman fell head over heels for him. I let go of all my inhibitions and ignored every logical thought that came through my head. He made beautiful promises and snuck me into Celadonia with him when the Council meeting was over a week later. I found out I was pregnant with you a year after that. His people didn't know that I was pregnant with his heir, but a few of his advisors knew and urged me to forego the pregnancy. 'A demi-fae child will destroy the realm,' they said … *repeatedly*. It didn't help that we weren't married. They thought me no more than the lover of the king and you would have been no more than his bastard child and his downfall. I was not a favorite amongst the court and lived in fear of them finding out about you. I had no idea what would happen to us both if they knew, but I feared it wouldn't be pretty."

Bastian stiffened at that notion. Her words hit him like one thousand barbs in the chest.

"That isn't at all true, Felicity. You had the love of the king and were therefore untouchable." He scoffed brashly.

Felicity's features grew harsh, her tone unforgiving. "Untouchable but not immune! Their words still reached me! I was untouchable by physical harm because of the king's threats to their lives, but the unforgiving words …" She shook her head, the pain in her features evident. "Their ill wishes on my life just because I wasn't fae … those were fervent … and words I would never allow my child to hear. *Never.* Darrin told me to let it go, the cruelness of the court. But words can do damage, Bastian. Sometimes words are deadlier than swords. You may have been a young man at the time, not of the rank I assume you hold now, but don't *pretend* you did not see the way I was treated by your people or your king. I had his love, but not his respect."

Her words found their mark, proving her point. Bastian could no longer look her in the eye, whether from anger or a deep seeded regret, Evangaline could not tell.

Evangaline noted the way Bastian grew withdrawn—for once not fighting back—and it thrust her brain into overdrive. She saw by the way the general shut up that maybe her mistrust and anger at her mom was misplaced. Sympathy took root in its stead. Evangaline began to see, with each word tumbling out of her mom's mouth, the courage that it took for her to protect herself and the child in her womb. It was … inspiring.

"So, you left," Evangaline murmured.

Her mom looked at her, really *looked* at her, smoothing out her features into a more emboldened and valiant visage. "Yes. I left. But to cross back to Vitalis, I needed to make a bargain—one that would protect me and you. It was the only way Darrin would let me leave. I was four months pregnant and could not risk anything happening to you. So, I made a deal, one that would ensure Darrin's people would not know you existed unless necessary. The magic that borders Vitalis and Celadonia is impenetrable unless granted access by the participating realm's leaders. I could not come and go freely, neither could Darrin. Since no trade occurs between our lands, I couldn't simply stow away on a ship and cross over either. I needed to seek permission. Darrin and I fought for what felt like hours. I wanted to go … needed to. We were done as a couple, and I needed you safe.

"Finally, he gave in, and we made the bargain. A bargain bound by magic I don't even fully understand. I was granted permission and safe passage to Vitalis and was able to raise you as I saw fit until you turned twenty-five, my age by the time of your birth. From there, your father, the king, if he had no other heirs and never married, could come claim you and crown you as his heir. He needed to secure his line, and I needed safe passage for my baby. I took the bargain. It seemed a fool's bargain on his part. Surely, he would find another woman and she would give him all the heirs he needed to secure the throne under his family's name, thus leaving you to your life here. I truly forgot about it as you grew up. I definitely didn't think he would send his *hounds* to get you the second you turned twenty-five." The barb to Bastian garnered a grunt of displeasure from the fae general and sent the room into a brief, tense silence.

Felicity finally spoke again once the tension simmered down, her voice breaking with pent-up tears. "I am so sorry, Evangaline. I never intended on surprising you like this. I never wanted you to be caught in the middle of anything. I did what I did—"

"For me. I know. *I know.*"

And she did. Evangaline was a lot of complex things, but she wasn't heartless or misunderstanding. She asked for the truth, and she got it. She knew as hard as it was for her to hear, her mom had to have struggled to relive her past, and to know that said past was bringing light to one of her biggest fears—losing a child—Evangaline wasn't going to hold the omission against her.

An omission that lasted twenty-five years. Evangaline could not even consider keeping a secret that long.

A feeling nestled into her gut that told her what she had to do and knew it would break her mom's heart, but it was the right thing. Twenty-five years of hoping Evangaline wouldn't be held to the bargain she made would be shattered with the next four words uttered out of Evangaline's mouth.

"I'll go with you," Evangaline said, her voice breaking as Felicity's sobs broke out.

Bastian dropped his arms and faced Evangaline. He looked surprisingly … surprised. The general seemed to expect more of a fight, but unfortunately for him, Evangaline didn't have any left in her. She was still tired from the night before and mentally exhausted from the revelation of the morning, and simply did not want to battle what seemed inevitable. She just wanted to shower and sleep for about a week and then, maybe then, would she give Bastian the fight he seemed to long for.

Evangaline looked at him and laced her next words with as much courage as she could in an attempt to sound authoritative. "You said we have till noon. I might need longer than that to get myself together."

"I'm afraid that isn't possible, Princess. The bargain between your parents starts doling out punishments at noon if it isn't fulfilled. Your mother will be the one collected on if she doesn't follow through on her end and a bargain this large, there's no telling what that payment will be if she doesn't meet her end of the deal. We must leave before noon and have you on Celadonian soil before the clock hits twelve. Magic this grand is fickle and granted the bargain they made, I wouldn't tempt the fates and challenge it."

With a heavy sigh and a tilt of the head, Evangaline stood facing him. "Well, don't I feel like Cinderella." Sarcasm sliced through her words with razor-sharp edges. "I guess I don't have a choice then. I'll be back down before noon, so get the carriage ready, Fairy Godmother. Oh, but just so you know, for future reference, I refuse to ride in a pumpkin." She sarcastically smirked at Bastian, "What should I bring?"

Felicity snickered into the hollows of Stephen's neck while Chloe giggled, all the while rolling her eyes with her hands firmly planted on her muscled yet petite hips.

Bastian stood sliding his hands into his pockets with the air of an unhindered man. His brows dipped low, brushing his dark eyelashes. His hair crested his elevated cheekbones and square jaw like a frame. If every fae male was this attractive, Evangaline was sure to be in trouble and could see why her mom fell hard and fast for the king of these creatures. He smiled at her, a little mischief in his eyes, as if sensing her thoughts. "Your wardrobe is already full, and your room is ready for you, so only important things, things that matter to you, stuff that you can carry."

She nodded and made her way toward the stairs when she faced her mom again. A silent stream of self-hatred milled about the silent sobs that filled Felicity's wary face.

"Mom, it's okay. I don't blame you. I'm a little pissed you didn't tell me sooner, but I'll make you proud. I'll fix this and I'll be back before you know it." She smiled at her mom, hoping Felicity could see just how grateful she was for all the years she gave Evangaline a normal life. Even if this surprise made for the shittiest birthday present ever.

In a flash, Felicity shot off the couch like a bullet from a gun, crashing into Evangaline. The two become an entangled blubbering mess in the matter of a few seconds.

"I love you, baby girl."

"I love you too, Mama."

Chapter Eight

With her small tote in hand, Evangaline made her way down the stairs, cherishing the touch of the dated wood banister. This home wasn't the one she grew up in, so leaving the house itself was easy. Her family, however, leaving them was a blow directly to her heart that she wasn't sure she could ever recover from. Everything remained so uncertain. The future she seldom liked to think about waited for her at the bottom of the stairs with no word of when she would return to her family or *if* she ever returned to them at all.

For the first time in a year, she was happy she lived with her parents. At least she would be able to hug them goodbye. She didn't know if she would be gone and living with the fae for one week or twenty-five more years of her life. But Evangaline knew magic was real, and she knew nothing about it. She knew nothing of magical bargains or the punishments they doled out should someone not uphold their end of one, and frankly, she did not want to find out about her mom's life. Evangaline needed to go with Chloe and Bastian and, even more so, she needed to cherish the next few minutes with her mom and dad.

"I didn't want to text all this shit to Katherine and Miles, so I, um, I wrote them these." She removed two bright red envelopes decorated with stars and hearts and in the center, her siblings' names were written in a delicate scrollwork. "I know they'll worry. It is too much of a story to make it out of here by noon—especially with as much as Katherine can talk—but please tell them the truth. I put as much as I could in here, but they need to hear the truth from you, Mom."

With a nod from Felicity, Evangaline crossed the room to her mom and handed her the envelopes. "They're old Christmas cards … it was all I could find." Felicity smiled shakily through her tears at Evangaline and latched her daughter into a tight embrace before the gates gave way and the sobs leaked out in a torrential downpour.

After a few moments, Stephen's warm arms encircled both women. The sobs echoed through the quiet room as Stephen squeezed tighter around his two girls until Evangaline squeaked out the last breath of air in her lungs.

Finally, they separated enough for Felicity to hold on to Evangaline's arms, her thumb gently caressing small circles around the worn in leather of Evangaline's jacket.

Stephen delicately draped his arm around Evangaline's shoulders, pulling her into his side and turning them away from Bastian and Chloe, who waited in the living room. "Do me a favor, Bug," A term of endearment Evangaline hadn't heard since she was a little girl.

She perked up at the word. *Bug.* She remembered being a mortified middle schooler when he called her Bug in front of her class on career day. After many taunts and verbal assaults from her relentless school bullies, she freaked out on the car ride home and begged him to never call her that again. He obliged.

As the word spilled from his mouth now, she wished she had never asked him to stop. Unable to choke down her ugly cries, she rushed into his arms once more, hugging tightly onto his waist like she did when he used to call her Bug. She hoped it wouldn't be the last embrace with him, the last time he called her that nickname, but with the way the realms operated, she feared it may very well be.

"Be courageous, Bug. Be brave. Be strong. Be bold. Be my fierce little bug! Okay?" he whispered into the top of her head.

She nodded as her tears stained his soft, light blue sweater. Letting his words sink in and grab hold of her heart.

Stephen pulled away enough to hold her face and gaze into her eyes. His tears cascaded in similar patterns to her own, fogging up his thick tan plastic-framed glasses.

With the last bit of strength coursing through her trembling body, Evangaline pulled free of Stephen's embrace and faced Bastian and Chloe. If she stayed one second longer holding onto her parents, she might not go with the fae at all. She might let her fear win.

Chloe stood no longer wearing her plunging silver dress, her hair no longer was a mess of floppy pink waves pulled up atop her head. Instead, she stood proud and tall, clad in a set of copper armor with a crest emblazoned on her chest that was hard to miss. A sword thrust through a heart encircled by a rose with thorny tendrils snaking its way down the hilt and blade of the sword and constricting the heart in a tight grasp. It was beautiful and terrifying at the same time.

Chloe's hair now sat delicately braided into a knot on top of her head, dozens of braids looped together, weaving a beautiful nest on her head.

A long sword draped down the center of her back. Resting atop the sword was a sparkling ruby gem nestled snuggly into the hilt. Amber shadows cast wherever the light refracted through the gemstone on Chloe's back.

As she stared in awe at Chloe, Evangaline finally saw the one aspect that separated her and the woman she thought was her best friend—Chloe's slightly pointed fae ears. Not at all harsh points like old Earth fables made up. They were just a delicate little point tapering right there at the top, like the gods just pinched her ears slightly. It was subtle but noticeable in comparison to Evangaline's rounded ears.

"Badass," Evangaline muttered through her sniffles and residual tears. Wiping her hand across her cheeks to eradicate the moisture taking residence on her skin.

Chloe broke her stoic visage and revealed a small smile as she eased toward Evangaline.

"How have you hidden your ears all this time?" Evangaline asked, touching the delicate point of her right ear.

"They were glamoured before I came here. Bash un-glamoured me when he un-glamoured himself. You ready?" Chloe's voice was tender but held a hint of grit that Evangaline had never heard before. *Authoritative. Badass.*

Cautiously, Evangaline peeked around Chloe and up at Bastian. His deep brown hair was now pulled up into a bun on his head. His own slightly pointed ears were now fully visible. His shirt, surprisingly, was void of any coffee stains. Squinting, Evangaline eyed him suspiciously.

"Didn't want to wear a stained shirt all day, huh?" She smirked at the man who called himself Hand of the King and General, raising a teasing brow.

"Oh, it is still very much stained. I glamoured it to appear clean. I can't look bad walking into the palace with the crown princess now, could I?" His lips ticked into a smile with a wink.

Evangaline huffed a breath. "If using me as an excuse helps you sleep better at night, go right ahead. But let's not pretend it wasn't your own ego guiding your actions."

Still staring at Evangaline, Bastian raised his hand once more and a portal formed. The beauty of it took Evangaline's breath away *again.* There's no way she will ever get used to seeing real magic like this.

Once the visual of a lush green landscape hazily formed through the iridescent opening, Chloe released Evangaline's hand. With sure strides, she eagerly stepped through the portal nodding at Felicity and Stephen as she disappeared in a cacophony of shimmering iridescent sparkles.

Bastian leaned forward and once more offered his elbow to Evangaline in a show of gentlemanly performance.

Hesitantly, she placed her hand in the crook of his arm. With a glance and smile at her parents, she whispered to them, "I'll be okay." She might have spoken the words aloud to her parents, but in reality, she needed to tell it to herself. She was terrified. Anxious. Excited. This was life altering, and she was too deep in it to turn back now.

Evangaline and Bastian took a couple steps towards the portal when Bastian pressed his mouth to Evangaline's ear, startling her from her cloudy inner thoughts. "I hope you brought that skirt, Princess."

She tilted her head to the side to peer up at his face incredulously. His taunting grin crinkled the corners of his eyes. Evangaline typically could abide by her stubbornness and strong will, but this male's shameless flirting broke right through her wall of bricks and mortar and practically forced a smile onto her face with an iron grip.

"Didn't fit in the bag …" she said with a shrug of her shoulders.

Bastian twisted his lips in a playful pout. "Damn. Never hated a bag more."

The air was crisp but not cold. Just had a refreshing bite to it that Evangaline soaked in with every deep inhalation she sucked in.

The sky above was a shimmering sunset of oranges and pinks. They might have been one planet converged, but the sky in Celadonia was somehow more beautiful than the skies in Vitalis. The clouds hovered overhead as though they were painted to stay in those exact places, their fluffy folds shadowed in the barest hint of violet. The grass beneath her leather combat boots seemed to swallow the dew that crested on each vibrant blade of green. Small yellow and pink flowers scattered on the plain before her, sprinkling the meadow in wondrous polka dots of golden and rose swells.

It was exactly how she pictured it, and somehow more.

Stuck in a state of awe, Evangaline released Bastian and made a small circle to take in the beauty of Celadonia.

To their backs was the edge of a forest. While shaded, the trees were a type of white bark bespeckled with little brown knots. They were so much like the spindly birch trees in Vitalis, except they were easily triple the size, if not bigger. As she studied the forest, she quickly felt the hum of the magic that surrounded her. The canopy of the trees sparkled with an enchantment that cycled through the seasons. From green to yellow to red and back to green in a slow fading rotation. It held the illusion that the leaves themselves were stuck in a slow cycle of transitioning through fall, spring, and summer every couple seconds, avoiding the death that would befall a normal tree in winter.

As Evangaline marveled, she felt a subtle ping in her chest, the same one she felt gazing upon the Velum with Chloe the night before. The gentle caress of a sharp talon right down the center of her sternum. As she rubbed her hand over the ache, movement in the distance of the trees caught her attention, distracting her from the stinging echo in her chest.

A breeze lightly ruffled its way through the trees, picking up velocity as it grew closer and closer, almost as though it were sentient and on the hunt. Directly for her, it flew. The rest of the trees abided by their slow movements and soft blinks, seeming not to mind the sudden gust of wind barreling forward.

Soon the breeze was upon Evangaline, and while she should have been scared, she felt nothing but a familiarity with the wind that charged at her being. It whistled through her hair and across her cheeks with a gentle caress that made her giggle. She came to note it was not a breeze at all—it was some form of wind creature. She couldn't see it, but its essence enveloped her every being. But before she knew it, the creature—with one last stroke to her cheek—flew back into the trees in the direction it came from, rustling the leaves in a way that created the most calming and sweet song in its wake.

"The elemental goddess likes you …" Bastian said, his eyes squinted in disbelief at Evangaline. "Interesting."

Those same eyes seemed to glow a brighter shade of green under the Celadonian sun despite their half-mast pursual of her face. Evangaline wondered if she looked any different or if she was still the suburban mom Chloe teased her about being.

"You going to stand there gawking all day? Let's go! I'm hungry!" Chloe yelled from up ahead. Her armor glinted rays of golden sun in Evangaline's eyes.

It was then, in that moment, that she noticed it, the palace in the distance. Even from their position at the forest's edge, it sparkled and glowed in the afternoon light like a diamond. A creation of white stone, possibly a type of marble if Evangaline learned anything from her parent's careers in architecture and design. A roof that shone the same bright refractions as Chloe's armor made it hard to miss.

Eager to see it up close, Evangaline secured her tote bag over her shoulder and began her trek to the impressive palace in the distance. Surprisingly, a smile cheated up the corners of her lips.

The entire palace could be described in one word—*Extravagant*. The way the sparkling fractals within the marble caught the light like tiny diamonds only added to the palace's extravagant elegance.

Carved into the walls and pillars around the front doors of the palace, just beyond the courtyard, were perfectly honed roses intertwining themselves with one another. The roses cascaded up and around an anatomical honed heart directly above the center of the massive copper doors—that of which—perfectly matched the tiles lining the elaborate roofline and all the many spires and eves of the palace.

It was more beautiful than she could have imagined. The closer she got, the more she really did feel like Cinderella. This place was too grand and opulent for her austere being. A game of tug-of-war engaged her mind as she took in the palace of the Supreme King of Celadonia. Should she thank her fairy godmother or wring the bitch's neck for sending her into a palace in combat boots and not glass slippers?

Not a single expense was spared on constructing the royal abode, that she knew for a fact, and she hadn't even seen the inside yet.

On either side of the massive doors stood two guards, dressed in the same regalia as Chloe. The only difference was the helmets resting on their heads. The same lustrous copper metal lined their chest plates and coverings. Yet the helmets sitting atop their heads were outfitted with a Mohawk of glittering ruby spikes that matched the ruby gemstones glistening in the pommels of their swords.

Chloe strode through the massive doors, as though it was *her* palace, and *she* was the hidden princess. Yet, again, she strode into their favorite coffee shop as though she owned that place too, so Evangaline wasn't all that surprised at her friend's fearless cadence through the palace doors. Chloe commanded every room she set foot in, something Evangaline always admired and yearned to emulate. *Maybe one day.*

As Bastian and Evangaline drew closer to the doors, the guards straightened and clicked their hands and feet tightly to their sides, bowing at the waist. The movement made Evangaline jump a little at the sound of their armor clanking in a loud *thwack* that reverberated through the courtyard.

"Do they know who I am?" she whispered, leaning into Bastian.

"No. The king has only informed me, Chloe, and Atlas—who you shall meet later—of your presence. For some time, you shall only be considered a guest of the palace, until you and the king have come to an understanding of your place here. You will learn the people are strong in their emotions and Darrin wants to do good by you and them both."

"… Don't pretend you did not see the way I was treated by your people or your King …"

Her mom's words echoed through her head as Bastian's words tapered to nothing. If the people of Celadonia weren't thrilled by her mom being brought to their land twenty-five years ago, they sure as hell will not be thrilled about Evangaline showing up after twenty-five years with a smile and her rounded ears screaming, *"Hey! I'm your princess! Bow down to me!"*

Not like those words or their flippant excitement would ever leave her lips. Nevertheless, the unveiling of her newfound title was a scary thought.

She knew little of the fae, but knew as a human she was at a serious disadvantage. She had no magic, no power, no enhanced strength, or senses, and, well, everything else that made the fae far superior that the humans weren't privy to. Hell, she was just caressed by an anthropomorphic gust of wind after stepping out of a portal she didn't know could be conjured out of thin air. What else was she not prepared for?

Be courageous. Her dad's words echoed in her head, quieting all the frantic thoughts that swirled in the dark recesses of her mind.

As she and Bastian stepped through the hammered copper doors into the foyer of the palace, Evangaline was taken aback. Her feet stopped of their own accord on the polished marble floors. And her eyes struggled to take in every detail of the palace around her.

Two carved stone glittering staircases swung from either side of the great hall. Both stairs were caressed with delicate ropes of pink and red roses lining the railings. How the flowers bloomed inside and stayed alive was beyond her, but she had no doubt magic was involved.

A massive chandelier hung from the ceiling that took her breath away. Delicate pink and purple blown glass flowers with green leaves covered the entirety of the light fixture. Correlating sconces lined the many walls that towered over her. The flowers having been blown into a state of blooming to cup a starburst of light as the glass leaves crept down the wall in a spiral. The walls glimmered and shined as servants and courtiers alike walked through the halls, occasionally stopping to gawk at Evangaline and Bastian with various looks of bewilderment.

Straight ahead, under a bridgeway connecting the two staircases, stood two gargantuan copper doors forged with the same heart and rose crest that was above the front door.

"The throne room." Bastian leaned in, following her gaze. "Come, I'll show you to your rooms."

"My rooms?"

Bastian did nothing but smirk and motion with an extended hand to the right staircase. Chloe was already waiting halfway up, her body slumped over the railing, watching Evangaline gaze slack-jawed at the more than impressive foyer.

They wound through the dusk lit halls at a steady pace, letting Evangaline peer into any room she could to investigate what was kept inside. A couple studies, a bedroom being cleaned by a maid in a dusty rose-colored gown, and what looked to be a meeting room of sorts furnished with a large painted table at the center, were all she could see while attempting to follow in Bastian's gait.

Occasionally, a courtier would pass and glare at Evangaline's black jeans, leather jacket, and white tank top as though they held the germs of a plague. She was a stark contrast to their sparkling gowns and decadent jewels.

Evangaline glanced down at her very mortal clothes, pulling her jacket closed in an attempt to close herself off from the leering eyes gazing upon her. As though that simple gesture would thrust an invisibility cloak over her, making it so no one would see her at all. Her very being within the walls of such an extraordinary palace felt wrong, especially with the few unwanted leers she received.

"Be brave, Bug." Her dad's voice echoed through her head at that exact moment.

As though he felt her sudden nerves, Bastian placed a tender hand on her back, his thumb making small reassuring strokes. His presence seemed to not only calm her, but scare away any other onlookers. Guards and maids alike curtseyed and bowed to him, being mindful to keep their eyeline directly at the floor as the three passed.

Quietly, Bastian leaned into Evangaline. "Just up here, to the right."

Evangaline nodded, letting him guide her.

After a moment, she found herself turning to a hallway lined with windows of stained glass. Possibly the most beautiful hallway she'd ever seen. Each pane detailed what appeared to be a union between a man and a woman. A love story.

The middle pane depicted a woman with blonde hair with a mighty sword strapped around her waist, her head topped with a sparkling silver crown. Her emerald green gown cascaded down a dais as she faced a man clad in a bright blue tunic. His hair was black with blue streaks in it. Their hands entwined within one another in a loving embrace.

The pane on the left of the couple depicted the image of a forest with animals cresting through the tree line. While the pane to the right of the man was shaded in dark purples and blues with the image of a cresting wave crashing on a foreign, dark coast during a storm. Where their hands were gathered, a bright white light flared up in strips of opalescent glass radiating upward toward the top of the pane, bathing the hallway in a rainbow of colors.

Its beauty transfixed Evangaline as she took in every cut piece of glass ever so delicately placed within the metal lined panes. All the while, Bastian continued his soft strokes with his thumb.

"Who are they?" she murmured to Bastian, unable to tear her eyes away from the glass, her attention drawn to the couple in a way she had never felt before. It was an odd feeling looking at the two ethereal fae upon their stained-glass dais. Like they were almost calling to her, begging her to ask the question.

It was Chloe who turned to take in the stained-glass masterpiece and answered. "Tuatha and Milesian. Their union ended the war of their peoples. Our kind. We used to be segregated, before the Convergence, that is, they each ruled their own realms. The land was divided right down the middle, separated by the rivers that led to the sea. Battles constantly erupted and diplomacy with the lords and ladies didn't end the war like many hoped. So, Queen Tuatha and King Milesian arranged a secret meeting to attempt peace talks. When they met on the border *where the forest meets the sea,* or so the legends say, they found they were fated. The truest form of mates. Their connection formed an alliance between the lands and two became one. *Literally,* Celadonia was born, and our peoples became one big happy family!"

Bastian moved past both girls during the story. The clearing of his throat drew Evangaline's thoughts from the couple in the stained glass. Swinging open the lone wooden door at the end of the hall, he revealed a small vestibule which provided all the same luxuries as the main foyer of the palace, just smaller.

She followed Bastian to the left into a massive living room and dining area. French doors lined the right side of the room, with a massive balcony waiting just beyond them. The floor to ceiling windows on the left side gazed out over what appeared to be a garden. Fae courtiers in glistening gowns of various jewel toned colors meandered the grounds talking and laughing in the dying sunlight of the beautiful day.

The room itself was something out of a dream. A marble fireplace on the far end of the room was flanked by two bookcases filled with various leather-bound books.

A mirror hung above the mantel that reflected her image at her—she looked so out of place it wasn't even funny.

It all was decorated in various shades of green. Her favorite color. *Did the king know that?* She asked herself before taking in the rest of the space with awe lining her eyes. Emerald green velvet drapes matched the settee and high-backed chairs in the living room.

A glistening table that could seat easily eight shimmered as though it was cut from a diamond itself. A golden chandelier was strung above the table, dripping in what Evangaline only could hope to be diamonds and emeralds. Ostentatious wasn't even a suitable word to describe the luxuriousness of the apartment Bastian called her "rooms."

Bastian nodded to Chloe and proceeded to make his way out of the room. All the while Evangaline took in every detail, her mouth trailing behind her on the wooden floor.

"I will leave you to get comfortable. Your bedroom is just on the other side, with the washroom. If there is anything you need, let Chloe know. I will be back when your—*the king*—wishes to meet with you. Until then, welcome home Princess." He bowed to her at the waist, but not in a mocking fashion this time. His movement was graceful and dignified. Once he straightened, he made his way to the door.

Chloe cut him off with a huff. "Where's my bow, asshole?"

Bastian stopped, his shoulders growing rigid. Evangaline tensed, waiting for another barbarian style eruption. Waiting for him to grow angry, breaking yet another door.

He surprised her though by throwing his head back, exhaling a laugh that echoed through the room. With an exaggerated motion, he bent at the waist and bowed to Chloe, his laugh shaking his shoulders as he made his way back upright. "Milady" he chastised.

Chloe echoed his laughter and punched him square in the shoulder with all her small but mighty force.

"Nice to have you back, Chloe." He pretended to wince at her punch. Then pushed her out of the way with one hand as he swung open the door, shaking his head. His laughter tapered off as he made his way into the hall once more, regaining the stoic impression of a mighty fae general as he closed the door behind him.

Chapter Nine

Sitting tucked into the cloud like folds of the light pink duvet upon the massive dark wood four-poster bed that was apparently all hers, Evangaline was still—after hours of sitting—perplexed at the grandeur of the room she sat in. *Her room.* Her *rooms*, rather, because she was now a fancy member of a royal family who could say pretentious things like that.

Hours ago, she was coming home from a drunken night with her best friend, hungover and tired. Now, like a fever dream, she sat snuggled up in the realm of the fae, apparently their princess, with that same best friend and a lot less confidence in herself than she did stumbling through the streets of the city. Still, however, very tired. At least some things are consistent from realm to realm.

The sun set an hour or so ago and took Chloe with it. The two girls sat silently while a stout and brash healer woman named Madame Chevalier tended to Evangaline's hand and fed her a tonic to help with the headache she was nursing thanks to her birthday celebration. Despite Evangaline never admitting her headache was due to a wild night of drinking, the healer seemed to know from the raised eyebrow and smirk on her rosy face.

The bright warm light that flowed from the healer's palms and seeped into Evangaline's cut hand was nothing short of awe-inspiring. The essence of the light was warm and gentle and tingled in the same way a person would feel when someone scratches their head. Comforting and soothing pulses of warmth that made tingles run down one's spine. If it went any longer, she might have fallen asleep. However, next thing Evangaline knew, her hand was healed, and the healer was packing her things. Not a scratch or scar was in sight. And then, just as quickly as she came, the Madame was gone without a backward glance.

Chloe left soon after the healer finished, eager to see her family and gather her orders from Bastian and the king. Evangaline simply nodded and wandered about the expansive room in the silence.

The staggering quiet of the space allowed her head to swirl with nervous thoughts. Questions and concerns about her place in the world, in the realm of the fae, more specifically.

She struggled to find her place at home in Vitalis and made peace with the fact that she might be okay being a ghost of a person. Soundlessly milling about her life until the day the dark came to claim her and then she could finally rest her weary mind.

It was a morbid thought, but it started to seem like a wonderful idea as the past year progressed. Clinging to the shadows of her consciousness, she could not help but feel a sense of longing for something greater. But the body and soul she was born into just could not be arsed to allow her to be the bold and fearless woman she read about in books and longed so much to be.

So, she made peace with the idea of being the silent observer.

But now, *this*. This palace and position guaranteed that there was no way that former life would take root. No longer could she sit silently by and watch people live while she clung to the background. She had to muster the courage to be exactly what Stephen told her to be. Courageous. Bold. Strong. Brave. Fierce. She at least had to try until the day she could go back to Vitalis and continue her phantom walk through life—if that life was still in the cards.

So much remained uncertain.

After Chloe left, a handmaid in a rose-colored gown and white apron came in and drew her a bath. Wren was her name. She was a black-haired young woman with freckles across her button nose. She appeared younger than Evangaline. However, with the immortal life span of the fae, she very well could have been triple Evangaline's age if not older, and Evangaline did not find it in herself to ask, for it seemed incredibly rude. After all, the young fae woman was kind and didn't sneer at Evangaline's bowed ears or heritage. Never once did she do anything other than joke about how excited she was to play with Evangaline's long brown hair.

"With length like that, I'll be able to braid and twist your hair into the most beautiful designs, if you will only allow me. Just ring for me before dinner and I shall do you all up!" Wren excitedly bubbled as Evangaline swayed on her feet anxiously.

When Evangaline asked for dinner to be brought to her room, Wren's smile faltered but she didn't back down, simply stating, "Tomorrow then!" Evangaline nodded with a half-smile, unaware if she would ever join the court for dinner. The thought sounded a bit daunting.

The handmaiden flipped the handles on the wall of the bathroom with a smile, not giving Evangaline a choice if she wanted to bathe or not. With a gurgle, water started filling the tub as Wren added all sorts of oils and bubbles that showered the room with both citrus and floral, calming scents.

Well, she claimed it to be a bath, but it was in truth a hot tub ... or a small pool. It was copper and nestled in an alcove of the bathroom, surrounded by windows. Evangaline was more of a shower girl, but being that the fae—it appeared—were behind technologically, the massive, elaborate tub would have to soothe her weary bones.

If she thought for a second that her new bedroom was over the top, it had nothing on the bathroom. A rose mosaic was even inlaid into the floor of the bathroom just before the white and gold sinks.

Evangaline's rough edges and dullness stuck out within the eccentric room surrounding her. But some part of her loved being showered in the room's glamorousness. It was a vacation she paid for, not in money, but in her very presence.

After about an hour of soaking in the tub, around the time her fingers pruned with moisture, and after allowing herself to relax into the bubbles that smelled of gardenia and lavender, she donned a silk green robe Wren had laid out for her.

Then she figured it was time to un-pack the meager canvas tote she packed.

Evangaline brought only a couple things with her, all of which reminded her of her family and the life she had left behind in Vitalis.

She packed away a small makeup case with her favorite cosmetic products, a couple of brushes, eyeliner, mascara, and her favorite shimmery eyeshadow. An irrelevant thing, in truth. But she didn't know if the fae had makeup and she only wanted to make the best impression she could … vanity aside. They did have makeup, however, making her small bag futile and irrelevant. Neat rows on the vanity showcased dozens of loose metallic powders, glitters, charcoals, and a few other makeup-like items … all of which Evangaline would definitely need Chloe or Wren's help to apply.

A photo album was the second and last of her belongings from home. She made it a couple of years ago and filled it with memories of her childhood and family. It was no wider than her shoe, but as thick as an apple. Filled to the brim with polaroid pictures from decades of her life. Some were of her and Chloe at a tiki bar in uptown New York that she recently added. Images of Katherine, her, and Miles dancing in a circle on Katherine's wedding day, a disco ball glistening overhead, oozed from the white pages. Dozens of photos Miles had taken with one of his favorite old grainy cameras of various Christmases and Thanksgivings, graduations and birthdays. Even photos of her and her ex-fiancé were stuffed into the book. In hindsight, those she should have been burned, but Evangaline couldn't find it in herself to remove them from the album … so there they sat … nestled between the pages of memories. Memories of a world out of her reach now, of a life she once dreaded living.

She tucked the photo album neatly in the single drawer of the gilded nightstand, barely getting the drawer to close over the hefty pages of the memory book, before she wandered the room once more.

For a bit, she gazed over the people walking within the exquisite gardens. She would have to have Chloe or Bastian take her down there one day. They looked so serene and peaceful and reminded her slightly of her pavilion in the park.

Even through the closed window, she felt as though she could smell the scent of the many roses and flowers filling her nostrils. Yet again, that might have been all the oils Wren put in her bath lingering in the air.

With no tv or radio in Celadonia, she decided a book would be the next best thing to take her mind off everything. It always worked in the past. Within the pages of a good book, she became whomever she wanted to be and currently she longed for something to overwhelm her brain with anything other than the many questions that were building up her anxiety.

She barely scanned the shelves before a title caught her eye, sending a small flutter deep in her stomach. Without hesitating, she extended her hand, reaching for the thick dark blue leather-bound book like it was begging to be read.

"A Kingdom of Shadows," she whispered, the title on the spine of the book.

The leather on the book was frayed on the edges and cracked along the binding, showing many years of use. The lettering sparkled in a bright silver embossment that was crackled in some areas, indicating this tome was indeed old.

On the cover was a foil embossed image of a dagger with the phases of the moon inlaid on the blade. A crown made up of stars encircled the hilt as though it was placed there in a hurry—askew and drooping.

She took the book, cloaked in curiosity, and made her way back to her bedroom. Nestling into the massive bed once more, Evangaline tucked her knees to her chest while placing the book on her thighs. As she opened the cover, it creaked like a door needing oil. It may have been used once, but clearly not in a long time. Yet as she opened it, she could not ignore the thudding of her heart in her chest. Something about this book felt right. It called to her singing a siren's song, luring her into the calming sea of its cream hued pages.

Nestled into the mountainside, a prince sits atop a throne crafted by darkness itself.

Just a few simple words and Evangaline could not help but feel like this was a story she was meant to read. Like it was important somehow.

The crown atop his head glistens from the light stolen from the stars themselves …

"Knock. Knock."

Chloe peered through the doorway to the bedroom, startling Evangaline enough to slam the book shut on her hand.

"Ow!" Evangaline shook her crushed hand out of the book. "Yeah?"

Chloe walked into the room apprehensively. Her armor was now gone and replaced instead with a simple pale pink chiffon gown.

Evangaline motioned for her to sit on the bed by patting the spot beside her while setting the book on her nightstand.

Chloe's pink chiffon skirt flowed around her ankles as she glided into the room and jumped like a kid up onto the bed. Not at all caring that she bore a resemblance to a fairytale princess in her own right.

"I always wondered what this room looked like. I tried to sneak in once as a kid, but a maid caught me and kicked me out before I got to the door," she said, laying back onto the fluffy pillows.

Evangaline, with a sweep of her arms and crinkle of her nose, motioned around the room and then laid back onto the pillows on her side to face Chloe.

She took in the contentment on her friend's face. She never considered—in the past few hours—that Chloe left her family to go protect Evangaline. She too was thrust into a world away from all she knew, and yet she always smiled.

"Do you hate me?" Evangaline whispered timidly.

Chloe sat up, staring down at Evangaline, eyebrows furrowed. "What? Why would I hate you?"

"Well, I took you away from your family and friends. *Your home.*" Evangaline sat up, crossing her legs, hands falling into her lap. She could not face Chloe, for the fear of Chloe truly hating her was too much to bear. The thought of her best friend leaving her was too much. She lost her family and home realm; all she had left was Chloe. The thought sent a tremble of fright through Evangaline's body.

Chloe cleared her throat and took the tone of a soldier, firm and adamant. "Ok. Let's settle one thing. Get this shit out of the way now! You did nothing wrong. No, I don't hate you. I could never hate you. I am a commander in the King's Royal Army, therefore I am sworn to the king and, in turn, sworn to you by law and oath. My duty sent me to Vitalis to watch over you and I would never take back my choice to go. Ever."

Chloe grabbed Evangaline's hands in her own, holding tight enough for Evangaline to peer into her piercing hazel eyes. "I was lucky enough that you trusted me with your friendship before you knew about any of this. I am still lucky to have you in my life, whether that is as my best friend or my princess. Or both. I don't give two shits, so long as you and I are together, I don't care. I have never, *never*, had a best friend like you! Plus, if one of us should be hated, it's me. You have every right to hate me. I didn't tell you the truth and I know how much you value that. I just knew it wasn't my truth to bear. Besides, it was I who practically stole you from *your home*."

A single tear streamed from Evangaline's blue-green eyes. "I chose to go, Chlo."

"Well, so did I. But unlike me, your hand was forced, Evie." Chloe's voice was unwavering in its stern tone.

"Yeah but—"

"But Bash *deserved* to be knocked out for just showing up like he did! He had no right. That wasn't the plan, and he knows it. King Darrin has already reamed him up the ass for how he acted, thanks to yours truly for getting her report in first." She chuckled at Chloe's cunning. "Your parents, all of them, deserve to be punished for their omissions, and you should not feel guilt for the burdens any of us have taken on. You didn't choose this, Evie."

Her single tear multiplied with every word spoken from Chloe's pink lips. Her words finally allowed Evangaline to make peace with the complex feelings of guilt and deceit. She forgave her mom before she left because she knew how hard things must have been for her. She forgave Stephen because it wasn't his story to tell, no different from Chloe. But she still harbored so many complex feelings. Grief for the life she lost in Vitalis. Nerves for the future that awaits her in Celadonia. Excitement for the new adventures she would get to have. Curiosity to know more about this land and her lineage. And about thirty other emotions she could not exactly pinpoint or latch onto.

All her many feelings, however, swirled around, mixing into the saltiness of the tears she allowed herself to cry.

Catching a lone tear on her finger, Chloe leaned in, kissing Evangaline on the forehead and wrapping her in her arms. Comforting her and holding her, allowing Evangaline to sit and cry for a good while until she simply had no more moisture left in her eyes to shed.

"A commander in an army? You've been a fucking badass this whole time?" Evangaline quipped, popping a grape into her mouth. "How many other women are commanders?"

After Evangaline left a stain of tears on Chloe's delicate gown, Wren showed up with trays upon trays of food, all brought in on a wooden trolley. The incredible woman not only drew baths and did hair, but she also delivered room service. The woman was a saint.

Wren sat everything on the crystal table swatting away Evangaline and Chloe when they tried to help. Once she finished setting up the feast, she lit a crackling fire and bustled out of the room, declining an invitation to stay and eat.

"It would be improper to dine with a guest of the king. I shall return later to clean it up." And then she left just as she said she would.

So, Chloe and Evangaline ate! And drank! And laughed! And forgot the past twenty-four hours had even happened with each bite and sip they took.

Hours passed as they sat at the table drinking fine wine and eating what Chloe deemed "*delicacies of the court.*" There was some form of meat pie that was so flaky and buttery, one bite had Evangaline falling in love with fae food in an instant. Plates of fruit, both human and fae, teased their delicate flavors over her tongue, and that was not even considering the divine appeal of the few desserts that were laid before them.

"Nope. I'm the only one. There are females in the army but none of high ranking like me!" Chloe touted cheerfully. "I agreed to join the army after my second decade. I've been there ever since. My family are all workers here in the palace. My mom works in the kitchens making these yummies." Chloe plopped a lemon filled tart in her mouth. "My dad tends the horses in the stables, and my brother is a messenger for the palace. I knew I wasn't meant for idle work. Being a maid didn't fit me. I can't cook for shit, and the horses make my allergies flare up. But fighting...that I was good at!" She slid a piece of chocolate cake over and plucked up two forks. Evangaline snatched a fork furiously and shifted closer to the monstrous dessert.

They both drove their forks into the cake with the tenacity of a ravaged bear. Scooping up the fudgy icing and spongy cake greedily. The second it touched Evangaline's tongue, her eyes went wide, and her body went slack.

Motioning with a fork to the cake. "That is for sure better than sex," Chloe groaned.

"Way better," Evangaline affirmed, her voice dropping into a sensual purr. "This cake would never cheat on me, would you cake?"

"Clearly, you two have had awful sex." A deep voice echoed from the doorway.

Bastian, arms and legs crossed, leaned on the wall of the vestibule. His eyes were wide with the visage of a predator playing with its prey. Pure animalistic amusement shined in the forest, green irises locked in on Evangaline.

"If good sex is anything like this goddam cake ... than you're right. I've had shit sex," Chloe replied coolly.

"No more coffee shirt?" Evangaline chided, reclining in her chair. Her face smug. "I can fix that if you would like? Though I only have wine and water ... so pick your stain!"

Bastian had changed and damn, did he look good. A sleeveless tunic of a dark burgundy now clung to his muscular chest revealing his sculpted tan arms. Copper embroidered filigree encompassed his collar like a fine necklace. A belt of matching copper snuggly clasped around his thick waist with a sword and dagger attached to opposite hips.

His black trousers fit every curve of his robust thighs and backside and tucked neatly into knee high black leather boots. His hair was clean and shiny and flopped delicately over the right side of his head as though he had just run his hands through it before entering.

In three long strides, Bastian made it over to the dining table just in time to let out a breathless snort of a laugh.

Realizing just then that she never changed from her robe, Evangaline straightened up. Clasping the robe together to cover the bit of her décolletage that was showing.

Bastian eyed her hands clasping the robe shut as he braced his hands on the table across from her. Sensuously, his gaze met hers after lingering on the area her hands clenched together. An uptick of his lips made her feel like she was laid bare before him, despite being covered with the thin silk of the robe.

His expression evened out as he swayed on his feet. "Your father wishes to see you first thing in the morning for breakfast."

"The king," Evangaline corrected with sarcasm and an eye roll.

Bastian snorted. "*The king*," he said with a sneer, "wishes to see you first thing in the morning for breakfast."

"Where do I meet him?" Evangaline responded after a lengthy sigh.

"I will come get you and bring you to him." Inviting himself to dinner, Bastian took a seat across from Evangaline. "He is excited to meet you."

Chloe scoffed. "And yet he can't meet her tonight? Real excited …"

Bastian finally broke his gaze with Evangaline and faced Chloe, grabbing a piece of a foreign-looking fruit and popped it into his mouth. Then draped his arm over the back of the chair beside him, really making himself at home.

"Your Majesty, had guests to entertain tonight and could not get away," he said with a flair to his voice that was … mocking?

Chloe cocked her head and raised her eyebrows. Setting her fork down and crossing her arms as she studied Bastian questionably. "He's drunk, isn't he?"

"He's *very* drunk," Bastian revealed, releasing a snicker. His façade of swaggering machismo slowly cracked. His bright forest green eyes sparkling with a hint of mischief.

Evangaline regarded the two of them in their exchange, not thinking too hard about the fact that the king chose to get drunk rather than meet his only daughter. However, she too was slightly tipsy eating cake that satisfied her better than any man she'd ever been with, so currently she wasn't one to judge.

Evangaline eyed Bastian speculatively, a conspirator's smile smearing across her face as she took in the dilated pupils and giggly demeanor of the massive general. His eyes narrowed back at her. Slowly, and rather sensually, he bit his lower lip in a challenge.

"You're drunk too, aren't you?" She chastised.

Bastian placed a hand on his heart. "*Me?* Never!" His smile matched her own.

A wail of laughter roared from Chloe, suddenly ripping Evangaline and Bastian's gaze from one another.

"She's right! You're drunk! The great general! *Drunk!*" Chloe managed to get out through her laughter, her own words slurring a bit. "Alert the masses! General Bastian unfit for duty!"

Truly, three bottles of wine between the two of them may have been a poor choice in hindsight. Luckily, despite her svelte frame, Evangaline could handle her liquor far better than Chloe.

Unable to help it any longer, Evangaline joined in on Chloe's laughter. Releasing her robe, she leaned forward, allowing her chest to be modestly displayed. With a great swipe of her arm, she grabbed her goblet of wine and raised it in the air. The red liquid lopped over the edge, splattering on the beautiful light wood floor beneath her feet.

"To being drunk!" She giggled out.

"To being *drunk!*" Chloe echoed, her jovial tone booming through the room.

Both looked to Bastian, waiting for him to join in the festivities.

He paused, eyeing them.

Then, with a shake of his head, he grabbed an entire bottle of wine sitting in a bucket of melted ice and tossed the cork across the room. The cold water from the long-melted ice splattered across the table, but none of them cared at all. He raised it equal to their chalices.

His face turned introspective and mischievous. "To the returned princess."

Evangaline's smile dissipated as the revelations from the day came swimming back into her consciousness. No amount of wine and sex-rivaling cake could make her forget her family and what happened today, despite all her fervent attempts at distracting herself.

Chloe grabbed her hand and, with a squeeze, murmured softly, "To Evie. Happy Birthday, babe."

With a clink of their wine, Evangaline downed the rest of the contents in her glass—not leaving a single drop behind.

Hours passed as Evangaline silently listened as Chloe and Bastian caught up on a year's worth of stories and travels. Their laughter and merriment filled the room until sleep found its way to claim them very late into the night. And with it drawing a conclusion to the most shocking birthday Evangaline had ever had.

Chapter Ten

With the morning sun not yet shadowing the lush green earth, a wash of orange and deep blue stained the watercolor sky. Somewhere the rays of gold and amber were peeking their ways above the foliage crusted land of Celadonia, however, said golden rays had not mercilessly shone upon Evangaline's room.

It was early in the morning hours, far earlier than Evangaline would normally wake. Despite her limited hours of sleep thanks to the three extra bottles of wine Chloe and Bastian ordered up to her room, she felt fully awake and ready to start the day.

Perhaps it was the looming presence of her upcoming meeting with the man that sired her or the surprisingly powerful urge that streamed through her veins beckoning her to go explore this new land. Either way, she couldn't bear to sit in bed a moment longer.

She found herself fully awake, gazing through the window at the flocculent clouds and dew-soaked grass that was waiting to be traipsed, eager to move forward with her day.

There was a restlessness to her soul that she couldn't seem to shake. Even through the wine and desserts the night prior, Evangaline still felt something deep within her chest, nudging her out of her room to go explore. A thrusting of her heart against the cage of her ribs guiding her towards something greater. It thrummed in a rhythmic beat to the breeze that swayed the trees and beckoned her to reach out and touch the soil of Celadonia.

Careful as to not wake Chloe, whom of which made herself far too comfortable tangled in the silky sheets and fluffy duvet of Evangaline's massive bed. Somehow, despite its size and ability to easily fit four people, Chloe was stretched out, arms and legs splayed like a starfish. Her delicate braids, released from their top knot, cascaded across her face and down her chest like a lustrous, twisting pink river.

Evangaline closed the door of the bathroom, tiptoeing the entire way as to not make a single noise, and drew a bath for herself.

Luckily, she had watched Wren fill the tub the day before and could remember which lever controlled what. After the tub filled, she turned on her heels and made her way into the attached closet at the far end of the bathroom to go pick her outfit for her breakfast with the king. For some reason, her curiosity never steered her to explore it the day before. But knowing she was to meet the king, her father, she wanted to look the part of fae princess and not lonely human.

Flicking the switch on the wall, the closet lit up with bursts of white light. One after another, three blown glass chandeliers illuminated the cavernous space. Their starbursts of luminescence shed light on row after row of gowns and garments. Some were made of simple chiffons and tulle. While some were made of the finest satins and silks. Others were massive ball gowns that could rival the designer ones Evangaline saw movie stars wear on red carpets—gowns that screamed *princess*.

Gliding her hand from one dress to the next, feeling the luxurious fabrics slip through her fingertips, she made her way slowly onto a section that was all sorts of tunics, corsets, and shirts. Next to it were trousers and leggings in cotton-like fabrics as well as various colors of leather.

Beside those was a shelf of folded leather and metal adorned garments that drew Evangaline's curiosity. Grabbing one, she unfolded it carefully. A body suit of sorts unfurled, equipped with sheaths for daggers, pockets on the hips, and a breastplate of copper. This suit was clearly made for someone going into battle, a warrior, someone like Chloe. Certainly not Evangaline.

She folded it back up with caution and made her way back to the simple gowns of chiffon at the front of the closet; completely ignoring the glass cabinets lined with velvet harboring hordes of jewels and tiaras.

One gown of a delicate light blue gauze caught her attention immediately. The bodice was made to imitate a corset and there was a subtle, yet classy, V that cut into the top and looked as though it would rest delicately between her breasts. Sleeves made of the same feather light chiffon that the skirt was made of draped and hung like sashes across the arms. A small and delicate silver belt clung to the waist of the gown just above the flowing skirts that were shaped like two swords crossing. Something princess-y, yet badass. She loved it.

With it in her arms and a pair of low-heeled slippers in hand, Evangaline was ready to bathe and start the day.

Roughly an hour later, the sun streamed fully into the windows, showering the room in the bright gold of day … and still Chloe slept like an ox. Evangaline, still trying to remain as quiet as a goddam mouse, made her way onto the balcony attached to the entirety of her suite—from living to bedroom—and regarded the sun that now stretched fully into the pale blue sky. The glowing ball of fire brought comfort to her. Warming her skin, reminding her of a new start to a new day, that the past was the past and fretting about her future was not worth the anxiety it caused. She took a breath, banishing any panic deluding her thoughts, and took in the surrounding sights.

When they arrived yesterday, the sun was already making its descent, casting the sky in dusky hues, so the land was painted in the pinks and purples of the setting sun. However, now, with the sun greeting the day, the vibrancy of Celadonia was unparalleled to anything she had ever seen before.

The forest with changing leaves twinkled in the distance with a newfound grandeur. The breeze softly ruffled the leaves, creating a soft hymn of tranquility. Evangaline gently closed her eyes, savoring the serene nature of the crisp air. No car horns blared, no sirens wailed, the sounds of children playing in the park were nothing but a distant memory to the breeze that flowed and the birds that chirped their good mornings.

With the gentle caress of a lover, Evangaline opened her eyes to the soft ruffling of her damp hair. The sentient wind from the day before twined itself around her neck like a silken scarf draped casually across her shoulders and softly glided across her cheek in light strokes. It was warm and calming, peaceful and loving. With a gentle curiosity, it snaked its way around her body and ruffled her skirts. Sparking a quiet giggle from Evangaline.

"Do you like it?" she whispered. "You think the king will approve?"

Almost in answer, the wind twirled around her in a quick cyclone that spiraled her hair straight into the air and twisted her skirts around her knees and ankles.

She knew, subconsciously, it should have frightened her; however, she could only feel calm and a jittering level of excitement around the sentient wind.

She interpreted its movements as though it replied, *"Yes! I love it,"* and smiled at where she assumed it hovered in the air.

Extending a hand to the open air, she tittered, "My name is Evangaline Rivers. Pleased to meet you."

Good lord, if anyone from Vitalis saw her they would think she, without a doubt, lost every last marble that occupied her mind! And perhaps she had, she was talking to the wind for crying out loud.

However, this was all very real. She made sure with a subtle pinch to her thigh.

The wind answered back softly, wrapping its force around her hand with a gentle squeeze.

With a wide grin, and a small laugh, Evangaline shook the phantom hand of the wind in greeting. With little warning, the gale twined through her wet hair, wringing the water from her brown tresses effectively—and efficiently—drying it in record time.

With a chuckle, Evangaline ran a hand across his silken hair, "Why thank you! The fae don't seem to own any blow dryers. I owe you one," she joked.

The wind softly caressed her hand once more and then was off flying through the ever-changing trees of the forest, leaving a wake of clattering leaves behind it.

"Bye friend," Evangaline said quietly, staring off into the direction of her new invisible buddy already growing cold without its reassuring presence.

"I feel like I should be frightened with how much the wind whisp likes you," Bastian commented from the doorway connecting to the living room.

Evangaline jumped and whirled around, her heart rate elevating at the surprise.

His shirt was wrinkled and unfastened halfway down his sculpted chest and untucked at his waistline. The metallic lined tunic from the night before haphazardly hung over his arm as he righted the hair that remained tussled from his sleep.

"Why? And did you sleep on the couch?" Evangaline asked quizzically.

Resting his forearm on the solid marble balcony railing beside her, he looked to Evangaline, eyes squinting in the sunlight as hints of a hangover shadowed his face. "I may have been too inebriated to find my room last night ... and from the looks of it so was Chloe," he said glancing back at the rather uncouth commander of his army sprawled across Evangaline's bed snoring loud enough to wake the dead.

"Sorry, I went to bed early last night. Though you two didn't seem to notice much ... I believe Chloe's beautiful rendition of the many pub songs I have yet to learn drowned out my hasty exit." Evangaline chided, giving a soft smile. "Why should you be concerned about the wind whisp ... thing? I like it."

Bastian straightened. "The elemental goddess is one of the most powerful gods the fae worship. *The queen of gods,* some call her. Many of the land's creatures respond to her and her alone, even other gods bow to her powers. The wind whisp being one of those creatures. The conifers another." At Evangaline's arched brow he continued, "They are creatures that hide in the trees. They are said to look like a man but fit their environment of the forest. It's said they are made of the forests themselves. If they choose to hide in an oak, they can change their coloring and texture to hide in them, a birch, or evergreen alike. Legends claim them to be her silent assassins."

His tone turned slightly mocking, like a child telling ghost stories around a campfire.

Enthralled, Evangeline leaned into him, ignoring his chiding cadence. "Have you ever seen one?"

"No. In fact, before yesterday I thought the wind whisp was a myth. The elemental goddess has not shown herself or allowed her creatures to be seen in a great many years, since the death of her daughter. Her approval of your arrival is not something to be taken lightly, Princess."

A sigh escaped her as she faced back toward the rolling greenery and shimmering sun.

"One more pressure to live up to," she muttered under her breath.

Bastian stood tall and faced her completely, eyeing her studiously, towering over her in an imposing stance as he did often, "All right, let me see it."

With her brow furrowed, "See what?" Evangaline asked.

"You. Come on, Princess," he said, creating a whirling motion with his hands, telling her to spin for him.

Evangaline rolled her eyes and then proceeded to twirl with a slight smile. The chiffon of her skirt billowed around her ankles just like it did with the whisp. Her smile broke wider—despite trying to hide it, she failed miserably.

It's quite fun to twirl in flowy dresses, she thought to herself.

"Do I look the part?" She asked, batting her eyelashes playfully.

Bastian didn't answer right away, his gaze searing into the skin below her shoulders and neck.

Still fixated on her, he buttoned his shirt and slipped his tunic on as he evaded answering. Evangaline wriggled under his perusal of her body but remained in place, smile and all.

Finally, after a bated breath, he took her hand, gently pressing a kiss to the back of it. "Magnificent, *Your Highness* … Shall we see the king?" He grinned up at her.

Evangaline slowly nodded, her smile faltering ever so slightly.

She tugged at her hand to remove it from Bastian's, but he gently resisted and placed it on his extended forearm. Not giving her the ability to walk on her own.

A chill crept down Evangaline's spine, but she ignored it, forcing her feet into motion alongside Bastian.

The two made their way out of the room, leaving a snoring Chloe nestled within the comforts of Evangaline's monster of a bed.

With each step, Evangaline reminded herself she was courageous, brave, bold, strong, and fierce … and she could do this … she had no other choice.

Chapter Eleven

The throne room was more magnificent than anything Evangaline's measly human brain could even conjure up. If the giant crested copper doors didn't scream, *this room is magical* before, they certainly did once they opened to her, revealing the splendor that was His Majesty's throne room.

Bastian guided her stoically into the space. Flying buttresses of solid shimmering marble soared dozens of feet overhead, holding up the multiple domed ceilings adorned with various angled panes of glass. The rest of the palace was outfitted with blown glass chandeliers of opulent flowers and foliage. The throne room, however, was simply illuminated by the rays of the sun and a few copper sconces on the walls.

A floral mosaic sat inlaid into the center of the floor with gold and silver tiles that shimmered flecks of light around the lavish chamber as they caught the morning rays of the sun.

Disco ball like reflections gilded the space and immediately made her think of her sister. *Katherine would love it here*, she thought as she took in the shimmering beams. Her sister loved anything that sparkled, and the throne room certainly did just that.

Climbing up the pillars and soaring across the buttresses of the throne room were more magically enhanced bright red roses. Their petals glistened with a morning dew that had no way of entering the room naturally and sparkled with the flecks of light from the mosaic's metallic pieces.

Courtiers were scattered around at various circular tables adorned with small bouquets of roses and towers of pastries and cakes. Some nobles sipped from steaming pots of tea while others indulged in the decadent towers of pastries, muttering amongst themselves with hushed debates and laughs alike.

The sight of a steaming, fresh croissant instantly had Evangaline's stomach grumbling with hunger.

Bastian took her straight to the throne room after a minor pit stop at his quarters so he could change from his sleep riddled attire. His new sapphire and silver tunic was in every way a perfect complement to her sky-blue gown.

They strode, wordless, down the throne room toward the elevated dais where an elegant carved dark wood throne sat atop the small riser. Small gemstones of emerald, ruby, and sapphires encrusted various floral elements in the seat back. Despite its beauty, it was the man that stood just before the magnificent bejeweled throne that caught Evangaline's attention almost immediately.

Suddenly, the attentive eyes and small sneers from the courtiers taking their breakfast dissipated into nothingness as she took in the imposing figure of King Darrin.

She saw quick clips of him years ago on the news in a Council meeting, but never really took note in him at all. At the time, it wasn't important. Yet now, knowing that he sired her, knowing this man before her is the biological father that her mother never wanted to talk about, she couldn't help but see the similarities between the two of them.

While her skin was the same pink tinted alabaster as her mother, she had her father's jawline. Evangaline's delicate heart-shaped face with high cheeks and an angled jaw, were the female version of his sharp lines and honed exterior. His hair was the same light brown color and in the glistening sunlight that streamed in overhead, the same red and gold streaks shimmered within his coiffed tresses. Evangaline always envied her mom's cardinal colored hair and assumed the red tints that shone in the right light were thanks to Felicity. However, staring at the king as she walked her way to him, it was his hair tried and true that she inherited.

With each step closer, her breathing became heavier. Her hands started to get clammy, and she could feel a single bead of sweat drip down the column of her back.

What if he doesn't like me? She randomly thought.

So captivated by the king, she hardly noticed the man standing next to him. All in white, with a tunic that drifted close to his knees. His long but groomed white beard matched perfectly to his ghostly white hair. However, the most alluring thing about him was his pale blue eyes that seemed to *also* match her dress. Guess she picked the right gown to meet the king in. Blue must have been the color of the day.

Several feet away from the dais, Bastian came to a stop, halting her with him. The king and the strange snowy man turned to face them. There was a warmth to both of their faces and a small smile on the white-clad man that eased some of her nerves.

Bastian began to bow at the waist.

Completely unaware of what to do, Evangaline quickly referenced every fairytale book she'd ever read and movie she'd ever watched, and dipped into a curtsy, to the best of her ability. Her attempt was not great. It was not at all graceful, but hey, she had only been a princess for barely twenty-four hours.

"Leave us!" The king's deep voice boomed over the cavernous room, startling Evangaline with his slightly harsh tone.

Immediately all the courtiers scraped their chairs back in a rush, taking last sips of tea and juice, shoveling in the last bites of their meals, before rushing off through the doors.

Evangaline, still in a curtsy, watched them all shuffle away out of the corner of her eye. Clinging to a breath that nestled into her throat and suffocated her with anticipation.

Finally, the doors slammed shut, reverberating through the room, sending a shock through her bones.

Warm, callused fingers jolted her eyes forward, settling to rest themselves just below her chin in an attempt to raise it slightly.

The king gazed down at her with the warmth of a seasoned father looking upon a daughter, however, the slightest hint of sorrow echoed beneath his pained smile.

His eyes were another attribute they shared. She was truly his daughter; it only took one good look at him to know that to be the truth. She was always told she had unique eyes. They were a medium shade of blue, however, just around the iris was a pale sage green that radiated streaks outward. Certain ways she did her makeup could draw out the green and others the blue. It all depended on her clothes and eyeshadow, she came to learn as she got older. Clad in her pale blue gown, her irises shone bluer, as did the kings, in his navy waistcoat and trousers.

"My dear daughter." He spoke almost in a whisper, like it was just for him and no one else to hear except Evangaline.

At some point Bastian had straightened to his full height, towering over Evangaline and the king. The visual of a seasoned general and courtier. His hands clasped behind his elongated back as he stood proud and tall.

The man in white, still atop the dais had a warm smile gracing his slightly wrinkling features, unfaltering in its happiness. His eyes sparkled with a burst of light as he took in the display before him.

"Evangaline. Umm ... Rivers. Evangaline Rivers." She seemed to get out in greeting and introduction as she straightened, sucking down a deep breath.

The king dropped his hand, a shimmer of water now lined his bottom lash line. He choked it back with a smooth hand on his jaw and a clearing of his throat. His raw emotion almost made Evangaline want to throw her arms out and bring him in for a massive hug. But she reminded herself of the fact that her mother left for a reason, and she was here simply to appeal to the bargain made before her birth. Nothing more.

"Your Majesty, Her Royal Highness has yet to be given a full tour of the grounds, I am told. Perhaps that could be arranged following your breakfast?" The man in white murmured from behind, snapping both Evangaline and the king out of their trances.

King Darrin half turned to face the man. "Yes, Atlas, that sounds like a lovely idea. Clear my schedule, Bastian, for the remainder of the morning. I should like to show my daughter her new home."

New home.

The term echoed through her head as Bastian spoke. "Of course, Your Majesty. Will you require anything else at this time?" His voice was hard and finite. A far cry to the man singing a vulgar song with Chloe about a bar maiden with massive breasts just last night.

"I shall appreciate it if you and Atlas join us for breakfast." Darrin motioned to a table just behind the dais, set before the giant floor to ceiling windows that overlooked the grounds and forest just beyond the greenery.

"As you wish," Bastian curtly replied as Evangaline looked up at him, eyes wary. Her emotions were all over the place and Bastian was the closest she had to a friend at the moment. He gave her a small nod and with that, she faced forward once more toward the king.

"After you, Evangaline," the king decreed.

With shallow breaths, Evangaline forced her feet to move and began walking silently to the small table with all three men in tow.

"Tell me something about yourself?" the king asked at his place across from her, taking a bite of his heaping helping of scrambled eggs.

Between bites of her delicious croissant, Evangaline cleared her throat. "What would you like to know?"

They had already addressed the weather and how beautiful the palace was. Bastian regaled them all on how efficient Evangaline was at wielding a coffee cup and the injuries the healer fixed for both of them. The story earned a salacious wink from the king as though to tell her that he was proud of her for knocking out his General and Hand, setting her nerves at ease just a little bit.

Thus, bringing their conversation to this point.

"Anything, truly, anything would delight me. Tell me of what you wanted to do in Vitalis, any hopes or dreams?" he replied, almost delighted.

Not be a princess, that's for sure! She replied in her head.

She knew not what the future held for her and never really gave it much thought. She lived her life predominantly in the present because the fear and anxiety she faced when thinking about her future terrified her. Her dreams consisted of being happy and healthy. Redundant and vague concepts that could easily be achieved day-to-day if she focused on them.

"Well," she said, setting down her croissant. "I've had quite the evolution. Five-year-old me was convinced I would be a marine biologist—despite not knowing that was what to call the people who took care of the seals and sharks at the aquarium. Or how to pronounce 'marine biologist', for that matter of fact. I loved the ocean as a kid, still do. Mom would take me to the aquarium all the time. I loved the sharks the most. To this day I don't know why, but I did." She shrugged with a reminiscent smile. "So, I told her I wanted to take care of them one day, but I grew out of that when I realized I wasn't built for scuba diving."

Her eyes fixed on the croissant beneath her fingertips, being torn into miniscule pieces. "Then I got older and realized that I enjoyed fashion. Window shopping in the city with my sister sparked that creative insight. So I wanted to be a designer … until I learned I was complete shit at sewing, so fuck that—" Realizing quickly she swore in front of the king, she raised a hand to her mouth, her eyes shooting wide.

His laugh at the slip up caused her to drop her hand.

Her face pinched. "Sorry, I'm still new to this whole princess thing. I didn't mean any offense."

Inclining in his chair, the king smiled at her. "You are fine. Believe me, any of the men before you have sworn at each other in much worse ways. I assure you this kingdom needs a princess with the ability to swear we have grown too prim in our ways. We need an *edge*."

She just smiled and nodded at the notion. She was likely not the princess with the edge he desired, but she would not be the one to tell him that.

"Please continue." He motioned with a wave of his hand.

To her right, Bastian sipped a cup of tea. The sight of it almost made her want to laugh. The cup was nearly dwarfed in his tanned hands making the whole visual seem almost comical. Hiding her laugh, Evangaline turned toward the king and Atlas.

"Uhm. After a designer, I realized I enjoyed my solitude more than anything, so when I graduated high school and went to university, I studied journalism. Books and, well, anything I could read were my constant companions as a kid, so I decided that was what I wanted to do—write. I just woke up one day and realized all the other things, the marine biology, the designing, they were all just infatuations. My true heart was always in literature. So, I got my degree in journalism and—"

"And yet you worked at a bookstore, I was told through Chloe. Why?" Atlas said, not in a condescending tone but rather in a hushed, quizzical one.

She studied his question and then decided honesty would be the greatest answer in this circumstance, so she gave it. Her mouth curved into a hard line as she nodded, "I was lost, still am truthfully. And confused. Quarter life crisis, I suppose. I was tired of being rejected by publishers and editors. It felt like any job I applied for I got rejected from despite being more than qualified. So I thought, why not just do the simple thing. Easier to stop trying and not face heartache than to keep trying and getting knocked on my ass. Anyway, I made a decent amount of money and was able to have a life, or somewhat of one. Before ... well ..." Evangaline motioned around the room, picking up her glass of orange juice and downing a hearty gulp.

All three men went silent. Studying her just as she did them at various moments of the awkward breakfast.

Unable to meet any of their eye lines, afraid she would see what they were thinking, she just set her cup down, gazing at the half-eaten croissant on her plate, no longer hungry.

She always wanted to be the strong, fearless woman that didn't take no for an answer, but with each no she got her soul crumbled bit by bit until it was easier to retreat into herself than to keep putting herself out there. Some might call it fear or cowardice, but Evangaline thought of it as self-preservation.

"You remind me of her," the king murmured in a somewhat longing tone. "Your mother. When I met her, her hair was just as long as yours. Her skin the same beautiful shade."

Finally, she met his gaze. His eyes were somber and somewhat withdrawn. She could tell in his tone and expression, he had loved her mom, maybe still did. Evangaline could not begin to imagine the pain of losing not only the person you love but also a child. That thought alone spurred her to reply. "She cut her hair. When I was a toddler, around when I was three. I twirled it too much when she held me, or so I'm told, I don't remember. So, she cut it one day to about here." She motioned just below her collarbone. "It's been there ever since. She says it's easier to maintain, anyway."

He smiled at her in earnest. Like the thought brought him joy and sadness all in the same complex emotional maelstrom.

"I know she told you of the bargain, and Bastian that of your position and title here."

Evangaline nodded.

"When we made the agreement, I did stipulate that it would be my wish for you to one day rule if it was left to you and now, I find myself the father to only one child, *you*. It breaks my heart, Evangaline, to throw all of this on you in such a rushed manner and I want to protect you as best I can. Aside from Chloe and Bastian guarding you, I have assigned Atlas to be your tutor. Anything you wish to know, he has the knowledge of it. He will help teach you our customs and traditions, and our history if you so wish it. I am to have a ball for all five kingdoms of my realm in three weeks' time. Come, that night, I wish to present you as my daughter, and more importantly, as the crown princess."

Evangaline sat forward, bracing her arms on the table in an unintentional show of un-princess like manners. "I agree to learn your ways and anything that is required of me. I actually think that would be fun. But I still don't understand. My mother said after twenty-five years you were to claim me, collect me, whatever the terminology was, but, and I may be forward in my approach, and I apologize … I don't mean it in a rude way, but at the end of the three weeks … am I … is the bargain fulfilled? Can I go back to Vitalis?"

She didn't realize that one question would send a bolt through his heart, but it did, and she saw it hit its mark with fatal accuracy.

"Perhaps we should discuss this further, just you and me. Please, walk with me."

The king stood, scraping his chair against the floor, dropping his napkin onto the plate of eggs he barely made a dent in. Bastian and Atlas rose alongside him.

Reluctantly, she stood and nodded. Following him without a backward glance to the other two men at the table. Their stares, however, fixated on the back of her neck, hot and searing, following her as she put distance between them. She could not figure out if it was a good or bad sign to have their attention so potently as she walked through a hidden passageway behind her father, but she had it, nonetheless.

Chapter Twelve

The garden was even more beautiful in person than it was through her windows. The rose bushes glistened in the morning sun, soaking up the rays like people tanning on the beach. It took everything in her being not to close her eyes and bask in the sunlight like a lizard basking on a rock in the desert right alongside the vibrant shrubbery.

She could see the wing of the castle where her room was situated and silently laughed to herself, picturing Chloe still up there sprawled on the bed, snoring.

Delicate rows of neatly manicured hedges were shaped into swirls, all lined and filled with varieties of flowers, encasing them in bright, exuberant colors. She was not particularly well versed in horticulture; however, she knew a lily from a tulip from a hyacinth and that was all she really needed in her arsenal of knowledge.

Their walk from the throne room to the gardens wasn't very long or far, but if someone asked her to get back to the throne room on her own, Evangaline would be lost quite easily.

Both king and princess made the trek to the gardens without a word. A tense silence filled the air in the place of words. She hated it. Sometimes the quiet was her friend, however, with him and all the questions she had, the silence was agonizing.

"I am sorry if my brashness hurt you," she said, finally breaking the tension filled silence.

He glanced down at her with a contemplative grin and then released a sigh. "There is much you've not been made aware of. I do not accept your apology simply because it is misplaced. It is I who is sorry, Evangaline. Truly. This bargain your mother and I struck. It was foolish, yet necessary. She needed you safe and please know, so did I. Our reasons were different for seeking the bargain in the beginning, but our intentions were always aligned to—"

"Me. I know. If there is anything I have heard on repeat, it has been that, Your Majesty."

The king nodded. "Call me Darrin. Though I will not stop you from calling me father or dad either," he said with a cheeky grin.

She simply nodded. Only Stephen was her father. Biology be damned.

"*Darrin*, this has all happened quickly … I asked this of my mother, and I need it from you too … the truth. Can you give that to me? Please?" She did not want to sound desperate, but, to some extent, she was.

He nodded. "The bargain will keep you here until you take the mantle as my heir, until the full court and realm know you are its crown princess. That is what the magic bound us to. We were sloppy with our wording, and the bargain is stated to expire once you take the seat of crown princess. That is why I planned the ball with all the kingdoms. It is the most effective way for the entire realm to know all at once, or as much of it as possible till word can spread—which I don't doubt will be quite rapidly. I would have had the ball sooner, but our friends in the south pushed for three weeks from now, so that is what we agreed on. From there, it will be your choice to abdicate or accept the role as princess and eventually queen."

"So, three weeks. After you present me to the kingdom as princess, I will be able to choose whether I go back to Vitalis or stay?"

A nod from King Darrin was her only answer. However, the hopeful gleam in his broken eyes did not go unnoticed.

Okay, three weeks was nothing. She could make it through three weeks with no problems! Then she could go back and resume her slow, silent life in the background.

"There is more."

Shit.

"If you do happen, at the end of the three weeks, to wish to stay and fulfil your role as crown princess of Celadonia, you will need to prove yourself to the people. They will not love you on the spot, that I know for certain. Along with that, we have a lot to learn about you. You have been suppressed by the wards of Vitalis for a long time. We will need to test you to see if you do have any magic in you or if you are more mortal than fae.

"Atlas and I, alongside Bastian, have been around this court, these kingdoms and their people for a great deal of time and in all of that time there has never once been a child born of both human and fae lineage. We don't know what Vitalis and your human side has done in conjunction to your fae side."

Evangaline stopped and faced Darrin. Her brow furrowed. Her expression quizzical.

"That can't be true. We've shared a planet for hundreds of years—you are telling me in that time there has been not a single fae and human child born until me?"

The king placed a hand on her back to urge her to keep walking as a couple sauntered by arm and arm, stopping to bow to the king and then continuing their procession through the garden without a glance in Evangaline's direction.

"Not one. The borders set between the three realms has prohibited the passing of each realm's citizens. Such is why your mother needed permission and my aid to bring her here, as well as to help her go home. It was complex then and frowned upon in both realms, me bringing her, but I..." *I loved her.* The words hung in the air as he regarded his shoes before he continued, "Not even the Vitalian government knew you were born of two realms. Your mother did well to hide it and protect you. Luckily, you inherited her ears, making the deception pass easier." He smirked at her conspiratorially.

"Until I sent Bastian to retrieve you and Chloe to guard you, both of which have been an affair that the Supreme President and her legislators had to agree upon. A fae never visited Vitalis aside from my appearance at the annual meetings. For her year with you, Chloe forfeited her fae gifts and was glamoured to appear human. Bastian was only allowed to open portals and remove the glamours when the time was right using a certain crystal that allowed partial magic. Anything else would have been considered an act of war against Vitalis. Both were watched rather closely by the Supreme President's guards. We risked, they risked rather, quite a lot to retrieve and protect you."

"Why send Chloe with only a year till the bargain was up? I made it this long without protection."

He sighed indignantly. His left eye ticked with a restrained anger. "We had an anonymous threat against your life some time before her deployment. Somehow, someone learned of your birth and the bargain your mother and I struck. They tried using it as leverage to get me to abdicate the throne or *'there would be war'*, so they said. I did not wish for war, nor was I willing to forfeit my birthright to people who wouldn't even make themselves known. So, I ignored it, but someone possibly knowing you were alive and vulnerable in Vitalis was a risk I could not take, no matter the laws of the realms. You are my heir and daughter."

An icy chill ran down her spine. Hearing that someone had a hit out on her and was using her just to get back at a king she never knew or met until now was unnerving. Her heartbeat quickened with new questions she was afraid to ask.

"What about now with me here? Will that not raise suspicions? Will more people use me to get to you?" She didn't know him, but she knew she didn't want harm to befall anyone in an attempt to get to her.

"There is no true way of knowing that." He motioned to a bench and took a seat along the gravel walkway. She followed his lead. "But that is why I would like for you to do the lessons with Atlas. He shall teach you anything and everything you need to know to thrive here, even if you wish to leave after your debut. The courtiers will be harder to win over than the regular civilians. They tend to be narcissistic in their motives and quite sheltered in their beliefs. Atlas, however, will teach you everything you need to know in order to thrive. He is older than the Convergence himself—"

Surprised, Evangaline whispered harshly, "He's what? He looks amazing! Shit!"

Darrin let out a brief chuckle, bringing a genuine smile to his otherwise somber face. "He would be thrilled to hear you say that. He is one of my closest friends. With his aid, you will be well educated enough to know what decision you want to make. However, I do ask that you remain in the shadows, unseen and unheard. Before your debut, you will simply be a guest in my court. Nothing more and nothing less. I want to keep you as secret as I can for the time being. If word gets out of your title before I have had the chance to introduce you, we will be at the mercy of the people rather than the two of us controlling the narrative. I do not want to place any unwanted targets on our backs."

Evangaline faced him, her blue skirt fanning out over the bench beneath her. As she turned, she could see the gaze of several members of the court watching her and the king from various places around the garden. "Lying low might be harder than expected." She motioned toward the windows to their side with a small nod of her head.

King Darrin followed her eyeline and nodded, glancing back at the members of the court spying on their king who sat speaking with the new mysterious human woman. As he turned back to her, his overly exaggerated eye roll made a laugh bubble within her throat.

"My mother mentioned the people of the land not being thrilled about her living here. Wouldn't they already know the only human here is potentially your child? It's not like we look wickedly different," she asked, genuinely confused and concerned.

With a sigh, he replied, "None of my court knew of your mother's pregnancy. When she left, she had barely begun to show—she hid it well. I felt you kick in her womb only once. To the other kingdoms and to my subjects, I banished your mother. Only Atlas and I had the knowledge of you until now."

"Not even Bastian? Mom said some advisors knew. Wait, you banished my mother?" Her anger came out sharp as the blade strapped to Darrin's waist on the last word.

Grabbing her hand, "Please keep your voice down. To the realm, yes, I banished her. I could not let the Council, or my subjects, believe that I simply allowed a human to go to and from Celadonia as she pleased. It would go against the code of the realms and not even I am exempt from punishment from those. In my heart, daughter, I never banished her. I need you to know that. It was the safest way to get her out. My old advisors were disbanded after they were critical of your birth, and I used my gifts to no longer allow them to be an issue." She quirked a brow at his ominous words, but he did not seem to notice the question in her eyes. "By the time I was done with them, they barely remembered their own names. They started their lives anew elsewhere.

"As far as Bastian, he was a young man at the time of your conception and not yet my hand or general. Just barely a grunt in the army. He, just like the others, never knew you were even conceived. I told him of you only when it became a necessity."

Evangaline simply nodded. Her hands wringing in her lap nervously. Her gaze fixed on the rows and rows of multicolored flowers around them in an attempt to regain some semblance of a clear head.

"I know this is a lot. I will be with you every step of the way and if you choose to leave, I shall not fight you, though I will not pretend to be happy about your departure. I wish more than anything for you to stay but you had a life, a mother and father in Vitalis who loved you, who still love you, siblings that I was not able to give you here. I am aware of that. All I ask is for a chance. To be here for you, to be the father I never got the chance to be when you were growing up."

She didn't know why, maybe it was his sweet words, maybe it was the strain to his voice, or maybe it was the fact that he acknowledged her dad, Stephen—that he did not try to erase her life completely—but silent tears fell down her cheeks and splashed onto her pale blue gown.

She stared at Darrin, as he too allowed his hushed tears to fall. Reaching out, she grabbed his warm, smooth hands and held onto them.

He began rubbing his thumb in small sweeps across the backs of her knuckles. Then forcing herself to not retreat within herself from the mounting anxiety she felt, Evangaline sat up straighter. *Be Strong*, she told herself. And so she gave him the most honest answer she could.

"I'll try."

Chapter Thirteen

Evangaline and the king walked around the palace grounds for a few more hours, discussing everything from Evangaline's childhood to the king's own upbringing. The anxiety and indifference she had, only yesterday, for the fae king slowly dissipated with each pass of the flowers and grand halls of marble.

As the king explained to her the history of the palace and how it was hewed from the marble mountains in the southernmost tip of the continent near somewhere named Pax, Evangaline found the sleep that evaded her for the past two nights punch her square in the gut. She tried to suppress her yawn as best she could, but it found its way to the surface despite her efforts, grabbing the king's attention.

With a gruff chuckle emitted from his content face, "I was bored out of my mind learning the history of the palace as a young boy too. You shall see the ballrooms soon enough…no need for it now. Come on, I shall escort you back to your rooms and have some food brought up. It's been a couple of long days for you. You should rest."

Evangaline did not protest. Food and bed sounded delightful.

"Get the fuck up!"

With a jolt, Chloe shook Evangaline awake. The sun began its descent into the luscious green earth, telling her she slept through the whole day. *Great.*

"We're going to miss dinner," Chloe quipped, rolling off the bed, her legs having been straddled around Evangaline's waist like she was galloping on a horse.

Evangaline stretched and yawned. "How long have I been asleep? What time is it?"

"Well, Bastian said the king returned you to your room just before noon and its nearly seven now."

Seven hours? And yet she still felt a lingering wave of exhaustion fogging her mind. Sauntering out of the closet, clad in a beautiful ivory gown encased in a breastplate of gilded gold vines, Chloe was the image of every mythical warrior goddess Evangaline read about.

In her hand, a sparkling gown of iridescent silver shimmered in the faint light of the bedroom. Adorned with rhinestone crusted ivy leaves that swirled about the skirt, the gown was nothing short of show-stopping. Evangaline hadn't seen a gown so beautiful in her entire life and wasn't quite sure how she missed it in her brief sweep through the cavern the fae called a closet.

Acting as though it were mere rags, Chloe heaved it onto the bed with a mighty thrust.

"Have you seen that damn closet?" Chloe motioned with her hand dramatically. "Get up and get naked, sexy lady." A sly wink finished off her sentence. "I am starving!"

Rising, Evangaline shook out her now wrinkled blue gown, her words coming out on a yawn, "The king didn't mention a dinner. Why can't we just eat here again? I'll call for Wren." She made to move to the doorway to call for the handmaiden with the small magical bell attached to the wall. But it was Chloe's tense body, leaning studiously against the jamb of the balcony door, that stopped Evangaline in her tracks.

"The king didn't request your presence. I do …"

Evangaline squinted. "Why?"

Chloe sauntered over to her, chewing on her thumb's cuticle. "Maybe I just want to stride in with a fine piece of ass on my arm." She finished off her crude statement with a pinch to Evangaline's backside. Evangaline squealed and batted her away, a smile wrinkling her nose.

"What is it, Chlo? I know when you want something and when you are lying, and both are at play right now." She gathered the gown from the bed into her arms while Chloe unfastened the buttons of her blue one.

"I just, I haven't seen everyone in a while …" Chloe quietly mused.

"Are you nervous about going in there?" Evangaline turned to her friend, holding onto her now unfastened gown. Evangaline's concern creased her forehead. "Everyone loves you. I'm sure the room will just erupt in cheers with your adoring fans begging for autographs at your feet." She tried to joke.

The joke fell flat on its ass.

Instead, Chloe just nodded as a cloudiness filled her eyes. Chloe was never nervous. If Evangaline needed one word to describe Chloe, it was fearless. This version of her was all kinds of disheartening and filled Evangaline with the feeling to move mountains just to bring the light back to Chloe's eyes. She would take on every fae in that room with a soup spoon alone if that meant Chloe would feel comfortable and happy.

"I would be honored to be your date for the night," Evangaline told her best friend earnestly.

In truth, Chloe might have been assigned to her as a protector, but in every way she pulled Evangaline out of the darkest point of her life. Even now, with all of the complexities of suddenly becoming a human-fae princess, nothing amounted to the depression and anxiety that plagued her a year ago. It was the worst it had been in her whole life. Evangaline was drowning. Then came Chloe, who threw her a lifeline and gave her something to look forward to each day. So, if Chloe needed her, she would be right there with her every step of the way. It was the least she could do.

"I have one condition, though." Evangaline grabbed Chloe's hand in her left while balancing her unfastened gown in her right. "I am supposed to meet with Atlas and learn about all of this fae crap … but I was wondering if you would train me, like train me, train me. Like fitness training. I don't want to be helpless or defenseless. Plus, with that orgasmic chocolate cake being so easy to request and no treadmill in sight, I'm practically begging to grow soft and weak. So, I wanted to know if you would teach me how to be as badass as a commander in a fae army?" A small smile began etching itself on Evangaline's face.

The words seemed to do the trick, lighting up Chloe's entire face. Her arms flung around Evangaline's neck, pulling her into a tight embrace almost absent-mindedly. "I would be honored," she whispered into Evangaline's hair.

"Good."

"Now get ready! Go! I want you to meet my friends." Chloe pushed her away, playfully swatting her ass in the process.

Evangaline held tight to the dazzling gown and ran into the bathroom, eager to put it on. She narrowly avoided her best friend's swatting hands with a laugh that filled the room with happiness.

Walking into dinner was just as foreign as she assumed it would be. The tables in the throne room were still in the same places they were during breakfast, but now *completely* filled with courtiers—lords and ladies—dressed in their dripping opulence. Excess spilled over faster than the wine that poured into their cups.

Music filled the air from a man with a lyre and a woman with a flute. The sound of the people reveling nearly drowned out their playing, but they still played, nonetheless. Their feet tapped merrily along to the beat that they strummed and performed, lost in their own rhythm. It was a jovial melody behind the murmurs and laughs of the patrons.

When they first arrived, many fae quieted at the sight of Evangaline in her shimmering silver frock and Chloe in her ivory and gold eveningwear. Chloe didn't seem to notice as she pulled Evangaline further into the throng. Her hair was pulled back with two silver and diamond combs, sweeping off her face in delicate swoops. However, it also drew attention to her rounded ears. No doubt that was Chloe's plan when helping her get ready, but the shock rippled on the many faces within the court as they caught sight of her circular ears. All the attention was discomforting, but Evangaline held her head high and carried on.

The king, sitting atop his brilliant, glistening throne, chatted with Bastian and Atlas. Mugs of ale filled to the brim rested in all three of their hands as they chided and laughed with one another. Even in the fae realm, a gathering of macho men with beer in hand still appeared—*shocking!* Aside from their lavish wardrobe, the men looked like they were tailgating at some kind of sporting event.

"We have to greet the king," Chloe whispered, ushering Evangaline forward, her arm looped firmly around Evangaline's elbow. "Then we eat!" Chloe smiled and wiggled her eyebrows.

As the two women approached the dais, the room slowly quieted, waiting on bated breath to see how the king reacted to the human in their midst. Aside from the musicians lost in the magic of their music, the diners and revelers all gazed down their noses toward Evangaline, taking her in from top to bottom.

The three men finally noticed Chloe and Evangaline making their way over and ended their conversation abruptly. Bastian raised his ale to his mouth, a smile tugging at his lips, eyes roving over Evangaline's gown, lingering quite obviously at her elevated bosom. His constant perusal of her body made her feel more like a piece of meat than a princess, but even so, she couldn't help but feel a hint of fire pool in her lower belly, knowing she was the one who caught his eye.

"Your Majesty," Chloe said with a bow.

Echoing Chloe's words and movements, Evangaline followed a bit more awkwardly, "Your Majesty."

"Commander Darrow, it is lovely to see you once more." Both women stood and faced the king fully. "Lady Evangaline, it is an honor to host you. Please ladies eat, drink, dance. Enjoy the evening." His mask of regality remained on, neutral, aside from the subtle wink he gave Evangaline.

She smiled back happily. It felt like she passed her first trial of being a crown princess—hidden crown princess, that is.

Chloe inclined her head to the king, looped her arm through Evangaline's again and whisked her away to a nearby table full of extremely good-looking men. Like *extremely* good looking. Evangaline was not even sure how so many attractive people could exist in one land together. But here she was. Surrounded by apparently a group of fae male models—if such a thing existed.

"Boys!" Chloe raised her voice over the chatter that was slowly rising in the room once more. "This is my friend, *Lady* Evangaline." Evangaline squinted at her sarcasm.

In unison, the men's heads snapped to Evangaline. There were six of them in total and all twelve eyes fixated on the odd human woman standing before them, glittering like a disco ball wrapped in leaves.

At first, her heart pounded with fear and dread. This certainly didn't feel like staying in the shadows, like Darrin asked. But here she was shimmering in the moonbeams that illuminated the throne room, waiting for the men Chloe deemed her friends to say something … anything.

Then one of the men rose and walked over to her. He was well over six feet, but not as tall as Bastian. His stunning ebony skin glistened with a golden shimmer in the pale moonlight. His hair was buzzed short against his head, but the ghosts of black curls were present. The gleam in his hazel eyes bore into Evangaline's soul and made her tremble under the weight of it. His stoic expression made her stumble a couple of steps back as he trudged toward her.

Stopping a foot or so away, the man's gruff voice filled the silence, "Commander?"

Chloe squared her shoulders and neutralized her face. "Yes? Is there a *problem*, Shaw?"

"Yes, there is, Commander," he said without remorse.

Chloe went from jovial to full on protector in a solid blink of Evangaline's blue-green eyes. How she got between Evangaline and Shaw was nothing short of a show of her abilities and fearsomeness. A small bit of pride rushed through Evangaline at the display before her. She would have smiled fully if

Shaw didn't scare the shit out of her.

"It seems in your time away, Commander, you have kept us from your rather radiant friends, and I take grave offense to being shunned from such beauty, Commander." The hard lines of Shaw's face softened, giving way to a smirk.

A sigh of relief whooshed out of both Evangaline and Chloe at the same time. Their rigid backs relaxed with the breath that whispered past their lips.

Shaw, with a shit-eating grin showcasing the deep-set dimples on either side of his chiseled face, bowed at the waist, then straightened and extended a hand to Evangaline.

"Lady Evangaline, there is a seat next to me if you would do me the honor."

Evangaline glanced to Chloe, suppressing her smile as best she could, her eyes screaming, *What do I do?* Chloe, in return, just shrugged, a sly grin tugging at her rosy lips. Entirely unhelpful, her friend was.

"For the record, milady, there is no chair by him available! He's just a flirt. Don't buy into his bullshit! Aside from his smooth words, he couldn't satisfy a pig in heat," a red-haired man shouted across the table, stuffing a dinner roll in his mouth with a careless charm.

Shaw stiffened. "There will be a chair by me when I knock your sorry ass out of it, Charlie!" Shaw retorted, staring at the moon through the glass windows atop the throne room.

Finally, Evangaline caved to her base instincts and began to laugh. Chloe followed suit.

"I like all of you already! But who's pouring the wine?" Evangaline asked, facing the men with her hands on her hips.

With a raise of a wine bottle, a small tan skinned man with dark hair and honey lined brown eyes laughed. "That would be me!"

Evangaline raised her eyebrows. "Then I shall sit by you!" She said with a laugh, pointing in his direction.

Shaw threw his hands in the air cursing, "Aadi, you are now first on my shit list." The dark-skinned soldier reclaimed his seat, shoving Charlie nearly out of his chair in the process.

The moon illuminated the throne room in a white glow that left Evangaline relaxed. She sat in awe at how the silver rays of the moon and the twinkle of the stars cast the grand space in a different kind of radiance than she saw the sun bestow on the space. She assumed the room would fall into darkness once the sunlight was devoid of the sky. However, she couldn't have been more wrong. It was only a different kind of light, one that brought forth revelry and mischief.

Her tablemates, Chloe's friends, were nothing but captivating and allowed the time to pass at a rapid pace, perhaps even too quickly.

At first, they bickered about who was better with women, a conversation Chloe informed Evangaline occurred over many campfires and within a great many taverns. Another similarity between fae men and human men, they still compared dick size and had pissing contests. Maybe the fae and humans had more in common than she previously assumed?

The remaining three men were introduced as Des. A stoic curly-haired blonde man who spoke very few words during the pissing contest but was voted by the rest to be the luckiest at securing a woman for an *"evening of leisure"*—their words, not Evangaline's.

Evangaline aptly noted a quick glance between Des and Chloe that seemed more than that of a commander and her comrade. *Definitely going to need to hear that story later,* Evangaline thought to herself, watching the interaction behind her wine glass. As Chloe's hazel eyes met Des's aquamarine ones, they both smiled at one another before turning back to Shaw and Charlie bickering over the last dinner roll.

The other two were introduced as Murray, an older black-haired and ebony skinned man. And Lukas, a lithe man with sun kissed skin and light brown hair. Those two seemed to talk amongst themselves. After Evangaline snuck a peek at the two men and saw their hands intertwined, Chloe informed Evangaline the two had been an item on and off for nearly three decades.

Finally, the table's conversation delved into topics of battles and long nights on the road.

Evangaline learned Chloe gained her role as commander after being taken as a prisoner of war in a battle between the Royal Army and a rogue group trying to gain control of the land through conquering small villages. The group was called The Heretics, or something like that.

Her friend took out an entire camp of her captors and seized the rogue leader with only her sword and her wits. Evangaline didn't hide her pride this time. Her eyes sparkled with it before Chloe changed the subject to some inside joke between her and her boys. Something about a cow and Murray and truly they lost Evangaline once the cow was brought into the equation, but she laughed regardless. Their laughter booming around her was too infectious.

Sitting surrounded by fae warriors should have scared Evangaline, but they were so warm and welcoming, it almost felt like they were all family. They welcomed her without question, as though they could feel the sense of belonging chime through their consciousness too.

The stories they told, though sometimes quite graphic and horrifying, were told with pride and ebullience. They made her feel as though there was no one else in the room except for the eight of them. With their laughter and kindness, Evangaline actually felt, for the first time in the last two days, that the next few weeks might go by *too* quickly. If every dinner was to be this enjoyable and everyone was this kind, she didn't know how or why her mom had problems with the fae.

"His whole ass was out!" Des quipped, garnering a roar of laughter from the entire table.

Evangaline glanced at Chloe to find the pink-haired commander lost in a fit of laughter, so much so, tears streamed down her face.

Chloe slammed her hands on the table. "How did you not know that, Shaw?"

Shaw, looking anything but mortified, sipped from his wineglass, pinky raised in the air like a posh little lady, and tutted, "I may have been so inebriated that I thought I was wearing a full set of armor—"

"Evangaline, the jackass only put on his helmet! He strode around the fire, balls—"

Charlie's words cut off as a looming shadow took over the table just behind Evangaline. The rose and bergamot scent wafting through the air gave away the owner of the shadow before she even saw his face.

Bracing his hands on the back of the chair she sat in, Bastian's face was as emotive as a rock. "Keep telling the lady about Shaw's balls, Charlie. I'm sure that is suitable conversation for a guest of the king."

None of the men or Chloe answered, aware of their general's presence. They all instinctually straightened and sobered up, glowering up at the man who gave them orders. Their change of presence around Bastian irked her so much she knew she needed to defend them.

A smile and snicker braced the smooth planes of her face. Evangaline glanced around the table, then tipped her head back to look at Bastian. As she did so, his face looked down at her, eyebrow cocked in a scolding manner as if to say, *"These are not discussions suited for a princess."*

"Do you have a better story, General? Any times you walked around in nothing but your helmet?" She cocked her head. "If not … you're killing our buzz." A raise of her eyebrows and smirk that had him squinting at her had his stoic mask breaking slightly with amusement. His lips tried hard not to tug into a smile with every tiny twitch of his jaw.

She could feel the cadre around her tensing until Chloe burst out laughing, drawing Bastian's leer to her.

"Anything to add, *Commander*?" He quipped with a raised eyebrow. That small smile he bore moments earlier vanished in a flash.

"Not in the slightest, *General*," she quipped back, sipping from her wine.

Evangaline laughing to herself, grabbed her wine and began mirroring Chloe. The glass had just barely made contact with her lips when Bastian's massive hand dipped down and removed the glass from her clutch. He began to drink the sweet red wine as he walked away. His sultry eyes meet hers with a wink. His long muscular legs strode leisurely towards a table of glittering courtiers.

Mouth agape, she muttered flummoxed, "That motherfucker took my wine!"

A beat of silence followed closely by a roar of laughter from the table echoed through the room, drowning out the musicians faintly playing their tunes.

Still fixated on Bastian and her wine as he socialized around the room, Evangaline was unable to look away. Returning her attention, he raised the glass to his mouth once more, earning a small shake of her head before she returned to the conversation before her.

Aadi filled another glass for her *like a true gentleman.*

Chapter Fourteen

WHACK!

"Really!" Evangaline cried out.

Chloe paced before her, sword in hand, twirling it like the opponent she was facing was one of equal skill. Her eyes glittered with a menace that Evangaline had never seen before. *This* was warrior Chloe, and warrior Chloe was a stone-cold bitch.

Warrior Chloe woke Evangaline just before the sun rose and dressed her in the Celadonia equivalent to yoga pants—leather leggings. Knee high black lace up leather boots were tossed at her next. Followed by a fitted halter top and of all the things that screamed "wear me during a workout", a leather hastings corset that fit her just under the bust and ended right at the top of her pants. It took a minute to rearrange her organs to a position where she would be comfortable working out, but eventually, she managed. Ignoring the pain of the corset squeezing her biological anatomy, as the screaming of her muscles bellowed a war cry of anguish.

Evangaline quickly threw her hair up in a ponytail with a hair tie she found at the bottom of the tote bag she brought over from Vitalis. She would have to learn how to tie her hair up with the leather strips provided by Wren another time.

Her day started with a three-mile run around the castle grounds, which was, to Chloe's surprise, relaxing for Evangaline. She had run in 5k's and marathons since she was a kid. Stephen was a health nut and went on his daily runs with a smile on his face and motivational quote locked and loaded. As a teenager, she joined him. Every morning they ran until she went to college. It was one of the only times where her brain turned off and all that mattered was the stinging in her lungs and the pavement beneath her feet. She both missed and craved the way the brisk morning air stung her skin as they jogged through the grounds. Sneakily, she used her run to learn the layout of the palace.

It was the fifty push-ups, fifty sit-ups, and the fifty squats that made every muscle in Evangaline's body scream at her to thrust her knuckles into Chloe's jugular.

When Evangaline finally laid on the dewy grass, allowing the water to soak through her top and turn the sweat dripping down her back to a cool reprieve, she thought the torture was over. Chloe dashed those dreams swiftly as a very real, very sharp sword landed onto her stomach, followed by instructions to learn how to defend herself.

"You may be able to outrun your enemies, but that is not the fae way. You must learn how to fight them off too," Chloe quipped, unsheathing her ruby hilted sword from her back. "Abs aren't gonna save your life. Skill is!" Chloe chastised as Evangaline grunted her way upright.

Evangaline didn't protest to the notion of training. She thought it was a great idea—hell; it was her idea! It was the notion that she would have to, in that exact moment, stand on her legs—that felt like pudding—that seemed like a bit of a problem. Finally, however, she willed her strength and stood, allowing her legs to harden with each determined breath. Pushing the pain into a box and shoving it in a far corner of her brain. She did as Warrior Chloe instructed.

For two hours, Chloe taught Evangaline how to ground herself, how to find balance, and how to properly hold and swing a sword. It wasn't too difficult, till they sparred, when Chloe, with all the force she could muster, thrusted the hilt of her sword into Evangaline's gut, effectively knocking all the wind from her lungs.

"I rescind my request for you to train me," Evangaline murmured, staggering up right.

With a scoff Chloe lunged, her sword slashing right, then left, then downward in seamless an arc of skill and precision—straight for Evangaline's boots. With the luck of every god out there, Evangaline blocked and dodged, narrowly avoiding the tip of Chloe's blade across her knees.

Then, out of nowhere, Chloe kicked out her leg, knocking Evangaline flat on her ass. In the process, knocking the remaining bits of air from her lungs.

In a single breath, possibly the last that was in her body, Evangaline muttered, "I surrender."

Chloe, satisfied with her victory, took a seat next to Evangaline, dangling her arms over her curled up knees.

"You did good, Evie. I might make a warrior princess out of you yet."

Sitting up on her shaky forearms, Evangaline side eyed Chloe. "Is that your goal? I thought you were going for *dead* princess?"

Chloe smiled, nudging Evangaline. The commander truly didn't have a bead of sweat on her perfect brow. It was disgusting. "Ha! This realm needs you alive, not dead. You kept up though! For someone who has never even held a sword, you blocked and parried better than half the rookies in my regimen. Didn't land any fatal blows, but its only day one."

Collapsing back to the floor, Evangaline didn't even want to think of day two … or three … or four … "Ughhhhh." She cried with her eyes closed in a wince.

Ten minutes later Chloe had Evangaline up and walking—or attempting to walk—with her shaking legs buckling under her weight, to her lesson with Atlas. Her muscles screamed at her with every step she took. Her feet ached for a massage. Evangaline hadn't worked out that hard in a long time and the proof of that was painted into each painful step she took.

The things she would give for a bath and her bed were insurmountable!

Evangaline followed Chloe aimlessly around the palace hallways, not paying as close attention as she should have. She and the king never made it on this side of the palace during their grand tour. Each hall and room they passed was foreign to her. Mentally she was scolding herself for not retaining every detail of her surroundings, but the exhaustion within her weighed heavily, making it hard to focus on what lurked behind each door and corridor they passed.

Chloe took her down two flights of stairs, which made Evangaline wish her friend had killed her on their makeshift battlefield in the meadow behind the palace. Finally, they turned down a hallway lined with no windows and one set of doors—a pair of large wooden ones with shiny copper hinges at the far end. Despite being in the subterranean levels of the palace, the hallways were still wide and the walls still glistened with the white marble that sparkled like stars through the clouds. The blown glass sconces still lit the hallway brightly enough to feel like the sun was shining around them.

Hung along the walls were many great of pieces of art. Some were of nature; one was a detailed pond with purple flowers and dragonflies hovering lightly above the water's edge. A painting of the ever-changing forest bordering the castle filled another golden frame.

Others depicted people. One couple was featured in a great many. As she took them in, Evangaline recognized the pair from the stained-glass windows outside her room, Tuatha and Milesian.

One painting depicted the couple waltzing amid a grand ball. Her glittering green gown sparkled behind her as she twirled, her blond hair whipping around the man holding her close. Another showed Tuatha in the same distinct green gown with her loose blond hair once again, sitting atop Milesian's lap, sensually gazing into each other's eyes. Both of their left hands were intricately lined in copper bands that the artist took precise care of drawing the eye to.

All of the paintings enhanced the already beautiful hallway, but these ones had Evangaline in a trance. The same pull from the stained glass held her rapt fascination, telling her these people were more than just a king and queen of old.

Evangaline didn't even notice the massive doors at the end of the hall draw closer until Chloe eased them open just enough to slip inside.

Just when she didn't think she could be awestruck anymore from this place, she found herself in possibly the largest private library she had ever seen. The easily twenty-foot ceilings showcased dark mahogany shelves lined with books and scrolls alike. Towering rolling ladders connected all the shelves by a golden railing that lined the vast walls.

While the rest of the castle was light and airy, the library was dark and mysterious. The dark teal walls and dim lighting gave the room a cozy feel. No windows lined the room, allowing it to remain shaded aside from the faint glows of the scattered lights about. It made her feel incredibly comfortable, even more so than her room did, which seemed entirely outlandish, but it did. If she had her way, she would lock herself in here and never leave.

This would be an amazing place for a nap! She thought to herself as her hand trailed over the spines of the leather-bound books closest to her, bearing titles like *The Battle of Cela* and *A Star Vow's Power*. As she moved down the row reading the enamoring titles, her intrigue and curiosity grew. Three weeks would pass so fast knowing she had so many books to read, plus the ones within her own room!

"It is something to behold, is it not?" Atlas pondered as he came up next to an awestruck Evangaline. "Wait till you see the libraries of Mirth."

With a warm smile, he welcomed her to the library. Atlas ushered her to one of the high-backed teal leather chairs nestled before the roaring black marble fireplace at the far end of the room. It was then that Evangaline got a tiny bit excited to learn about Celadonia and all the magic it held. No one from Vitalis knew the secrets of Celadonia, and here she was within the fae stronghold with the opportunity to learn everything that she could about a land that seemed, only a few days ago, like nothing more than a fairytale.

She took an excited breath and then smiled back to Atlas. "This is amazing."

Chapter Fifteen

After bidding farewell to her torturous fitness instructor with a curt nod and two-finger salute, Evangaline followed Atlas beyond a few mahogany tables all the way to the high-backed chairs that sang her a siren song to nestle into their sweet cushions.

Situated on a table between the chairs was two clear crystal cups and a crystal decanter. A ruby stopper nestled just into the top of the decanter. An amber liquid resided a quarter of the way down, where it too beckoned to Evangaline's weary bones.

Atlas, dressed in his signature white, gazed at her happily with his pale blue eyes illuminated by the golden glow of the fire roaring just beyond them. As he took a seat opposite Evangaline, claiming the chair to the left of the fireplace, he sighed like he too was in desperate need for some comfort.

"Would you enjoy a drink, my lady?" He motioned to the amber liquid, noting Evangaline's eyes, glancing longingly at the bottle. "I can retrieve other beverages; this one is my personal favorite when I am here, which is most of the time, truthfully. It puts me at ease, between the liquor and the environment—"

The giant chair swallowed Evangaline whole as she sunk into it. Its cushions worn in from decades—maybe even centuries—of use. It fit her aching bones and muscles to perfection.

"I would love some!" She interjected, perhaps too eagerly. "I can see how you would be so comfortable. It's perfect here." She softly spoke, remembering she *was* in a library after all.

Atlas nodded in agreement. "Commander Darrow certainly didn't receive her ranking due to idle work. I assume she did not go easy on you?" His piercing blue gaze sparkled at Evangaline, a smirk playing on his lips in a teasing manner. "I was thrilled to hear from her that you two would be training. One is only healthy when both mind and body are well fit," he said, pouring two glasses, handing one to Evangaline before sitting back in his chair.

Wincing, she scoffed, "Oh no, she didn't. Go easy, that is." Evangaline sighed as she reclaimed her sunken state within her new favorite chair.

"I can send for a healer. They can give you a tonic or something to ease the pain."

The way the healer simply held her hand out and the wound from the coffee mug closed right up, all the while Evangaline stared at her in amazement—quietly soaking in the magic—was incredible. The power Madame Chevalier had was something out of a movie. If only the borders were down and the fae could heal humans from cancer and other ailments, the world might be a safer and happier place. However, it seemed silly to abuse the healer's power for some sore muscles.

"No, that's alright. But thank you for offering. It means a lot." She took a sip of the amber fluid and winced as the smooth burn glided down her throat, heating her insides. Whiskey. She never was a fan of whiskey, but somehow *this* whiskey was just what her aching body needed. "What have we in store for us today, Atlas?"

A smile tugged on his barely age marked face. "Let's get right to it! I wish to begin with the Kingdoms of Celadonia. I assume they do not teach you of the kingdoms that make up Celadonia in your Vitalian schooling. Besides, soon enough, the rulers of the Kingdoms will be upon us, and I want you prepared for all of them. They can be quite a handful if not prepared."

Evangaline set her glass down on the small table between them and grabbed the rather large burgundy book that Atlas began handing to her.

"Open to the first page, please," he softly instructed, all the while sipping his whiskey tenderly.

Obeying instructions, she opened the dusty tome, suppressing a cough as a slight puff of grime clouded the air.

The book had no title or author; it had no dedication, or anything that would detail what its pages spoke of. Even so, just like the many fantasy novels she read back home, the first couple of pages consisted of a black and white map of the realm of Celadonia.

Smoothing down the page, she ran her finger down the map, noting the five kingdoms. Starting at the northernmost tip of the massive continent was the Kingdom of Frost. Then, as she trailed her finger south noticed the Capital and the forest of changing colors.

Before she could form any words from her own mouth, Atlas cut her off. "That is where we are now. The Capital. It is where the king and his court live, alongside a small village to the south of us. It is mainly run by and inhabited by those of the lesser members of the court and the folk who work here, but a few others do reside there as well. Other than that, nature claims the rest of the land around the Capital."

Silently, Evangaline nodded and continued down the map.

To the right of the Capital lay the Kingdom of Leaves, bordered to the south by the Kingdom of Fire.

Ominous, Evangaline thought with a shudder, quickly running her finger to the direct left of the Kingdom of Fire to a region called the Kingdom of Mirth.

Then she saw it. Her finger rose from the page as she looked up at Atlas, her eyebrows squeezing together on her forehead in question.

"The Kingdom of Shadows?" She murmured quizzically.

The southernmost part of the continent and the largest of all the kingdoms. There was even an island off the coast tucked neatly into an inlet. All of it bore the unmistakable words scrolled in a delicate script—The Kingdom of Shadows.

She only made it two sentences into the book in her room but in the moment it called to her. An odd shutter echoed deep in her stomach, like something was pulling her toward this mysterious *Kingdom of Shadows*. She just assumed it was a clever name for a fictional story. Even the opening lines sounded fabricated in fable and fiction, but it wasn't fiction at all. It was not only staring at her in black and white script across the pages of the book she held, but it was evident in the terse silence that echoed between her and Atlas.

As she stared at the kingdom on the map, she couldn't ignore the flutter deep within her belly. Like her body was telling her something she couldn't quite decipher.

"That's an actual place?" she asked Atlas.

Atlas looked at her, just as confused as she looked at him. With a cock of his head to shift his snowy locks, he nodded and leaned forward, closer to her. "Yes dear. Why would you ask such a thing?"

"There's a book in my room. I didn't get through more than the first page, but I assumed it was fiction. I didn't realize it was real, that's all." She tried to soften out her features to pretend the elusive kingdom didn't send a thrill through her body for reasons she didn't know. For reasons she definitely couldn't tell Atlas of, merely because she didn't want to sound crazy.

"Shall we start then?" She plastered a fake smile on her face, despite her blood pulsating in her suddenly warm veins. *It's just the whiskey*, she told herself, trying to ignore the many odd things her body was doing, unable to stop staring at the Kingdom of Shadows on the gray-scaled map.

"Yes, let's. We shall start with your new home, the Capital," Atlas instructed, gesturing to flip the page.

Four long and tedious hours passed.

But Atlas was everything the king said about him and more. Despite his age, his memory was sharp and his quips even sharper. He was delightful to be around. Warm and cutting, just like the whiskey he continued supplying her with.

She learned just enough information about each kingdom and their leaders to secure her a gold star for the day. Despite there being *"a plethora more of knowledge needed to imbue the brain with,*" as Atlas reminded her when she finally felt confident in her day's studies.

There were five royals that ruled the kingdoms, all of which served under the Supreme King, her father. Four princes and one princess. Only her father's line could be a king or queen, as they ruled over the entire realm, while the royals of the kingdoms presided over their individual kingdoms.

Prince Tunit ruled over the Kingdom of Frost, a land of snow and ice. Their crowning achievement being that of their esteemed fishermen and enriched sea.

Prince Conall was the ruler of the Kingdom of Leaves. His land was closest to the Capital. His subjects mainly consisted of farmers and in that provide a lot of the realm with their food supply. An important kingdom indeed as they farm the grain and till the flour that helps to make the dreamy cake she has been yearning for since Chloe left her earlier that morning.

The Kingdom of Fire had in its disposal some of the land's greatest blacksmiths and swordsmiths. Craftsmen of the highest rankings call the Kingdom of Fire home all under the rule of Prince Surtis and his husband Taris, the latter being the greatest bladesmith in the land, according to Atlas.

The Kingdom of Shadows was the land of the last prince of the realm, Prince Ryder. Despite the cagey description of the land, Atlas simply deemed it as a place for both "creatures and dreamers alike." A description Evangaline was still working around. Despite her intrigue, Atlas did not go into depth about the southernmost kingdom, stating, *"Ryder tends to not involve the monarchy in his rule much anymore, so we don't need to worry too much about the Shadows. He will come and go and you, my dear, will not even notice he was here."* The old fae said, moving along in the lesson, despite Evangaline's need to sate the need to learn more.

Last but certainly not least, the Kingdom of Mirth. A land presided over by the only other ruling princess in Celadonia, Princess Ophelia. Alongside her wife Helena, the Kingdom of Mirth was described as "the land of art and sciences", or so Atlas deemed it. Housing not only the continent's greatest schools but also the largest library of the land, as well as various theatres and museums. It sounded like a dream.

"Have you been to all of the kingdoms?" Evangaline asked, curled in her chair, sipping on another cup of whiskey, taking her time to nurse its soothing warmth as the fire blazed to her side.

Relaxing with his glass on his chest, Atlas replied, "As old as I am, girl, I've seen them all and reveled in *all* of their delights."

She laughed, smiling at the notion of a young Atlas traveling the land. "Which is your favorite?"

"Mirth is always a nice vacation. I am a sucker for a night out at the theatre! I'm not one for heat, so Surtis's land isn't my cup of tea. Too warm. However, I was born in the old south, before the Convergence. Where the ancestors of the Kingdom of Shadows ruled. But even so, the new Kingdom of Shadows still feels like home, despite making the Capital my home at present."

Surprised by his admission, Evangaline thought to herself, *new?* "If you don't mind me asking, how old are you are exactly … for this version of the Kingdom of Shadows to be new?" She nervously asked, setting her cup down, nestling her hands in her lap, and curling into the smallest little ball.

Atlas laughed off the question at first, then his face grew solemn, the shadows of a sad memory clouding his vibrant eyes. "I was born a few decades prior to the Convergence when our great many kingdoms were expansive. You see, child, prior to the joining of our realms, much like Vitalis, our lands were vast and our houses mighty."

Evangaline nodded, taking in the information. It made sense. If half of the old Earth was wiped away and merged, it only made sense that Celadonia would have suffered and shriveled as well. "Is that why the princes and princess still preside over their kingdoms? Is it almost like how we have our states back in Vitalis?"

"Mhmm. Just like your states indeed. Each Kingdom was ruled by a family long before our land was known as Celadonia. In truth, there used to be many more, the land more divided and riddled with kingdoms. The ones that stand now adapted and are ruled by the most powerful of the fae rulers." He shifted in his seat, sitting with his arms on his knees at the front of his chair. "You see, every fae has enhanced abilities, smell … sight … movement

… breathing, even. However, some fae have gifts on top of their abilities. Commander Darrow, for example, has enhanced abilities, but no magic. The great houses and the rulers of the kingdoms descended from lines of the most powerful of fae magic."

"How did they get such gifts?"

"That is a question not even I can answer. Some believe they were gifts bestowed by the many gods, or maybe even the fates themselves. Others believe it was through the act of breeding with magical creatures. Others just believe it to be a part of nature, creating bigger and badder beings. In all honesty, the magic of this land predates even I. It is not something we question, just an aspect we covet. Magic is power, in more ways than one."

Evangaline rubbed a hand over her nervous chest. The conversation scared and fascinated her all at once. Magic wasn't something other than pulling a rabbit out of a hat at home. Science was where the real power lied. But in Celadonia, those in places of power were those that harbored magic. Just another reason she was ill-equipped in this land. She had no magic *or* enhanced abilities.

She let out a silent breath of disappointment. "And you? Do you have any *gifts*?"

A smirk was his first tell. "Aside from my handsome face and charisma? Very few." With that, he snapped his fingers and a ball of light, bright and white, just as bright as his beard and clothes and hair, glittered out of his fingertips. "More of a party trick than a gift."

Dazzled by the light, Evangaline laughed. "I can't even tell you what I would give for a party trick like that. It's incredible, Atlas!"

With a flick of his wrist, the orb disappeared straight into the tips of his fingers. Atlas's bright eyes twinkled with excitement and gratitude. "I suspect you have a great deal of party tricks tucked away inside of you, my lady." He said with a wink.

With a flourish of sarcasm, Evangaline snapped her fingers and smiled. "Tada!" Silence. The only lights flickering were the flames to her right in the hearth. "Nope … see no cool party trick. I used to be able to burp my ABC's … but I don't think that would fall into the princess category." She giggled to herself.

Atlas laughed heartily. "No, I suppose not."

A knock on the wooden doors startled both out of their laughter.

"You may enter," Atlas yelled, rising from his seat. Clasping his hands behind his back, he faced the door.

Bastian entered clad in his evening attire. His shiny black boots were muffled by the soft dark teal carpet, but his heavy gait was still audible in its thud.

"If you are finished for the day, the princess has been requested to attend dinner tonight with the Commander," Bastian spoke sternly, bowing at the waist to Evangaline.

With a huff, Evangaline rose and faced Bastian with a sarcastic smile. "I swear she's obsessed with me ... Alright." With a slight turn on her heels, she faced a beaming Atlas. "Thank you for today. Same time tomorrow?"

Atlas simply nodded at her, claiming the large leather-bound book off the table and holding it to his chest.

"She is all yours, General." Atlas said as Evangaline approached Bastian, trying her hardest to cover the slight limp from her screaming muscles.

"All mine?" Bastian uttered in a low whisper down at her. "I like the sound of that." A cheeky smile plastered on his hewed face, his evergreen eyes twinkled with amusement and possessiveness.

"Good God," she muttered, walking past him and straight out the massive doors.

Chapter Sixteen

Bastian relaxed on the lush green settee in her living quarters, his booted feet propped up on the coffee table, head reclined back. The luscious chestnut hair of his fell over the back cushions. He brought her straight to her room, only to crash on her couch and immediately take a nap while Wren helped her get ready for dinner.

Choking down a bit of jealousy, Evangaline approached the couch and peered down at Bastian. His eyes were closed, his broad arms crossed over his chest.

Today had been long and physically draining. Her legs were still aching and throbbing. Every step felt as though she was being sliced by a hot blade straight through the muscles that held her up and yet, here she was, standing in a pair of heels watching a man on her couch sleep soundly.

"Didn't anyone teach you staring isn't polite?" He muttered.

Smirking a bit, she fiddled with a bracelet made of rainbow diamonds and stones. "Didn't anyone teach you it wasn't polite to take a nap on a stranger's couch uninvited?"

His forest green eyes flicked open, and for a moment they just stared at one another, eyebrows raised. A standoff.

He rose off the couch with a sigh. "Let me," Bastian motioned at her miserably, failing to latch the glittering bracelet she was trying desperately to clasp.

She obliged, way too tired to keep trying on her own.

"You look very beautiful tonight," he said, watching as his large hands consumed the dainty bracelet.

Evangaline's cheeks flushed with color. She had to bite the inside of her cheek to not smile up at him like some idiotic crush addled teenager.

But she did feel beautiful tonight and Bastian saying so just made her feel even more so.

Her gown was an ivory chiffon that draped into a low V neck just above her navel. The back mirrored the front, except it had two long pieces of fabric that hung from her shoulders to the floor. An ombre rainbow effect was delicately died into the chiffon, creating two waterfalls of the purest pastel rainbows. A single layer of a glittery fabric shimmered with holographic flecks a few layers under the top chiffon layer that gave the gown just the right amount of shine.

Wren pulled her hair back into a low bun and placed a few flowers in it to distract from the oils that were making it greasier as time went on. She had no time to wash it, so they worked with what they had.

Bastian fiddled with the bracelet for a couple of seconds, then finally secured it. His hand remained gently caressing the inside of Evangaline's wrist for a few moments before sliding down to hold her hand.

"Sit with me tonight." It wasn't a question, but more of a command from the fae general.

Neither one of them made eye contact, their gazes fixated on their joined hands.

Evangaline knew deep down she didn't feel anything for Bastian. It was nothing against him as a man, it was the lack of a spark. She had been with a man once before that she felt no spark towards, and she wasn't interested in wasting more time sparkless. Bash was good looking and he sure as hell knew how to flirt with a woman, but she didn't feel anything else for him. He was her ally in this clusterfuck of a situation and she didn't want to string him along or cost him his position.

"I can't. Chloe. I prom—"

"She will be fine." Finally, his eyes met hers. "Plus, she got you last night … and this morning."

Squinting up at him. "And do I get a say?" she said mockingly.

A devious smirk tilted his lips. "Not on this."

Unfortunately for Evangaline, her stupid girl brain overrode all common sense while lost in his eyes. The word escaped her mouth before she had time to really process the condescending and arrogant tone in his statement. "Okay," she whispered.

"Okay." His smile crept up to meet his eyes before he placed her hand on his arm and ushered her to dinner.

Chloe was not thrilled at all when Evangaline informed her, Bastian asked for her to sit with him. Aside from a sigh, eye roll, and punch to the arm, Chloe also added in a whispered shout of Evangaline's personal favorite quote. One that set the cadre laughing to the moon like a pack of wolves, "Chicks before dicks!" she grunted harshly at Evangaline.

Bastian overheard and whisked Evangaline to his table just as Evangaline was replying angrily, "Hypocrite! *Mr. Brooks?*" Which shut Chloe right up. By the look on Shaw's face, she would not get away without elaborating on that little tale.

For most of the dinner, Evangaline sat with Bastian and a few lords and ladies, and pretended the distrustful stares and whispers weren't affecting her. Her anxiety crept up her spine and made her hands tremble at the sudden feeling of becoming the outcast amongst the very people she was tasked with winning over. She surely did not belong with *these* people. Their diamonds dripped from their hooped ball gowns and shimmered even in the absence of light. They made her beautiful chiffon dress look nothing grander than a hand-me-down nightgown.

The night prior, with Chloe and her cadre, Evangaline felt welcomed, at ease. The rest of the room melted away in their laughter and comradery. But here, with these particular fae—the nobles—she could not feel like more of a stranger. The way they stared her down, taking in the shape of her ears with down-turned lips and squinted eyes, made Evangaline want to duck under the table and hide.

"And what is your business here, *Lady Evangaline?*" A black-haired and waif thin fae woman sneered at her.

Swallowing a gulp of wine and squaring her shoulders, Evangaline opened her mouth, reminding herself to be brave…she was the princess after all…they just didn't know that yet!

"She is a guest of the king, is that not business enough, *Lady Whittell?*" Bastian sneered, sipping from his wine, not allowing Evangaline to answer.

Gently he placed a hand on Evangaline's bobbing thigh, stilling her jostling. She hadn't even realized she was doing it till his callused hand engulfed her leg. It was a nervous tick that drove her mother—and apparently Bastian—nuts.

Softly, he began sweeping his finger back and forth in a nurturing movement. Her body felt all sorts of conflicting emotions. His touch sent chills of discomfort down her spine while simultaneously calming her active nerves.

Lord Whittell leaned forward, his stocky frame leaning on the table, making the small floral centerpiece slide toward him, the water sloshing about the vase. *Okay, so not all fae are wickedly attractive,* Evangaline noted in the journal of her mind.

With a tsk, Lord Whittell let his voice be heard. "We are members of this court, General. A human woman has entered *our* land, took reception with *our* king, trained with *our* soldiers, all in two days' time. We are entitled to be privy to the king's motives. Don't think we do not see and hear everything in this court." A quick glance at Bastian's hand on Evangaline's leg had the lord smugly sitting back in his chair. "Are only the king and his advisors aloud human slaves, Bastian? Is that what this is? The last time the king sampled human filth, it did not end up well for either party." Lord Whittell laughed to himself.

That was her mother he was talking about. Evangaline almost lunged across the table and stabbed him with her salad fork right then and there. She had no desire to win over this court if they all were like this pompous ass. She would prefer to stick to her idle life in Vitalis and let Darrin's throne burn to the ground than appease the Whittell's and their cronies.

While Evangaline's heart raced with disgust and anger, Bastian seemed thrilled by the challenge of dealing with Lord and Lady Whittell. The arm, not caressing Evangaline, rested on the table casually while his hand sat on his wineglass, making idle circles around the rim.

The smile that tugged at his face did not at all put Evangaline at ease.

Retreating into her better nature, she sucked inwards, longing for a bath, book, and bed. The three heavenly B's.

She simply gazed down at Bastian's hand and the slow movements of his thumb on her thigh. Trying with all of her might to gain her composure and not dive into a full-blown panic attack right in the middle of a crowded dinner service.

A solid thirty seconds of silence passed, Lord and Lady Whittell reclined in their seats, while the rest of the table sat quiet in anticipation. Their heads shifting uncomfortably between Bastian and the Lord. The two courtiers were all too smug in their self-proclaimed victory of making Evangaline feel out of place and less than she was. It lit a fire within her very core and made her so angry she didn't even notice herself speaking before it was too late.

"I am no one's—"

In one swift movement, Bastian rose, nearly knocking over his own chair.

"Quiet Evangaline," he commanded harshly down at her.

Bastian whirled around to King Darrin whom of which was sitting on the dais chatting a little too closely with a beautiful blonde-haired fae woman.

"My King," Bastian boomed, bowing, silencing the entire room with his words. "It would appear, Lord and Lady Whittell, doubt your motives in welcoming Lady Evangaline into our court and seek an explanation as to why she has entered *their* land, took reception with *their* king, and trained with *my* soldiers."

Clearly Bastian didn't speak to Darrin about not putting Evangaline in the spotlight and harboring unwanted targets on her back. Cause now every eye in the entire throne room was fixated on her, many of which lighting with offense at her presence.

The musicians stopped their music. The servers stopped pouring wine. And Evangaline just sunk into her seat, her embarrassment clouding her vision. Or maybe that was her tears building? It did not take long to realize it was both.

She never was the kid in school to volunteer to present a project. She was always the one who waited till the end and was basically dragged to the front of the class kicking and screaming.

The man who sired her remained silent for a moment. His eyes bore down at them in a way that conveyed he, too, was ready to strike Bastian down for drawing unwanted attention to the daughter he fought to hide. His lips twisted from a tight line to an overly forced smile and back to a neutral façade.

But like a true monarch, he stood slowly, dismissing the woman he was wooing, and faced the couple doubting his actions. He did not look happy, but he also did not look angry. He just simply was.

In that moment, the crowd's heads were on a swivel, looking back on forth between Evangaline and Darrin. She couldn't help but hope no one saw the similarities that she now saw every time she gazed in the mirror. The hair, the eyes, the face shape.

"Lord and Lady Whittell, and any others for that matter that dispute my hospitality, hear this once. Lady Evangaline is a guest of my home and, therefore, yours. If you do not like my choice, by all means, find accommodations elsewhere. I hear the Kingdom of Fire is lovely this time of year." And with that, he sat back down and motioned to the musicians to spark up their tune once more.

That was it.

Once the music filled the air, Bastian slowly turned and sat, his arrogance wafting through the air like mustard gas. His meaty hand once more found its place on Evangaline's lap. However, between the anger and embarrassment that was blurring her vision and the shallow breaths she was trying to take to avoid her surging panic attack, she had no willpower to swat it away as much as she wanted to, so there she sat.

Staring at the half-eaten dinner on her plate, conversations echoed around her, but Evangaline only heard the voices of two men echo in the chasm of her mind. Lord Whittell calling her mother "*human filth*" and Bastian telling her to be quiet. How dare he not allow her to stand up for herself and her mom. No, instead he embarrassed her. Made her feel a fool … made her feel weak … as though she needed a man's validation and protection. She needed to get out of there. Needed to get away from the Lord and the General before they both took a utensil to the eyeball.

Coming to her senses, gathering a calming breath, she spoke, "Apologies. If you would excuse me. Thank you once more for such *fine* company." Shooting Bastian a glare that mortal men would run from, she pushed her seat back and walked out of the room. Her pace getting faster and faster as she closed in on the copper doors of the throne room.

Chapter Seventeen

Rainbow chiffon billowed behind her in an effervescent streak of light against the whitewashed backdrop of the palace. Evangaline ran up the stairs in the foyer and down the hall she thought led to her room. Her hot and angry tears pricked her eyes with an unfathomable rage, each one straining to drip their way out. The anxiety and panic shaking her from the inside out made her hands tremble as she fisted the many layers of her skirt.

She just wanted to go back to Vitalis. She wanted to call her sister and vent. She wanted coffee from that godforsaken French press. She wanted to not have to be a princess of a land that despised her and thought her nothing more than "human filth" that was using their realm as nothing more than a vacation spot. Evangaline didn't ask to come to the realm of the fae. She did not ask to be the sole heir to the throne. She did not ask to be a crown princess. All she *wanted* was to be free. Free from the burdens of others. Free from the soul-crushing weights of society. Free from the plague of darkness that clouded her mind in moments like these.

Her breathing became tighter, and she felt as though she was drowning and lost.

Quite literally, though, she was lost.

In her haze, she must have made a wrong turn and now, as her panic attack consumed her, she stared down a hall lined with wood and copper doors she had never seen before. Tapestries of foreign creatures and fruits hung on the walls. She had never seen this hallway before, but was too tired to find her way out.

She was alone, and that was all she needed.

Slowly, she slid down the wall, cupping her face in her hands.

"Honey, there you are! Come here." Chloe uttered from down the tapestry ridden hallway panting out hollow breaths. Wrapping her arms around Evangaline, she sank to the floor too, squeezing Evangaline in tight. The cold bite of her armor burned into Evangaline's shoulder. "It's okay," she murmured into Evangaline's hair, placing her cheek on the crown of the broken princess's head.

Unable to remove her face from her hands, Evangaline whispered, "This was all a mistake."

"I told you not to pick dicks over chicks …" Chloe smirked. "What happened back there?" Chloe's hand smoothed calming strokes down Evangaline's arm.

Looking up at Chloe, tears streamed down her face, Evangaline chuckled, "I was so mad, Chlo. I *am* mad. Those people … those fae … they aren't like you and the guys. I don't know how I am going to win over anyone from this kingdom when they refer to my mother … whom of which they don't know *is* my mother…as *human filth*." Evangaline shook her head. Her rage-soaked tears stained her cheeks. "Then Bash … I was just about to defend myself … the bastard told me to be quiet, literally said *'Be quiet,'* and then threw me to the wolves instead. Made the whole room look at me. He gave them a reason to judge me even more than they already are. I don't think I can do this."

Chloe shook her head, unable to cover the annoyance gathering in her eyes. "The Capital courtiers can be assholes. The entire realm knows it. They think they are entitled to the world because their ancestors had money and passed it down. I'll gladly shoot an arrow into the gelatinous oaf that is Lord Whittell. He will be great target practice. Better yet … I'll teach *you* to shoot an arrow through his fat ass!"

Evangaline laughed, wiping her tears. "Deal. Do I have to go back in there, Chlo?"

"No one is making you. I'm sure the king will understand." Chloe said softly, brushing Evangaline's face clean of the remaining evidence of her tears.

"But I should, shouldn't I." Evangaline chided. Resting her head on the block of cool marble behind her. "I can't let them see they got to me. I am their goddam princess after all, even if they don't know it." She smirked, feeling her anxiety subside with each second that Chloe held her.

Chloe smiled at the notion. "I think that's the first time you've admitted it out loud. And for what it's worth, Evie, there is no one better suited to do this."

"Ugh, Chlo. Will you do it all with me? I'm scared shitless …" Evangaline sniffled.

"Absolutely, and if you ever need to cry some more," Chloe patted her shoulder, the metal clinking in return. "I've got a perfectly good shoulder to cry on … and a very sharp sword to cut some bitches with."

With a sigh and laugh, Evangaline crashed her head thoughtlessly back into Chloe's armored shoulder. "Ow," she said, laughing through the slight pain now sweeping across her forehead.

Chloe and Evangaline walked back into the throne room arm in arm thirty minutes later, as though nothing had happened. Some heads turned in their direction, but not nearly as many as Evangaline thought would. Certainly, Lord and Lady Whittell were not thrilled with her arrival, but they could sincerely fuck right off.

Across the room, the king sat in his throne alone, his face held a hard edge to it as his knee mindlessly bounced. Like father, like daughter. As he swept his gaze across the room, he caught Evangaline's eyes and smiled demurely. She could see his appreciation and pride for coming back into the room. She didn't realize how much she sought his approval, but apparently, she did. It eased her anxiety monumentally to know that she did right by him. Maybe Chloe was right…maybe she could do this?

Chloe steered her toward the table with her comrades and pulled out a chair, ushering Evangaline in.

"The lady of the hour! We are honored you have chosen us once again." Shaw chastised, despite the ominous glare from Chloe.

"Aadi, you got that wine again?" Evangaline sighed.

Aadi smiled and flicked up his thick black eyebrows. "Glass or bottle?"

Taking a seat in the pulled-out chair, Evangaline puffed her cheeks out in her best imitation of a puffer fish, really considering her options. "Both?" she laughed somberly.

Chloe's cadre spent the next hour cheering Evangaline up and making her laugh. In hushed tones, they told Evangaline embarrassing facts about the courtiers filling the room. Followed by more stories of depravity and battle filled escapades.

Slowly, Evangaline was reassured once more that not everyone in Celadonia was a distrustful asshole, just apparently the nobility. From that moment on, she made herself a silent vow. She would not try to win the hearts of the nobles, no matter how much Darrin wanted her to. They weren't the vast majority of Celadonia, anyway. It was the workers, the families, the people who stayed in the village and helped her settle into this new land that she owed her thanks and attention. Not the glittering twats who looked at her as beneath them just because of where she was born. If Darrin wanted their approval, he could beg for it himself, but Evangaline would not—in good conscious—let them take up space in her brain, making her feel less than she was.

From the corner of her eye, Evangaline saw Bastian rise from his table of jerks and start to make his way in her direction. She rolled her eyes and sighed, trying to ignore him as best she could.

"Evangaline, I need a moment." Bastian murmured from behind her.

Beside her, Chloe stiffened. Glancing up at Bastian. "We were just on our way out. Right Evie?" The hostility in her tone showcased her anger at the General and Hand of the King. If the scowl on Chloe's face didn't already tell Bastian he wasn't welcome, that tone sure did.

"Thank you for that information, Commander, but I was speaking to

Lady Evangaline." Bastian's hostile tone matched Chloe's.

Evangaline shook her head. "Shall we take the matter up with the king? Alert the room? Let's make a spectacle of it!" Evangaline murmured under her breath onto the rim of her wineglass.

Des snickered at the breathy sarcasm, and Charlie took a wide-eyed sip of his ale. The only indicators to Evangaline that her angry comment was louder than she expected it to be.

Choking down the swell of anger that filled her at the sight of Bastian, Evangaline kept facing away from him.

His anger, however, swept in a wave over the table. The presence of the man set Evangaline on edge. His beauty sure did a good job of concealing his darkness.

His signature bergamot and rose smell grew stronger as he pressed in closer to her ear. "We need to talk. I would like it to be in private unless you would prefer it here and now." His breath was hot in her ear.

Evangaline swallowed the last of her wine and set the glass down with enough force to rattle the silverware on the porcelain dishes before her.

"Gentleman, Chlo, thanks for the lovely evening. I shall be retiring to my room now." She punctuated her sentiment by pushing her chair out straight into Bastian's groin. His contained grunt of displeasure swiped a completely sincere smile on her face.

"Will we have the honor of seeing you tomorrow, milady?" Shaw asked, the slightest hint of humor in his eyes.

"Sure," Evangaline said with a forced smile. "See you bright and early, Chlo."

Giving Chloe a kiss on the cheek and waving her goodbyes, Evangaline made her way out of the throne room once more, keeping well ahead of Bastian and his temper.

Chapter Eighteen

"Talk to me, Princess," Bastian demanded. His agitation echoed in his voice as he banged on the bathroom door.

The entire walk back to her room, Evangaline masterfully ignored his presence. Now, with a somewhat clear head, and more than enough anger to last her a few rounds in a boxing ring, she decided she would sequester herself in her bathroom and try to relax. The added bonus of holding up in the palatial bathroom long enough for the general to get the hint and leave her alone sat idle in the back of her mind as well.

A bath sounded wonderful, maybe even a face mask—there had to be one somewhere around here?

"If I was a face mask, where would I be?" she whispered to herself as she riffled through the drawers in the vanity, ignoring Bastian in the process. Random bottles and jars were neatly stacked in military like rows. She sifted through them all until a jar labeled "rose scented face balm" caught her eye.

She tried to drown out Bastian with the sound of the water filling the tub, but that plan was already failing. He was persistent in his pursuit of her attention, banging on the door the second she closed it in his face.

"You have *nobly* returned me to my room. You can leave now." Evangaline shouted from her closet as she gathered the most luxurious silk crop top and short pajama set and made her way back into the bathroom.

"That's not going to happen," he shouted back, banging harder.

Evangaline scoffed. "Make it happen."

"Is that an order?" He retorted through an arrogant breath.

With a newfound authority, Evangaline channeled her inner Chloe and replied, "Yes! An order from your princess to kindly fuck off."

Beyond the door she could hear Bastian's haughty laugh and then finally, *finally*, his footfalls grew quieter, and the room became silent.

She took a deep breath and then began to take down her hair, allowing the flowers Wren placed in it to fall in the sink.

Her relief was short-lived.

Over her shoulder, the makings of a glittering, opal-hued starburst sprang from a portal.

Stepping through and closing it up in one angry flick of the wrist, Bastian faced her. Arms crossed, legs firmly planted. Ready for battle. Luckily, for him, this evasion of her privacy set all the anger she shed coursing right back through her veins and primed her for a fiery war.

"You are seriously twisted. Did your mother drop you on your head as a child because there are definitely a few marbles loose up there?" Evangaline asked sarcastically. Charged with the flames of her fury.

Icy indifference crossed Bastian's eyes. Yeah, he wanted a fight. "You have no idea how twisted I can be, Princess."

Turning back to the sink in a show of dismissal, and murmured a hushed, "Lovely."

Evangaline planted her hands firmly on the counter, watching Bastian in the mirror. Waiting for him to take the hint and leave. Yet as he stood staring back at her, it was evident the brute was just as stubborn as she was.

He stepped closer to her, a wicked look glinting in his eyes. "Tell me Princess, what exactly is pissing you off? Your attitude started after I confided in the king. Or was it my touch on your skin that flustered you?"

She whipped around so fast she didn't realize how close to her he really was. Only inches separated them, but Evangaline was too angry to care. "Confided? That was you *confiding*? Good God, Bash, the whole goddam room was involved in you *'confiding!'*" She punctuated the last word with some air quotes. "You would benefit from looking up the definition of that word!"

"Okay, sure, I wanted a spectacle. I wanted the room to know those comments weren't tolerated. I wanted Darrin to know the princess was being questioned. I wanted the entire room to look at you sitting next to me and know ..."

Shoving him back in a fit of rage, "They don't know I'm the princess, Bash. Darrin told me to fucking lie low! I can handle myself...I *was* handling it myself when you told me to be quiet! When you steamrolled me. Ignored me. You didn't think about anything other than showing your own authority and stroking your own ego! You were selfish!" She screamed at him.

With tears of rage forming in her blue-green eyes, she shoved past Bastian's towering frame and made her way out of the bathroom, only stopping to turn off the water filling the tub. There was no bath in her future now. Relaxation be damned.

She was not entirely sure where to escape him since he seemed keen on just making a portal into her private spaces now.

Barreling onto the balcony, Evangaline managed to choke back her tears just a little bit before two large, cool hands wrapped around her waist, making her flinch. Bastian's chin rested on her head, locking her into the hard press of his body. "I'm sorry, Princess." He sighed, as though apologizing for his actions physically pained him.

Evangaline just stood there, hands braced on the stone railing, silent tears falling down her face. Slowly, Bastian turned her around to face him. With a finger hooked under her chin, he tilted her head up to bring her eyes to his, his other hand curled possessively around her waist in a bruising grip.

"I wanted everyone in that room to know the human woman sitting there was *mine*. From the moment you ran into me in that club in that sexy little skirt, to the moment you cracked my head open with a mug, I knew you would not belong to any other man. You are mine Evangaline." His voice was measured and bode a possessive nature.

Staring up at him, she felt nothing but fear course through her body. She searched his face to find if he was telling the truth, but couldn't find anything other than harsh lines and searing eyes. She scoured the wrinkle furrowing his brow for lies and came up empty-handed. Her eyes gazed at his lips and their slightly parted stance, waiting for him to say anything else, but he didn't.

"I only plan to be here three weeks, Bash. I can't be yours. And I don't belong to anyone—"

"I want you and I'll have you." His voice rumbled through his chest in deep reverberations, cutting off her words completely.

Suddenly, his mouth was on hers. A kiss filled with nothing but raw need and sin. His hand tangled in her hair while his other one held her close to him around her waist.

At first, Evangaline resisted, but his kiss was intoxicating. Finally, she gave herself to him. Reveling in the feel of recklessness. Caving to the needs of her body and not the wiles of her head.

Savoring the need coursing through his veins, she leaned into his touch and allowed him to fist her hair, tilting her head up so he could draw the kiss even deeper.

This was careless and stupid, but she needed a release. She needed a minute where she only cared about herself and not all the things currently going on in her life. So Evangaline let him kiss her with a recklessness she never knew lived inside her.

She had never been kissed with so much desperation before. It was primal … animalistic, even.

But he needed more. In truth, so did she. It had been over a year since she had a man touch her in any intimate way. She should have cared that she was seeking it through Bastian, but she didn't care at all whatsoever.

As though he could read her mind, the hand on her waist dove south, grasping onto her hip. The hand in her hair dropped to knead her breast through her gown, searching through the thin fabric for her pebbled nipple. Slowly, with measured and dominant steps, he backed her up, pressing her back into the cold, unforgiving stone railing.

All the hairs on her body stood at attention. The sensation of his touch was cold and exhilarating.

"Say you want me," he grunted breathlessly onto her lips.

Slowly, she opened her eyes and took a much-needed breath. Her heart pounded in her aching chest while her brain failed to grasp onto logic.

"I want you." *Just for tonight.*

That was all he needed to hear. Bastian's arms crashed around her, hauling her up. Her legs wrapped instinctually around his waist, the light material of her dress hiked higher around her thighs in the process.

His hands were firm as they held her close to him.

She wrapped her arms around his neck and plunged her hands into his silken strands of hair as she kissed him again, this time being the one supplying the need.

Lost in his touch and taste, she didn't feel him walk them back into the bedroom. He laid her onto the bed and stood at the foot and let his animalistic eyes feast on her. He was a predator, and under his unrelenting stare, a small zap of nerves pinched in her chest. With the motion of his hand easing up his body, she shoved her nerves deep into a box and sent them away. Her already damned logic to hell might as well ride her reckless wave to completion.

Slowly, he unbuttoned the deep purple jacket that covered his broad chest, tossing it to the floor. His white shirt followed, leaving nothing but his toned and tan chest to glisten in the faint light from the bathroom.

Good lord, the man was a sight to see. In her lifetime, Evangaline would not imagine talking to a man this good-looking let alone kissing one. Let alone whatever was about to happen. And she had a pretty good idea what he wanted if the bulge in his trousers was any indication.

With a great tug, he shucked off his boots, tossing them atop his now mounting pile of clothes in the corner.

"Come here," he demanded with his gruff voice. Deep, sultry notes clung to those eight letters and two words.

Evangaline paused, eyeing him warily.

"Now." He commanded.

Swinging her legs off the bed, she padded over to him, his eyes not missing a single second of her walking to him.

He grabbed one of the ribbons of chiffon hanging off her shoulder and twisted it in his hand, letting the fabric tangle through his fingers.

She tried her hardest to keep her breathing slow and controlled, to not let him see she was nervous.

"This gown is beautiful on you, Evangaline."

"Thank you," she whispered through barely parted lips.

A provocative smile graced his lips. "But I don't want you wearing it anymore."

"Oh?"

Possessively, he ran his hands down her shoulders, over the sides of her breasts, and down her waist, leaving an icy trail of goose bumps along their wake.

He softly pulled her in close to him, wrapping his hands around her back, bracing themselves on either side of the buttoned-up enclosure of her bodice.

Her heart thundered in her chest as her hands clenched at her sides.

Bastian bit his bottom lip, hiding the devil's smirk gracing his face. All the while, his eyes situated on the swells of her breasts. "Yeah, Princess. I want it off."

A sudden yank of the soft material at her back jolted Evangaline forward, crashing her into his chest. Through brute force and his superior strength, he ripped through the back of the delicate bodice, pulling apart every ivory button that kept her inside the beautiful gown.

Dozens of pearl buttons flung in various directions around the room and onto the floor. Some rolled under the bed, others flew onto the balcony, one rolled clear into the living room.

She let out a quick yelp that had Bastian laughing through the kiss he was crashing onto her lips. His tongue took her prisoner.

His skilled hands made quick work of the gown, leaving it a useless rainbow puddle on the floor. In turn, leaving her completely bare to him, aside from a pair of silk underwear that covered very little.

The cool air from the open French doors settled over her now exposed skin, warring with the fire in her blood.

"Holy shit, Evangaline." Bastian whispered onto her lips as she made quick work of unfastening his trousers while he did away with her silken undergarments. Their hands flying at lightning speed. There was no savoring the moment. High emotions thrust them into the arms of one another and those heated emotions were pushing them to fighting for their own releases and pleasure.

Their bare bodies pressed firmly against one another a moment later. Their hands roaming across the vast array of exposed skin in torrid exploratory movements.

Bastian's hands situated themselves in her hair once more and held it in a tight grasp as their maddened kiss became more frantic. Pulling till her scalp tingled in slight pain.

In one swift movement, Bastian scooped Evangaline into his arms and threw her on the bed, only breaking their kiss to situate himself over her.

"You are so sexy, Princess."

"Thank you?" She said, twisting a piece of his hair in her fingers. "You're not so bad yourself," she quipped, biting down on her lower lip.

"Something tells me you don't believe me," he said in a low purr, laying a trail of kisses down her jaw and neck.

Breathy, "Truthfully? I don't. I think you just said nice things to get into my pants." Evangaline replied.

Clamping her nipple in his mouth ferociously, drawing a gasp and moan from Evangaline, Bastian snickered, "So far it has worked."

Arrogant asshole.

Then, before she had a chance to retort, he took her nipple into his mouth once more, caressing it with his tongue, soothing the ache from his bite. Every sarcastic comment and argument swirling in her head was nullified with the frenzied pulls of his lips on her overheated body.

She fisted his hair in her hand as she arched her back, unable to tell him to slow down. He was sending her right for the edge. Quickly.

This wicked man was going to be her undoing.

Slowly, he trailed his hand up her leg. His finger making idle serpentine motions while he worked his magic with his mouth on her breast.

Her aching need for him grew stronger and stronger with every swipe of his tongue and trail of his fingers.

That wayward hand of his gripped her thigh, prying her legs apart as he continued his trail of kisses from her breast to her stomach, stopping right above the part of her that ached for his attention. His head tipped up, revealing an absolutely sinful grin as a soft mewl escaped her closed lips, begging for release.

"You like this, Princess?"

"Fuck yes, why'd you stop?" is what she wanted to say. However, all that came out was a breathy, "Uh, huh."

Pleased with himself, he let out a mischievous laugh right into her inner thigh as he began kissing and teasing around all her most sensitive areas. Never touching the part of her that pulsed and ached for his touch.

The skin on her entire body pebbled, and a shiver coursed up her spine, locking her muscles tightly in an atrophy like state.

"Then you're going to love this," he joyously murmured as he stopped teasing her with kisses to her inner thigh and rose back up over her, smashing a kiss back onto her lips in a fierce claiming that had her grasping onto his shoulders in sheer surprise.

Just as he was with all other aspects of his life, Bastian was not gentle. His kiss, his grip, his force was harsh and filled with a possessive need to own, to claim.

And with one mighty thrust, he plunged himself deep inside of her.

Her gasp shot out as he growled from pleasure.

His claiming of her was sudden and swift. Her body struggled to welcome him, but as she relaxed into the chill of his skin, every muscle and nervous beat of her heart mellowed out under his weight.

He kissed her neck and throat as he pulled out and thrust back in again. Over and over.

Each movement filled with more need, more want, in an attempt to leave his feral mark on every inch of her body.

Evangaline was positive this was not lovemaking, this was pure primal sex. There were no tender kisses or whispered sentiments of admiration.

It was something she had never experienced before. Bastian's need for her body and hers for his was all that mattered in that moment.

The sting of pain with each thrust of his body made her lose herself in him just that much more.

Her breathing grew into heavy pants and moans as he tenaciously ground his way inside of her.

She grasped tightly onto his shoulders, her nails sinking into his tanned flesh as his own fingers moved to hold tightly onto her hips, giving him greater access to her.

"You're so perfect," he finally breathed onto her lips.

Slowly, she could feel herself unraveling. Her toes curled with pleasure, and her body tensed with each pulse of him.

"Bash," she moaned into the lustful air around them.

Driving harder and faster into her, Bastian moaned as he kissed and bit her neck, "Go ahead Princess, I want to feel it. Let go. Let me feel how good I make you feel."

At his command, she let go of the tension in her body. A moment later, release hit her. A tidal wave of pleasure crashing into a shore. Her orgasm hit a crescendo with just as much force as he was relentlessly thrusting inside of her.

All her muscles clamped and tensed around him in a tight and unrelenting grip.

"Fuck," he ground out, never stopping his unabated pace.

She rode each wave of her release with breathy moans, her body twitching with ecstasy.

Finally, Bastian's head dipped into the crevice of her neck and shoulder. His teeth clamped around the flesh at the base of her neck just above her collarbone, stifling his own moans and masculine grunts of bliss. The pain of his bite was unexpected, but as he found his release, plunging deep and slow into her body, she found herself riding another unexpected wave of nirvana.

Chapter Nineteen

Once the libidinous frenzy settled and their heart rates returned to a steady melodious rhythm, Bastian curled Evangaline into his muscular arms and held her close to his chest in a tight, unwavering grip.

Her breathing was still slightly labored as she continued to regain conscious thoughts. *I just fucked Bastian.* The realization hit Evangaline in frantic repetitions as his hand squeezed her backside. Her sweat glistened on the skin of her back in a luminous glow, reflecting the rays of the pale moonlight that shone through the windows.

"I need you to be honest, Princess."

Evangaline flicked her eyes up at him, resting her chin on the hand she had rested on his chest.

"Okay?" Her brow furrowed.

His face was wan. His brows furrowed in anticipation. "Please tell me that was better than that goddam chocolate cake?"

Evangaline closed her eyes in relief and laughed, burrowing her head into his chest out of pure embarrassment.

"Ehhh," she taunted, wiggling her hand back and forth in a seesaw motion.

Bastian's brows shot up on his forehead while his mouth grimaced into a tight line. His hardened gaze met Evangaline's, sending a deep pit into her stomach.

Suddenly surprising her, he squeezed her into his arms, flipping her over onto her back. Twining their legs together as his body pressed on top of hers, pinning her to the plush mattress.

With a huff, "I guess I'll just have to try harder."

She giggled as he smothered her with another deep and possessive kiss that left her gasping for air.

Evangaline laughed harder as she pulled away to gather air into her lungs. "Practice does make perfect …" she whispered onto his lips.

Smiling against her mouth, he asked, "Is that a command from my princess?

"Absolutely," she growled, gathering his lower lip between her teeth.

"As you wish, *Your Highness …*" he hummed, grabbing onto her legs and wrapping them tightly around his waist.

And they were off for round two.

Finally, sometime after their third bout, Evangaline nodded off to sleep in Bastian's arms.

That chocolate cake was still pretty high on her list of great things in Celadonia. Bastian's primal desires were a good rival to its velvety chocolatiness, though she would never tell him she still held the cake in such high regards. Bastian's ego was too important to him. She would hate to wound it, especially with his swift temper.

He filled her so fully each time he claimed her, that by her final release she practically forgot her name, which was just what she wanted. What she needed.

She didn't want to remember her obligations or fears. She simply wanted a distraction … an escape. And his lust provided just that. She never used sex as a reliever of stress, even in her previous relationship. However, somehow, the way she threw caution to the wind and ignored every red flag was oddly liberating. She allowed herself to take what she wanted and damn, did it feel good to put herself first.

"Oh, gross!" Evangaline heard from the doorway to the bedroom.

Shit!

Bastian didn't hear—or at least didn't react to—Chloe's yelp of terror. The string of curses at seeing her best friend—her princess—and her boss slash general in the same bed, completely naked, tangled together between the crumpled sheets, gave Evangaline all the insight she needed to know the mindset of her best friend.

Evangaline shot straight up, smacking Bastian on the chest as she heaved herself from the bed, hauling the wrinkled sheet with her.

Her hair was a jumbled mess, their clothes were all over the floor, and her sweat beaded down her forehead thanks to the mortification filling her lungs.

Chloe remained in the living room, aptly cursing Bastian out through a variety of very creative and colorful phrases.

Hastily, Evangaline flung Bastian his pants as he lounged in bed, arms behind his sleep tousled head, looking every bit the proud male he was.

Unable to find her robe and unable to salvage the gown from the previous night—being that the buttons were strewn about the floor, creating quite an obstacle course of pearls—she panicked and grabbed Bastian's shirt. She threw it over her head in a last-ditch effort to clothe herself. Evangaline swam in it, but it covered her naked flesh. So it would have to do.

Behind her, Bastian let out a low groan of approval. "Shit, Princess. Get back over here." He purred, flinging his arms out in a failed attempt to get her back in bed.

Evangaline looked at him, eyes wide. "No, get up. Chloe is in the living room! Besides, I have to train!"

"Tell her to go. I'll train you myself ... while wearing my shirt, if I'm lucky." He said with a wink.

"Good God. Put your pants on!"

Standing out of the bed, Bastian stretched his hands over his head. Every impressive bit of his body was on display as he made his way to Evangaline.

She must have been gawking because the next thing she heard was, "Keep looking at me like that and I'll bend you over this bed with Chloe here or not."

Planting a kiss on her lips while cupping her face in both hands certainly did nothing but make Evangaline want to see if he would live up to his word.

Just then Chloe's voice echoed from the living room shaking the lust off Evangaline, "Chicks before dicks, stop doing whatever you are doing in there and get dressed!" Chloe's voice was every bit the army commander. There was no softness or playful beat to her tone. She was pissed, and rightfully so. Evangaline was reckless and whatever this thing was with Bastian was surely a mistake … despite it feeling so good.

The soft clinking and clacking of Chloe's armor as she paced in the living room echoed within Evangaline's skull like the ticking of a clock. A steady count down until Chloe came in the room and either castrated Bastian or slapped Evangaline senseless.

Carefully, Evangaline peeled her body away from Bastian's and turned, walking toward the bathroom and closet.

"Chlo, give me ten minutes and I will be ready! Promise," she yelled to Chloe.

"Please wash all the smell of Bash from you! It'll make me vomit!" Chloe yelled back, earning a hearty laugh from the general. His muscles rippled as he situated his hands on his toned hips.

For the life of her, Evangaline couldn't fathom why in that moment it was so hard to walk away from him. Maybe it was the rippling pectorals, or the causal arrogance, or maybe it was the way that when she was under him, all thoughts and responsibilities vanished, and she could just *be*.

So, silently—and rather stupidly—Evangaline turned back to Bastian, this time with mischief glistening in *her* eyes. As quietly as possible, she jumped up in his arms, planting a kiss on his pillow soft lips. His hands gripped her thighs with a tight squeeze.

"What can you do with five minutes, General?" She whispered into his ear, hoping Chloe's fae hearing wasn't *that* good.

Smiling from ear to ear. "A great deal, Princess. No promises you'll stay quiet, though." He shot a glance in the direction of the living room, where Chloe continued her pacing.

She was certainly not thinking properly as she began peppering kisses to his jaw. "No promises *you* will stay quiet," she shot back at him, wiggling her brows promiscuously, biting down on her lower lip. "You're quite noisy."

Bastian growled in response and carried her into the bathroom, where he proved just how difficult it was for Evangaline to stay quiet.

Ding, ding, ding! Round number four!

Chapter Twenty

After a four-mile run and two sets of workout circuits, Chloe's distaste of seeing Evangaline's post coital deeds shone through in their workout regime. Chloe was shooting from the hip with one goal in mind—Evangaline's eternal suffering.

The tiny pink gremlin did not hold back any of her lingering feelings during their sparring session. Each swing of her sword was brutal and deadly, if not avoided. Luckily, Evangaline's always been quick on her feet and could dodge almost all the attempts Chloe made to take off her head. *Almost.*

"I still can smell him on you, by the way." Chloe grunted, bringing her sword crashing down in the direction of Evangaline's left shoulder with a faked gag.

Evangaline parried and threw her sword up to block the blow, arms screaming in a shaking pain. "I genuinely don't know what to say to that," Evangaline spat out, retaliating with a dodge and blow of her foot to Chloe's armored abdomen.

Chloe staggered back, her face wringing with confusion now. "It's Bash though."

"I'm fully aware of that, Chlo!"

Without warning, Chloe swung again, this time softer. The two swords met once more in a way that allowed Evangaline to deliver the offensive blow. Swiping from right to left, only to be blocked by Chloe once more. Their steel sparked as they collided with each maneuver.

"Why?" Chloe asked, genuinely confused. Finally, dropping her sword to her side.

Evangaline lowered her sword. Her breath was heavy with exhaustion. Her sweat dripped down her forehead and onto her cheek in rivulets of icy fire. "I don't know Chlo. I just ..." Evangaline shook her head, noticing the shift in Chloe's stance.

Chloe charged without a word, her movements quick and merciless. But Evangaline anticipated her move, saw the way her feet shifted into position as she spoke. Chloe's eyes glanced down, just briefly, to Evangaline's lowered weapon and her vulnerable position and in that moment, Evangaline knew the hit was coming.

Dipping low, Evangaline swung around to Chloe's back, extending her foot square into Chloe's backplate, sending her friend toppling forward rather ungracefully.

Junior year of college, Evangaline took some self-defense classes after a string of on campus assaults. Fucking frat guys couldn't handle their alcohol, apparently—pigs. So, a bunch of girls from her English lit class decided it would be good to learn some basic self-defense skills at a local boxing studio. Those basic skills were now coming in handy.

With a grunt, Chloe sat up on her knees. Her armor scuffed from the grass, leaving streaks of green and brown on the otherwise pristine copper sheathing. Her ruby hilted sword now lying a few feet away, discarded in the grassy meadow they claimed for their training grounds behind the palace away from prying eyes.

Just for a split-second Chloe's mask of authority slipped, and Evangaline could see her mirroring exhaustion ... and a small bit of pride.

"The student has become the master." Chloe smiled as Evangaline pointed her practice sword at Chloe's exposed throat, "You bested me and it's only day two. You *bitch*."

Evangaline let out a small titter as she marched over to retrieve Chloe's discarded sword. It was heavier and far longer than the one Evangaline was practicing with and perfectly balanced—something she didn't notice till holding both swords in her hands.

Sneaky little bitch gave Evangaline an unbalanced sword to practice with. Feeling how perfect Chloe's sword was made Evangaline's victory that much sweeter.

Extending the pommel down to Chloe, Evangaline gave a wayward smile.

Once Chloe took the sword, Evangaline looked away at the leaves in the distance, slowly changing colors in the breeze. "You know … for the first time in three days … I forgot … about *everything*. I know it's weird. And so, SO stupid. I know he's your boss, technically, but I just—"

Chloe finally stood up, using her sword as a cane of sorts. "Well, it's a few days late, but you got a belated birthday lay, I guess." She mused, laughing under breath.

"Good lord!" Evangaline's amused laugh was swept away, carried with the breeze as she looked away from Chloe. Her thoughts all came back to fill her head and made her face hard and solemn. Apparently, her belated birthday lay only quieted her thoughts for so long, and their shelf life had expired. "How did you do it?"

Chloe stepped toward Evangaline, taking a shaky deep breath. "Do what? Bash? I never have *done* Bash—"

"No! Goddam." Evangaline chuckled, "Good to know, but no! God no! How did you … adapt … to Vitalis after growing up *here*? Did you feel this anxious, this confused, and scared … curious even?"

Chloe blew out a sarcastic breath. "Oh, are you joking! The king and your new fuck buddy hand-picked me to go protect you and I only said yes because the king asked me personally." She sighed before gazing out at the forest that continually drew Evangaline's breath away.

"Evie, until your presentation to the realm, my own mom can't know I was in Vitalis. Do you know how hard it is to not tell your mom something so crazy? Everyone simply thinks I was away in Sedna, freezing my ass off, sucking up to Prince Tunit! None of it was easy in Vitalis. Fortunately, you didn't tell me to fuck off right away and I didn't need to stalk you to protect you. You don't realize how much you helped me this past year, too. You're my princess, yes. My job even … sworn to protect … blah blah blah, but Evie, you made my year there bearable. I told you I'll be here for you. Every step of the way, the same way you were for me."

Evangaline smiled at Chloe, a smile laced with gratitude and fear, laced with a sense of newfound belonging. As she looked at Chloe and the expanse of land that surrounded the palace, the sun now high in the sky, Evangaline felt her chest constrict. A small pulse right there in her heart, like a string being pulled taught. She wanted to be in Vitalis, where it was safe—familiar. Where her family was. But this place filled her with curiosity and intrigue, and she could not help but want to learn more. To push her boundaries and step out of her comfort zone and dive headfirst into the anxiety that plagued her when new things arose. She wanted to battle the darkness and explore the gift she was given of a new life full of wonder and … magic.

Suddenly, her eyes shot over to Chloe, wide and dilated. Evangaline threw her sword into the sheath on her back and spun around to the palace, dirt splaying onto her black laced up leather boots. "I'm gonna be late for my lessons! I have to go!"

"Old Atlas will be fine. You and I have a lot to discuss." Chloe scoffed, angling her eyebrows inquisitively, throwing her arm around Evangaline's shoulders, nearly needing to stand on her tippy toes to do so.

"Chloe." Evangaline warned, knowing exactly where Chloe's mind would go. The gutter.

Chloe laughed. "Don't play coy on me now. Clearly, Bash wasn't that good. You ran four miles and—"

"Nope, no! Not a discussion we're having," shaking free of Chloe's grip as her face turned a tomato shade of red.

"Come on! Well, speaking of …" Chloe laughed to herself.

An embarrassed smile crept its way onto Evangaline's face. "Don't!" She warned Chloe.

Despite her embarrassment, her body tingled with the memory of Bastian trailing kisses up her legs and down her chest. His hands roaming aimlessly around her skin, his lips claiming hers in possessive strokes.

What was she doing? This whole situation was insane. And Evangaline just topped off the crazy sundae with a hot fae man to screw her brains out till she forgot her troubles. Nothing could go wrong. Right?

She knew whatever was happening with Bash, it certainly wasn't love. That notion was completely foreign to her, all Evangaline's previous attempts at love were only met with heartache and grief. There was even a discarded wedding dress in her closet in Vitalis to prove it.

No, what she felt with Bastian was completely lust. Every time she thought about him, it normally ended up in a vision of him pinning her to a wall or exploring her body with that cheeky mouth of his. Or some other depraved sexual act that colored her porcelain cheeks an intense shade of red. It was devoid of all tender emotions and centered around their mutual need for release. Nothing more, nothing less.

Chloe nudged Evangaline's side, shaking her from her sexual delusions. The look in Chloe's eyes as they walked off the field was all taunting. She knew the memories of the previous night flooded Evangaline's mind. Evangaline could see the many intrusive questions bubbling to the surface under Chloe's warm, brown skin. They gnawed at the cotton candy haired fae like dozens of blood thirsty leeches. Chloe shimmied and nudged at Evangaline, biting her lip, flaring her eyes, hoping for any details on Evangaline's previous night with Bash.

Itching to change the subject as they entered the shade of the palace, Evangaline opened her mouth and asked without thinking, "What's up with you and Des?"

The playful nature suddenly drained out of Chloe's face, and she became the stoic commander once more, grounding her feet in place. "What about Des?"

Evangaline raised her eyebrows as her mouth dropped open. "The two of you have for sure boned! I see the little glances you give each other at dinner."

"We … girl … I would watch it if I were you!" Chloe's finger pointed in her face. She didn't deny it though, and that gave Evangaline hope.

Laughing, Evangaline pushed, "Oh, really? Tell me, you little dominatrix!"

"You first! You tell me a juicy secret and I'll tell you one." A smirk spread across Chloe's smug face. She knew Evangaline well enough to know that Evangaline was not forthcoming with information on her sex life. But Evangaline's curiosity about Chloe and Des outweighed everything. To hell with it. Chloe saw her naked practically on top of Bash this morning. There's very little more to know.

"The chocolate cake was good … but shit Chlo … it's got some competition!" A smile tugged at her lips. "The general is … tenacious—"

Genuine shock washed over her face. "No! I've heard rumors about the man's stamina, but better than that cake? I'm sorry, but I don't buy that shit one bit!"

Neither did Evangaline … that cake was fucking good. "Do I want to know these rumors? Also, you aren't free of answering. Tell me about Des."

"Des and I are, I don't know. Before I left, he and I started *having fun,*" Chloe suddenly went coy herself.

Evangaline angled a brow at Chloe speculatively.

"Fine, I've liked him since I was a young girl. He was a little older than me, only a few years, and those pixies never went away. We started hooking up one night a few weeks before I left. He made it clear he didn't want anything more than what we were doing, and I was fine having even the smallest piece of him. Then I left. That is all to tell."

Evangaline grabbed her hand, swinging it between them as they continued on their way. "You should tell him. Or at least go get him to have some more *fun.*"

"I can't. It's too complicated now. I tried to forget him with other guys like I know he's done with other girls, but I always just think of *him.* You remember that one guy in Vitalis, the guy with the fancy yellow car?"

Chloe, back on Vitalis, didn't have too many lovers, but the few she did rope in were always either unbelievably hot, incredibly rich, or a mix of both. It always amazed Evangaline just how skilled Chloe was at securing the most eligible of New York bachelors. *Cough, Mr. Brooks, cough.*

"Yeah, the blond guy. Ran some hedge fund or something, the nepotism baby."

"Yes, that guy! Well, we stopped *having fun* because I screamed … like *scream* screamed, Des's name out in bed." Chloe laughed. Her cheeks turned an adorable shade of pink that had Evangaline unable to peel her eyes from her friend.

Evangaline was now the one to stop dead in her tracks, her jaw practically scraping across the polished marble floor.

"No fucking shit!" Evangaline practically yelled down the cavernous hall, "That's why he stopped seeing you! I always wondered why you wouldn't tell me. I get it now," she said, motioning to the palace and pointing at her own face.

It was evident, if Chloe had told Evangaline about Des, she most likely would have needed to tell her about Celadonia and the whole being the crown princess thing. She started dating the hedge fund guy nearly three months after she started working at the bookstore. She could not risk giving up the bargain and lie that was woven over the course of Evangaline's life, because as her friend said already, it wasn't Chloe's place to reveal an age-old lie.

"Yep." Biting her bottom lip. "Legit, it was so embarrassing. I thought being away from Des would mean I would forget all these annoying feelings, but seeing him at dinner. Ugh, Evie, it's like I'm a stupid lovesick girl again. The first dinner we went to, I was so afraid to see him again. All I could think was 'what if he is with another girl?' I would have been crushed." Chloe exhaled a defeated breath.

Resuming their slow walk to the library, Evangaline pulled Chloe in tight to her side and embraced her friend. Evangaline herself never fell for someone where she felt butterflies in her stomach. That feeling where every other man was ruined for her, like Des had become for Chloe. Even her ex-fiancé, now looking back on it, never gave her the good kind of butterflies.

"Those pixies fluttering around your stomach, does that happen when you are with Bash?" Chloe asked earnestly, reading Evangaline's mind. Concern marred her pitched eyebrows and crinkled her forehead.

"Is it bad if I say no? I enjoy looking at him and sleeping with him is … nice. I enjoy him holding me and giving me an escape from my own brain—but I can't say I've felt the butterflies or pixies around him. At least, not yet." Evangaline's honesty flowed from her lips so quickly that once the words settled into the air, she felt bad. Like, in some way, she was using Bastian.

She knew it wasn't love from the second Bastian kissed her, she already admitted that to herself, it was lust through and through. The fireworks never lit in the background. Her heart never lurched. The world never stopped spinning at the sight of him. In truth, aside from the lust, she didn't know how to feel around Bastian. She trusted him as far as she could throw him, so calculating size and weight, not far at all. She knew next to nothing about him, and yet, somehow, she still selfishly craved the way he relaxed her body and mind.

She always dreamed about someone that would hold her without kissing her or saying anything at all. A partner that would surprise her with flowers on random weekdays and talk about growing old together. Something that was beyond sex. Beyond the typical transactional exchange and stereotypical prototype of marriage. A bond that couldn't be broken by time or space, a love that would outlast the stars in the sky.

Guilt clawed at her, but she did not need to think. Bastian was not that man.

You are probably leaving in three weeks, you can't get attached anyway, so stop thinking about all of this, Evangaline told herself. Warding off all thoughts of love and futures.

The what ifs and other impossible questions floated around her head until Chloe cut off the swirling vortex of doom that became her brain.

"Bash has never been in a long-term relationship, that anyone knows of, that is. He's had trysts with some of the ladies of the court. He's even gotten into trouble in some other kingdoms for his inability to keep his dick in his pants. He once had an affair with Lady Barrow's betrothed daughter. Rumor has it the lady herself walked in on the two going at it. Apparently, she was so surprised seeing whatever they were doing she passed out and came to a day later with a concussion and amnesia. Her daughter got married to a wealthy swordsmith in the Kingdom of Fire and Bash never once confirmed or denied the affair.

"Of course, all his soldiers, male soldiers that is, bought him rounds of ale for his *'tenacity and bravery in the bedroom.'* So I guess, now thinking about it, that was him taking credit for it. Hmmm." Chloe pondered something silently to herself before shaking her head clean of the thought. "Meanwhile, the women began to spin tales of his crazy stamina and size. Which no doubt got back to him and inflated his ego tenfold."

Evangaline sighed. "Why are you telling me this, Chlo?" Evangaline couldn't help but feel a little grateful to hear that Bastian was nothing more than a fae fuckboy. It made the thought of using his body for pleasure, then leaving him with nothing more than a fist bump and goodbye easier. Perhaps he was using her for the same reason.

Chloe raised her brows and pursed her lips, heavily debating vocalizing whatever words sat on the tip of her tongue. "One, I am a notoriously curious being and I need to know if he really is a rockstar in bed, and two, I just want you to be careful. Bash is practically a brother to me, ok maybe not brother but like a … distant cousin twice removed," she smirked, "he gave me all the opportunities I've gotten. I care for him in a weird fucked up way, but I also know him well enough to know he always has his own agendas and is not the best at feelings. Sex is just a hobby for him. He collects as many notches in his bedpost as he can, and he flaunts them like conquests and not actual living beings. I don't want you to just be one of those conquests. At least not an unknowing one. If you want to ride that horse till you can't walk anymore, girl, giddy up! But I…I just love you and want the best for you. So if Bash is that, then I'm happy for you two."

Evangaline peeked down at her and Chloe's now entangled fingers and drew in a deep breath. "Well, I am a notch in that post now, four notches actually," she laughed, gaining an amused gasp from Chloe. "So, too late to take that back, but … thank you, Chlo. I love you too. Also, as your princess, I need you to do one thing for me. Will you promise to do it?"

Chloe cocked her head and rolled her eyes. "Ugh, I hate that. *'As your princess,'*" she mocked in a high-pitched squeal, making Evangaline laugh.

"Okay, what is it?"

"Talk to Des. You deserve to be happy, too. And I see the way he looks at you, not just how you look at him. He feels it too. Trust me on this."

A genuine smile bloomed, tickling Chloe's voluptuous black lashes, her skin heating with a timid orangey pink hued blush. "Okay, *Your Highness.*" Chloe quietly and extremely sarcastically murmured under her breath.

Evangaline, without hesitation, let out a laugh and, with a massive grin across her face, pulled Chloe in for a monster of a hug. She squeezed Chloe so tight that even through Chloe's armor, her friend let out a brief *oof* noise as the air rushed out of her lungs.

The two remained that way, giggling and hugging, until Atlas came to the door, opening it slightly.

"Ready for lessons, my dear?" He chided, adding a subtle smile that reached his sparkling blue eyes.

Chapter Twenty-One

Five days passed of the same routine.

Wake up, train, lessons with Atlas, dinner with the boys and Chloe, occasional evening activities with Bash, sleep, repeat.

It wasn't by any means a horrific way to spend one's days, but it was tiring, nonetheless. Evangaline slowly felt herself growing stronger. Her muscles ached less and became more defined with curves and lines that she had never seen before, nor thought possible, even with the occasional piece of orgasmic cake she shared with Chloe. Okay, they shared the cake most nights. Every night. The cake was a new nightly tradition for her and Chloe.

Her skill with a sword was deemed *tolerable* by her commander slash trainer, so they incorporated work with knives and blades, which slowly became Evangaline's favorite. She learned how to throw them with near fatal accuracy, as well as wield them in close combat fighting. She was slightly better with the knives than her trusty practice sword, but she was learning and trying her best, which had to count for something.

If anything, the company and the physical outlet cleared her head for a few hours, even if they were skills that were meaningless when she returned to Vitalis. The anxiety she felt constantly looming in the background of her mind was nearly non-existent as the days ticked on. And any sadness she once felt because of her previous depressive episodes was gone completely.

Of course, she knew that it never stayed that way without her putting in the work, so that was what she did. She felt content and happy in her monotonous new life.

She took minor risks here and there, be it in training or introducing herself to people around the palace. Maids, the cooks, a few of the less narcissistic courtiers. If she felt a twinge of trepidation and anxiety creep in, she tugged on the part of her brain that embraced the Chloe method of living and just went for it. She even one night, after a few glasses of wine at dinner, asked Darrin if he would dance with her. His startled expression and glance about the room showed his own anxieties. Just as Evangaline apologized and began turning away, he relented and lead her in a fast-paced skip about the room that made them giggle and joke—mainly about Evangaline's lack of skill on the dance floor. It provided them with a moment that, if she had a camera, Evangaline would have loved to add to her photo album.

Atlas dove in with lessons on etiquette and the daily duties of a crown princess once he felt she knew enough on the kingdoms to get her by. At times, his type of training felt more difficult than that of blade training. *"Sit this way." "Do that." "Say this."*

It took two days alone to memorize every courtier in both the palace and the royals of each Kingdom's court in the way Darrin suggested would be good for her.

To add onto her workload, much to Atlas's surprise, Evangaline asked to learn about every servant and their families residing within the Capital. As well as the owners of important shops and businesses in the town. It was tedious and a pain in the ass to learn about everyone, but she knew it was important.

She wanted to know everyone, not just those of wealth. Plus, it was a good way to get Atlas sidetracked. He often strayed, telling stories of the many courtiers and civilians alike. How one male caught his wife with another woman. How this couple's child married some far-off noble in another kingdom. How he knew someone's ancestor long ago and how similar they look. He was an encyclopedia of knowledge … and gossip. All of his stories thrilled Evangaline and allowed her time to relax in the library's coziness, sipping her warm whiskey with a graceful ease before dinner filled her with laughter and wine.

Each night was fruitful and certainly without boredom. The boys enjoyed the fact that they had hundreds of stories to tell a new set of ears. Each tale was filthier and more depraved than the last. Having someone new to Celadonia allowed them the perfect opportunity to recount their exploits with wicked detail that sometimes had Evangaline wincing in horror.

Chloe still hadn't approached Des. However, the longing stares across the table continued night after night. Evangaline suspected Lukas knew, but he was a hard nut to crack. He caught Des one-night staring at Chloe between supper and dessert. Evangaline simply raised her shoulders, gaining an eye roll in return from the brown-haired soldier, followed by a knowing smile. Nothing else was said or done, and Chloe and Des continued their longing glances, secretly in love with one another.

Four of the five nights, Bastian warmed her bed. His stamina was more than Chloe's rumors even knew. He dominated her and she allowed it, longing for those couple hours of a silent mind and trembling body. She let him drive the pleasure from her, taking anything he needed along the way. He knew exactly what her body craved to turn off her rapidly firing mind, and she was far from complaining.

In those moments, her brain cleared. All she cared about was the feel of him and the ecstasy that he filled her with. He might have gotten his title by being a general on the battlefield, but he earned it by being one in the bedroom as well. He was tenacious and vigorous.

Despite her nights of brainless sex, as each day rolled along, Evangaline slowly felt herself seriously questioning her motives. She thought it wouldn't be easy to live here, to follow her daily routine until it was time to go. But that was far from the truth. It was the easiest thing to wake up and start her day. It felt more natural than her old routine in Vitalis and felt more fulfilling, too.

She just had to learn what Darrin wanted her to learn, stay in the background, and play her part to the best of her abilities. Then she was free of her parent's bargain, and she could make her final decision. She could stay in Celadonia and keep living as she was doing now, but that came with questions. How would her peaceful routine change once the realm knew she was the crown princess? Would Bastian really accept her 'no strings attached' mentality if she stayed? He already was a bit controlling sometimes. Would he take well to Evangaline voicing her dis-interest in anything other than sex? Or she could not worry about any of it and go back to her whitewashed bedroom in the Upper West Side, her job at the bookshop, and her family, which she was missing like crazy.

With each day, the idea of home became more and more blurred, and it became harder to make a finite decision on where she wanted to plant her roots and grow—because that is what she planned on doing from this day forward. Growing. Not withering.

She felt a sense of belonging in both Vitalis and Celadonia, and yet, somehow neither.

Vitalis was her *home* because her family was there. Over and over, she told herself that her family was her home, and she needed to go back to them. But as the days turned to night, she couldn't help but remember how alone she felt, even at what she thought was *home*. Katherine was starting her own family. Miles was thriving in college. Her parents had each other and even after twenty-five years of marriage, were still madly in love with one another. And there she was, twenty-five, a career she all but gave up on and no place to call her own. She loved her family so much it would make her heart quiver and ache just thinking of their names, but was Vitalis really her home anymore?

Celadonia was still new and foreign to her, but the second the crisp air hit her skin and filled her lungs she felt charged with an electricity she did not even realize she could feel. Here she had Chloe and Bash and the boys of the cadre. She had King Darrin, whom of which, despite the very few encounters between the two, one on one, was warm and welcoming. And yet, Celadonia also didn't feel like her home. It felt more so an obligation at times.

With every day that trudged on, she could not help but feel as though no matter the choice she made, it would be the wrong one. Seven days ago, her mind was seemingly made up—she was going home to Vitalis. Now though … She didn't know where she wanted home to be.

Chapter Twenty-Two

Day nine brought a new kind of trial for Evangaline. Halfway through her training with Chloe, right as she was about to deliver the fatal blow in their sparring session—a blow that would have resulted in her fourth consecutive win—a cramp hit her like a bullet to the gut.

"Shit," she spewed as she gripped her side in pain, dropping her sword to her side.

Of course, she would get her cycle now. In her rush of packing, she didn't even think to grab any feminine hygiene products. Not a single pad or tampon for safe measure.

Chloe rushed over, looking for a wound or gash, but soon found nothing to fret over. Evangaline calmed Chloe by telling her it was just mother nature kicking her ass. Chloe laughed and surprised Evangaline, saying she only got hers once every six months. *Lucky bitch.* Apparently, Evangaline's uterus decided to take on the human side of the family when it came to periods and shunned the bi-annual period favored by her fae half. Great.

Despite her protests to keep going on with training, Chloe walked her back to her room, calling off training for the day. The look on Chloe's precautious face was one of great worry. It was as though any second the elevator doors of Evangaline's womb would open and the red seas from *The Shining* would come flowing out and consume the palace whole. She propped

Evangaline's arm up around her shoulder to carry Evangaline's weight and slowly helped her into the palace, ignoring Evangaline's protests.

Evangaline laughed when she processed the worry in Chloe's eyes as she stretched out her newly aching back. Clearly this was not something fae women have a lot of experience in.

In Evangaline's many years menstruating she grew used to it, and subsequently passive regarding the tithe taken out on her body for not producing a baby. It was not that she was not in pain. She was in a lot of it, in fact. Since the first cramp hit, her entire back began to ache and an incredibly invasive amount of nausea set in. But these were things she had been feeling for over a decade and despite the pain, she found them to be more annoying than anything else.

Chloe sat with her in bed for a while after supplying Evangaline with the fae version of a pad, which, incredibly, was more comfortable than the plastic diaper like creations they had on Vitalis.

The two talked and gossiped and drank tea while they figuratively spilled it. They sat that way for a couple hours. Chloe sent word to Atlas that she was calling for a girls' day and that Evangaline would not be present for her lessons. That was until Bastian came barging in through the door, his hair pulled half up, his white flowy button up halfway undone like he had just thrown it on in a haste. Even with cramps, the sex appeal of the man called to her, making her ache in places she very much so didn't need more aching.

"I was told you returned to your room early and canceled your lessons with Atlas. Why?" He clamored; his hands restless at his side as he strode toward the bed angrily.

Sipping her tea, "I'm fine. Nothing's wrong. You okay? Where were you?" She said with a slight smile.

Coming to her side, completely ignoring her question, his tone came out condescending. "It's not any of your business." *Okay then* … "Nothing is wrong with you and yet you are here in bed, sipping tea in a robe and not training or abiding by your father's wishes."

She set her tea down and gave him a sidelong glance, slowly blinking up at him, confused. She ignored his cagey response to where he was and focused on his judgmental tone.

"Am I now training for battle, General?" Evangaline asked sarcastically.

"No. Of course not. You would be useless in a war. Why are you in here if nothing is wrong?" Agitation rode his words.

His comments sent a shock of anger and sadness through her. She flinched back as though he struck her. He was being cruel for no reason. Bastian spoke as though she was a new recruit who fell out of line and not the woman he fucked almost every night.

Besides, her training with Chloe was her idea and something the king found to be useful, so *the king* allowed it. Never once was it required. Therefore, Bastian's arrogant prodding into her current incapacitation was highly unnecessary and slightly invasive.

From beside her, Chloe scoffed, whispering into her tea, "It's her room. Why are you here?"

His head snapped so fast at Chloe, Evangaline thought that just for one second, he might have given himself whiplash.

"You are excused, Commander." His voice was deep and hauntingly serious. "I'm sure you have maneuvers with the recruits to take care of."

Chloe laughed, shaking her head. "Better yet, answer her question. What were *you* up to, Bash? It *reeks* of infidelity in here."

Bastian's upper lick ticked with anger. "You are to leave the premises effective immediately, Commander."

Evangaline let out an irked laugh. "Like hell she is. Don't listen to him Chlo." She picked up her tea and took a sip of it, glaring at Bastian over the rim. Chloe's comment of infidelity sent a nauseous wave through her that had nothing to do with her womanly issues.

"She is to listen to me; I am her General. Now Chloe, *go*. I need a moment of Evangaline's time," He barked back.

Abruptly, Evangaline stood, knocking over a plate of cookies, slamming her tea on the nightstand. If he wanted a fight, he would get one. Her hormones were all over the place and she was ready to either cry or punch someone. Bastian was coming extremely close to getting the latter.

"And I am her *princess*. *She* stays. *You*, General, can fuck off!" She snarled back at him, her face a deadly shade of serious.

If Evangaline were in a cartoon, there would certainly be steam rising from her ears in thick white plumes. Her face would be fire engine red, and the sound of a train whistle would be echoing through the room.

Bastian, however, was not in one of his few good moods, nor was he appreciating her throwing out the princess card. *Get used to it, buddy!* Evangaline held her ground, meeting his stare. Despite having to look up at him, she was, in every way, looking down on him and his childish attitude.

"She got her period, you fucking asshole." Chloe snipped from the side, "Can we not just have girl time without you coming in here swinging your dick all over the place?"

Eloquent, her best friend was always so eloquent. She was, however, incredibly correct. Bastian and Evangaline weren't dating. They were somewhere in that gray area of friends with benefits and work colleagues. She owed him no explanation, and that was not even considering the fact that she was by blood, his princess. According to her lessons with Atlas, she could technically have him jailed or beheaded for defying her orders. The fae laws surrounding the crown leaned more towards harsh and unforgiving than benevolent.

Obviously, she enjoyed their fun together, so cutting his head from his body would be a bit of an over exaggeration, but by blood and law she did not have to endure his insolent behavior. A notion Bastian had seemed to forget in their short time together. He was not her owner or master and therefore she owed him nothing.

His face never softened with Chloe's quick barb. If anything, it grew angrier. His rapid blinking and the muscle that flickered in his jaw were the only sign he was uncomfortable with the insight provided to him.

"That was information I did not need, Chloe. Nor do I need your opinion every time I am around Evangaline. I can deal with my woman myself and right now, both of you will do what I say." Bastian replied, his tone softer but still deep and filled with menace.

Evangaline flinched at his declaration of ownership over her. "I'm not your *anything,* and I certainly don't take orders from you."

Chloe chuckled to herself. "Sure thing, Bash. Sure thing." She rolled her eyes for added impact, sipping her tea but remaining in her place on the bed.

His eyes fixed on Evangaline once more, there was a malice hidden in his green irises that sent a chill down Evangaline's body. "I will be gone till the autumnal equinox. Chloe, you will be responsible for the safety of the princess. I expect you to train and continue your lessons, so you won't be seen as a useless heir once you are unveiled to the realm. How you are perceived will be a direct interpretation of the king and, therefore, me. You will train and do as I say and once I return, we will discuss your lessons and training further. I will see you at the feast. There is a black gown with red stones on it that I expect to see you in at the celebration."

Evangaline stood, mouth agape, staring at this man who was nothing like the one she had gotten to know over the last week. He was cold and unfeeling. Arrogant on a level that he had never been, which was saying a lot since Bastian held an award for narcissism and self-assuredness. This version of the man she gave her body to was all around awful!

Chloe in an over exaggerated manner saluted Bastian sarcastically. "Yes, sir!"

Bastian ignored Chloe, still fixated on Evangaline. His breathing was heavy in his puffed-up chest, his telltale sign he was pissed, and frankly Evangaline didn't care. He was being an ass. His eyes held a malice deep within them as they watched her like a hunter.

He reached out slowly to grab her waist, but Evangaline stepped out of his grasp.

Angry, she spit venomously his way, "Have a delightful trip, General."

He scoffed and leaned further into her, grabbing her waist with force, pulling her flush against him, squeezing hard enough to leave a bruise. "We will discuss this when I return, and you aren't in a mood." And then, in front of Chloe, he kissed her like a depraved beast going in for the kill. She didn't return the kiss nor revel in it as she normally did.

Evangaline pulled away, uncomfortable, angry, and disgusted, only to be greeted by his smirking face.

The flags all waved as he stood before her, acting like he won a battle that was never waged. Their crimson red banners flickered in the breeze around his head, warning her to stay clear of the man she thought was there to help her.

Chloe scoffed at him. "See ya later, Bash!"

After a tense moment, he turned on his heels and stalked out of the room. The door closed with a soft thud behind him that shook the chandelier in the foyer.

Evangaline remained standing for a few moments before turning to Chloe, who was placing the displaced cookies back on the plate and sweeping up the crumbs to the floor.

"That was ..." Evangaline murmured, brows pinched. "He was ..."

"Odd. A dick." Chloe filled in. "Covered in the scent of another woman ..." she muttered under his breath. "All of the above."

"I figured that from the rumpled shirt. But he acted like I personally offended him by sitting in bed. He fucking called me *his woman*," she said, crinkling her face in disgust. "I am *nobody's* woman. And then the orders ... like ... I ... What the fuck?" she stammered.

Chloe leaned back, grabbing her tea once more. "Some fae males are fucking assholes when it comes to women. Well I guess, women can be too with men they claim. Whatever, just ignore him. Better yet ... dump his ass. *Even* better yet ... tell Darrin to send him on a mission to the Kingdom of Fire to sweep the inside of the volcano!" Evangaline breathily chuckled at Chloe. "Clearly, his panties are in a twist. He's probably just pissed he has to go away on a diplomacy mission, and he can't send someone else like he normally does."

"Do you know where he is going?" Evangaline sat back on the bed, grabbing one of the cookies from the plate.

"No. Probably something for the king, though, before your grand unveiling. I sometimes forget he's the king's right-hand man as well as general. He probably just has to schmooze a royal into doing the king's bidding. Bash always gets pissy when he has to go to the other kingdoms. He thinks they should come here when '*the sovereign needs them*' and bend the knee like they are some paupers or some shit. It's not how Darrin works and believe me, the royals would sooner tell King D to shove it before becoming his pets, like Bash wants. It's all about power for them. Bash too."

Evangaline's chest did the thrumming ache thing it's been doing off and on since she came to the fae realm. She rubbed at her chest, breathing until the pressure subsided.

"Evie, you okay, Hun?" Chloe mused. Her face pinched, studying Evangaline's now worried countenance. Evangaline had a haunting feeling as though something was wrong but could not for the life of her figure out what.

Evangaline snapped out of her transfixed daze and muttered, "Yeah. Yeah. Sorry, I'm good," while plastering on a fake smile that she mastered at a young age. However, she could not help the feeling that wherever Bastian was going wasn't for the good of Celadonia. He was too moody and unpredictable, fae male explanation aside, Evangaline couldn't shake the sirens going off in her head telling her to run the next time she saw him. However, she didn't tell Chloe any of that, opting for the fake smile. "I should start to get ready for dinner. I'm feeling a nice long bath today. Can you braid my hair for me when I get out?" Evangaline asked.

It was Chloe's turn to plaster on a fake smile. She could always read right through all of Evangaline's bullshit and the slow nod of her head gave away her apprehensions, but she smiled anyway. "Of course." Chloe said, sliding off the bed.

The halls of the palace at night glowed with each gentle caress of the moonlight that seeped through the gilded windowpanes.

Her feet were bare as she padded through the slumbering halls on her way to ease the uncertainty within her soul. Ever since Bastian left that afternoon, she could not shake the feeling of something being wrong. Of a fate waiting for her that was riddled in shadow and mystery.

After schmoozing the royal fan club at dinner, a dinner that Darrin actually ate beside her, she feigned an excuse of exhaustion and retreated to her rooms to change from her opulent gold gown into black trousers and a matching sweater.

"This is so stupid," she whispered to herself as she stopped outside of Bastian's door. "He was just grumpy. It is an off day. You're gonna find nothing and go right back to letting him defile you … I'm talking to myself. *Fuck,*" she cursed as she jammed the butter knife she stole into the door.

After two hard pushes, the door eased open; the lock tumbling open with a soft *thunk.*

She shuffled inside and promptly relocked the door.

She had come to Bastian's suite a couple of times after being summoned for a few rendezvous sessions.

His room was smaller than hers. His massive bed was clad in black and white sheets with blankets of the softest fur hanging from them. A wingback chair sat beside the bay window that faced the front courtyard of the palace where there were now guards in their copper armor making their rounds.

With the lights off, it was increasingly difficult to make out anything suspicious, but she knew she wanted to scour his desk for answers. Answers to where he went off to in a huff. Answers to his attitude. Answers too well just about anything she didn't know about the man she shared a bed with the past week. The sirens in her head never stopped blaring. She knew from past mistakes to never doubt her instincts, and right now, they were urging her to scour Bastian's room for answers.

Chloe's words played through her head as she tiptoed through the room. It was true Evangaline truly had no clue how the fae men operated. Hell, she barely understood how human men operated, but the prickling unease that slithered through her body and filled her with anxiety pushed her to find answers for herself. Knowing Bastian, he left all the answers she sought in plain sight with a big sparkly bow just waiting for her to see them. He was cunning, but not exactly smart.

His massive ebony desk sat opposite the bed against the wall. The expansive table was littered with random papers and sealed letters waiting to be opened.

After a quick fruitless sweep of the room, Evangaline picked up the stack of letters on his desk, looking for ones that had been opened by the broken seals on the back. Only two had been opened and, by their position on the bottom of the stack, hidden. Bingo. The rest did not seem important, anyway. The labels in the top corner indicated a couple of the unopened correspondences were from Des. One was a report from Chloe. And the final ones were labeled from Prince Tunit and Prince Surtis. The two opened ones, however, bore no labels from their senders. Making their existence more curious.

Evangaline opened the first correspondence. Dated for two days ago and filled with a delicate feminine script.

My Love,
I have ached for your touch since you last left my chambers yesterday morn.

Great. Chloe was definitely right about the other woman. She should be livid, angry, grossed out—anything! Knowing the man she gave access to her body was sleeping with other women should fester emotions that make her weep or smash something, but truly, she felt nothing. If that wasn't a sign of just how much she didn't love Bastian, she didn't know what was. It was, however, a wonderful fact to note. The two of them weren't exclusive, so she could use that to cut the cord and release him to the wild. "Go fuck all of Celadonia, you big bastard. See what I care," she mumbled. She should have put the letter down, but couldn't seem to do it.

The heat of your skin was a privilege I hope to encounter more often. I know you are besotted with that human girl, but her mortal sensibilities cannot take the amorous responsibilities of a fae male. Let the king have his plaything. I will be yours and yours alone in a way she will never be. Call it fate, my love, but I feel my heart yearn for you. However, if it is only my body you want, it is yours. I will be in the palace in two days. See you soon.
Sincerely,
Waylay Whittell

Whittell? Was Bastian sleeping with Lord and Lady Whittell's daughter? Well, this was some gossip Chloe and the boys would *love* to hear! Evangaline's stomach hollowed out as she sat on this new information. Not out of jealousy, but out of pure revulsion. The lord and lady were nothing but pompous and arrogant nobles, hell bent on their own selfish needs. Their daughter did not even live in the palace. She and some friends shared an apartment in the village, according to Atlas and the boys. Hopefully, she was nothing like her awful parents.

"He's all yours Waylay. Good luck with him." Evangaline whispered to herself as she refolded the letter and shoved it back under the stack.

The second letter bore a crest of gold and was embossed with a leaf and stalk of wheat. A fox head was engraved in the expensive stationary at the header.

B,

I'm happy to hear you are finally fulfilling your plan. The king would be a fool not to agree to your proposal. You know I have always supported you and I would be delighted to bend the knee to you one day.

I heard that there is a human residing in the Capital Palace from my sources. Is that true? How in the heavens did a human pass through the Velum? Also, if there is, have you had a bite of that apple? What am I kidding? Of course you have! Fae women fall to their knees to suck your cock with just a wink at you in their direction. Of course a weak human would drop to her knees without even thinking twice! She must know she is no match for the great general of the Royal Army! Either way, have some fun with her before the king tosses her back across the border or buries her in the sea off Tunit's border. That is what I would do.

See you soon my friend. I look forward to catching up in a few days.

C.

"So long for staying in the shadows," she shook her head, taking in the date of the letter. Three days ago. At least she knew Bastian was not gone on the king's orders. Yet, where he went was still a mystery and yet part of her could not seem to care at all.

Re-folding the letter and placing it back in its spot, Evangaline let out an exasperated sigh.

Who is C?

What did Bastian propose for the king to decide on?

How did this mysterious C know she was here? That was a silly question, the nobles gossip too damn much. That's probably how!

Evangaline expelled a breath as she scanned through the papers on Bastian's desk, looking for anymore answers. Expense reports, invites for the king, replies to citizens and nobles declining and accepting requests for aid—nothing of intrigue. Nothing that gave her any answers beyond that of knowing Chloe was more than right—she was nothing more than a notch in a bedpost—and that even Bastian's random friends are sex- crazed assholes. Oh, and that she was certainly done with Bash. From here on out, they would be professional acquaintances and nothing more.

In a way, she felt relieved. Her heart didn't hurt because she never even liked him in a romantic way, so maybe him going all possessive alpha male and reading those two letters was good for her. Aside from the tumultuous number of questions they gave her, she knew for certain that her instincts were right. The chocolate cake was better than Bastian, tenfold. It never claimed her and talked down to her.

"Fuck men," Evangaline whispered to herself as she eased the lock on the door and slipped from Bastian's room back into the dark hallway, feeling oddly lighter than she had before.

For the next four days, Evangaline resumed her schedule as though nothing was different, just how every woman had ever done since the dawn of time. Continue on … just do it while bleeding. Push the pain away and carry on. She went to her training every morning, ran every single mile planned and sparred with Chloe despite her cramps and nausea.

Despite the pains ricocheting through her muscles and bones, the questions that she had garnered after leaving Bastian's room lingered at the forefront of her mind. She kept her ears open, listening for any insight into where he went and if something was happening in Celadonia, but heard nothing. Deep in her heart, she knew something was brewing. Her doubts in Bastian singed in everlasting flames against the back of her mind. And yet, just like her womanly circumstances, she carried on, pushing the dubious thoughts about the man she took into her bed to the deepest recesses of her mind. Instead, focusing on the things she needed to do and the bargain she agreed to fulfill.

She went to her lessons with Atlas and continued her training of royal protocols and the various laws of the realm as though nothing sinister was plaguing her psyche. She knew something bad was going to happen but had no evidence, only the nagging feeling deep in her gut that she trusted more than the words of men. She was being left in the dark and she did not feel comfort in that fact. Subtly, Evangaline asked Atlas questions about the realm and any tensions thriving. Yet just like everyone else, he simply smiled and waved off her question with a laugh and assurance that the realm was fine.

In spite of it all, Evangaline found luck to be on her side as she got Atlas, veering on a tangent after she admitted to not knowing how to play cards. Following a grueling workout, the last thing Evangaline wanted was to study fae laws. So when Atlas brought up his fondness for card games, she jumped on the opportunity to drink whiskey and play cards. Even Chloe stayed for the poker lesson that ensued for the next three hours. Apparently, the ancient fae was a card shark and, man, did he rejoice in wiping the floor with Evangaline. He taught her the basic rules of the game and then, as he did with everything, turned the game into a lesson. "A valuable skill for a future queen," Atlas remarked with a smirk as he dealt her a losing hand following a lengthy discussion on steeling one's face to not show emotions in times of duress.

Evangaline found solace in the old man's ability to turn a simple game into a life lesson with nothing but a deck of cards and a smile.

As the sun set on the thirteenth day of her stay in Celadonia, her cycle thankfully ended. If she had to hear Chloe fret about the *"fucked up way human women were punished every month for not procreating crotch goblins"*,

Evangaline was sure to drive her practice daggers into her own ears and twist.

Evangaline watched the sun sink below the lush soil and found that she couldn't bear another dinner, getting dressed up and mingling with the court. She only had so many false smiles loaded into her chamber.

Last minute, she practically begged Wren to call for dinner in her room. Chloe hadn't made her way to the daily feast in the throne room, but the boys had. However, once Wren conveyed Evangaline's invitation, the king's feast was abandoned without a second thought. Without the leering eyes and the inquisitive murmurs—typically coming from the direction of Lord Whittell, *asshole*—Evangaline could enjoy her food and drink without remembering to be a lady. She simply was Evangaline.

Chloe sat at the table with Evangaline, both women foregoing gowns for trousers and corset tops. Evangaline proudly kicked up her favorite lace-up boots onto the crystal table—a gift from Chloe for her training. They were covered in dirt and sweat, but they made her feel powerful and were insanely more comfortable than the heeled boots the noble women wore with their pants.

Sipping wine leisurely, they stared out after the six men singing a raucous pub song in the living room. They sang about, well, if Evangaline was being honest with herself, she had no clue what the song was about. They all sang off-key and over one another, creating a jumbled mess of a ballad that was entirely too hard to understand.

"You have to admit, music in Vitalis is so much better than whatever this is." Evangaline grinned, waving her wine glass toward the impromptu concert happening in her living room.

"Oh, there are beautiful songs and musicians here in Celadonia. Mainly in Mirth. These six idiots are not amongst that category." Chloe rebutted in a low volume.

Evangaline knew as she followed Chloe's eyeline where it would end up … or whom it would end up on, rather. Des stood tall and proud, his arm slung around Shaw, a beaming smile gracing his handsome face, as he sang out, laughing as he did so.

"You still haven't talked to him, have you?" Evangaline asked quietly.

"Nope, and I'm not ready yet."

Evangaline had seen Chloe bang a guy she didn't know simply because of his name. The fact that she was nervous about telling Des her feelings spoke volumes about how badly she had it for the soldier. Seeing Chloe so secretly in love stirred up a plethora of emotions within Evangaline. Happiness for her friend, anger that she wouldn't tell Des, and oddly enough, a sense of longing to feel as deeply for another person as the two of them clearly felt for one another, despite their inability to convey said emotions. Chloe was in love. It shone across her dark complexion and twinkled in her eyes.

Des might not know Chloe's feeling's yet, but Evangaline knew once he did, he would hold on to Chloe and never let her go. The way he stole brief glances at her pink haired friend showed how much he admired her. With every smile and wink, his love prowled to the surface of his aqua eyes. He thoroughly respected her, and would no doubt worship the ground she walked on … if they only admitted their feelings.

"I'll be here when you get the courage." Evangaline said as she dropped her feet from the table and placed a kiss on her friend's cheek.

Chloe smiled at her, and that was the last of it.

As the evening wore on, Evangaline taught the guys how to play some human games like charades and Pictionary. Chloe's suggestion of poker, however, turned into a ruthless death match. Thanks solely to Atlas's teachings Evangaline won multiple times and walked away with the small pot of two gold pieces, a handful of silver coins, and Charlie's ruby earring—which she was going to return to him after he was done pouting about his loss. Her poker face was perfect, and in so many ways, she wished Atlas could see her with her winnings.

Finally, as the midnight sky darkened the room, they all laid in the living room. Chloe snuggled on Evangaline's lap. Evangaline's legs were propped up on Shaw. Shaw was leaning on Des. Murray and Lukas were curled up on the floor with Aadi sitting with his back to the sofa, next to an extremely drunk Charlie. Like a family, they snuggled in close and reveled in their friendship. It should have felt odd for Evangaline, having not known these men for long. However, the way they lounged and talked was the most natural thing in the world.

Slowly the wine ran out, and the laughter turned to musings. The cadre were all surprisingly philosophical thinkers, musing on the stars and how they believed great change was coming purely by the constellations twinkling in the night sky. It was all so beautiful to listen to.

With each bit of their ruminations, Evangaline's mind wandered onto the changes in her life. Of course, her fae heritage was a massive change. But in Vitalis, Katherine had to have been close to her due date. Evangaline was going to miss the birth of her niece, which broke her heart in two. Her mind lingered there for a while as Des discussed a constellation of what he called the Lovers. The last time Evangaline saw Katherine, her older sister was just about six months pregnant and terrified. Evangaline wished she could be there to hold Katherine's hand just as she promised, but luckily Katherine had James.

Evangaline loved her brother-in-law. From the first day he walked into their hostile Christmas dinner full of bickering and sarcasm a few years back wearing an ugly Christmas sweater—the only one wearing one—Evangaline knew he was a keeper. James also loved books and horror movies just like Evangaline, they bonded the whole day about their mutual interests. By the end of the night, Evangaline told Katherine that if she didn't lock James down, Evangaline was claiming him for herself. Six months later James proposed, and they've lived happily ever after since.

The day Katherine called Evangaline and said she was pregnant; Evangaline wept, then laughed, then cried some more when Katherine started to cry. The first word that came out of Evangaline's mouth in response to the news was "Why?", which made Katherine laugh harder, which made Evangaline laugh harder—Katherine's laugh was infectious. "James, that's why," Katherine responded once they both regained their composure and that was all Evangaline needed to hear to know her sister was going to be just fine. It was what Evangaline reminded herself of as she sat in the living room within the stronghold of the fae realm, thousands of miles and a magical border away. Wishing she could be there for her sister. *Katherine has*

James, Evangaline told herself. Katherine didn't need Evangaline anymore.

Before she spiraled too deep, Evangaline squinted down at Chloe, remembering something. "What is the autumnal equinox?"

"The first day of autumn. The king will have some fancy dinner to celebrate, which you already know of after Bash's outburst." Chloe responded, twisting a strand of Evangaline's hair between her fingers.

Leering down at Chloe. "Darrin hasn't invited me. Is that a bad thing?"

Des laughed under his breath. "He probably just assumes you will go. I don't know why. You sit with us almost every night and …" His deep gravelly voice drew Evangaline's attention. "None of us go to the king's celebration."

"Where do you go?"

"There's an annual feast outside the village. Everyone brings food and spiced ale. We dance and revel around the fire and pray to the gods that this harvest will be bountiful. Or some shit like that we tell ourselves." Shaw said. His flirtatious voice lilting over the crackling fire.

Charlie with a sly grin on his face mumbled. "Really, we go to drink, dance, and fuck."

Evangaline burst out laughing. "Well, I know which feast I'm going to tomorrow!"

Chloe shot straight up, staring at Evangaline, a worried air filling her hazel eyes. "Evie you can't." Her eyes said what her mouth couldn't, *"You're the princess. You can't go to the village gathering."*

"Chloe, I'm fine." Evangaline's tone became uncommonly assertive as her own eyes blazed at Chloe, saying what *her* mouth couldn't. *"No one even knows I'm the princess. I'm going."*

"It's settled! Lady E," Shaw quipped. He started calling Evangaline *Lady E* about two days ago randomly. The moniker rapidly became Evangaline's favorite nickname. It made her sound way cooler than she actually was. "Tomorrow at 8, we will introduce you to the real people of Celadonia!"

Evangaline looked at the group, ignoring the frustrated stare Chloe was boring into her skull, and then with a smile proclaimed, "Tomorrow at 8!"

Chapter Twenty-Three

They were late.

It was tomorrow. And it was well past eight.

Chloe spent twenty extra minutes fiddling with Evangaline's hair, kicking Wren out of the room like a petulant child. The high ponytail Wren did was curled beautifully, but to Chloe it needed something extra, something that made her look like a princess without a glittering tiara resting upon Evangaline's head.

"In a week when people learn you are the crown princess, don't you want them to remember you looking like a princess and not some disheveled slob?" Chloe asked when Evangaline tried different hair pins and clips. Evangaline scoffed at the insinuation.

After a brief argument, several clips, pins, and baubles later, the two women decided on a bow of crimson crushed velvet. The tone off-set Evangaline's rust colored cotton gown and brown corset. Her off the shoulder long sleeve shirt allowed a bit of coverage against the slight chill that took over the air once the sun went down.

Chloe was nervous. Her nit picking and perfectionism were one sign she was truly nervous about the night and how it might unfold.

Evangaline, however, was itching to see the village and meet all the people Atlas had taught her about. Her excitement shadowed the anxiety that weighed in her stomach.

On the way out of the palace, Evangaline asked Chloe to swing by the kitchen so she could grab something to bring to the feast and bonfire. Felicity once told her to never show up empty-handed to a party, a rule she tried to live by. Not like Evangaline got invited to a lot of parties. But if she knew one thing, the best way to win over the people of the Capital, was going to be through food … and alcohol.

Not knowing a thing about what the fae favored, she grabbed a couple of bottles of wine and some spiced cookies, chocolate, and some thick, fluffy marshmallows. Shaw did say there would be a fire and where there is to be a fire, there should be s'mores!

With their offerings nestled into a small wicker basket, Evangaline and Chloe made their way across the meadows and fields at twenty minutes past eight.

As the palace became a distant shimmering copper twinkle behind them, booming with the sounds of courtiers gossiping in their frivolous frocks, the quaint village of white tumbled stone and orange ceramic shingles took shape. But that was not the girl's final destination. In fact, they were not going to be going into the village at all, much to Evangaline's disappointment.

Chloe guided Evangaline around a massive white and gray stone wall. The Guardian Angel, she called it. The massive structure surrounded the village, with a gate situated in each of the cardinal directions. A precaution taken by the crown after the rebirth of the realm following the Convergence. The Guardian Angel was erected to protect the people from any potential threats or attacks. Atop various parapets and watch towers, royal guards kept their eyes glued to the horizon. Their copper armor and shining ruby swords caught brief glances of moonlight and shined like mirrors displaying morse code.

Occasionally, a guard would recognize Chloe in her flowing gown and incline his ruby and copper clad head in a curt greeting.

Walking quietly, the sound of music glided to Evangaline as though it traveled on a phantom carriage straight to her ears. Softly at first, it moved toward her until the melody picked up and enveloped her in its jovial tune. She could not help but to close her eyes and let the sweet song sink into her skin in warm vibrations. Opening her eyes with a flutter, the scene unfolded spectacularly, a dreamscape even her vivid imagination was incapable of painting.

Butted up against an outcropping at the edge of the ever-changing forest sat a pyre of yellow, orange, and blue flames. The smoke billowed in tumultuous white clouds through the air. The smell of firewood and cinnamon wafted through the breeze, smelling of all the comforts of autumn.

Dozens upon dozens of fae gathered around—more than Evangaline even knew lived in the village on the outskirts of The Capital Palace. Some of the fae were dancing in wild formations, being spun in circles and heaved into the air in complex moves that fooled her as not being choreographed. Some villagers feasted on lush spreads of food splayed out on blankets upon the ground surrounded by cloud like pillows, drinks sturdily in hand. Others were cooking food over small braziers, roasting meat and vegetables alike, all the while laughing and drinking with the masses of smiling faces, waiting for the decadent delights being cooked. Despite them all being fae, it seemed so human, so normal.

"Oi Oi! Look who decided to show the fuck up! *Finally!*" Charlie shouted from a massive blanket laid upon the ground casually with a small blonde woman neatly tucked under his arm.

Des jumped up to greet Chloe and Evangaline, a massive smile lifting the apples of his cheeks up to his aqua eyes. His sleeveless shirt was untucked, oozing every last bit of casual sex appeal that would drive any woman insane. Especially Chloe, if the wide-eyed stare of her friend was any indication.

As he grew closer, Evangaline saw Chloe's hands tighten into a white knuckled grip on the necks of the bottles of wine she held onto. Every ounce of restraint and nerves Chloe was clinging to, however, disappeared as soon as the tall, muscular fae grabbed the bottles from her petite hands and planted a kiss on her cheek. She melted into his hold with the ease of a woman besotted in love.

Evangaline bit her lip to stop the spread of her smile.

Holding both bottles in one hand, Des grabbed Chloe's in the other. Smiling back at Evangaline, he shouted over the music, "Come this way! We've got plenty of room."

And that they did. All eight of them plus the blonde fae woman and a gorgeous red haired-fae woman, whom of which was precariously sitting on Shaw's lap feeding him grapes like a king.

Children enjoyed themselves on the fields surrounding the cadre, running and playing tag. The sound of their youthful laughter only added to the merriment of the evening.

Shaw was right, they may have celebrated the equinox to thank and pray to the many fae gods, but this night was more a celebration of community more than anything—at least to Evangaline it was. A moment to appreciate the friends and family around one another. And for the briefest of moments, Evangaline saw how her life could be if she stayed. Ignoring Bastian and the king, forgetting her duties, and the bargain her parents made … *this*. This sense of community—of belonging—was a foreign comfort she did not want to let go of.

Never once did any of the reveling fae look at her as though she were a steaming pile of human garbage, like many of the nobles did. Despite her ears being on obvious display—the single indicator she was not fae—they welcomed her with open arms and beckoned her to share in their traditions like she was one of them.

Jeremiah, the owner of *"the best pub in town"*, his words not Evangaline's, taught her how to roast a pig over a spit. All the while, his adorable and formidable wife Dolores told stories and jokes at her husband's expense. Surrounded by the warmth of the fire and subtle jazz like melody of the band, Evangaline fell into an effortless tranquility.

She ate and drank and danced, never once caring about anything but the surrounding celebration. It was magical. It was the most alive she had felt in a long time.

Chloe spun her around to the sound of the lyre playing a fast-paced melody, nearly making Evangaline sick from both too much spiced ale and laughing too hard.

Once they tumbled to the ground in a fit of laughter, Shaw invited Evangaline for a "proper dance"—again, his words not hers. It was fast and difficult, and she stepped on his toes more times than she cared to admit, but he didn't care in the slightest. He simply laughed and continued teaching her the paces, holding her upright when she faltered, encouraging her to keep trying.

"Did they teach you this in school?" She laughed as she stumbled into his arms.

His laugh shook his chest. "Not at all. All fae are just gifted dancers. Perhaps your mortal is showing, Lady E."

She punched his arm and ushered him to keep teaching her the dance.

Once they finished, a small fae boy with straw-blond hair neatly tugged on Shaw's loose sky-blue shirt and asked if he could have the next dance with Evangaline. Her cheeks swelled with flattery and excitement.

Evangaline accepted the invitation with great flair and an over-exaggerated curtsey to the young boy, extending her hand. As he twisted his hands in anticipation, watching her show, his cheeks flushed an adorable hue of pink, only growing redder and redder as he skipped her around the dance floor jovially. Her curled ponytail whipped around her shoulders as they turned in circles past other dancers, not at all minding the choreographed dance happening around them. Evangaline's laugh filled the air as the song came to a close and the dancers clapped their hands appreciatively to the band.

"Would you like to learn how to make a treat from Vitalis? It involves ooey gooey chocolate," she asked the boy ruffling his hair, all the while struggling to gain her breath. His eyes lit up at the sound of chocolate and he ferociously nodded his shaggy blond head.

"Alright, go grab your friends. Oh! And each of you find some sticks for me, okay? Long ones!" She shouted as he ran back to his small group of gossiping young boys and girls.

Jeremiah allowed her to use his brazier while she taught the children and the small crowd of party goers gathered round how to make a s'more.

Sure, the spiced cookies held no comparison to a good old fashion human graham cracker, but they weren't bad. They held up enough for Dolores to decree them as a new fixed staple on the pub's menu, in fact. Pride swelled through Evangaline as the fae around her embraced her Vitalian traditions.

Her mind couldn't help but think of Chloe and their conversation the night of her pre-birthday partying. What would the New World look like without the borders? Could the humans and fae truly embrace one another in the same way the folks before her embraced her as one of their own, or would the Lord and Lady Whittell's of the world cast judgment on their non-magical counterparts with prejudice and hatred? Would humans be open to living alongside beings that could overpower them with flawless ease?

She shook herself free of her thoughts and went back to distributing chocolate and marshmallows to the children tugging at her skirt with a smile that shone with gratitude and happiness.

After quite some time, the band's music slowed and the fire began to quell. The flames flickered around four feet tall as compared to the gargantuan ones that towered over Evangaline mere hours ago. She wandered the meadow alone, sipping her wine, taking in the now quieting party.

The children were all ushered to bed by their parents once the moon reached its peak and ushered in the midnight hour. With that, the evening soon become one for the lovers and poets as the stars dotted the sky in groupings of swirling constellations.

Shaw and the rest of the cadre laid out on the blanket, gazing up at the stars while Des and Chloe danced slowly—and closely—as the band played their tranquil ballad. Chloe's head rested on his chest and his cheek rested on her plaited pink hair. They swayed so peacefully with their eyes closed, holding one another tight, slowly rocking in the breeze like time and duty did not separate them for a year. As though they were the only people the Earth spun for and the only ones the stars shone upon.

It made Evangaline's heart ache. *That* was what every little girl and boy wanted when they grew up. To be held. To be loved. So wildly and unconditionally that even the thought of speaking it into reality was scary.

Standing across the pyre, her back to the forest, Evangaline scanned the crowd that was left behind. Couples danced and kissed, others laid out on blankets or in the chill dew of the grass.

She took in the scene with keen eyes, taking small sips of her wine. She felt so at peace, so alive and cherished. It made her heart constrict and pulse in fluttering beats.

Until her the muscle giving her life stilled altogether, shocked into a state of fear and unease that made her breath lodge in her throat and her fingers tense in uncertainty.

Chapter Twenty-Four

Directly across from Evangaline stood a being … a creature … a demon. Its preternatural stillness sent a wave of unease through her whole body that begged her to run.

She drank in the sight of the ghastly creature through the heatwaves and haze simmering about the quelling fire. The fire's emissions slightly distorted the being's towering frame, making it hard for her to inspect the details of the creature.

What she could see was that of a crumpled silhouette shrouded in a swirling darkness, claws cascaded down its long-pointed hands, and bright red glowing eyes-fixated directly on her, unblinking. Eyes that pierced into her soul and seared their image on her retinas like a tattoo.

Folks walked around as though it was not there at all. For a split-second, Evangaline thought the ale and wine was getting to her head. But it was there. She knew it was. All the hairs on Evangaline's arms stood at attention as her breathing turned to heavy pants. Her chest ached and thrashed in fear, so much so she felt acute pains ripple through her breastbone and down her arms. She clutched the space right over where her heartbeat in a raucous staccato.

Despite her unease, Evangaline couldn't peel her eyes from the monster. It paralyzed her and fogged her mind, obscuring the part of her brain that should have told her to run or scream. It was as though she was locked into a staring contest with a demon sent straight from hell.

In the blink of an eye, the creature disappeared with the uptick of a flame.

One second it was there, the next it wasn't—disappearing into a cloud of smoke.

She wanted to run to Chloe and tell her what she saw but she found herself glued to the spot she stood, from fear or dread, she could not quite place it. Whatever that creature was, it was looking at her, *hunting her.*

Before she could allow her brain to decide on an action, a hand slipped over her mouth from behind. Then another wrapped around her waist, pinning her arms to her sides in a well-fortified grip.

Her cup of wine clattered to the floor—spilling all over the front of her skirt—as she was dragged deeper into the forest.

She tried to fight back; she tried to bite the hand that covered her mouth, but she was not strong enough for either. The force of the being's hold was more powerful than she could even attempt to immobilize. Hard muscles pressed into her back and restrained her completely.

Smaller and smaller, the festival got as she was hauled deeper and deeper into the ever-changing leaves. The copse of trees blinding out any sight or sound of the equinox festivities, until she could see no more fire and the darkness took over beneath an unforgiving moon.

Evangaline forced herself to take deep breaths. The last thing she needed was to have a panic attack right now. She needed a strong mind—if her physical abilities could not defeat this monster, perhaps her mind could. She just needed her wits about her. With each deep breath, Evangaline's head cleared, and her adrenaline became something that could power her rather than hinder. Chloe taught her how to fight. She could do it. She could fight this creature. She just needed to not let her fear get in her way.

Closing her eyes, she took one deep breath, followed by another.

Suddenly, with a jerk, her assailant released his grip on her torso and pushed her up against a tree, scraping her shoulders with a pinch of pain. That was when she recognized it, the smell. It was faint covered by the heavy stench of alcohol, but it was there—*bergamot and rose*.

"Bastian?" She mumbled through the hand still pressed to her mouth. Her eyes flung open wide as saucers with recognition.

And there he was. Hair pulled back into a neat little bun. His maroon vest glittered in the moonlight, buttoned up just enough to show his sculpted chest, leaving his arms exposed to the elements. A wicked glint hung in his eyes as his mouth quirked up in a taunting smile.

The hand that gripped her waist bore down tight enough for her to gasp in pain just as he released his hand from her mouth. And before she knew it—before she had a moment to spew the venomous thoughts lining the tip of her tongue—his lips crashed into hers. Frenzied and rough, he claimed her against her will.

Pressed against the tree, she was trapped. She tried fighting him for a moment before his kiss grew passionately hostile and punishing. Gripping his arms, she sunk her nails into his flesh, drawing a bit of blood. She willed him to stop while pushing with all her might against his brawn.

Finally, she was able to pull away, turning her cheek to him. "What the fuck Bash?" Her words were a sharp whisper in the night.

His eyes were feral, absolutely feral. "You defied me. You weren't at the feast. And you certainly aren't wearing what I wanted you to wear. Once I learned where you went, I decided I didn't want an audience and wanted you alone. So ..." he said, starting to kiss her jaw and neck with possessive pecks and bites. As though that was an explanation for the attack he was waging on her.

"Bash, stop!" She responded, trying to push his massive body away from hers.

He didn't listen, continuing his assault of kisses across her collarbone that he no doubt meant to be sweet but was anything but. His hand began to mindlessly untie the small bow keeping her white blouse together under her corset.

"Bash! Stop!" she yelled more aggressively, shoving him with all her might.

He stumbled back a couple of steps. His lips were full and swollen, the wild look in his eyes grew dark with anger.

"Princess ..." he hissed in a mocking tone, cocking his head to the side.

Evangaline knew he wouldn't hurt her—*right?* She *hoped* he wouldn't hurt her, but she also knew in that moment he scared her. Possibly more than the red-eyed creature. She didn't want this.

Whatever the red-eyed creature was had frightened her, but it didn't attack her. The line Bastian crossed scared Evangaline more than the menacing demon her mind conjured across the fire.

Bastian was every bit the apex predator playing with his prey that she always saw him as. He knew he had size and brawn over her. He knew with the flex of his muscles he could snap her in half if it so pleased him. It showed in the taunting creases of his eyes and the slack stance his body stood in.

"I've missed you, princess," his eyes still fixed on her. Smile still ticked up in the corners, forming a menacing grin. "Be a good girl and show me how much you missed me."

Her stupid girl heart, despite her fear, fluttered at hearing that he was thinking about her. But she quickly reminded herself, this wasn't how a man showed a woman they missed them, nor was the wanton letter begging for his attention on his desk. But he didn't know she knew of that little nugget. No, Bastian was bad news. Chloe was right. It was fun, but it was time to kick him to the curb. That volcano pitch sounded better and better with every unwanted pet and touch Bastian swiped across her skin.

"You need to stop, Bash. This—us—we can't do this anymore," she murmured quietly, the words falling out of her mouth in a plea.

He cupped her face, tilting it up to meet his eyes, "I wanted you four days ago, but Chloe ruined that—"

"What, Waylay didn't take care of your needs enough before your trip?" Evangaline spoke so fast her words failed to pass through the scanner built into her brain that told her if she should truly speak or not. For a moment, Bastian blinked at her, confused, but the intensity of his eyes grew clouded with a relief that Evangaline knew meant nothing good.

"Not even close, Princess." He embraced the affair with a smile instead of denying it. "Yet, here I stand, having wanted to feel you every day since I left. You are like a drug for me, Princess. There is no escaping this."

"No. We can't. We *won't!* Not anymore. I don't want this … especially not this way, Bastian."

Bastian's lip tugged up in a salacious grin. "Don't blow things out of proportion, Princess. I'm here now. Where neither of us should be." He raised a scolding brow at her. "You know the king was expecting to see you at his feast tonight. He was a little angry at you, which means he was a little angry at me. Which makes me a lot angry at you. I told you I would see you at the feast and yet I had to hunt you down. You have a lot of explaining to do." He began kissing her neck again, this time slower. Grazing his teeth over the places he kissed.

"I like these people. I like them better than anyone at the king's feast." Evangaline angrily exclaimed, grabbing Bastian by the jaw, making him face her. She wanted him to see the truth in her statement through the hard look in her eyes.

He straightened, bringing his forearm to rest above her head on the tree. His other hand moved, gripping her throat possessively in a grip that was almost bruising. Gently, he pressed up against her, crushing her body between the trunk of the tree and his towering frame.

He was menacing and dark. Shrouded in feral wickedness. He felt so different from the man she first met. Was this who he really was?

She could feel him through his pants, hard and ready to take her. Deep down, she knew he enjoyed this little game he started.

Regret hit her hard and fast for ever letting him dominate her in the first place. She was reckless, caving to the whims of her body and not thinking things through. That night on the balcony was a mistake. She knew it then, and she knew it in the force of his body now.

"I was at that feast. And here I was thinking you liked me." He breathed into her ear. "You are mine, Princess. You just don't know it yet."

She braced her hands on his chest, trying to push him away. "Bastian, you're scaring me. Now let me go."

His eyes were laser focused on her mouth; his breathing became heavy against her chest. Slowly, he ground into her, his eyes closing as he pressed his hardness against her waist.

Whispering, "This is your fault, Princess. Take some responsibility for your actions." Bastian slowly and sensually dropped his hand from above her head to her thigh. Gathering up her skirt until his cold, callused fingers pressed way too close to her sex, making her squirm in discontent.

Evangaline knew what *he* wanted and that at any second, he could overpower her and take it, but she would fight like holy hell to not let that happen.

"Go ask Waylay to take care of you."

His fingers grazed the soft skin of her thigh as he chuckled against her skin. "If you cared about me, Princess, you would let me take you right here. Like this. Show me how much you care for me."

That was the thing. She didn't care about him. They were complicated, yes. Somewhere caught in the gray area of friends and lovers. Their relationship was all flirtation and sex, nothing more. *You owe him absolutely nothing;* she reminded herself through his gaslighting. *You have done nothing wrong.*

He looked back up at her, his forest eyes glittering in the starlight. He was strikingly attractive in a haunting way. Where his touch and glances once filled her with lust, they now filled her with an overwhelming nausea.

This was truly not the man she thought he was, but she was glad his true colors showed themselves before she got in too deep. Evangaline doubted this was the man even Chloe thought he was, because if it was, Chloe would have castrated him already for even breathing near Evangaline.

All Evangaline needed was the perfect opportunity to break free of his grasp and run like hell back to the festival. She knew fighting her enemy wouldn't work. She simply wasn't strong enough, so running was going to have to do. She would run all the way back to the palace and surround herself with the entire Royal Army if that meant staying out of Bastian's grip tonight and every night thereafter. Someone had to be searching for her by now. Someone must have found her abandoned cup or heard her muffled pleas for help. At least she hoped that to be true.

Suddenly, without warning—as though it read her mind—the wind whisp darted through the air and barreled into Bastian with the force of a freight train, sending him straight on his ass.

This was her chance.

She threw a sidelong glance at Bastian and ran like hell. The wind whisp billowed through the trees at her side, keeping pace and egging her along with gentle gusts of wind at her back to help her speed along faster.

Panting and crying, Evangaline gasped, "Thank you, friend." The whisp kicked up leaves and dirt as it billowed in her wake.

The slow burn of the fire took shape as she heard Bastian swear somewhere in the distance behind her.

Evangaline barreled through the trees with the whisp never leaving her side. With a soft caress of her face, just as she slowed down at the forest's edge, the whisp careened off back in the direction of Bastian. The sight of the fete quietly ambling on sent a torrent of relief crashing through her shaking body.

A soft gasp had Evangaline twisting her face to the side just in time to see Chloe running toward her, wide-eyed and desperate. Des, Shaw, and Charlie were on her heels. Genuine fear etched on each of their dashing faces.

Evangaline put her hands on her knees, taking a deep breath through the tears cascading down her face. Choked sobs escaped her as Chloe approached.

With gentle hands, Chloe grabbed onto Evangaline's cheeks, pulling her face up to her own, brushing aside the tears marking them, "Evie, what happened? What's wrong?" That was when Chloe looked down at her untied blouse, her fair skin glistening with sweat and red marks from Bastian's teeth and hands.

Unable to catch her breath, Evangaline stood up, taking in her friends. It hadn't hit her till just then in that moment, but they *all* were her friends, ones she always dreamed of having but was never lucky enough to have. A new family that Evangaline was forming all on her own. Chloe gave her that. Chloe gave Evangaline not just *her* friendship but also the friendship of those she herself cherished most. Lost in her emotions, Evangaline lunged and hugged Chloe with the desperation of her fear and love. Crying harder into her friend's shoulder.

Des, Shaw, and Charlie stiffened as they looked past Evangaline into the outcropping of trees. They watched with terse expressions as Evangaline's perpetrator closed in from the darkness of the forest.

"There you are. I thought I lost you! That training is proving fruitful. Good work Commander." Bastian's deep voice echoed through the tree line, followed by his haunting laugh.

Evangaline's stomach hollowed out. *"You are mine … you just don't know it yet."* The words repeated in her head like they were a riddle she needed to solve. He would be relentless in his pursuit of her, and that terrified her.

Her heart shuddered, thinking of his words as his heavy footsteps grew nearer. She quickly sobered herself. Drying her tears making her eyes grow distant in the way Atlas taught her while playing cards. Evangaline didn't want Bastian to see he hurt her, *weakened* her.

Throwing an arm around her shoulder, Bastian hauled Evangaline out of Chloe's grip roughly. "That damn whisp scared you again. It's alright. I've got you … *I've always got you.*"

"Whisp?" Des asked Evangaline, something lighting in his eyes.

Evangaline opened her mouth to speak to Des, when Bastian cut her off, "Yeah, the wind whisp seems to have taken a shining to my lady here," he said playfully, shaking Evangaline's shoulders.

Evangaline glanced away from all of them, the words swirling in her mind with anger but not making their way to her tongue, *"I am not your lady!"*

Shaw stepped forward to Chloe's side. "Shall we escort you back to the palace, Lady E?"

Evangaline stepped out of Bastian's grasp up to Shaw and spoke before Bastian could control her narrative any further. "That would be great. I don't want to ruin all of your evening, though. Chloe could take me."

Bastian stepped up to her side once more. Evangaline could feel her repulsion and anger streaming across her face, no matter how hard she tried to hide it. "I can take you, *Lady E*." Bastian spit toward Shaw in a demeaning bite.

Des then stepped up, looking ready for battle, on Chloe's other side, his hand braced protectively on her lower back. Charlie stepped to Shaw's side. An impenetrable wall of fae warriors stood before her. All willing to protect a human woman, they had no idea was their princess. Nor did they know how grateful she was for their friendship. But she would tell them later once she her mind cleared, and her heart stopped racing.

"We will all go." Des said finitely, "Evangaline?" He amended, extending his elbow for her to grab. He never once took his eyes off Bastian. His distrust of the general shining through in every last ember of his glistening heated eyes.

Evangaline grasped Des's arm before she could be forced onto Bastian's and began walking with lead covered feet.

Chapter Twenty-Five

"Lady E, did he hurt you?" Shaw finally said, breaking the sullen silence that filled Evangaline's living quarters.

Chloe, Des, Charlie, Shaw, and Bastian all escorted Evangaline back to her room. A somber processional of tension that walked through the many drunken and dazed courtiers celebrating the equinox.

On the walk back, Des quietly instructed her to say she was tired once she entered her room, then they would all walk out with Bastian in tow. After a couple minutes, he said the cadre would return, and they did. How he knew his plan would work was the least of Evangaline's worries. She trusted him explicitly. His plan worked flawlessly, and once they came back into the room, they all gathered in the living room without a word. The snapping of the fireplace was the only noise for a long while until Shaw spoke.

Evangaline was so deep in her own head, replaying everything that had occurred, she barely heard Shaw's hushed words. She thought she was safe with Bastian. Unfortunately, he had to go dispelling everything she believed. He had to go and live up to the muttered rumors and hushed warnings. She was so angry with herself.

"No, Shaw, he didn't hurt me." Evangaline murmured, staring at the crackling amber fire.

"So was it really the whisp that scared you? I've not seen it, but I don't fault you if it did." Charlie asked, concern riding every syllable of his thick accent.

Evangaline swallowed hard. Chloe grabbed her hand and gave a soft squeeze, reminding Evangaline she was safe with them—all of them. However, Evangaline knew without Chloe's reassurance. She felt it in her heart. Her friends warmed the vital organ in her chest and made her feel safe. It was the secret royal bullshit that made her quiver with guilt. They should know. She wanted to tell them a dozen times but could never find the words or courage to go against her word to Darrin.

"No, the whisp didn't scare me. The wind whisp is my friend. It helped me to get away," she curtly replied. Her voice was so sinfully hollow.

Des stopped his pacing and focused on Evangaline, "The wind whisp is your *friend*?"

Evangaline looked up at him, eyes searing. "Yes."

Des nodded, accepting her vow without further questions. At the finality of her words. He turned and resumed his pacing, clearly contemplating something. What that was, he never elaborated. He simply just kept walking back and forth, his face scrunched together in thought.

Chloe laid her head on Evangaline's shoulder for a brief moment. "I never should have let you go tonight. It was dangerous."

Evangaline walked to the window overlooking the dim garden. Unnaturally still, she watched the lights twinkle above the pathway faintly illuminate the spiraling rows of shrubs and flowers that brought her peace.

"Bash would have found me either way. If I was at the palace, I would have been closer to him. For whatever reason, he thinks I'm *his*. Why, I will never fucking know. But he was quite offended that I did not obey his orders." She folded her arms and turned around to her friends. Her voice growing in anger and volume, "I will never regret going tonight and I don't want any of you feeling bad for inviting me or taking me. I had the most fun I have probably ever had in my life. Those people—you guys—are not to blame for one stupid prick who doesn't know how to keep his dick in his pants."

Chloe jumped at the hostility in Evangaline's voice, her eyes wide with panic. She looked toward Des, who once again stopped his pacing. Shaw's mouth cracked open, brows furrowed at Charlie, who mirrored his expression.

"Evie," Chloe whispered. "Did Bastian … Did he … please tell me he didn't …" Her soft voice breaking more and more with each word. Her faith and trust in the man she believed was a friend dying with her pleas.

Evangaline fixed her sight on the floor. She bit her bottom lip, and she breathed down her anxiety, anger, and loss of trust. The realization coming to her stronger than before, the man she gave herself to willingly, just assaulted her. For some reason, the assault paled in comparison to the breach of trust, the comradery she once shared with the man she lusted for. However, seeing Chloe—hearing her strong voice die with pain—Evangaline fully digested the events that occurred. Fully understood the weight of the situation and just how awry it could have gotten had the wind whisp not allowed her a chance to run.

She cleared her throat. "He dragged me into the forest … I was … he pinned me to a tree and tried. But no, he didn't … go there." She crossed over the room to Chloe, who began to cry, her tears streamed down her slightly tangerine hued cheeks. Evangaline grabbed Chloe's hands and pulled her close, hoping her words would soothe the ache that broke in Chloe's chest. She knew the tears weren't for Bastian. No, Evangaline was positive. The only emotion Chloe felt for him at the present was the overwhelming urge to tear his favorite appendage from his worthless body. No, these tears that cascaded in pained rivulets were because she failed. Chloe's sworn duty was to protect Evangaline—her princess—from any harm and in the time she took to revel in her own wants, Evangaline was nearly taken advantage of. Chloe took her duty to heart, and this broke her. But it was Evangaline's fault—correction, it was Bastian's fault—and she needed Chloe to know she was not at all to feel bad for the events of the night. Nor any of the guys. "He touched me and kissed me and said I was his but Chlo, look at me. *Look. At. Me.* I am no one's but mine. I should have listened to you about Bash. I should have and I am so sorry I didn't. You were right, I was a notch in a bedpost … another name to add to his list of conquests. But I'm so much stronger than he thinks. And that is solely because of you." Chloe and Evangaline wrapped each other in a tight embrace and cried into each other until they had nothing else to cry about.

Occasional muttered apologies and then dismissals of said apologies floated through the air but died out in the crackles of the flames that burned at Des's back.

Nobody said anything else for the remainder of the night.

As sleep began to claim the group, Des insisted on staying with Chloe and Evangaline in Evangaline's rooms, making himself comfortable on the couch. Shaw and Charlie promised they would not say a word of what happened to anyone and would carry on as though nothing had occurred. Which they were not happy about at all. If it were up to the boys, they would have woken the king from his drunken slumber and had Bastian's head served on a nice silver platter. Which was one of many punishments for mistreating royalty in Celadonia, however barbaric and gory.

Neither man knew she was the crown princess. Yet they still insisted on alerting the king, for she was a guest of his and should be treated with the respect of a person of his standing. It was noble of them to say so. But their declarations only drove her guilt through the roof in knowing they could follow through on their motivations should she reveal her true identity to them. However, they left with gentle hugs and soft smiles, swearing their loyalty and secrecy. Before they left, they kindly asked their commander to be brought onto Evangaline's security personnel, along with the others. Chloe agreed and sent them off with a weary wave.

As Evangaline stared at the ceiling, listening to Chloe breathe deeply and soundly, she found herself replaying the night. The creature with red eyes and claws. The creature with a silver tongue and forceful body. The creature that clawed in her chest making it thunder with fear, anxiety, and anger.

At the end of the day, she was only human. She tried to fight Bash and couldn't win. Not even with all of her training. The fae would always be faster, stronger, cleverer, and she would always just be… human. No matter the half of her that came from the realm of the fae, she was not blessed with fae gifts or abilities and certainly had no magic, which meant as long as she stayed in Celadonia she would be vulnerable. She couldn't very well have the cadre always surrounding her, protecting her, they had jobs of their own. Plus, Evangaline didn't want to be helpless all the time.

The events of the evening solidified a plan in her mind. In one week—after she was presented as crown princess of the realm—she would return to Vitalis and leave all this behind for good. No matter how painful the thought of leaving her new friends and Chloe behind was, she was not equipped to live among the fae.

Chapter Twenty-Six

"I really am sorry, daughter, but with the arrival of the kingdom's royalty and the many nobles beginning to portal in, I cannot allow you to attend the welcome feast." The king quipped, pacing the floor of the elaborate ballroom. His jewel encrusted tunic shined off the freshly polished blinding white floor tiles as he moved.

"But we have three days before my debut and Chloe's eager to go and I, besides, would be lying if I said that I didn't want to see a bunch of regal-ass fae make their fancy ass entrances." Evangaline pushed back hurriedly. Her tone a mixture of soft but jovial.

During her lesson with Atlas, the day before, Evangaline learned her debut ball would mark the first time in nearly two decades that all five royals from the five kingdoms would be together in a time of peace.

Every get together before were in times of unrest. Battles or skirmishes had been pulling the land apart in one instance. One of the royals didn't feel like showing in another. But now Evangaline was here, with a front-row seat to witness Celadonian history. She was too curious for even her own good.

"Evangaline, there will be people from every court, *plus* the royals. This is not a normal Capital dinner. I need to focus on the royals. I do not want to worry about reassuring more of my subjects of the harmless intentions of the human in our midst and lie any further!" The king all but shouted. His voice was low in volume but carried through the room in soft reverberations.

She shuddered at his curt statement before coming around him to face him. "You brought the 'human into their midst.' I will stay out of the way! If that is really what you want. But please, Chloe wants to go. She just doesn't want to leave me alone and abandon her duties. The other guys are working the event tonight, but she has off. She's been working too hard and could use the break. Please."

The king sighed, pinching the bridge of his nose before cupping her face, "Evangaline, you are my greatest creation. Truly. I only want to keep you safe. In three days' time, you will be the surprise of the century for this realm. Just please, stay in your room tonight. Bastian will be busy. I would have him escort you, but can't risk the distraction for anyone. And there will be too much happening for me or the guards to watch you properly."

Evangaline cringed at the mention of Bastian. "At least let Chloe go. She has a dress picked out and everything." Evangaline pleaded, giving her best attempt at puppy dog eyes. "You wouldn't deny a young woman the honor of seeing her king host the most spectacular welcome reception on this side of the Velum, would you?" She batted her eyelashes.

The king tipped his head back and sighed, squinting at the beautiful baroque gold trimmed dome ceiling of the ballroom. "Fine, Chloe may come, but you must stay in your rooms! Promise me this Evangaline. There will be no guards to watch you, especially if Chloe is attending the dinner!"

He looked the most fatherly he had ever looked. His face was that of a dad getting asked by their teenager for more money. A face that of which Evangaline had seen a great deal of time plastered on Stephen's face. The sight of Darrin's fatherly countenance made her laugh. Her heart warmed slightly at the vision of her fae father.

As he lowered his head, she leaned into him and placed a kiss on his cheek. "Thank you," she whispered before leaving the ballroom, both elated and deflated at the same time.

Chapter Twenty-Seven

Standing in a cobalt blue silk robe and matching nightgown, Evangaline gazed out the window at the few fae meandering through the swirling gardens below her room.

The sun set a few hours prior, exposing the sky to a beautiful cascade of stars.

Without the lights and skyscrapers of the city, she could see every celestial body that stretched across the expanse of the great black sky. The moon shone like a beacon of the night, somehow calling to Evangaline like a signal to explore and revel in its white light.

Chloe left around the time the sun did, clinging to Des's arm—of course. Both clad in the most beautiful of ivory silks stitched with gold thread that sparkled as though spun by the sun itself.

Chloe's pink hair was out of its signature braids and masterfully sculpted into a waterfall of curls down her head by Wren.

She was beautiful.

Evangaline felt like a mom sending her daughter off to prom, all misty eyed and proud.

Now, however, several hours later, she stared out the window, and found herself searching for Chloe and Des. Bored out of her mind and insanely restless. She hoped to get a peek at her friends reveling in the jubilant night she wanted to attend so badly. Though knowing the two of them, they would be close to wherever the wine or ale was being stocked. Which was certainly not in the garden she now stared off into.

Instead of her friends, Evangaline saw many new faces from the different kingdoms during her time people watching. Each one unique in their styles and fashions.

The Kingdom of Frost's citizens were covered in luxurious furs of various types, despite the slightly warm temperature of the night. They were the easy ones to pinpoint and identify.

The court from the Kingdom of Leaves stood out in their ensembles consisting of natural elements. Whether it was flowers or leaves, wheat, or barley, they represented the land they coveted and tilled. Some even donned hats and fascinators with animalistic qualities just for an extra flair.

The others were harder to place. But the courtiers of the Capital in their glittering ballgowns stood out even amongst the costumed new arrivals to the court, drawing all the focus to them. No doubt their primary intention if Evangaline knew their narcissistic qualities well enough.

Crossing the room, Evangaline stood on her balcony and anxiously gazed out over the expanse of grass and forest beyond her. Taking in the faint distant echoes of the band playing below her.

As her mind swirled, she was caught off guard by movement in the trees. A soft rustle of leaves high in the canopy of the trees. Where she knew rationally, it was probably only an animal or even the wind whisp. She strained her eyes to look. Unable to find any sign of anything suspicious, she took a breath and looked away from the forest.

A dark, red-eyed creature that she could not seem to forget swam in the recesses of her mind and latched onto her fear, escalating it anytime she saw something out of the ordinary. A rustle of leaves. A random shadow. She startled at nearly everything.

Perhaps it was just another of the elemental goddess's creatures. Evangaline thought to herself, itching to see more of the goddess's allies. Bastian told her about a couple of the creatures the goddess called friends, but not all of them. Perhaps the creature she saw at the equinox was just another friend of the goddess?

In all her lessons over the past two and a half weeks, Atlas never taught her about the many gods and goddesses that the fae once looked up to. The only one she knew of was the elemental goddess and that was only because of the whisp. Yet that was all she knew. She didn't even know her true name or what powers she held—though by her title, her powers were pretty self-explanatory.

Now wrought with curiosity, Evangaline walked to the books on her shelves, itching to know more. She ran her finger along the spines to find that, despite the absurd amount of literature in her room, not even one referenced the fae gods.

Defeated, she plopped on the couch, hoping that she might be lucky enough to fall asleep. If not only to ignore the fact that she was dealing with some major FOMO at the moment.

The library. She sat up quickly as the thought popped into her mind. She could easily make it to the library without anyone seeing her. The hallways that led there were in the opposite direction of the banquet. She would only have to sneak past the throne room once, which she could easily manage if she stuck to the dark shadowed area under the stairs.

Besides, the party appeared to be dying down with each hour that passed, which meant many people were either quietly getting drunk or they were back in their rooms already.

Excited for an adventure and an excuse to shake off some of her frenetic energy, Evangaline jumped up, foregoing slippers to remain silent across the marble floor. She was no spy, but she watched enough espionage movies to know the gist of staying out of sight.

"Let's go on an adventure!" She whispered to herself as she made her way to the door of her room. A smile spread so far across her face, her cheeks pained her as she crept into the dim hall.

Chapter Twenty-Eight

She made it to the library with only one person seeing her.

A young servant boy who went by the name of Colby—if she remembered correctly. She recognized him from the many dinner services she had gone to. He was always nice and provided the table with more than their fair share of wine.

Yet even though he saw her tonight, he paid her no heed in her nightgown and robe. Offering a simple smile as he continued on his way, as though it was a standard occurrence to see her in her nightclothes wandering the dark parts of the palace. Yet, she didn't dwell on his knowledge of her breaking her word to the king and simply kept creeping along till she was at the wood doors that marked the library.

Once she was there, she could not help but feel an overwhelming feeling of unease. Her chest ached far under her ribs as though it was screaming, *"we shouldn't be here!"*

Ignoring her body's nagging to turn and run, Evangaline scanned the many shelves of books, searching for anything that would talk about the gods and goddesses, but there was nothing. With thousands of tomes in the library, there had to be at least one that would entertain her, anything to satiate the annoying need to learn more about the elemental goddess.

Unfortunately, Evangaline was the kind of person who, once she set her mind to something, she couldn't let it go. It nagged at her until it either consumed her or she quelled the ache with knowledge.

As she scanned and scanned, an hour passed without her feeling a second fly by.

In that span of time, a pile of books got stacked on one of the nearby tables. Titles she wanted to take back up to her room for weeks but never got a second to squirrel them away. Atlas's warning eyes and constant supervision warned her not to remove even a single book. He was quite protective of the library, never allowing her to steal a book or two. He always welcomed her should she want to simply sit and read, but as far as taking a few books to her room … that was a big fat nope!

However, if she was going to be locked away for a few more days, she might as well have some books that tickle her fancy, none of which though talked about the gods. Atlas would never know she stole a few books until she was gone. Besides, her stack was filled with cheesy fictional romances that she had been surprised to find tucked between tomes and scrolls of science and art.

Evangaline's fingers trailed on the bindings of ancient books as she scoured the titles. Until a noise filling the quiet cavern nearly made her topple off the ladder she was about to mount.

"What are you doing?" A jarringly familiar voice asked behind her in the doorway.

"What are you doing here?" She snapped at Bastian. Her back was turned to him, leaving her vulnerable. She didn't like that he caught her out of the blue … again. Whenever she let her guard down, he appeared.

She had spent three days void of his presence and yet the feeling of fear from that night lingered in the back of her mind. Between him and the creature she saw, she was unable to forget how quickly her celebration turned to fear.

"I thought I saw you sneak past the throne room." His voice was haughty and taunting. "The servant boy verified my suspicions. I knew this must be where you were headed," he answered, not making any advancements toward her. Thank the many fae gods she knew nothing about!

"Colby. His names is Colby," she huffed. None of the nobility ever took the time to learn the names of anyone they thought of as beneath them. It pissed Evangaline off to no end.

"Whatever you say, Princess."

Finally, she turned around and stepped away from the bookshelf, putting the ladder to her back. The sight of him was both breathtaking and aggravating. A red jacket lined with black scrolling on top of ivory trousers clung to the chiseled curves of his thighs. He looked good, and that really pissed off Evangaline. Knowing someone so evil could look so pretty should be illegal.

Willing all her strength, she calmly and sternly stated, "I don't want to see you, Bash. Please go away. Leave me alone."

He moved toward her but stopped when he saw her flinch, "Forgive me Evangaline. I was drunk that night. I would never hurt you, you know that."

Evangaline remained still, staring at him. She wanted to forgive him for some stupid reason but knew she shouldn't, so she just didn't respond. Standing there like a wraith, her face and body defiant in their stance. If it happened once, it would happen again if she allowed him back in. Abuse was a cycle that was hard to escape.

"Please, Princess. I…"

"You, what Bash?" She cut off his half-assed apologies. "Admit to me what you did, and maybe, just maybe, I can—"

Then, from her right side, she heard a noise that cut off her words and drew her eye. An unnatural scraping sound filled the quiet room. She shifted her sight from Bastian, only to feel the air thicken with a dark wave of black mist drifting across the room.

Soon Bastian was before her, drawing a blade from his boot.

Fear quivered her voice, "Tell me you see that too, Bash."

The black smoke drifted to the top right corner of the room directly across from Evangaline and Bastian, where it manifested into a shape. No, not a shape, a demon. *The* demon.

Long talons protruded from large fingers that scraped across the dark wood. The opaque black creature cocked its head in a robotic movement that allowed Evangaline to get a good look at the bright red eyes sheathed within its angular skull. Eyes Evangaline could not forget even if she tried. She couldn't forget the horror that stared across the fire at her. The very one that stared at her now, cocking its head in slow, appraising rotations.

"I've seen that thing before, Bash." Her voice grew shakier and more frantic. Her anxiety clogged in the back of her throat, not allowing a full breath of air into her lungs.

"When, Evangaline? When did you see *that* thing?"

The creature just stared at them, still as death. One claw scraping on the wood.

"That night, right before you ..." She couldn't finish the sentence and with it, she could feel Bastian tense. His body going ridged as he watched the creature effectively sharpen its talon on the wooden bookshelf.

Slowly he turned to face Evangaline, putting his back to the creature and blocking her view of the monstrosity staring down at her. "I am sorry for that night, Princess, but I need you to run now, okay? When I tell you to, charge the door ... got it?"

Glancing between Bastian and the red-eyed demon, Evangaline nodded rapidly.

Bastian then cupped her cheek tenderly. Slowly, as though he was an entirely different man, he placed a delicate kiss on her lips. Call it adrenaline, or recklessness, but her body clung onto his and she kissed him back. It was stupid, but her fear often made her stupid and reckless. Perhaps it was staring death in the face that made her yearn for a love that would never exist, but she threw caution to the wind and kissed him back despite the revulsion coursing through her system.

Pulling away slowly, he flashed her a smile, and quietly whispered, *"Go."*

Chapter Twenty-Nine

Evangaline lunged forward, sprinting past Bastian. Tears of fear filled the backs of her eyes. She ran as hard and as fast as she could toward the door, pushing her legs to their brink. When she heard the scraping of claws growing closer to her, she released a determined scream and pushed her muscles to run harder.

Stupidly, she took her eyes off the creature for two seconds to run, hoping Bastian had her back. Yet, before she knew it, the damn thing was leaping straight for her after running across the walls, using the bookcases as though they were the floor beneath her feet. The demon defied logic and the simplest rules of gravity. As it ran to her, its deadly sharp claws extended out, making Evangaline flinch with every flick and flash of its ebony talons.

Bastian, with a cry, threw his dagger at it as the beast lunged even closer. It struck straight into the back of the beast and sent it tumbling into the door. The exact door Evangaline was running to.

She skidded to a halt and watched as the creature rose, its towering frame dwarfed her in its shadowy silhouette.

It certainly didn't appear so big a few days ago. While she stood at a casual five foot six, the build of the demon rising over her made her look three feet tall. Even Bastian was dwarfed by the shadow of the beast as it stood to its full height.

Reaching its long gangly limbs behind it, the demon scratched and clawed at its back, trying to retch free the dagger protruding from its leathery skin. Eventually it did, gripping the blade and stabbing it into the table to its right. Black goopy blood dripped down the hilt and blade, leaving it to pool on the wooden table in a puddle that churned Evangaline's stomach. The smell of sulfur and death wafted from the creature, turning Evangaline's stomach even more.

Evangaline knew that running from a bear was a bad idea. And in dinosaur movies, people always froze, so the carnivores didn't see them. This unholy beast couldn't be too much different, *right?*

So she froze.

She maintained eye contact as the form of the monster seared into her retinas like an unwanted polaroid. The demonic red eyes blazing with the fire and promise of death.

Its dark black skin was cracked and wrinkled in the same way old worn leather appeared over time. Those neon red eyes glowed unnaturally, like two red holiday lights shining in the empty cavern of one of hell's finest concoctions. She could see ribs through its leathery skin and the claws that adorned its crooked fingers were made of a transparent black crystal. A living nightmare. That is what it was. It was a living nightmare.

"Hello, Princess of the realm."

It fucking speaks! Her brain shouted as her eyes flared open into two dinner plate sized circles.

Not just did it talk. Oh, Satan would not allow his finest specimen to crawl from the pits of hell just to speak like any *normal* human or fae. No, it spoke without a very important component of speech. A mouth. The noise of its voice reverberated through its body in vibrations and echoes that formed words.

"Hello ... creature from hell," she responded, her nerves riding each word. "I don't suppose you will tell me why you're stalking me."

"I am but a soldier of death, not a messenger." The creature creepily projected in a grave whisper. "You are my mission."

"Wonderful," Evangaline muttered while taking small steps backward toward Bastian, until she was pressed firmly against him with his arm wrapped around her waist like a seat belt.

Trapped between two monsters. Yet this time, Bastian was the lesser of the two evils.

They stared each other down as the creature clearly grew agitated with the evasion tactic and began slashing its talons out. Releasing a hideous screeching noise that rattled the room.

Evangaline ducked down instinctually, covering her ears as the crystal decanter her and Atlas bonded over exploded at the decibel of the shriek.

As she dropped down to protect herself, Bastian lunged at the dagger lodged into the table. Pushing Evangaline out of the way in the process.

The creature, though, was smart and fast and new Bastian would go for the dagger. Without hesitation, it grabbed one of the books Evangaline stacked up and hurled it at Bastian, knocking him out cold from the force alone. His body slumped motionless behind the table, out of her sight. Evangaline cursed to herself, scrambling to her knees.

"Finally," the demon vibrated as it barreled into Evangaline as she tried to rise from the floor to make another attempt at an escape.

The two tumbled across the dark carpet. Shards of the crystal decanter wedged themselves into Evangaline's skin as her robe slid off her shoulders and onto the floor. Sharp claws dragged through the flesh on her left arm, leaving burning shreds of flesh in their wake.

Her scream of pain echoed through the room. Tears stung her eyes, but she fought to hold them back.

Reaching down, she fisted her hands into the carpet, searching for any sort of broken glass. She needed a weapon. The creature sat on top of her, pinning her to the floor with its gangly limbs and gargantuan body.

Slowly, as though it was being unzipped from the inside, a mouth appeared. Rows of spindly teeth stacked one after another—like a shark— sat crooked and coated in saliva and grime.

A bead of black tinted saliva dripped onto Evangaline's chest as she fondled the floor for anything to use as a weapon. It burned slightly, but she paid it no attention as she struggled to free herself.

There! She grasped the ruby stopper of the decanter and plunged it as hard as she could into one of the fire red eyes of the creature, causing it to rupture.

Deep gray blood, viscous and putrid, exploded onto her as the beast backed up, grasping at the stopper wedged in its eye socket.

Her nightgown was covered in both the demon's gore and her own blood as it seeped from her wounds in slow, pulsating streams. Her head grew light, but she fought on; ignoring the echoes of pain within her body.

The creature scurried backward, clutching its eye, releasing a series of grumbling screeches. Giving her a chance to get away from it.

Evangaline ran to Bastian, grabbing hold of his dagger.

Shaking the unconscious general, never once losing sight of the creature huddled in the corner wailing like a banshee. "Wake up! Wake up, you fucking asshole!" Evangaline screamed at Bastian, forcing her voice to rise over that of the demon screeching in the distance.

"Princess?" He muttered, his eyes squinting in the dim light of the library.

"Not now, Bash, up! Up!" She gathered him to his feet.

He stumbled slightly but was able to steady himself. He wasn't bleeding, but he was going to have a nice bump on his head come morning if Chevalier didn't heal it.

Evangaline angled herself before Bastian, facing the creature as it prowled toward them, slow and angry. Bastian's dagger was gripped in her hand with a white knuckled grip.

Suddenly, the door swung open, her white knight appearing. Clad in her ivory gown, she was an angel sent from heaven.

Chloe froze in the doorway, eyes wide, staring at the hunched over monster prowling bloodily toward Evangaline and Bastian. Slowly, Chloe drew out a long dagger that was concealed on her thigh under the layers of ivory silk.

"Bash, once this thing is dead, you and I are having words," she angrily bit out, staring down the demon.

Bastian reached his arm around Evangaline again, tightening his grip.

"Deal," was all he said in response. Clearly not paying any attention to Chloe's threat with the demon stalking them.

"Evie, you, okay?" Chloe asked, slowly creeping to Evangaline's side and grabbing her unoccupied hand.

The three of them stared at the demon. "I'm doing great, lovely evening, don't you think?"

Bastian and Chloe both let out a tight mouthed chuckle right as the creature sprang forward. Its back haunches acted like springs to propel itself so fast, Evangaline barely had time to release the hilt of the dagger in her hand. She should not have thrown a perfectly good weapon, but she took the chance, knowing the alternative would be hand to hand combat with a nearly eight-foot creature that bled black. The risk was worth it.

Sinking dead into its other eye, the dagger hit its mark perfectly. Her training with Chloe coming in handy. The creature swung its boney arm out in a last-ditch effort to get Evangaline, swiping just as Chloe jumped in front of Evangaline.

Chloe's dagger plunged deep into the creature's chest, sending it falling backward and crashing into the floor with a force that shook the tables beside them.

The once dark teal carpet slowly flooded with the dark gray blood seeping from the demon's eyes, chest, and back wounds.

As Evangaline lifted her gaze to look at Chloe, her breath of relief turned to a scream of horror.

It got her. It got Chloe. Evangaline watched in horror as ruby-red blood cascaded in a waterfall down the front of Chloe's ivory satin gown. Chloe gasped for air, clutching onto the rugged gash marks on her throat. Her eyes were wide with not panic, but something akin to regret.

Evangaline rushed forward, catching Chloe as her knees buckled underneath her, taking Evangaline down to the blood-soaked floor.

"I've got you Chlo. You're gonna be okay. It's all okay!" Evangaline turned around to Bastian. He stood over her with eyes dark and somber, glazed over with the knowledge that Evangaline did not want to allow herself to think. Chloe was dying. "Go get a healer! Get help! Get Des!

Go!" Her tears fell as her screams echoed the hallway.

"Evangaline …" Bastian said quietly, putting a hand on the shoulder of her shredded arm. She shook it off.

"Don't you fucking dare, Bash! Go get a fucking healer! Now!" she screamed as her tears fell down her blood-soaked face.

Bastian didn't fight her for once and took off in a sprint down the hall.

Evangaline held Chloe in her arms and rocked her, a hand firmly around Chloe's wounds, hoping she could stop the bleeding.

"Do you remember that time, when … when … we went out to the beach over in Jersey? We walked on the boardwalk and ate taffy, and I … I got that hideous sunburn in the shape of a flower on my back because of that stupid swimsuit. Do you remember that? I told you that day, as you put all that goopy aloe on my back, that you were my … my … Chloe … you *are* my lifesaver. I needed you then and I need you now."

Chloe's eyes began to close as her breathing slowed, but she still smiled up at Evangaline.

With her hand caked in her own blood, Chloe raised it and placed it on Evangaline's heart. Right in the center of her chest where her heart was currently thrashing at her ribcage. A pain settled deep within her bones with each shallow breath she took. A choked sob escaped Evangaline as Chloe's hand fell slack onto her motionless body. With her throat in tatters, Chloe couldn't speak, but that one simple gesture was the closest she could come to saying, "*I love you too.*" Evangaline felt Chloe's love mingling with her own sadness as she clung to a small ounce of hope.

"No … No … BASTIAN! SOMEONE HELP! PLEASE! PLEASE!"

Evangaline's screams were blood curdling. Her throat ached, and her jaw throbbed, but she still yelled until she heard footsteps, dozens of them.

She looked up as Bastian rounded the corner and drew to a stop, dozens of royal guards halting behind him. Their eyes were all wide, looking at the display before them.

"Fucking move!" Des shouted, pushing through the guards knocking past Bastian. "Chloe?" he said in a whisper, his face going white.

Evangaline screamed her anger, her tears soaking her face. Her sobs echoed through the cavernous hall, nearly shaking the foundation of the palace.

Resting her forehead on Chloe's, she whispered, "I love you, Chlo. I'll be brave … and strong … just like you. I will be the warrior you want me to be, I promise. Just don't leave me."

Opening her eyes again as Des crouched before her, looking over Chloe's lifeless body. Silent tears streamed down his handsome face in realization. The woman he loved was gone.

"I am so sorry, Des." Unable to choke back the sobs that sprang from her throat. "It's my fault. It's my fault. It's my fault …" Evangaline repeated in a heartbreaking melody.

Des said nothing as he stood and moved to Evangaline's side. He placed his arms around Evangaline and motioned to two guards to come take Chloe's body from her lap.

"No … please … no …" Evangaline squeaked out, trying to cling to Chloe.

As they lifted Chloe onto an unfurled white cloth gurney and draped a matching shroud over her, Evangaline screamed and cried. Her body shook in denial and anger.

Des sat on the floor with Evangaline in his arms and they both grieved.

They cried for their friend. For their loved one. They cried for all the moments they shared with her and all the moments that were stolen. They cried for the small bit of light that died that night and the hope that went along with it.

Chapter Thirty

Hours passed, but the hollowness that made a home inside Evangaline was unshakable. Ruptures lined her heart and cracks marred her soul.

There was an ache in the pit of her being that would not go away. She stayed in Des's arms well after Chloe was taken to the crypt beneath the palace and the demon hauled off with her.

Des only let her go once Darrin himself came to fetch Evangaline, practically prying her from the soldier's grip. She didn't want to let go of Des but did reluctantly as she looked into Darrin's commanding eyes and guilt marred her conscious.

Now, standing in what Bastian called the strategy room, coated in her blood, Chloe's blood, and the demon's blood, she stared at the fire roaring out of the carved marble fireplace.

Her fingers idly traced the intricate carvings of ships and waves etched into the mantel. Leaving flecks of dried blood behind with each pass, while the fire beneath scorched her bare, blood-stained feet.

The heat of the fire matched the heat taking place in her heart. The anger that was starting to bubble deep within her was akin to a spark in a dense and dry forest. She was ready to burn the entire realm to the ground. It took everything from her, and she would never forget that.

Bastian and her fae father stood behind a massive table painted with a map of the three realms. Small figurines of each ruler and army sat scattered around.

"She's gone," she murmured, letting the marble soak up the gore staining her fingers.

For a moment Bastian and the king fell silent and faced Evangaline.

Those were the first words she'd spoken in hours aside from her tears that neither man comforted her over.

Even when the healer went to heal her, all she did was shake her head and dismiss the old woman with the wave of a hand.

It was foolish, really, but Evangaline could get her wounds healed later. Right now, the stabbing ache she was feeling in her cuts and bruises felt justified.

She deserved to feel pain. Chloe was gone because of her idiocy, because she couldn't just stay in her room like she was told.

Chloe was gone.

The king made to speak before two men entered the room, flinging the doors open with a bang.

She had never seen the men before.

One was abnormally tall and wide. He was a mountain of a man. His long crimson curls bounced on his forehead as his boots boomed across the floor with each hulking step he took.

The other man was maybe four inches taller than Evangaline. He was muscular and by no means was he a small man, but compared to his companion, he looked like a child. His well-maintained cropped golden blond hair fell recklessly on either side of his head, parting in the middle.

Both men clearly were woken from sleep, if their clothes were indicators. They had to be visitors from the kingdoms since Evangaline did not recognize either one of them.

The king met them halfway to the strategy table, extending an arm. "Surtis, Conall. Sorry to disturb your slumber. We have a great deal to discuss." The king motioned for them to join around the table.

Never once did they notice Evangaline, despite her watching them intently. Which was probably for the best. She was caked in blood and bore a striking resemblance to a victim from a horror movie.

Surtis and Conall gathered around the table. "I think you need to put more girth on my figurine Darrin, he's looking a bit tiny." The large red-haired man quipped, putting the figure back on the table with a hearty laugh booming from his throat.

Bastian and the man named Conall exchanged a greeting with a laugh and a quick hug. They seemed close, but Evangaline had never seen the blond man before.

Evangaline pondered the red-haired man and noted where he set the figure ... Surtis ... Conall. She knew those names and they have figures on the table?

Holy shit! It hit her all at once. *Prince* Surtis from the Kingdom of Fire and *Prince* Conall from the Kingdom of Leaves.

The realization hit her like a bolt of lightning, clearing a path through her mournful fog. The king called a meeting of the royals. *Tonight?*

That was when the anger filled her even more. The princes stood there laughing with the king and Bastian while Chloe laid in the crypt mutilated and *gone.*

She opened her mouth to speak her mind when the door flew open, and three individuals filed through, silencing her before she even spoke.

A beautiful dark-skinned woman with golden necklaces wound around her neck stepped through first. Her hair was a beautiful black afro that subtly bounced as she kept pace with the men she walked with. Her billowing white robe trailed behind her, making her look like a goddess.

There was only one other royal princess presiding over the realm, Princess Ophelia—Princess of the Kingdom of Mirth. That had to be her.

She was in a heated discussion with the man that strode to her side. A man with sepia colored skin and hair white as ice. His beard, eyebrows, even his eyelashes, were a pure white, almost so white they came across transparent. His silver eyes flashed with white light as he glanced over at the Princess of Mirth. His heavy fur-lined boots gave away his identity as soon as Evangaline noticed them.

Prince Tunit, Kingdom of Frost.

That left the man who followed behind them. Far enough away to not be part of their conversation, but close enough to keep stride. His face was grim, angry even. His hair was darker than the night sky and fell gently onto his forehead. His sapphire blue eyes seemed to swirl with hidden depth behind them as he glanced over and took in the ghastly sight that was Evangaline. Sweeping his eyes from her head to toes then back up again in a piercing assessment that made his jaw tick.

Something in her chest stirred and tightened as he held her eyeline while walking to the strategy table. He was the only one who looked at her. The only one who saw her.

Slowly, her stomach filled with a nervous patter. The flutter of butterfly wings.

He was distressingly beautiful, even more so than Bastian. His black shirt was undone just enough for Evangaline to see what appeared to be black tattoos stamped on his honed and bronzed skin. By the time Evangaline noticed them and tried to identify the design, his back was to her, and even that was attractive. However, the sudden loss of his eyes made her immediately feel cold and alone.

There was only one royal she hadn't accounted for—the Prince of Shadows, Prince Ryder.

"Ryder, Ophelia, Tunit, please," the king greeted them—verifying her assumptions—the same way he did with Surtis and Conall.

Prince Ryder made his way to the table and crossed his arms as he stared down, not making a point of saying hello to Conall and Surtis. He just simply planted himself there, powerful arms crossed, feet braced firmly on the floor to show he had already had enough of his companions and this meeting.

Evangaline couldn't tear her eyes away from him.

"We are sorry to call you all here at such a late hour, but there has been a breach of the palace, and we wish for you all to be notified." Bastian started the meeting, ever so much the voice of authority that he pretended to be. He changed from his blood-stained clothes, even bathed, in the time it took to call the meeting and bring Chloe to the crypt. No one would ever know by his appearance that he was, just hours ago, lying motionless on the floor due to a book after failing to immobilize a demon creature.

"What sort of breach?" Ophelia asked. Her voice was almost melodic.

"One of the members of my court was attacked earlier this evening in the royal library." King Darrin somberly replied, unable to meet Evangaline's gaze as she watched them all.

"And are they alright? I assure you, waking us for one member of your court is not means to sound an alarm, Darrin." Conall asked, almost sounding annoyed. "People get injured every day."

Immediately, Evangaline herself got annoyed, glaring at the Prince of Leaves. All she could do was shake her head at the prince's insolence. His inability to care. Was one life, Chloe's life, not worth more than a somber farewell?

Prince Ryder scoffed, bracing his hands on the table. "Ask her yourself. You all walked right past her. Unless blood covered lingerie is the new fashion trend of the Capital. She's by the fire." His voice was smooth and yet rough, authoritative yet gentile.

Suddenly all eyes were on her, and Evangaline felt herself stiffen, her breathing going heavy with anxiety. All eyes except Ryder's. His muscular back was still to her, his eyes instead studying Bastian with a predatory intent.

Biting her bottom lip and swallowing her fear and anguish, she let her anger rise and give her the strength to carry on. Evangaline straightened her spine and proceeded to the table, fixing herself between Bastian and Darrin. She promised Chloe she would be a warrior and so that meant pushing her anxiety aside and doing what scared her. Like facing some of the most powerful fae in all of Celadonia.

So long for staying out of the watchful eyes of the realm's royals. She stepped directly out of the shadows and into the limelight. Directly across from her was Ryder, his eyes roamed to her wounds and the bloody handprint on her chest, then up to her face. She could have been mistaken, but for a brief second, a flash of worry creased his brow and flooded his blue eyes before his face returned to its unamused state.

"Poor thing." Ophelia muttered into her hand, barely able to take in all the blood coating Evangaline.

"No." Evangaline said somberly, but assertive, never breaking Ryder's eye contact. They were mesmerizing, his eyes. She could swear deep within his irises, shadows swam. They were like churning deep blue pools of shimmering water.

Bastian slowly smoothed his hand along the base of her spine, shaking her free from the trance she found herself in, gazing at the Prince of Shadows. She flinched at his touch but did not pull away because she had nowhere else to go. Plus, making a scene with Bash just seemed like too much energy. A fight with him at this hour was not worth it.

"No, I am not fine," she amended, regaining control of herself.

At this, Ryder stood straight again, crossing his arms along his chest once more.

"Darrin, she is a human woman. Maybe the assailant was displeased with your breach of the borders. *Again.*" Each word out of Prince Conall's mouth held an icy bite. Surprising for the Prince of Leaves, ice wasn't his thing.

Ready to show what this human woman could do, Evangaline said without remorse, facing Conall, "I was not the only one attacked, *Your Highness.* General Bastian was at my side and my assailant lies breathless, alongside a commander of *your* king's army beneath us in the crypts."

Just then Evangaline noticed from the corner of her eye one of Prince Ryder's tattoos shift and swirl, the black ink gliding across his chest. It was not a tattoo at all … it was a shadow—lithe and serpentine. Her eyes shifted to it, watching it move at the base of his throat.

Her mind then remembered the dark mist that formed the creature, that too started as a shadow. Questions and accusations flitted through her head at lightning-fast speeds.

In the few seconds of silence, Ryder shifted, his hands falling leisurely into his pockets. "If the attacker is dead, why couldn't this meeting wait? There are many more pressing things to attend to—"

"Prince of Shadows?" Evangaline interrupted, her voice cold and smooth. He turned his sights back on her with an uptick of his brows. "Your pressing matter, whomever she is, will be there when you stride back into your suite." Her tone grew more and more hostile. "*This* is very much your concern." She shifted her weight nervously. "The demon that attacked us took its form after appearing first as a *shadow*."

The prince's eyes turned cold and distant as he stared down at Evangaline. His strong jaw grew tight.

"Ryder, do you know of a creature that can take the form of a shadow first?" The king softly asked, as though he was afraid to.

Atlas had told Evangaline the Prince of Shadows was one of the most powerful fae in the realm, but in this moment, Evangaline couldn't give two fucks. Her best friend was dead, her whole body ached, and she had basically three days till she could get the fuck out of Celadonia. She wanted answers, and she wanted them now. Never mind the slight ache of jealousy that clouded her when the prince's eyes squinted in a knowing shock when she mentioned the woman most likely waiting for him back in his rooms.

Evangaline stared down the prince, her teeth grinding with anger.

Slowly, he smiled, revealing a very charming dimple in his left cheek that she suddenly couldn't stop looking at.

Get your head together, Evangaline!

"Bastian, I would control your human whore. She sure knows how to start controversy," he said, glancing up at Bastian before returning his gaze to Evangaline, "Yes, Darrin, there are creatures I know of that can manifest from shadows, a great many in fact." Ryder said with his entertained smile still on his handsome face.

Evangaline wanted to claw his beautiful eyes out and slap that smug smile clean off with the insinuation that she was Bastian's anything. Forget being a whore that she could not care about, but to be linked to Bastian in such a way was aggravating.

Her anger was not limited to the prince, no Bastian and the king would have their asses kicked later for not correcting Ryder on calling her names. That shit simply would not fly.

Leaning forward, "Of course, I will need an image of the creature you speak of." The prince continued.

Evangaline snickered, bracing her hands on the table, leaving Bastian's hand lingering in the air. Thank God it was finally off her. "Oh yes, give me five minutes. I'll make sure I give you a painting of it. Would you prefer watercolors or oils, *Your Highness?*" Two could play this game.

Darrin then leaned in and grabbed Evangaline's mangled shoulder. She briefly winced, but relented to his touch. Ryder noticed her discomfort and immediately dropped his smile and glared at Darrin.

"I see why you claimed this one, General. She is a firecracker!" Prince Surtis said, laughing.

Glaring at Prince Surtis, "I belong to no one." If only she could shoot lasers from her eyes, she would sear all of these assholes.

Cockily, "Point taken, now I would love to have a one-of-a-kind watercolor to have a souvenir of this fine evening, but a simple description would do just fine." Prince Ryder said with that dimple gracing his all too smug and beautiful face once again.

Evangaline shrugged free of the king's hold on her shoulder and choked back any lingering barbs she wanted to throw the prince's way.

"Black leathery skin, long dark crystal-like claws, bright red eyes." Recounting the image of the creature was the equivalent to dumping a bucket of cold water on her. Evangaline's body trembled from the image of the beast and Prince Ryder noticed.

Her agony came flooding back with jolts of images of Chloe lying dead in her arms. She closed her eyes, holding them tight for a moment as the images faded behind the fireworks exploding behind her eyelids. Then she opened them and fixed her gaze on the table before her before meeting Ryder's again.

"It was tall, freakishly, could rival Surtis." Bastian finally spoke jovially as his hand meet her lower back once more in a possessive way.

Evangaline knew he meant for it to be reassuring, but his touch seemed to do quite the opposite. His contact felt toxic to her. The feel of Bastian's hand on her made her want to swat it away and turn out the contents of her stomach. But she already made enough of a scene tonight, so instead she let it stay there. Grinding her teeth at the feel of the circles he was rubbing.

Ryder's smile slowly faded as he glanced from Bastian to Evangaline.

A stagnant pause filled the air.

Where he once saw a defiant and angry woman before him, he saw exactly what she was—broken and wounded.

Evangaline's downcast eyes blocked the single tear that was trying to spring free from her lash line as she recounted the mental images of Chloe lifeless in her arms—unable to escape them.

"My king, I apologize, but that is no creature of my kingdom. I know of none with red eyes. Besides, almost all shadow manifesting creatures are harmless unless provoked. They would never seek out trouble. Let alone venture this far outside my kingdom." Ryder said, his condescending tone gone entirely.

Evangaline simply shook her head, trying to will back her anger and push aside her grief.

It didn't work as she wiped a tear from her face. All the eyes in the room quickly landed on her. Willing her strength once more and failing, she glanced up at Darrin and Bastian.

If the fae in this room did not know what the demon was, then she feared she would never find out. But she wouldn't give up. Chloe deserved that. She needed answers.

"I saw the same creature the day of the equinox. It was brief, and it never charged me. It just stared and then vanished into the flames. Tonight, before it attacked, it said things." Evangaline said quietly, wiping another tear from her blood speckled cheek, unable to stop them from falling.

Darrin came to her side, his hand spinning her to him, sending a jolt of pain through her wounded arm. A brief growl escaped Ryder, but she ignored it as she faced her fae father. Clearly Bastian didn't tell him that little nugget of information as the king looked more confused than anything. "It spoke to you? What did it say?"

Evangaline tilted her head, another tear streaking her cheek as she blandly smirked. "Eh, you know, normal first date stuff. What's your favorite color? Where were you born? I'm a soldier, not a messenger. You know, real icebreakers."

As she turned back around, tearing free of Darrin's painful grip, she earned a giggle from Tunit and a genuine smile from Ryder. Though it faded fast as he smoothed his thumb over his bottom lip, clearly lost in contemplation.

Darrin, however, was not pleased. "Eva—" He smoothed over his face and released a sigh. "It said it was a soldier?" He finished.

Bastian finally removed his hand, throwing them into his pockets, saying, "Yes, Your Majesty. It knew her. Said she was its mission. It greeted her by her … title."

Darrin threw his hands into his hair angrily. "Godsdammit Bastian, why didn't you … this … It's them … The Heretics. It has to be. They're the only ones …" He muttered to himself, clearly worried.

Evangaline glanced around the room. All the royals stiffened, their faces turning dark with various levels of anger. Ryder's shadows, the peculiar ones on his chest, swirled faster. He looked down at Evangaline, catching her staring at his exposed chest.

Evangaline turned to her father; she knew that name but couldn't place it. She knew it was not something Atlas taught her about, but it wasn't coming to her at that moment.

"If it was the work of The Heretics, why were they after your general, commander, and human concubine?" Tunit asked, his voice airy with a slight lilt.

Ew. That was so much worse than human whore. Evangaline winced at the words, "Not a concubine," she grumbled through clenched teeth.

Darrin's face was equally as repulsed by the insinuation as he spoke. "The Heretics once captured the commander, did they not, General?"

Bastian cleared his throat, "Yes, sir, one of their battalions did. She escaped after slaughtering the camp and their apparent leader. It was on their attempted conquest into the Kingdom of Leaves."

That was where Evangaline knew the name! The boys told her of Chloe's daring escape after being captured as a prisoner by the rebel group that was hell bent on overthrowing Darrin.

Conall, finally appearing visibly shaken, practically shouted at Bastian and Darrin, "What? When were The Heretics marching in on my land?" He asked, anger riding his tone.

King Darrin sat back in the chair behind him, gripping the armrests, "Oh, don't get so worked up, Conall. The Heretics were never in your land. They were on the outskirts of The Capital. The Heretics have tried to invade all of your kingdoms at one point or another, and my armies have stopped them before any of you were the wiser. Ryder was the only one who managed to know of a coup in his kingdom and deal with it on his own."

The room fell silent once more with the admission.

"Perhaps they were after your commander for revenge. It seems they got it," Surtis added after a moment.

Evangaline shuddered at his words. They weren't after Chloe, she was caught in the crossfire trying to save Evangaline, they were after the princess, *her.*

"Perhaps." Darrin said studiously, then he looked up at Evangaline and said quietly, "I got another threat. Three days ago."

Evangaline's heart sank. She knew what he meant. Every word he didn't speak hung in the air between the two of them like static electricity. A year ago, someone threatened Evangaline's life, demanding a king's ransom. Three days ago, on the equinox, he received another threat the day the creature first appeared. Then the creature appears? These Heretics, they were the ones who knew about her birth, the ones with the hit out on her—they had to be. "Why didn't you tell me? They're the ones who …" she whispered, catching herself before she leaked her secret early.

"What kind of threat?" Ryder asked harshly.

The king stood, unable to tell the full truth, but unable to lie. "A threat against my people's lives and demanding my abdication of the throne. I received the first a year ago, right before the failed conquests started. The last came three days ago on the equinox."

Evangaline stood solemnly at the table around five royals who were seething at being left in the dark, *"Wait till Friday, when you learn this human whore is your princess!"* she yearned to scream at the top of her lungs.

Ophelia then stood forward. A beacon of grace and dignity, her words flowing off her tongue like the finest song, "You have kept us in the dark too long, my king, and tonight you and your people have suffered for it. To lose one life is to lose the hope of the people."

Evangaline looked away, her eyes stinging with the unshed tears that now managed to find their way down her cheeks silently. Chloe was Evangaline's hope, she was light, she was happiness, she was her beacon in the dark, and she was dead.

"From here on out, your battles are our battles. Your troubles are our troubles. We are one realm, and we will fight as such. These burdens are not yours to bear alone, my king." Ophelia continued.

The Princess of Mirth enthralled Evangaline. Her grace and beauty were nothing compared to the wisdom that she clearly had. Her eternal youth didn't give any hints to her actual age, but in mortal years, she looked no older than thirty. Although she spoke with the same knowledge as someone as old as Atlas. If Evangaline wasn't a physical and emotional mess, she would for sure fan girl over the gorgeous fae princess.

Tunit braced his arm around Ophelia's shoulders. "The Kingdom of Frost agrees."

Surtis grunted, "Kingdom of Fire stands with you. We are one. Our forges are your forges, Your Majesty. We fight together."

Conall nodded, "For your eternal protection, the Leaves stands with you." His face did not match his words as he whispered beneath his breath, "I guess."

The room was silent as the four royals looked eagerly to Prince Ryder, but he looked at Evangaline as though he wanted to say something just to her. Her chest thrummed as she looked at him and her stomach fluttered in ways she had never felt before.

"The Kingdom of Shadows stands with *you*." Ryder's head dipped to Evangaline, with his piercing eyes locked firmly to hers.

He did not say it to the king, or the general, but to the wounded human woman surrounded by the most powerful fae rulers. A woman he did not even know was his realm's princess. A woman whose heart and mind were a disregarded mess at present. He said it to her because he knew she needed to hear it most.

Evangaline swallowed, her throat working through its burn. Her tears silently fell on the war table beneath her fingertips.

Without a word, she turned and took her father's hand in her own, squeezed it goodnight, and walked out of the war room. No one tried to stop her, no one tried to say anything to her, but as she left, she looked at Prince Ryder and inclined her head in thanks. His eyes never left her as she left the room with her head held high.

All the emptiness in her body swallowed her in a black hole. Closing in on itself in an agonizing realness as she walked out into the silent, glittering halls with a royal guard close on her heels.

"Take me to the crypt," Evangaline said, turning to the guard, not leaving any room for him to debate her.

So he did.

And there, beneath the shimmering pale castle, there laid a hidden princess among the dead. Beside the only true friend she ever had, crying into the brisk night air, she finally drifted off into the land of small death, hoping to never wake again.

Chapter Thirty-One

It should have been easier to focus, but for some reason, the ghost of the woman covered in blood with tears in her eyes lingered within the confines of the Prince of Shadows' memory. There was grief lining her waterline. Yet, behind the blue and green irises that reminded him of nature—the earth and the sea merged—there was such soul deep pain and sadness.

Once she left the strategy room, an icy coldness crept over his being and bumps lined his skin. His shadows shuddered from her loss, and he found himself dispatching a few to follow her. Never once in Ryder's life had he found himself attached to a woman the way the human woman—*Eva*—ensnared him in her grasp.

To say she was caked in blood was an understatement. He faced minor battles in his five decades of life and seen the bloodied results of death firsthand. He, himself, had been coated in more gore than she bore this evening at one time and yet, despite it all, she was a beacon in the dark. The most wondrous creature he had ever seen. It was like his body knew hers intimately, despite never having met before. His heart began beating at a rhythmic pace he had never once felt it beat at. Time slowed when he saw her by the fire, bloody but so insatiably beautiful.

"Are we done here?" Ryder interrupted Darrin as the King spewed excuse after excuse. Intemperate reasons as to why they all mustn't worry about The Heretics—despite Darrin being the one spooked enough to call a meeting at this ungodly hour of night and have it last for hours. Eva must be more than some plaything for him and the bastard general if her attack spurred him into action so urgently. Ryder could not tell if that relieved him or set him on edge even further.

Ryder's hatred of Bastian went back decades. They both were young when Bastian first came into Ryder's home as nothing more than a spindly soldier in the Royal Army. While Ryder met with Bastian's superiors, the bastard tried to make a move on Lilith, Ryder's younger sister. She was no more than a child, barely over a decade and a half, and Bastian was well … damn well old enough to know better.

Between Ryder and Lily, Bastian and his drunken brigade of buddies found themselves face down in the mud with a stern warning not to return to the Shadows. That, of course, didn't last long. After some time, Bastian weaseled his way into the king's good graces for reasons unknown to Ryder. He was part of the reason the Shadows took care of their own matters. A King who would put his trust in a man like Bastian was either naïve or an asshole in his own right. And Ryder wanted as little to do with either of them as he could. The realm deserved better than Darrin and Bastian. A coward and a cunt, he always thought of them as a pair. Maybe one day the realm would be lucky enough to bow to someone worthy of a bent knee. Until that day, Ryder enjoyed the solitude of his homeland and little else.

Yet, now, he could not help but hope he enjoyed the company of a certain strong willed human woman. One who pushed his buttons and filled him with an electric buzz he hadn't ever experienced before.

She truly stepped up and accused him of murder, hadn't she?

A smile tried to light up his face at her ferocity. Women normally tossed themselves at his feet, begging for attention without trying to know him as a person and not just a prince of the realm. It drove him mad. For nearly the last two decades, his father pushed for him to marry, "You must secure the line, Son. If we lose the kingdom from your inability to marry and produce an heir, you will become a tarnish on your mother's memory!" The ghost of a smile dropped from Ryder's being with the repetitions of the words his father threw at him every time he refused a proposal or proposition.

Call him weak, but the Prince of Shadows, beneath his hard exterior, was nothing but a romantic. Love was the foundation for a marriage in his mind. That was what his parents had, and while their marriage benefitted the Kingdom of Shadows, they married for love and not obligation. Nothing and no one would force him into something he did not choose for himself.

Ophelia nudged him from his thoughts, using her gifted power to read his aura to see he was wound tight. The Princess of Mirth was practically a sister to him. But even her taunting smile could not erase the urge in his bones to hunt down the human warrior that stood before him hours ago.

Eva's tears broke his heart and for the first time in his life he wanted to hunt down a woman to simply hold her and ensure she never cried again. Though he would not fight the urge if she wanted more than that. "Eager to return to that redhead you took back to your room?" The Princess of Mirth laughed. Tunit chuckled but shut up as Ryder pierced the Prince of Frost with an icy gaze of his own.

"No." Ryder quipped finitely. "Is there anything else to discuss Darrin, or shall we reconvene this meeting when the sun returns?"

Darrin eyed Ryder as he always did, like a petulant child he wanted to lock away and never look at again. It made sense. Ryder never bowed and kissed the king's ass the way his father did before him. "I suppose we have discussed the breach enough. Just remain vigilant and if anyone has any insight as to the creature's origins, let me or Bastian know we would appreciate it."

Bastian stood tall, staring daggers at the Prince of Shadows.

Ryder made to turn around and leave but Darrin stopped him with his words. "And I must put this into the ether before any of you decide it is proper to make insinuations again. The human you met tonight is here as my guest. One more ill-favored word thrown in her direction or any action I deem unfitting will result in a permanent stay within the dungeons and a swift death at my hand."

Ryder's head turned to lock eyes with the king over his shoulder. Bastian glanced at the king, his face a mask of indifference. However, there was a gleam in his eyes that looked a lot like surprise.

The king was awfully protective of this Eva. Never once had Darrin threatened the royals with punishment. There had been plenty of times each one of the royals, Ryder included, that could go against the laws of the crown. And each of those times, the king looked the other way or grunted his disapproval and moved on.

It made Ryder remember something he had suppressed. Years ago, the king invited a woman from Vitalis to stay at the palace. She was as close as any woman got to being the king's consort, but was banished not long after. The Shadow court dined with her and Darrin once, her name forgotten with time. All Ryder remembered was her phoenix red hair and her soft smile. She was kind, but the king never once stopped the murmurs coursing through the room of her being a salacious stain on his reputation. Darrin even laughed along with some of the quips and barbs being thrown at the poor woman. It put a foul taste in Ryder's mouth, seeing his king treat her so. But what about this human was different?

The two stared at one another in a terse silence. The soft tingle of one of Ryder's shadows drew his attention from the king. Its cool presence coursed up his leg, winding around his body till it sat in its place at the base of his throat.

The whispers of the shadows were a type of solace he seldom felt in the quiet. *"The object of your desire sleeps, carried by a soldier with blond hair, up to the wing in the east."* They whispered to him and him alone. No one else could hear the call of the shadows. Only a few in history could command them. All of which were Ryder's distant ancestors. Neither of his siblings inherited the gift. When the shadows started following him as a boy, many within the kingdom looked at him like he was a wonder of god-like proportions.

Ryder faced back in the direction of the doors, not dignifying the king with a comment. He was quite rude to Eva, but it was she who deserved an apology, not the king. So with a determined gait, he strode out, ignoring the murmurs of conversation picking back up behind him.

He turned fixated on finding the woman that held his attention but instead came face to face with a man clad in royal armor. Hair blond and shaved close to the scalp. *The shadows did talk of a blond man*, Ryder thought.

"Where did you take the human woman?" The Prince of Shadows commanded. His tone was harsh enough to make the soldier jump—eyes wide—and drop into a bow.

He stammered but gathered himself despite being scared shitless of the Prince of Shadows, just how many were when they came to stand in Ryder's presence for whatever reason. He was tall and broad and could cut an imposing figure, but he always assumed it was the shadows that frightened people the most. "Um, the crypt, your highness. I left her in the crypt." The soldier managed to say.

Ryder's heart jumped. "Alone? You left her alone in the gods forsaken *crypt*!"

No wonder she was attacked in the first place. It was evident she had the spirit of a warrior, but without magic she was an easy target in Celadonia.

The soldier's eyes went wide with terror. "No ... no ... I ... she was not alone, sir. I stayed till her friend brought her to her chambers."

Ryder sighed. Half out of frustration at the incompetence of the soldier before him and half out of relief knowing she was not alone. He pushed past the man murmuring a soft, "Pathetic," before calling on the shadows that watched over her to return to him. Once they did, he made them show him the way to where she slept.

He needed to see with his own two eyes that she was okay. His guilt at taking out his frustrations on her started to eat away at him, and with each measured step up to her room, he grew anxious. And that was not factoring in the urge to protect her that stirred through his body.

"*Past the colored glass ...*" the shadows whispered as he turned a corner to be greeted with a hallway of stained glass illuminated by the rays of the fading moon.

Two guards stood at the end of the hall before the door, talking quietly. Neither noticed Ryder as he ducked from the hallway, clinging like his shadows to the dark corners out of sight.

"She is fragile now, but that isn't in the lass' spirit." The red-haired guard claimed.

An ebony skinned guard nodded solemnly. "What even attacked them? I asked some of the pixies when I went to Christoff's, but they had no clue of what it could be. Never saw any creature like that in their travels. It's not from the Shadows?"

Ryder's back straightened at the mention of his kingdom.

"Naw, apparently little lady brought it up with the prince herself. The other guards said she went toe to toe with the brute." The redhead chuckled to himself. "The brass balls on that one, but he claimed to not know of it. If the shadow prince doesn't know … we're shit out of luck."

They stood in silence for a second before the door creaked open and two more guards joined them in the hall.

"She okay?" the black-skinned guard asked. His voice was so small, and his heartache was clear.

A tall man with golden curls shook his head. His aqua eyes were bloodshot and puffy, his skin marred with the trails of tears. "No. But she says she is." He sighed. "She is our focus now. Whatever Chloe had with her, it is our burden to uphold now."

All the men silently nodded and stood in their silence until the blond one turned and reached for the door.

"I am going to stay here from now on. With Bastian and this demon beast, I don't like the thought of her being alone."

A smaller tan skinned man chuckled quietly, "She could kick my ass with no issue. If it weren't impossible … I would think she had a little fae in her."

Ryder smirked at the comment, certain from his brief meeting with her that the man's statement was true. Her soul echoed with the essence of the fae.

"It isn't a matter of *if* she can fight. She has been trained well, but she is *not* fae and that is the problem. She came close enough to death tonight and I will not allow her body to enter the crypt next." The blond man said with a terse sort of finality.

No one responded. They just let him re-enter the room. A click of a lock turning into place made some of the rigidness in Ryder's chest ease. He may not have seen her exactly, but clearly these men cared for her, whomever they all are, and with that he knew she was safe. That was all he wanted.

As a group, the three other men turned and walked from the corridor leading to Eva's room.

Eva.

The name felt like warm hot cocoa on a wintry day. It felt right. *She* felt right.

He shook his head at how crazy that thought sounded.

Once he was alone in the hall once again, Ryder made his way back to his chambers on the opposite side of the palace.

He turned the key to his room and entered, letting out a string of quiet expletives as the woman he left sprung up from his bed. Her clothes had been discarded since he left and for some reason, despite her body being pleasurable to look at, there was a sense of wrongness looking at her.

Ryder turned his head from her to avert his gaze as she swayed her hips over in his direction.

"You are tense, my Prince—" she tried to press her hands to his chest, but he grabbed them within one fist.

"Out," he demanded.

She startled back, "What?"

"Out! Get your things and leave." The command was simple, and yet she stayed in her place.

He opened his palm as he let her go, gathering a ball of dark shadow magic, "Five, four, three—"

She bristled and shot around the room, gathering the gown and shoes she haphazardly kicked around. As he got to one, she threw the door open and ran out, leaving him once again to the quiet that made his thoughts ache in his skull.

Maybe that is why people are afraid of you, asshole. He thought to himself.

Tension lined his muscles, and a lack of sleep rimmed his eyes. As he stripped his shirt over his head and laid his midnight hair on the pillow, surprisingly, only one thing flitted through his mind. *Eva.*

Chapter Thirty-Two

They buried Chloe the next morning atop a dew-soaked hill under the sunshine. Shaded only by a flowering oak tree with strong limbs and pink flowers that hung down in delicate ropes. Evangaline had no say in where her best friend would be laid to rest. However, the tree looked like a living extension of Chloe gifted to the rich soil of the Celadonian earth. It was perfect.

Chloe's body was shrouded in hand-spun iridescent silk that delicately blew in the autumn breeze as it covered her small frame.

The ruby hilted sword Evangaline knew so well draped down the center of her chest. A talisman to bring with her into the world of eternal slumber.

Darrin stood by Chloe's parents and when they were ready, after presenting them with the copper and ruby helmet of Chloe's armor, the king elevated his hand. With a gentle and mournful wave, he guided Chloe's body softly into the earth with his magic. Shutting her away from the world, never to be seen again.

Her laugh would never echo through a room. Her brightness would never rival the suns. Her warmth would never touch Evangaline ever again.

The whole cadre stood by Evangaline, far from the crowd of soldiers, courtiers, and villagers at the bottom of the hill.

Their copper armor and helmets reflected the sparse rays of the sun that shone through the clouded sky.

Evangaline tried not to cry, but her tears still found a way out. She wanted to stay strong, to not show that she was cracking apart, but her grief was too potent and her tears too strong.

When she woke that morning broken and falling apart, she grabbed black gown after black gown, but none felt right. She put on her training attire—leggings, blouse, and corset—yet still she did not feel she was properly dressed to put Chloe in the earth for eternity. Nothing felt right. Her own skin felt itchy and claustrophobic.

Then, just as she was ready to give up, the light caught the glitter of the copper attached to the battle leathers folded neatly in the corner of her closet.

"I'll make a warrior princess out of you yet!"

With the sound of Chloe's optimistic praise ringing in her ears like their very own death bell, Evangaline donned the black leather outfit adorned with copper accents and leather bands. Her chest shone amber streaks around the closet. The breast plate was etched with the same rose, sword, and heart insignia that Chloe wore proudly. Small pieces of metal covered her elbows, and a strip ran down her spine like scales.

She grabbed the practice sword that she discarded in the corner of her closet and fitted it to her back neatly in the built-in sheath of the suit. A basic blade, not one of perfection, or topped with a fancy ruby, but one that would protect, one that she came to know intimately. Each of the many blows and knicks she took at the hands of the woman being fed back to the soil made her heart lurch with pride and sorrow.

That is how she stood at the funeral. Not a soldier or a princess, but a warrior. Just for Chloe. Just for today, at least. Tomorrow she would figure out how to breathe with her head below the water. Today, in the present, she would welcome the crash of the waves over her head and the stinging in her lungs and sink to the bottom. Feeling all the pain that thrummed through her body.

Today, amongst the armored guards she called friends, she stood and silently wept.

Des remained by her side; their pain equally as palpable. The best friend and the lover. It would make for a remarkably heartbreaking painting. Two souls brought together by another, silently weeping but standing tall despite the sorrow in the air.

Evangaline slid her hand into Des's and held it until the ceremony was over. Until they both wiped their armored arms over their faces, allowing the chill of the metal to soak away their tears.

Once the grave marker was laid and the crowd dispersed, Evangaline could not bear the pain of confronting Chloe's parents and apologizing for their loss. So, she did what she and Chloe did best first thing in the morning, while the air was crisp and the breeze stable—she ran.

In many ways, she ran from the reality of Chloe not strolling around a corner, making a joke, or hitting her in the ass with her sword. But she told herself she ran because it was her routine. It was something Chloe enjoyed doing with her, something Chloe was *proud* to do with her. So, Evangaline ran.

Halfway through her trek, it was as though the gods themselves felt Evangaline's anguish and they too wept. Her feet pounded upon the soggy earth for hours in the rain until her lungs burned with the fire of a thousand suns. She ran until her leather boots squished with mud and water soaked into their well-worn soles.

When she got to her normal training grounds around the back of the palace, she found Des waiting. He said nothing at all, just lifted his sword and got his stance ready.

In the pouring rain, she and Des trained. The two didn't speak because words were not what either of them needed, nor wanted, instead they channeled their anger and sadness into fighting.

Des filled into the role he knew Chloe would want him to do without a second thought, the same way Evangaline ran.

She didn't say it, but, in that moment, she was eternally grateful for Des.

And so they trained.

Parries, blocks, stabs, and lunges, until it became a part of Evangaline. Until her muscles ached with the pain of her sorrows and fears. Until she no longer wished for death to claim her, too.

The king tried to get Evangaline to cancel her lessons with Atlas or to take them in her room at the very least, but Evangaline protested. He wanted to lock her away until the debut ball like some defenseless damsel, especially now with the attack on her life. Her rage propelled her in her protests and eventually he just stopped fighting her and walked away muttering profanities about her stubbornness, shaking his head in defeat.

That creature and these Heretics, whoever they were, already took her best friend. She would not allow them to take a place she felt at ease, a place she felt at peace. That library and the time she spent with Atlas became a sacred part of her life, one she needed now more than ever.

It was the same reason she still did not see a healer. Using a hand mirror and tweezers, she removed all the crystal shards from her back and bandaged her arm to the best of her abilities.

The bruises and scratches were still on full display on her face and shoulders. Evangaline wanted to see them, she wanted to remember her pain every time she looked in the mirror, at least for today.

In some fucked up way, Evangaline felt like the second those cuts and bruises were gone, everything with Chloe was gone too. All her memories and heartbreak would be cleared of her body, and she couldn't quite follow through with that purging of sins just yet.

She needed to keep any part of Chloe with her just a minute longer. *Maybe tomorrow*, she told herself.

So, just as she did every other day, she made her way through the hall towards the doors of the library, leaving a muddy, wet trail in her wake. Her leathers and hair dripped puddles onto the pristine white stone with the rainwater that chilled her to the bone.

She opened the door to the library with a tenacious ease.

She knew what she would find, blood stains and awful, horrible memories.

But as she eased open the massive doors with a soft groan, she found it as though nothing happened. Fae magic was truly special if it could get that much blood and grime out of the carpet.

The sound of Atlas bellowing out a deep laugh from his chair filled the air of the royal library, reverberating off every book, wall, and table.

Was he here with someone? He had to be. He was old, but he wasn't crazy enough to talk to himself.

Evangaline continued forward as though she were being pulled by a magnet of curiosity as she heard Atlas talk about someone she did not know. Something about dark hair and tattered rags of clothes. She stopped short, knowing she was disrupting a conversation, that in and of itself was beyond rude. Scuffing her muddy boot on the floor to make a U-turn and leave, she bumped her hip on the side of a table, knocking over a golden lamp in the process.

"Oh, my dear!" Atlas jumped up, startled. "I did not expect to see you today!"

Evangaline forced a smile, righting the lamp, "Surprise … I can leave though if you want. If I am disturbing you."

Just then, startling *her*, standing from the chair she normally claimed as her little leather sanctuary, stood the Prince of Shadows himself.

Clad in all black with his hair neatly combed, unlike the previous night. His fitted jacket tapered from his broad shoulders to his fit waist, garnished with a sash of black and silver.

Evangaline swallowed. "I'll come back tomorrow."

Atlas rushed to her as she made to turn around. "No, dear." He put his hands on her upper arms, narrowly missing the wound wrapped on her left one. His pale blue eyes seemed to say, *"Don't be alone now."* His sorrow leaking through his icy gaze.

"Sorry about the decanter and the whiskey." Evangaline said, nodding toward where the ruby topped decanter used to sit before it shattered and eventually ruptured the eye of the demon creature, saving her life.

Atlas smiled at her sympathetically. The usual bright light behind his eyes dimmed slightly and, for some reason, that broke her heart just a little bit more. With a fast movement, he waved his hand and motioned to the chairs. "We were overdue for a new one, anyway. You did me a favor."

Walking over to where Ryder now stood, Evangaline tried to keep her eyes fixated on the floor but found herself drawn to the prince's cerulean eyes as they made a steady sweep along her face and body, leaving a trail of flutters in their wake.

"Take my seat, dear. I will grab another chair." Atlas murmured.

Ryder then stepped aside, snapping his eyes to Atlas like he was freed from a trance, "No. Please. Atlas, sit."

He faced the fire and, without even moving a muscle, another high-backed chair, in black though, not teal, manifested out of dark swirls of effortless magic.

Evangaline was entirely impressed and a little scared. She turned to Atlas as she unsheathed her sword, discarding it on the floor, and sat with a grimace. "Now that's a party trick."

And it was. Conjuring chairs from thin air seemed like a useful trick and only made her think of what else he could do. She practically accused the man of murder last night, not caring what his powers were, but now, she didn't know if pushing his buttons was a good idea.

As she settled in her favorite seat, squeezing the water from her braid, she couldn't help but take a deep breath inhaling his smell. Salt water and firewood. He smelled like a beach bonfire on a brisk night. Calming and yet edged in darkness.

"I saw you this morning … training. My suite looks out over the field behind the palace." Ryder said, catching Evangaline entirely off guard as he sat back in the ebony leather seat he conjured out of thin air.

She did not know what to say to the prince. "May I?" she asked Atlas, pouring herself a drink out of the brand-new green crystal decanter that now rested on the repaired table between them.

Atlas inclined his head in a small nod.

Her tone was somber and quiet. "I used to train with Chloe every morning. Des filled in today," she replied to Ryder, handing him a glass of whiskey, then Atlas, then settling into the chair stained with Ryder's scent. She held her own glass close to her chest, like a child with a teddy bear.

"Where was Chloe? She afraid of the rain?" Ryder chided, with a roguish smirk on his handsome face.

Evangaline sucked on her lower lip, and sat a little straighter, "Commander Chloe Darrow ... is ... *was* ... who we buried this morning. Who I lost last night." Her voice broke on the last words, but she kept her tears in.

Ryder's face went pale, his eyes softening, the roguish smirk disappearing beneath a mask of sympathy that she felt was no mask at all. "I'm ... my deepest apologies. I did not know."

Evangaline reclined into the chair, giving him a curt smile as to say it was okay.

"We almost made it three weeks, Atlas. Almost three weeks without a hitch, so close." Evangaline snapped, tears dangerously lining her eyes.

She took a big sip of her whiskey, her throat scorching as it traveled down. The burn felt nice, though. Its simmering heat made the cool tears in her eyes evaporate.

She finally peeked up at Atlas. "I came here looking for a book last night. Something to bide my time while I waited for Chloe and Des to get back and regale me with their tales of debauchery and woe." She smirked with sorrow. "I was curious about the gods and had no books about them in my room. So, I came down here ..." She smiled, her head rested on her hand, as she looked up at Atlas to see his face twisting in various shades of sorrow. He still smiled back though, as to say, *"it's not your fault."*

He never took a sip of his whiskey, which was unlike him, also a sign he was vaguely uncomfortable.

Ryder was nursing his whiskey, albeit slower than Evangaline, but he was drinking it, nonetheless. He sat reclined in his enormous chair, ever so the model of sophisticated grace. His legs braced on the floor spread apart at the knees while one hand idly made circles on his thigh as he watched Evangaline with intrigue lining his squinted brow. He looked like he was studying a painting in a gallery.

"Eva? Was it?" Ryder asked, swirling the amber liquid in his glass before setting it down on his lap.

"Evangaline, actually. Evangaline Rivers," she replied, meeting his intense blue stare.

Something inside of her thrummed when she gazed into his deep ocean eyes, the same way it did the night before. Unlike the red eyes of the demon that paralyzed her in fear, or Bastian's green irises that filled her with nausea—the Prince of Shadows' eyes were soothing and sensual.

What a time to feel pixies flutter joyously in her stomach. If only she could tell Chloe.

"May I call you Eva? It suits you."

Evangaline huffed a laugh, "It's better than human whore, so sure!"

Atlas, after finally taking a sip of his drink, let out a cough as he choked on the murky amber liquid. He studied Evangaline with a determined pain in his face. His features hard set and angry.

"Who on this good green Earth called you a human whore, child?"

Evangaline cracked a smile and began to laugh, flashing Ryder a wide-eyed glance.

He returned the smile, much to her surprise, his dimple coming out to play. He was the most beautiful man she had ever seen…but when he smiled, he became breathtaking. "That would be yours truly …" he said coquettishly, raising his whiskey glass in the air.

Atlas looked back and forth between both of them. His eyes filling with confusion, and a slight twinkle of amusement, "Prince or not, your mother, rest her soul, taught you better than that boy!"

Enjoying the sight of a mighty fae prince getting scolded, Evangaline smiled into her glass of whiskey, "It's fine, Atlas. I've been called much worse."

"Not under my watch, you will not. You may not be my daughter, but you will have my protection. Got it? Both of you, play nice!" Atlas finished by pointing at Evangaline and Ryder.

"Yes, sir," Evangaline replied by saluting Atlas. "How do you two know one another?" She giggled, raising her glass to her lips.

"Atlas is my uncle." Ryder replied, as though it was a known fact.

Evangaline sat up, mouth agape, and braced her forearms on her thighs.

"What? You never told me that? Are you also a prince?"

Atlas briefly chuckled. "No, just a consort to one. There should also be a couple greats somewhere before 'uncle'. My husband, whom I lost some time ago, was Ryder's great uncle, Prince Dimitri."

Evangaline's body softened. "Would you tell me about him?"

Atlas's eyes sparkled and his lip quirked up, almost as though he was recalling a pleasant memory. "We met, Gods, eons ago now. When our realm was no realm but a world of its own. When the Kingdom of Shadows was a land all on its own. Dimitri and I were both very much free spirits. He tried to escape princely duties, like someone else I know." He glanced at Ryder, who only raised his eyebrows at Evangaline, a small uptick of his lips appearing.

"As a young lady, with a preference for males, you will understand when I say he was tall, dark and handsome, and I fell in love with him the second I saw him. We were smack dab in the middle of the Great War, however, between the two realms at the time. I fought for Cela, the realm the old Kingdom of Shadows belonged to. Dimitri came one day to my camp on a diplomacy mission. I looked worse than you do now."

Evangaline stilled, raising a hand to the bruise on her cheekbone, then raised a sarcastic eyebrow. "I bet, because I look absolutely gorgeous right now, don't I, Atlas?" She said in a forced sarcastic tone that tried to hide her crippling emotional pain.

Ryder sipped from his drink and snorted into his cup.

Evangaline side eyed him, "I heard that."

Atlas rolled his eyes, continuing, "Anyway, I fell in love with him before he even knew my name. I made it a priority to find the nearest lake and bathe. I found clean clothes. Then I waited. And waited. And waited. I never was the type to go take what I wanted, besides he was practically untouchable being of royal lineage.

"Finally, a day later. Now keep in mind I'm fighting in a bloody war. I come back to camp coated in everything from mud to blood to gods only know what, just caked in it. Absolutely filthy. My previous bath was long gone. I come trudging up back to my tent and I see him sitting there, by himself, in the dark. It was fate, and he was gifted to me in a moment when I really needed him. So, I plucked up my courage and took out my *party trick*." He flicked his fingers, and the little white orb appeared bright and constant. Drawing a warm smile across Evangaline's battered face. She really loved his *party trick*.

"Him and I talked until I had to go back out and fight and then he left. I never thought I would see him again. Weeks later I was wounded, took some shrapnel to my leg during an ambush. It took weeks for the healers to get every little piece out. But on my third day in the infirmary, Dimitri came, said he heard of the ambush and couldn't stop worrying. He sat with me every day while I healed, and when I got better, we got married. Soon after that, Tuatha and Milesian were fated. They combined the realms of Cela and Ceradonia, and made one realm united, *Celadonia*. And we were happy for a long while until I lost Dimitri in the Convergence."

"I am so sorry," she muttered, holding her glass tightly to her chest. Her own loss was a wound not yet healed.

"We had a wonderful time together. Five hundred and seven years, to be exact. He was my sky and moon and if I had to live through the heartbreak all over just to repeat those years with him, I would in an instant."

Evangaline stayed still, thinking about Chloe. Would she risk this pain all over again just to have that one amazing year with her friend again? Probably … no … she absolutely would.

"Tuatha and Milesian. I see them all over. They're in the window by my room, the paintings in this hall. Chloe told me a little of them, but not much. Aside from their union and ending a war, why are they so special?" Evangaline asked, trying to change the subject.

Atlas set his cup down and leaned back real deep in his chair till his face was slightly shadowed. But it was Ryder who was the one to surprisingly speak, "Tuatha De is the daughter of Danu."

"Danu?" Evangaline asked, a pulsating feeling taking over her chest, a knot constricting.

"The elemental goddess. She is the most powerful of the gods. She controls the land and, well, all the elements. Earth, wind, fire, water, ice, rain, you know the lot of them. If it is a natural occurrence, Danu is the force behind it." Atlas added.

Ryder cleared his throat, gaining Evangaline's attention once more. "Danu mated with the King of Cela. The myth of it being love or strictly for breeding is convoluted in history. I like to think a child wasn't conceived like chattel, yet it is up to you to fill in those blanks. They're unnecessary plot points."

Evangaline smirked at the notion that a prince with literal moving shadows on him, always surrounded by darkness, could be secretly shipping an ancient goddess and a fae king. It was kind of cute.

Ryder continued, "Their … relations … resulted in Tuatha De. She was a fae princess with all the powers and gifts of her mother. She could do something as small as make a sapling grow or create a fifty-foot wave out of thin air. She was the power of the land and sky personified. Milesian, on the other hand, was a powerful fae prince and the only legitimate son born to the king and queen of Ceradonia. The king slept around and had some bastards here or there, but Milesian had both his father's gifts for telekinesis and enhanced strength, as well as his mother's powerful gifts of compulsion.

"So, the son of the most powerful fae couple, then king, and the daughter of a goddess, then queen, came together at the height of the war and made a treaty. One to end the bloodshed and set peace to their two realms. One that would separate their lands with a warded border sealing the other out." He finished, his face growing distant as he sipped from his whiskey.

Well, that sounded oddly and eerily similar. The boarders that separated Vitalis, Munbra, and Celadonia were the initial idea based on a treaty made by Tuatha and Milesian, centuries upon centuries ago? That fact alone shook Evangaline's world. There was so much the humans didn't know, living in their blissful ignorance.

Atlas then, cut in, "However, when they went to shake on it, the touch of their skin to one another awakened the bond of the fates. The small attraction and pull they felt guiding them to one another was amplified as they were fated, soul to soul, for eternity."

"What's so important about being fated?" Evangaline pondered out loud, squinting her eyes and crinkling her brow.

"It is considered a blessing of the gods and fates themselves to a lot, but to other old romantics like me, it is something deeper. It is two souls choosing one another, a perfect match. It is love in its purest form. Unbreakable. Undeniable."

Leaning forward, "Were you and Dimitri fated?"

Atlas smiled, "No. No, we were not. Tuatha and Milesian were the last fated couple to grace this realm. I could count the number of fated couples on my hands alone. They are couples of greatness and traditionally, a great omen for a monumental change."

She shook her head, "Jeez. I get why their portraits are everywhere then." Evangaline said, releasing a breathy laugh.

"This is their palace, young one," Atlas chuckled back, throwing her a knowing glance. "The king is their direct descendant. If Darrin had a *child*, they would carry the blood of the fae *and* goddess in them." Atlas smirked, sipping from his whiskey, winking over the rim of the glass.

It took everything for Evangaline not to drop her own glass on the floor. She froze, lifting the cup halfway to her lips as she could feel the blood pumping through her veins and into her cold little heart.

A descendant of a goddess? That can't be true. She then had a random thought. The wind whisp was her friend. But she didn't have any powers or gifts? She had no discernable fae attributes. Maybe that side of her lineage skipped her?

Lost in thought, Evangaline's brain began to race. If she abdicated the throne after her debut, the line of Tuatha and Milesian would end with her father. Did she want that?

The reign of this triumphant couple would end, her apparent super great grandparents, and it would be her fault. They built the realm upon their own blood, sweat, and tears. Her head felt ready to explode. The day was proving to be more than she bargained for. Her thoughts about leaving in a few days were now being picked apart. This was the reason she seldom planned out her future.

"Eva?" Ryder questioned, his eyebrows knitted in a contemplative knot.

Evangaline flicked her eyes up at the beautiful dark-haired prince. "Yeah. What's up?" her voice was still jaded and foreign.

Before Ryder could answer, Atlas cut him off. "A story for a story, I think. Evangaline, regale us in a tale of your greatest love, since that appears to be the theme of today's lesson."

Evangaline, still shaken from the juicy little nugget of her ancestry, realized what Atlas asked of her. She never talked about her love life to anyone except for Chloe and even then, Chloe got the spark notes version, no matter how hard she pried. Even her family didn't know the exact reason she ended her engagement, just that it was bad, and she didn't enjoy talking about it. But Atlas bared his soul to her and, well, fuck it. She truly had nothing left to lose. She might as well bare her soul to a friend and a hot ass stranger.

Downing the rest of her whiskey in one mighty gulp, she faced the men before her. "This isn't gonna be as good as you and Dimitri. Or Tuatha and Milesian, for that matter … but it sure will be entertaining for you two," she said, setting her glass down with a clink on the table.

Ryder looked oh so entertained indeed. His dimple nestled onto his cheek as he settled into the back of his chair, practically laying down. Atlas was not much different. His legs delicately crossed, and arms folded, but equally reclined. The old man nodded his head for her to begin.

With a sigh, she spoke, "Once upon a time … just kidding. I had one actual boyfriend my entire life. Back in Vitalis, the notion of love is a bit different. We don't have fated couples and epic love stories aside from those written in fiction. Dating is casual and messy and awkward. I struggled a lot with my mental health growing up, so school was difficult for me. When other girls my age were dating and having their first kisses, experiencing everything the dating world had to offer, I was normally in my room with a book. My head lost in the stories of made-up characters instead of me being out living my own life. I had no social life at all. I enjoyed my own company and was far too anxious in social settings, anyway.

"It wasn't until I went to college, and I was able to figure out who I actually was, that I started to go on dates and … you get it. Umm … that was when I met Harry. He was in one of my literature classes and for some *crazy* reason liked me. We dated throughout college and when we graduated, we moved to California after he got a job writing for a big paper. He proposed two months after we moved, and I said yes."

She noticed Ryder eye her left hand, searching for a ring, his face pinched in what came across as concern.

Holding her hand up to him, "Ah, context clues. You are ahead of me, Prince. I planned a whole wedding. One I didn't want to have, by the way. I was fine going to the courthouse and calling it a day. But I planned a whole goddam wedding. Bought a dress I hated, ordered a cake that tasted like sugared cardboard, the whole nine yards." She grinned, releasing a small breathy laugh.

"I spent the next nine months planning because he wanted a reason to get drunk with his friends. Anyway, that is beside the point. I came home early from work one day, a month before our wedding, to find him and not one but two of his work colleagues in *my* bed having a hell of a time. Apparently, he was having an affair for months with one of them and well; I didn't care to ask how the other fit in to the equation. He blamed it on me, of course, and asked for the ring back in case he ever 'needed it again'. I was so pissed I threw the damn thing in the ocean like a true psychopath. Then quickly moved back to New York while he was at work a few days later. Fast forward a year and I am here burying my friend and sipping whiskey with you two fine gentlemen!"

Atlas and Ryder just sat quietly staring at Evangaline as though she were a charity case. Like she was one of those sad puppies on the commercials that tried to get people to give fifty cents a day to help a dog in need.

"God, guys, I'm good. Well, I'm not good. It's taking all my restraint not to get completely shit faced on this whiskey right now, but that's what love is, right? It's messy. I did warn you before!" Evangaline chided, pouring herself another hearty glass of booze.

"Atlas, you remember Cecily?" Ryder said, surprising Evangaline. Atlas nodded, confused.

Ryder then turned to Evangaline, smiling so wide his pearly white teeth were peeking out of his luscious mouth. He looked on the verge of a laugh, forearms rested on his knees, "I once had a girlfriend when I was young, who I was head over heels for. She was a couple of years older than I was. Her name was Cecily. We courted for about a year."

He cleared his throat. "One day, she comes to me and tells me she is pregnant. Rightfully, I panicked. As any young man would, a fae child is extremely hard to conceive. Some are never lucky enough to conceive, so I freaked out. I was young and we weren't married, but I was happy about it, scared, but excited. With my title and birthright, I couldn't risk a scandal, so we vowed to keep it a secret for a while. I had not inherited the kingdom yet, thank the many gods. I went away a couple weeks with my father on a trip around the kingdom, only to come back to Cecily and the stable hand having a *hell of a time*, as you called it. Right there in the horse stall I was leading my horse to. My father and I bared witness to the whole thing. In my haze of child induced panic, my daft brain neglected to remember I was taking a tonic to prevent such a fate. Didn't even consider it, just took her word for the truth. Was only thinking about her and the kingdom. Cecily later admitted to the affair, which happened to be her and I by the way, and an entire scheme for the palace coffers. She and the horse boy were on and off for years, well before I even met her. The babe was never mine."

Atlas's face was distorted and entirely unreadable as he choked on his drink. "You never told me any of this …" he said, swatting Ryder with a book that was tucked away in his chair.

Surprisingly, Evangaline felt a twinge of jealousy laced with her condolences for a young Prince Ryder. However, a small twinge of contentment bubbled up, knowing the prince was not spoken for by a wife or child. She banished the thought before she allowed it to fester like an unwanted maggot into the hollows of her brain. She didn't need another mistake like Bastian.

Ryder dodged Atlas, kicking his foot out to knock the book out of the old fae's hand. "I was embarrassed, plus I didn't want to sully her name. Her, the baby, and the stable boy now live in Mirth, from what I hear."

Evangaline sighed, a massive smile gracing her face. "Good to know even the fae have fucked up dating lives." She laughed, sipping from her whiskey. "For what it's worth, she was a shitty person to you *and* the horse boy, even if she is still with him."

For a brief minute, Ryder just gazed at Evangaline, admiration shimmering in his eyes. "So was your fiancé, Eva."

She nodded and sighed, pursing her lips. "Oh well. His loss. I'm a real fucking catch!" Evangaline joked, the side of her mouth curling up mischievously while she shrugged her shoulders. Throwing her drink back, "I should be off and leave you two to your catching up. I've imposed enough, besides I have a whole bottle of wine waiting for me to drown my sorrows with. And a bath ... I smell like whiskey, mud, and sweat."

She stood, sheathing her sword, and walked away before turning around, "Thank you for making me feel less ... alone ... I guess," she said to both men who had now risen to their feet and watched her cross the distance to the door.

The oddest thing was, she meant it. She came into the library feeling more depressed and alone than she had ever felt in her life, and somehow Atlas and Ryder made her feel somewhat normal. Not better, but more normal. They reminded her that life was often filled with more turmoil than sunshine. Yet, the few rays of sun that were gifted to us should be cherished and held onto for every last fleeting moment.

"Same time tomorrow, Atlas?"

"Same time tomorrow, my dear."

Chapter Thirty-Three

She saw the red eyes first.

Easing her eyelids from their sedentary state, she saw them. Bright and glistening, as though she had not ruptured them a day before.

Surrounding her was an eternal darkness shrouded loosely in a wispy gray fog.

Ruby-red blood pooled at her feet and coated her hands.

The smell of decayed flesh filled her nostrils, sending a jolt of fear straight down her spine, quickening the pace of her rampant heart.

Death. The smell of charred smoke and the ashes of death swirled around her in the foggy clouds. It was almost a sulfuric smell, but one that was even more nauseating.

"Hello, Princess," a demonic voice filled the air in a quiet whisper. It was a different voice from the creature before her. It was smooth yet cold, unlike the demon that sounded like nails grating down a chalkboard.

Evangaline's bare feet were glued to the onyx floor beneath a shallow pool of blood as she stared at the demon that killed Chloe. The ruby stopper was no longer wedged in its eye, but Chloe's dagger, shimmering with its golden handle, protruded from its emaciated chest. The killing blow. Streams of black blood streaked down its leathery flesh as its nails flicked in a foreboding tick.

Her arm began to burn with a fiery intensity as a sharp nail from behind her cut the bandage away from her wounded arm. The presence of the being to her back was thick and heavy. His essence radiated nothing but fear.

So much pain swept through her arm with his slow clipping of her bandage.

Unable to fight the pain, she screamed in agony, dropping to her knees.

Her hand clutched firmly around her wound. Oozing blood and an oily substance that was black as the darkness that surrounded her, but with an iridescent twinge. An iridescence that reminded her of the way the wings of a dragonfly glisten in the sun over a lake.

"You're wound will kill you eventually if you continue your wallowing. Like your friend, you will join the dark stony soil, your body will feed the monsters you so fear. I can't have that, Princess. I need you at your peak, not your weakness. You will never fulfill the purpose I need you for if you kill yourself with self-sabotage." The voice whispered into her hair from behind her.

Cold, dark talons gripped her throat from behind. Her body pressed against the lithe, muscular form of the being at her back.

It laughed. "See you soon, darling."

With a crack, her throat collapsed in on itself, her breath caught mid-gulp as she choked on her own blood. She could feel the veins in her head straining, her body numb and alien.

He then let go of her, releasing her body to fall through a chasm that was not there before. She fell down and down into the blackness where the pool of blood once laid at her feet.

Her vision blurred as her lungs burned for any bit of air. Tumbling through the thick black expanse until she collided with the hard earth, all of her bones broke in the way glass shattered when stepped on.

She shot straight up, gasping for air, hands grabbing at her throat and then feeling her arm for the bandage that was still perfectly intact on her arm.

"A nightmare. It was only a nightmare." Des reassured her, as he ran his hands through her sweat soaked hair.

He did not know Evangaline was the princess, but he knew Chloe was her personal guard. After the attack—well, attacks—with both Bash and the demon creature alike, Des repeatedly stated he did not feel comfortable leaving her alone. So, he started sleeping on the couch.

"Are you okay?" He asked, throwing his shirt over his head to cover his exposed chest.

In the two nights since Des started sleeping on her couch, Evangaline saw why Chloe fell in love with the man. While his countenance most of the time was nothing more than a stoic soldier—not to mention he was more stubborn than any person, Evangaline knew—he cared about everyone and everything so deeply that it pained him at times.

For two nights, they ate with the cadre in Evangaline's room instead of the throne room. Despite the royals seeing Evangaline, all of them, aside from Ryder, still assumed she was nothing more than either the king's or Bastian's paramour. So she assumed it would be best to stay away. Plus, the thought of mingling with the nobility was more of a task than she wanted to take on. So, the cadre ate and remembered Chloe in Evangaline's suite the best way they could … through food and booze.

She hadn't seen Ryder since their time in the library, but she did often think about him for some odd reason. He left an unshakable imprint on her that filled her with a nervous excitement.

The day she left the library, she went straight to her room, drank an entire bottle of wine—got delightfully drunk—and then read the entire book about the Kingdom of Shadows in her bath.

She learned a brief history of the kingdom, lots of which didn't get logged into the files of her memory thanks to her inebriated state, but she did remember its beguiling creation. Apparently, before the Convergence, the Kingdom of Shadows was home to many noble houses that often battled, until Prince Ryder's family took the royal mantel and brought peace to their land. His ancestors worshiped the stars and, according to the book, "drew their power from the celestial bodies themselves". Whether or not that was true was a mystery, but it sounded cool.

She learned about the island of Pax, the capital city—post-convergence—

and how its bays and gulfs are home to the Undersea Kingdom that governed itself outside of Caledonia's reign. Their only Celadonian ally being that of the Kingdom of Shadows. Basically, for some ought reason, the Undersea Kingdom told the rest of the land to politely fuck off.

She learned a great deal of the kingdom's history, but what it did not go into was Ryder and his immediate family. All it spoke to was the ascension of Ryder from his father Tryamon, who from the sketch provided in the book looked nothing like Ryder. It spoke of how the "young prince" began his rule once his father abdicated after the untimely death of his mother. Other than that, there was no information regarding the Prince of Shadows, his powers, lovers, battles, nothing.

It did go so far as to include a sketched photo of his handsomeness in his crown of stolen starlight sitting atop his throne crafted of darkness itself. *Stern Regality* was what she would name the piece if she were an artist.

She felt a tad stalkerish reading about a man who insulted her, then kind of complimented her, confided a very personal story to her, and then well … made his presence in her head as steady as the beat of the many wings of the pixies and butterflies fluttering in her stomach.

It was annoying.

Bastian, on the other hand, she saw in passing a couple of times during her training. Well, not quite passing. He would lurk in the distance until Des, being her noble watchdog, quickly barked Bastian away. Another reason to be grateful for Des.

She still couldn't face Bastian without feeling as though she were covered in filth and grime. The memory of his touch was forever tainted from ecstasy to sludge in one horrid night.

"You okay?" Des asked, sitting on the side of her bed.

Evangaline dropped her head into her curled up knees, shaking. She had panic attacks both nights since the attack. Unable to close her eyes without seeing Chloe smiling at her through her bloody gurgles. Evangaline would stare at the ceiling waiting for the weight of absolute exhaustion to take her, however it didn't, no matter how hard she tried. She would stare and stare until her brain would shout how much it was her fault that Chloe was gone. How she effectively killed her best friend. With each image and replay of that horrendous night, she wanted to leave this nightmarish fantasy of a realm and get a hug from her mom. Thought after thought, question after question, until she had to lock herself in her closet and sob it all out. It happened two nights in a row. Both nights since Chloe was laid to rest.

She stayed strong all day, but couldn't fight the helplessness that came at night. She let her tears carry her lifeless soul into the abyss and let them cradle her as she sank deeper and deeper into her depression. She stopped, trying to breathe through them. Stopped trying to quell the ache. Evangaline was so close to being able to go home and cry in her mom's arms, but for now she had herself … and Des.

Last night, Des heard her crying in her closet and all but shattered the door. He sat with her curled into his chest and let her cry until she fell asleep in his arms. She woke the next morning tucked back into bed, Des in a chair to the side wrapped in his blanket from the couch.

He was a good friend to her; one she did not deserve.

Des wrapped his arm around her shoulder and rested his cheek on her head, "It's okay. I get them too sometimes."

Evangaline turned her face up to him, tears streaming down her face. "How do you get through it?"

He pondered for a moment. "I don't. I cry. I want to burn the whole realm down for taking her away from me. I would walk into the pits of the underworld to get her back."

Evangaline swallowed hard and said very seriously, "Can we do that?"

Des snorted and pulled her in close. "No. If it were possible, I am sure many would have done it by now."

"Instead, we are left feeling like *this*, huh?" She paused taking a breath to quell her trembling fingers, "I feel so broken, Des." He didn't know her title or the burdens she felt from the crown looming above her head, or the guilt she felt for lying to him and the boys. He didn't know why she was here or that she was most likely going to leave him and this place and go back to her family soon. He didn't know that thinking about leaving now made her feel like a coward, but the thought of her staying filled her with unimaginable fear. And still he never pressed, he never asked. He accepted her as she was, broken and worthless, and for that she would always hold him in her heart no matter where she was.

Tiny fissures were breaking down her will to live long before she came to the land of the fae. But when Chloe died, the fissures that the pink-haired commander helped to mend grew into deep cavernous cracks. With each day since Chloe's death, those cracks had deepened, leaving Evangaline with the want to take a hammer right into the wall and let it tumble down, burying her beneath the rubble.

Des pulled away from her and brought his stern eyes to hers, his golden blond hair mussed from sleep and falling across his cheekbones.

Softly but forcefully, he cupped her face, his aqua eyes intense and searing, "Look at me Evangaline. This pain you feel, this heartache, you use it. You got that? This pain, *your* pain, is your power. Never forget that. You draw from it to fight. You channel it when you want to succeed. You tap into it when you feel like your whole world is collapsing, because it, *it* is the only thing that can either shatter you or push you to be the wonderful and strong woman Chloe knew you to be. That I know you are. You don't give up on me, okay? I lost one warrior, I refuse to lose another."

"Okay." Evangaline shakily said through her tears.

Nodding, he pulled her back into his chest. "Okay."

They sat holding tight to one another for a good thirty minutes before Evangaline saw a glimpse of sun peek underneath the heavy velvet curtains of her room.

Des had fallen asleep holding her, his head unevenly leaned on the headboard at an awkward angle.

She didn't have the heart to wake him, despite her mind not allowing her to drift back to sleep, lingering on the way her arm ached in her nightmare.

Feeling horrible, Evangaline wiggled free of his hold and pulled the blanket over him.

She quickly changed and scribbled a quick note to him, leaving it on the pillow beside his sleeping form.

Went for a run, then to the healers. No training today. Get some rest.
Thank you.
-E.

She snuck from her room just as the light streamed through the intricate stained-glass windowpanes displaying her ancestors. She stared at Tuatha and Milesian in the bright morning light and contemplated everything Atlas had told her about the people who built the foundations of her family. Even in glass, they were regal and strong. The exact opposite to how Evangaline felt.

They had courage and strength, sure they had fae abilities and magic to help them, but they were strong … and they were *her* ancestors. Their blood ran through her veins. So she could be strong too, even if it was exhausting.

Contemplating everything, she made them a promise right then and there just like she made Des earlier, "I'll make you proud. I'll keep fighting."

Chapter Thirty-Four

Dripping in sweat, Evangaline made her way to the healers' quarters. It only took three weeks, but she finally learned how to navigate the palace without someone telling her where to turn.

The run she forced herself on eased the tension from her shoulders. The sun barely hovered above the earth by the time she made it outside the walls of the palace. Not even the maids were readying the throne and ballrooms for breakfast services. Quiet filled the air in an anticipatory breath. Her anxiety nagged at the back of her mind, telling her it was careless to venture out to the forest alone, but once her feet moved in their steady pace, all her anxiety drifted away. She clung to the forest's edge, sometimes dipping within the shade of the ever-changing leaves to cool off. Occasionally, a far-off rustle would sound, but she never worried, knowing, with some foreign knowledge, that the wind whisp was running alongside her, protecting her.

It felt good to feel the breeze on her skin. Evangaline's thoughts and grief took a back seat to the burn of her lungs. With each impact of her boot on the grass, small zings of pain echoed in her bruises and cuts—nothing unbearable but enough to become annoying. With each pinch and zap, Evangaline pictured Chloe kicking her in the butt or poking her in the rib, making fun of her for being stubborn. For holding onto the physical pain to torture herself. Chloe wouldn't want her to suffer, and while her mind would take time to heal, her body certainly didn't. It was time to heal her wounds and bruises. Des was right her pain was the catalyst behind whatever power she could manifest. Yet, Evangaline didn't need said pain displayed on her skin, not when she was about to be debuted as the princess of the realm that very night. She needed to be strong and look stable, Atlas preached that particular lesson time and time again. Although she was shattering with grief, anxiety, and fear, she would do her best to be what Darrin expected of her.

Her heart thumped inside her chest with anxiety at the thought of the ball. She wanted to get it over with. She wanted the bargain to be fulfilled more than anything.

Tonight, it was imperative to remember her training with Atlas. To be the princess Celadonia required her to be. One night to either be welcomed or one night to be booed mercilessly. Not that it would matter long term. While she loved the boys like brothers, there was still a fragment of her being that knew she was not built to coexist amongst the fae. No matter the reception she received at her debut ball, Evangaline would most likely be heading out first thing in the morning to the warm embrace of her family.

But first, she needed to heal her wounds, especially being that her nightmare centered around them. Evangaline chalked it up to her subconscious, telling her to not be stupid any longer and to see the healer. However, she could not forget the pain she felt in her dream. Could not forget the voice that whispered in her ear. It all felt too real. But she reminded herself that, when she woke, her bandage was in place and her hands void of the blood that felt so sickly real. There was one thin red mark marring her neck where the phantom's hands gripped, however that could have been from sparring with Des or just a bruise from the attack she didn't notice before.

The healers called the highest tower of the castle home, keeping far away from the court and prying eyes, hoisted high up in the sky.

Evangaline bristled through the palace corridors, greeting servants and courtiers by name and title, plastering on the largest of fake smiles.

The servants always had an appreciative expression when she addressed them by their given names. Expressions that filled her heart with an immense happiness tinged in the bitter taste of sadness. Just hearing their name brought a smile to their faces—it was appalling—they deserved better.

The courtiers, however, always came across disgusted as though their name falling out of the mouth of a human woman was foul and improper. Which was exactly why Evangaline kept doing it. She loved the way she got under their skin. It only made the surprise tonight taste that much sweeter. She hoped when they learned the woman they practically spit on as she passed was their princess, their faces would contort in the most delightful ways. Call her petty, but those were the fae she did not care to piss off with her royal title.

Rounding the hallway, with a determined swiftness to her step, Evangaline crashed straight into the hard binding of a book. The force of her impaling herself with the top of the book's spine forced the air out of her lungs, enough to where she felt embarrassed and unable to speak for a second.

"I am so sorry," she sheepishly wheezed, rubbing the pain she suddenly felt in her chest.

"It's alright, Eva." Ryder quipped with a jovial lilt to his voice, closing the book and holding it to his chest.

Evangaline looked up, surprised to see him wandering the halls so early in the morning.

His black shirt was unbuttoned, revealing the slow swirling shadows lurking beneath on his bronzed skin.

His hair was tussled with the effects of him just running his hands through it. A couple strands fell delicately across his brow, somehow making him even more attractive.

Evangaline stared up at him for a moment before speaking, her nose slightly pinched. "Why are you here? Wait, did Atlas really let you borrow a book?" Her voice turned jealous at the end. Atlas never let her take a book from the library, no matter how many times she pouted her lips and batted her eyelashes. She even used the princess card once … it did not work.

He smirked, opening his eyes slightly wider. "What my uncle doesn't know won't hurt him." He winked conspiratorially. "And don't worry my lady, you shall be rid of me tomorrow and therefore won't need to worry about me ruining your early morning walks through the halls of the palace like a wraith."

Evangaline stammered and swallowed hard, regaining her composure. "I was … *rude*. I do not wander like a … never mind. Arguing with you is pointless. I didn't mean it like that. I meant why are you in this wing of the palace? All of the other royals are in the main hall?"

"My suite is just beyond the tower entrance at the end of the hall. I prefer to be where it is quieter."

Evangaline simply smiled and nodded and began to walk again when Ryder fell into step beside her, heading in the opposite direction of the one he was going in.

Leaning his tall frame down closer to Evangaline, arms twined behind his back, clasping the red leather book in his hands, he whispered, "Why are you here?"

Evangaline shot her eyes up to him, unable to focus on anything besides the handsome boldness of his features. Forcing her gaze away, she cleared her throat and spoke, "I have to go see the healer."

Ryder straightened, his eyes suddenly fell on the many bruises still covering Evangaline's body and face. His eyes lingered on the putrid green and purple one creeping up her back, peppered with many little cuts where the shards of the decanter were once lodged.

Noticing his gaze, "I don't want to look like a bruised apple going to a royal ball. Being a human seems to draw enough unwanted attention." She shimmied her shirt further up her shoulders to hide her marks from him. For some reason, she desperately did not want him to see her as weak. "Hi Elain," she said to a maid passing by with fresh linens in her arms.

"Oh, Hello Evangaline. Your Highness. Beautiful day, isn't it Miss Evangaline?" The maid replied, far too bubbly in her cadence. It should not have bothered Evangaline, but it did. A simple hello should not be a gift. "Will you be training in the yard today? The breeze will keep you nice and cool!"

Evangaline smiled, continuing her walk. "Yes, it would. But no training today. I told Des to take the day off. I did do my run though, and the breeze was wonderful. Oh, and before I forget, thank you for the lavender oil you gave Wren. It was perfect." Evangaline smiled, waving back at the maid.

Half shouting, "Anytime, love. Enjoy your day!" the maid quipped.

Evangaline giggled under hear breath, gazing down as her feet struck the glimmering white stone floors.

Ryder's sapphire blue eyes fixated on her, twinkling with awe. Evangaline felt his stare deep within her very being and faced him, mushing her features with confusion.

"What?" she spoke finitely.

"I've been around a great many courts, including my own, and have never seen such respect given by the staff," he said as that goddamn dimple appeared next to his bright smile.

Evangaline stopped in front of an arched doorway with no door. Straight through it was a staircase covered in climbing pink roses that lead to the healers' wing. An infirmary sat just behind the stairs with a few beds for emergencies.

She looked up at him quizzically. "I'm simply treating them with the respect they deserve. Maybe you will gain the respect of your staff by doing the same." She turned sharply and made her way up the winding staircase.

Below her, Ryder tipped his head back and laughed. Deep and sensuous. His laugh echoed in the staircase, followed closely by the clicking of his boots as he hastily climbed the stairs two at a time. Once more falling in stride with Evangaline.

She would be lying to herself to say the prince did not entertain her. In fact, every second in his presence was thrilling. He was the finest of strategy games that she wanted to play forever. From their initial meeting, he met her barb for barb. Even in his insults or jests, a kindness lurked behind his swirling cobalt eyes, whether he wanted to admit it or not.

Her stomach did acrobatic performances around him, as much as she did not want to admit it, and a small thrill coursed through her veins when he persisted to stay by her side.

"And you now know how my kingdom operates, do you?" He chided.

"I never said that I did."

Ryder, with one mighty stride, beat her to the next stair, cutting off her pathway. Towering over her as he stared down at her, utterly amused. His eyes sparkled with what looked like tiny stars, and she found herself lost in the small galaxies beneath his irises.

His eyes dipped to her lips briefly before he spoke. "You are a curious creature, Eva."

She tilted her head further up to him, "How so?" Evangaline breathed.

Ryder's eyebrows pinched slightly but a small grin stayed on his face as he answered, never once removing his eyes from her own. "You go toe to toe with the highest rulers in the land. Vanquish some odd shadow beast thing. Laugh in the face of failed love. Train with swords and knives in the rain. And continue to undermine my authority … Does nothing scare you?"

Alright, Evangaline's turn to tip her head back and laugh. *If he only knew,* she thought.

Smiling up at Ryder, "Is your main conundrum the fact that I *'undermine your authority'* or that you secretly enjoy it?" She said in a sensual purr, stepping up onto the same stair, mere inches away from the Prince of Shadows. One miscalculation of a breath and their chests would meet. Their skin would touch where it was exposed and whatever electric charge that hummed in the air around them would ignite with a bolt of lightning. "What, Prince Ryder, are the women falling to their knees at your beck and call, not satiating your needs? Not keeping you humble?"

They stared at one another. Their eyes boring deep into the others as a guttural noise echoed in the prince's throat as he swallowed. Something crackled between them. To close the distance, to put her hand within his hair and claim his lips would be so easy—just a slight lean forward would do the trick. But she didn't cave to the desire coursing through her body at his proximity to her.

She stepped around him before she did something she would regret, careful to not touch him for fear she might enjoy the feel of his body on hers too much. The simmering heat of tension beginning to ripple between the two of them was too much to bear. Her mistake of taking Bastian to bed haunted her. She did not want to use Ryder in the way she used Bastian to drain her anxiety and fear. Ryder was different. Evangaline felt that in her gut—he wasn't Bastian—but still she needed to focus on the bargain and where she would end up in the morning. The weight of a realm rested on her shoulders. She wasted enough time with her lustful thoughts. So, she plastered on a smile that barely caressed her cheeks. "As far as my fears, I live in fear of a great many things, Prince, but to tell you would be to give away my secrets … and we can't have that now, can we?"

Ryder sucked on his bottom lip, watching Evangaline climb the remaining stairs to the healer, a delighted tug inching his smile higher.

Evangaline made it to the landing, trying her hardest to hide the grin that the Prince of Shadows' smile brought to her face. All the while, Ryder lingered on the stairs behind her.

She knocked on the door to the healer's office, which was slightly ajar, "Madame Chevalier, do you have a moment?" Evangaline murmured.

Madame Chevalier bustled and slung open the door, revealing the stout woman with rosy cheeks and black hair peppered with glistening strands of white.

Placing a hand on her robust hip, just under her worn in gray apron, "I've been wondering when you would stop being so stubborn and let me fix you!" Chevalier huffed.

Evangaline toed the doorframe, her cheeks flushing with embarrassment enough to not notice Ryder glide up to her.

Madame Chevalier's face grew so taught her eyes practically popped from her tiny head at the sight of the gorgeous prince. Suddenly—startling Evangaline—she dropped into a low bow. "Your Highness, I shall see to you after the misses, if that is alright with you." It wasn't a question. It was a statement.

Evangaline looked back and forth between Ryder and Madame Chevalier. "Where was my curtsy?" A breathy laugh escaped her lips.

Glancing at Ryder, Chevalier turned her attention toward Evangaline, trying to shield her words from Ryder. "I'll bow to you the day you wear a crown on your head like him. For now, you're a rose's thorn in my side!"

Evangaline shook her head and whispered under her breath, "Careful what you wish for." With a squint to the old woman.

"I do not seek your services madam, just was passing by and wished to escort Eva to your care." Ryder replied to the lively healer then softly whispered in Evangaline's ear, "So, maybe you don't have *all* the staff wrapped around your pretty finger."

Evangaline rolled her eyes. "Don't sound so thrilled. Thank you for your *escort* though," she whispered back.

"Very well, my Prince, it was an honor to be in your graces. Evangaline, come in." Madame Chevalier moved behind Evangaline and practically slammed the door in Ryder's face. "Please tell me you were able to remove all that glass?"

Stepping into the office, Evangaline began unfastening her corset. "Yes. I also bandaged my arm ... and before you ask, yes, everything has been sterilized and cleaned around the clock. I have taken the tonics and chews that you gave Wren that night, as well. Thank you, by the way."

Madame Chevalier assessed Evangaline's back, ignoring her gratitude. Evangaline walked to the bed in the corner, both women completely unaware that the door did not completely close behind them, nor did Ryder leave. Instead, he stood leaning against the doorframe, closely analyzing Evangaline's wounds with a ferocity in his eyes and a scowl on his face.

His shadows swirled in a cloud around his chest and neck.

Evangaline shimmied her left sleeve off, exposing the bandage on her left arm. Slowly, she unwrapped it.

"What the ..." Evangaline whispered.

The bandage that was fresh and a pristine white was now smeared in an oily black substance and blood on the inside. The same substance as her nightmare. Her anxiety spiked and her desperation leached the color from her face.

Suddenly Evangaline became frantic. She peered up at Madame Chevalier. "This ... it wasn't ... it hasn't ..."

She was so caught up in her head she did not feel Ryder move away from the doorframe to her side. He stopped himself short of touching her, tossing his book onto the bed.

"Healer, what is that?" His deep voice echoed, startling Madame Chevalier and Evangaline both.

"My Prince, I asked you to leave." Chevalier was stern. Call it healer-patient confidentiality, but the tone in the healer's voice was nothing like the obsequious tones Evangaline heard the staff apply to any of the royals.

Evangaline looked back at her arm oozing black, "Please get out," she said toward the prince. Harshness and fear riding her tone.

"No," he growled, not looking away from her gashes. "Now, what is that healer? Eva, did the shadow demon do this to you?"

She didn't fight him … she had more to worry about. Like, the fact that her arm was effectively spewing what only looked like crude oil after she had a dream where a demon made her bleed something that looked much like said crude oil. She was freaking out. Her voice trembled as she answered Ryder with a simple, "Yes."

"You're wound will kill you eventually if you continue your wallowing." The mysterious phantom told her within her nightmare.

"I think it's poison … or venom …" Evangaline murmured under her breath.

"I've never seen anything like this before." Madame Chevalier said, reaching out to touch the liquid slowly seeping from the gash mark on Evangaline's arm.

Grabbing the healer's wrist, "Don't!" Evangaline gazed back down at her arm and up to Ryder. "No one knew of the creature that gave it to me, but I think it's a type of venom. Don't ask me how I know I just—"

"It will be alright." Ryder cut her off, his face softening for a moment to just reassure her.

She was panicking, but she needed to stay levelheaded. Just that morning her arm looked fine, as though it was on the mend even. It was beginning to scab and everything. Her training with Des the last few days didn't disturb it. She cleaned it and took care of it. She chewed the herbs and drank the tonics that were given to her to ease the pain, even though their bitter taste made her want to vomit.

The being warned her in her nightmare. The demon creature poisoned her. How? Why? Was she dying? Was her nightmare real?

"Its claws had to have been filled with poison," she stammered. "I think … please don't touch it." Evangaline told the healer.

"How would you know that? Have you felt nauseous, or lightheaded, have you felt at all susceptible to poison, Evangaline." Chevalier said, almost angry.

"I just know!" Evangaline snapped, "And not at all. I've felt … fine."

Ryder started rubbing his jaw. His chest began moving up and down in heavier and heavier movements. He was either freaked out or in seriously deep thoughts. Either way, Evangaline didn't need him seeing her this way.

She looked up at him with pleading eyes. "Prince—"

His hands dropped to his waist. "Don't even tell me to leave. It is not happening. Madame, do you have any poison testers, the tablets typically used for the king's drinks?"

Chevalier stood up, confused, and hustled to a giant wooden chest with drawers of various sizes on the other side of the room. She shuffled through assorted bottles of potions and herbs and tablets until she found what Ryder requested. "Here." She rushed it back to Ryder, dumping a cluster of chalky mint green tablets into his hand. Then over to Evangaline with a small bottle of an inky purple liquid. "It's passionflower. It's for calming. I can feel your nerves clawing through you. It will be okay, dear." Chevalier whispered to her.

Ryder glanced over his shoulder as she downed the vial before striding over in two big steps to a table full of medical instruments. He scooped up a small wooden bowl filled with suture needles and thread and dumped the contents out, not caring where they flew and tumbled. Then, with a swift movement, handed the bowl to Madame Chevalier. "Scoop some of … whatever it is into here …"

"Let me." Evangaline interjected, grabbing and bringing the small wooden dish to her arm as the passionflower swept through her body like a warm wave, calming her nerves and anxiety. Gently, Evangaline squeezed the lacerations, drawing a few drops of the blood. She let out a small cry as a white-hot pain radiated through her arm and into her shoulder. It felt as though her muscle was being burned and her skin was being melted clean off. Even so, she squeezed till enough of the oil and blood sat in the bowl.

She opened her eyes to see Ryder and Chevalier both staring at her, dumbfounded. Evangaline peered into the bowl and at her arm and suddenly became nauseous. Every vein in her arm was black against her porcelain skin, from her shoulder to the tips of her fingers. Like various decrepit roots were nestled under her skin.

Evangaline forced a shaky smile. "That can't be good …"

Ryder went to grab the bowl from Evangaline, but she jerked it back. "Tell me what to do. I don't want you touching it."

Shaking his head in annoyance, he placed a glass of water and the tablet on the desk. "Combine it with the water and drop in the tablet. It is made to detect poison in drinks. It might not work, but if it does, and this is a venom or poison, it will let us know."

She nodded. Her arm shooting out a sharp pain that she was doing quite poorly at ignoring. Her face was smashed in a concentrated agony as she did as the prince instructed and combined the water with the shiny black venom. The black liquid rose to sit at the top of the water, congealing instead of combining.

Evangaline glanced up from Madame Chevalier's desk to Ryder, "Is that okay? Or should I try to mix it?"

He simply nodded. "It's fine."

As the mint-colored tablet left her hand and glided into the wooden bowl, Evangaline felt the air grow thicker. The same way she felt the night of the attack. The tablet tumbled into the dish in slow motion. Her chest grew heavy with anticipation, and her throat closed up with each bated breath. Evangaline flexed her hands at her sides and watched as the tablet dropped through the substance, coating itself in the glistening black sludge and floated to the bottom. The effects of the passionflower kept her anxiety at bay, but she could feel it battling with the components of the tonic.

They stood there for what felt like a lifetime before the bowl began to smoke. The same gaseous substance that formed the demon creature swirled before her, drawing a gasp from Evangaline's lips.

A whirl of black putrid plumes lifted out of the bowl and into the air, carrying the scent of death with it.

Ryder reached to his hip and drew out a black dagger with a silver inlay of the phases of the moon in the blade. The same one that graced the cover of the book from her room. Evangaline gawked for a second as though she saw a celebrity and then quickly refocused on the emission of the bowl.

The whirl of smoke, in an instant, shot back into the water as though it was dragged back into the black sludge forcefully. Before any of them could speak, the bowl released a blinding green light that had them all stumbling back and shielding their eyes.

As the light dimmed, Evangaline edged toward the bowl cautiously. The black liquid was glowing green at the surface of the water.

She looked up at Ryder, her eyes wide with fear.

"What does that mean?" She asked, her heart thundering in her chest.

Tucking his blade into the waistline of his pants and taking a deep breath, "That means you should have been dead days ago."

Evangaline sat back in Madame Chevalier's chair and rubbed her face with her hands. Her arm still burning and throbbing.

"What now?" Evangaline asked, sitting straighter. "Is there anything to be done?"

Madame Chevalier moved about the room like a small tornado, her little feet moving in a rapid succession as she gathered all sorts of jars and bandages.

Evangaline tracked her around the room while Ryder simply stood on the opposite side of the desk. His eyes were always on Evangaline, despite the whirlwind that was Chevalier bustling behind him. His jaw was set in a hard, terse position—ticking with a restraint that appeared painful to the naked eye. His eyes swam with fear as they grew darker with each sweep of Evangaline's body.

"Alright, now that we know we're dealing with a venomous substance, I am going to need to extract that first. It's gonna hurt like the gods above, but you are a big tough girl … you can handle it. Then I will heal it, and then I will heal the rest of your ailments." Chevalier said confidently, setting all her many accoutrements on the table. She swapped her worried and puzzled demeanor for her typical strong and fearless one that brought a sense of calmness to Evangaline.

Evangaline went to stand, wincing in pain before Chevalier tsked at her. "Stay there. I can access your arm better here than in the bed." She then stared at Ryder with a grateful expression. "As for you, my Prince, I thank you for your quick thinking, but I need to tend my patient. She comes first, so I would ask you to either seat yourself on the bed over there, or you can see yourself out. I am too old to be watched over like a hawk. Your brooding can go elsewhere."

Despite her pain, Evangaline smiled and let out a tight-lipped giggle as she glanced up at Ryder.

The unamused prince obliged the adamant healer, begrudgingly so. Like a child, he dragged his booted feet over to the bed and sat with one hand firmly planted on a thigh and the other covering his mouth.

He sat staring at Evangaline like the most gorgeous gargoyle to exist. Dark and brooding, but intriguing all at the same time. He too was a curious creature and if she survived this, she would tell him so.

No one spoke as Evangaline chomped down on a bit of leather Madame Chevalier handed her. She sucked in her screams, clenching down on the leather, as the seasoned healer stuck a massive syringe into her arm and drained out the black liquid vein by vein.

Slowly, the insufferable pain caused Evangaline to tremble as Chevalier extracted load after load of poison and blood from the three gashes in her arm and squirted them in a bucket below her feet.

Through her muffled groans and screams, Evangaline felt the burning sensation ease with each load emptied and before she knew it, felt no pain at all. A little dizzy, but no pain.

"How's that? Still burning?" The healer said after quite some time.

Evangaline looked into Chevalier's eyes, her face gaunt and white as a ghost. "No. None." She sighed, leaning her head against the back of the chair, tossing the worn bit onto the desk.

"Good. That means I can start."

Before Evangaline could question her, Chevalier placed her hands on Evangaline's arm, releasing the soothing ivory light from her palms. It took quite some time, but eventually Evangaline's arm looked as though no monster tore open her flesh and no poison coursed through her veins.

Chevalier ended up kicking Ryder out of the room completely so Evangaline could remove her shirt and allow all the bruises that lined Evangaline's torso to be healed. He was certainly not a fan of being kicked to the curb and talked at like he was just any old fae, however, he obliged.

Evangaline's body was a map of her mental pain. Of course, the stubborn healer didn't recognize that and swore her up and down for not getting fixed sooner. But with each blemish healed, Evangaline felt Chloe drift further and further away.

Evangaline was too much of a coward to admit to the woman healing her that she felt she needed to be punished for that night in the library, suffering through the pain of her wounds in payment for costing Chloe her life. So she simply let Chevalier chastise and reprimand her.

Ryder waited outside the door until Evangaline finished and then insisted on walking her back to her room. Evangaline protested, but just with the healer, he adamantly insisted, and she relented. A little bit giddy to spend some time alone with him.

"I can either walk with you or I will follow behind you. Either way, I will be around you. Your choice," he said when she pressed him to take his leave.

The man aggravated her, and he knew it. He knew just where to push Evangaline's buttons and appeared to enjoy the thrill of her sarcasm and quick wit. The two bantered all the way across the palace grounds, trading barbs and backhanded compliments.

Truth be told, she enjoyed his company and appreciated him being there for her back with Madame Chevalier.

"You are the least lady-like lady I have ever met," Ryder chided, combing his hand through his floppy black hair.

Evangaline smiled, "Oh, I'm no lady! And lucky for you, I take that as a compliment."

Ryder chuckled as they rounded the hall toward her room, "I am surprised you are joining us for the ball this evening."

"Why?" Evangaline asked, raising an eyebrow.

Ryder's eyes darted down to his feet and paused a minute. He opened his mouth and then closed it. Then finally opened it once more. "I have looked for you at the dinner feasts over the past few days and have not found you to be in attendance."

Evangaline took a deep breath and exhaled despite the butterflies gliding in her stomach. "It's just been a long few days. I've taken dinner in my room with my friends instead. Besides, I don't need to dress up or act a certain way when I'm with them, don't need to be subjected to the *leers of the aristocracy*." The last words she punctuated with a sarcastic swirl of her hand in the air.

Ryder chuckled. "I understand what you mean."

"You do?" Evangaline asked, rounding the corner to her suite. She gazed up at Ryder, her features softening as she took in the slight pain behind his enthralling eyes.

He looked down at her sympathetically. "I do compl—"

"Evangaline," a far too familiar and unwanted voice boomed from her doorway, cutting off the prince's words.

Chapter Thirty-Five

"Prince of Shadows, what a pleasant surprise. I heard whispers that you were escorting *my* lady. Lovely to see you again." Bastian said with the venom of a thousand snakes.

"General Bastian, I wish I could say the same." The prince said, straightening his spine, his jaw flickered slightly in irritation.

Evangaline didn't say a thing as she took in the two men.

Bastian leaned casually on her doorframe, his legs crossed before him. The look of the hungry predator clouding his eyes once more.

She stared at him, hoping he would see her repulsion and kindly fuck off. Yet he didn't. He was an apex predator who enjoyed playing with his food, and he would not stop until Evangaline succumbed to his wills. Unfortunately for him, she could be a stubborn bitch and would not go to him without a fight.

"Thank you for escorting *my* Evangaline back to her room." Bastian jovially threw into the air.

My Evangaline. The sound of her name on his tongue was more painful than getting the venom sucked from her arm. *My.* Two times in a matter of thirty seconds, he had called her his something. His lady … His Evangaline. It set her on fire. The possessiveness was unwarranted and unwelcomed.

"Where is Des?" Evangaline asked, fire coating her tongue.

Bastian smiled wider. "I sent him away to train some new recruits. I needed a word with you … alone." The last word was geared at Ryder. So was the ice-cold glare.

Evangaline squared her shoulders and cocked her head, stepping between the two men. The rainbow of colors from the stain glass window streaked her features. "Unfortunately, I don't want to talk to you. Alone or otherwise."

Bastian stalked closer to her, placing his hands on her waist, grinning from ear to ear, a carnivorous smile etched onto his face. Dropping his voice so only she could only hear it, "Have I not apologized enough? Why are you so keen to talk to Prince Ryder and not me? What is he to you, Princess? Tell me, does *my* girl think of me at night when she's alone or are you getting your needs met elsewhere?" He said, flinging his eyes up towards Ryder.

My girl.

Evangaline shook her head. "I was never your girl, and I will *never* be your girl."

Bastian glared down at her. His hands sliding down her back till they rested at the base of her spine right above her backside. Slowly, he leaned down and whispered in her ear, his smile tickling the lobe, his eyes fixed on Ryder in a triumphant glare. "We will see what fate says about that princess."

Evangaline studied him as he straightened. Her jaw was tight, her breath heavy with her anger and nerves. Every second his hands were on her, she felt sick to her stomach and the urge to knee him right in the balls grew more and more.

Ryder's presence behind her was fervent. She could almost feel his shadows swirling on his expanse of muscle, could have sworn she felt his jaw ticking with rage. He, too, was an inferno. For some reason, he hated Bastian, too. But at the moment, he was letting her fight her own battle. However, Evangaline knew by the heaviness in the air, his power was thundering through his veins. Never in her life had she felt so protected and overwhelmed by a presence as she was with the Prince of Shadows at her back.

From down the hall, footsteps sounded. They grew louder and louder, rushed even, and yet Bastian did not release Evangaline. They were locked in a battle of wills, and both were too prideful to concede.

"Lady E, I have a special …" Shaw sang as he rounded the corner, "delivery …" his voice grew quieter as he digested Bastian holding onto Evangaline.

Des growled low and angry next to him.

"General, I have finished with the recruits. I believe they await your further orders." Des said cautiously. His tone maintaining a diplomatic cadence, but a hard-edge rode through his posture.

"Your Highness," Des and Shaw said, finally acknowledging Ryder standing there watching Bastian with lethal accuracy.

The prince didn't respond.

Evangaline put her palm against Bastian's chest, slowly digging her fingernails into his pectoral muscle. "Your soldiers need you, *General*," she purred not at all sensually but rather with a fire strong enough to rival the sun.

Bastian leaned in close to her ear once more, "I want you so bad, Evangaline, and I will have you, no matter what you say or think. You are my key to everything." He then kissed her on the cheek the way sweethearts did. Slowly, his hands peeled away from her back as he strode down the hall with all the arrogance of a man who won a game only he was playing.

"Gentlemen," was all he said as he left, striding past the prince and Evangaline's friends.

Evangaline stood stoic at the end of the hall and willed herself to resume breathing without throwing up.

"Fucking prick." Ryder said, earning a brief chuckle from Evangaline.

Des side eyed Ryder rushing to Evangaline. Placing his hands on her cheeks, he took her in, inspecting her for anything wrong. Instead, all he saw was her now unmarred skin and small traces of sleep deprivation clinging to her under eyes. Her face was clear of scrapes and bruises. The anger deep within her blue-green eyes bore into the worry in Des's aqua eyes.

"Did he hurt you? I came back as soon as I was told you left the healer." Des whispered, bending at the knees to look into her eyes.

"No, Ryder was with me the whole time," Evangaline replied, grabbing Des's hands and smiling up at him weakly.

Des peered over her head at Ryder, "Thank you for staying with her," he said graciously, "I owe you, Your Highness."

Evangaline turned around and faced the prince, her eyes softening at his presence.

Ryder took a moment to soften his own, but once he did, he smiled. It wasn't the same smile that filled his face with joy and intrigue; it was the same smile she bore—one concealing emotion too heavy to be voiced in public.

"Um, these are my friends, Des and Shaw." She pointed at the two men, eyeing the prince suspiciously.

Ryder regarded the two soldiers clad in their royal regalia with familiarity. "The lady is lucky to have friends like you. It is an honor to make your acquaintance." All the joking and softness he had with her was suddenly gone from his voice, having been replaced with the stern demeanor of a royal prince doing his duty.

Shaw juggled a massive pink box with a green ribbon and shakily extended his hand to Ryder. "The honor is ours, Prince Ryder."

Ryder politely shook his hand and Evangaline could see Shaw glow with pride.

Shaw once told Evangaline how he grew up very poor and worked extremely hard to get his position within the Royal Guard. He spoke of his fondness for the royals, seeing them as celebrities. Basically, to state it plainly, he was a royal fan boy.

"Is that for me?" Evangaline asked Shaw, motioning to the box.

Almost dropping it, "Oh shit, yes, sorry, yes, a gift from the king." Shaw jogged the massive box over to her. "Do you wish for me to put it inside?"

Evangaline nodded hesitantly, smiling.

Shaw smiled back and made for the door.

"Wren will be up in an hour to help you get ready." Des muttered to Evangaline.

She continued smiling weakly, "Did you guys eat? I can call up some lunch?"

Des smiled and shook his head, "When do Shaw and I pass up food? I will ring for Wren and order some up."

"Thank you," she said to Des, not entirely facing him. "I will meet you inside?"

Des glanced up to Ryder and back to Evangaline. "Of course. Once again, thank you, Your Highness," he said, bowing at the waist before turning on his heels and striding in through the door, leaving the Crown Princess of Celadonia and the Prince of Shadows alone in the hall.

For a solid twenty seconds, the hidden princess and the Prince of Shadows stared at each before Evangaline spoke.

"Thank you. For everything." A shadow of a smile graced her face. A show of strength. She was a crumbling, dilapidated structure held up by sheer pride and pain alone. The events of the day—of the week, really—were crashing down on her emotional barrier. All it took was one Bastian sized bullet to pierce her hide. She didn't want Ryder to see her breakdown. So, she forced the smile. "If you want … you can join us for lunch. You don't have to … if you don't want to … I get it … the other guys will probably come by once they hear food is on its way," she nervously giggled.

Smiling back at her half-heartedly, "I would love to, but I am already running late to meet Atlas. Thank you, though. I would, truly, I don't pass up a good meal and company, but you know how Atlas can be."

Evangaline nodded at him.

He looked down, "Bastian—"

"Is nothing but an entitled prick who won't take no for an answer." Evangaline bit off.

His eyes met hers and nodded. "I won't let him hurt you."

His words shattered a part of her heart that she was not aware existed. She knew she was strong, but the sincerity in Ryder's eyes gave her no room but to believe he meant every word. She was surrounded—daily—by the greatest soldiers Celadonia had to offer. She trained with them, ate with them, learned from them, and yet in one simple sentence by a man—a prince—she barely even knew she felt safer than she had ever felt.

Her lips opened of their own accord, prepared to tell him she would not let Bastian hurt him either—a vow she felt all the way into the pit of her soul—but Ryder filled the silence first.

"Here." He handed her the book he was carrying, the one he stole from Atlas. She took it reading the title, *A Twist of Fate: The Legend of Tuatha and Milesian.* An arrow pierced through her heart, reading the title. The weight of her decision to abandon the throne her two ancestral fae built upon the bridge of their love was unbearable. Ryder spoke before her tears of anxiety formed. "You inspired me. I hadn't read about Tuatha and Milesian in a while. That one is less about the hardships and more about their love. I think you will enjoy it."

Her heart thrummed a beat of admiration for the prince before her. She looked up from the book to the stained glass of the fae in question, then back to the prince.

"Thank you," she whispered. "See you tonight, then?" Her smile faltered, but she regained it. Why was she disappointed at his rejection? They barely knew one another? And yet it stung, nonetheless.

Ryder nodded with a sense of sadness ghosting his enthralling eyes.

Evangaline turned to her door and entered the bedroom with her false smile still on her face, leaving Ryder in the hall.

She did not know why his rejection and kindness was the final straw in destroying the dam she built, but they were. The cracks of Bastian's abuse and possessiveness fractured further alongside the rupture of her heart at losing Chloe. Mix that with the weight of letting down Darrin and an entire realm, plus her guilt at lying to her friends. She was weakened. The foundation was cracked too much, and the burdens weighed her down until they were nothing but rubble beneath her knees.

Her chest ached and vibrated with every slow thud of her heart. She rubbed at her chest till the pain eased.

Long strides carried Evangaline across the room to where Des and Shaw stood before the beautiful gift from the king. She set Ryder's book atop the table and then collapsed to the floor in a heap of tears. Her hands cradled her face as she sat there on her knees, weeping. Des and Shaw wrapped her in their arms, the cool kiss of their armor stinging her freshly healed skin the same way Chloe's did just a few weeks ago, making her cry harder at the memory.

Everything from the past three weeks crashed upon her and held her head under the water.

Right there in the dining room, held by her friends, she cried away her sorrows.

Chapter Thirty-Six

Once her tears cleared, Evangaline felt lighter, airy even. The vibration in her chest remained—a steady humming—but she ignored it by pushing it to the furthest recesses of her mind. Life was barreling forward, whether she wanted it to or not.

Wren came to her room after she and the boys ate lunch—just as Des said—and beautifully styled her hair. Sweeping up the sides and delicately pinning it back away from her face to expose her rounded ears just the way that Chloe liked to do. Those very same rounded ears were adorned with delicate diamond ear cuffs that made it hard for anyone to *not* look at them. Her long, straight, brown hair was softly curled at the bottom and cascaded down the length of her back like a waterfall of sepia to rest right on the crest of her behind. Gold metallic powder dusted her eyelids and was accentuated with a soft wing from the bag of cosmetics she brought with her from Vitalis.

Wren was transfixed with the eyeliner pen and mascara tube and begged to be taught all about human makeup. The smile that graced her handmaiden's face when she was in her element, surrounded by hair pins and cosmetics, was all Evangaline needed to etch a genuine smile across her own face. The events of the morning were forgotten to a bonding session full of glamour and laughter.

"Well, that is easier than charcoals for sure!" Wren exclaimed, watching

Evangaline with exasperated awe as Evangaline swiped her mascara on with two surprisingly steady flicks. "And so much darker! Let me try! Let me try! Let me try!"

Wren had become a good friend despite her inability to let Evangaline help her with any task. She meant well and always kept Evangaline's best interest in mind with zero qualms or hesitations. If all Evangaline had to do to show her gratitude was spend thirty minutes teaching Wren how to apply winged eyeliner with a pen instead of the ink pot contraption the fae used, then Evangaline would do it in a heartbeat!

Wren picked up the art of a cat eye in nearly two seconds flat. Painting her own eyes with huge Egyptian style wings that brought out her stunning narrow almond-shaped eyes. Evangaline was slightly envious of Wren's ability to gain the skill so quickly. Being that Evangaline spent all her college years looking like a drowned raccoon. But Wren's excitement only made her smile grow wider and wider till their laughter filled the gilded bath chamber.

Finally, after her girl time with Wren—which Evangaline needed desperately—she donned her gift from Darrin. A gown made of a sparkling fabric so black it swallowed any light that passed through it. Faint flicks of holographic gold sparkles glittered as though the stars themselves were bestowed upon the dress, twinkling with each swish of the gown. Every constellation and shooting star flowed around her hips and knees till it cascaded in a pool of liquid darkness at her feet.

The bodice dipped into a slight v with off the shoulder sleeves that cascaded down the backs of her arms and draped to the floor like waterfalls of pure night.

Adorned with shimmering gold crystals that swirled up the center of the garment—as well as down the pooling sleeves—in an intricate baroque style scrollwork, Evangaline knew she would stand apart from the bright colors the Capital nobility tended to wear. A slit in the center of the billowing ball gown allowed freedom of movement as well as a little glimpse at her dazzling lace up gold and black heels.

She didn't admire her reflection in her mirror for long. The image staring back at her was beautiful and regal. Not at all how she felt. But she still stared ahead anyway, hoping that somehow, she would find the courage within her heart to feel one day as powerful as she looked.

Once she was ready, adorned in all her finery, she walked out to the living room. Greeted by her cadre of boys, their warm, smiling faces hid nothing as they took in her regality.

After Shaw and Des let her cry and mess up their armor with her tears, she ordered up some food and wine and told them to start pre-gaming. She said nothing to give away her secret but told them it was going to be a long night and they all needed to let loose a bit before.

Of course, like moths to a flame, the other boys showed up in full force. Especially after Aadi heard through a gossipy servant that "General Bastian and Prince Ryder had a standoff by the human woman's quarters." How the maid even knew was beyond Evangaline's knowledge.

The boys were practically six older brothers and the second their little sister was even close to danger; they swarmed like a pack of hungry lions to a zebra carcass. They said they showed up because of the food, but Evangaline knew they all didn't want to leave her alone, knowing Bastian was trying to claim her again.

Something apparently many fae did when they were attracted to another. A concept that was both primitive and disgusting in Evangaline's opinion. Yet again, maybe if she loved the man claiming her—or even felt a fraction of admiration—she might find it endearing. *Might*, being the key word!

Despite it all, the boys were to be working the ball, so they all only had a glass of wine with lunch, but promised to get hammered once the ball was over. Having neatly stacked the bottles on the table in a formation that reminded her of bowling pins, they instead chose to gorge themselves on food.

She laughed with them, indulging in a piece of her favorite cake while describing what bowling was and how fun it would be to install an alley in the palace. "When we drink all the wine from the bottles later, I will show you!" She quipped before running off to get ready with Wren.

"Damn, Lady E." Shaw whistled as she walked out into the living room.

Shaw was her hype man through and through. She loved it. And him. All of them. She loved all six of the men who stood before her, beaming with pride and happiness.

All of them were clad in their shimmering copper armor. The ruby hilts of their blades peeked over their backs, reminding Evangaline of the first time she saw Chloe in her royal regalia.

If only Chloe were here to see this.

No doubt Chloe would be beaming, too. However, knowing Chloe, her gown would hug her curves and sparkle with the rays of the sun just to steal all of Evangaline's limelight.

Des approached her with a knowing glance. He was thinking the same thing, too. He didn't need to know she was the crown princess to know that she was missing Chloe. By the slight glossiness clinging to his eyes, so was he. "Shall we?" He asked, extending an arm.

She plastered her best fake smile back on her done up face, suppressed her nerves, and took his arm.

Time to become a princess. Officially.

Chapter Thirty-Seven

The halls were bustling with an exuberant energy. More people hustled around the palace grounds than Evangaline had seen in the three weeks she had been in Celadonia. Faces passed in blurs of movement, too fast to pinpoint names and stations. She took in the madness with one sobering thought—it was all for her. All these people buzzed around the palace, summoned by their king, all to learn she was their crown princess. She worked hard to contain her panic and focus on taking deep breaths.

It will all be over soon. She heard her mother's voice in her head like a ghost of calming energy, reminding her of the ending to the prison sentence of the bargain.

Her mind still teetered on a saw of uncertainty. Return to Vitalis and live her life in the background where she felt safe in the shadows? Or stay and commit to her role as Crown Princess of Celadonia and battle her natural instincts to *not* command the spotlight? She shook the thought free and focused on the scene before her, pressing the matter off until tomorrow when a safe return to Vitalis was even an option.

Courtiers glided to the ballroom with their dazzling opulence from every kingdom.

Servants wandered aimlessly, trying to get a glimpse at the festivities, while others ran food and wine to and from the kitchens.

The armed guards took up their posts and paced around the castle in meticulously choreographed formations.

It was no surprise Darrin took extra precautions, having every guard working the event, knowing the significance of the night. The recent attack and threat didn't give anyone warm and fuzzy feelings. Plus, there was no telling how the kingdoms and their royals would react to Evangaline becoming heir to the throne. Would Ryder suddenly hate her? Would he stop looking at her with his gentle, sparkling blue eyes like she was something special? Or would he look at her with disdain, the same way he looked at Darrin?

"Why do you care what he thinks?" Evangaline whispered to herself as she entered a dimly lit room where Darrin stood waiting for her. Des bowed to the king and winked to Evangaline with a cheeky grin before taking his leave.

"My little princess, all grown up," the king said as a single tear streamed down his face at the sight of Evangaline. He wiped it quickly, covering his emotions. Though, the pride that he had for her shone like a beacon of light from a lighthouse on a cloudy night.

He might not be her dad in actions. He didn't raise her or see her grow up, but she couldn't help but feel something for him, as much as she denied it weeks ago.

Pity? Remorse? She could not place the mixture of feelings, but whatever it was, it filled her with a warmth that made her beam right back at him. She wanted to make him proud. From the first day they met, she had the nagging urge to make him see the potential she had. Sure, she might have been a reserved person by nature, but she longed—*no*, felt deep within each and every strand of DNA in her body—that something great was waiting for her.

He clearly loved his only daughter and wanted to be there for her in her adolescence, but the cosmos had other plans for them.

Despite it all, the fates worked their magic and brought them together now, and the present was what she wanted to focus on. The past was heavy with regret and the future was looming with fear, but the present was up for interpretation.

Evangaline did not know what tomorrow was going to hold, but she had this moment now. With the man who gave her life and loved her despite never knowing her fully, who protected her when she did not even know she needed protection. So if this were to be her last chance to be his little princess, she was going to cherish it.

Evangaline wiped another tear from his face. "Thank you for the gown," she muttered as she gripped his hands, smiling gratefully.

"Only the best for my daughter," he whispered. "Oh, that reminds me."

Abruptly, he dropped her hands and motioned for a man she hadn't seen standing against the door. In his hands was a wooden box carved intricately with a tree. The roots of the tree were carved deep into the top of the dark oak box and wound down around the sides, slithering into a heart-shaped lock in the center.

Once the servant presented the box to the king, Darrin removed an emerald flower shaped pin off his robe and delicately took her pointer finger. "Forgive me," he murmured as he poked her flesh to draw a bead of bright red blood. Evangaline winced as he smoothed her finger over the heart-shaped lock, covering it completely with her lifeblood.

One by one, the roots of the tree receded into the trunk on the lid and the box flung open with a miraculous whip, nearly blinding Evangaline with the contents.

Laying on a bed of blue silk sat a crown of sparkling diamonds that shone bright despite the low light of the room.

A lustrously encrusted rose sat nestled in the center of the tiara, flanked by rows of carefully crafted filigree leaves in circular clusters. Thousands of diamonds winked up at her, stealing the breath from her lungs.

Gently, the king retrieved the diadem from the box, excusing the deliverer of the treasure in the process. She peered at the young man's confused face as he hurried away from them before facing Darrin.

"This tiara was forged for the last crown princess born to this realm and has been the only tiara forbidden from any queen married into the bloodline through a quite nasty ward. Hence why I needed your blood to open the case. Mine would not have worked. Only a true female heir can wear it. You are the first since Tuatha herself daughter," the king told her, beaming with pride as he examined the crown in his hands.

She looked up at him stupefied, "There have really been no other daughters before me?"

Letting out a closed lip laugh, "I'm afraid the royal bloodline found the formula for princes and did not master that of the stronger sex till you." Darrin said with a sly wink.

He raised the taira and placed it on Evangaline's head with grace and honor shining brightly in the red blotches marring his upturned cheeks.

She thought it would weigh more with the many diamonds that filled the fine silver details, but it was oddly light and comfortable. She hated just how right it felt once it settled onto her head. The aching tremor she had been feeling in her chest seemed to sing along with the whispered song of the tiara resting in her hair. In that moment, she felt all her anxiety rush back into her body. She couldn't do this. Maybe she could tell Darrin she felt unwell? A headache? A stomach bug? Diarrhea? Anything that would make it so she did not have to step out before the most elite fae in the realm and be announced as their crown princess. She'd grown comfortable in the shadows.

"The room is ready, Your Majesty." A guard called out as he bristled through the door.

Darrin nodded at the guard, excusing him with a grin. Her time to make up an excuse was over. She scanned Darrin's unwavering excitement and realized there was no escaping the threads of fate that brought her to this moment.

A lifetime of comfort in the background would never be possible again. The murmurs in her brain whispered, sending a course of jitters through her body. Evangaline clenched her hands into the starry fabric of her gown, trying to regain her composure.

"Alright, it's time." Darrin beamed and with that, her fate was set.

"All hail, His Majesty, Supreme King Darrin De of Celadonia, first of his name, son of Kalinite De and Mara, Ruler of the Realm."

A royal crier decreed as the massive copper doors of the beautifully decorated ballroom swung open to reveal Darrin and Evangaline.

Shit, that's a lot of people.

The domed room was adorned with golden candles and garlands of red, orange, and yellow roses that snaked along two massive tables interwoven with strands of diamonds and crystals alike. Every person had a place along the table, aside from four chairs that sat on a slightly elevated dais at the center of the room. A smaller version of Darrin's throne found itself nestled in the center, glinting jewels and all. Another jewel adorned chair—daintier, smaller—sat beside Darrin's. The back was carved in the shape of a rose covered in pink and green crystals and, of course, diamonds. *It wouldn't be within the Capital Palace if it did not have diamonds!* She thought, taking in the scene before her. Two other plain wooden chairs flanked the bedazzled ones, fading into the background compared to their counterparts.

Courtiers from all five kingdoms and the Capital filled the ballroom, dressed in their finest fashions. Some more opulent than others, but beautiful, nonetheless. Diamonds, and chiffon, and furs—all the finest varieties of garments that took Evangaline's breath away.

Evangaline began to sweat as all the eyes in the room fell on her. The human girl on the king's arm sporting a treasured royal tiara.

Did they know about the tiara, or was it just another secret her family harbored?

Her throat tightened with fear.

The king stopped just inside the massive doors and waited a beat.

A smile beamed from his face as he peeked down at Evangaline and then back up to the people of his realm.

No going back now!

"For the past twenty-five years, I have held a secret from my people, from you all." His voice echoed through the ballroom as he projected it loudly enough for all to hear, despite the room falling silent with his arrival. He could whisper and every single finely tuned fae ear would most likely hear what he had to say.

"I hope you accept my sincerest apologies in my omission. However, it was in the best interest of the kingdom. I did so, and I do not regret it one bit."

Squeezing Evangaline's hand lovingly, he looked to her as he spoke.

"Tonight, I present to you all my most prized treasure, the *first* daughter born to the entire realm of Celadonia. Tonight, I present to this realm Crown Princess Evangaline Rivers. Daughter of Supreme King Darrin De and Felicity Rivers of Vitalis, the first daughter of Celadonia, and the rightful heir to the throne."

For a brief moment, the room remained still. The words left to hang in the air. Not a breath was heard or the ruffle of a skirt. No one shouted or booed, which seemed like a good sign. But no one applauded or cheered either, not a good sign.

She stood in a purgatory of her people.

Evangaline didn't know what to do or think. So, she gazed around the room with her heart thrusting in vicious pulls against her chest. As she scanned, she could hear the blood thrashing through her body in her ears. Her mouth became incredibly dry and hear palms became incredibly clammy.

Catching wayward glances of various courtiers, she began to fear the worst. Why did she allow even a small part of herself to assume the fae would accept *her* as their crown princess? It was foolish.

Slight movement caught her eye from the back left side of the ballroom close to the dais. She turned in time to see Ryder sink to a knee, placing a hand across his chest and bow his head.

Evangaline stood in shock.

One by one, courtiers and royals alike curtscyed and dropped to their knees following the Prince of Shadow's lead, their left arms crossing over their chests, heads bowed.

Evangaline looked up at her father. Worry flooded her delicate features.

"It is a show of allegiance to you. To us. A sign of respect. You are the start of a significant change, daughter. I can feel it." The king then surprised her as he leaned in and kissed her on the forehead. It was the first time he openly showed his affection for her. That one small peck of his lips to her head calmed every anxious beat of her heart. For a brief second, she sank into the warmth of his love. "I am so proud of you," he whispered to her.

Her shoes clicked on the marble floor and propelled her forward on the king's arm as she trembled slightly. She felt as though at any moment someone would hiss at her and pelt her with a ripe tomato. But they didn't.

As they passed, those who bowed rose. One by one, taking her in with fresh eyes.

Some muffled whispers broke out in their wake, but still no tomato or any other ripened fruit. So, so far, so good.

Once they were at the front of the dais, Darrin turned to his people, released Evangaline, and threw his hands in the air, clapping them together with a jovial laugh. "Celebrate the arrival of your princess. Feast, drink, dance! We have much to celebrate tonight."

And with that, the band started playing and people buzzed about the room once more. Many acted as though they did not just hear the news of her becoming their princess.

She did it. Bargain fulfilled. There was no pulse of magic or anything to signal the bargain was fulfilled, but she could feel a weight be lifted off her shoulders. She felt lighter. She wondered if Darrin and her mom felt the same way?

"I shall be right back, daughter." Darrin whispered before he left to go speak with Bastian and a few other members of the court.

Bastian looked put together in his dark purple jacket and white pants. His hair was slicked back behind his delicately pointed ears. Despite how good he looked, his eyes were dark with ill intent. Something evil lurked behind his wicked smile as he watched Evangaline wring her hands nervously. A dark-haired fae woman clung to his meaty bicep like a leech. Her slender frame, her dark hair, and taut features gave her away as she sneered toward Evangaline. Instead of sneering back, Evangaline shook her head in a laugh. "Good luck with him, Waylay," she muttered under her breath.

Breaking Bastian's stare, Evangaline turned around, spotting Atlas and

Ryder both watching her with their own tenacious intent. The latter with a very unreadable countenance. But he looked every bit the beautiful prince she began to admire.

A circlet of black and silver carved with the phases of the moon, same as his dagger, sat upon his brow, just barely dipping into a shallow point on his forehead. His dark black glittering jacket nearly matched Evangaline's gown, save for the sparkling gold crystal detailing that adorned her dress. Instead, he opted for a metallic silver embroidery in an oddly similar swirling pattern.

His shadowy tattoos peeked slightly over the collar of his jacket, barely moving.

Gold and silver rings adorned many of the fingers that rested firmly on his bulging biceps as his arms crossed over his chest.

Atlas was the prince's opposite in every way. Clad in his signature white, he chose to wear a shimmering white jacket belted with an icy blue sash that perfectly matched his eyes. He reminded Evangaline of a fresh and sparkling sheet of untouched snow.

Evangaline's feet started walking to them before her brain could quiet. They drew her in with their magnetic pulls. There was a part of her that wanted nothing more than to run into the Prince of Shadows' arms and scream, *"I did it! I kept the secret!"* But she really didn't know him and that would be highly inappropriate no matter how much she craved his hold, so she opted for cool indifference instead. And a smile.

Unfortunately, halfway there, she was cut off by Lord and Lady Whittell. And their sneering daughter. *Delightful.*

"From the moment we saw you Evangaline, we knew you were special. Allow us to extend our hospitality and entertain you in our private residence some time. We are so fortunate to call you a dear friend, are we not Waylay?" Lady Whittell spewed, dipping into a half-assed curtsey. Her fraudulent face sneered into a smile that her daughter mirrored. The lady certainly did not mean anything that flowed from her viperous lips.

Evangaline wanted so very much to laugh and tell them to fuck right off and eat a bag of dicks instead of the meal provided, but she was now a princess, *formally*. She couldn't let her first impression be that of telling members of the royal court to choke on a dick. No matter how amusing that would be.

Lifting her chin to look down on the insufferable family, "That is most hospitable of you. I will be sure to stop by sometime in the future. I'm quite busy being a princess and all, but I will call upon you some time. Enjoy your evening." She walked away from them, rolling her eyes before they could open their treasonous mouths again, but the small scoff from the youngest Whittell was not lost to her ears.

She pointed at Ryder's almost matching jacket with a playful wince. "Apparently, we both have excellent fashion sense. But one of us is going to have to change …" she joked, shrugging her shoulders.

Ryder cocked his head at her with an almost angry air about him. "You are no lady indeed …"

Raising her eyebrows, "Nope," Evangaline said, popping the P.

"I mean no disrespect but calling you princess or Your Highness just doesn't seem right knowing how often you swear. That and how fitting a sword looks draped across your back. I still like Eva, it suits you. Strong, simple, beautiful. Unless you've come around on human whore …" Ryder said, the left side of his mouth quirking up, revealing that adorable dimple she knew lurked beneath all that brooding.

"Beautiful, huh?" She rose a mocking brow, "I'll allow Eva. I am, however, banning human whore. From existence. Forever. I'll make it a royal decree if I must," she said, smiling up at a grinning Ryder.

His smile sent butterflies soaring in her stomach alongside the pixies that Chloe once spoke of.

Atlas cut in, grabbing Evangaline by the shoulders, "*I* am banning that insufferable term! No decree necessary. Now, let me get a look at you!" He grabbed her hand and spun her around. Her sleeves and skirt twirled around her as a jovial giggle escaped her light pink lips.

It really *was* way too much fun to twirl in a ball gown.

She always admired Vitalian fashions but playing dress up was fun. She could get used to twirling in big dresses.

"I don't look ridiculous?" She muttered, coming to a stop.

"Absolutely not." Ryder spoke without a moment's delay, his piercing eyes trailing the length of her body and back up to her eyes, leaving a hot tension in their wake.

He slid his hands into his pockets coyly. A second later, Princess Ophelia pushed past him, followed closely by a lovely woman with golden braids that curled with gems just at the ends.

"Move you two! Quit hogging her! You have no idea how long I have waited for another princess to grace this bloody realm and take command. Lily and I are dying in this cesspit of testosterone. This one won't yield the crown to his sister, so I'm stuck alone at the top." She pointed over her shoulder to Ryder, who rolled his eyes with a laugh. "Your Highness, if you need anything please, I am at your service. Oh! How rude of me! This is my wife, Helena." Ophelia's words flowed like a song out of her mouth, mesmerizing Evangaline with each vowel.

Helena leaned forward, curtseying with her Grecian style lavender gown cascading across the floor.

Rising, Helena leaned into Evangaline. "We were growing tired of the sausage fest, can you tell? You are sent from the gods, I tell you!" She joked, pointing back at Ryder the same way her wife did.

"I heard that," Ryder quipped, cocking his head at the beautiful consort of the Princess of Mirth.

Evangaline laughed. "Thank you. Both of you. My best friend …" she paused, swallowing hard, "… My best friend liked to joke and remind me to always put 'chicks before dicks'," Air quotes surrounded Chloe's favorite phrase. "So, you two are already pretty high on my list just by not being dudes." Evangaline heard Shaw snort off to the side, where he took his post along the wall. "Anything *you* need, please don't hesitate." She laughed a breathy laugh.

Helena and Ophelia both laughed along with her, they were a gorgeous couple, holding onto one another with a love that transcended any love Evangaline had ever seen. Truly mesmerizing.

"Oh Ryder, you are no longer my favorite of the royals."

Ryder squinted at Ophelia. "I was your favorite?"

"Naw, you were just the prince who pissed me off the least." She laughed, hitting him in the chest. She was so lying. It was obvious they were close.

Evangaline laughed. "We are going to be *great* friends," she said to Ophelia and Helena. Winking up at Ryder.

"I'm wounded!" Ryder groaned, grasping his powerful chest playfully. It was a breath of fresh air to joke around with him and Ophelia. They welcomed her so easily.

Helena turned to him, rolling her eyes. "You'll heal."

Atlas peered up to the dais and nodded to the king, catching Evangaline's attention.

Sitting on his throne was King Darrin, beaming at Evangaline behind a golden cup of wine. Dulling the visual, however, was what sat next to the rose chair a seat away from her fae father, Bastian.

That left two chairs and Evangaline had a vague foreboding sense she knew exactly which of the chairs was hers.

Atlas leaned in. "Time to take our seats, dear."

"Alright." Evangaline replied with a shaky smile.

"Ladies, nephew, we shall see you later. The princess is much too busy to deal with the riffraff." Atlas joked with a wink, making Evangaline snicker. He steered Evangaline up the dais to the rose chair, right where she didn't want to be … next to Bastian.

Chapter Thirty-Eight

Six courses into the meal and they were showing no sign of slowing. Evangaline's bodice grew tighter and tighter with every bite she took. The idea of fitting another morsel of food into her mouth made her want to heave up the previous six dishes and splay herself on the table like a spit roasted pig, apple and all.

As she sat upon the dais, she expertly avoided any interaction with Bastian. He attempted conversation, but she shut every attempt down with a smile for show and clipped or one-word answers. Occasionally, a grunt found its way out if words failed.

"You look ravishing," he purred in one attempt.

"I know," she replied.

"The meal is delightful, is it not?" He said on another.

"Yep."

"Dance with me later?" Was his last try at gaining her favor.

"Shut up," Evangaline whispered with a smile.

Luckily, Darrin entertained her the majority of the time, saving her the task of shunning Bastian. He told her about various fae from other courts and descriptions of the various delicacies they were eating. Menial conversation topics, but ones that she was grateful for because they kept Bastian away.

As she sat there in her jewel encrusted seat, she searched around the room for the cadre in her spare time between courses. It was like a game of *Where's Waldo*, but with her attractive fae friends instead of a svelte man in red and white. She found Aadi and Charlie by the doors instantly thanks to Charlie's bright crimson hair. Murray and Lukas, ever the pair, were stationed beside one another to her left, with Des and Shaw to the right in the same positioning. Hands clasped behind all of their backs and those very backs against the wall.

Conveniently, Des was positioned right behind the Prince of Shadows and Princess of Mirth, with Shaw just over Ryder's left shoulder.

Catching her watching him, Shaw gave Evangaline a wink and a wry smile. Then mouthed *"Princess* E, sounds good." Evangaline grinned back, shrugging her shoulder, sending her own wink back at the guard.

Ryder, not-so-secretly, watched Evangaline play her little eye spy game and followed her sightline to the source of her smile.

The prince sat casually with his arm draped on the back of Princess Ophelia's chair, his other hand preoccupied holding his reflective copper chalice of wine.

He turned, seeing the royal guard smiling back at Evangaline, catching Shaw completely off guard. Wiping the bright smile on Shaw's face into an expression of stoic nervousness instead.

Ryder said something to Shaw and then shook his hand as though they were good buddies.

After that, Shaw fell back into formation, releasing a puff of air that made Evangaline laugh to herself.

Evangaline looked away from the two men and went to reach for her wine glass when the king spoke, drawing her attention to her left as he stood. She held her breath under the gaze of the people staring her way and focused instead on her fae father.

"As you may remember, earlier this evening I said we had much to celebrate." He placed his hand on Evangaline's shoulder, "With all of you in attendance I am happy to not only announce the arrival of my beloved daughter—who finally returned to me—but also her betrothal."

Betrothal?

Evangaline's smile disappeared in an instant, her brows furrowing with silent questions. Her hands fell to her lap and began to shake. Her hearing grew fuzzy, as though her brain was sending out signals to the rest of her body saying, "*stop paying attention!*"

Was she even breathing?

Darrin turned to Evangaline and smiled, then he looked past her, "General Bastian, you shall make my daughter exceptionally happy."

Bastian!

There was no way she heard that right.

She was going to throw up. Yep, all six courses were coming up!

Evangaline looked around the room to her friends with a frantic look. The cadre all grew tense, their faces wrought with the same surprise that graced her features.

Des's face grew so dark and full of hatred that death itself would tremble in his presence. His golden features dulled into a putrid gray as he resembled a vengeful god, ready to draw first blood instead of a soldier sworn to protect.

Evangaline swallowed hard, her breathing becoming so heavy she felt her lungs physically constrict in pain as she tried to gather as much oxygen as possible.

She looked at Atlas down the table as the crowd cheered. Bastian grabbed her hand, hauling her to her feet with a tug, tearing her frantic eyes from Atlas.

Atlas was clearly just as surprised as Evangaline, but did nothing to stop the announcement. Did he know?

Was this what Bastian's correspondence was alluding to? Was this the proposal he had for the king? Was this what he had planned all along? To weasel his way into becoming royal through a marriage to her? All the signs were right there in front of her and still she was blind to see his plan.

She thought back to their time spent in lust and suddenly felt dirty. Felt used and betrayed. Even as she reminded herself she used him as an escape, he used her and took from her to gain fame and wealth. To gain a crown upon his head.

"The next celebration we shall all have together shall be for the wedding of the crown princess." Darrin's voice was drained out in her ears as a sharp high pitch noise began taking over. Her hands went completely numb, and she felt the tears of hate and scorched trust resting on her eyelashes, ready to splash down her face at any moment.

They betrayed her. The king and Bastian both. They did not give her a choice as they promised. They all but forced her hand, like she was a goat, to be sold to the nearest farmer. She was chattel to them. She was nothing more than a pawn in the game of men.

Lost in her own introspection, she didn't realize Bastian had wrapped his arms around her waist and kissed her. His frigid grip soaked through her gown, locking her in place for him to use further.

Once she noticed she was being kissed, she backed up and placed her hand on Bastian's chest to push him back. Her hands shook as she applied pressure, but all he did was smile.

"I told you. You are *mine*." Bastian whispered in her ear as he turned them to face the crowd, eating up the well wishes and congratulations from the many courtiers applauding his conquest.

As the music picked back up and people began mingling and dancing, Evangaline slipped her hand free of Bastian's and made her way down the dais to the exit.

Briskly, Evangaline raced past Shaw and Ryder. As the prince pushed his chair back, standing abruptly to face her, she dodged him, not able to look into his worried eyes. Des reached for her hand, but she drew it away, out of his reach, and kept walking.

An obstacle course of males trying to block her path to fresh air.

She smiled half-heartedly at courtiers as they approached her and uttered their welcomes and congratulations in one breath, ignorant of the panic attack latching onto her nervous system.

Suppressing her shuddering and tears, Evangaline politely thanked them and excused herself.

The room began to tilt and shake with each shallow breath she took. Her heart was beating in her chest so fast she could hear it in her ears. Her blood sloshed about her body like thick mulled wine shifting in a tumbling barrel.

Finally, after what felt like hours, she made it into the hall and threw the back of her hand over her mouth to suppress a sob. Evangaline turned left where she knew there was a small verandah and started walking so fast her feet seemed to barely touch the ground. She needed the fresh air, desperately.

Chapter Thirty-Nine

Evangaline's heels rapidly clicked on the marble floor, trembling her legs with each reverberation. The lights were dim as she jogged her way to the verandah. It took every bit of strength to remain upright, but she carried on.

She could see her destination in the distance. Her pulse eased slightly at the thought of being outside in the fresh air, just as a hand grabbed her arm and shoved her into the wall, cracking her head on the stone.

Aches pulsed through her skull from the force of the impact. Her vision blurred slightly, making her see stars as she squeezed her eyelids shut.

His scent hit her before his words. Just as it always did.

"Where are you off to, *wife*?" Bastian crooned into her ear. Each breath he took was hot and prickly against her sweat slicked skin. "Getting cold feet already?" he laughed.

A single tear slipped free of its cage and streamed down her face.

Shakily, she whispered, barely containing her rage, "What did you do, Bash?"

"I asked your father for your hand. Told him I already enjoyed the taste of his sweet little girl. May have told a few lies like you were madly in love with me, but those obstacles can be overcome with time. He wanted you here … I want power. It was a win-win. Plus, there wasn't going to be a line of eligible bachelors yearning for a sullied human who opened her legs to anyone, now was there?" She opened her mouth to argue his false accusations, but he beat her to vocalization, "Not after I've already claimed you publicly. Besides, I told him it would make you happy … you weaken him, you know. The second I told him you said yes to my proposal already, he welcomed me to the family with open arms and a glass of century old whiskey. You should be thanking me, really, the other suitors were way worse."

Pinning her arms to the wall with his hands, he dragged long, tedious kisses along her jaw and down her neck. Then slowly, in a punishing display of possession, his tongue darted from his traitorous lips and licked the tears from her cheeks like a heathen.

Evangaline struggled against his grip. "Bash, you're hurting me. Please stop. Let me go. We can talk about this."

It was then she could feel it, even beneath all the layers of her gown, just like the last time in the forest. He pushed into her, his hardness pressed against her stomach as he growled low and menacing, "As my wife, it is your duty to service your husband."

She struggled to free her hands but was unable to. His grip only got tighter and more painful with each attempt to gain freedom. Evangaline felt weak, emotionally and physically, and she hated it. She bucked and tried to pull free, but his grip was unrelenting. Chloe would be so disappointed in her.

"I am *not* your wife," Evangaline growled through her tears.

"Eh, semantics. We can talk … *after* you show your *fiancé* some respect." He breathed against her chest as he assaulted her with more languid kisses and bites.

With all the force she could muster, Evangaline thrusted her knee into his crotch in a last-ditch effort to disengage his taught grip on her wrists.

But he dodged the crippling strike, forcing her knee to contact the hard expanse of his thigh instead.

"Get off me Bash! Now!" she demanded, steeling her voice the best she could as the tears streamed her face.

Bastian laughed, then crushed his lips to hers, quieting her sobs and pleads.

She struggled some more, throwing her knee into his thigh, her heeled toe into his boot, and biting down on his tongue as it explored her mouth. Anything to get him off of her. Her brain began preparing for the worst. Her eyes clenched tight as she locked up, becoming dead weight against the wall.

Suddenly, Bastian was hauled off her with enough force to rip the air from his lungs and cut her lip on his teeth as he sought purchase in her kiss.

Evangaline tried to regain her breathing but was unable to. She didn't want the whole ball to run out and see her being sexually assaulted by her recently betrothed. Her lungs had other ideas, however, and she couldn't seem to regain her composure. Not even a little bit.

Would they even believe me if I told the people of this assault? She thought to herself, thinking back to all the applause Bastian got moments ago at the announcement.

A small touch of a finger to her cheek ripped her from her thoughts. She flinched. Through her tears, she saw Atlas, along with Des and Ryder.

Des grabbed Evangaline's elbow, helping her stay upright as Ryder slammed Bastian to the floor and let his fist connect with the general's nose. A sharp crack echoed through the hallway, followed by a grunt of pain.

Des quickly glanced over his shoulder, eyes wide at the sight of Ryder looming over Bastian, then back to Evangaline, looking her over for wounds.

Her wrists were aching, no doubt would bruise in the morning. Red marks marred her wrists where Bastian held them against the wall. Evangaline's head throbbed, but was only a distant ache compared to the way her heart was pounding in an agonizing cadence within the hollows of her chest.

"Get. Up." Ryder growled with his back facing Evangaline, Des, and Atlas. She could see the tension in the firm line of his shoulders. And the rough grit in his voice gave away how much he longed to maim Bastian. There would be no objections from Evangaline should Ryder decide to decimate Bash in a cloud of shadow and rage.

Slowly, darkness crept up the walls, snuffing out the starbursts of light shining in the glass sconces. Ryder's shadows swirled around his torso and neck all the way through his fingertips, where balls of dark ether gathered in cyclones.

Bastian slumped himself against the far wall and laughed, as though the menacing silhouette of the Prince of Shadows was a joke. From all Eva could see through her tears, Ryder was the exact opposite of a joke. He looked more like a harbinger of death and darkness than a joke.

Des stepped before Evangaline as a shield, watching as Bastian rose to his feet as commanded.

"Times haven't changed, huh, Prince? Still brawling over bitches. Aren't we?"

Ryder didn't respond to the taunt, he simply prowled closer to Bastian with a regal grace. His steps remained silent with a deadly purpose.

Nose to nose, the men stared each other down. Bastian had more bulk than Ryder, but Ryder was more powerful in every sense of the word and was not small by any means.

Suddenly, surprising Evangaline as she peered out behind Des's shoulder, Ryder smiled. He shifted as though he was going to back away when his hands thrust forward, balling up Bastian's purple jacket. Where his dark cyclones touched, material burned with a black flame. Lifting the general into the air and slamming him into the wall, cracking the stone beneath Bastian's bulbous head, Ryder growled low and deep.

Rumbling into Bastian's ear, "Call her a bitch one more time and I will let my shadows feast on you, *General*. It will be slow and painful, and you will beg for my mercy before death finally claims you." He let the threat hang between them for a beat. "Now, I am going to set you down and you are going to walk back into that room as though nothing happened here. You aren't going to *speak* to Eva. You will not *touch* Eva. You will not *look* at Eva. Got it?"

Bastian didn't answer, his face wringing with unrestrained anger. The promise of retribution lurking in his swampy eyes.

Evangaline flexed her hands at her sides, trying to regain any semblance of feeling. Willing herself to breathe despite her chest throbbing incessantly. A feeling so intense within her body sang, begging her to release the fury and fear that sunk deep within her.

Somehow, her tears stopped falling, and she had settled into an anxious sort of rage. The same rage she found herself in the night she lost Chloe and met Ryder.

Des remained before her, feet planted sturdily, his back inches from her chest, caging her in against any potential attacks or fall outs. A white handled blade graced his fingers, ready for a fight.

Atlas stood still, facing Ryder and Bastian, but to her side. His hand slightly grazed her own in reassuring strokes that felt paternal and caring. He knew better than to get between the two powerful fae males ready to end one another. His party trick held nothing compared to Ryder's shadow magic and Bastian's brawn.

Slowly, Ryder placed Bastian on the floor and smoothed out the general's coat before stepping back.

Bastian snarled and looked up at Ryder, then over to Evangaline.

"Eh … what did I say?" Ryder snarled at Bastian, almost like he was training a dog. His voice was powerful and almost taunting in its convictions.

Without another glance or word, Bastian ran his hands through his chestnut hair and sauntered back to the party as though nothing happened. Following the prince's orders like the obedient dog, he was trying to masquerade as.

Once Bastian was around the corner, Des relaxed. He let out a long breath as though the entire time he was holding it balled up in his chest. His blade found its sheath on his thigh.

Evangaline put a reassuring hand on his back and then stepped around him. Trying to get her breathing in check as well.

"My dear, please tell me you are alright." Atlas finally spoke frantically, grabbing her hands.

Evangaline flinched at the contact but did not pull her hands away.

As Ryder turned to face Evangaline, his shadows slowed, and the darkness slid from the walls, letting the lights pop back up with their dim yellow starbursts until all the darkness seeped across the floor and back into the Prince of Shadows.

His eyes landed on her hands in Atlas's and the bright red marks marring her wrists. Beneath a hint of worry, shadows of vengeance swam. His jaw held tight and ticked with the anger he was holding in for her sake.

It took a moment, but finally Evangaline realized what Atlas asked her. She gazed perplexed at the white-haired fae before pulling her hands from his and speaking, "Like fuck I'm alright! Did you know?" Silence lingered in the hall. "Atlas tell me. Did you fucking know?" She yelled.

Atlas remained quiet. His down-turned gaze gave away his guilt. He did not need to speak for her to see the truth written on the pinched features of his face.

Evangaline shook her head and turned on her heels towards the verandah.

"Fuck, Atlas!" She said, her anger singeing each word. "And to think I thought we were friends."

She flung the French doors open, allowing the bitter chill to seep into her skin and pebble the flesh that trembled with rage and fear. Her body began to hurt, and her tears began to cloud her eyes once more.

The arches and pillars surrounding her were clad in beautiful mosaics of climbing roses and trees that enamored her the first time she saw it. Now each mosaic piece held the sickness of her evening. A beautiful masterpiece covered with grime.

Silently, the three men joined her. Allowing her time and silence to compose her thoughts, but not the privacy of being alone.

"Did he honestly tell the king I slept with him to secure the marriage?" Evangaline quietly asked, unable to look at the men behind her.

"I am unaware of that. I knew your father tossed about the idea of a marriage to get you to stay prior to your retrieval from Vitalis. I knew not to whom or why. If Bastian assured your father of the union and of your entanglement, then I am sure your father saw no other options but to wed you to Bastian." Atlas replied, as though he were giving a lesson. Maybe he was a lesson as to how naïve she was. She trusted blindly. She allowed beautiful words and kind smiles to guile her into handing over her body on a silver platter.

Evangaline laughed as she bent down to take off her shoes. "Three weeks. I was supposed to fulfill a bargain that I didn't have a say in. Claim my crown and decide if I wanted to go. And in three weeks, I have kept my word and every promise I made. Yet, in the fucking process, been attacked by a demon beast, assaulted *twice now*, buried my best friend, and now married off like I am someone's possession. To the very man who sought to take what was not freely given, might I add."

Finally, getting the straps untied, she tossed her shoes on the floor with the force of her anger. She turned to Atlas. A simmering fire lurked behind the blues and greens of her eyes. "I will say this once, Atlas, and you can relay it to Darrin. I am no one's possession or pawn. No promise of marriage will seal my own decisions. Now, I will be leaving tomorrow, whether my *father* or *fiancé* likes it or not. I am going back to Vitalis. And that is the end of it!"

Des stepped forward, grabbing Evangaline's hand, "Please Evie …" His voice broke. A tear streamed down his reddened cheek. "I know you are broken. So am I. So are Shaw and Aadi, Murray and Lukas. Hell, even Charlie, despite him still acting like an ass … but we need you here. We need each other. We've already lost Chloe. We can't lose another member of the group. And the realm can't lose their princess. You are our heir." He tried to smile through his pleading words.

Seeing Des cry shattered Evangaline. The last bit of her soul she thought wasn't broken obliterated the second that tear streamed down his cheek. He had been her rock through everything. Since Chloe passed, he remained strong for her. She never considered how she might have been his rock, too.

She lunged and wrapped her arms around his waist, nuzzling her cheek into his chest plate. "Des, I am so tired. I don't want the little voices in my head to win, but they are *winning*, and I can't fight them anymore." Evangaline somberly choked, allowing her tears to mirror Des's. "I can't stay here. I am not safe."

She pulled back reluctantly, bent down and picked up her shoes in one hand, dangling the glittering heels by the strap on one finger.

She faced the expanse of grass and then the forest with its ruffling leaves envisioning the whisp out there watching her. She loved the forest and the land surrounding her.

"I can't tell you how many times over these last few weeks I thought I could make this place my home. Don't get me wrong, there were just as many times that I dreamed of going back to Vitalis. Hell, my sister probably had my niece already, and I missed it. That thought alone hurts," Evangaline smiled at the thought of her sister becoming a mom. Then faced Des, tears leaking down her cheeks through puffy red eyes. So much for Wren's masterful makeup.

"The truth is, Des, I have been running toward this notion—this feeling—of *home* my entire life. The safety of it. The comfort and warmth that only authors seem to accurately describe. I have been searching for this missing piece … for this part of my heart that has always yearned for more. I have waited for good things to fall into my lap, and then this all happened, and it was scary and hard. I never wanted power or fame. I wanted strength, yes. I wanted to be bold and fierce. I wanted to be courageous. I wanted love. I wanted to be happy. God, I wanted to be happy so bad. I started to want to be happy *here*. But it turns out I'm just as broken here as I am there. I tried to channel my pain into some kind of power like you told me to, but I am just too tired to try anymore."

"There's still so much here for you …" Des added quietly. "Don't let them ruin all the good that can come from all of this. Evie, you are someone they will write stories about one day. That's how epic you are. I knew it the moment Chloe brought you to our table. You just need to keep fighting those voices in your head that are telling you that you aren't worth all the good that awaits you."

She walked over to the soldier before her and placed a hand around his cheek to rub away his tears while a shattered smile shook her face. "Chloe was so lucky to have you. No wonder she loved you as much as she did. Even if she was too afraid to tell you. You have been an amazing friend and I will never, in my life, forget you, Des. But it's best if I left. I am not as strong as you think I am."

He sniffled, "No. You are stronger."

She dropped her hand and stared into the sorrow of her friend's tears. Evangaline spent her entire life perfecting her mask of stability. Of showing the world she wasn't cracking. Very few saw through her façade. The fact that Des had firsthand accounts of her pain and still believed with his whole heart that she was some noble warrior was earth shattering. It felt like a lie. The metaphorical foundation beneath her feet once more cracked open and threatened to swallow her whole. She did not feel capable of becoming the woman Des believed she could be. She did not want to disappoint him, and that fear alone forced her to take a step back.

Celadonia was beautiful. It held a warmth she never felt in all of her years in Vitalis. But it also brought forth a peril that, in only three weeks, proved she was not strong enough, physically or mentally, to withstand.

Swallowing heavily. She wiped her face and made her way to the door, ready to pack her things and request the next portal to New York City, when Ryder reached out, grabbing her left hand with his own, "Wait!"

Chapter Forty

The moment Ryder's hand wrapped around her own, a torrent tidal wave of shimmering golden light rushed forth surrounding them in warmth and peace. A light so bright, their eyes strained to focus, forcing them closed. The rays of the sun itself shot from their conjoined hands, encircling them in its steady calmness.

Evangaline's arm started tingling. The thrumming in her chest echoed so loud she felt seconds away from a heart attack. Her previous grief and anxiety washed away under the wave of light, leaving only the security of Ryder's hold and the caress of his skin.

She felt the ground tremble under her feet and Ryder's hand tighten on her own in response.

Finally, Evangaline opened her eyes and peered up at his annoyingly perfect face and incredulously felt her heart thump even faster within the confines of her meager body.

The butterflies in her stomach fluttered with a renewed vigor, as though Ryder's touch alone inspired them to dance about her chest and core.

Dimming lighter and lighter, the gold glow faded until the only light once more was coming from the moon high above them. The air shifted from the chilly autumn air to a warm, breezy caress on the exposed skin around Evangaline's collar bones. She felt safe, warm, at ease despite the events of the day. The feeling she just told Des she longed for sank deep into the hollowness of her bones. Filling her with a satisfaction she had never felt before. *Home.*

The puzzle piece of belonging that she searched her entire life for settled into place.

Ryder's eyes never left her own, his beautiful cobalt blue irises twinkling with hidden galaxies.

Both of their breathing was labored as though they ran a marathon.

For a moment, they were lost in one another.

In their own euphoria, the world around them stopped spinning. The stars froze in their state of twinkle and the florescent glow of the moon became a spotlight focused just on their beings. It was a divine moment designed just for them.

Evangaline felt as though she had run fifteen miles, heavy and exhausted but also strangely whole.

Evangaline gazed at Ryder like he wasn't a stranger from a foreign land but like he was a sanctuary, someone safe and familiar that she had known intimately her entire life. Her pulse thrummed a beat identical to his through their conjoined hands.

"Holy shit," Des whispered, snapping Evangaline and Ryder out of their hypnosis and sending the universe back into its rotation. Their spotlight fell away and the Earth began to spin again.

Evangaline studied Des's stupefied expression, following his eyeline to hers and Ryder's joined hands, still firmly clasped around one another.

"What is that?" Fearfully, she pulled her hand free of Ryder's and dropped her shoes to the ground in a shuttering thud.

Around her left arm was a marking, a tattoo … but also not.

Starting from her shoulder wrapping down to her hand spiraled a winding copper line. The metallic band shined and glistened with an iridescent glow as she examined the mark marring her porcelain skin.

Leading down her arm and stopping right at her ring finger where two bands now shimmered with an eight-pointed star joining them, right in the center. They shimmered and gleamed in their metallic state, aside from the star that twinkled on its own like the diamonds resting in the crown atop her head.

"What did you do?" Evangaline muttered, studying her arm.

Ryder studied his hand closely, examining the same markings on his ring finger. "Eva …" he rolled his sleeve up his forearm quickly exposing his own line of glistening copper ink shining against his tanned skin.

His shadows swirled around the mark as though they were curiously trying to determine the new addition to the prince's body.

Atlas stepped forward, taking Evangaline's hand, studying her arm like it was an ancient relic long buried beneath time within the crust of the earth. "He did nothing to you, dear. I can't believe what I am seeing." Atlas began to chuckle to himself, giddy like a little boy. His low breathy excuses for laughter only bolstered Evangaline's growing distress.

Ryder stepped forward, gently removing Evangaline's hand from Atlas's and holding it tight in his own, blocking Evangaline with his muscular form from his old uncle.

"Do you not feel it, boy? Hell, you are acting like it, blocking her away from me. Protecting her from the gaze of any other male." Atlas said with a genuine smile growing on his face, his tone haughty and coated with an edge of repugnance.

"Feel what?" Ryder snarled at his uncle.

Atlas laughed again, rubbing the back of his head, messing up his snowy hair. He walked over to a bench and sat down, covering his gaping mouth with his hand, rubbing his jaw in indignation.

Des then stepped forward with his hands up in surrender to Ryder, his look of awe and merriment changing the tears that once beaded in his melancholic eyes to ones of bewildered joy.

In one breath, Des whispered, a single tear cascading down his reddened cheek to the corner of his mouth that was ticking up in a smile. "You've been fated."

Chapter Forty-One

The corners of Evangaline's lips started to slant upward as she glanced back and forth between Des, Ryder, and Atlas. Not from a sense of joy or happiness, no, not from that at all. Instead, she smiled with the realization that she was in a bad dream. All she had to do was wake up at any moment and return to her life as usual. No crowns, no betrothals, no bargains, no being fated. *This is all a bad dream,* she told herself as she slammed her eyes closed and took one deep breath after another.

It was when she opened her eyes and took in the six-foot something fae man before her that reality slapped her in the face yet again.

Pure astonishment radiated from Ryder's face as he took in Evangaline. His eyes sparkled with a hopeful kind of fear as he took her in. Staring at Evangaline, occasionally glancing at their matching markings, he scanned her, almost contended. If the smirk gracing his lips was an indicator, this recent development was somehow good news to him.

The look on her face and the tug of her supple lips made his stomach do flips on itself, but the sad fire burning in her eyes filled his heart with a sense of dread. He knew what was about to come, and a small part of him broke at the face of the woman that fate gave to him as a blessing from the heavens. Evangaline's hands tremored, and her eyes took on a disbelieving grace, but it was the small joking smile that spread across her lips that gave him pause.

Not obeying his instincts to wrap her in his arms and hoard her for himself. Ryder simply watched her.

Evangaline was in utter disbelief.

Bubbling from the depths of her throat, Evangaline laughed. Her laughter echoed into the night as the thrumming in her chest grew louder and louder. She had cried and suffered enough torment for one night. This was just the whipped cream on the shit sundae. She could only find herself with the ability to laugh at the twists and turns fate has thrust upon her.

"You're fucking joking, right?"

Swaying on her feet, her laugh faded as none of the men surrounding her joined in. They didn't laugh, didn't smile, in fact they barely moved.

It was always in the silence that words spoke the loudest. This wasn't a dream to wake up from. It was in that moment of silence, staring into the pale blue eyes of Atlas, that she knew the fates and gods decided for her. Once more, her choice was taken from her by a force bigger than her. Evangaline was left at the mercy of others once more. She felt trapped.

A bargain forced her to the land of the fae and just as she was free of that binding magic, just when she was free to return to a life without the gravity of a realm weighing her down, she was thrust into a completely new type of binding magic. One that meant a lot to the fae of Celadonia.

Sure, Ryder was hands down attractive, his strong angular face and high cheekbones, made her weak in every part of her body not just her knees.

Curiosity of his shadows alone made her want to reach out and touch them as they glided on the hard planes of his chest. All she wanted to do was run her finger down his muscles and see how his shadows felt under the pad of her finger, to see how they reacted to her touch.

And his eyes! Gazing into his gorgeous, intoxicating eyes, had her lost in the depths of their sapphire blue churning seas. His changing irises filled her with a warmth that did nothing but give her hope.

But this, *this* was absolutely insane! There was no way that the two of them were some great omens of change. That they—a fae male and half human woman—bore a love grander than any other kind of love. That they were two souls entwined in fate—destined for one another. It all sounded absurd. Her brain could not wrap itself around the mark on her arm. Could she grow to love the Prince of Shadows? Sure. Possibly. *There's no debating it, you will,* her subconscious spoke as she tried telling herself how crazy the notion of being fated was.

Evangaline looked up at Ryder, searching for any kind of assurance. Maybe he had an answer to this madness? He was older, had more knowledge of the fae.

She gazed into those mind splitting eyes, begging him to do something or say something that could fix this. That could make sense of what had just happened, but there was nothing. A small shake of his head was her only assurance of his loss for words.

Throwing her gaze up to the ceiling and closing her eyes, as a tear slowly fell down her cheek, Evangaline knew deep inside her aching chest the answers she was searching for were stamped in copper on her left arm and hand. Things she wasn't willing to admit to herself just yet. Her place wasn't in Vitalis, her place was in Celadonia, and the gods just quite literally forced her hand.

Over the last three weeks, she grew to know that fact. She could feel it in the pain in her chest and the pixies in her stomach. She knew she belonged here, but then all the bad things started happening and she told herself that the feeling was wrong. She forced herself to ignore the sense of belonging that called to her in Celadonia due to her fear and gave into the homesick feeling and the familiarity of her quiet life before being a crown princess.

Taking a deep breath and steeling her expression to allow the mask of a happy princess to slip into place after coming to terms with the gravitas of her decision to stay.

With a nod to the gentleman silently watching her, Evangaline turned on her heels and left before any of them could catch her. Once more, she ran away from the hard conversation before her. Ran away from her problems because that was what she knew how to do.

Evangaline walked straight through the glass French doors as though nothing happened. She pretended Bastian hadn't been two seconds away from defiling her moments ago. She ignored the iridescent copper starbursts of light that reflected each whisp of light from the sconces she passed from her new permanent accessory. Evangaline made believe that there wasn't a fae prince that set her stomach on fire, a fae prince that the fates bound her to for eternity, standing speechless on a verandah.

Her gown swished behind her as she methodically passed through the grand white halls of the palace and straight to her rooms.

Her night was over.

Welcome home.

Chapter Forty-Two

The diamonds of Tuatha's tiara glistened against the pale streams of moonlight as Evangaline held the diadem in her left hand, her right holding the neck of a blue wine bottle. So long for having an afterparty with the boys. So long for bowling with wine bottles.

An hour turned into two, which turned into three, and still she sat on the floor of her balcony with her back pressed against the frosty glass of the French doors. The slightest echo of music pulsed through the air from the ball still raging deep within the palace.

The fireplace was crackling and burning when she made her way back to her rooms thanks to Wren, but she wished to be outside in the chilly air. Somehow the heat from the fire made Evangaline feel as though she was suffocating.

She needed the air to fill her lungs with the smell of the trees and dew of the grass filling her nose. She needed to hear the distant ruffle of the ever-changing leaves and the soft hum of the crickets singing their love songs to distract her from the present.

Surprisingly, she didn't cry or punch a wall upon returning. She just *was*. Still and un-moving.

It was an odd sensation—her mind being quiet. Her anxiety didn't flare up, numbing her fingers. Her depression didn't sweep her into a puddle on the floor. She just was. For the first time in her life, her problems and fears didn't consume her because they didn't truly scare her. Disbelief still clung to her psyche, but no fear or hatred.

The dull ache in her chest echoed the beats of her heart and thrummed a vibrating calmness that almost reassured her as opposed to pain her.

"Any room for one more?" Ryder's deep, velvety voice crooned from the open door.

Evangaline nearly dropped the tiara from her hand she jumped so hard at his sudden presence.

The Prince of Shadows certainly lived up to his moniker. His feet glided across the floor like the shadows that swirled about his chest, not leaving even the smallest noise in his wake.

"Holy shit!" Evangaline rasped, clutching the wine bottle and tiara to her chest. Earning a roguish smile from Ryder. "Sure," motioning to the floor.

As he crouched to the floor, he made a noise halfway between an exhale and a sigh.

A smile tugged on Evangaline's lips, "How old *are* you? You sound like an old man getting out of bed."

Ryder narrowed his eyes at her and leaned in, their shoulders touching. "Old enough to know numbing your pain with alcohol is only a temporary fix." His eyes flashed to the wine bottle being white knuckled between her fingers.

Pursing her lips, she turned to him and extended the bottle. "Speaking from experience, are we? You aren't wrong though, but it does help sometimes." She grinned. "And that doesn't answer my question."

He smiled at her, a genuine sorrowful smile, and grabbed the bottle, bringing it to his lips, taking a hearty gulp. He had discarded his jacket and circlet and rings. A black collared shirt clung to his muscles and let Evangaline know he, too, didn't return to the night's festivities.

Returning her gaze to the tiara, she placed it gently on her lap, letting it rest in the black and gold expanse of her gown.

"I'm five decades and three years old, to answer your question." He took another sip of wine as she hummed, a response clearly lost in thought. "So, how'd you like your first royal ball?" Ryder said, nudging into Evangaline's side.

Turning to face him, Evangaline gave the prince a face even the devil would run from. Ryder wasn't deterred, though. His dimple remained out despite the incredulous look. A chuckle even briefly escaped his lips.

Softening her features, "Well, I can tell you being *fated* to a fae prince wasn't on my bingo card for tonight."

Ryder's brows furrowed and he cocked his head. She giggled. "Right, of course. The fae don't have bingo. It's just a human game. Ignore me."

A moment passed before Ryder spoke. "The ball will end soon. There's still time to go see if you can go snag yourself a different prince. I hear Conall has a penchant for women with brown hair, some gross fetish with the soil or something ..." His sultry laugh quaked through her bones.

Rubbing her face with the palms of her hands, "Ugh, no thank you. Also gross," she rasped.

Ryder laughed and sarcastically quipped, "Oh, come on, Eva. He was all but swooning over you at dinner, or maybe he was glaring? His face does seem fixed in a position akin to someone taking a shit. He's said to be a generous lover, however, so—" His eye peaked at her as a taunting smile crooked his mouth upward.

Cocking her head in the prince's direction. Meeting his sparkling gaze, she contained her laugh. "You know a lot about Prince Conall ... are you sure *you* don't want to snag him? Tell me now if dirt is a turn on for you cause, I don't know if I'm into that ..."

His chuckle was warm and alluring. "Eh, you're safe. Dirt isn't my idea of foreplay." He replied, taking a big gulp of wine, eyeing her from the corner of his eye.

Ignoring the tremor of heat that rocked her core, Evangaline sighed and forced her eyes back to Tuatha's crown.

There was a brief pause between them, where the only noise that flowed through the breeze was the soft chime of the leaves rattling from the forest and the crickets that sang their songs.

"Where have you been?"

It was Ryder's turn to sigh. "Drinking Atlas's whiskey in the library with Des."

Evangaline snorted, a soft exhale of laughter out her nose.

"What do we do, Ryder? What does this mean?"

He took a deep breath, exhaling slowly through his nose. Then set down the wine bottle and rested his hands in his lap. "First thing, Eva, you need to know I'm not mad at … *this* …" Gesturing to his copper tattooed arm. "I'm not disappointed in it, or ashamed, and I don't think you are either. This … it's … it's bigger than the both of us."

"I know," she whispered, staring down at the diamond tiara in her lap, then her tattooed finger, thinking of how her ancestors felt on the night of their fating.

"I'm going to follow your lead, though." Ryder continued. "We might be fated to one another, but that means nothing to me if you are not happy. I will never force you into anything you do not choose for yourself. If you feel nothing for me, that is okay. I'm a grown man and I can handle the rejection. I understand the pressure you are under. Believe me, I do. I understand that you have only been here a short time and have endured more here, in that short time, than many will in their entire life spans. But Eva, I will follow your lead. Always."

She let his words sink into her skin. Let his gaze search her face as she tried to understand what it was that she felt exactly.

"What if I don't know what to do or what I want?"

"I think you do, Eva." He kept his eyes on her as he sighed. "Okay, do you want to hear a secret?"

With her brows furrowed, she stared at the dark and stunning prince, offering up a bit of himself. "Okay …"

She angled her body to face him as he spoke. "The first night I met you, I wasn't alone, as you so *expertly* guessed. Ophelia is still making fun of the fact that you guessed right, by the way." He raised his brows at her and smirked. She smirked back. "But I couldn't sleep that night. I bailed on the dinner early and my head was swimming with different thoughts. Things

I had to do, people I needed to meet, problems I needed to fix, and this nagging feeling in my stomach that something was wrong. So, I went for a walk around the grounds and took the first courtier back to my room who threw herself at me—"

Evangaline's face smooshed into a confused interlacement. "This, my Prince, is no way to start off a relationship. Fate-ship? Fating? Fate-lationship? I don't know what to call it, but this is no way to make me want you. If that's what you are trying to do."

He darkly laughed. "Keep listening. Shhh …"

"Did you just shush me?" Evangaline smiled.

He turned, smiling back at her, "Yes. Shh! So, anyway, I met this courtier … she was alright, much like all the other lords and ladies, eager to rise the ranks by jumping into the bed of a royal. She was pretty but was just a body to warm my bed and ease my racing mind."

Evangaline's smile faded as she tried to ignore her jealousy at the thought of Ryder bedding another woman, but then she thought about Bastian. That's all he was for her. A release. He silenced the thoughts in her head through passion and held her close when she needed a warm body. He was never anything more. *And look at where that has gotten you*, she chided herself.

"We had just barely got back to my quarters when I heard a rap at the door. I was furious but also slightly relieved, and I did not know why I was relieved. Now, thinking about it, it makes perfect sense." His eyes seared into hers with a passion she had never seen before. "But either way, I was. Angry that I was bothered but relieved I did not need to carry on with the woman." He turned to face the copse of trees in the distance. "The second I walked into that room, Eva, and saw you standing by the fire, battered and bloody, my mind quieted. Every nagging thought I had racing through my head was doused and suddenly a million eager questions flowed in, all about you. You were covered in gore and bruising and yet you were still more beautiful than any woman I've had in my bed … more intoxicating than any woman I've ever met."

Evangaline froze. Her heart thundered in her chest.

"But I got so angry seeing you hurt. The fact that we were in a palace filled with guards and powerful fae and you were bleeding and hurt. It set my hackles rising. And then the second Bastian touched you, claimed you before all of us … I thought it was just pent-up lust clouding my mind and told myself to ignore it. All of it. The anger, the attraction. I pushed it away, denied it. Then you spoke, and I felt my heart shudder. The shadows all started talking and moving about the minute you opened that mouth of yours. You woke them, which is not an easy feat for people other than me. I assure you."

He smiled at her briefly before looking away. "I stood there so mad at you for allowing Bastian to touch you in a way that I wanted to, and I didn't even know your name. I unjustly took out my feelings on you. Even so, with all our crude comments, you stood up to a room full of the most powerful fae in the realm. Bloody and mightier than many warriors I have seen in battle. You enthralled me and then I saw that mightiness slip. I saw the tears fester in your eyes and it almost broke me, Eva. Right then and there. I could not think of anything else but making sure you were okay.

"When I got back to my room, back to that courtier in my bed, I made her leave immediately. I couldn't stand the thought of her hands on my body or mine on hers, not after I met you. I couldn't stop thinking about you and all the questions that clouded my mind. I wondered what you looked like not covered in blood. Wondered what your smile was like. What it felt like to be in a room where you laughed and not cried. I wondered a great many things until I drifted to sleep. I stopped thinking of all my burdens and only thought of you. Then, like a wonderful gift from the gods, I woke to swords clashing outside my window and rain pouring, muddying the earth. I watched you battle and fight, and there she was, the warrior from my dreams."

He took a breath and shook his head. "You are stronger than you know. Braver and bolder than you recognize. There is a fierceness coursing through your blood. You just need to allow yourself to see it. Eva, I am not upset at being fated, only because I have been fated to you."

Evangaline's eyes burned with stinging tears. Okay, so he wasn't just beautiful, he was blessed with the gift of speech as well. If the romance book about Tuatha and Milesian didn't give it away, his beautiful speech did—the Prince of Shadows was a romantic at heart. She swallowed hard, her throat contracting in a strenuous attempt to keep her tears sheathed in her eyes.

Ryder gazed down at his now copper tattooed ring finger, prideful and happy. A sense of safety flooded through Evangaline, seeing him wiggle his hand, catching the light of the metallic bands that wrapped around his finger. He was hers. She just needed to claim him.

"I got butterflies," Her throat bobbed. "When I saw you that night. I felt it too. I got butterflies in my stomach and somehow, I couldn't look away from you. You saw me. You were the only one who saw me standing there. When I started … when Bash and I … fuck. Chloe warned me. She asked me if I got *pixies in my stomach*' when I was with him and I told her the truth. I told her no. Honestly, I've never felt that with anyone, until you walked in looking all dark and brooding and—"

He laughed. "I was not brooding!"

She faced him, a smile gracing her face, forcing her tears to retreat. "You were so brooding! And SHH! I'm trying to be sweet and endearing! Don't ruin it!"

He threw his hands up in concession, smiling, allowing her to finish. "But then you called me a human whore and I deflated inside a bit. Got pissed as hell, don't get me wrong, but I was sad you only saw me as some dirty human, like some of the other nobles did. Yet somehow, I still couldn't bear to look away from you." She nudged him with her shoulder. "And just so you know, I only let Bash touch me that night because I didn't want to embarrass him or cause a fuss by swatting his hand away. But his touch made me physically sick. I just had more pressing matters to attend to. Like accusing a mighty fae prince of murder." She smirked as he huffed a laugh.

"I am not mad, Ryder, or sad, or embarrassed, to be fated to you. I truly know very little of you … only what the book here in my room said, which wasn't much …" she smirked.

"You read about me?" He asked coyly, his dimple gracing his left cheek.

Smiling, she answered with a blush rushing to color her cheeks. "There was a book here in my room, but that isn't the point. What I *am* saying is that being fated to you isn't what upsets me. It's the fact that I kind of want it and that feels selfish. If I accept this fate, which I don't seem to have a lot of a choice over, no matter how kind you are to give me the option, I won't ever see my family again. Not to mention I will formally be the crown princess of the realm and I don't even know where to start with that!"

"Do you want to … to leave … to return to Vitalis?"

"I thought I did. Then I didn't … then I did … then I didn't. Then everything with Bastian and Chloe and I did again was pretty certain of it, especially after the fiasco tonight. I mean, you heard what I told Des. I meant it. I've never really told anyone outright as much as I told him tonight, but it's the truth." She sighed. "The truth is, I have never felt at home. I was starting to feel it with Des and Chloe, Shaw … the ache of losing my family was not gone, but it became tolerable. Then I lost Chloe for good, and my world broke. She helped patch up the parts of me that I never thought would be fixed. She saved my life in more ways than I can count. And then she was just gone. And I didn't break. I shattered." A tear fell from her eye as she stared off into the darkness. The ache of losing Chloe echoing louder than it had since that fateful night.

"Then I learned I was the last descendant of a real baller fae line that I didn't—don't—want to disappoint and I felt small. Then tonight happened with Bastian, and I felt used. I felt cornered … but now this …" She held up her arm and took in the simple markings, "and it almost feels safe. I'm even more forced into a cage of someone else's making, but for the first time, I feel like I *want* to stay here, and not just *need* to. It hurts to say that cause I will never hold my niece or see my brother graduate. I won't see my parents, or let them meet *you*. I can never show them this place, or any of it. But that doesn't mean I'm mad or disappointed at being fated to you, Ryder. So please don't think that."

Suddenly, the pain in her chest became so pungent that she winced from a pinch of pain. Smoothing her hand across the ache in circles, she took a breath.

Ryder shifted closer to her, his face contorting with worry.

"What's wrong?" He bit out.

"It's just a pain. It's fine. It's probably just an anxiety attack rearing up. I just have to breathe through it."

He cocked his head and smirked. "Eva, how long have you felt pain in your chest? Before the attack?"

She looked at him shrugging and shook her head, "Aches here and there since I got here but it spikes, like now. It's just anxiety, I'm fine. I've just been stressed. Don't worry about it."

Gently, with a lover's caress, his warm hand covered the hand on her chest as he gently smiled and said, "Well, that is too bad. I will always worry about you. Good or bad news first?"

Pinching her brows together, she embraced the heat that pulsed through her body at his touch. "Good?"

"Good! Okay. Good news is we are in this together. I will be by your side *if* you want me to be. If you don't … well, you will never know I existed … aside from the fashionable matching tattoos we now share, can't get rid of those, I'm afraid. Also, if you choose this, I want you to meet my family too." He winked at her. His large hand engulfed hers on her chest. She reveled in how it felt.

The heat that rushed through her body with his touch was intense. However, it was not a sexual heat, well some was. He was gorgeous, and she was a heterosexual woman with two working eyes. It was like being wrapped in a warm blanket. A subtle and comforting warmth that encased her in a cocoon of peace. Was that the fating bond, or was that just him? She leaned toward the second option.

She blushed and placed her other hand on his. Smiling up at him.

"Now the bad news! You are going to be in a lot of pain unless you listen to me carefully, okay? Do you trust me?"

She eyed him warily; her smile was weak and looked more like a grimace. "Unfortunately, I think I do."

"Okay, good." He chuckled, pulling his hand away from hers. "Baby steps."

Gently, he grabbed the tiara from her lap and placed it on her head, then pushed to his feet, pulling her up with him.

He then cupped her hands into a bowl, his hands gently caressing under hers, holding them up in the air between them.

The feel of his touch sent a jolt of electricity through Evangaline. Despite the pain in her chest, Evangaline couldn't help but savor every bit of his warm, tender touch.

"Okay, that ache in your chest is a normal thing for fae to feel. Looks to me like you inherited some of Darrin's side after all. Though now, looking, I'm surprised I didn't see the resemblance sooner." He smirked, taking in her features until she cleared her throat. "Right. Typically, us fae feel it when we are going through pubescence, but you grew up in a land without magic, so you never would learn about it or have the resources to know you could die if not properly taught."

Evangaline ripped her eyes away from their cradled hands and stared up at him, worried. "What is it? What could kill me? I'm only half fae though, and please don't tell me I have to go through puberty again. I can't. Once was enough," she babbled.

His face was entirely too excited as he laughed, "Not entirely, think of it like … a half puberty? You'll learn. Just trust me, I'll be here with you."

"Learn what, Ry?" she asks quietly.

He stared into her eyes, then placed a hand on her chest over where her thundering heartbeat was. Pinpointing the exact place the pain thrived. "How to control your magic, Eva. Power as great as our bloodlines can consume you if you don't use it and the warning signs manifest in pains in the chest. You were warded against using your own magic in Vitalis. But here, especially now, with us being fated, I think your magic has had enough of being contained."

"You're saying … I have powers … magic … like what? Can I make a chair appear out of thin air, too?" She taunted excitedly.

"I formed a chair from shadow magic, not out of thin air. But being that you are a daughter of Tuatha, that is what we are going to see." He smirked and removed his hand from her chest and suddenly she felt cold. "Close your eyes and imagine a string connecting that pain in your chest all the way to your hands. Now we don't know what your powers are, but just think of slowly releasing the cork that is holding it in and send it down the string to your hands. Any magic you can grab onto. It sounds difficult, but once you latch onto your pocket of magic, it will do the rest. You just have to control it. Let down your walls and allow your power to be a part of you. Once you give it permission to manifest, it should feel like an extension of yourself. Accidents rarely happen, but I'm here to help you in case it goes wrong."

"Oh, reassuring," she muttered.

Evangaline, despite her nerves at this new breakthrough—one more thing to add to the list of events for the night—she took a steadying breath and thought of *her* magic.

She pictured her power in the same form, the glittering opalescence that the Vitalis border, the Velum, was made of. She pictured it gliding through her chest and down to her hands like a trickling brook. Evangaline remembered how her, and Chloe looked out over the Velum on the night before her birthday and how Chloe talked about a world free of borders. Chloe's ever-optimistic presence—even in Evangaline's memories—gave her the serenity to pull on the string and let her magic wash over her body.

As she relaxed and focused on the magic, she grew warmer and warmer.

Evangaline furrowed her brow in concentration. And slowly the ache in her chest eased as a tingling warmth flowed through her extremities.

Ryder leaned close to her ear. The caress of his breath tickled the soft part of her earlobe and sent a chill down her spine. His hands remained firmly around her own cupped hands.

"Open your eyes," he whispered.

As her eyelids fluttered open, what she saw was the most exhilarating, terrifying, and beautiful thing that words failed her for a moment.

Glinting in their cupped hands was a single flame dancing in the breeze. Evangaline's eyes grew wide, but her smile grew wider.

"I did that?"

"You're *doing* that." Ryder chuckled, removing his hands from hers, stepping back, allowing her the space to enjoy the little flow of magic escaping her. "When you want it to stop, just will it to stop? It should feel as though you are replacing that cork. It is yours to command. Never forget that."

She bit her lip and curled her fingers at his instruction, effectively extinguishing the little flame.

Her smile spread to her eyes, crinkling the corners, her eyelashes tickled her high set cheeks while she laughed.

"Will you teach me more?" she asked, trying not to sound as though she was begging, but she knew she was desperate for him to say yes, for many reasons.

Once the thrumming and tender vibration ebbed in her chest, it made room for a new feeling. One that made her heart constrict in glee. One that made the pixies begin to flutter in her stomach in a raucous dance. One that made her excited to have the mark of the fates spiraling down her arm. A small bit of anxiety beat a soft drum in the background of her mind, but she told it to go play its tune somewhere else. She wanted to bask in all the good things happening in the present. No doubt come morning she would have a panic attack as she forced herself to do what she hated doing—planning for the future—but for now she wanted to enjoy her magic and her Prince. She wanted to forget about the shit cyclone that tried to ruin her night before. It's what Chloe would have done, and what Des would do too. So, with a deep breath, she committed to embracing the happiness she felt in her soul.

Ryder looked at her, gleaming with nothing but pride and hope. His stunning face warmed her heart as the two beamed at one another. "Okay … But does that mean you are staying? Do you want to try to see where this goes?" He motioned to his tattoo, something both of them tended to do now when they were at a loss for words.

She stared at him, thinking through everything that had happened in the last three weeks as quickly as she could—especially within the past few hours. His confession of admiration. Her confession of her pesky little butterflies. The magic he told her he would help her hone. Even her family … and his. She stared into his endless ocean eyes and knew the fates had put her on a path right to where she needed to be. It wouldn't be easy, but life never was and never would be. But with her friends and her newly fated partner, she knew she could at least try. Try to be Ryder's fated. Try to be the crown princess the realm deserved. Try to not let her fears and anxiety dictate how she was to live her life. To try to fight to be the warrior, everyone told her she was the warrior Chloe wanted her to be.

"I'm staying." She murmured as she smiled at *her* fated prince.

Chapter Forty-Three

"For the love of the gods, can you stop with the pacing?" Des exhaled through his flared nostrils as he leaned his toned frame against the carved marble fireplace of the strategy room.

With her eyes fixed down at her feet, Evangaline snickered. "Nope!" And with that retort, she continued her pacing. Painted with intricate details of Celadonia with two nondescript blobs on either side, the table she paced behind portrayed the three realms—sort of.

Celadonia was the largest of the lands, sitting smack dab in the center of the table. The Velum and The Mist flanking either side of the continent. Vitalis was to the left in a semi-shapeless formation that was painted a dull green color. Black script bearing the human realm's name in the center. A black shapeless mass sat to Celadonia's right in a somewhat lazy attempt to construe what little was known to the fae of Munbra. The table was massive, to say the least. As she paced behind it, Evangaline pictured it being surrounded by chairs. It could easily seat ten people comfortably. However, that was not the purpose of the table or the room. She found herself anxiously pacing around.

One lone dark wood chair was reserved for the king that sat dead center of the table facing the entirety of Celadonia, quite literally putting the realm at his fingertips. Or in this case, Evangaline's fingertips.

Evangaline sat in the chair briefly when she first got in the room, dizzy with anxiety at the reality that was settling in on her calling a meeting for the first time. But as soon as her backside settled into the carved wood of the seat, she quickly jumped up with realization as to what chair she was resting in—or whose chair rather—with her legs thrown over the arm haphazardly.

She was terrified. Anxiety writhed through her bloodstream and made standing still hard. She wanted to crack a window to let in the breeze, but unfortunately the strategy room's windows were fixed shut. The night before started strong, took a turn, and then consumed her with an excitement she hadn't felt since she was a kid.

Ryder stayed with her in her room for only a little while before excusing himself to go talk to his advisors. He did not travel to the capital with many from his court, but he wanted to ensure the safety of the few that did travel alongside him back to his home Kingdom. Ryder was just as eager as Evangaline to learn about the powers that thumped in her chest, but he was a ruling prince first and foremost. It was intoxicating to see him get serious and commanding, but she refrained from telling him how attractive he was when he turned all broody—which he was, no matter how many times he denied it!

Once he left, Evangaline found herself unable to contain her excitement for her magic. She played with the fire she already knew she could conjure a bit longer before wanting to test what else she could do. An errant flame nearly torched her eyebrow, so she thought, why not try to summon water, the opposite of fire?

She was able to get a single drop of water to hover in her palm just as the fire did, but only for a second. Over and over she conjured her droplet before Des entered her room, scaring her to the point that she flung the tiny droplet straight into his face. Accidentally, of course!

He didn't see it that way, at first, but once she conjured another drop, he was more intrigued to learn she had magic and quickly forgot about the drip of water gliding down his forehead.

It was only a drop, anyway. She thought as an idea for a conjuring a storm crossed her mind.

That night she slowly fell asleep, tracing the line of her fated mark, unable to look away from the markings that reflected the starlight. For the first time in days, Evangaline enjoyed a solid eight hours of hard, un-labored sleep.

Only to be woken with an anxiety attack that had her running outside onto her balcony so her lungs could fill with air.

She couldn't belabor her problems and wanted to claim Ryder and their fating before anyone else could speak of it. It was their story to tell, and she wanted to be the one to tell Darrin. She also wanted to wring the king's neck for promising her to—bleh—Bastian. Whom of which was a whole separate problem, whom of which incited her wrath.

So, as the sun rose, messages were sent straight to Ryder, Atlas, Bastian, and King Darrin to meet her in the strategy room at precisely ten o'clock. She needed to accomplish her tasks before she chickened out and hid in her room, playing with her newfound magic.

Before she sent the letters—after she enjoyed a brief conversation with the wind whisp on the balcony—Evangaline decided it was time for her to stop sitting in the background and to start taking initiative. Since she told Ryder she was going to stay in Celadonia, she had a lot still to learn, especially regarding magic. All these weeks, she had power inside of her. She just didn't allow herself to embrace it by dwelling solely on the half of her that was from Vitalis. That would end today. She was the crown princess and blessed by the fates. It was time to stop sitting on the sidelines and jump into the game. Despite the imposter syndrome that was playing tag with her anxiety.

You can do this Evangaline. Fae up. You are a strong, independent woman who is capable of almost anything. No! Fuck that … you are capable of everything! She repeated her hype speech over and over in her head until finally a small part of herself believed it.

In what had to have been her five hundredth time pacing along the massive table, Evangaline glanced up at the small wooden clock resting on the mantel beside Des's armored arm.

Nine fifty-five. Five minutes till they were late.

Daunting thoughts swirled in her head. One after another as the seconds ticked by on the clock. Maybe they don't think she is serious about wanting a meeting? Maybe the messenger did not deliver the messages? Maybe, just maybe, they don't think of her as respectable enough to call a meeting in the first place? Maybe Darrin was mad she bailed on the ball he orchestrated just for her?

Maybe ... maybe ... maybe ... NO! You are capable of anything and everything; they will come and listen whether they want to or not! Even if you have to drag them by their ears to the strategy room. Evangaline took a deep breath. "You've got this," she whispered to herself, cutting off the derailing train in her head.

"Talking to yourself now?" Des side eyed her, a smirk playing on his otherwise bored face.

"Shut up," she said as she continued her pacing.

Still very mad at her biological father for practically selling her to Bastian without her consent, the message he received consisted of a few words. She tossed them over in her mind as she waited for him.

Strategy Room. Ten. Be there.
-Evangaline

No doubt he would be angry to be ordered around with little explanation, but Evangaline did not care in the slightest. Until she had a solid understanding of what was going through his thick fae skull, she remained pissed at him. He deserved to be ordered around. One meeting being called at her hand would not be the end of the world. For him, at least.

Bastian's note was even shorter and if she could have, it simply would have read "Fuck you!" but she needed him complacent for her plan to work.

Strategy Room. Ten.
-E

Was all it said.

Once Des saw her address the letter to Bastian, he didn't even give Evangaline the ability to fight him on his presence being known at the meeting. And much to Des's surprise, she didn't put up one.

She wanted him with her, anyway. He was her rock and her most trusted protector. She could not imagine doing any of what she planned without him. Especially with so much at stake.

She was going to ruin Bash, claim Ryder and accept her place as crown princess all in one meeting. It was a big day for the human-fae princess pacing along the white marble floor.

Wren helped her braid her hair, possibly in the most beautiful braid Evangaline had ever seen. The handmaiden wove in small golden arrows. "For strength," she said quickly, noting Evangaline's bouncing nervous knee.

Des returned to her room not long after Wren left, looking suited for battle. Presumably to kill his general if Bastian even looked at Evangaline in the wrong tone. Yet again, as she thought it over, she knew that should that happen, Ryder's shadows would be unleashed on the prick before Des could even unsheathe his sword. However, Des's copper armor still shone brighter than the sun, regardless of Ryder's protectiveness. The ruby hilt of his sword rested high above his back within close reach, two copper daggers strapped to each of his muscular thighs—a new edition—were sheathed in black holsters, and just for a little extra something, a bandolier of small throwing knives was draped across his chest like a deadly pageant winner.

"That's a little much, don't ya think?" Evangaline asked when he entered her suite.

Stoically, he responded, "Not to protect my princess. This isn't even *close* to enough."

Evangaline rolled her blue-green eyes and grabbed Des's arm, shaking him into a nervous smile. Then they slipped back into their icy facades and made their way to the strategy room.

That was thirty minutes ago and thousands of steps ago.

The clock moved both in slow motion and fast forward.

Two minutes passed since she last checked, and still none of the men were stalking through the giant wooden doors. Evangaline's heart began to both sink and thud faster simultaneously.

She turned to Des, wringing her clammy fingers, "Do you think they will—"

Before she could finish her sentence, the door creaked open.

Evangaline stilled in anticipation.

Unfortunately for her, the most punctual of the men was the one she least wanted to see.

Bastian strode through the door, determined. His pace was heavy and fervent. Though the brief glimpse of surprise at seeing her and Des in the room gave her enough confidence to face him. She rattled him just in her presence.

Evangaline put on her mask of boredom and shut away all her hatred and anxiety. It was oddly easy to slip on the mask of a scorned royal when steaming hatred bubbled within one's gut.

Despite her nerves and Des now firmly at her back, she crossed her arms behind her so Bastian wouldn't see the faint shimmer of her fating mark beneath her gossamer sleeve. Shoving an imaginary steel rod in her spine to force herself to stand as tall as she could, she met his gaze as he approached the table.

"Princess," he said, bowing at the waist.

"General," she replied, trying so hard not to punch him in his smug face.

Des's presence grew in intensity. The heat radiating from his metallic armor was almost stifling at her back.

Bastian assessed the guard by scoffing and rolling his swamp green eyes. Somehow, the green she once thought was beautiful became putrid. From crisp summer leaves to rotting vines and decaying flesh in a single shitty night.

As the door opened again, two distinct voices echoed through the hall. Atlas and King Darrin.

They sounded to be in a heated discussion of whether cookies were appropriate to serve at a breakfast for royals. Real riveting stuff.

Evangaline squinted at the nonchalance of the conversation, her blood heating slightly at the lack of urgency at her calling for a formal meeting.

Eventually, their conversation died down as they entered and regarded Evangaline. For a moment she thought she saw joy flash across her father's face, but then it died into a mask of stoic royalty matching her own. Except his was much better, she would have to practice better in the mirror later.

"I assume you have called this meeting, daughter, to discuss your upcoming nuptials to the General. I do not believe I had the opportunity to offer my congratulations as you made a hasty exit from the fete last night." He said with an amused smirk that told her he thought he won.

Evangaline narrowed her eyes and choked down a cough of indignation. "Yes, *father*," she said with force and anger. Wielding the term, he wished for her to call him as nothing but a weapon and not a term of endearment. Its impact landed straight in the center of his chest, and oh boy did she see it, effectively deflating his mask of authority. "That is precisely why I called this meeting. Along with a bevy of other things that we must all discuss."

By the look on Atlas's face and the small uptick of his mouth, he expertly neglected to tell the king of Evangaline and Ryder being fated. *Good.*

Bastian also noted the look on Atlas's face and turned to Evangaline, brow furrowed.

"Eager to start the wedding planning, are we, *sweetheart?*" Bastian said to Evangaline, his tone a deep mix of condescending and brutal sarcasm.

He rattled her just slightly, but Evangaline didn't falter. She held her ground perfectly. Her feet were firmly planted on the white marble floor, taking the fighting stance both Chloe and Des drilled into her head. Her hands were clasped tightly in a knot behind her back. And she kept her chin high.

Evangaline's intense stare locked into Bastian as a small, narcissistic smile tugged on his lips.

Bastard.

The king resigned, his body relaxed almost to an indignant level. "These are all discussions for another time daughter, I shall send the planners to you, and you can start designing your gown and discussing flowers. Evangaline, I shall spare no expense for my only daughter. Just pick a date and you two shall be wed. But this is no need for a meeting for us all."

Evangaline stood still and smiled. Her eyes sparkled with a disobedience that thrilled her. She simply did not speak, and that silence echoed through the hall louder than if she screamed with every ounce of oxygen in her lungs. She knew firsthand how stifling silence could be, and she was going to use it to her advantage.

Bastian stood taller, his hands falling in his pockets as his cocky smile turned to a scowl. He could see her defiance, and he hated it. His ideal woman was not one with a quick wit and a strong sense of self. "You, Princess, have a duty to your realm to wed and continue on the line—"

Evangaline's brows rose as she cut him off. "Is that what I am, General? Some sort of breeding stock? Someone for you to sully further and fill with your seed just to *'continue the line'* or am I just a pawn to gain the power you crave oh so much? I never said I won't marry, nor did I say I will never have children. What I *am* saying and why I called this meeting is to say that I will do none of it, with *you*."

Bastian slammed his hands down on the table, knocking over multiple figurines that represented the different royals and their kingdoms.

Evangaline blinked and glanced down at the table, her mask never once slipping at Bastian's temper tantrum. She smiled wider when she noticed the only figure to remain upright was Ryder's, right there in the center of the Kingdom of Shadows. It stood as tall and proud as a little wooden figurine could stand.

Des unsheathed his knives, twirling them with a sardonic smile for an added emphasis and taunt. It was a nice touch.

"Now, Bastian, what did I tell you about even looking in the princess's direction?" Ryder's deep voice crooned from the doorway, bringing the smile that graced Evangaline's face even wider. He was late, but man did he make one hell of an entrance.

Across the white floor darkness and shadows flowed like black silk from Ryder's body, swirling up Bastian's tall frame, coating his face in fear and darkness. The shadows made their way onto the table, righting the fallen figurines that were strewn about.

One little shadow, as it passed Evangaline, swirled and shimmied as to say hello before it picked up a figurine and hovered it in the air as Ryder strode across the floor.

He looked so good. Everything about him was effortless and yet somehow perfectly put together. He casually cut over to Evangaline with an air of arrogance and charm that made her cheeks flush a rosy color. She was attracted to him before, but now, being fated to the prince, her body and soul sang for him and only him.

His black hair was falling delicately on his forehead but was soon swept away by his left hand, which was proudly displaying his fating mark. With his black jacket sleeves rolled up to his elbow it was so beautifully on display. Just the sight of it made Evangaline's heart thud with excitement. Her entire body felt like it was floating on a cloud as she drank him in.

This man, who she barely knew, made her heart beat in her chest and her blood warm like the summer sun touched it with one of its rays. Those damn pixies started fluttering around her stomach in twists and twirls simply because Ryder looked at her and smiled before returning his eyes to Bastian, putting on his own royal mask of indifference.

For a moment, as she took in the searing eyes of half the room, she was struck with a lightning bolt of nerves. She took a deep breath and instead of letting them shut her down; she soaked in their zap of electricity and used it to fuel her.

Atlas stood up taller and Des sheathed his weapons at the sight of the prince, while the king and Bastian looked lost and dumbfounded. Anger flared in the twin flames behind their eyes.

Subsequently, neither man noticed Ryder's new markings as they turned their stares at Evangaline. Her own hands remained clasped behind her back; her matching marks largely remained concealed except for a bit at her shoulder. She had a plan. Hopefully, the testosterone in the room didn't erupt into a battle for dominance before that plan could be executed. She was growing fond of surprises, especially ones at the expense of men who saw her as nothing but a trinket.

"Ryder, what is the meaning of this interruption? This is a closed meeting. You were supposed to be off at dawn, back to the Kingdom of Shadows. What are you playing at!" her father barked out; his tone was more hostile than Evangaline had ever heard.

The coldness in the king's tone only made Ryder smile and hum to himself as he grabbed the levitating figurine. His shadows quickly retreated into his muscled frame and fluttered across his chest, neck, and shoulders.

"I was leaving and now I am not. No games. Is this meant to be Surtis? He looks … *tiny*?" Ryder asked, wiggling the figure of Surtis in his hand before placing it on the map within the heart of the Kingdom of Fire with a soft pat on the head. "I would encourage you, Darrin, to stop trying to infiltrate my head. It is very impolite to use your powers on a guest, is it not? As far as to my presence here, I have every right to be here as it was my crown princess's wish and truthfully, there is no place I would rather be. My presence at this meeting has more merit than others." He glanced at Bastian, who was practically foaming at the mouth with anger. However, Ryder's taunting smile never faltered. "Bastian, I do believe *your* presence here is unnecessary and I think I speak for us all when I say you may excuse yourself."

Bastian huffed into the air and narrowed in on Ryder, "Like hell I will! You keep overstepping your boundaries, Ryder and I will—"

The sight of someone threatening her fated stirred up all kinds of emotions within Evangaline, ones she had never felt before. It was like being fated took her emotions about Ryder from a simple crush to that of a stage ten clinger in two point five seconds. Her blood turned as hot as lava upon hearing Bastian's threat. Its magma seeped through her veins and illuminated her eyes, turning the once blue-green hue to a fiery bright copper orange and red. She was too angry, however, to notice, too protective.

"And you will what, Bastian? You have repeatedly forgotten *your* place with me and those around me. If you threaten the life of Prince Ryder, you will not only have the contention of the Kingdom of Shadows to deal with, you will also have that of the crown princess and the Royal Army. Is that what you want? You have already made yourself a viable candidate for a beheading, but being that I am not the one currently ruling, your worthless head is still attached to your worthless shoulders."

The king glanced around with an alarmed visage smeared across his face. Cautiously, he stepped toward Bastian. "General Bastian? Is there something I must know of? Evangaline, how dare you—" His tone was both worried and harsh.

"I have every right to speak to Bastian the way I am," Evangaline snapped at the king before he could admonish her.

Bastian bit his bottom lip, then laughed, a hollow and threatening laugh that charged the room with tension. It filled her bones with dread, but she maintained her ground.

"You weren't complaining, Princess, when my *worthless* head was between your pretty little thighs." Bastian snapped.

Then Ryder snapped.

The room suddenly darkened in a way that made it seem as though the sun and moon hid from the world, casting it in a perpetual darkness.

The pristine white walls seeped black in swells of shadow magic. The fire cracking in the fireplace was smothered with shadows, and darkness emanated from Ryder. Though his face remained impassive, a stone-cold look grew in his eyes that made them dark and murky. The shadows on his chest began to swirl and thrive, yearning to answer their master's call and be set free.

Growling, "Say that again, Bastian," his voice was low and hostile. The simmering fire that filled her veins quieted as the darkness consumed Evangaline's vision. Before total darkness claimed her, she turned to Ryder.

There goes her plan. Right in the garbage.

Bastian, being the smug asshole he was, didn't even notice in that moment what the king saw as Evangaline unclasped her hands in the dimming light.

Darrin gasped and shuddered. His hands fell to the back of his head and his expression mirrored Atlas and Des's from the night before.

Evangaline slowly placed her left hand, revealing her fating mark on top of Ryder's right hand. Which was firmly gripping onto the table. His fingernails dug into the wood. As her hand made contact, the darkness ceased its progression. The dim lights from the sconces flickered through the shadows enough to illuminate them.

Des shifted with every movement Evangaline made. His daggers thrived in his hands, once more eager for a fight.

Bastian pressed into Ryder's side ever so, the taunting asshole he was. He leaned into the prince's ear, forcing Ryder to tense with anger and disgust. Ryder's fingers gently wrapped around Evangaline's possessively, but also to seek comfort from her. He was trying his hardest to force himself to calm down for her sake. His thumb smoothed over the soft skin on top of her hand in slow circles.

Ignore him, Ryder, he is not worth it. He thought to himself as Bastian leaned in closer to his ear.

Whispering, Bastian crudely chuckled, "Tell me, Prince, did you enjoy her too? When she rode you did she make that little ... whimper ... it is deliciously hypnotizing, isn't it, our little siren. Or has she not spread her legs for you yet?" He finished with a wink and a laugh a mere inch from Ryder's face. He was goading Ryder. Everyone, except for Darrin, in the room could see it. The king was stuck, mesmerized, staring at Evangaline and Ryder's fating marks.

Evangaline tensed as Ryder's hand grew tauter in her own. She could feel his anger on a visceral level. It mirrored her own, but that was exactly what Bastian wanted.

With an explosion of darkness that clouded the room in a dark black haze, Ryder threw Bastian back into the wall. His power did all the heavy lifting. Pining Bastian's limbs to the white stone with his shadows.

Evangaline could not see anything. She only knew Ryder was no longer close to her. Coldness swept across her skin, and she longed for his touch once more.

Fear pounded through her heart. Not at what the Prince of Shadows was capable of, but at what Bastian was. He was cruel and conniving, and she knew he would stop at nothing to make Ryder the villain in the narrative. The general was cruel in his greed.

She was able to hear Bastian's air leaving his body as he was hurled against the wall. The sound of stones cracking echoed through the spacious room. Sound was the only thing giving away their position in the dark cloud surrounding them.

Des was right behind her, daggers drawn. She only knew of his presence the second his arms threw her behind him, his body becoming a shield around Evangaline.

But she panicked. The darkness was so black she could not even see her own hands. She could not make out where the two men hellbent on destroying each other were, aside from the sounds of hushed threats and grunts. As awful as it sounded, Ryder could tear Bastian's heart clean from his chest and Evangaline wouldn't weep for the man who assaulted her. But Ryder. She couldn't even allow her brain to think of how she would feel if she lost him so soon after getting him.

"Enough!" Atlas yelled into the darkness, flaring up his party trick, illuminating his frost white beard and wolfish eyes until he was a shining beacon. The orb in his hand grew larger and larger illuminating the king flanked by his private guards. The orb of light slowly expanded to illuminate Evangaline, Des, Ryder, and Bastian.

"Tell the king, Bastian. Go on, or shall I tell him why his daughter did not return to the ball last night?" Ryder's voice boomed through the strategy room with nothing but a silvery darkness riding his words.

Bastian's head was slowly dripping blood onto the tile below his feet. Ryder held him up by his throat as his shadows pinned his arms and legs to the wall.

Evangaline slipped from behind Des and hurried her way to Ryder. His body was rigid with the grace of death.

Softly trying not to startle him, she put her hand on his shoulder, as though she were petting a rageful lion. Trepidation and nerves lined her every movement.

As soon as her hand made contact with Ryder's honed shoulder, the darkness began to fade bit by bit. His shadows removed themselves from Bastian's limbs and retreated onto Ryder's frame.

The fire reignited in the fireplace, and with the whoosh of the jaundiced flames, Ryder slowly lowered Bastian to the floor. The death grip he had around Bash's throat held strong, leaving the men now eye to eye.

"My fated will *never* be even a thought in your head, aside from her benevolence to you. I should have killed you a long time ago. But let me remind you …" Ryder darkly chuckled, "I am the prince of the most feared kingdom in the realm and have every right to execute you without even a motive or approval from the king. No matter of your station or title. Don't test me Bastian."

Ryder finally released Bastian physically, but his eyes were locked into the general with a severe ruthlessness.

Bastian looked down at Evangaline and then to her hand. His eyes grew wide and then his face turned wary, as though he was searching her eyes for mercy and answers alike.

She was fated; she was the princess, and she was so far out of his reach it wasn't even funny. He tried to take advantage of the wrong girl and he knew it by his expression. His hollow eyes glistened with what looked like resentment and fear.

Bastian shook his head, "No. It can't be. *Princess*?"

Softly but loud enough for all in the room to hear it, Evangaline said, her hand still holding onto Ryder's shoulder, "Whatever deal you and the king made regarding this engagement is over. You, General Bastian, are nothing more than the monster you have proven yourself to be. Your assaults were only the nails in your coffin. I was never yours. I will not marry you. And I will not so much as think of you from this day forward, but I will make sure that every day of your very long life you remember me. Remember what you did and said, and I will ensure you remember how you pay for those actions."

"You don't mean that." Bastian muttered, almost sounding hurt, but more frustrated than anything.

Evangaline removed her hand from Ryder's shoulder and stepped in front of her, fated, situating herself inches before Bastian. She would have been scared had it not been for the firm mountain of muscle resting at her back. Bastian wouldn't be a threat to her or Ryder so long as she breathed.

Ryder didn't move or touch her but with every deep shuttering breath he took, Evangaline felt it against her temple, reassuring her that he was there, and he was only restraining himself for her.

From the corner of her eye, she could see as Des inched closer while the darkness fully withdrew. The brightness of the room gained jurisdiction once more and bathed them in the light of morning.

Des had his sword drawn and his gaze firmly locked on Bastian. His hate simmered through his beat red face.

"Guards, please apprehend General Bastian and take him to the dungeon." Evangaline calmly beckoned.

"What is the matter of this? Guards, you shall do no such thing!" the king shouted.

"I can and I will. Any member of the royal family may call for the apprehension of a criminal. It is your choice, however, as king to make the sentence. Is that not right, Atlas?" Evangaline retorted, her eyes never leaving Bash's. Weeks of learning names, and laws, geography, and nuances of Celadonia left her with the knowledge to rid the realm of Bastian for good. According to a royal decree that was enacted pre-Convergence, should a member of the royal family believe they have been wronged or harmed, they may have the suspect or criminal apprehended and housed in jail without question until the reigning monarch judges the crimes and decides a punishment. Admittedly, there were some flaws with the law. Even so, once she remembered learning about it, she knew that she must call on her right as the crown princess and use the law to her will. If not for her, for all the women Bastian probably preyed upon. Once a creep, always a creep.

Bastian rolled his eyes as a defeated smile filled his face.

"That is correct, Your Highness. Also, My King, there are witnesses to his crime against the princess." Atlas leaned into the king's ear and whispered what had transpired the night before. The old man didn't even know about the instance in the woods on the autumnal equinox.

With each word, Darrin's eyes grew wider and wider and eventually he broke on a gasp, "Guards! Take him to the dungeons. I shall deal with him personally later. There will be no trial. You are hereby stripped of all of your duties and titles Bastian. Guards! Now!" The king was downright pissed, as he should be.

Despite it all, Evangaline never broke her gaze from Bastian. A small feeling of guilt situated itself within her stomach as the guards rushed over and grabbed Bastian's arms and secured them with shackles that glowed a faint purplish-blue.

The second they clasped around his wrists, Bastian winced slightly, but then looked back up at Evangaline with a devious smile gracing his strong, handsome face.

He leaned down into Evangaline's air and snickered, "You are playing a dangerous game now, Princess. You should have run back home when you had the chance. I'll make you regret this."

Evangaline leaned into him, their lips a hairsbreadth away from one another, "Unfortunately for you, General, this is now my home and *you're* gonna regret making that threat."

Bastian then smiled even more and looked up at Ryder with a wink. Ryder growled a warning, and then Bastian was hauled away through the doors.

He would never hurt her again and with that thought, she breathed a sigh of relief.

Next manner of business, the Prince of Shadows still breathing heavily down onto the nape of her neck, his rage still a cauldron of intensity.

Good lord, why is it always up to a woman to be the diplomatic, sensible one calming down all the raging men? She shook her head and then turned around.

"Ryder, it's okay. We're okay. We're going to be alright," she said, gazing into his eyes while cupping his cheek.

He slightly nuzzled into her hand, his eyes closing softly. With a great effort on his part, he breathed in and out, slowly regaining his composure. His eyes slowly blinked open while his lips tugged up in the corners.

Transfixed on one another, the entire room faded away and it was just Evangaline and her fated Prince of Shadows, until Atlas crept up beside them and spoke. "I thought Milesian and Tuatha were possessive of one another, but gods above, the two of you take the cake." He giggled, drawing her attention from Ryder to his giddy visage.

Evangaline flashed a hesitant and quick smile while Ryder simply stared down at her. His ocean blue eyes swam with their shadows and sparkles. He was still on edge, but not as much. He slipped his fingers through

Evangaline's and gave them a slight squeeze.

"Daughter?" Darrin said from the place he had been rooted in by the table.

Evangaline blinked slowly and released her hands from Ryders, reminding herself of the other important reasons she called the meeting.

She smiled up at Ryder and then stepped around the beautiful prince to make her way to the king.

"Yes, Darrin?" She acknowledged plastering the resigned mask on her face once more. It wasn't hard to appear aloof to him because the comradery the two of them built was shattered with his choices. It would take a lot of work on his part to regain her trust.

His face was one of pain incarnate. "I had no idea. You are to stay then? That is what you are choosing?" He asked, glancing at her tattooed arm, then over to Ryder briefly.

"I had every reason to leave last night after the stunt you pulled. Bastian's abuse aside, you really thought you could force me to stay through a *marriage*. Have you no sense at all?" Evangaline said, allowing the mask to slip and her pain to show. "I was starting to trust you."

"Love, Evangaline, please forgive me. He told me you two were in love. He told me he had you ..." He swallowed the words acid in his throat, "He told me ... He ... You ..."

"Had me in his bed?" Evangaline snapped.

"Yes, I never knew it wasn't consensual. I never would have allowed him to propose."

Evangaline chuckled in disbelief.

Ryder crossed his arms as he situated himself behind the table with Des. His huff and eye roll showed his temper was not all gone and was eager for an excuse to come back out.

"He never proposed, Darrin. Whatever he told you was not true. Last night, from your lips, was the first I heard of any marriage. And it was consensual until the night of the equinox. He tried to hurt me then, for the first time. Claimed I was *his*. He never listened to me pleading to stop. The wind whisp saved me that night. Then Ryder, Des, and Atlas saved me last night." Her face was impassible.

Darrin's face crumpled, "The wind whisp? It saved you?"

"Yes. It is my friend. It greeted me the second I stepped from the portal. Why is that what everyone gets hung up on?" She just admitted to being assaulted multiple times and yet the wind whisp was what stunned the man. She shook her head and crossed her arms as she grew more and more pissed.

Darrin looked to Atlas, confused. Atlas's returning gaze of perplexity then turned and seared into Evangaline. "The whisp only responds to those with the powers of the divine goddess. You are a…" Atlas murmured rather harshly before his words trailed off. His eyes, though, gave away his judgment as they fixed onto her un-pointed ears. *Human.*

The side of Evangaline's mouth ticked up as her gaze met Ryder's softening face at the insinuation from the king and his ally. She was a human—and she was damn proud to be. But she was also Darrin's heir and with that carried the blood of the fae—blood of Tuatha. Blood of Danu.

Then her prince did the most remarkable thing.

He tipped his head back, exposing his strong throat and laughed, which despite her attempt to remain poised and stoic, made her smile genuinely.

Once he was done filling the room with his deep, honey laced laugh, he made his way around the table to Evangaline's side.

"For being the people around Evangaline the most, you really do miss quite a lot," Ryder rather pointedly quipped. His Cheshire cat grin grew, exposing his bright white teeth.

Evangaline then gazed up at the man bound to her and smiled. She held up a palm and reached inside the thrumming in her chest, right past her heart that was fluttering methodically to its own exuberant tune. With a mental nudge, she allowed the small flame to reappear and dance around her hand, flickering in the morning sun. It wasn't second nature yet, as Ryder promised the night before, but each time she conjured the flame, her body hummed in encouragement.

Raising her other palm, she manifested a small drop of water and threw a taunting smile at Des. He rolled his eyes, but his smile held a mirth that she hadn't seen in him since before Chloe's death. It made her fearless to have the support of those closest to her. This power she had in her thrived with her courage.

The flame and the water danced in her hands in simultaneous movements, a magically choreographed waltz. The water glistened with each flicker of the small flame.

Dropping her gaze to her hands, Evangaline focused in on the fire and water in her palms and willed them to come together, to intertwine around one another without snuffing the other out.

It was an experiment, in all truth, one she hoped would impress the men surrounding her, but she knew deep inside she could do it. So she did.

Evangaline delicately transferred the water to stand beside the flame. Within a second of conjuring the idea in her mind, the form of the little water droplet and flame took on the shape of two elemental people. Then they danced. A delicate tango of flame and water twirling around her hand, both contained in their own elemental state, yet combined in a melodic symphony as she willed it. Sweat beaded down her back at the effort to contain the dancers in her palms, but she was doing it.

Ryder placed his tattooed hand around her waist and whispered in her ear, "Well, that's new."

Evangaline smiled widely and chuckled. Never in her whole life had she felt this complete.

She always felt like an outsider, even among her family. Katherine and Miles were always so fearless and independent. Even as children, if her siblings wanted something, they found a way to achieve it. Without fear or reservations, they got what they wanted.

Meanwhile, Evangaline was shy and introverted. Her fear always stopped her from taking what she wanted. She stayed in the confines of the gilded cage of her anxiety and fright.

Not any longer. Now she had power. She had a purpose. She had friends. She had a man by her side, whom, despite not choosing one another, was thrilled and proud to be there. His hand was a steady presence on her side. The glow of his smile beamed onto her like a thousand stars—bright and steady. She felt confident to fight the fear in her body, to take her place in a world that seemed to ignore her once upon a time. She waited long enough for something good to happen to her, and it did, but it would take hard work and determination to keep that good thing. She had to work for it and goddammit she was going to work her ass off. Never again would she hold herself back.

She looked forward to the future instead of dreading it. Eager to wake up and practice her magic, travel the realm, meet with the people. She finally had a purpose, and she was not going to squander it. She found her courage and bravery all in one crazy, eventful night.

Evangaline knew what it took to be strong and bold by watching her best friend live her beautifully short life. With each new morning, she would attempt to be fierce and unfaltering like she dreamed she could be. Starting now with the little elemental dancers thriving in her palms.

"We have much to discuss, *father.*"

Chapter Forty-Four

For the first time in days, Evangaline was gifted with an afternoon of solitude. She had spent days in meetings, scheduled appearances, lessons, trainings, and dinners. After Darrin came back from the dungeons hand delivering Bastian a life sentence within the underground cavern prison beneath the palace, he was unrelenting in making sure her days were packed with things to keep her busy. For a man who wished to see her stay permanently through a sham marriage, Darrin certainly did not want her spending any time with Ryder. However, his attempts did not work. Evangaline blamed it on being fated, but she simply could not stay away from her prince even if she tried … and she tried. Were they ever alone? Not very often. Seldom, in fact, did they barely even get five minutes alone without someone interrupting them? If they were gifted with more than that, it became a magic lesson or fate related study session thanks to Atlas's excitement.

Evangaline's only alone time in the last few days consisted of the late-night hours that she crawled into bed and crashed within minutes. Only to be woken too quickly by the sun to start bright and early with her training.

To say she was reaching a level of burnout in less than a week was an understatement. Her body was strong thanks to her training. Ryder was helping her powers excel, but her mind, well, that was chugging along on its last leg. She desperately needed time to recharge.

So when Wren told her all the men in her life were otherwise preoccupied, she thanked whatever god would hear her and dedicated herself to curling up on the couch with the book Ryder gave her, *Twist of Fate: The Legend of Tuatha and Milesian.*

Ryder had an emergency meeting with a member of his court. Atlas was tied up returning correspondences for Darrin—who was off visiting the Kingdom of Leaves. And Des and the boys were running drills for the Royal Army.

She hadn't had a free moment to just relax and read a book in, gods, she couldn't even remember.

Evangaline spent hours reading about Tuatha and Milesian. How they met in the last decade of the old fae world before the Convergence thrust them into the New Ages. She read about how they spoke little of the intricate nature of being fated, but their sudden love for one another outweighed the hatred of their peoples. The novel was informative in many ways but seeing as she too bore the mark of the fates; it was in the minor details that the author described her ancestors' relationship, that Evangaline felt seen.

Her and Ryder spent much of their free time scouring the library looking for any information on being fated. How it will affect them, what it means, prophecies, diaries, anything that would allow them the opportunity to know more about the turn their lives had taken, but they came up short. As they soon found, not a single fae soul truly knew every in and out of being fated. There simply weren't enough couples blessed with the mark. It would appear Tuatha and Milesian simply did not have enough free time to write it all down for the future generations. Ending a war and then immediately picking up the pieces of the Convergence, *apparently* consumed their entire schedules. Even the stories about the couple were not very detailed in regard to being fated, but Evangaline picked up on quotes or nuances the author wrote and dissected them with a meticulous eye.

In the early days, Tuatha herself was quoted talking about the secret meeting with her fated and how an overwhelming sense of rightness enveloped her. Her exact words were, "I felt the stars themselves smile down on me as to say that for once I made the right call". It was exactly how

Evangaline felt when she and Ryder's hands met nearly a week ago. He became a sort of home, a solace of warmth and guidance. Of course, she still battled her grief, anxiety, and fear, for she simply didn't become a different person just because she was blessed with Ryder. But knowing she had his support made the impact of choosing Celadonia over returning to her family in Vitalis more bearable.

Evangaline knew he cared from the small glances, warm smiles, and tentative hand holds. He gave hugs that enveloped her in a way that made her want to curl into his lap and ask him to never let her go. They both knew the need for each other's companionship was an effect from being fated—at least that was what they told themselves in an attempt to not come across as psychopathic clingers. She wanted to take it slow, get to know Ryder before jumping him—she made the mistake of trusting her libido once before and vowed not to do that again. Evangaline wanted to get to know Ryder before she jumped in bed with him, despite how difficult that was proving.

As she flipped to the end of the book and took in yet another sketch of Tuatha and Milesian sitting in their thrones—her father's throne—movement caught her eye in the corner of her room by the fireplace. It was brief, quick, and dark. She didn't turn immediately toward the splash of darkness that scurried across her floor. Instead, she reached under her silk dress stealthily and unsheathed a small knife she concealed there on her thigh. Between Des and Ryder and their protective natures, she made an effort to keep a small blade at the very least strapped on her person at all times, especially when alone.

Clutching the small knife in the palm of her hand, Evangaline pretended to return to the book in her hands. Again, movement shifted in the waning light of the sun by the French doors. Her heart pounded with memories she was unable to suppress. Had the same demon that killed Chloe come back to claim her again? Was she strong enough to kill one on her own? If she screamed, would someone hear her and come running? Would her magic work on the vile creatures?

Flashbacks of Chloe's blood dripping down her skin flashed before her eyes. The grief pooled in her gut and anger filled her blood. Her palm warmed her blade with fire magic until it became a red-hot brand of her fury. She would make the murderer pay in blood and ash. She would bring them to their knees before watching the life drain from their eyes.

The second movement caught her eye again. Closer to the chair beside the couch, Evangaline jumped up, hurled the book toward the inky intruder and wielded her small knife. "Show yourself!" She demanded. Nothing happened. No scratching noise. No misty fog transforming a beast. Just a toppled book, a fiery blade, and an angry but scared princess.

Evangaline crept slowly around the chair; knife held aloft, ready to strike whatever lurked in her room. But as she rounded the chair, her shoulders dropped, and her anger morphed into a guilty embarrassment. There, huddled under the book, shook a tiny little shadow. It was only a streak of silky darkness, but the moment she eased the book up, she immediately recognized it as one of the shadows that prowled her fated's chest. It was smaller than the rest of his shadows.

"Did Ryder send you to spy on me?"

It shook harder and curled itself into a little ball, ashamed.

The turn her life took … first she spoke to the wind and now to a shadow … *one ticket to the looney bin, please!*

She took in the cowering shadow, and her heart sank. "I'm sorry I scared you. You scared me too, though. I thought you were what killed my friend. Please don't tell that to Ryder, though."

Evangaline sank down to the floor, allowing her dress to pool on the hardwood. The shadow eased a little toward her like a dog greeting a new owner. Slow tentative slithers across the floor until it sat right before her in a way the shadows only thrived on Ryder. It wiggled a brief hello that made her chuckle.

"Hello. So tell me … He sent you to spy on me, didn't he?"

The shadow curled in on itself in embarrassment.

She sucked on her lower lip, an idea springing to mind. "I have an idea. Go report back to him that you saw me in here in the arms of another man. He deserves a little payback for scaring the shit out of both of us!"

The shadow wiggled excitedly and then tore away from her, gliding across the room and under the door with a silent ease.

Evangaline shook her head, flexing her festering panic attack away. It was bad enough dealing with regular everyday anxiety, but the PTSD she was trying to work through from Chloe's death was numbing at times. It got better with each day, but occasionally, when something would startle her or her mind would play tricks on her, images of that night flooded her mind, incapacitating her completely. The fear that took over her body when she saw the shadow made her frustrated at herself. *You will not live in fear!* She told herself.

Of course the thought of one of the demon creatures manifesting again was bone chilling but she couldn't help the way the nausea and cold sweats gripped her when the images of Chloe's mangled body flashed in her mind the moment she thought she was in danger. Whoever said a person's life flashes before their eyes in the face of danger was a dirty fucking liar. She didn't have a montage of the times they spent laughing over drinks or watching Chloe sell books she knew nothing about, but selling them, anyway. None of the good times came to mind first when Evangaline panicked. It wasn't her life or any of the positives that flickered in her eyes; it was her regrets that surfaced first. Her fears. The things that made a pit form in her stomach and her eyes sting with tears. Two seconds of panic was all it took to see the horrid flashback at the sight of Ryder's little shadow.

She rose to her feet, dragging in a deep breath to calm down.

You're safe. She told herself on repeat until stomps manifested down the hall outside her door.

A ghost of a smile stretched across her lips the moment a barely restrained fist knocked on her door. She waited a minute, gathering her book from the floor, righting her skirt, slipping her pocketknife into the garter on her thigh.

Another knock sounded, this time a bit harder. A sigh of frustration almost made her crack apart with laugher. *That's what you get for spying!*

Slowly, Evangaline wandered to the door, wondering if her fated's fae hearing could hear the soft pitter patter of her feet on the hardwood.

Just as she reached her arm out to undo the lock on the door, a shadow—

not the same little one as before—slithered under the door and up to the lock. She squinted down at it just as it stilled, clearly being caught. With a finger raised to her lips, she shook her head. Another accomplice joined her ranks as it bobbed in a nod. *Take that, Ryder!* The shadow slowly unlatched the lock and made its way under the door.

With her book clasped behind her back, Evangaline took a step back, knowing exactly the level of restraint Ryder was exhibiting.

Five, four, three, two …

Bang!

The door slammed open, revealing Ryder. His hair was in disarray. His shirt was untucked and unbuttoned nearly all the way. His feet were bare, just as hers were. Had he been napping?

"Were you taking a nap?" She voiced out loud, her tone held a hint of ridicule. A smile stretched across her face so much that her cheeks hurt.

Ryder stalked in the door, his eyes swimming with darkness. "Where is he?"

"Where is who?" She played coy.

Ryder took a breath before stepping closer to her to close the door behind him. They were so close, no more than a couple of inches separated them. She could smell that summer beach bonfire scent that clung to him. She could feel the heat that radiated off of his body like a furnace. The book in her hands got clenched tighter as he dipped his face to hers. If she had any balls whatsoever, she could easily step onto her toes and press her lips to his, but unfortunately, she was ball-less. His proximity short circuited her mind and all she could do was stare into the depths of his eyes.

"Who is he, Eva?" He meant business. Was he jealous of an imaginary man?

Evangaline let out a breathy laugh and looked down on his exposed chest. Little shadow was the only one of his parasitic friends that wasn't writhing across the field of tanned and toned skin of his chest. "I don't like being spied on," she whispered, meeting his eyes again.

They stood a hairsbreadth away, looking into each other's eyes. The tension was palpable between the two of them, but not as much as the lust clouding her mind. What about fae men made her want to throw caution to the wind and climb them like a goddam tree without a single thought? Yet again, Ryder wasn't like Bastian. He was broody, yes, but he was kind and sensitive, he was a romantic, and hers. He was *hers*. And she was *his*. That thought alone made heat pool in her lower belly.

Realization dawned in his eyes as they grew lighter in color, fading back to their pristine, flawless sapphire hue. He leaned closer to her, his nose coming within an inch of the skin just below her ear. His hand met the wall above her head just as he inhaled. "There was no other man, was there Eva?"

She shook her head slightly. "I don't like being spied on …" she whispered again.

"Did you know you smell like evergreens in winter? Fresh, airy. What you don't smell like is another man." His eyebrow arched as he looked down at her.

She arched her eyebrow back. "That's because there is no other man. I'm kind of insulted you would actually think I would cheat on you." She swung her head under his arm and walked back into the living room, flipping her book to the page she left off on. "If you wanted to know what I was doing, all you had to do was ask. You didn't need to send one of your little spies to check up on me. Don't be mean to little shadow either, it was my idea to prank you … not theirs." She sat on the couch with her back to the prince, that of which she left standing in the vestibule by the door with his mouth agape and an ashamed look in his eye.

It took a second before the couch dipped beside her. Ryder's head rested on the back. It took a moment, but his hand reached out to grab hers. "I trust you. It's everyone else I don't trust. And the idea of another man around you makes me—"

"Feral?" She giggled. She glanced over at him. Her fingers tightened around his as he laughed. "It's okay. I get it. The other day at dinner, when Lady Hightower checked out your ass, I may or may not have thought about stabbing her with my soup spoon." Ryder's eyes narrowed as he glanced back at her with a smile cheating across his face that sent her heart into flutter territory.

"You did not?" He huffed a laugh.

She winced jokingly. "I absolutely thought about it."

"My curious little creature. One minute you are looking radiant in a ball gown dining with courtiers, then plotting their deaths with blunt ended utensils in the blink of an eye."

Her cheeks flushed with a pink blush. She scooted closer to him, tossing her book onto the coffee table, scrunching her knees under her bum. "Woah, woah, woah, I said 'stabbing', not killing. Just a little enough wound where her and every other woman know not to stare at your ass. It's impolite to stare, that's all. Don't get a big head about it. I wouldn't be doing it for you!"

Ryder laughed as he unlaced their fingers and put his arm around Evangaline's shoulders. "Of course not! Why would I even think you too would go 'feral' for your fated? Silly me."

She rested her head onto his chest, his heart beat in perfect synchronicity with hers, his breath was even and calm, her hand splayed on his stomach. It was the first time they sat cuddled into one another. It felt … nice.

"You were definitely taking a nap, though, weren't you?" She joked.

"Mhmm," he hummed. "My meeting finished. And reading dossiers is incredibly boring." His voice was sleep riddled. She tilted her head up, smiling as she saw his eyes closed.

She nestled her head into his chest and listened to sleep claim him. Eventually, laying in the warmth of his arms, sleep claimed her too.

"They're so cute all cuddled up wike two wittle cutie pwies,"

"Shut the fuck up, Des." Ryder's voice rumbled through his chest and into Evangaline's ear.

Shaw and Charlie echoed Des's laughter.

"Fuck off," Evangaline added with a flick of her middle finger in the air.

Ryder's snort of laughter shook her head, but still she kept her eyes closed.

Charlie laughed harder. "They're perfect for one another. Dunno why we waited till they were fated to see it."

"Dinner is all set up, guys!" Wren called out from behind them in the dining room.

At the handmaiden's voice, Evangaline opened her eyes and peaked over the back of the couch.

"I didn't call for dinner?" Her groggy voice barely squeaked out.

Wren eyed Evangaline with a blush on her cheeks and a smile on her lips. A small wing of eyeliner played around her almond-shaped eyes. "You missed dinner, ma'am. Des asked me to bring some up."

Evangaline straightened up, suddenly feeling the warmth of Ryder's hand as it rested up her skirt and around her thigh. She looked down at the exposed skin of her leg and up to Ryder, whose eyes were still clamped shut. Small, mindless sweeps of his finger across the soft expanse of her leg sent chills up her spine. Chills that told her if she didn't get up, she was going to do very naughty things in the company of her friends.

Her eyes found Des's and the taunting grin on his face told her he knew what she was thinking. With a quick flick of her wrist, a drop of water, alright a splash of water, crashed into his grinning face. Her magic smacked him right on the dome of his head and washed away every last joke he had brewing. "Son of a bitch!" He shouted, jumping away from her small wave.

Ryder's eye peaked open as a laugh escaped his lips. His hand clenched tighter on her leg and his arm pulled her closer. "Your lessons are certainly proving fruitful," he rumbled.

She giggled and sank into his chest again. "Did we really miss dinner?"

"Yep! And seeing that you two were conveniently the only two not there … good luck combatting the new rumors that are now swirling around about how you can't keep your hands off one another." Shaw plopped onto the couch beside Evangaline with a wink.

Ryder scoffed, "We're fated," he said, as if that was validation enough. "Besides, now Eva doesn't need to stab anyone with a spoon …"

Evangaline swatted playfully at his chest, "Shut it." Ryder pinched away her argument, making her squirm upright. His hand fell from her leg, pulling her dress down to cover the exposed skin in the process."

"Did you guys eat?" She asked gratefully, smiling down at Ryder before looking up to Wren. "Are you hungry? Will you stay? Save me from all of this testosterone!" Evangaline pouted her lips playfully, garnering a laugh from Wren.

"Oh, I … no my lady I am … I have …"

"Does the little lass have a date?" Charlie taunted.

Evangaline shut him up with a pillow to the face. "Leave her alone."

"That, soldier, is none of your business!" Wren quipped, earning a smile from Evangaline. "I will be off. If you need anything, Elain will be on duty."

Evangaline nodded with a smile. "Have a good night, Wren. Love the eyeliner, by the way." She winked as Wren bristled bashfully from the room.

Des laughed, "We ate. Dinner is for you guys."

"Speak for yourself. I'm still hungry! What did the little darlin' bring us?" Charlie breathed, lumbering over to the dining table, rubbing his hands together menacingly.

Evangaline rolled her eyes and extended a hand to Ryder. He reluctantly grabbed it and stood upright. They smiled at one another with admiration coloring their eyes. Unspoken words that both clearly felt, but were too timid to speak aloud.

"Uh-hem," Des coughed, shaking the residual water from his hair. "Evie, you going to eat or are you two going to eye fuck each other all night?"

She took a deep breath. "Lord, help me," she whispered into Ryder's chest.

With her hand in his, he led her to the table. Side by side, they sat down. His long frame filled the seat to her left, the same one Chloe used to sit in. For the second time in the day, her thoughts spiraled to the final images of her best friend. She closed her eyes, trying to erase the images floating through her mind in a rapid-fire montage.

Breathe, Evangaline.

"You okay?" Des whispered across from her. His face dripped with concern.

She nodded, "Mhmm."

"Eva?" Ryder asked rubbing his finger across her knuckles.

"It's nothing." She opened her eyes smiling at her boys. "How was your day?" She plastered on a smile and focused on the squinted aquamarine eyes of her friend. "Seriously, I'm good! What'd you do today?"

Des's eyes never wavered from her own. He knew what was plaguing her. It plagued him, too. They shared an unspoken bond of heartache, but he didn't push the matter. He simply nodded and flashed a quick look at Ryder before relaxing in his chair. "Trained some new recruits. Had a meeting with Atlas. Oh, which reminds me! You two lovebirds—"

Evangaline snickered, cutting him off. "Des—" she warned with a smile.

Des smiled back and nodded backing down. The asshole loved to poke fun at their being fated and the up in the air way that they approached their relationship. "Atlas scheduled an interview and portrait session with The Golden Prophet," Ryder growled his discontent. Evangaline returned her own strokes on his hand to ease the rigidness that consumed his body. "The king wasn't a fan of the idea, but Atlas did it anyway." His eyes spoke the word he did not want to say aloud, *Sorry.*

Evangaline held tighter onto Ryder's hand. "Do we have to? I'm sure everyone in the realm already knows?"

Des nodded, "I know." His facial features pinched the moment his shoulders raised indignantly.

Ryder squeezed her hand before settling his grip on her thigh. "Is my uncle *trying* to kill me?"

"Not a fan of interviews?" Des said, grinning around the piece of fruit speared on his fork.

Ryder rolled his eyes. "Interviews, I don't mind. The assholes at The Golden Prophet? I mind. Greatly."

Evangaline stiffened. "Are they that bad?"

Des snickered while Ryder let out a sigh that bore the weight of many years of aggravation. "They enjoy twisting the stories they report. When I took my father's place as the Prince of Shadows, that twit of an editor twisted all my words. It made me look like a fool. It took weeks of interviews with other papers to undo what he did. Fuck, when Ophelia and Helena got married, they did a whole piece about the choice of gowns they wore at the ceremony and how they weren't virtuous by not wearing white, leading to the headline *'Are two women cut from a morally ambiguous background truly fit to rule Mirth?'"* Evangaline giggled at the way Ryder spoke in a pretentious accent to quote the paper. His thumb made circles on her thigh as he grinned down at her, "All I am saying is when we meet with them … say the bare minimum. They can be a bunch a prick."

"I'm a writer. I have a fancy journalism degree and everything! Why can't I just write an article and have The Golden Pricks publish it?" The idea of writing an article to announce her and Ryder's fating excited her a bit.

Ryder hummed thoughtfully, "It's not a bad idea …" he looked to Des hopefully.

"No can do. If we had more time, maybe, but the reporter and artist will be here bright and early tomorrow. So, training will have to be canceled."

Evangaline deflated, "Ugh, fine. I'm still going to get a run in before they come. I need a clear head before."

"Care for company?" Des pleaded, "I could use the air?"

She nodded, about to tell Des the time she would be ready when food started flying through the air across the table, back and forth between Shaw and Charlie. The two men giggled childishly as they exchanged pies and pastries through aerial assaults.

"Oh, shit, Lady E … try this!" Shaw interjected with a mouth full of food, clearly not caring about the conversation beside him. A small meat pie landed on her plate with a thud. She laughed and took a bite, giving Des a grateful smile. Shaw was right. It was delicious. Suddenly, another pie came flying at Ryder without a word, luckily his hands elevated at just the right time, catching the meat pie before it smacked him in the face.

"Thanks?" He muttered.

Shaw grinned, elated with himself. "Eat up, Prince Man!"

Ryder obliged, sighing once he took a bite. "Okay … it's good," he muttered.

They ate until Evangaline felt ready to burst. She was exhausted despite taking an hour-long nap on her prince sized pillow. Her eyes barely held themselves open as the men around her talked and laughed.

The way Ryder fit in with the boys was refreshing. He relaxed around them, filling in conversations and returning their banter tenfold. His willingness to get to know her friends filled her heart and made the tension in her shoulders ease. The last thing she needed was her friends and fated to be at odds. Between Darrin's expectations and the people who doubted her abilities, she was grateful to have all of her favorite men getting along.

Finally, her eyes drifted closed, and her head dropped to Ryder's shoulder as she yawned. Sleep called to her. *Who knew being a princess was so tiring!*

She did not know how long she rested on his shoulder, nor knew how much time passed, but when she woke in the morning, she was neatly tucked into her bed in the gown she wore the night before.

On her nightstand, resting on her book, laid a beautiful black rose that sparkled with a glint of the cosmos. It sung with Ryder's shadow magic. Its petals were kissed with starlight. Its leaves glinted with moonbeams despite the sable base of the rose.

She smiled as she took in the flower her fated made with his magic just as Wren bristled through the door. "Good morning, Princess! You have a couple of hours before your interview." She beamed.

"Good morning." Evangaline murmured back, knowing the moment the article reached the furthest corners of Celadonia, there would be no turning back. Every citizen would know who she was down to the very last glint of copper lining her arm. She breathed deep, ready to start her day with a run and her first sit down interview as the Crown Princess of Celadonia and fated to the Prince of Shadows.

Chapter Forty-Five

Two weeks flew by faster than the wind whisp that visited Evangaline early in the mornings as she ran through the forest. The hands of the clock twirled by faster and faster each day; relentless in their rotations.

Maybe it was Evangaline's newfound commitment to her new role or her eagerness to learn more about her power, but she found herself desperate to wake in the morning and savor every last second that her eyelids remained up. The fact that she knew there would be a certain six-foot five dark haired prince waiting for her when she finished training always helped get her out of bed. Not only did she have so much to learn, but she had a whole new world to discover. She had work to do, and people to make proud!

Evangaline spent her days practically the same way. Her primary goal, however, was to acclimate herself with the intricacies of the court and the day-to-day activities of a crown princess of the fae. That of which included, but was not limited to, civilian matters, politics, and taking notes of the necessities that the king and his advisors needed to tend. She was determined to be the princess everyone needed her to be. No matter how much that terrified her. And bored the shit out of her at times.

Atlas taught her the basics of Celadonian royalty in her first three weeks, but their lessons dove into more rigorous territories now that Evangaline accepted her new political role. Understanding political structure, hierarchy, and a plethora of other things that kept the realm and their relations to the New World functioning properly were at the top of her course curriculum.

All of which were extremely boring. She tended to lots of correspondences and sat in on meetings with allies and dignitaries from the kingdoms almost every day. All of which she was a silent observer for, taking notes in the background like a good little protégé.

"The Leaves ask for the king's aid in securing funds to pay for a new school in the village of Cidus."

"The Kingdom of Fire is eager for His Majesty to approve the new design of the new weapons for the Royal Army."

"The Kingdom of Mirth extends an invitation to the orchestra's opening night at The Einsmod Theatre."

The king was happy to hand over some responsibilities to Evangaline. Sorting through his junk mail was not entirely her favorite pastime, but she found it to be her job more often than not. Despite it all, the tedious work allowed Evangaline an insight into the realm and gave her the opportunity to learn about the key players within the kingdoms and their courts.

Every day, though, before the sun even rose high into the sky, she would wake and train, just like she did before she formally accepted her title and role. It was important to keep some aspect of her old routine intact, so she didn't entirely lose herself. The monotony of her training kept her sane and despite Darrin trying to pack her schedule with his snooze inducing encounters, Evangaline was adamant in keeping her mornings free for training. It might have been a coping mechanism, but it made her feel healthier in not only body but mind. For those few hours, the pounding of her feet on soil and blades clashing gave her a clear head. In those hours, her anxiety disappeared and the weight on her shoulders eased. It was only her and the burn within her muscles. It was her safe place.

Throwing on her worn in leathers and strapping on her dingy practice sword, Evangaline would set out ready to tackle the day with a smile and determination in her heart.

Des was typically there waiting on the field behind the palace once she returned from her run, but now, with Bastian rotting in an iron cell far beneath their feet, Des had many additional responsibilities. He was promoted to General of the Royal Army, a role and title he thoroughly fought Evangaline over. However, without Chloe to rise the ranks and a lot of the other commanders and high-ranking members voicing their support for Bastian, Des was the rightful choice—and the safest one for Evangaline. He was loyal to the crown and a fierce warrior with empathy for anyone he met. After a week of pestering him, and wearing down the king, the role went to Des—begrudgingly.

Meanwhile, Atlas got the role of Hand of the King, something he should have been from the jump, but somehow Bastian beat him to it. Atlas, with his demure smile, was rightfully promoted and excelled.

The court in general was … *surprised* when the news broke of Bastian's imprisonment and the crimes he committed against their newfound crown princess. The article with her and Ryder was published two days after their joint interview and while some bits and pieces were taken out of context, she spoke the truth and they wrote the truth. *Thankfully.*

Evangaline knew it would be hard to tell the people of her relationship with the ex-general, and it was, but she did not want to start her tenure as a monarch by lying. Darrin had done enough of that for the two of them and she wanted to earn her people's trust, even if that meant offering up a hard truth.

The court was shocked when they heard of Bastian's multiple assaults— or at least they pretended like they were. The gasps and mewls of the crowd were anything but comforting, but Evangaline knew well enough than to be shocked. Bastian was someone the courtiers looked up to, someone meant to protect them, so hearing the news of the new princess sleeping with him then throwing him in jail for assault was not quite the turn of events they saw coming. It didn't help that the word of a woman was always questioned. Even with the fae, men still dismissed her claims as the angry rantings of a woman scorned. But they simmered down when Evangaline and Ryder announced their fating. The good outweighed the bad, she supposed.

Many of the court looked at Evangaline and Ryder as some form of the gods. Handshakes tended to last longer with many of the courtiers and civilians, seeing them as holy figures. They would run their fingers along the copper markings like the tattoos were a genie's lamp, and Evangaline and Ryder would grant their wishes if they hovered long enough.

Ryder never allowed the lingering touches, saying they freaked him out. Instead, a quick, solid, simple shake of the hand was all the Prince of Shadows allowed.

But Evangaline could see the wonder in some people's eyes. Many—almost all—hadn't been old enough to see Tuatha and Milesian be fated, Ryder himself was old but not that old, and well, with the lack of other couples bearing the marks, the notion seemed like a myth or fairytale to many people of The Capital. Yet, Ryder and Evangaline stood before them, bearing the mark of the fates, bonded for life, and it enamored them.

Other members of the Capital, however, were not convinced of the soul binding union. Mainly all the men who looked up to Bastian as their own seriously twisted god. The misogynistic and egotistical fae of the court, including Lord Whittell—*shocking*—liked to challenge Evangaline and Ryder's fating and would complain, almost non-stop, that Evangaline herself was planning a coup of the realm. *"For the mortal trash of Vitalis, she works. Taking out the General was only the first of her demented plans. The fae will fall to ruins at her feet, I tell you."* The pompous oaf would murmur under his breath to his group of cronies in a way reserved for broken records.

Ryder had no problem one particular night, allowing his fate-provoked protective nature to come out and play. When he heard the insipid rantings of the nobles, his shadows thrived, and a wicked gleam came over his eyes. Lord Whittell didn't utter another word after one of Ryder's shadows happened to slip from his grasp and crawl up his chubby leg and around his flabby torso, constricting ever so slightly. Whittell swatted at it like a bug until Ryder pulled it back at Evangaline's request. They laughed about the exchange later in private, that was until the king interrupted and reprimanded Evangaline for her so called "insolence".

Since the day after the ball, the king had been off edgy even. His ego was inflated and his tolerance severely deflated. The article detailing Evangaline's time in Celadonia and subsequent fating to Ryder only made

Darrin's attitude sourer.

Everything Evangaline did was under constant scrutiny. If he didn't ream her himself, he sent Atlas to do it. Atlas was much kinder and made it more of a reason to drink some whiskey in the library, but he still told her to behave herself. Despite ninety-nine percent of the time not doing anything worth condemning. Laughing with the boys? Reprimanded. Holding Ryder's hand in public? Reprimanded. Asking questions during meetings? Reprimanded. Nothing she did was done right in Darrin's eyes. It was aggravating, but she took a breath every time she was told what she was doing wrong and tried to forget about it. Tried to be the bigger person.

Atlas even saw the changes in the king, but assured Evangaline that it was just a stressful time with her debut and *"everything"*. Evangaline never pushed, but she knew *"everything"* couldn't be a good thing, but she had enough on her plate. All of Darrin's burdens could stay his own.

So, Evangaline turned to her daily training as therapy and thankfully, the whole cadre pitched in. She saw little of them with all her new obligations and meetings, but even if it was a quick dinner or a training session; they made it a point to spend some time with one another. They never spoke of it, but Evangaline could tell the loss of Chloe affected all of them and made the entire group more in need of companionship than before.

On some days, Evangaline was lucky to be blessed with them all feeding her—most of the time—incredibly unhelpful comments such as "don't get hit." Or her personal favorite, "try to duck next time, it will sting less." That little nugget came from the otherwise quiet Lukas, when Aadi, who was surprisingly quiet and fast, ambushed her and clubbed her on the head with the pommel of his longsword.

Despite her raucous trainers, she was improving rapidly. Even her skill with a bow—which was a surprisingly difficult skill—got better. Nine out of twelve—*almost*—bullseyes were pretty good in her book.

"You're damn elbow!" Charlie screamed from two trees over.

Evangaline sighed, lowering the bow and arrow. "What's wrong with it now?" She screamed back.

"It's sagging." Murray amended, reclining against another tree, sharpening his sword.

They had gone deep into the forest and hung a target for her to practice her archery. The whole cadre had the morning off and instead of doing something useful, they decided to be gigantic pains in Evangaline's ass.

Des walked over, his steps heated. He had been in a bad mood since Evangaline bested him in their sparring session earlier. His male ego was a little wounded. "Like this!" Des picked up the extra bow and nocked an arrow. Staring Evangaline down, he raised the bow and released it.

"Oh, you fucking show off!" Evangaline breathed as Des's arrow sank deep inside the bullseye, puncturing halfway out the backside and into the tree.

Des smirked, his aqua eyes chiding her with their sarcastic glow.

Evangaline smirked back, snapping her finger and conjuring a small little rain cloud just for Des. With a small crack of thunder, the cloud rained right on Des's smug head of golden curls.

"Jokes on you. I needed a bath." Des quipped, strumming his hands through his hair as his clothes became soaked through.

Evangaline laughed, "I know I smelled you from twenty feet away. My eyes started watering and everything!"

"Are you sure you two aren't related? You bicker like siblings." Aadi questioned as Lukas, Murray, and Shaw laughed from their blanket on the leaf sodden ground at Des's expense. The laughter sent what little of Des's pride right out the window.

"Best three out of four?" Des challenged her.

"Oh, you're on. What do I get when I win?"

Des snickered. "A swift kick in the ass."

"Well, that makes me not want to ask what I get if I lose."

"A swift kick in the ass," Des repeated, his little rain cloud thundering above his head. "Can you make this go away?"

"Nope … I think it stays. It's your handicap. You have what, five hundred years of training on me?"

"I'm a little over thirty years. I'm not that old. I'm younger than your …" He flicked his hands at her tattoo, "whatever you two are."

Truth was … Evangaline didn't know what she and Ryder were. They never talked about it further after the night of the ball. She had feelings for him that she could not even explain, and he admitted feeling something for her. But they never put a formal name or title on it aside from being fated.

They hadn't been on a date or kissed. Aside from the one day they napped, cuddled into one another, Ryder only wrapped his arm around her a few times. He held her hand and occasionally she would get a Ryder hug here or there—which made her insides weak. His touch alone sent those pixies in her stomach on a carnival ride. The rollercoaster that they screamed on tended to numb every part of Evangaline's soul. Mainly the part of her being that missed her family and grieved Chloe, which both happened daily, but somehow not as much when Ryder was around, let alone touching her.

Despite not having a formal name for their relationship status, the Prince of Shadows was with her every day. She could see him occasionally, like earlier this morning, from his window as he watched her train. Sometimes, to her amusement, he would be sleep mussed and shirtless. His glistening and fit torso displayed all his perfectly sculpted abs. The shadows stationed on his chest and shoulders slumbered while his fating mark glinted in the sunlight as he sipped his morning tea.

He was otherworldly and seeing him right out of bed made Evangaline weak and hot all over. Her heart pounded with the urge to visit him late at night and see every inch of his toned and tanned skin up close for herself. Her body practically hummed with an insatiable desire to be with him, under him, on top of him, any way he wanted her, truly, she wanted to be for him. But she restrained her womanly desires by telling herself to get to know the prince before jumping into his bed like some sex crazed animal— despite every fiber of her being wanting to do the exact opposite. Evangaline was desperate for a moment that was just the two of them without it being a lesson or an exploration into her powers. Without the pressures of the realm or their peoples.

"Shut up and figure out an actual prize for me to win when I kick your ass, *General Des!*" Evangaline quipped after growing flushed with a strawberry pink hue, thinking about Ryder watching hours before at his window, shirtless and groggy.

Des pushed her softly, "You just want to pick a fight today, huh?" His face was a lethal mixture of taunt and provocation.

"Ha! We already fought and I kicked your ass!"

"Rematch, Rematch, Rematch, Rematch!" the rest of the cadre chanted, shit-eating grins smeared across their far too entertained faces.

Evangaline smiled and shook her head, "It's what my people want …" she shrugged and eyed Des with a smirk.

"Take the cloud away and fight me like a real warrior."

"Some would say a real warrior fights with all the tools in their arsenal." Ryder's deep voice crooned from behind the cadre.

Evangaline whipped around just as the men all scurried to get their weapons in their hands. Until they noticed it was only Ryder and, well, he could kill them with or without their swords.

As they scurried to their feet, Ryder chuckled, "Guys, you don't have to stand to greet me. Sit. Please don't tell me Eva makes you bow whenever you see her?" He glanced tauntingly at Evangaline.

Charlie huffed, "The second I bow and kiss her wee ass will be the day I shite out a goblin!"

Evangaline, mouth hung open, eyes squinted, looked to Charlie, "What the literal fuck did you just say? How much wine have you had so far this morning? Also, thank you … my ass is *wee*." She laughed.

Des huffed, "Evie. Cloud. Now!"

"Jesus! Someone woke up on the wrong side of the bed today." Evangaline waved her hand, dispersing the small cloud and then pursed her lips slightly to blow a puff of air on Des, effectively drying his clothes with a magical blast of cool air.

Des shivered. "Could you make it warmer next time?"

"I guess I can cross off rain and wind from the list of Tuatha and Danu's powers." Ryder smiled at Evangaline.

Evangaline nodded. "Yeah, I figured out the whole cloud thing in the bath last night. Long story short, I wanted a shower, so I thought I'd just make one. It worked!"

"A shower?" Des asked.

The fae had a lot of things, magic being one of them, but where they made up in beauty and fantastical elements, they lacked in others. The fae had magic and therefore, science kind of lacked. Furthermore, they still took baths despite having plumbing and heated water. Overhead faucets were not quite a thing in Celadonia. Evangaline had it on her list of things to introduce to the realm. Baths every morning were tedious and often made her tired, but a good shower … that would wake her right up.

"Yeah, essentially what I just gave you. Picture it like a bath that you stand in. The water rains down on you from overhead instead of you soaking in it."

"Well, that sounds ridiculous." Murray quietly whispered.

Lukas squinted. "Not only ridiculous, but stressful. Doesn't it just get in your eyes? Why would you want that?"

Evangaline blinked away their aversions to a warm shower and faced Ryder, shaking her head. "Why are you here? I didn't think I was to meet you and Atlas till later?"

Ryder looked at her and shrugged. "I guess without Des's rain cloud, I'm here to see him kick your ass."

Evangaline gaped at his taunting smirk, unable to decipher if she heard him correctly.

"Yes! C'mon, Prince! Saved you a front-row seat!" Shaw happily patted the blanket next to him.

"You son of a …" Without a second of thought, Evangaline raised her bow in the air and released the arrow nocked in its quiver.

"What the hell are you doing—" Des yelled, searching the sky for the arrow as it came crashing down-to-earth right at Ryder's feet inches away from his worn in boots.

Lukas scoffed. "The target is that way. You could have killed us!"

Evangaline smiled sweetly and shrugged. "I hit my target perfectly."

Ryder stared at Evangaline, his eyes glittering with amusement.

Des was not at all amused, however, "Sword … Now!" He drew his sword and brought it crashing toward Evangaline before she could remove her beat-up rusting practice sword.

She threw up the bow in her hands as a shield. The string snapped in two and the wood groaned under the pressure of Des's blow.

With her boot, Evangaline swung out, knocking Des square in the ribs just hard enough to knock him off kilter. Thus, giving her just enough time to drop the bow and roll out of the way, unsheathing her new favorite daggers from her thighs.

One day when she needed air, Evangaline begged Des and Shaw to walk with her to the village while Ryder was in a meeting. They were having an outdoor market that day and it was there that she saw the most beautiful set of daggers. Their golden blades were long but not too long, with a slight curve at the ends, perfect for her to hold in a reverse grip. Their hilts were bound in an emerald green leather embossed with leaves and flowers alike. A small diamond rested in the hilt and called to her like an old acquaintance.

The salesman said they were made by Taris himself from the Kingdom of Fire, Prince Surtis's husband and the greatest swordsmith of the realm. The salesman verified the story by showing her the small embossment of Taris's insignia, a small T surrounded by a flame. He gave them to Evangaline for practically nothing, asking only for the golden butterfly clips in her hair that day. She obliged without hesitation.

Those very daggers were now drawn on the princess's closest friend and confidant.

"You could have counted us down!" She yelled as she ran, swinging her blades at Des.

Blow after blow was blocked by the new General of the Royal Army with his pristine Royal Army issued sword.

"Knives against a sword are stupid. You would be better with the bow!" He spit out as he swung for her legs.

Des and Chloe were such a perfect match. Every time Chloe thought she could catch Evangaline off guard, she would try to swipe out her legs. Des did the same thing. That mistake was what costed him their sparring match earlier. He went low, Evangaline swiped high.

Evangaline jumped over the sword, swinging across the dirt as though it were nothing but a jump rope.

"My daggers a fucking awesome! You're just jealous!"

She swiped her hands, right, then left, then right again. Des leaned back and dodged her strikes. Of course, they weren't battling all out, just till either first blood—only a minor scratch was permitted in their sparring sessions—or until someone surrendered. Which was certainly not going to be her!

Des lunged, dropping his sword to the ground and grabbed for Evangaline's wrists, locking them behind her back. Pinning her back against his chest.

"Tap out." It wasn't a question. It was a command.

Evangaline smiled as she took in the cadre and Ryder now with his ass firmly planted next to Shaw, knees bent with his fate marked arm draping over, smug as smug could be, "Naw … Tap in actually …"

Des squinted, confused, "Wh—"

He was cut off by the heel of Evangaline's boot, swiftly kicking him square in the balls.

All the men winced, breathing out multiple variations of "Oh!" and "Owww!"

"Low blow, Your Highness!" Aadi muttered loosely, grabbing his crotch.

Evangaline laughed and readied her stance for the retaliation, spinning her knives in her hands. "It's not my fault all men have a weakness smack dab between their legs! Woman up! I've trained with all of you idiots bleeding!"

Des steadied himself, grabbing his sword while licking his lower lip, "You are brutal. And I don't need to know your—"

Evangaline lunged first, knives in hand, "Grow up!" She shouted as she swung her dagger adorned hands.

Blow. Block. Blow. Block. Blow. Back and forth until Evangaline had one dagger and Des lost his sword completely.

"Des!" Ryder shouted, tossing her opponent his trusty black blade.

Evangaline scowled at Ryder. "What the fuck? No outside help!"

Ryder laughed, "Eva, that mouth of yours!"

Evangaline blocked a kick from Des before parrying and delivering her own kick that freed Ryder's intricate black blade to the ground. She gathered it from the floor and threw it straight into the tree behind where Ryder and the cadre sat. "You'd be surprised what my mouth can do, Prince." She sarcastically smiled and winked before being tackled by Des to the ground with an "Oof."

"Stop fucking flirting while we're sparring!"

"Ouch! I'm not flirting! You two stop cheating!"

Ryder huffed in her direction with a laugh. "You were absolutely flirting."

Evangaline managed to punch Des just hard enough for him to ease his grip and for her to roll him over and find her blade. She held it to his throat, scratching the delicate skin above his Adam's apple just lightly enough to draw first blood.

Ryder, with his quiet grace, managed to walk behind her as she rolled off Des's defeated form. "I'm not complaining though," he whispered in her ear, sending chills down her spine before offering a hand to Des. "I tried, my friend," Ryder sighed as he hauled Des to his feet, patting him on the back.

Des shook his head and threw his arm around Evangaline, tugging her close to his side. "Chloe would be so proud of you right now."

Evangaline laughed through her heavy breaths. Her body now aching and sore, "She would be happy I kicked your ass. She would also give me a stern warning about kicking you in the dick." She chuckled and winked.

"Which brings me to my next point, don't ever kick me in my dick again. *Please*."

Ryder laughed, watching the two of them.

Evangaline sucked in a breath. "I don't know if I can make that promise … but … eh, for you, Desy, I'll try."

Des physically recoiled and winced. "Bleh. Never call me *Desy* ever again."

"Oh … now I'm calling you Desy all the time." She hugged him. "Thank you. For saying that about Chlo. It means a lot." All her sarcasm and laughing died from her voice in her earnest gratitude. Hearing from the only person Chloe ever loved with her whole heart, that Evangaline would have made her proud, made Evangaline want to cry. But she held it in and stayed composed.

Des hugged her back, "It's the truth. She would be. About everything." He peeked at Ryder. "Even you, Your Highness. She'd be proud of it all."

Ryder nodded silently, giving a grateful and polite smile.

A single tear tried to slip past Evangaline's defense. But she held it in. She was having a good day, a day free of tears so far. She wanted to keep it that way!

"I should get upstairs to get ready. Wren's probably already waiting. Do you need me to send Chevalier for that?" She motioned to the small cut on Des's neck.

Des shook his head. "Naw. I'll keep the scar. It will remind me not to piss you off in the future."

Evangaline smiled. "Ha! Okay."

"Prince Ryder, would you mind filling in for one of us and escorting Evie to her rooms? I promised these idiots a round at The Gilded Rose." Then, surprising Evangaline, Des winked at Ryder conspiratorially.

Evangaline eyed both men. "Well, now you're flirting with him!"

"Go!" Des laughed, then walked to the cadre who were already beginning to heckle the poor man.

"Eva, after you," Ryder smiled and extended his arm in a playful bow.

Evangaline laughed and then began her hike back to the palace with a jovial Ryder in tow.

"Wren, is there any way that you can help me tie this?" Evangaline held up a navy-blue velvet ribbon that perfectly matched the corset she chose to wear. Wiggling the ribbon in her hand, she gave Wren her best 'please help me, I'm useless' smile.

"Of course, Your Highness." Wren happily quipped, dropping the towel she was folding and securing the ribbon in Evangaline's hair perfectly on the first try.

"Thank you. I can fold those when I get back. I just have to go meet Ryder and Atlas, and then I can do it. Go take the rest of the day off. You work too hard."

Wren smiled. "No ma'am, you will not. I enjoy my job. It is an honor to serve you."

Evangaline winced at the notion. She hated having people wait on her hand and foot. She couldn't believe it, but she actually missed doing her laundry. Having someone else wash, fold and even *press* her underwear was just plain odd and made her feel fifty different shades of embarrassed. But this was her life now, pressed underwear and people waiting on her hand and foot. She begged Wren to let her help with so many things, and every time Wren shot her down. All the staff did.

"Fine. It was worth a try. But Wren … I will write it into a royal decree if I have to, but you're my friend and with that, please stop calling me *Your Highness* or *ma'am*. Evangaline will do just fine."

"Yes, Your Hi—Evangaline." Wren smiled, wincing at her almost mistake.

Evangaline began to walk away.

"Oh Evangaline," Wren snapped, "Prince …"

Evangaline's stomach hollowed out at the jumpy tone in Wren's voice. "What's wrong with the prince?" She quickly shot out in a nervous tone, cutting off Wren's words.

Wren's face softened. "Oh, nothing ma'am—Evangaline—he's been waiting for you in your living quarters. That's all. Startled me half to death when I came in the room but insisted on staying."

"He's been here this whole time?"

It had been an hour and a half since Ryder slowly walked Evangaline back to her room. They joked and talked. Evangaline knew the palace well enough to know Ryder was walking her the long way to her room.

"The entire time." Wren added, her brows drawing nearly to her hairline as her smile speared across her delicate features and her cheeks reddened slightly.

Evangaline took a deep breath and mentally told her pixies to go ride on the merry-go-round in their mental carnival. Something slow and monotonous. Not the damn roller coaster they insisted on riding whenever

Ryder was nearby.

He sat on the couch in the same place he napped, his powerful body enveloped the green settee. His dark essence was so out of place in the light green room. The same way the room almost was too proper for Evangaline. Ryder's hard edges and darkness stuck out like a nail laid amongst a pile of feathers.

"You didn't have to stick around." Evangaline said, drawing up behind him with a grateful smile from ear to ear. That was until she saw what he was reading. "Where did you get that?" She rushed around the couch, reaching for the photo album in his hands.

He leaned away from her so she couldn't grab it. "It was on the nightstand."

She crossed her arms, fuming. "And you just snoop through people's bedrooms?"

Ryder smirked up at her. "Only the bedroom of the woman I am fated to for eternity. Tell me about these." He tilted the album so she could see the photo he was lingering on. "This isn't a painting?"

Evangaline softened, looking at the photo as she sank onto the couch beside him. "No. They're photos, we take them on a camera. It's a device that captures the moment exactly how it is in real time. This was Christmas almost four years ago now. We were opening presents." She pointed at the people in the photo. "That's Miles, my brother, and my mom and dad. My sister Katherine. And that oaf in the light up sweater is James, Katherine's now husband." She laughed to herself. "That was the first time we all met him. He didn't celebrate Christmas … wait, do you celebrate Christmas?"

Ryder shook his head. "I don't even know what you're talking about." He chuckled.

Evangaline followed suit, "It's a holiday, one that used to be dictated by religion really, but as science became more popular in Vitalis, religion kind of took a backseat. We aren't a religious family anyway, so we celebrate it like most humans and use it as an excuse to eat lots of food and give each other gifts. Either way, James is slightly religious. He's Jewish and celebrates another holiday—Hanukah. But he wanted to 'make a good first impression' on the family and, well, he came in this Christmas sweater that lit up and played music. It was ridiculous. And *amazing*. We were all fighting that day. The second we woke up. *Fighting*. Miles was grumpy cause his girlfriend at the time was out of town. There was a blizzard and my dad nearly got frostbite shoveling the driveway. Which leads to my mom yelling at him to and I quote, 'stop being a pig-headed fucker and get your ass inside'. You can see where I get my foul mouth from." Evangaline laughed.

"Then the ham burned, the lights on the tree wouldn't work, and then James showed up and quite literally lit up the room. He made it one of my favorite Christmases because it wasn't perfect for once. He ordered pizza after the ham burned and we busted out some board games. Oh, shit, you don't have pizza here either! Pizza is like bread with tomato sauce and cheese. It's amazing. I will make it for you one day! Between showers, Christmas, and pizza, the fae are really missing out!"

Ryder laughed. "I like seeing you like this," he said, looking back down at the photo album. "You look—"

"Happy?" Evangaline cut him off before he could finish his sentence.

He nodded. "You look so relaxed. You rarely look that way here. I may be presumptuous, but the smile you wear most of the time here is forced."

Evangaline nodded. She did force her smile most of the time. Going from zero to princess with all eyes on her, and the corresponding expectations to go along with it, made her nervous. "I wasn't. Relaxed or happy. I was a ball of mixed emotions. In that moment, I was content, though. You remember weeks ago I told you about my ex-fiancé?"

Ryder growled, "Unfortunately." His poorly hidden jealousy made her smile a bit.

"Well, he took the picture. It was our senior year of college. He had just got a job offer a few days before and that morning I got my rejection from the same company. I wanted to write for them so bad. He only applied because I was nervous and didn't want to apply alone. We had a massive argument about him getting the job and not me. We barely talked all day. He told me he just 'worked harder', which was bullshit. His daddy had a name, and he wasn't a woman. Plain and simple. It pissed me off. I was in such a bad mood until James came. He and I have the same taste in books, and James bought me a collector's edition of Frankenstein. It was my favorite thing I got that year. That is what I'm holding in the photo."

Ryder gritted his teeth as two little hairs fell onto his forehead. His possessiveness made Evangaline smile even more. "Why wasn't your fiancé in the picture?"

"He didn't like being in pictures all too much, especially not with my family. Insisted on 'capturing the memories instead of being in them.' Which I guess was a relief in hindsight. I only had a few pictures we had to cut him out of."

She grabbed the book and flipped to the back, where she kept her engagement photos with Harry. "I think that is the reason I haven't been able to let these go. They're some of the only ones I have of us."

Ryder took the photos from her and examined the shaggy blond haired man holding Evangaline on the beach at sunset. Evangaline's hand was delicately held up to the camera in one photo, showing off the sparkling diamond on her finger. In another, they were kissing. And in another Harry was kissing Evangaline as she was sitting on the counter of their new apartment, surrounded by moving boxes and mounds of bubble wrap.

Evangaline knew the pictures made Ryder jealous as she watched all the shadows on his chest move with an agitated and shaky pace. He was trying to contain them from destroying the photos and any evidence that Evangaline once loved another.

Why do you still have these? She thought to herself as she took in Ryder's profile.

"The more time goes on, the more I see just how much I never loved him." She broke the silence, "I think I was just young, and he was the first boy that showed me any sort of kindness outside of my family. So, I dove in headfirst. Ignored all his faults. At best, he was a lesson. One that I needed to go through to get me *here*." She grabbed the photos from Ryder's hands and replaced them with her hand. "They might be some sneaky little bastards, but the fates gave me everything I never knew I needed." Evangaline smiled up at Ryder.

His thumb stroked the back of her hand in soft gentle sweeps that sent heat coursing through every nerve and blood vessels in her body. For once, he didn't look back at her, but instead fixed his gaze on their hands. It was written on his face, but he too was savoring this one quiet moment between them.

Finally, his eyes rose to hers, before dipping to her lips. They were suspended in a moment of pure belonging. Ryder's hands tightened on Evangaline's as their breaths became heavier. She leaned slightly, and he mirrored the movement perfectly. She wanted to kiss him, hell, practically since she met him, and it was finally going to happen. The pixies were doing a disco in her stomach. Her heartbeat like a drum, and her cheeks flushed with a light claret hue.

"Ma'am, I am going to head out now. Is there anything else you need?"

Evangaline shot her eyes to the ceiling with a sigh. *Great timing Wren.* Ryder must have thought the same thing because the gruff exasperated chuckle that came from his throat mirrored Evangaline's thoughts exactly.

"No, you're all good! Thank you! But Wren …"

"Yes, I know! Evangaline! My Apologies!" The handmaid said as she bustled out the door.

Evangaline took a breath and then rose to her feet, dropping Ryder's hand. No kiss today. *Fan-fucking-tastic.*

She clenched the pictures of Harry in her hand and with a careful precision let them turn to ash within a fire of her own making. Hungry flames devoured the memories of another time, another person. She let the pictures fade to nothing but soot before turning to Ryder. The act made her feel lighter, happier. Like she was getting rid of old baggage so Ryder could move his own into her heart.

"There's something I want to do. Will you come with me?" She asked her Prince of Shadows as he stared up at her with the light of the stars in his eyes.

They stood at the edge of the ever-changing forest, their backs to the palace, and their fronts to the expanse of the rolling greenery of the Capital.

"Are you sure about this?" Ryder asked cautiously. "You are still new to having magic. You don't want to go too hard too fast. It takes many years for a fae's magic to fully develop."

"I think I can do this, though." Evangaline gritted her teeth as she felt the swell of her magic course through her veins.

Through Atlas's meticulous research over the past couple of weeks, they found a single scroll tucked up high within the library that described many of Tuatha's powers and, in return, Danu's. One by one they went down the list, checking off what Evangaline was capable of.

They already knew she could manipulate fire and water and as she sat in the bath or beyond the flames of the fireplace, she would practice those powers. Plus, those were the ones Ryder focused on since they were the ones she called to first. "Better to hone what you know then start in on multiple different ones recklessly," he said one day in a stern professor like voice. It was hot. She told him so. It was the first time she made him blush.

But today, after her little show with Des's rain cloud, she took her fated out to the meadows eager to test more of her magic. The *"powers of the earth"* were what the fae called Danu and her daughter's abilities to manipulate plants and nature. Evangaline thought, with her fated in the uncommon spare time they had, it was as good a time to train with the earth as ever. She had been itching to try since she read the scroll and learned how Tuatha was able to grow her own flora and fauna.

Yet after half a day and the beginning of a splitting headache, Evangaline was so done with trying to change the color of a single flower and manipulate the earth. Over and over, she pushed herself to change the yellow daisy into a white one.

"Let's just go. I can't do this," she finally conceded. "I'm tired, hangry, and disappointed."

"One more time. You've got this. I believe in you. My fated isn't a quitter." Ryder placed his hands on her shoulders, kneading the muscles below her shoulder blades. "Feel that string of your power and channel it toward the earth. Picture what you want in your head, then send it down the string."

Evangaline breathed deep and closed her eyes, thrust her hand out and did as Ryder said. And when she opened them, she didn't change the color of the damn flower … again. It was useless.

"Ugh! Let's go. Seriously. I'm starving," she snapped in a tone that was somehow even more tired and deflated.

They almost ticked off earth manipulation as a dud, thinking she might have only inherited a few of Danu's powers, when the ground around them trembled as she turned away.

Evangaline stared out at the ground with fear mingling in her eyes. *What had she done?* Ryder grabbed her hand, holding it tight and drawing her close to his chest just as something amazing happened.

Rising from the splitting earth, approximately two feet in front of them, right where she was trying to change the color of the flower was the sapling of an oak tree. Its trunk was no more than six inches in diameter. Its height was only four feet or so. But there it stood surrounded by dozens of yellow daisies and one that, in the process, Evangaline turned purple. Its dark trunk and green leaves swayed in the subtle autumn breeze like a subtle wave of hello.

She grew a damn tree! Forget the flower, she grew a tree! Accidentally, but still.

Ryder was so happy he started laughing uncontrollably and spontaneously grabbed her from behind, launching Evangaline into his arms and straight into the air.

He spun her around, "You, Evangaline Rivers, are the most spectacular little creature I've ever seen!"

She laughed and smiled, unable to truly grasp an understanding of what she just did.

"I grew a mother fucking tree!" She shouted into the dusky sky as Ryder hugged her from behind with his chin resting atop her head with his muscular arms wrapped snuggly around her shoulders.

His light laughs vibrated through his chest and sunk into Evangaline's heart in a beautiful symphony.

They stared at her little sapling as the stars twinkled into existence in the header of the night sky just as the sun sank over the horizon. And with every moment that he held her, telling her his plans to help hone her power, Evangaline began to fall harder and harder for the Prince of Shadows. Now she just needed to work up the courage to kiss him.

Chapter Forty-Six

"I've never been outside the palace grounds before." Ryder muttered almost to himself, embarrassed in his sudden realization, drawing Evangaline's blue-green gaze. "My whole life, even as a boy with my mother and father, we portaled right into the palace and portaled right out when it was time to leave. I've never been to the village at all. I'm not even sure if my father has been."

Evangaline cocked her head and took him in. She stared at him as though he grew four more heads. It was so hard to believe someone who had been alive for decades more than her had lived such a cloistered and sheltered life.

"Seriously?" She asked earnestly.

He chuckled deeply, situating his hands in the pockets of his trousers, his down turned gaze watching his worn in boots keep stride with Evangaline. "I promise. It's the truth. I always wanted to. The palace is so ... I don't know ... *fancy*. But the Village always seemed—"

"Normal? Warm? Welcoming?" Evangaline added, giving him a smirk. "Any of the above?"

His endless ocean eyes locked with hers. "Yes." There was a hidden depth in the single word. Each syllable screaming its own story of longing.

It was a long day of training and schmoozing with snobby courtiers that had Evangaline drained mentally and physically. Her bones ached and her head pounded. The last thing she wanted was to sit and dine, rubbing elbows with Lady Whittell and the other nobles. The kissing of her ass and gawking over her and Ryder like they were tigers at a zoo was insufferable at times. The people always had questions about their fating and future, questions neither of them had even remotely discussed nor knew the answers to. Truly, they were flying by the seat of their pants.

So instead of dressing in her finery, Evangaline stopped by Ryder's room and asked if he would like to join her for a drink in the village. She didn't stop to think about what she was doing until her fist was connecting with the slick wooden door and Ryder was opening it. Impulse rode every last one of her decisions in that moment.

He looked as though he had been lying down or working—if the papers scattered across his bed were any indication. His hair was messed up from his fingers no doubt trailing through his ebony tresses, and his shirt was wrinkled in more than one place. At the sight of him, Evangaline panicked and blurted out the dinner invitation like it was a warning instead of a question.

For a second, as he stood filling the doorway. Arms crossed, face stoic, it looked as though he was going to say no, but then in true Ryder fashion he allowed the moment of anticipation to dissolve and put Evangaline out of her misery. The corners of his mouth ticked up into a wide smile. He only replied, "Let me grab my jacket," before he returned to Evangaline in the hall, throwing on a black jacket with silver buttons.

As they left the palace, they were cornered by the new General of the Royal Army. After a very lengthy argument, trying to assure Des they would be safe on their own without a bevy of guards following them, they walked to the village.

That argument cost her an extra hour of training in the morning, but it would be worth it. Just to have a normal dinner date with the man she was fated to spend the rest of her life with. The added bonus of getting away from the glittering halls of the palace would be worth any extra hours of training.

So with that, they wandered to the village, silently taking in the crisp autumn air. The half-light of dusk painted the sky in hues of purple and orange as the sun wavered in the sky, making way for the moon.

Evangaline was barely through the archway of the Northern Gate when the first of the villagers started their attentive staring. It was no surprise the women were all transfixed on Ryder as he took in the many sights of the village with apprehensive, wide eyes.

"You're being stared at Ry," Evangaline whispered, nodding to a group of young girls with baskets full of fruit and groceries. They couldn't have been any older than fifteen—that was at least how they appeared due to the slow rate of fae aging—by their blushing faces and insistent giggling. No doubt did they fancy Ryder, regardless of age. And who could blame them? He might call her a creature, but he was a specimen.

He cast a roguish glance at the giggling girls, nodding at them with a polite smile and simple wave.

"Jesus." Evangaline laughed.

"What?"

Evangaline gave a lopsided grin at Ryder, raising her eyebrows mockingly. "Can you please not make all the women in the realm spontaneously combust just at the sight of you?"

Ryder blushed. "I am not." He smirked. "Besides, the one woman in the realm who did catch my eye didn't even crack a smile at the first sight of me." He returned her mocking eyebrows.

It was Evangaline's turn to blush. They were shameless flirts, each waiting for the other to make a move. "I'm immune to your charms, what can I say?"

"Who said I was talking about you?" Ryder laughed, winking as she shoved him in the arm.

With a mischievous smile, she chided, "Oh, really? Care to tell me something—"

"Miss! Lady! Miss!" a small urgent voice shouted from behind them, cutting Evangaline off before she was able to make fun of Ryder for practically exploding the ovaries of the young female population of the village.

She turned to the voice quickly, her brow knitting in confusion and concern. The skirts of her navy gown twisted into the velvet maroon cloak clasped around her shoulders and for a moment constricted her movement.

Instinctively, Ryder reached for her arm, clasping his fingers around her hand. He held her hard enough for Evangaline to look up to him for reassurance. The protective gleam in his eyes shone as he searched for the commotion, only softening his grip when he saw the danger in question was only that of a small boy.

A smile bloomed on Evangaline's face as she saw the shaggy straw-blond hair of the child come into view. The tiny face full of freckles that reminded her of a map of the stars belonged to the young boy she danced with at the autumnal equinox gathering.

"What's the matter?" Evangaline asked, bending into a crouch to be eye level with him.

As he came to a stop before her, skidding on the heels of his dusty shoes. His face became a flush of red she could only equate to that of a strawberry. His eyes darted to the stalwart hand clasping onto Evangaline's and the massive man attached to it.

"I, umm … I … I …" the blond boy stammered, gaping up at Ryder.

Evangaline cocked her head and softened the features of her face. "What's the matter?" She repeated her tone, grew a bit sterner but still full of compassion.

"I … I … well … I am happy to see you again. That's all. Oh, and to say thank you. Mom told me not to come up to you … you being princess and all … plus …" His eyes flung back to Ryder. A hint of fear crossed his tiny face as he tucked his head into his shoulders like a cute little turtle.

Evangaline followed his gaze and tugged at Ryder's arm to get him to shrink down beside her.

With a roll of his oceanic eyes and a small sigh, Ryder obliged and crouched beside Evangaline, dropping one knee to the ground.

Some people stopped and stared, others rubbernecked as they saw the crown princess and a prince of a powerful kingdom kneeling to speak to a young peasant boy.

Apparently, being kind and attentive to the common folk was a relatively new concept for the nobility of the realm … a change Evangaline was passionate to rectify.

"I am happy to see you, too. I've yet to find a better dance partner than you." Evangaline said, smiling at the red-faced boy. "Is that all, though? Or is something else bothering you? Are you alright?"

He peeked at Ryder once more before dropping his eyes down to his feet. "Well, mom and dad talk. They don't think I hear things when I'm in bed, but I … well … I'm not a small child anymore!" he shouted.

"Of course not!" Evangaline replied with a grin, crinkling her eyes and nose. "Are your parents alright?"

"Well, after they found out who you really were, and that you danced with me, and ate with us … well, it just meant a lot to them. For you to … I don't know … dad works at the palace … says you are really nice … they like you. He's happy you're our princess. Me too! I just wanted to let you know." He then leaned into a whisper in her ear. "Though, with respect, my lady, he's kind of scary."

Evangaline sat back on her heels, squeezing Ryder's hand before throwing him an apologetic glance. The prince definitely heard the boys' failed attempt at a whisper. His slight smile and shake of the head gave away how little he cared about being interpreted as scary. And yet something inside Evangaline creaked with a sadness. He wasn't scary or mean. Her fated was nothing like the rumors she would hear in passing about his fearsomeness or his callousness. He was stubborn and hated bullshit, but he certainly wasn't scary or mean.

Evangaline leaned into the boy's ear and whispered loud enough for Ryder to hear, "He's a lot nicer than he looks. He's a big teddy bear when you get to know him. But you have to promise not to tell him that, okay? I don't want him to get a big head." She winked slyly.

"Really?" He replied, his tiny nose scrunching in disbelief. His small face contorted as though he had just smelled rotting trash.

Evangaline nodded conspiratorially.

The boy stepped back a few paces and then shot out his hand in Ryder's direction. His attempt at courage was commendable, but also a façade made of glass. His trembling fingers were inches from Ryder's chest. "Theo March, Your Highness!"

Ryder threw on his stoic cold hearted prince mask and straightened, never dropping Evangaline's hand. "Nice to meet you, Theo March," His hand dwarfed small Theo's shaking hand, immediately making the boy stand taller. "I hear you are my competition when it comes to enthralling my fated on the dance floor, is that true?"

Theo, now scared out of his mind, looked to Evangaline, who smiled back, winking once more, "Yes sir! She is a really fun dance partner." Theo said, standing as tall and proud as his tiny frame could allow. The tips of his small, pointed ears turned pink.

"I'm flattered!" Evangaline gasped, throwing her hand playfully to her chest.

Ryder's mask slipped for a moment as he caught his laugh in his throat, just before he leaned into young Theo. "Be careful, Theo, all this praise might go straight to *her head*, then she will dance with neither of us."

Evangaline elbowed Ryder in the side with her hand still in his. "I heard that. Don't listen to him Theo. I will always dance with you! Maybe not him … but *always* you!" She said, garnering a laugh from Ryder.

The villagers began to regard the interaction more intently with smiles, laughing when Ryder and Evangaline laughed.

Theo went on to tell Ryder how his dream was to be a soldier in the Royal Army one day. Not surprising, being how the young boy held himself, and how he wanted to protect his future queen. "Don't worry, Mr. Prince of Shadows, sir, your fated is safe with me! I'm going to be a guard one day. She'll be safe with me, you'll see!"

Ryder smiled at Theo, then at Evangaline, squeezing her hand tighter in his, "That makes me very happy to hear, Theo. She would be lucky to have a guard as brave and fearless as you."

Evangaline stared at Ryder as the words flowed from his mouth and saw how his eyes sparkled in the way that happened when he was happy or proud. He meant every word he said to Theo. Every word. Her heat skipped a beat.

Suddenly, with a yelp, Theo's mortified mother barreled out of a shop that sold soaps and other cleaning essentials. Bundled in her arms was a small baby and a basket of home goods.

"Theo! Oh my! I do greatly apologize, Your Highnesses. He is a slippery one, my boy. I greatly apolo—" Mrs. March said, bowing at the waist.

"No need. Theo is my friend. I would have been upset if he didn't find me." Evangaline said, standing up tall to meet Mrs. March's wide-eyed gaze.

Ryder remained stoic as he raised to his full height, flashing Theo a quick smile before becoming princely once more. "You have your hands full. Please let me help," he said in his rich silvery voice, extending his vacant hand.

"Oh no, Your Highness. I am content. Plus, Theo is a nice help. Aren't you, babe? He enjoys carrying my basket."

"It makes me strong!" The young boy flashed a wormy muscle, garnering a laugh from Evangaline and Ryder and a few villagers watching close by.

"That's what his pop assured him, right?" Theo nodded, then she dropped her voice lower in volume. "It was a good ploy to get him to do his chores and help around the house."

Evangaline smiled and laughed and then glanced at Ryder. His sapphire eyes were locked into her with a simmering look of pride and admiration. A hint of fire lurked in his blue eyes, that tingled her skin in small warm bouts of white noise. She loved that look, it set the pixies and the butterflies aflutter.

"We should be off, but it was lovely to see you, Theo, Mrs. March. Come find me next time I'm in the village, alright Theo?" Evangaline said as she inclined her head at the adorable family.

Theo smiled wide and nodded rapidly.

"The pleasure was ours, Your Highnesses. Have a lovely evening." Mrs. March ushered a beaming Theo away, his hands struggling to hold up the full basket.

Ryder and Evangaline turned to make their way to the pub, when, like the bell of an alarm clock, Evangaline's stomach growled so loud, she halted mid step.

The bellow of the prince's laugh filled her with warring emotions of embarrassment and glee. She loved the timber of his laugh.

She would sell her soul to hear that laugh for the rest of her life, which, luckily, the fates had already gifted her. No selling of souls necessary.

"Let's get you some food." He laughed as he wrapped his arm around her shoulders to pull her into the safety and warmth of his side just before escorting them through the crowd once more.

"Ok … Ready? Rock, paper, scissors, shoot! Fuck!"

"Ha! Go ahead … another fun fact!" Ryder chastised as he raised his frosty mug of ale to his smug lips.

"Shit …" Evangaline sighed, a frown eating at her lips.

For two hours, they sat at a table in the back of The Gilded Rose. The quaint village pub owned by Dolores and Jeremiah—the sweet couple that welcomed Evangaline around their fire during the autumnal equinox—was just the reprieve they both needed.

Ryder and Evangaline already were treated to fresh bread, meat pies, stew, and now generous frosty rounds of ale. Dolores practically fainted when Evangaline stepped through the threshold to the pub. Her round cheeks went red, but she pretended their presence did not affect her by showing them to their table with just a wave of her hand.

Evangaline and Ryder were halfway through their first round when Evangaline introduced Ryder to rock-paper-scissors. There was only one slice of bread left and only one civilized way to figure out who got it.

An hour later and they made it into a game. Whoever lost a round of rock-paper-scissors revealed a fun fact about themselves. It seemed like a fun way to get to know one another. Little did Evangaline know they both shared quite a competitive side that absolutely could not go unchecked.

Unfortunately for Evangaline, Ryder happened to be surprisingly good at knowing what she was going to draw and in turn thumped her far too many times in a game he happened to just learn. Not like it took any real skill, but even so, he was far too good.

So far, she had revealed her favorite color—green. Superficial fears—clowns and spiders. Her impression of a crying baby—which turned all the heads in the pub. And finally, her appreciation for seals, which were not an animal in Celadonia apparently, so she had to paint the mental image of one to Ryder. To which he frowned and replied, "They sound *useless*." Evangaline pleaded her case by telling him, "They just lounge around and look like sacks of chocolate with whiskers and cute little flippers." He still wasn't sold.

Ryder, in all two of his turns losing, happened to reveal he had two siblings. Evangaline knew that already. And that his favorite color was black, sometimes dark blue, but mainly black. Real intriguing and insightful information from The. Prince. Of. *SHADOWS*. One fact she knew and the other, well, it wasn't a surprise since his entire wardrobe consisted of those two shades entirely. She shouldn't have been so aggravated that he kept his secrets close to his chest, but she was. He knew so much about her and even in a silly game he wouldn't give her anything other than two piss poor factoids about himself. Still, she played on, determined to crack him open sooner or later.

Sipping her ale, she pondered, "Hmmm … what do you want to know?"

Ryder chuckled, "You said your sister was due soon with a babe. Do you have other nieces and nephews?"

The thought of missing her niece's birth suddenly sobered Evangaline up faster than should have been logically possible, considering the amount of alcohol she had just gulped down.

Staring into her ale with a fading smile, "No. She is the first. My mother's dreams of one of her kids having a baby finally came true." She darkly chuckled.

Ryder set down his mug and regarded Evangaline. Her pain was written on her face, and she didn't try to hide it. Seeing her eyes grow weary and dark shattered Ryder. It was as though her sadness threw a rock straight through his fragile glass heart. The shards flew apart and punctured his very soul, allowing his own sorrows to seep through to the surface of his dimming eyes.

His own face grew solemn and contemplative.

"Do you want them? Children?" Ryder asked quietly.

His words sprung Evangaline out of her foggy daze, "Umm … I thought about it. Once upon a time."

"With Harry?" Ryder cut her off, gulping down the last of his ale with pinched brows.

Evangaline noted the sharpness in his voice. Could it have been jealousy? Whatever it was, it made her smile.

She looked up at Ryder, meeting the endless depths of his eyes. "He wanted them and convinced me I did for a time. My mother *loved* the idea. But I feel like I have too much I need to learn about myself first. Too much I need to fix up here before I take care of the future generations." She tapped her head. "Plus, I think I would be a horrible mother. I know I'm twenty-five and am technically a full-blown adult, but like, I almost don't feel old enough … does that make any sense at all? Do you, especially after what you went through with your horse girl, want kids?" She knew the name of the woman Ryder thought he got pregnant, but for some reason the thought of Ryder loving anyone else sent acid straight into her throat and refused to say her name. Evangaline knew damn well she was jealous. "Because if you do, with this whole—" she began rambling.

"First off, you would be a great mother. I watched you with Theo this evening, and that was only one example of how great you would be. I have never seen a woman, let alone a royal so attentive to her subjects—"

"Ugh," faking a gag, "I hate that word. *Subjects*. Like I am better than someone else. They're people I was born to protect and serve. If we want to get technical. Not the other way around. Besides … I used to eat leftover pizza for a whole week in a room I shared with three other girls in college. I am certainly not better than anyone here, no matter the fine dresses I wear or the crown that sits on my head." Evangaline retorted with an edge of disgust, riding her words.

Ryder squinted and leaned back in his chair, his muscular arms crossed over one another. The corner of his mouth curved up as he watched

Evangaline. He took in the way she sat curved over her mug, her white knuckled grip holding it firmly, showcasing how she truly detested the idea of being well … royal. More specifically, being treated better than others for a title alone. She accepted the role with grace and dignity, but the implication that she was above someone else and was, therefore, gifted opportunities and gifts for it turned her stomach into a knot.

His eyes sparkled with the same essence as someone dropping glitter in a glass of water and shaking it. A couple pieces of his raven hair fell onto his forehead and rested just above his furrowed brow.

Evangaline stared back, releasing her ale. Loving the glitter that filled his eyes. She studied every single piece of him as he studied her. "What?" she said in a whisper.

"I meant it when I told you that you were a curious creature," He finally said after a lengthy pause. "I will never tire of learning about what makes you … *you*."

Ryder bit his lip and leaned on the table. If Evangaline wasn't already taken by the man, that small nibble of his lower lip would have done it for her. He truly was breathtaking, inside and out. Even with all of his bottled-up secrets.

Her entire body heated up and her heart sped up just a bit faster.

Before she could realize what she was even doing—which was becoming a natural occurrence around Ryder—she leaned across the small carved up, sticky wooden table and brushed the two pieces of hair on his forehead back into his trimmed but flowing mane of black tresses.

For an all too brief second, Ryder's eyes fluttered closed, and his head dipped slightly into the warm embrace of her hand as it circled to cup his jaw.

Once his eyes opened, the glittering irises of endless blue bore deep into Evangaline's soul. The warmth of his gaze felt just as comforting as the warmth of his delicate touches. The safety she felt in his presence was like a piece of a jigsaw puzzle finally finding its place. She knew deep down if fate had not pushed them together, they would have found a way to one another—that she felt deep in her bones. Two souls cut from the same cloth.

One cloaked in shadow and one cloaked in nature—both with an equal understanding of the other, despite their differences. Her heart shuddered under his gaze. The world around her vanished. All her senses were only tuned in to him. *Kiss him now!* She leaned ever so slightly more—

"My Princess! I thought you would enjoy the adjustments made to your recipe!" Dolores shouted over the laughing patrons of the pub as she excitedly burst out of the saloon style kitchen doors. A plate of desserts raised in her palm.

Evangaline broke her eyes away from Ryder's, a harder task than one would think, and half smiled toward Dolores, begging her pulse to quiet its roaring.

Does the universe have something against kissing? Really?

The pleasantly plump older woman made her way to the table and set down the plate. "Alright, Your Highnesses. My Princess, I took your biscuits, marshmallows, and chocolate, and added one of my world-famous brownies. Then I covered them in more chocolate because I'll be damned if I can't cram as much in there as possible."

Ryder glanced at the decadent but messy plate with his eyes squinted in thought as he took in the sinful dessert.

This was definitely not the meal of a prince. There were no fancy cakes or pastries with elegant piping, no servings of game hens or roasted vegetables, nothing prim and proper about it. But by the raise of his brows and the slow smile gracing his face, he was more than happy to dive into the chocolate-covered monstrosity.

"Go on! I want to see your reaction on the first bite. People have flocked here just for these little puppies! Go on!" Dolores chided, waving her hands at Ryder and Evangaline.

With a deep inhale, Evangaline reached and picked up one of the warm brownies. The bottom was a graham cracker-like crust, then the fudgy brownie, then a small toasted layer of marshmallow, topped off with Dolores's favorite—drizzles and drizzles of chocolate. It was certainly not at all a clean meal to eat, but it was truly delicious.

Evangaline took a bite and set it down on her plate just as Ryder took his first bite.

Calmly, Evangaline stood and wiped off her mouth and hands. Keeping her face unreadable despite the heaven that was gracing her tongue.

She waited for a second till Dolores began swaying on her feet anxiously. A little payback for interrupting the kiss that Evangaline wanted so badly.

Ryder, meanwhile, was lost in his s'more's brownie. The building could have collapsed around him, and he might not have seen it happen.

Evangaline then smiled and wrapped her arms around Dolores, bringing the older woman in for a hug. "Dolores, you've outdone yourself!" She laughed as the old woman wrapped her arms around Evangaline's back and jumped with her up and down in excited little hops.

Breaking away from Evangaline, Dolores turned to the rest of her patrons and shouted from the top of her lungs, "The princess likes them, you hear that! Desserts on Jeremiah and me tonight!"

She then turned, without another word to Evangaline and Ryder, and laughed her way back into the kitchen, clapping her hands with the largest smile on her face.

The men and women of the pub began to applaud and shout their thanks at Evangaline. Misplaced gratitude, but she did not have the fight in her to tell them so.

Evangaline couldn't help herself but laugh as she took her seat again.

Wiping his fingers on a napkin, Ryder smiled at her and then stole her unfinished brownie off her plate. She swatted at him, cursing in several volumes, but the second the dessert entered his traitorous grip, it was lost forever. Goodbye, *delicious friend!*

The volume of the room grew as people from the street piled in, hearing of free desserts. Many, however, swarmed the pub just to get a glimpse of Evangaline, but kept their distance the moment they saw Ryder across the table from her. No one wanted to challenge the Prince of Shadows, especially not a fate marked Prince of Shadows.

Evangaline took a sip of her water, regarding the people living their lives in the pub. The moon came out shortly after they arrived and brought out the people looking to have a good time. The only lights within The Gilded

Rose were the flickering bursts of the many candlesticks that lined the walls on various shelves and the single candle lit chandelier.

It was loud, without a doubt, but it was also peaceful. It felt like going to some of the seedy bars Chloe would find downtown to blow off steam after a long work week. It felt … normal. It felt homely.

She peeked at Ryder, drawing his attention from the patrons now playing fiddles and flutes in the front corner of the room, "I miss them."

Ryder looked at her with his face drawn into a knot. "Who?"

Evangaline looked around the room, smiling wistfully. "My family. Chloe. I miss Chloe a lot. Choosing this, these people, I had to give up so much. I can't go back. I made a promise to them …" she nodded to the patrons. "By accepting my title and not fleeing after the debut, I promised the people of Celadonia that I would protect them and be somehow worthy of inheriting Darrin's throne one day. I can't ever just decide to call it and go back to Vitalis when things get hard. Not now that I've given them my word to be their princess. And that's not even factoring in you."

She leaned her arms on the table and took a breath. "I'm not worried about my future or kids or anything like that. Truthfully, I don't think too hard about it. But when you asked about my sister's baby. It made me sad to know I will never meet her. That's what hurts the most, missing those little things. The things that I never thought I'd miss, the ones that felt like they were written in stone. Unchangeable."

Her eyes met Ryder's as he wove his warm, callused fingers through hers on top of the sticky table. "You will, Eva. You will see them all again. I can't tell you when or how, and I hope you don't see Chloe again for a very, *very,* long while, but you will." He squeezed her hand. "Besides, eventually, I am going to torture you with meeting my family. You will need to return the favor someday. And I refuse to not be in some of your Christmas pictures." He darkly chuckled. "In fact, I plan on being in every single one from here on out."

She smiled at the implications of his words and sighed; they meant the world to her. Maybe she wasn't actively planning their future, but he was. Ryder was her future. "I suppose I do have to meet your family, being that we're in a *fate-lationship*." She said, wiggling her brows. She didn't know what to call their entanglement, but Ryder hated every odd term she came up with. She loved to tease him with her made-up words.

Ryder looked down and with a breathy laugh and shook his head. "Okay. No … That's not what we're calling it."

Evangaline gaped her mouth open. "So what would you call it, *Mr. Eloquent?*"

"We are *fated*. You are my fated, you are practically my wi—" He began to say before being cut off unexpectedly at a commotion shuffling through the door.

A young man with muddy brown hair, dark skin, and a sweat slicked brow panted in front of their table. A messenger of the king if Evangaline were to guess right by his sweat stained tunic bearing the royal crest.

Once more, Ryder's grip on Evangaline's hand tightened, ready to pull her away from the stranger at any moment. The prince's eyes grew as dark as the deepest depths of the ocean, the glittering amusement having faded into the shadows now swirling deep within his irises.

"My Prince. My Princess. I have been sent to retrieve you. It is of the utmost urgency." The messenger said, panting through his heavy breaths. *Did he really run from the palace?*

Ryder stood towering over the young messenger, practically hauling Evangaline with him. Once he had a protective grip on her hand, he never let it go. If she wasn't feeling kind of frightened, she might have felt giddy and annoyed at his protective touch. Evangaline was perfectly capable of defending herself, but Ryder's protective nature was an added comfort. "An urgent message from whom? What is your name, boy?" Ryder grunted.

"General Des has requested you to return immediately, Your Highness. My name is Christoff Darrow, sir, at your service. You too ma'am. I am the lead messenger." He said, flashing Evangaline a small smile before facing Ryder once again.

Evangaline's breath caught. He was not just any messenger; he was Chloe's younger brother. She did not know what to say or do. She did not see him at the funeral, yet again she noticed very little at the funeral. He could have been right in front of her, clucking like a chicken, and she would not have known, nor cared.

Ryder noticed the shift in Evangaline's posture and slowly put the pieces together. His grip on her hand tightened to just a step below bone crushing. It was his way of saying he knew what she was struggling with, and she appreciated it. So, she did what she could to tell him she was okay and squeezed right back.

"Lead the way, Mr. Darrow." Ryder replied, taking a handful of gold coins from his pocket, placing them on the table for Dolores. The old tavern owners told them their meal was on the house, but Evangaline and Ryder already agreed that was not happening.

In a somber yet hastened pace, the three made their way out of the crowded pub and back to the palace as fast as their feet could take them.

Chapter Forty-Seven

Ryder paced the length of the strategy table restlessly. Now littered with all new figurines, all dark and faceless, the table bore a striking resemblance to a game of high stakes chess.

He discarded his jacket hours ago, having tossed it on a chair by the fireplace that he conjured out of thin air, just as he did in the library. His movements were graceful and yet full of an unadulterated rage. His strong arms crossed one over the other, allowing his sculpted muscles to press strenuously against his now half unbuttoned shirt. With his finger resting on his chin, he stared at nothing but the path he was slowly wearing into the floor.

Evangaline and Ryder were escorted by Christoff through the quiet palace into the strategy room where Des stood still as death. His back faced the door as he hunched over the table, shaking his head. Darrin stared out the floor to ceiling lead paned windows without a readable expression nor a faint greeting at their arrival.

The room was cold as ice. Despite the raging fire and the warm, callused hand clutching her own, Evangaline could not suppress the shiver that skated down her spine. Something was terribly wrong.

In the few hours they were away, battalions of Heretic soldiers marched on multiple kingdoms, laying siege to many cities and villages. Leaving an unknown number of fae dead. All under the cover of night. They clung to the darkness to set their fires and slaughter innocents without even a single suspicion being raised. What started as a peaceful night ended in a blaze of fire and destruction.

It was the start of a war.

It didn't take a veteran of conflict to see the signs glaring at her from the table.

Ambushes began a couple of hours prior to Christoff fetching them. Every attack came from the coasts, all from unmarked and unknown vessels that sailed in undetected. Dark ships camouflaged against the dark night sky and even darker sea. The ships held countless numbers of Heretics with one purpose in mind—total destruction.

Tunit sent word from Sedna, the capital city of the Kingdom of Frost, informing of a naval battle just off their shores. The white icebergs and frost covered seas allowed them to spot the dark vessels prior to them making landfall. They were holding up, the Prince of Frost said in his brief message. Having the advantage of the high ice-covered glaciers the city was built on, Tunit was given the advantage, thus allowing the Frost Army's soldiers the opportunity to cut off the head of the snake while keeping visual of the body. However, they were grossly unprepared and unable to stop the demolition of five of their naval ships. The battle had just barely begun when he wrote.

Evangaline's gut told her what no one else wanted to hear … this foe was no snake but a hydra waiting to spurt more heads from its deceit filled body.

Then Princess Ophelia's message came moments later from an exhausted Christoff. A coordinated attack off the beaches of the Kingdom of Mirth occurred just after nightfall—at the same time Tunit's message indicated. The lighthouses off the coast of Mirth spotted the ships of Heretics approaching and were able to ready their defenses on land, but were still in the heat of battle with no further updates as Christoff delivered Ophelia's message.

The Kingdoms of Leaves and Fire remained intact and unbothered on the eastern coastline—for now.

The Kingdom of Shadows was a ticking time bomb. Unlike the other two battles, the message that came from Ryder's brother, Niall, in the Kingdom of Shadows, detailed a battalion of Heretics off the coast. An hour later a message came—hundreds of soldiers were camped on the southern shore, readying their formations but not moving. They were just waiting, lurking in the distance, allowing the kingdom to ready their army and await Ryder's orders. It was odd, but Evangaline focused on the fact that they still had time to save the Shadows. Luckily, no Heretic's surrounded nor threatened the capital of Pax. Ryder had given orders to start evacuating villages and towns and relocating those residents to the capital city, but refused to leave Evangaline's side and travel there himself.

"What do we do? We've waited hours and still no word from anyone. Surely, we can ready the Royal Army and—" Evangaline broke the sullen silence of the strategy room before Darrin cut her off with a silky bite to his tone.

"That is easier said than done."

Ryder stopped his pacing, throwing mental daggers at the king. His glare was harsh and unyielding and anyone with a weaker demeanor would have cowered, but not Darrin. Both men were lit fuses waiting to ignite.

Evangaline, standing opposite Ryder, continued to scan the table and the prince before her. There had to be a way to stop the Heretic Army and end this melee before it got worse. All the figures marking the enemy on the Kingdom of Shadow's shore were nothing but black shapeless blocks. Black shapeless blocks the table was now littered with, subduing the realm like defenseless prey. The entire western seaboard was practically covered in the enemy markers, and that was based on nothing but a couple of letters and a few royal spies. This was bad and she knew it. The blood of the fallen would be on her hands. It was her family The Heretics despised, after all.

Des came to her side, his hair tussled and ran through from his hands, fisting it for hours on end, pulling at the blond curls until his scalp was red and aching. His armor cast bright copper flares off its pristine exterior, refracting in the pale moonlight streaming in the windows behind Darrin. "Our armies would take nearly two weeks to get to the coast of the Shadows by foot. To open a portal that long and that big would no doubt expend the magic of even the strongest fae. We are operating on hours, at best."

Growing peevish, Evangaline turned to him, "Should we not try, anyway? Send one group to Sedna, and then another larger one through Mirth and down to the Kingdom of Shadows. Even if this is over by the time they get there, we will be dealing with massive losses and catastrophic damage. Ryder and Darrin have to be strong enough to hold open a substantial portal, and I can try. Should we not be there to help the people?"

Des warily glanced at her with the same visage as though he were looking down at an uneducated child. The look on his face made Evangaline angrier than anything. He had never looked at her with such annoyance before.

"I know I am not knowledgeable in war, but I've watched *people* long enough from the sidelines to know what we *should* do. I am not a stupid child, so don't treat me like one." She all but yelled, wiping the look clean off Des's face.

The king scoffed, "Not a child, just naïve," he muttered under his breath.

Hearing the insult, Evangaline spun on her heels so rapidly she nearly would have teetered over if it wasn't for Des's hand grabbing her shoulder.

She felt Des sigh and shake his head next to her, but his reaction was not the bothersome one.

Ryder started to cast the room in a slight darkness, not enough to snuff out all light, but enough to draw attention to the shift in mood.

"Oh, call back your shadows, *Prince*." The king huffed toward her fated.

The prince, however, did no such thing. Instead, he braced his arms on the table, shoving it forward into Evangaline's backside, and it was then that Evangaline turned around to face him.

It was like déjà vu of the night they met. A small hole in her heart echoed a painful murmur, knowing she met Ryder on a night she lost her lifeline, her best friend, her Chloe. But that ache also came with a newfound sense of hope and safety in knowing her heart's match. She took a breath and, just like Chloe always did; she chose to see the bright side. Standing in this equally shitty circumstance, she thought through everything they knew so far. There had to be something to learn, a way to fight whoever this elusive army was.

The bright side?. Think Evangaline. What the fuck could you learn? Is there even something to learn?

They've sat warily waiting for messages showcasing the dark and grim facts of the night, but what if they looked at things from the bright side? A different angle may be a key to wiping all the little black blocks off the map. Or give them an insight into how to handle said little black blocks?

"Ok, what do we know about them?" Silence. *Thanks, boys!* "We know the might of The Heretics. The fact that they aren't some small rebel groups scattered around the realm like we once thought, they are an army of their own. That is good, right? Maybe that will tell us where they are coming from or gathering?" Evangaline said, facing Des. Her voice was quiet and hopeful.

"Is any of this really *good*?" He asked quirking an apprehensive brow.

Shrugging, Evangaline added, "Well, the circumstances are grim and fifty shades of fucked up, but still, we know the brunt of what we are dealing with, sort of. We can see how they fight, what magic they might have on their side, hell we can see, finally, who leads them. It *might* possibly allow us to cut the head off the beast. For good. We must have the advantage again. Somehow, we need to find the upper hand."

"We will be able to see the might of their forces and gain important knowledge, possibly. We might even know if there is more planned or if this is their first and last stand." Ryder stared at his kingdom on the table. There was a dark muskiness to his tone that Evangaline had never heard echo in his words. It reminded her of a forest cast in moonlight. It was haunting and calming all at the same time. He was aggravated but unlike Des and the king, tried hard to not take that out on Evangaline. Many times through the past few hours, he reassured her with simple clutches of her hand or gentle circles traced onto her back. "We just need access to their camps and a few prisoners to help us gain that upper hand." Her fated murmured, studying the board at his fingertips. "It might work."

An annoyed huff passed through the king's lips.

Evangeline turned to her father, cast in his moonlit haze, "We aren't going to help anyone sitting on our asses. So, if you have knowledge of these asshats, let us know now. I'm done playing proper princess waiting in my ivory fucking tower, not when people are being slaughtered. Darrin, either give us information—the information you are *clearly* harboring—and help or go sulk and be rude somewhere else."

Ryder straightened, his darkness and shadows pulsing against his bronze skin. His eyes were trained on his monarch's back as he fought a slight grin.

The king, darker and more menacing than Evangaline had ever seen, turned to her. He stalked forward with a slow gait that had everyone tensing. His posture was different, straighter, broader, scarier.

Evangaline felt her limbs lock into place from an unseen force, commanding her actions. She tried to move, but it felt like a cold metal chain was slowly being wrapped around her, pinning her arms to her side. Her mouth tried to open as she attempted to scream from the pressure building in her muscles, but she was unable to. Her lips wouldn't even part to take in a breath. She was a living statue wrapped in Darrin's magic. Evangaline knew Darrin had the ability of telekinesis and telepathy but was gravely unaware of his ability to make one a slave to their own body.

Des lunged to grab her arm, only to suddenly pull his arms to his side. He stood at attention, like the same chains bound him too. A statue of a perfect soldier.

Ryder cast his shadows out, darkening the room. His power thrummed through the room, vibrating the blood in Evangaline's veins. "Enough!" he barked, only to be ignored. He made no move to go to Evangaline. Instead, he drew his dagger and held his ground, knowing the king would use his power over him too if he got too close.

Darrin got within inches of Evangaline, snarling, "You want insight. Here are the facts. I am the Supreme King of Celadonia, and you are my heir. If I choose to let this realm burn to ash and leave you nothing, then so be it, but I will not take orders from some insolent human child. Keep that in mind the next time you open your mouth and make demands."

Finally, the grip on Evangaline and Des dropped. Her limbs gained movement but felt atrophied. Evangaline caught her weight on her trembling hands as she gripped onto the table for support, sagging into its splintered edge in a tenuous attempt to not crash onto her knees.

The king had never used his power on her before. She had only ever seen him use them for small things. His willingness to use compulsion on her was, at the very least, unnerving.

Evangaline's brain ran with the speed of a cheetah. Thinking of the threat Darrin tossed against her, thinking of the insults hurled her way, but she could not keep her mouth shut, not when he forced all of this on her. She knew she was stupid, but she did not deserve to be called names and threatened when she wasn't the one pouting like a toddler in the corner. Weeks, she spent weeks dealing with his holier than thou attitude, and she was done! She could not tolerate it anymore.

Shaking with anger and fear, Evangaline barely noticed Ryder rushing to her side as she watched the king rush to make an exit from the room. *Coward.*

Ryder's hands held her close to his chest. He looked so worried. So scared. It broke her heart. And filled her with rage.

His darkness never eased around the room but didn't consume it completely, either. It sat poised—a cobra ready to strike at any moment.

"I may be naïve. I may be insolent. I am no doubt your heir. But I am not the one who brought me here or made a bargain with powers they didn't fully understand. If you have a problem with me suddenly being a princess and taking the initiative that you are too much of a coward to take, you should have thought that through before you fucked my mother and forced me here!" She yelled at the back of Darrin's head.

With a conniving smile, a blast of bright, cold energy blasted from his fingertips and straight into Evangaline. She flew back out of Ryder's arms and into the glass windows Darrin stood gazing out of moments.

Ryder was at her side, instantly flanked by Des. Worry marring their handsome faces.

Evangaline's nose was bleeding, and her head was pounding. Her eyes barely focused before she saw the two men stand in front of her blocking her view of the king.

Darrin snarled, a threat she could not hear above the ringing in her ears. Ryder snarled right back. His magic grew darker, his shadows more frantic. They swirled from his body in a cyclone of darkness, enveloping him in a tornado of vengeful spirits.

Evangaline made her way onto unsteady and aching feet. Blood dripped from her nose and a small cut on the back of her head leaked red onto the pristine white floors through her long hair.

The king raised his hand, casting forth a cold shard of energy, this time in Ryder's direction. Darrin looked truly evil, with a smile across his face and a chuckle deep in his sternum. He was releasing all his anger at Ryder.

Evangaline lurched forward, nobody not even the king, would hurt her fated. She allowed her fate blessed instincts to take over and let her rage and fear control the magical flow of power through her veins.

Before he could even blink, Evangaline blocked Ryder with her body, barely covering his enormous frame. Still, she tried her best to stand tall.

With a scream the floor trembled, the stones beneath their feet began to seizure and cracks formed in vine like movements all hurtling in the direction the man who sired her.

The chandelier overhead swung in pendulous movements, slowly keeping pace with the fervent beat of her heart.

A cyclone of wind formed a shield around herself, Ryder, and Des. With surprising little effort, Evangaline threw out her hand and sent forth a blast of wind so hard and ferocious it made Darrin's cold power seem like child's play.

She conjured a tempest especially for King Darrin. Evangaline allowed her powers to take flight. Weeks of emotions poured from her being, clouding the space in the harshest aspects of the elements.

Rain fell, dousing the flames of the fireplace. The already cold room froze over with a glacial chill as ice coated the marble floors and walls.

Hurricane style winds ripped from her hands, scattering the players on the strategy table, and toppling the king's chair onto the floor behind her, cracking its back in two.

The guards looked on in horror from behind shields of air, unable to move from their positions. Despite her power taking on a frightening level of chaos, Evangaline still had the wherewithal to protect those around who were innocent. She threw out blasts of wind shields around the few guards along the walls to keep them safe from any potential danger. With only the smallest thought, her magic answered to her call, like an obedient servant. Obeying her wish for a tempestuous storm for the king and the king alone.

This was between her and the king, a battle weeks in the making between father and daughter. With the finesse of a puppet master, Evangaline elevated her arm, allowing a hurricane of power to swirl out and straight into the king. Throwing him back through the room, to land on his back with a mighty wallop. The sounds of his rain-soaked body hitting the now cracked and icy floor was heavy and powerful. The sound of bones breaking was enough of a victory for Evangaline to release the wind shields and evaporate the rain.

Bit by bit, Evangaline pulled back her power, and with each pull of magic, the sharp pain coursing through her seeping skull magnified. Her eyes grew blurry and before she knew it, she was falling to the ground. Ryder's arms softened the fall, but his screams bellowed out, tightening the pain in her head.

"Eva! Eva! Look at me, Eva! Look at me! Keep your eyes open, love!" Ryder's muffled voice echoed in her ears as though he was shouting through a vacant cave. "Get the healer! Now!" He called out. But his efforts weren't enough to stop the darkness from creeping into her vision, lulling her to sleep. As her eyes closed, the pain writhing in her exhausted body quieted till there was only darkness and quiet.

Chapter Forty-Eight

Blinking open her eyes slowly at the expense of the dull ache in her skull, Evangaline woke to the sun glistening and bouncing off of something metallic. A shimmering aura shining right in her face like a beacon in the early morning sun. Her eyes were so hazy they struggled to adjust to the light creeping in even through her furrowed brow and squinting eyes.

She slowly sat up, blinking away the haze, and there he was, her prince. His metallic tattoo cast light like a faint copper mirror around the pale green room. *Her beacon.*

His large frame somehow managed to nestle itself in a small chair from the dining table at the side of her bed. Using his jacket as a blanket, he looked so incredibly uncomfortable. His ebony strands of hair fell onto his perfectly angular face and tickled his cheekbones with each deep exhalation he took. He looked so peaceful despite the lack luster sleeping arrangement; it felt like a sin to wake him.

So Evangaline tried her hardest not to.

Easing her feet from the covers of her bed and pulling down the nightgown she certainly was not in the last time her eyes were open, she padded to the bathroom on pins and needles. Avoiding the squeaky planks of wood that she had grown accustomed to.

Evangaline's whole body ached and screamed in a festering dull throb.

Her chest felt unbearably tight. And her head … her godsdammed head throbbed with what felt like the staccato of a bass drum. Her eyes felt heavier than they ever felt. Each blink was a battle to open them once more. She felt like she could sleep one thousand years and it still would not be enough.

"You're up." Ryder muttered from the doorway, rubbing his eyes with the palms of his hands. His voice was delightfully gruff with the disuse from morning, just how she pictured it every time he watched her train from his window.

Evangaline turned to face him, trying to plaster on a smile even though each of the muscles in her face was weighed down by lead. Suddenly, she realized she was on display in her slightly sheer satin nightgown. Timidly, she threw her arms across her chest to block out any potential sight of her breasts and body, but was failing miserably.

Ryder never even glanced down to gawk at the sight of her body through the pellucid negligee. Instead, on heavy legs, he padded forward to grab her robe off the hook by the bath and draped it around her shoulders.

She slipped her arms through and fastened it around her waist, and once more trusting her impulses, wrapped her tender arms around Ryder's waist in a silent act of gratitude.

For a moment, he didn't move, and she thought she may have overstepped an unspoken boundary. But then he exhaled a breath, one that was echoing with relief and contentment. Gently, he wrapped his arms around her shoulders and hugged Evangaline in closer. Resting his cheek on the top of the bird's nest that some might call her hair, he breathed deeply.

"What happened?" She asked into the flexing muscles in his chest.

In the silence between her question she listened to the steady beating of his heart as it conducted a philharmonic melody that steadily became her new favorite song.

He sighed. "You and your father had quite a reckoning. Even the gods would have liked to have seen the two of you throw down."

"I remember that part. Is he okay?"

"Yes, he is okay. Despite your show of power, you held back. I could tell. I've seen you channel your power enough—you controlled it just enough.

He, on the other hand, did not. You were much worse off. If you weren't as strong as you are, he could have killed you. It scared me half to death, Eva."

Evangaline eased back and met his eyes. He looked down at her through his thick black lashes, a soft gloss coated his tired eyes. "I was afraid he would hurt you and Des. I honestly didn't think I just *did*."

"Your eyes glowed. Bright silver this time," he mused in a hushed tone.

She squinted up at Ryder. "This time?"

A grin appeared on his face. "Yeah. When you grew the sapling, they were bright green like the grass. The day you confronted Bastian and protected me from his petty threats, your eyes burned bright orange. What was going through your head then?"

Evangaline stood back, dropping her hands to only have them caught inside Ryder's. She tried to remember back to the moment Bastian threatened Ryder the day after they were fated, what she felt.

Squinting. Her brows drew close together in though, "Lava. My blood felt hot, like lava. I was searing with it, like I could set the bastard on fire for threatening to harm you." She met Ryder's gaze again.

He bit his bottom lip and nodded his head. "And last night?"

"My mind felt like … it felt foggy and cloudy. I was so mad. My mouth tasted like rain, like a summer storm. I … I … conjured a storm, right?" She muttered, lost in thought.

Ryder pulled her close, wrapping her arms around his back and cradling her face in his hands. "With the blood of Tuatha coursing through your veins, it comes as no surprise that you would be this powerful. Last night even had Des thankful he only got a small rain cloud when you sparred. The sheer power of the magic you have, Eva …You are just as powerful as Danu herself." He shook his head. "That would explain the whisp that's been pacing the balcony all night." A slight smirk eased onto Ryder's pensive face.

Evangaline chuckled. "The whisp is here? How do you know?"

Ryder huffed deep within his chest, dropping the handsome smirk that brought out his dimple. "You expended your power too fast. It would be no surprise if you couldn't channel your power for the day."

She backed up slightly, her brow pinching in confusion. She felt her power just the same as every other day. Her physical body was sore and piqued, but inside her power writhed with a newfound vigor.

Evangaline opened her palm, summoning a flame and looked up to Ryder in question, "My magic feels fine?"

His brows pinched in confusion, but dissipated as he shook his head. "Either way, your body wasn't used to the pressure of it, and you passed out once you drew it back in. The second you fell into my arms, a banging started happening at the windows. Des and the guards were ready for a full-blown battle thinking The Heretics finally came to the Capital, but it was the whisp. Little guy … or gal … do we know?" He chuckled, not giving her time to answer. "Either way, they threw themselves through the pane on the third bang and went straight to you. I nearly pissed myself seeing it nuzzle into your hair. It even stayed as Chevalier came and healed you, even as Wren changed you, and then it stayed all night on the balcony. That's why the door is open. It would bang on the glass when I would shut it. I've been freezing my ass off all night."

Evangaline laughed as Ryder cloaked her once more with his warm body. He nuzzled into her hair, ensconcing her in the safety of his embrace.

"First Theo, now the whisp … you really are giving me good competition, Eva," he added with a chuckle that vibrated through his chest and into Evangaline's cheek that rested right where his heart played its wondrous tune in her ear.

"There's no competition." Evangaline sighed.

Ryder squeezed her, sending a singe of pain through her bones. She refused to tell him of her aches for the sheer fact that she never wanted him to let her go. "Good."

Evangaline smirked. "Why are you happy? I pick the whisp … it doesn't call me a human whore."

Ryder laughed deep within his chest. It was horse and gravelly and deep and so, so perfect. "I'm never going to live that down, am I?"

"Nope." Evangaline snickered, burying her head in his chest once more.

The wind whisp followed Evangaline around the same way Ryder's shadows trailed him. Surely, if the whisp could be tattooed on her chest like the prince's shadows were, it would choose to be etched right onto her bosom. She couldn't even pee without it banging on the door. It was a protective little thing, even more so than Ryder. Whom of which also stayed close to her, never taking his eyes from her. Constantly checking her temperature. Supplying tonics and medicines, Madame Chevalier left. He also offered to carry her around for the day, and while the offer was tempting, she needed to use the aching muscles in her legs.

After they held each other for a while, Ryder drew Evangaline a bath and went off to find out any new information on The Heretics and the battles. He stayed away for an hour gathering intel and that was the longest he was gone. Unfortunately, with no new updates and the sad reminder of the reality and war staring them in the face, they remained in a terse holding pattern.

Des came and went, checking on Evangaline here and there, but had too much going on that he could not stay for long. However, he kept Shaw and Aadi as her royal guards and threatened them with their positions and the loss of their manhood should anything happen to Evangaline on their watch. Even though the attack the night before came from the king himself, Des insisted on protecting "not just the princess but his friend." Evangaline didn't fight him. He felt bad enough for snapping at her the night before, anyway.

Plus, it was charming knowing she was surrounded by a bunch of overprotective males, despite her being more than equipped to protect herself. Evangaline was a feminist, born and bred, but seeing all the guys worried broke her heart. If all she had to do to make them feel better was to let them mother hen her for a day, she could tolerate it.

Evangaline, Ryder, Shaw, and Aadi made their way to the throne room halfway past noon at the request of Darrin.

"Eva, if he does anything or you simply want to leave. We're gone. Okay?" Ryder stated, his voice nervous yet steady.

"It'll be okay. He won't hurt me."

Shaw choked on air, as Aadi grumbled from behind them, "E, he threw you into a window and compulsed you and Des for no reason. He already *did* hurt you. He's … I don't know. Unstable."

She looked over her shoulder at Aadi with her eyes squinted. The sight of Ryder's raised brows condescending her as she looked back forward, made her concede.

"Fine!" She gave up. Her bones still ached, and her head still pounded, even with everything Chevalier did to heal her. She was done fighting for the day, anyway. While her pride would never allow her to tell them … they were right. She was too weak, and the king was too volatile to be trusted at present. "Do we need a code word … should I tug on my ear to let you guys know I want to leave?" Evangaline queried sarcastically. She tried her hardest to alleviate the mood, yet her smile cracked across her face without reciprocation.

They turned past the embellished copper doors and into the throne room.

The only thing within the cavernous hall was the dais, where atop sitting in his jeweled throne, a glittering, gaudy gold crown, and matching jacket, was the king. Or a version of Darrin she had never met before. He rarely wore a crown, for him to wear one now was certainly a show of force.

He once told Evangaline, *"A crown only reminds the people who is in charge should they waver in faith. Its importance is a show of the time.,"*

To which she replied cheekily, *"So I take it as a good sign I never see you in one?"* His smile was the only answer she needed. But now, with a towering spiked diadem resting on his head, he looked imposing. He wanted to make a point, especially for her. She was the one who wavered in faith, and he wanted her in line.

Ryder had told her she did not hurt Darrin, however, she still feared she did. Seeing his indifferent and wholly put together self sneering down his nose from atop his throne, he honestly looked better than ever. His eyes were bright. His skin glistened like the top of a fresh dinner roll. But it was his smile that alluded to his complete disregard for everything that had occurred the day before.

Shaw and Aadi peeled off to the sides, watching from their posts on either wall. Ryder grabbed Evangaline's hand and strode to the dais. His head was held high, and his expression was full of disgust. Evangaline watched him as he moved with a feral grace before fixing her eyes forward to the throne, which held a man she once respected. Shoving a steel rod up her spine, she faced down the imposing figure of the king with nothing but fierceness.

Evangaline opted for her training leather pants and corset combo, leaving her shoulders exposed. A true warrior princess, Chloe would be proud. Both of her knives were strapped to her thighs, their diamond hilts sparkled in the sunlight streaming through the glass domes of the ceiling.

Wren placed a circlet atop Evangaline's brow of pure copper just to solidify her power and ranking. The king wasn't the only one wanting to show off. The handmaiden did not outright say it as she braided Evangaline's hair, but her twisted brow and the rare scowl across her face gave away her frustrations at Evangaline's birth father.

As Evangaline grew close to the Wren, she couldn't help but notice her always accessorizing Evangaline in mementos of strength. Despite never admitting it, they did help Evangaline feel more powerful. She made a mental note to tell her as soon as she saw her next.

Word spread of the fight between the Supreme King and his daughter through the servants and to the court like a wildfire. Talk of the fight overshadowed the battles with the Heretic's.

"Princess. Prince," The king drawled.

"King," Evangaline quipped. "Have you any news on The Heretics?"

The king stood to his full height, adjusting his shining silk gold jacket, plucking imaginary flecks of dust from his shoulder.

Ryder didn't waste any time being protective at the sudden elevation of the king. It just came natural to him. A natural born leader and protector. One second, he was beside her, and the next half his body was covering her lithe frame from Darrin's view. His hand was firmly within hers, nearly crushing bone.

Evangaline's eyes were fixed on Darrin until she felt a slight pressure wrap around her ankle and flow with a static-like grace across her stomach and onto her exposed shoulder.

By her feet she could feel the cool wind of the whisp coil itself around her leg. Holding her in a position of defense, just like Ryder. But that did not explain the tingling on her shoulder.

Slowly, Evangaline glanced down to see one of Ryder's shadows coiling along her collarbone. Not just any shadow, her prank accomplice, her little shadow.

In a whisper, she smiled down to the whisp, "Hi, friend." Then looked over her shoulder. "Hi, little shadow."

Simultaneously, the shadow wiggled with the wind whisp as though they were saying their greetings before fixating themselves in a slightly reassuring and domineering grip.

Evangaline chuckled, squeezing Ryder's hand. "Well, that's new," she whispered exclusively to him. His eyes dropped to hers and his lip quirked up for only a second before returning his death stare to the king.

"If you have no news of The Heretics, we will be off. I don't have time for your childish displays again, Darrin." Ryder drawled.

The king stepped down from the dais with his hands held up in surrender. "Please, if you scowl like that any harder, Ryder, that pretty face of yours will be stuck with the wrinkles that come along with it. I simply needed to start by apologizing to you both. My anger at the current situation got the better of me. However, I am glad I finally got to see the full scope of your powers, Daughter. You have been holding out on me. You are a treasure many will seek, Evangaline."

Evangaline scooted around Ryder. "It is in the past now. We will keep it there." Her tone was more regal than anything. She had been practicing her royal voice and wave in the mirror. Without *Netflix*, a girl had to find ways to entertain herself.

"Your Majesty, a message for the Prince and Princess of Shadows." Christoff ran in, waving a small piece of parchment in his hand.

Princess of Shadows?

"Well, that *certainly* is a new one. I'm gaining new titles by the second."

Evangaline muttered under her breath.

A breathy chuckle came from Ryder as he released her hand to meet the messenger halfway across the room. Unfurling the folded note, he stood with his back rigidly toward Evangaline.

Evangaline swayed with anticipation. "What does it say?"

"My brother has written to say The Heretics have begun to sail in the direction of Pax. The Undersea Kingdom agreed to help and is surrounding the waters, prepared to fight with us. And they've begun on the land …" He paused, then looked to his monarch, his eyes growing distant and wild. "How long, *Your Majesty*, have you known they've sought to end your reign and in that to harm the princess? My fated? You have yet to tell me of the anonymous threats you mentioned … pray do they involve my Eva?"

The threats on her life. The threats for the king to abdicate. She completely forgot in the whirlwind of her new life to tell Ryder about the threats to her life. With their fating and the discovery of her powers, it was the last thing to cross her mind. The night Chloe died, the king insinuated it was all the work of The Heretics but never went into detail. Only saying the psycho anti-royalist fanatics purely wanted his removal from the throne. But with their armies on Celadonian shores and the destruction they've laid at the monarchy's feet, it was time for the king to turn over whatever information he had. It was time Ryder learned why Chloe was sent to her and the magnitude of whatever the threats against her were.

While one side of her brain was swirling with questions and concerns about The Heretics and how she would play into their entire scheme, the other side of her brain was filled with a whole bevy of emotions that sent those pixies right to her stomach. They played a jovial tune that let them dance around their maypole of happiness and contentment among the fluttering butterflies. *My Eva*. Ryder called her *My Eva*. Through her fear and anguish, she blushed. Bad timing? Absolutely. But did she like the words flowing from his lips? Fuck yes.

When Bastian said it, it was possessive and demeaning, but when Ryder said those words, his tone—however angry in the moment—was filled with admiration and warmth. He said it from his heart, not his lust, and that made all the difference.

The king's face did the opposite of blush, however. He turned white as the stone dais at his feet. Was it fear of The Heretics? Or because he was caught in another lie by omission? Evangaline was leaning toward the fear of being caught for yet another dishonesty.

"You will believe the words of The Heretics and not your King, Prince Ryder?" Darrin said, trying to deflect. "How could you possibly have that information?"

Ryder pocketed the message along with both of his hands. He sucked his lip between his teeth and began his steady approach back to Evangaline's side.

"I don't trust The Heretics at all, nor do I, in this moment, trust you, but I do trust the author of this message, my brother. Are you claiming him to be a liar, Darrin? Our army received intel that the threats you received were not just threatening your life, but also the life of my fated. No matter how we got that insight, is it true? Was Eva the target of the attack that claimed Commander Darrow? Did you drag her into *your* battles unprepared and untrained?"

Darrin floundered like one of those basses that sang on the wall of a grimy bar, his mouth flapped open and closed in a silent opera, words not falling out.

"I suggest you answer, *father*. Spill whatever you know before more innocent lives get hurt on your doorstep. How exactly were the threats worded?"

"Don't act innocent, *daughter*. I told you there were threats against your life. I only neglected to tell you exactly the severity of said threats. They want you. They wanted you as a babe, they wanted you in Vitalis and *he* wants you *now!*" the king blurted with a sneer. "You are the first woman born to a line where the women are more powerful than the men. Cursed with sons for centuries, we simply rule because it is our birthright. If the prophecies and fables are true about the women of the Supreme Crown, which according to last night, you *Princess,* have been blessed by Danu herself, as will any other females birthed in this family's line. You are a threat to many, but for many, you are a tool of great power. There have been those who have sought to destroy this line and claim the throne for themselves. With you here now, and your power so fierce, The Heretics grow bolder in their attempts to destroy my reign and take you for themselves."

Ryder wore his anger on his face. His bold brow pinched in the center. His dimple only showed because of the way he kept clenching and releasing the muscles in his jaw. His chest heaved in deep breaths, like he was trying to steady his lungs, but he was one pull of a brick before his tower of blocks came crashing down. "All this time? You've known they've wanted her?"

"Since Evangaline's birth, *my Evangaline's* birth," the king threw her name out like a slur, "With her comes great power. And those great powers want her."

Evangaline swallowed, forcing her throat to work. "Did my mother know of The Heretics?"

If her mother knew and didn't warn Evangaline before allowing her to cross into this realm, Evangaline might never forgive the woman who birthed and raised her.

The king sighed, "No, Felicity did not know of The Heretics, to my knowledge. She was more scared of the sneers of the court than anything. It preoccupied her time."

"I can see why, your courtiers are awful," Evangaline muttered under her breath while releasing a sigh of relief.

"All the hidden attacks. The anonymous threats. They were the start of a war we are yet to see if we can win, all because you hid vital information from your people!" Ryder's tone boomed through the throne room, making Evangaline and many guards flinch. "All because you refused to tell us all the threat to you and Evangaline!"

Evangaline closed the distance between them and looped their fingers in a reassuring squeeze. "Ryder, look at me. It's okay. We—"

"No Eva, it's not okay." His tone was harsh, but not intentionally to her.

"I hid vital information that kept *your fated* safe. Yet again, before you craved her touch and felt her warmth, you certainly did not care for her at all, shall I remind you?" the king challenged.

Ryder ripped his hand from Evangaline's with such force she nearly toppled forward. Before she could right herself, Ryder was gripping the lapels of Darrin's golden jacket. His shadows swirled around her birth father's legs, awaiting their master's call.

"I cared for Evangaline well before I even heard her speak. Being her fated is an added bonus. I will gladly lay my life down to protect *your daughter*, to see her grow into the woman you stifled and hid away with the humans. You are not her savior and will never be. You are just a man who donated his seed to her creation. She will be a greater queen sitting on that throne for one second than you have ever been in your hundreds of years of pitiful existence."

Before Evangaline could let the words that Ryder spoke seep into her subconscious, before her brain could absorb the soul he laid bare in her defense, the palace rattled and shook. An explosion of smoke, ash, and flames billowed through the foyer and into the throne room.

Evangaline was thrown forward onto her stomach. The wind whip struggled to drag her leg to the side out of the way as the blast barreled into her back. Her bones wilted under the force of the explosion that shook through the palace, crashing her to the stones at her feet. Splayed out on the cold floor, Evangaline crawled to her knees, trying her hardest to regain the breath that was sucker punched from her lungs. A tight high-pitched buzzing shocked her ears, a small trickle of blood seeped out her right ear, hearing became all but useless.

Without her hearing coming through in nothing but echoing whirs, she looked up frantically in a failed attempt to get her bearings. She could not see but two feet in front of her, eliminating two of her five senses.

She searched around in the haze, unable to see anyone, coughing and wheezing as she inhaled the thick gray smoke. She gripped tight onto one of her daggers. A small breeze billowed from her other hand to clear away some of the fog. It didn't help.

"RYDER!" She screamed against her protesting vocal cords.

Nothing.

"RYDER!" She screamed again. Her panic coated each letter of his name. She was in pain and yet all her mind cared about was him.

Still Nothing.

"No ... Ry—"

Evangaline shoved her dagger back in her holster and raised her hands, fully prepared to sprinkle rain from her power alone but was cut off. Two hands wrapped under her aching arms, and for the briefest second, relief barreled into her at the soft touch.

The small lapse in fear and anxiety led way to her exhaustion. She was so tired, as the ringing in her head thumped in perfect harmony with the beating of her heart. She didn't even struggle against the person hauling her to their chest, but she knew by the feel of his hands, it wasn't her fated. His chest wasn't as big, his hands weren't as adoring, but his actions were protective instead of malicious, so she didn't struggle.

Muffled, "I've got you Lady E."

Shaw. It was Shaw. He picked her broken body into his arms and cradled her as he ran through the frenzied halls of the palace as though she weighed nothing.

With each step he took, she bobbed and bounced. Her bones were made of glass and, one by one, they developed fissures that, under the right pressure, would shatter.

They barreled through the chaotic palace. The smoke tapered as they flew up the stairs and down the secluded hallways. Figures blurred by Evangaline in hazy apparitions as Shaw flew at a determined cadence.

"Here! Now!" Aadi shouted from just beyond them. His tanned face was covered in ash and speckled with flecks of blood.

"Are you okay?" She croaked looking upon her friends with tears in her eyes.

Shaw obeyed Aadi, with blood and ash across his armor, and before she knew it, the door was slammed behind them.

Carefully, as though he understood her brittleness, Shaw set down Evangaline on a sofa that was familiar but not her own.

Struggling to get to her feet, Evangaline finally spoke through broken tears, "Ryder ... Shaw, where is Ryder?" She managed to get out, despite her voice cracking under the weight of her fear.

Shaw frantically ran around the room, closing curtains, checking under the bed, securing the room until he was satisfied.

Finally, steadying herself, Evangaline took a few deep breaths. *"Be courageous. Be brave. Be strong. Be bold. Be fierce."* Stephen's voice echoed in her head in a calming, steady beat, grounding her as an anxiety attack surged through her body, numbing her from head to toe. She could barely feel her lips as they opened and closed, searching for the strength to face the situation.

Then she stood tall and wiped the tear cascading down her cheek, "SHAW!" She shouted, finally grabbing his attention as he looked out the window through the curtains, "Answer me!"

Shaw stilled at the harshness of her tone. "Lady E … I don't know. Please sit down. You're bleeding. It's okay. He gave us instructions that, in case something happened today, to bring you to his quarters and to wait here. That's all I have to offer you. He'll be fine. He's the toughest bastard I've met—"

"I don't know if I should be flattered or not, Shaw." Ryder quipped, covered in ash, soot, and blood. His dagger had been drawn as he stepped through a portal behind Evangaline, but quickly tossed it onto the couch.

At the sight of his ashen covered face, relief struck Evangaline like one thousand arrows to the chest. And yet, seeing him in disarray made her tremble with rage and fear. Her already weak knees gave out, her strength sizzled like the dying embers of the fire in the hearth.

She threw her hands over her face, concealing her blood and tear-soaked face and sunk to the floor, allowing her anxiety attack to consume her whole.

Her relief mingled with her fear and anger, manifesting in shaking waves of hysteria and tremors.

She knew she needed to be strong, with this attack and the battles still hanging over their heads, but the fact still remained, she was only a girl from New York. Not a knight who has trained her whole life to take on traumas like explosions and war. She was scared out of her mind.

Ryder's warm, soothing hands wrapped around her waist and pulled her onto his lap. He held her tightly to his chest. He stroked his hand down her hair in a gentle sweep as he tried his hardest to comfort her. Soft shh's and murmured whispers traveled into her hair as he held her close to his body. She laid her head across his chest under his chin and drank in the steady beat of his heart like an addict. He was alive. That was all that mattered.

Evangaline breathed in the smoky, crisp ocean smell of him with each deep breath she took as she tried her hardest to regain her composure.

Through her tears she grumbled, "You fucking bastard …" She wiped her tears with the back of her hand. "You don't get to give instructions for me to be whisked away … Don't do that. Ever again."

"Shh. I'm sorry. I won't. I won't. I promise." Ryder cupped her face and whispered into her hair as he gripped her tighter.

She hiccupped a laugh through her tears. "Did you just shush me?"

Ryder smiled onto the top of her head, reminiscing about their conversation after they were fated. "Shh …" he whispered softly, steadily.

Shaw stood at attention and watched them by the door. As he did, his heart broke at seeing Evangaline undone. Covertly, he wiped a tear from his own eye, drawing Ryder's attention.

Nodding at Shaw, Ryder softened his facial features but gathered Evangaline even closer to his body. He needed to hold her. To feel her heartbeat. Even the feel of her tears soaking his skin brought him relief. He hated seeing her upset, but he would take five thousand days of her being upset and alive, then her being gone. He held her in a tight grip and gave a reassuring—yet weak—smile to Shaw. The sibling-like bond all of the cadre had for his fated was a bright light in the mess that was their current situations. So long as they were with her, she would be okay. That Ryder knew for a fact. "Thank you Shaw. Des needs you in the dungeons. He's called for you and Aadi specifically. I've got her. She's safe, thanks to both of you. I am eternally grateful."

Shaw swallowed hard and straightened his back as he tried his hardest to drop the visage of a worried friend and replace it with that of a royal guard. "Of course … of course." He made to turn away before halting with his hand on the door, "Lady E …"

Evangaline looked up, her face red, eyes puffy. She knew she looked like hell, but she could not give two flying fucks at the moment. "Yeah?" she whispered.

"He's right, you know." He tipped his head at Ryder. "You will be the best damn queen this realm has ever had." Then he turned on his heel and left the room, leaving Evangaline and her inconsistent emotions to start crying into Ryder's chest again.

Shaw's words struck her right in the heart. He believed in her. Ryder believed in her. Des believed in her. Everyone believed in her; except for *her*. And that fact she could not deny, not even to herself. They all were people who had only, practically, just met her and yet they put their utmost faith and trust in her abilities to rule a realm. It warmed her heart, but also hollowed out a gaping pit in her stomach filled with the eternal darkness of fear.

After a minute, she composed herself … mostly.

Evangaline agreed to stay in Celadonia. Therefore, she couldn't feel sorry for herself. She was a servant of the crown and to the people; she needed to be strong. If not for herself, for them. There were too many horrors occurring within the realm that, as the crown princess, needed her to be a symbol of hope and strength for the people. If Atlas hadn't drilled that into her head before, an explosion and looming war certainly reinforced the notion. Despite growing quite content within the hollows and curves of Ryder's embrace, she forced herself to be strong, and sit back.

"Why did Des need Shaw in the dungeons?" She leaned back. "Oh shit, I'm sorry about your shirt." She swiped her hand over the soft black shirt that was now stained with her tears and tiny blotches of blood—*was that hers? Or his?* Like smearing her soot covered hand across the wrinkled fabric would actually do something to help, either way. She only made it worse.

"Eva…" Ryder's tone turned somber as he stopped her hand in its frantic movements and held it still on top of the skin that housed his heart. His melancholic eyes did not meet her own when she looked up at him.

She sat up straighter in his lap, moving her legs to either side of his thighs, ignoring how good it felt to be pressed against him. "Ryder … what happened in the dungeons?"

The shadow that remained coiled around Evangaline's shoulder began to move. Its slithery movements created tiny tingles along her chest and back that mirrored the fear coiling in her stomach.

Ryder watched the little shadow with unwavering focus. Its serpentine movements mimicked the same ones the shadows made on his own tanned skin.

"They took him Eva. The Heretics, they broke him out."

"What? Who …" Her words trailed off as she remembered something.

"You are playing a dangerous game now, Princess …"

Just when she thought things couldn't get worse, this had to happen.

Bastian was a Heretic, and he was now free.

"How?" She asked, not sure if she wanted to hear the answer. Her hands shook more with each new revelation.

Ryder swallowed heavy. His throat bobbed with wariness. His normally dazzling ocean eyes now were a vacant and dark navy-blue.

Evangaline cupped his face in her hands, forcing him to meet her gaze.

"How, Ry?" Her voice shaky but stern.

Ryder nuzzled into her palm before shaking his head. "The explosion, Des thinks it was a decoy. They detonated it in the courtyard. That's why we felt it so closely. He must have had other Heretics planted inside the palace; this wasn't a small feat, Eva. They planned it. Took credit for it even … they left a flag behind in his cell. Either way, during the commotion, they took him away. Freed him."

Evangaline dropped her hands. Her lungs constricted inside her chest in deep, wringing movements. "No one saw him running out? Or the people helping him? He's not exactly small."

"The only things in his cell were his chains and the pennant. They must have used a portal. I don't know how or why, but they have him. Why Darrin just didn't kill him when he visited all those weeks ago is a mystery for the ages. Bastian was stripped of magic—it would have been easy."

After Bastian's apprehension, Evangaline learned the blue-purple glowing chains were made of a special gemstone found in the Tenebris

Mountains within the Kingdom of Shadows, named iolite. For magic wielders, the stone suppressed whatever power courses through one's veins. Apparently, they were the inspirations for the wards the leaders of Vitalis asked the fae to put in place after the Convergence. In every way, they act like kryptonite for magic wielding fae.

Evangaline leaned into Ryder's warmth once more and began to darkly chuckle. Light airy noises escaped her lungs as she snickered. Ryder's arms wrapped around her hips, squeezing tightly in a reassuring embrace.

"This is a fucking mess and it's all my fault," she said, closing her eyes to prevent the tears that threatened to fall.

Ryder put his chin on the top of her head and let out a sigh, "It's your father's fault—"

"The king is not my father! He made that evident yesterday." Evangaline bit out, albeit a bit too harshly.

Ryder tightened his hold on Evangaline, their bodies sat flush against one another. In any other situation, it would have been incredibly intimate. Ryder's hands held onto her hips as if he were holding onto a buoy in the middle of the sea, clinging to her for his life.

Evangaline nuzzled into his chest; his heartbeat thumped next to her ear. Just as many people could fall asleep to the sound of rain or waterfalls, the sound of hearing Ryder's heart steadily beat could lull Evangaline to sleep. The melody of stability and homeliness—a tune to remind her that he was alive. He was there, holding her.

A notion deep in the shadowy pit that was now her gut began to feel like a clock slowly ticking. A doomsday clock inching to zero.

"You have to go, don't you?" Evangaline whispered, not wanting to delay the inevitable.

Ryder inhaled a deep breath and then exhaled. His breath tickled the top of her head as his fingers traced idle circles on her hipbones. "I am going to need to. But *honestly*, I don't want to."

Evangaline pulled away and looked up at him, "Honestly? I don't want you to." She then bit down on her bottom lip. She was trying to create a dam, so the next words didn't flow out, but she couldn't stop them. "But I know you have to and as your crown princess, I wouldn't want you to stay. You have people to take care of. I understand that. They need you more than I do."

A tear that did not fall earlier slipped past her lower lashes, streaking down her face and onto the skin of her chest, right on the—now still—shadow twined around her collarbone.

She looked down at the tear resting on the shadow. "Sorry, little shadow."

The shadow wiggled, shaking off the droplet of water. Evangaline giggled under her breath. The sensation tickled, like a feather lightly caressing her skin.

Evangaline brought her eyes back up at Ryder. He looked so sad, so tired. Which he should be. Being that he slept in a chair awkwardly next to her all night, now all of this, he had to be exhausted already.

She whispered, "I can go with you. I can fight *with* you." Her words were laced with hope as she looked into Ryder's mournful sapphire eyes.

Ryder shook his head softly, closing his eyes. A few strands of his onyx hair fell onto his forehead in the process. She pushed them away, "No Eva. It's safest here even despite what happened today. I can't let you risk your life, your future, on an unpredictable war in my homeland. I won't allow you to risk it. I *can't* risk *you*. I dislike the bastard, but the king is right. If The Heretics really do want you, I don't want you marching in with a target on your back. Besides, if you got hurt … you're still, from what we know, mortal Eva, still part human. If you got hurt …" The little strands of hair resting on his brow jostled as he shook his head, withdrawing his gaze from Evangaline in agonizing thought.

"Ryder …" Pleading. "I can't stay here wearing fancy gowns, eating, and drinking, as though you aren't fighting in a war that the king himself won't even fight in. He was eager to fight the small battles when he thought The Heretics were some small anti-king groups. When he was harboring his secrets. But now, they have ships and a whole army. They now have Bastian and all he knows of the realm's secrets …"

She swallowed, trying her hardest to push down the lump growing in her chest.

"I will always have a target on my back, Ryder, always. With or without you, Vitalis or Celadonia, I have a target on my back, regardless. I can't allow them to hurt my people, *our* people, just to get to me, *please*. I can't leave you to fight alone."

Ryder's left dimple appeared as he stared into Evangaline's watery, pleading eyes. The rich, vibrant sapphire sparkles swam up to the surface of his endless gaze.

"You are an incredible woman, you know that?" He said to her in a hushed, loving tone.

Evangaline rolled her eyes, making Ryder laugh.

He grabbed her face between his tender hands. "I mean it. You are truly my curious little creature. I know you aren't going to like it, but you need to stay here. I need you here. *The realm* needs you here. I will come back and get you as soon as it is safe. As soon as I know, the only threat you will face in Pax is from the five hundred questions my siblings will bombard you with. Stay with Des and the guys. Train. Lead. Keep getting answers, keep asking questions. I've fought for decades. Battle is second nature to me. In fact, it is quite tedious and boring at this point. Don't worry about me or the Kingdom of Shadows—we're a hearty lot. I only just got you Eva, I'm not risking you."

Evangaline opened her mouth to fight him, but she closed it again when she knew her argument would be useless. Instead, she pleaded, "Promise me, Ryder, promise me that you won't face death alone. Going to battle is one thing, but if it looks bleak, if that stupid, annoyingly noble part of you takes over, don't let it lead you straight into death's arms. You are immortal, not invincible, and I only just got you, too."

He nodded, a small smile playing on his lips, "I promise."

"Good."

"As long as you promise to keep working with Atlas, to hone your powers more. I don't want to leave and something like last night happen again. It scared me half to death, Eva. Power is complex and dangerous when not understood. And truthfully, I don't understand yours at all. Promise me you will stay safe, even from yourself. Promise me, Eva, you will be strong and brave. Be the fearless princess that had no problems accusing me of summoning a shadow demon." He laughed at the memory.

Evangaline smirked and nodded. "I promise. I'll stay safe and I will practice. I promise."

"Good."

"Ryder?" She asked, laying her head back against his chest.

"Yeah?"

"If you see Bastian out there … kill him."

She could feel Ryder's smile against her forehead. "Without hesitation."

"Good."

Chapter Forty-Nine

Ryder stepped out of the Capital and into Artemes—the capital city of the Kingdom of Mirth—the next morning at sunrise. He decided the night before at dinner with the boys to visit the Kingdom of Mirth as it shared a border with the Kingdom of Shadows. With no correspondence from anyone yet, he wanted to gauge the enemy on his own shores by seeing their previous destruction on another. And he was worried about Ophelia. Apparently, Ryder and Ophelia shared a bond like Evangaline and Des. He wanted to check in on her and ensure she was safe. Though he only spoke of that as he held Evangaline on the couch long after the boys left her room.

He claimed he had seen battle enough to know you could learn just as much from the rubble as you could from the front line, and who was Evangaline to argue that logic.

Evangaline watched him go. Without a kiss or hug, with nothing but a squeeze of the hand and the weight of their promises, he was gone.

She clutched her hands tight to her sides to stop them from shaking.

As the sparkling black opal hued portal closed behind her battle-ready prince, Evangaline felt a piece of her heart go along with him. The part of her that felt safe and warm. That little puzzle piece of her heart that fit into its place oh so perfectly when he was near, that small but vital piece that kept her heart beating and her body warm, suddenly fell away and she was left cold and feeling un-whole. She did not know how she would cope with the unrelenting nerves that she felt knowing what sat on their plates, but she did not have a choice. She took those nerves and used them to keep her busy, to propel her forward.

The wind whisp curled around her on the breezy hill outside the palace, as they watched the morning sun offer its greeting over the horizon. Casting yellow streams of light through the purple and pink sky. Evangaline didn't know when she would get another moment to breathe in the fresh air of the Capital without it being tainted by the fumes of war. She embraced the bite of chill and the sound of the leaves alongside the wind whisp.

"We've got this," she muttered to the whisp, "one day at a time. Right?"

The whisp wiggled its agreement against her shoulder.

Then with a determined set to her spine, Evangaline began her walk back to the palace, holding her head high. She locked her tears firmly behind her eyes despite their valiant attempts at lodging themselves free. The breeze blew through her diaphanous purple gown and empowered her to keep taking the next step forward. Placing one foot in front of the other, despite the overwhelming urge to curl into a ball and cry. Evangaline had work to do and promises to keep.

Day Ten

The capital received word of the first battle taking place in the Kingdom of Shadows, only a couple of days after Ryder left.

The Heretics waited to attack the Shadows with all their might just after nightfall, the same day Ryder was set to return to Pax.

Led by her prince, the Shadow Army pushed The Heretic Army back to the coast before The Heretic's ultimately retreated from the battlefield altogether.

"The army consists of fae, human, and unidentified creatures alike, all trained and well equipped to do serious damage." Christoff, Chloe's brother, read aloud. The message had been written by Ryder's brother, Niall. He wrote as soon as he had word from Ryder at the battlefront and provided all he knew to date. Insights filled his letter that were both hopeful and damning at the same time. The other kingdoms who got attacked only reported seeing fae battling, however, Niall reported members of the human realm being present on the battleground. The first mention of humans beyond the Velum since she arrived in Celadonia.

"How could that be? Humans and fae? Together?" Evangaline asked the table of men surrounding her, "I didn't think that was possible with the borders."

Des, King Darrin, and Atlas called a meeting to discuss the war surging around them. Des brought along the cadre to assist in war discussions. All being high-ranking members of the Royal Guard and Army, he wanted their opinions too. Evangaline was not, however, invited. But, after she heard the meeting was called at dinner with the boys, she showed up anyway.

Des shook his head, his face wan with exhaustion. A slight scruff appeared around the taut outline of his jaw. "I don't know. An army this big we would have—should have—noticed training from the scouts. None of this makes sense. From all of his records, or the ones I was given, Bastian noted nothing off within the land."

"It seems the bastard was one of them. He wouldn't very well leave his traitorous secrets lying about," Evangaline quipped, crossing her arms across her chest.

"You are excused Christoff." The king sneered, seeing Christoff from the room.

Evangaline sighed. "We should have known humans were somehow involved. The first threat you received from The Heretics proved they knew who I was and, more importantly, where I was. They knew too much information about Vitalis to just be fae."

On day three after Ryder left, Evangaline weaseled her way into the king's private study and scour through the few letters and threats he received from The Heretics. Everything was kept under lock and key, of course. However, with her growing powers, she learned she could simply freeze some ice into the lock and fashion a makeshift key.

Disturbingly, the freaks Ryder battled knew where Evangaline worked, who her ex-fiancé was, they knew where Miles went to school, where her parents worked. They knew her entire life. The fact that they didn't include her social security number and a lock of hair in the letters was a surprise.

Atlas leaned forward to the strategy table. "Do you think Vitalis could be capable of this level of deceit?"

The king raised his eyebrows and shrugged his shoulders, seemingly unbothered, "I couldn't imagine it. The Supreme President is mindless, but not stupid enough to wage a war against us."

Shaw stepped forward clearing his throat, "Does my king wish to have the armies readied and distributed through the realm? We can plan to march to each of the five kingdoms to ready for battle and offer aid."

The king leveled a look of pure disgust at Shaw. He was not happy at Des's insistence of the cadre being present, but chose his battles carefully.

"I don't think it would be a bad idea. The ships have retreated, thank the gods, but we all know it won't be long before they are spotted again. Even if the army goes to assess the devastation, it is not a bad idea to have our men and women ready should our foe make landfall again." Des added.

"No! That is final. The Royal Army stays here under my command!" Darrin yelled for no reason other than to hear himself shout.

This same fight had happened between Evangaline and Darrin nearly every day and the stubborn bastard wouldn't budge on his stance. He didn't want the army to fight, nor did he want to help in any way. He simply wanted the realm to struggle under the attacks. Which made no sense at all. Many from Mirth were displaced from their homes. With battle only just starting in the Shadows, it would be inevitable that many more would be without food and shelter, and yet the king didn't waver in his stance to sit idly by and watch their land fall to the waste side. Afterall, he was bedecked in gold and diamonds, had food at his leisure cooked by the best chefs in the land, and kept a steady rotation of women passing through his quarters at night. What would he care if others suffered when he lived luxuriously?

"I will write to Niall, ask him for more information on the humans and creatures fighting. Maybe he will know more that will help us." Evangaline quarried, gripping onto the table with white knuckles. She nodded at Shaw and Des. They nodded back to her. They all knew she was changing the subject and they would discuss the matter of aid privately later.

Selfishly, Evangaline wanted to write to Niall because she needed to know how Ryder was.

They had never shared a bed, never even kissed, but the hollowness that surrounded her at knowing he wasn't close made her toss and turn at night. She felt a part of her soul become hollow with each day they were apart thanks to their fating. It was excruciating.

She even asked Atlas days ago to help her understand being fated better. She needed to know if it was normal for fated couples to feel so alone without the other close by. Of course, like almost everyone, the notion of being fated still was outlandish and, therefore, he only knew very little. However, they were able to find a single tome that detailed what it meant to be fated, as told by Tuatha and Milesian. It contained no more than ten pages and nearly half of said pages were diagrams and details about the mark on her arm and the way it felt when said mark was placed upon a fate marked fae's skin.

"As a couple is joined by touch, they accept the will of fate. Their separate souls shall entwine, combining into one." The tome read. *"The power of fate is one unexplainable and at time unpredictable, yet the copper mark of the fate blessed, is a symbol of two souls choosing one another by powers, not even the Gods themselves control. Destined Love. Souls are marked at birth for only one another and only fate itself will drive them together when they need one another most."*

"Very interesting. You two are bound by fate, but also in your souls. I was not aware of some of this with Tuatha and Milesian." Atlas pondered.

"That doesn't help at all." Evangaline added with a side eye as she finally changed the color of a rose. A task she did as she patiently waited for Atlas to finish reading his tiny, very unhelpful book.

Atlas laughed. "Your loneliness is partly due to your souls entwining with one another. If I had to guess. Though I have a feeling your feelings, the ones you've yet to admit to yourself are the ones making you feel such loneliness."

"What do you mean?"

Atlas just winked at her and left the library without another word, laying the open pages down in front of her. She stared at the book written in an old fae language and the diagrams drawn of the mark on her arm, and immediately felt worse than when she came in seeking answers.

Atlas left her with far more questions that day than anything else, and she hadn't the courage to ask for more information or to even seek it out. The situation was hard enough, and she needed to focus on her promises to Ryder first and foremost. Ask questions. Get answers. Lead. Stay safe.

"Yes, write to Niall, see if he can offer any insight. We will have it sent out as soon as possible. Any word from Surtis or Conall? Are they still spared of this madness?" The king answered, drinking his wine as he relaxed in his chair.

Des leaned forward. "Conall claims to have seen nothing off the coast. But his army is ready in case they arrive. But he doesn't seem worried. Surtis believes the mountains are protecting them but still are ready should the enemy fall on their kingdom as well. His army is also ready to march alongside the Royal Army should you request it, Your Majesty."

Darrin nodded with his brow pinched in a contemplative visage. "Hmm … Fine. And the others? Frost, Mirth?"

"Ophelia informed us a few days ago that they have ceased their battles. The enemy on their shores fled with the others and the remaining ones on land have been exterminated. Artemes was vaguely unharmed, minimal damage unlike some of the neighboring villages and towns. Tunit responded this morning. His shores remained untouched, but they lost half their naval fleet in battle. He also claimed in the heat of their skirmish on the sea, The Heretics unleashed a creature beneath the waves. That was all he wrote. No details on the creature," Des recounted. Evangaline couldn't help but note the wariness to his voice.

Des barely slept since The Heretics began their siege. Whether he was with the soldiers readying them for battle or training Evangaline harder than ever, he barely got any sleep. Round the clock he was working. The purple bags under his eyes were the physical indication of his exhaustion, but the mental exhaustion was evident in the wariness of his voice. His solemness matched only her own. They often ate together in silence, needing company but not wanting to talk.

Darrin stood from his chair at the center of the strategy table. "Alright. We shall meet again in two days' time. Evangaline, gather as much as you can about your Prince's kingdom." At those words, her heart lurched, and she did not ignore the fire that edged the way he spoke of Ryder. "The rest of you carry on doing what you have been doing. Whatever that is."

And he stood and left as though there weren't lives at stake.

Day Twelve

Wren un-braided Evangaline's hair. Allowing her long brown tresses to cascade down her back.

Evangaline sat in another war council that morning, with no updates from the Kingdom of Shadows. She wrote to Niall immediately after leaving the meeting two days prior and had the letter sent out within the hour.

Dear Niall,

Thank you for writing and updating us here at the Capital. I greatly appreciate it. We greatly appreciate it. We are trying to understand more about the report of humans battling alongside the fae. You were the only one to mention it in your letter. Were they clothed and trained alongside one another or were they two separate battalions? Any information would be helpful in knowing Vitalis's involvement in the battles ahead. As far as the creatures, are they identifiable? Have you or your people seen them before? Any insight would be gladly welcomed.

Sincerely,

Evangaline

p.s. Please tell Ryder to stay safe.

Two days and she had yet to hear from the Kingdom of Shadows, and boy, did the king remind her how useless she was. He seemed to take the lack of communication personally. "Clearly, all being fated is good for is some matching tattoos," he scoffed, laughing to himself when she reported that there was no response yet to her letter.

It took everything for Evangaline to not singe the edges of his gilded coat with her flames or conjure a rainstorm above his head. She even considered at one point in the meeting how fun it would be to blow him around the room like a kite. However, she settled for a simple apology from her lips and let it go. Or *tried* to let it go, rather.

Her powers had grown stronger during her lessons with Atlas. She made waves in a nearby river that stood taller than her own frame. Not a tsunami but large, nonetheless. She trained her flames to grow larger, making burning waves of their own kind. The wind whisp enjoyed teaching her how to manipulate the air around her. And sapling after sapling was sprouting up where her and Ryder were when the first one sprouted from the ground, making a small forest of her own design.

"Are you sure you wouldn't like a bath drawn?" Wren asked, snatching Evangaline out of her thoughts.

Evangaline smiled her gratitude. "No, I am just going to go to bed. Long day."

Wren nodded. "Of course. I will leave you for the night."

"Thank you, Wren. Good night."

Chapter Fifty

"Your prince is a valiant fighter, cherub."

Evangaline looked around frantically. Where was she? Something wasn't right.

The ground was an onyx black stone with flicks of gold and silver embedded within. The endless black depth of the floor appeared beneath her uncovered feet as if she was standing on top of the night sky itself.

She could not make out any walls or anything surrounding her thanks to a hazy gray mist that encased her.

"Who are you?" Evangaline shakily hissed, fisting the thigh length silk skirt of her pale green nightgown.

Her breathing grew heavy and hear heartbeat thudded louder in her ears as she stared into the foggy abyss without an answer. Anxiety pooled in her lower belly.

As she stood in the quiet, the looming presence at her back grew heavier. She took in her surroundings one more time. Then glanced down at her state of dress. It did not take long to realize another nightmare was seizing her within its grip. It had been a while since the demon of her dreams came reaping, not since Chloe's death, to be precise. Even then she chalked the entire bad dream up to her subconscious telling her to get her wounds fixed. But now, with the being at her back, breathing down her neck in soft pants, his presence was unmistakable. He was real. She just did not know how, or why, or who he was, but he was not just a figment of her imagination.

Then, with a spontaneous whoosh, the fog to her left side parted its swirling tendrils, and her heart stopped beating entirely.

"Ryder?" She asked softly.

His towering frame strode through the fog. A helmet was tucked neatly under his arm. His handsome face was speckled with blood and dirt. Her favorite two pieces of jet-black hair fell onto his sweat and blood-soaked brow just how she remembered.

Ryder bore armor in a rich matte black that was dinged and dented, but from what Evangaline could see, he was whole. Disgustingly dirty, but whole.

She stalked toward him when the phantom's hand grabbed her shoulder, halting her mid-stride. The demon's ice-cold tipped talons gradually dug into her shoulder. Evangaline froze at the touch, her limbs going numb with fear.

A breath tickled her ear, hot and unwelcome. "He dreams of you often."

It was a painful voice, each word like a nail on a chalkboard. Grating and raw, but familiar. She had heard it before, months ago, in the nightmare she survived after Chloe's death, but this time it was taunting. It wasn't scolding her for lingering wounds; it was enjoying the sight of her squirm and writhe under their forceful touch. The being soaked up her fear and pain with a sinister grin she could not see but rather felt through his words.

"What do you want?" Evangaline croaked as she tried to steel her voice and shake away the debilitating fear that was coursing through her bones. It was a hopeless endeavor.

"What he wants …" the pale black tipped hand released her shoulder and pointed forward to the image of Ryder past her face. It was the most Evangaline had seen of the phantom at her back, but it was enough to make her not want to see more.

She watched as Ryder stopped walking and inclined his head back, taking in a lung full of air. His free hand, the one marked by the fates, was braced firmly on his hip. He looked exhausted. He stood unnaturally still, just breathing with his eyes closed. His black armor reflected the glow of the moon onto his weary—and handsome—face.

It took everything for Evangaline to not run up and wrap her arms around his waist. Everything inside of her longed to hear his laugh again. To feel his hand in hers. She missed their talks and the way it felt so natural to open up to him. She even missed the tingle on her skin of the little shadow he placed on her in protection.

"I want *you* too," the voice said before pushing her to her knees. "For different reasons, of course, but you, nonetheless. However, we would make a powerful duo, you and I. Maybe keeping you by my side wouldn't hurt." He hummed. "I will think it over."

Her knees cracked against the inky black floor as the figure to her back pushed her down. Evangaline looked up, not wanting to take her eyes from Ryder. Her fated was approached by a younger man. Smaller in stature, his hair tied up in a leather, but the same color as Ryder's, an unmistakable midnight black. He handed Ryder something—a piece of paper—before patting the Prince of Shadows on the shoulder. Ryder took the paper and the two dimly smiled at each other. Ryder's grin was less bright than the young man, but his eyes gained a sparkle to them that set Evangaline's heart a blaze. They walked away until they were engulfed in the cloud of swirling gray mist that surrounded Evangaline.

"Ryder, wait!" Evangaline screamed, only to hear her voice die into the emptiness, unheard and unfelt.

Suddenly the phantom hands pushed Evangaline to the ground, her face smashed into the same starry surface under her knees. The ghastly hand clasped firmly around the back of her neck, nearly piercing her skin with its sharp nails, "Don't grovel, it's unbecoming on a daughter of Danu." He sneered venomously. "You will belong to me, one way or another, Princess. I'll give you the choice now to cooperate. All this suffering will end. Come with me."

As the hands released their ice-cold grip, Evangaline shot up screaming, "No!" waking herself, in the process, from her sleep.

The moon was still high above the soil below the palace. She had no idea how long she was asleep, but she knew she certainly wouldn't rest again anytime soon.

Evangaline swung out of bed, fisting her palms into her eyes and rubbing until she saw fireworks. As she stood, a sharp pain shot through her knees.

A ping of fear tinged her stomach and froze her to the very spot she stood.

Streams of blood dripped down her right knee, leaving a crimson path in its wake. She was afraid to look down, but she did. Her knees were scuffed and bruising already, bleeding from tiny pores now etched into her milky skin, right where she had fallen in her nightmare.

Day Fifteen.

For three days, Evangaline was unable to sleep. At some point her under eye bags matched Des's—the ripe purple of an aubergine. The nightmare scared her enough to not close her eyes for more than half an hour increments. The words of the creature followed her throughout the day. The underlying threat and ultimatum.

She called them nightmares, but in truth, they were more than that. They were attacks and she was defenseless against them. It was a purgatory of lucidness where she found herself unable to feel any of her magic. Only fear clung tight and unrelenting to her body as the demon taunted her and fed from her pain. Luckily, she was only haunted in her sleep. As long as she didn't sleep, she needn't worry. *Easier said than done.*

Finally, Evangaline told Des about the nightmares, considering both of their lack of sleep. Leaving out the parts where she was injured in real life, she told him she was haunted by a demon who apparently wanted her and threatened her. Des just looked at her like she was drugged out of her mind and reassured her that everything would be alright. "It is just a stressful time," he said. If she had a quarter for every time sometime told her that over the past fifteen days. "It's just a stressful time. That is why the king is moody." "It is just a stressful time, no need to worry." "It is just a stressful time. Your body is just channeling your anxiety into your sleeping state." Every time the phrase left someone's mouth as an excuse, Evangaline wanted to hurl a chair through a window. At the end of the day, Des told her to tell him if another nightmare happened, but Evangaline knew there was nothing he could do, nor was it at the top of his priorities.

As the fifteenth day since Ryder left drudged on, she couldn't shake the gaping hole that erupted in her soul, seeing Ryder in her sleep. Her sleep induced demon never just tortured her with physical pain. He played in psychological warfare, and somehow he knew Ryder was a pressure point he could press on. Unsure if it was the fating or her ever-growing feelings for the prince, Evangaline felt part of her soul shred when he would appear through the gray fog that encompassed her nightmares.

Surprisingly, the pain she felt in her knees before Madame Chevalier healed them was nothing compared to the gaping wound left in her heart at seeing Ryder in her sleep. It felt so real. Despite the logical side of her brain telling her it was just a nightmare, Evangaline couldn't shake the notion that what was presented to her was happening in real time. Ryder's exhaustion and pallid face, the blood and the dirt, they all felt so real.

Unable to find comfort anywhere around the palace, Evangaline stood dressed in her training leathers before Chloe's grave. This was the first time she visited since the funeral, but found it was the only place she could finally breathe. Outside, shaded by the flowering oak tree behind Chloe, she felt oddly at peace. Like somehow, despite her not physically being around, Chloe's warmth permeated from the soil in a gentile hug.

"Hi Chlo …" Evangaline's voice was shaky as tears began to stream their far too familiar path down her cheeks. "You'll never guess what's happened since you left. For starters, I'm fated. I know. Insane right. To Prince Ryder of the Kingdom of Shadows, but I suppose you know who he is. So, why am I saying his full title?" She rubbed at her face, clearing the tears, "Also, for what it's worth, you didn't tell me the Prince of Shadows was insanely good-looking. Like beyond Mr. Brooks level hot." She paused, choking down a sobbing laugh. "I've missed you like crazy." Evangaline whispered into the air.

Lost in Chloe's spiritual warmth, Evangaline sat for an hour, telling

Chloe everything she missed. She told her best friend about Bastian and the king. About Des and how she picked a good one in the new General of the Royal Army. All to top it off with Evangaline blushing in her stories about Ryder. About his hair and eyes, how she hasn't seen him naked yet but knows that he is just as impressive as her imagination could conjure. There was no way he wasn't. She told Chloe everything that echoed through the chasm that was her brain. Spewing everything to Chloe's ghost in a therapy session for just the oak and wind to hear.

"I miss you, Chlo. Sometimes I feel like you're right here with me, just as you were back in Vitalis. No one can replace you, ever." Evangaline sighed. "I like to think that you would like Ryder. He's a good man. I surprisingly miss him … *a lot*. It's crazy how I could only know him for so little time and miss him this much. I actually understand all of those princesses in the cartoons I grew up with. I get how a person could fall in love with a complete stranger. I just hadn't found my stranger. Yet again, those bitches weren't *fated* to their princes, now were they!"

Evangaline played with the lace on her boot, breathing deep and heavy. "I really hope you are proud of me, wherever you are, I hope I can be the warrior you wanted me to be. I try. Some days it's easier than others, but I try because I know that is what you would have done. Things aren't the same without you. I love you, Chlo. I miss you, you crazy bitch. I'm so mad you had to go, being all plucky and shit. I miss you every fucking day, more than anyone will ever know—"

"Your highness?" A quiet voice startled Evangaline upright.

Spinning up to her feet, Evangaline ripped away one of the daggers sheathed in her boot and pointed it straight at … Christoff?

"Oh, my god. I am so sorry Christoff. I … I'm … on edge. Please forgive me," Evangaline sputtered, noting her error and sheathing her dagger as fast as she could.

"No, I snuck up on you. I apologize," Christoff contended as he approached Evangaline.

The closer he got, the more Evangaline thought he looked like Chloe. His little button nose and full lips were identical to Chloe's. Their hair was the same curly texture, just his wasn't dyed bright pink and purple. The same rich black skin, unmarred and smooth.

He nodded to Chloe's grave. "I haven't wanted to bother you since it happened, but she spoke nothing but great things about you since she returned. Of course, leaving out the fact you were—are—the princess."

Evangaline's lips tugged into a quick smile as she hummed a small sound of sad amusement. "She was too good for this." Pointing at the grave marker "She saved me in way more ways than just shielding me that night. Your sister was … she was my everything … I never said how sorry I was to your parents. To you," her tears fell.

Christoff gazed at Evangaline and smiled. He really smiled. Standing before his dead sister's grave, he had the courage to smile. Something Evangaline could barely do without tears. She tried but failed.

"Your Highness—"

"Evangaline, please. Your sister would be on her ass hysterical to hear you calling me 'Your Highness,'"

"Evangaline." He then turned to face Chloe's grave, securing his hands behind his back. "My sister was the bravest of us all, not afraid of death. She taunted it with open arms, even. Laughed in the face of it. What she was afraid of, though, was not doing something meaningful with the life she got. She loved helping people. Loved being a pain in the ass while doing it, but she lit up when she could help someone." He took a breath. "Your presence means a lot to the realm. Many feared the future with the lack of an heir. She would be proud of you. You've done nothing but put others first, every chance you get. I don't need to be around you all the time to see it. It's felt. Down in the village more than anything."

Evangaline allowed the words to settle over her for a few moments before smiling back at Christoff. "Back in Vitalis, working at the bookstore, Chlo was awful at stocking shelves or doing the menial tasks—but she was great at helping customers. She could convince someone looking for a cookbook to leave with six romance novels and a biography on some random celebrity no one cared about. She loved helping people that walked through the door even if she never said it out loud. Her face lit up when she talked to someone new. I never got to tell her truly how much she helped me. She knew, but still, I didn't say it enough. It was her gift, I think. Maybe she didn't have any magic, but her ability to help people—her empathy—that was her true power."

"Yeah, yeah it was."

Christoff and Evangaline stood staring at where Chloe eternally rested before Christoff cleared his throat and faced Evangaline, "Now, I come baring a message from the Kingdom of Shadows for *Your Highness*." He finished the last part with a wink that made Evangaline laugh.

He extended his arm giving her the letter and brushing off her thanks before turning on his heel and heading back in the direction of the palace.

Once he was out of sight Evangaline ripped open the letter so fast the wax seal flew off into the grass meters away.

Dear Princess Evangaline,

Thank you for your letter. It is not every day the crown writes with thanks personally; I feel extra special. Unfortunately, our knowledge on the monsters encountered on the battlefield is faint. We have enclosed a sketch of the ones we have encountered in hopes that the royal library might have any record of the beasts, and my Uncle Atlas can offer his help. They appear on the battlefield as though they manifest from the very shadows we cherish. However, they have only engaged a few times with our forces, preferring to be spectators rather than participants.

As for the human's fighting. They have been placed at the front lines, clad in the same armor with the same weapons. They appear to be without reason and simply fight to kill. They do not talk or even flinch before death. They have been the first to be slaughtered despite Ryder's efforts to not engage with them. It is as if The Heretics are placing them there on purpose, a purpose we have yet to find out. But the human men and women fight with the same fervor of their fae and monster counterparts.

Please tell the king the ships off the coast have retreated but sailed to the eastern seaboard in the direction of the Kingdoms of Fire and Leaves. I have written to said kingdoms but wish for the king to be notified as well.

As for our battles on land, my brother continues to push and kill his way through the enemies like the showoff he is. After their retreat, the enemy has now set up camp along the mountains, where we suspect the next battle will take place soon.

I hope any of this helps.

Yours Kindly,

Niall

p.s. My brother says he expects a few rounds and a game of rock, paper, scissors at The Gilded Rose once he returns. And to stay safe, too.

Evangaline would have chuckled if her heart didn't hurt so much. "I will get you as much ale as you want and answer all of your silly questions. Just come back to me." She said to herself.

Folding the note, Evangaline opened the drawing of the monster.

There it was. Red eyes. No mouth. Gangly limbs. Sharp black claws. It was the same type of demon that killed Chloe. Staring at her right there on the paper in black and red charcoal.

Evangaline's heart lurched into her throat.

She had to warn everyone. She lived because of her power and ancestral blood, according to Madame Chevalier, but others might not be as lucky.

With fear pushing her on, she raced back to the palace, making a B-Line for her room so she could write Niall back and warn him.

Dear Niall,

As your brother's fated, please don't call me princess, it's weird. Please call me Evangaline. However, that is not why I write in such a haste. Those monsters, I have encountered them. I don't know where they come from or what exactly makes them so lethal, but you need to tell Ryder that those creatures are the same demons that killed Chloe. He will understand. Their claws are laced with a lethal poison your brother has seen firsthand. If any of your men are wounded by one, tell your healers they only have so much time and to extract the venom before it can mingle within the bloodstream. Ryder will know what to do. I will have my healer, Madame Chevalier, write to you with instructions. I will try to do more research to find more about them. Atlas and I have already tried looking for their origins in the past, but came up empty. I will try to see if I missed anything and do as much research as I can.

Sincerely,

Evangaline

p.s. Ryder has a cold ale waiting with his name on it when he returns. Possibly a s'mores brownie if he's lucky. My treat.

Day Twenty-five

Ten days and Evangaline had still heard not a single update from the Kingdom of Shadows regarding the ongoing battle or the demons that lurk on their battlefield. She was on edge. Anxious. And all around, not pleasant to be around. Her fear laced with a healthy dose of shitty sleep, which left her restless and moody. She snapped at Des, blew off lessons with Atlas in favor of some peace and quiet, and rolled her eyes at Darrin when he, yet again, admonished her relationship and intelligence. Her indifference resulted in a tongue lashing that had Shaw and Charlie tensing. Evangaline just stared vacantly at Darrin, letting his cruel words slide off her skin. The realm was at war. Nothing he could say to her would be worse than standing idle while many Celadonians were suffering.

She still slept fitfully, if at all. Despite there being a clear ebb in the battles that were raging, nothing she did helped her to sleep at night. Thanks to the nightmares she had consistently. The moment she closed her eyes, her tormentor was there, ready with taunts and riddles. She had become numb to it all.

The ships that sailed away from the other kingdoms were spotted off the coast of the Kingdom of Leaves two days ago. However, they made no advancements, nor were they getting closer. They simply anchored out at sea and sat. Docked like omens of death and destruction.

Conall wrote every day, updating the king on the enemy off the coast. With the Leaves directly bordering the Capital, Darrin didn't seem at all bothered by the battle getting closer to home. His temperament remained cold and distant, which shocked nobody when it came time for meetings or dinners.

Cold silence would fill a room like a welcomed guest during dinner service since the battles raged. Where there once was music and laughter, dread and a lack of hope lingered instead. And with each day that passed, Evangaline began to stop shunning it away. Instead, she welcomed the cold numbness with open arms. Allowing the frosty silence to coat the ache in her heart and further hollow out the pit in her stomach.

Was it her destiny to lose everything she cared about? Her family to the segregation of realms, her best friend to death, Ryder to war. The thought of *actually* losing her fated coated her body in a hollow daze every now and again. The only thing that would pull her through the agonizing loneliness was the mental record she made of all the sweet things he had said and the promises they made to one another.

Ryder might have looked tough and brooding, but he was exactly as Evangaline told Theo. He was nothing but a big teddy bear, at least he was to Evangaline. When she felt weak, she remembered the night on the balcony of her room, the night her life officially changed. His voice was soft but firm. *"You are stronger than you know. Braver and bolder than you recognize. There is a fierceness coursing through your blood. You just need to allow yourself to see it. Eva, I am not upset at being fated only because I have been fated to you."*

That night, he gave her the choice to leave, but also gave her more reasons to stay than she even saw at the time. She felt the way her body reacted around him, the way he made her feel safe and wanted, like she was the strongest person on earth. And for him, she would try to be. For Des and the boys, she would be their toughest activist and greatest friend. Evangaline wouldn't allow herself to forget the courage and strength that she had housed within her cold, aching soul. If they all thought of her as a warrior before they knew she was a princess, before Ryder knew she was his fated, before she held magic in the palm of her hand, then she knew she had to try, at the very least.

Keep trying no matter how hard it is, she would tell herself when she felt herself losing a grasp of who she was. If Ryder could go out and fight monsters and armies, she would fight the monsters in her head until he came back to her. And then they could fight it all together.

Day Forty-Five.

Day forty-five came along with a snowstorm of epic proportions. It had been thirty days since she last heard from the Kingdom of Shadows and since she last wrote to them regarding the monsters they faced on the battlefield.

They were the only kingdom brutalized with such force by The Heretics. Evangaline wasn't naïve enough to know why. Once the news of her and Ryder being fated spread across the continent in The Golden Prophet, the Kingdom of Shadows became more than just a domain within her realm. It wasn't her *home* necessarily, but it had the closest thing that felt like home battling on the front lines with his men. He became her Achilles heel thanks to their fating and The Heretic Army knew it just as the phantom in her nightmares did.

Evangaline had other nightmares, but only two that left her with scrapes and bruises along her body. She still never saw her nightmarish assailant's face, but he held a giddiness at showing her visions of Ryder. Or perhaps it was the fact that after each image he showed her, a piece of her wilted just a bit more.

The first of the nightmares showed her Ryder atop a grand gray and black speckled horse. At first it just appeared as though he was riding through a muddy field until the first red armored fae came into view—a Heretic. Wielding a sword made of black crystal, the Heretic swung straight for Ryder, not a deadly blow but one that would cause enough damage to immobilize him for a bit.

Evangaline's heart nearly ended as she watched his horse buck, throwing Ryder to the ground. He rolled onto his back only to thrust his sword into the Heretic with the same ease as skewering a chicken kabob. He was confident and fierce, but it never stopped Evangaline from bellowing his name with a false sense of hope that he might hear her, eventually.

His helmet landed in the mud with its shining black wings thrust into the soggy earth. He stalked forward with a tenacity that scared even her. His shadows seeped from him and swirled like a tornado at his feet as he walked, sword in hand, toward an eager group of human Heretic soldiers.

His hair was longer than she remembered and under all the dirt and blood on his face, she could see just a hint of a shallow beard.

Despite it all, his sapphire eyes still set her at ease—despite their darkened shadow filled state.

Another time she saw Ryder, he was asleep on a pallet of furs. A fire brazier flickered feet away under the awning of a canvas tent. She watched his chest dip up and down in steady, even movements. He was alive, and that was all that mattered. His glistening naked torso was visible and bore small bruises and scratches, but ultimately was pristine. All things a healer could mend with ease.

She didn't even feel or hear her tormentor taunt her about wanting her. Not even as the phantom drew its claws down her back in sensual teases. She ignored the pain of his nail, because her fated was safe, Ryder was safe and sleeping, and that was a gift the devil at her back didn't even consider. She was thankful for once that she saw Ryder peaceful in her nightmares and not tense or in the heat of battle. She never even called to him for fear that she might wake him. She just watched him sleep while her tormentor drew blood from her back with tally mark like scratches.

She hadn't had another nightmare since seeing Ryder peacefully slumber on day forty-two, but the fear of another one happening never went away.

So, sitting in her room—bored out of her mind, antsy, and afraid to take a nap—staring out at the fresh white snow now covering the supple green earth, Evangaline picked up a sheet of paper and a quill and began to write.

Dear Niall,

It has been some time since our last correspondence, but I wanted to check in and see how things were going. You would be in your full right mind, sitting in my gilded cage of a palace, to tell me to fuck right off. With your kingdom in the state that it is in, I would not blame you one bit. Believe me, though, when I say, if I could, I would be battling with you all. I'm only here because I promised your brother I would stay. So blame him if you must.

The other kingdoms have remained quiet, thankfully. The ships disappeared off the coast of the Kingdom of Leaves without even a stray arrow on their shore. Tunit and Ophelia have begun to rebuild, which I am grateful for. But my heart still lies in your kingdom. Every day that goes on, it gets harder to sit idle.

I've been unlucky in finding anything on the monsters you face. I've scoured almost every tome and scroll, to no avail. The library looked ransacked at one point; I thought Atlas was going to have a heart attack when he came in that day for my lessons. But I haven't given up hope. I have been visiting the library in the village regularly. The scholar who resides there has been trying to locate anything on the otherworldly creatures, so hopefully we will have our answers there. I also sent the picture to Ophelia in hopes that one of her scholars would have something in their many libraries. I am eager to hear from her and will write to you as soon as I do.

Truthfully, if it were me, the Royal Army would have marched down to help Ryder by now, but I've been unlucky in securing aid. But I am here to help, in any way I can. I am here for you all. I will always be.

Yours,

Evangaline

p.s. Ryder still has his beer waiting for him. Also tell him, there's a whole new forest growing where the sapling was. He will get it. Oh, and to stay safe.

It was times where Evangaline sat in the quiet with no technology that she yearned for a cell phone in Celadonia. Any form of communication that she could just say reach out to Ryder without writing letters and having Christoff send them out. Just to hear Ryder's velvety voice, even if just for a millisecond, would put her fretful mind at ease.

Instead, she wrote her letter and handed it off to Christoff for him to get it to the Kingdom of Shadows at his earliest convenience.

And then she resumed her routine of waiting, practicing, and arguing like a good little princess.

Chapter Fifty-One

Ryder's heart pounded as he made his way back to the camp on the outskirts of the muddy battlefield. The Shadow Army had managed to veer The Heretic soldiers away from two small villages with minimal casualties. With the help of his sister, Lily, both villages were safely evacuated and brought to Pax—his capital city and home. Plenty of wards and enchantments were erected to keep the people within the island safe from outside attacks. Not to mention the regular patrols made by the merfolk of the Undersea Kingdom. For now, Pax was as safe as he could make it.

Night had fallen and the stars twinkled overhead as the smell of muck and death clung to Ryder's being. A perfect dichotomy, beauty hung above his head while the despair of the blood trodden earth sat beneath his boots. Never once had he seen a battle like this. The sheer stamina of the fae and humans that fought on the side of The Heretics was commendable, but in every way worrisome. They were fearsome and relentless. Even when staring down the sharp blade of death, they did not blink or falter. They greeted death as an old friend and walked into its embrace with such ease that it sent a shiver down Ryder's spine.

His life was not always easy and shimmering with the veil of royalty, but never once had he even thought of death as a friend. Especially now. His copper lined finger twinkled up at him, reminding him to grab forth the small tattered journal from the pocket hidden beneath his armor. The pencil that he fastened to the binding slipped between his fingers as he flipped the book open.

To anyone else, the first pages in the notebook would present him as a madman. Tally marks of various thicknesses and lengths marred the pages. Mud and blood occasionally splattered about from where it seeped through his armor and onto the worn parchment.

He drew another tally with a sigh. Fifty-seven in total as of that morning.

Fifty-seven days since he last saw his fated. Fifty-seven mornings where he woke to the sounds of a rising war and not the clinging of Eva's sword against Des's. Fifty-seven days waiting to see if the king neglected his kingdom and people.

Ryder had battled these heathens once before, but that skirmish was off the coast of Pax and consisted of one single ship. He barely regarded it as a skirmish. It was nearly a blip in the radar of his days. The king's scouts had spotted the vessel from his envoy and tried to bargain with Ryder. Darrin claimed he would handle The Heretic ship in exchange for Ryder's help on a mission where the king needed the prince's shadows. Ryder refused and took the ship out on his own. Only a few of his men were wounded from debris and the ship sank to be dealt with further by the Undersea Kingdom.

Anything off the coast was theirs to do with as they so please under the treaty between the Shadows and the Sea. Ryder thought he saw the last of The Heretic's that day. After all, they paraded themselves as just another rebellious upstart against the crown—easily squashed and dealt with.

Yet, climbing the hill to the circular tent where his comrades and General of the Shadow Army, Everett, were meeting, he felt deep into the marrow of his bones that this "rebellious upstart" was something far more sinister. He just could not peg what. Ryder simply feared that their interest in the woman that bore the same copper marks as he did was more involved than even she believed. She was too pure to be dragged into the world he found himself wading through at present.

He tucked the notebook back into his pocket as the sounds of aggravated discussions reached his ears. A grunt of unsatisfied annoyance left his throat as he muscled his way to the flap in the tent.

"We don't know what we face! Barreling across the land to the coast would be folly and you damn well know that!"

Ryder sighed as he crossed his arms. "We will not be heading to the coast. If they want a fight, they know damn well where to find us."

All the heads in the room snapped to him.

Everett, with his light brown skin caked in the blood of the fae and humans he faced earlier, let loose a smirk, accepting his triumph over the old stubborn ass that was Commander Fandroc. Ryder never cared for the old bastard and clashed with him countless times. However, seeing as the commander was best friends with his father, Ryder was pressured to keep him within the ranks of the Shadow Army. Everett, however, was ten times the soldier Fandroc was. The two grew up with one another and when they turned two decades old, joined the army under Fandroc's command.

Ryder was told not to as "an heir does not need to dirty his hands as a recruit." But he wanted to see first-hand what it took to be a soldier before one day commanding the whole Shadow Army as their prince. Plus, he enjoyed the excuse of getting away from home. But that was a fact only he and Everett knew. Ryder served for a few years but left to resume his duties as the heir to the Shadows. In that time, Everett stayed on, rising the ranks and growing into a fearsome soldier. The day the crown was placed upon Ryder's head, he knew exactly who would take on the role as his General of the Shadow Army.

In many ways, Des reminded Ryder of Everett. Perhaps that was why Ryder admired Des so much? The two soldiers—generals now in their own right—would get on perhaps too well.

"This is madness—" Fandroc started.

Ryder slammed his hands on the circular table strewn in various topographical maps of the Kingdom of Shadows. "What is madness is the fact that we are still fighting endless days with a foe we know nothing of! What is madness is the fact that you think it wise to continuously debate your superiors because you believe age puts you at an advantage. Well, it does not work like that here. The plan stays as is. We push them away from the civilians and seal off any retreats that would give them access to the other kingdoms, the same way Ophelia and Helena did for us."

Fandroc scoffed indignantly. "Your plan has us lying in wait to be killed!"

"And yours has us blazing into death with open arms!" Ryder returned.

Silence befell the tent as they all stared at the two men glaring at one another. Ryder's shadows pulsed across his chest and neck and magic gathered angrily within his clenched fists in warning.

He promised Eva he would not willingly court death and, therefore, played each one of his hands safely. No risks were taken. Besides, there were too many unknown variables. The Kingdom of Shadows would play it safe. End. Of. Story.

"Lily ensured that both villages were safely brought to the refugee camps in Pax. The Heretic Army is looking weaker with each day. To risk the lives of the Shadow Army any further would be a mistake." Ryder attempted to calm himself down, peeling his eyes away from Commander Fandroc and fixing them back on the table. "We keep them here to the best of our abilities, where there is nothing but open space. They cannot retreat into the forests, nor can they escape to the mountains, as we have blocked both passes. Lieutenant Clarkson, how far have you gotten with the prisoner we took? Have they spoken about their leaders or motivations?"

A powerful young woman stepped forward. Freckles dusted her cheeks as well as dirt. Her throat bobbed with the inhale she took as she looked up at her prince, "No, Your Highness. We barely got the first question out before the man … well, he killed himself, Sir."

Ryder gaped at the lieutenant with a squinted brow, "How? He was bound and human?"

Everett cleared his throat, "He threw the chair back and cracked his head on a rock."

"He did not even think twice about it. In fact, he smiled as he did so … it was … disturbing," she amended.

Ryder rubbed at his face. That was the second prisoner they took. The first was a fae with minor powers to manipulate fire. Before iolite shackles bound their wrists, they set themselves ablaze. Taking a human prisoner was better as they were weaker in every way, however, that too went awry. Apparently, the man was smarter than he appeared. And they were back to square one. The Heretics remained a mystery for another day.

"Okay. We will find our answers elsewhere." He groaned. "Get some rest. Everybody. The night guards just took over. The battle has ceased for today. We shall resume tomorrow when word comes from the scouts of The Heretic's movements."

One after another, the men and women nodded and bowed to Ryder as they made their way to their tents. Fandroc was the last to leave, brushing past Ryder as though the prince was worth nothing more than a grain of salt. It was another long and grueling day. Ryder should have forced the commander beneath him, on his knees and groveling for penance, but he was simply too tired of fighting. By the looks of the wan faces around him, everyone needed a bath and sleep, himself included.

"Nothing from the princess?" Everett asked, dropping his elbows onto the table and glancing up hopeful at his prince and friend.

Ryder shook his head. "No. Last I spoke to Niall, she hadn't found anything else about the beasts. And the king is still being an ass so—"

"No Royal Army," Everett surmised.

The crackle of the brazier was the only thing that filled the air for a moment as the two men stood in a vexed silence. The air breezing into the tent was balmy and held the essence of winter. Snow had not fallen on the flatlands of the Shadows, but small dustings coated some of the mountains to the south. Rain fell more so than snow in these parts, but the air of the night held the promise of flurries.

"And what of your fated?" Everett quietly asked.

Ryder tensed, peering at his friend with a scowl. "What about her?"

Everett cracked a smile and laughed, "Easy, boy. I'm only asking how she is? None of this can be easy for her."

With a sigh, "No, it can't be. But she is strong. Fuck, I'm starting to think she is stronger than me. I can tolerate her father for no more than a day, yet here she is tolerating his broodiness for weeks." Ryder sank into a canvas chair, dropping his head lazily off the back. "Not to mention the fact that she puts everything on her own shoulders. The guilt she holds for anything—*everything*—that goes awry ..." He took a deep breath. "Once this is all over, I think I'll take her to the cottage on the coast."

Sinking into a chair beside the prince, Everett breathed a laugh. "Mmm. A vacation sounds nice. Perhaps you will need security detail." He winked, making Ryder laugh.

"Between her friends, you, and my siblings, I have a feeling getting a moment just between her and I will be more painful than extracting a tooth." Ryder chortled.

"Have you written her yet or are you still suffering from writer's block?"

Ryder's head lolled to the side to look at his friend with a roll of his eyes. "I can write a letter to every citizen in my kingdom in a day tops, but for some reason writing a letter to the woman that fate has bound me to is the absolute hardest thing I've ever had to do! I don't fucking get it. And then my brother ... don't get me started on that little shit and how he corresponds to her with ease."

Everett laughed, drawing a smile to the Prince of Shadows' tired face. "You've got it bad, my friend. Wait, I've got it!" Everett exclaimed, rising from his seat in one fluid motion, "What you must write is this! Take notes! Ready?" He took a breath, then stood tall, pretending to be a classically trained actor. "My dearest princess, my love, my heart and soul, how fine thy eyes, and hair, and breasts—"

Ryder grabbed hold of a paperweight and flung it at his friend with a grimace. "I will warn you just once, never speak of her body. You know what just never speak of her at all, how about that? Dick."

Everett laughed. "I'm just joking! Calm down! Godsdamn you fate-provoked asshole!" He sat back down and reclined in the chair. "Seriously though, just write to her what you feel."

"Oh, thanks for the advice. Has anyone told you, you have wasted all your scholarly potential as a fighter?" Ryder quipped sarcastically.

They both chuckled before settling into the quietude of their camp. For a moment Ryder's eyes eased closed, but a sudden feeling of unease settled across his skin.

He peered up at the top of the tent. "*Search,*" he whispered to his shadows. One by one, they seeped from his skin and across the walls of the tent outside.

"That will forever be gross to me." Everett shivered. "*Search.*" He lowered his voice to mock Ryder, but the prince did not smile. He did not even react to his friend's mocking. His senses prickled and raised the sweat soaked hairs on the back of his neck. The feeling sank into his bones and rattled his core. He didn't need the shadows to report back that the camp was too quiet. No sounds of the wounded, no sounds of fires crackling, or soldiers enjoying a pint. Nothing.

"We're under attack." He rose from his chair and grabbed the sword from its holster at his side.

Everett jumped up, never once doubting his friend. A long bow and quiver graced his back in seconds as he exited the tent on Ryder's heels.

It was dark and still as death.

No fire crackled because there was no longer a fire lit. Not a single member of the Shadow Army was around. Ryder's pulse beat quicker.

"*In the forest beyond the skull shaped boulder.*" Little shadow whispered back to him. Eva's favorite shadow was quick and agile. He trusted it and lead Everett through their abandoned camp and straight for the tree line in the distance. By the time they approached the skull shaped boulder, the rest of his shadows lined his body and clung to his frame like a remora clinging to a shark. They all whispered the same things. "*The enemy has taken their wills. But they live.*" "*They attack their minds, not their bodies.*" "*Watch for the zealots in red. They trick the head.*"

"They must have at least one fae wielding compulsion." Ryder did not like their odds, but knew he had no choice but to attack. "*Where are The Heretic soldiers stationed?*" He asked the shadows in a whisper.

"*Two in the trees, four on the green, three you will see,*" a shadow responded quickly.

Ryder peered up into the canopy of the giant pine trees that surrounded him and Everett. "Get your bow ready. There are two somewhere in the cover." He didn't need to squint like Everett was doing in order to see in the darkness that they clung to. Luckily, his shadow magic gave him enhanced eyesight in darkened spaces, a perk of his power he thanked the gods for at present. "There! At two and seven o'clock. On my signal, shoot them out of the trees. Shadows, you will take out the three surrounding our soldiers, split up, and leave nothing behind. Make it quiet. I will go for the four surrounding on the grass. Everett, once you are done with the scouts above, help me … Scratch that, get the soldiers out. I think the three soldiers the shadows are going after are the ones keeping the soldiers compulsed." Authority rode Ryder's tone and with-it Everett and the Shadows readied.

Everett knocked four arrows, one ready to fire after the other. He was an expert archer and taught Ryder all the ins and outs of the skill. No doubt he would only need two of said arrows. However, he knocked four just in case.

Ryder held tighter to his sword as he crept around the boulder. A clearing sat nestled in the trees. Hundreds of his soldiers sat, compulsed out of their goddam minds, on their knees with heads bowed as three fae—two men and one woman—stood around them. Their heads tipped to the sky in concentration. All three of them were needed to hold such a large crowd hostage, but they were weakening. Their power and strength were being drained with each second that ticked by, but what were they waiting for? The entire battalion could have been slaughtered easily, and yet they sat on their knees like worshippers.

"*Feast,*" He told the shadows.

One by one, they slipped away, slithering through the grass as snakes would. A sick sense of power always filled Ryder when the shadows did what they did best. They were creatures of death, no matter how cute Eva found them. They thrived on the hunt, enjoyed the fear as it gripped people. The relationship they had with Ryder was symbiotic. He gained their eternal aid, so long as they had a host that knew their power. The shadows followed him before his magic even manifested. Drawn to one another like magnets. At first, the constant whispers were maddening, but as he grew, Ryder learned how to wield them, and then when his shadow magic emerged, the shadows clung to his skin and became an eternal source of power.

A synchronized dance of darkness eased up the power wielding fae. So deeply consumed in their magic, they did not even feel the shadows easing up their bodies. By the time the shadows constricted their necks, their fate had been sealed and all that remained of their bodies was polished white bone.

As his soldiers gained the jurisdiction of their minds, Ryder slipped from the shadows and threw Everett the signal.

Everett struck true in only two shots. *Show off.* The bodies of two human Heretic soldiers tumbled from the trees and landed on the ground. The sounds of bones crunching and flesh impacting had the four Heretic soldiers on the perimeter turning to Ryder.

His first opponent was felled in only a second. They bore no skill with the freakish blade they wielded. With two swipes of his sword, the man's head rolled to the feet of the second soldier. She, however, leapt over the body of her comrade with a catlike agility. She was quick and trained well. Her hair whipped around her in two long braids that matched the color of her armor. She swung with purpose, but not nearly enough. Ryder briefly smiled as he thought of his fated, as the woman swung her sword in a horizontal arc toward his legs. Des always tried to get Eva by taking out her feet, but Evangaline was smart. Every time he did, she jumped high. Sometimes remaining on the defensive, others taking the offensive and kicking Des in the chest.

"You may be good, but Eva is better," he grunted as he jumped over her sword and kicked the Heretic square in the face, imitating his girl. She tumbled back with a sickening crack. Her life ended and faded from her eyes as her neck snapped at an unnatural angle.

The confused murmurs of Ryder's soldiers carried to him in the distance, just as Everett shouted a pained cry.

Ryder spun to see his friend with a gash marring his thigh—deep and viscous. Everett stumbled back, but never stopped swinging his broadsword. The man he faced—though human—was far bigger and broader than Everett, bigger than even Ryder. A flail twirled in his hands as his dead eyes settled on Everett.

The Heretic soldier swung fearlessly. Everett's sword went flying just as Ryder cried out. Ryder's feet pounded against the grass and dirt. Sweat dripped from his brow as he threw up his arm, shielding his friend from a no doubt fatal blow. The flail wrapped around his forearm, skimming the side of his face with the spike tipped ball. Blood seeped down the groove in his cheek, but he kept eye contact with the monster of a man.

"*Feast*," he commanded. And this time, the attack was not quiet or subtle. The shadows jumped the man in a cyclone of darkness, ridding him of his flesh. For the briefest second, Ryder looked into the Heretic soldier's eyes and saw what he could only describe as grateful acceptance.

One foe remained and as the shadows clung back to their prince's skin. Ryder fixed his gaze on the Heretic soldier being pinned to the ground by members of the Shadow Army.

Ryder stalked forward. "General, get these men and women back to camp." He scoured the group, finding a healer. "Heal his leg if you can. He will be a stubborn ass about it, but I need him well."

The healer nodded; his svelte frame was dwarfed in his standard Shadow Army black armor. A sash of white wrapped around his forearm was the only indication of his healing abilities. Everett and the healer made their way out of the clearing, hauling the confused mass of soldiers behind them.

A human woman laid on the grass, her limbs pinned by three of Ryder's soldiers. Her face gave the impression as though one day it might have been pretty and round. However, now it was pale and gaunt. Her eyes stared at him, distant and dazed. Freckles lined her forehead and nose, but so did bruises and scars. She looked far too young to be a brainless soldier, willing to die for a cause her kind had no shares in.

"Who is your commander?" Ryder asked, kneeling in the grass next to her.

She sneered a vengeful smile and then spat on his boots.

He took a breath, "Do you feel better?"

A small laugh escaped her lips, "He will come for her and then none of this will matter. We will be free."

"Who is coming for who?" The Prince of Shadows demanded, however, deep inside, he knew the answer. Fear licked down his sweat lined skin in bumps.

"When it is death you wish for, your eternal damnation is life," she whispered.

Ryder peered down at the woman with a crease etching his brow in confusion, his lips moved to open, a question poised on the tip of his tongue. Before he could ask any more, an arrow soured through the air, impaling the woman right in the throat.

The three shadow soldiers holding her down jumped up and whirled around just as Ryder did. His heart pounded through his chest as he squinted into the distant dark. Red armor and white blond hair strode away from them without even a backward glance. His mission was to silence the woman, and he did. The man stalking away cared not for his opponents sitting exposed. He simply whistled as he walked away, content in his murder.

Blood spurt from her mouth as she choked on the last dregs of air in her lungs. The ruthlessness of the murder wasn't what disturbed Ryder the most, it was the gratitude filled smile that filled the woman's face. Another soldier happily walking into death's embrace. Another soldier that left Ryder with more questions than answers.

He sat back onto the grass and watched over her as her life was snuffed out in gurgles. His hands threaded through his hair as his eyes clouded with confusion and grief. The entire night was befuddling. Why control the minds of an entire army, then let them live? Why does death look like a release for The Heretic soldiers? And finally, who wants his Eva badly enough to wage a war over it?

"Your Highness? Should we head back to camp?" One of the soldiers that stayed behind for the interrogation asked.

Ryder looked up at her slowly. "What did you see or hear? How did they lure you away?"

"It was more of a feeling," another soldier answered.

The first soldier cleared her throat. "One second I was by the fire, the next I just *needed* to head out here. A voice just told me to come and sit. Everything else is a blur."

"No one hurt you? Or asked you to do anything?" He asked.

She shook her head.

Ryder released a sigh, "Alright head back to camp. I will clean this up. If you think of or remember anything else, come find me immediately."

He stood as the three soldiers left him alone in the clearing. With the moon shining overhead and the stars twinkling, Ryder released his shadows on the deceased.

The Prince of Shadows remained under the stars for a long while after. He had been to the forests of his kingdom many times as a boy. He had many fond memories of climbing the trees and playing with his brother and father in many groves similar to the one that surrounded him. Life seemed so much simpler then.

Alone in the forest, he removed his armor. The shirt that clung to his skin stank with the day's sweat. He tugged it over his head and tossed it on his pile of sheathing. The second his skin was free, he traced the copper line of his fate marking contemplating the events of the evening. Around and around his muscles, his finger glided until he landed on the permanent ring on his left ring finger. Two bands connected by a symbol of the fates, an eight-pointed star. He wondered if Evangaline gazed at her marking as much as he looked upon his. It was simple and yet utterly breathtaking.

Decades worth of tales spoken about Tuatha and Milesian, decades of believing their story to only be myth and legend. Something parents told their children to believe in peace and not war. To believe in love. And yet he was chosen. Out of thousands of fae, he was *blessed*—rather—to bear the mark of fate. Sometimes it felt surreal, but then he remembered the feeling of Evangaline curled upon his chest as they napped on her couch, and it felt so right.

She had a way of understanding him that no one else had. Even in their short time knowing one another, the need for her has been insatiable. He rushed to her that day in a fit of panic and rage only for her to endow upon him one of her beautiful smiles—the ones that did not happen enough— and grace him with the warmth of her body. Every day he cursed himself for not kissing her even once, for not holding her tighter, for not sharing a bed with her. Since their fating, being away from her felt unnatural.

His brother gave him every letter she wrote. Even in her correspondences, she had a magnetism that could not be matched.

P.S. Ryder still has his beer waiting for him. Also tell him, there's a whole new forest growing where the sapling was. He will get it. Oh, and to stay safe. Her last letter swirled in his head.

When he read her postscript, a surge of overwhelming pride came over him. So much so that he could not shake the smile from his face. In fact, when Everett asked, "What has you in a good mood? The misses send you a nude portrait?" Ryder didn't even wallop him over the head. Instead, the prince grinned and cooed, "Nope, she grew a fucking forest!" and then walked out of the dining tent like the happiest bastard alive.

A newfound determination settled into his bones. If he could slaughter grown men with just a sword and his wits, he no doubt could write a letter to the woman he loved! He was such a fool for not taking her with him. She could have stayed in the Palace of Stella, his home, and he could have visited her every day by portal. Instead, like a dunce, he forced her to stay where she suffered under the lecherous commands of her birth father. Never again would he part from her. Especially now, knowing just how valuable she was in the eyes of their enemy. Once The Heretics ease their efforts, as soon as Everett was able to handle the foe by himself, Ryder would be at the front doors of the Capital Palace with his arms open and ready to take Evangaline far away. Somewhere safe and quiet.

Oh shit, Everett was right … you have it bad! He thought. Then for the first time in weeks he earnestly smiled and laughed up at the stars.

"I'll be home soon, baby." He whispered, hoping that somehow Eva would hear it.

Chapter Fifty-Two

Day Sixty.

Still no word from the Kingdom of Shadows.

But on the sixtieth day, Evangaline smiled for the first time in a while.

The snow fell in a light dusting, as if someone was slowly sifting powdered sugar on the realm. Relentless blizzards raged for days on and off, and the bitter chill in the air was nothing but brutal. But it looked like a picture-perfect snow globe out her window when she woke on day sixty.

Restless and tired, luckily not from any nightmares, Evangaline took the cadre and went out for a snow day. Just as she, Katherine, and Miles used to do when they were kids. She knew she needed air and to get away from the constant talk of Heretics and war echoing within the halls of the palace, and time in the crisp winter air would do them all well. So she dragged each of their ornery butts outside!

The ships reappeared outside the Kingdom of Shadows, all of them. The entire fleet. Six days ago. The palace spies detailed their re-emergence as "an apparition through fog and darkness." The description alone terrified her. The knot that wrung itself in her stomach as to what Ryder would be facing grew tighter and bundled her nerves into a wicked tangle. But luckily, Ryder was accustomed to the darkness. He wore it like a beautifully tailored suit and even in these dark times, she hoped it would remain his friend and not his foe.

Evangaline and Des continued fighting daily to send the Royal Army down south, but every time they brought it up, the king threw a temper tantrum. He was a kid who was hell bent on getting his way. He sneered and hollered until they relented. He constantly reminded them of his rank and said it was Ryder's problem to deal with. The latter argument made Evangaline's blood boil, but she kept composed and brought up the argument the next day in hopes that the king would finally come around. He never did.

The Shadows had a few days' reprieve from what the royal scouts had heard before the Heretic naval fleet emerged. They finally defeated the last of The Heretic's that were camping in the Tenebris Mountains and across the flatlands. Ryder's men began to make their way home when they were ambushed by the squadrons from the ships a day ago. The Undersea Kingdom had yet to emerge to help their earth trodden ally, but Evangaline was hopeful they would destroy the ships and help Ryder out a bit.

With the news of the ships and the attacks, Evangaline grew tireless. She could not sit inside scouring books and dining with courtiers, all the while pretending her fated's land wasn't getting battered because of his affiliation to her.

Just thinking about Ryder battling made her sick to her stomach. No matter how tough and powerful he was, or how many times he reassured her that, "bloodshed was more a nuisance than something to be fearful of," he was still a man that could easily be felled by a blade that cut too deep.

So, to take their minds off everything, on day sixty, Eva took the cadre and decided they needed a minute to unwind. Henceforth, the snowball fight that she started once they made their way to a clearing just outside the village. Each round grew more and more intense, but it brought much needed smiles to their faces.

Before she knew it, many kids from the village, including Theo, joined and soon it became the boys vs. Evangaline … and children.

Though smaller, the younglings had many brilliant strategies. They carefully built snow mounds as barricades to deter the boys. While others dedicated themselves to making ammunition. All the while, Evangaline used her magic to build an igloo to hide in and for her team to catch their breath—much to Des's chagrin. She made it so even his brute force strength couldn't collapse the snowy blocks; it was wonderful ... and he hated it. Which made her love it more.

She trained her powers, so they became an extension of her like another arm or leg—at least that was how she thought of the magic coursing through her veins. She would use it for little things throughout the day so the thrumming in her chest wouldn't appear so taught and she wouldn't burnout as Ryder feared. Evangaline wanted to stay poised and ready to strike in case she needed to use her powers to protect people or fight. Lighting a candle, preserving a rose against the cold, building an igloo ... all little things to exert a little pent-up magic and stretch her power muscles.

Evangaline was just about to lob a snowball right into Shaw's unsuspecting face when movement caught her eye over the hill in the direction of the palace. Christoff waved her over with his mittened hand frantically.

"Theo ... Take this and get Shaw!"

The young boy did as she said with a sardonic smile gracing his rosy cheeks. Hitting Shaw square in the forehead with fatal accuracy. Bright white snow dusted over the soldier's entire face, coating his thick black lashes, and getting stuck in the stubble on his chin.

If the kid could aim that good now, he would be a shoe into the Royal Guard by the time he's of age! She thought as she walked away, hands up in surrender.

Her pride beamed through her laughter as she climbed up the hill to Christoff. Seeing everyone smile and let loose released some of her tension and relaxed the ever-present ball of anxiety in her stomach. *We're going to be okay,* she told herself as she took in the rumble of activity between the soldiers and kids.

"Oh, I'm gonna get you for that! Yeah, you better run, Theo!" Shaw shouted, tearing off after the boy, a massive handful of snow fisted in his massive palm.

Evangaline continued laughing and sauntered up to Christoff, brushing her gloved hands on her skirt. She stopped anticipating letters from Niall.

She had, however, begun to write to Ophelia out of restless boredom and even heard from Tunit a couple of times. In truth, she wrote to all of the royals, but heard from only the two since her correspondence with the Shadows petered off.

As relieved as she was to hear back from them both—apparently, to the surprise of the king—the royal's appreciated being asked if they need any help. Even offering support by way of writing a simple letter brought gratitude. The gratefulness and surprise from both royals was a little discomforting, despite their gracious tones.

When she first arrived in the realm of the fae, everything seemed picture-perfect—like there couldn't be anything wrong. However, between the civilians and royals alike being surprised and grateful for the smallest act of kindness by the crown, Evangaline feared things were more fractured beneath the surface. Not even the kaleidoscope skies and verdant soil beneath her feet stopped her from noticing just how disjointed the crown and people were.

Tearing off her gloves, Evangaline smiled at Christoff. "Did Ophelia write back? I told her I would see about getting her some of Dolores's brownies for her winter solstice celebration. Dolores needs a head count," Evangaline told the messenger, who remained oddly stoic. His usual smile and witty banter lost to the furrowed brow and wriggling bottom lip that he now held.

He peeked over her shoulder at the snowball fight and then back at her.

"You can join us if you want. You always have a standing invite, you know?" She professed.

Christoff gave the weakest of smiles. "Thank you," was all he said, extending her a letter. His face remained neutral as he held it in his gloved hand.

Unlike the rest of the correspondences she had received, this letter was not on a crisp white parchment. There was no emblem on the seal clasping it closed, or any indication of who it was from.

In every way, this letter had been through hell and back. Its faded yellow color, the dirt marring the edges, even the weak morsel of navy wax sealing it shut, was misshapen and hurried almost, having splattered across the back. This letter was different from the rest.

Her smile faltered back into the neutral expression that she had worn quite frequently lately. This particular message allowed the gaping hole in her stomach to grumble and gurgle with dread. Her magic ached to be released deep inside her chest as she grew nervous.

Cracking open the seal, her heart stopped.

Dear Eva,

It can't be, she thought. Only one person called her Eva. She drew the letter closer to her face puffing out a cloud of foggy relief riddled air.

Dear Eva,

I implore you to stop writing to my brother, as his head has inflated enormously. His ego has now swallowed whole his humility, and he already has deemed himself "the crown princess's favorite member of the Kingdom of Shadows" and I simply will not tolerate that.

Eva, I am so proud of you. I cannot wait to see your forest and everything else you have achieved. I apologize for not writing sooner. Every time I picked up some ink and parchment, the words never conveyed what I wanted them to.

We have made progress with The Heretics. Sealed off any retreat to the mountain ranges and kept them away from the cities and villages. We still haven't had as many casualties as we imagined, but even one life lost seems like too many. But Pax is safe and the civilians relatively unharmed. So far, none of the fae of our opponents has had devastating magic that stupefies us, so in that we have a bright side, as you sought to find. We had one compulsion riddled hiccup, but we handled it easily. It has mainly been those trained in hand-to-hand combat that have worn down the men and women. Since we defeated the army in the mountains, we haven't encountered any more of your monsters. Which, might I add, you never said the night we met, talk without their mouths! However, your identification did save the lives of many of my soldiers and has not gone unrecognized. They sing your praises, as they should.

I have counted every day apart from you and don't know if it is the fating bond or not, but, Eva, I can honestly say, I miss you every day. I am man enough to admit that I have never, in my long life, missed someone as much as I miss you.

I will be back soon enough, and I will gladly take you up on that brownie and ale.
Yours Forever,
Ryder

Evangaline's eyes began to water as she held the dingy letter close to her chest. Her voice was nothing more than a whisper. "I miss you too." The tears froze to her cheeks, but they did not cease.

One single dirty, mangled piece of paper held so much of her heart in it that she simply could not bear to let it go.

With the sound of Christoff clearing his throat, Evangaline sprang back into her body, allowing the incessant thrum of her heart to propel her.

"Christoff, If I write to the Prince of Shadows, do you know where to send it? Do you know where this came from?" She asked with determination lacing her every word.

"Yes, ma'am, the pixies can deliver a letter anywhere." Christoff replied.

Brow creasing, she asked, "Pixies?"

"Yes ... little winged fae ... part of the little folk. They are our royal avian messengers. I oversee them. You didn't know that? They are the fastest messengers in the realm. The best of the best!"

"Hmmm," was all Evangaline said before she stalked off toward the palace. Now was not the time to consider pixies and whomever the 'little folk' were. The fact that they were very real and not just the annoying little figments of her imagination that swirled in her stomach whenever Ryder was near was shocking. Yet again, their existence should not surprise her. She talked to a wind whisp frequently, so ...

Ryder,
I apologize for the increased size of your brother's head. That may be a serious medical condition that a healer needs to see to. As far as him being my favorite ... who says he isn't? I can neither confirm nor deny ...
I am glad to hear the Kingdom of Shadows is not suffering great losses, but I agree, one loss is too many. None of the scholars or libraries I reached out to had insight on the monsters you face, and I have almost entirely lost

faith that I will ever learn what truly killed Chloe.

I am so sorry for all of this, for everything you are enduring. If I would have known this would happen with me staying, I would have left.

Today is day sixty as I write to you. I've tried to tell myself to take it one day at a time since you left, but truthfully, with each day it gets harder and harder to smile. The cadre and I had a snowball fight today. We all needed air and to let loose, the wine stopped numbing emotions weeks ago. Des has a beard … that should say enough for all of our mental state. We may not have been in physical battles like you, but the mental ones here are exhausting.

Darrin has remained cold and as stubborn as an ass. Even the courtiers are beginning to notice and gossip. It's like he has given up, not on himself but his people—on Celadonia. We have regular war councils to discuss what to do. Every day I fight him to send you soldiers, to send you rations, clothes, anything, and each time he tells me I'm a naïve girl thinking with my heart, not my head. I argue I am ruling with both, unlike him, who uses neither.

He's remained tight-lipped about much, though I was able to read the letters he received, the threats against him and I. They knew everything about me, too much about me. Honestly, it was creepy. But nothing that would help you annihilate these fuckers.

I'm keeping my promise to you. I train every day in combat and magic. I've gotten stronger, checked off every power on Tuatha's list. Twice, I'm a real-life Santa Claus! Atlas was thrilled seeing my power manifest, till we had to test to see if I could conjure a tornado. He didn't like that one, but I did it! One swirling vortex of wind and storms, about ten feet tall that twirled around the ballroom for a solid minute till Atlas said it was enough.

I will be here waiting with desserts and lots of beer when you come back. But Prince, if this battle keeps raging on, I'm disobeying you and coming down there to kick their asses myself!

I miss you more than I care to admit. Truly, it might be pathetic how much I miss you. I asked Atlas to help me do research on being fated, and all I got out of it was that our souls are intertwined. Whatever the hell that is supposed to mean! Atlas wasn't much help. Sometimes he can be so vague or cryptic. How have you put up with it all these years? Anyway, I am rambling, but what I mean to say is that I miss you, too. A lot.

Yours Always,

Your curious little creature

p.s. It's _our_ forest, not just mine. You're gonna love it.

Chapter Fifty-Three

Day Eighty.

"It is tradition to wear something blue tomorrow for the Winter Solstice Ball," Wren said eagerly as she placed the many little baubles and trinkets in Evangaline's hair before dinner. "I will look to see what is in your closet and give you a few options, if you would like?"

With a nod, Evangaline answered dryly, "That sounds lovely." The last thing on her mind was fashion.

A dozen little swallows were delicately pinned into the intricate braided bun surrounding Evangaline's head. Wren topped off the style with a simple gold circlet resting on her brow.

Evangaline found it hard to wear a crown on the days where her imposter syndrome was too much to bear. The insanity of her situation hit occasionally, making her feel odd wearing a glittering crown and dripping in diamonds—she did nothing to deserve them. But the simple circlets were easier to wear while still showing her station, which suddenly was something that Atlas and Des told her was important.

With the king raising eyebrows around the court for his erratic behavior, both her best friend and mentor felt it was important for everyone to see her embracing her role as crown princess. Solidifying the understanding amongst the nobles that she could do the job better than Darrin. Not that she wanted to inherit the throne anytime soon, but she at least had more empathy in her pinky finger than Darrin was exhibiting through his entire being.

Her off the shoulder long sleeve burgundy satin gown did very little at keeping out the blistering cold, but she didn't really care. It was comfortable with its lack of a corset or boning. The simple sheath shape hugged her curves while cascading to the floor in a simple swath of shining fabric.

Her day had been exhausting. She handled both hers and Darrin's correspondences to the other kingdoms. Had a lengthy argument with Darrin regarding the assistance of aid to the kingdoms hit by the battles. Plus a trip into the village to scour the books in the library for anything that might help Ryder with his little Heretic problem. Evangaline had been up since before the sun to take a freezing run through the forest and train, and up until she sat before Wren, she kept moving—working.

She thought the letter from Ryder twenty days ago would help her get some sleep—but it did the opposite. She got her letter into the tiny hands of the pixies right away. The tiny yellow hued pixie who was to make the trek to deliver the message was named Lucy. Evangaline stressed to her the importance of the letter nearly a dozen times.

Lucy was Christoff's best deliverer and when she returned a couple of days later, she confirmed she hand delivered the message to Ryder at his camp. Which only left Evangaline sitting on pins and needles to hear from him again. Twenty days later, and still no word from her fated.

Yet, Evangaline was still holding out hope.

Scouts came back from the south reporting a bloody battle but one victorious for the realm, with the enemy forces scattering to the wind, their ships sailing off to God knows where. Meanwhile, the whole of Celadonia sat eagerly wondering where they came from and, more importantly, where they went when they fled.

Des and Evangaline had their own meeting a few days prior following a war meeting with Darrin to discuss possible locations the fleeing army would go. The princess and her general mapped out how they could secretly ready the Royal Army to deploy if The Heretics were spotted again. If she had to go over Darrin's head, she would. Damn the consequences. She knew Ryder would be mad, but she would personally march at the front of the army should she not hear from him in the next coming days. She hit her limit on sitting idle.

At times, it felt as though the weight of the war rested on her shoulders alone. And no matter how hard she tried, she could not shake the feeling that this was only the tip of the iceberg. She should have cheered, learning of the departure of the enemies on Ryder's homeland however, all she felt was dread. This war couldn't be over that easily. Nothing was ever that simple, especially with the fae, as Evangaline had come to learn.

"Do you wish for any cosmetics? Perhaps that fancy eyeliner?" Wren asked with a wiggle of her shoulders, making Evangaline give out a half smile. Wren could see the pensive sadness that began to fill Evangaline and, bless her, she always tried to make Evangaline smile. Wren sought to make Evangaline feel powerful and strong even when exhaustion clung to her body.

With a shake of the head, "No, we will save it for tomorrow. Lord only knows I have more of a role to play at the ball."

Evangaline hated the Winter Solstice Ball with a fiery passion. For the last ten days, the king had only focused on it. On *putting all this Heretic stuff aside and celebrating the solstice properly.* Evangaline asked if it was appropriate with the Kingdom of Shadows still plagued by battles on their shores and many still displaced in Mirth, but her question died the moment it was spoken aloud.

She was meant to sit pretty in her blue gown, with her tiara resting atop her royal head. All the while, her heart yearned and lurched across a land she never got to see with her own eyes or feel under her own feet. She felt useless.

A small part of her was furious at Ryder for making her promise to stay in the Capital. For making her sit by while he battled an army hell bent on ending *her* family's rule. It felt selfish and wrong. His men were dying for her and yet she was to sit by night after night and drink wine and eat roasted pheasant like nothing was wrong or even happening, for that matter of fact.

She was cursed to live in the same ignorance that plagued the king despite having knowledge of the cruelty in the world.

It made her sick to her stomach, but she went on anyway. To another dinner. To play the role of the crown princess dutifully. To kiss the assess of courtiers who only wanted to kiss hers for their betterment. All so the land could see a stable heir sit on the throne and not the crumbling, broken woman sitting beneath Tuatha's revered crown.

"How much do you yearn to see my face?" The ominously cold voice called out to her in the dark.

There was no image of Ryder greeting her when the monster to her back made her lucidity light her sleep deprived state. No sparkling floor or mud-covered battlefield. There was nothing. Infinite blackness beneath her feet and infinite gray mist before her eyes. Still, her nightmarish torturer remained at her back. *Coward.* His hot breath trailed down her neck, chills and tremors cascaded across her alabaster skin.

She had no concept of time when he took over. While her pulse quickened in something akin to fear, the attacks on her subconscious became so frequent she was accustomed to the way time stilled within the dark void of her nightmares.

Despite it all, this nightmare felt as though it dragged on for hours and felt so different from the others. More foreboding. More sinister. The endless darkness stretched around her and yet she could not shake the claustrophobia plaguing her lungs.

The torture didn't come from seeing Ryder battle and sleep. The torture came through the silence. It was quiet enough to hear her own blood rush through her rapidly pumping heart.

One after the other, the fog formed tentacle like tendrils. Slowly they approached Evangaline and wrapped around her arms and legs. Pinning her to her knees on the ground despite her inability to move from her exhaustion alone. Finally, a misty rope constricted her throat like a noose. She had awaited their moves, unable to stop them without the pressure of her magic coursing through her veins. She watched in a horrified anticipation as she sat on the ground before the fog as the tentacle like smoke writhed like a sentient creature. Finally, once it struck, the searing pain and force of the fog's sinewy fingers ground her bones and strangled her muscles with a strength it should not—scientifically—have.

"N-not at all." Evangaline managed to grit out through her gasps for any sliver of air.

The tendrils were unrelenting, wrapping tighter and tighter with no reprieve.

Tsking the phantom at her back leaned in, his putrid hot breath skated across the side of her face hot and stagnant, "Beautiful little liar, you are."

He wasn't entirely wrong. She wanted to put a face to the creature that found joy in her suffering. Who wove threats like silk and ultimatums like gold.

The tendrils wrapped tighter as the putrid hand of the phantom in her nightmare slowly lowered the thin strap of her nightgown down her left shoulder. His icy fingernails skated against her fate, marked skin in a perfunctory threat as his hard body pressed against her back.

Her already tense muscles grew even tighter. She tried to dip away out of his touch, but the tendrils of smoke held tight. Even the smallest movement had them growing more taut, strangling her further.

Gagging, Evangaline could feel the veins in her head pulsing and bulging at her temples. At any moment, she felt as though her brain would combust within her skull.

Just when Evangaline thought this nightmare was the worst yet, the phantom behind her ran its tongue up her neck right above her collarbone. Slowly and meticulously, not leaving an inch untouched by his repulsive claiming. Not only was the tongue at her throat hot and foul, but its end was forked. Both prongs wrapped around either side of her throat, effectively locking her in place.

Evangaline clenched her eyes shut and held her breath until he no longer tasted her.

"I will have you soon enough, little princess. You will learn to not struggle with me. One day, you will come to me willingly, without the lies and stubbornness." He whispered in her ear with a dark laugh. "I learned a long time ago that if I cannot have love, I will have power. You are my ticket to that."

Evangaline saw spots in her vision.

Her body convulsed, shaking back and forth in the nightmare … or was it?

No! She was being shaken in real life. She just needed to wake up. This was a dream. A really bad, fucked up dream but a figment of her imagination, nonetheless.

"w-wake … up … wake up!" She pleaded to herself as her eyes closed, pinching out a tear.

The phantom returned to her back with a sneer. "What?"

THUD!

Her body landed on the cold wooden floors of her bedroom with enough force to knock the air from her lungs. Her entire body jolted with a lightning bolt of pain that struck her fragile bones. Her heart raced and pounded as a force pushed her up onto her knees.

Just like that. A simple shake and she escaped the hellscape of her dreamland.

"Thank you," Evangaline gravely muttered, reaching out to the person who woke her. But her hand swiped through the air.

Her eyes fluttered upward to see no one there. "What?"

With a great effort, Evangaline pushed herself onto the bed, the stinging in her bones screaming with an exaggerated and lengthy moan.

Just as she thought she was losing her mind, the wind whisp nuzzled into Evangaline's hair and settled around her neck in a comforting hold.

Its normally warm presence was now cool from the winter breeze. Acting as an ice pack, it wrapped its essence gently around her reddened nape and settled in.

She didn't need a mirror to know she would be bruised in a few hours. Nearly every other nightmare resulted in injuries she could easily go to Madame Chevalier to fix. *"Fight training. You should see the other guy!"* she said one time to the ornery old healer when she questioned the bruises on Evangaline's knees. Or a simple *"I'm clumsy"* would seem to suffice before her cuts were healed and she was sent on her way. Easy white lies to conceal the truth. Evangaline couldn't very well tell the healer that a phantom with black tipped hands, and a forked tongue, was touching her in her sleep. *Hurting* her in her sleep. It sounded crazy, even in her own mind.

Des knew of the nightmares, but he was not aware of the brutal implications of them. Evangaline was diligent in getting to Chevalier without the general or her friends knowing. After Des dismissed her weeks ago. Evangaline pretended the nightmares did not happen at all, just because it did not seem worth it to make him fret about something else.

She was alone trying to understand her night terrors, except for the whisp. It had stayed with her some nights when she couldn't sleep. They would talk, or Evangaline would talk rather, and the whisp would listen. She told it everything.

"Thank you, friend. How did you get in here? I didn't leave the door open tonight?" She asked, laying her head on the hollow cushion of the whisp.

Evangaline was so out of it, she didn't feel the crisp bite of winter nipping at the exposed skin left out by her pale green silk nightgown.

The whisp proudly turned her head to the now shattered French door windowpane. Faint morning light seeped in through the broken glass, where snow piled on the floor.

"Well, how am I supposed to fix that now?"

The whisp responded by nuzzling into her neck reassuringly. The sensation was so different from the slate tendrils of the nightmare. The whisp was a refreshing scarf, delicate and loving, unlike the torturous and agonizing tendrils of the fog.

"Hmmm ... maybe we can ..." Evangaline stood on shaky legs and tiptoed around the broken glass at her feet. She held her hand over the pane busted by the whisp and willed her magic to help her. As she moved her hand around the broken window, ice formed. Thin iridescent fractals shot from her palm, wave after wave till the now frosty blue pane cut out the snow and the chill.

"Maybe that will hold it till I can get someone to fix it?" She questioned, cocking her head. A wiggle of the billowing wind whisp at her nape was her only answer. "Yes, it will work," it seemed to say.

"Now that I'm up. You want to go for a walk? I need the air."

Another wiggle set her in motion.

"Day eighty-one," she muttered as she walked into the bathroom, taking in the early morning sun.

Chapter Fifty-Four

Day Eighty-one

Day of the Winter Solstice Ball

Winter solstice was definitely not as pleasant as the autumnal equinox. The day held nothing but frost and chill—not at all surprising. The shocking part, however, was the fae's ebullience in ringing in the winter solstice by doing everything outside. In the snow. Eating outside, walking outside, talking outside, basically any activity—aside from using the bathroom— was done outside.

"Why?" Evangaline asked.

"It is important to embrace the cold as well as the warm and give thanks for the frost that coats the earth and renews the soil and rivers," Wren explained as she helped Evangaline out of the damp clothes she wore on her morning stroll.

If Evangaline knew that little factoid, she would have remained in her room, nestled by the fireplace. Instead, she explored the frost covered gardens in the wee hours of the morning, unfreezing all the beautiful ice-covered roses.

With a groan and a bit of hesitation, Evangaline put on her princess smile and got ready to head right back out into the glacial gardens to dine with the nobility.

Wren dressed her for the frosty luncheon in a gown of thick sherpa lined brocade with a matching coat delightfully lined in warm white fur. It was toasty and kept out the chill for a bit until the breeze picked up and sent a debilitating rattle across her skin.

Evangaline meant to stop by Chevalier to heal her ailments and bruises but thought that the bruise that was forming around her throat from her nightmare would alert the old bat to something being awry. So, instead, Evangaline went back to her room and was cautious to not let Wren see the mark on her throat with a high-collared shirt and a bit of makeup.

"The roses are splendid, Your Majesty. You have truly outdone yourself!" Lady Whittell crooned from across the banquet table nestled in the heart of the flowers and shrubs of the gardens.

King Darrin smiled. "Yes, I believe I did. Their beauty it is eternal even in the snow."

Evangaline rolled her eyes at the blatant lie. *His Majesty* did not even have the power to keep a weed alive, magic or not.

The man that sat beside her with the spike adorned crown atop his head was hardly the man she met when she first arrived. No wonder her mother left. This version of Darrin was insufferable.

Since the meeting after Evangaline and Ryder's fating, the king had been off. Withdrawn, angry, temperamental. He used to be understanding and kind—if not a little brash. Now, since Evangaline found her place within the realm, he became no better than the man her mom painted a picture of. And after the bombing, he somehow became even worse. The gleam in his eyes was selfish and malicious and turned her stomach into a nauseous mess.

Evangaline sat quietly with the ghost of a smile gracing her face, mentally picking apart all who sat around her and the narcissistic ways they moved through the world. So long as their pockets were lined and their glasses full of wine, they cared not that war was ravaging parts of their realm.

She muttered a "Thank you," here, a "Wonderful to see you again," there, but never sought out conversation. She had nothing to say to anyone. Her thoughts were confined within the jail of her own head, anyway. Thinking of ways to help the realm instead of sitting on her ass sipping bubbly wine by the barrel.

It had been eighty-one days since Ryder left. Eighty-one fucking days since she felt the weight of the—now blue opal—crown resting on her head.

Wren chose the tiara today for the lunch specifically. It was far smaller than Tuatha's crown with its simple silver scrollwork. Standing no taller than an inch high, it featured a rather impressive blue fire opal the size of a quarter and perfectly round like a marble. It was beautiful, understated yet powerful, like everything Wren chose for Evangaline to wear.

Lately the handmaiden had been having fun, using Evangaline as a human sized doll. For weeks, Evangaline just hadn't felt like herself. The task of dressing in fancy gowns felt tedious—it felt disingenuous. She would pay far too much money for a t-shirt and jeans and her favorite black leather jacket. Something casual and comfortable that she could fight in or relax in—not that she was doing much of either. She just didn't feel right knowing Ryder and his army were probably in a trench with sweat dripping down their backs battling and here she was in fine silks and jewels. So she let Wren play by separating herself from the reflection in the mirror. "*Imposter syndrome is a bitch,*" she told Des one day over lunch. He breathily laughed and agreed. He felt the same way about being general.

"If I may be so bold as to ask, Princess Evangaline, how is the Prince of Shadows doing? We hear he is quite the renegade on the battlefield," Lady Whittell asked, surprising Evangaline with the change of topic. The lady's tone was nothing cruel or demeaning like it had been in the past. In fact, for the first time, she sounded genuine. The mention of Ryder set Evangaline on edge, an auto response triggered by her constant fear that he would not return to her.

Since the day he left, people rarely asked about him. A few inquired about the battle he fought or the status of his kingdom, but few asked about him as a person.

"Oh … umm … busy. He's been busy, but last I heard from him he is hopeful for all this to be over soon," Evangaline tried her best to sound strong, but she felt so weak. Her tears glistened on her waterline. A faint silver shimmer that conveyed all the unspoken fears she could not tell the nobility that sat before her.

Lady Whittell noticed the pain in her eyes, however, "He's battled many times before, Your Highness. These scoundrels are nothing for a warrior of his status." She flashed a sympathetic smile and for the first since Evangaline first met Lady Whittell, she was grateful for the flashy courtier. If a table wasn't separating the two of them, Evangaline may have given her a hug and thanked her quietly for her support. However, all Evangaline could offer was a smile and a nod in return.

The lady's words weren't thrown out to kiss Evangaline's ass. No, they were said to comfort her. Something Evangaline needed greatly. Her loneliness was an animal of its own these days. Always lurking in the distance. She had felt its razor-sharp teeth sink into her throat and its claws dig into her back—she didn't fight it. The boys had been busy. Ryder was away. Her family was in a realm she could not get to. Even in a room full of people, she felt as though she could scream at the top of her lungs and not a single person would turn to check on her.

But here she was, being comforted by possibly the last fae she ever imagined. It surprised her enough to claw her way out of the recesses of her own mind and truly take in her surroundings and, most of all, herself. Sometimes she felt alone, but she wasn't. Not in reality. They all were just driving over a speed bump. It wouldn't last forever … hopefully.

She shook herself free of her thoughts and refocused on the people around her. For them, she would smile today. However, after the solstice ball, she would talk to Des and make her way to the Kingdom of Shadows. Her time waiting in her ivory tower was over. She would enjoy the ball tonight, dance, and drink her bubbly wine, because come tomorrow Evangaline was going to war.

After the luncheon, Evangaline returned to her room and sat before the blazing fireplace on a pile of pillows from the couch. Her bones were chilled to their marrow from hours in the snow.

Fuck the winter solstice if all it meant was freezing your goddam ass off all day.

She sat watching the flames flicker in the hearth. Using her power, she made it twirl and dance, remembering how she used to play with the tiny flame in the palm of her hand. She willed two of the flames into humanoid forms and watched them tango in the form of a fiery man and woman. The woman's hair twirled above her head in a twirling tornado of fire and with each movement the man spun her around the fireplace with passion and integrity.

Evangaline watched her fire people dance, somber and solitude, until their dance ended in a sinew of ash and smoke.

Evangaline took in the room around her—bored and restless. Des was doing last-minute preparations with the Royal Army and the rest of the boys on their secretive maneuvers. Readying rations and equipment just in case they decided to march out should The Heretics return. She had yet to speak to him about her new plans to go to battle. No doubt he would put up a fight, but she was determined. A unit was readying to head to each kingdom if it was needed and she would join the unit headed to the Shadows come morning. Princess's orders. Oh yeah, she was prepping the princess card!

As she scanned the quiet room, a book glistened on her shelf in the sunlight, the same way it did the first day she came to this strange and foreign land.

A *Kingdom of Shadows.*

The cracked silver lettering glittered down at her. Evangaline took it as a sign of the fates, telling her it would all be okay.

With a sad smile, she took the book back to her makeshift pallet of pillows and slunk into them. Her sherpa lined gown pooled around her in a light blue brocade lake.

Once nestled in snuggly, ignoring the slight breeze of the open French door, Evangaline flipped to the last few pages of the book right where she knew she would find him.

"The eldest son of Prince Tryamon and his consort Princess Aria, Prince Ryder. The most powerful of the Oberon line, first of his name."

The words read in a fine script under the watercolor portrait of Ryder.

His starlight crown sat atop his onyx hair. He donned a beautiful black coat with silver embroidered thread that fit close to his broad shoulders and toned chest. His shadows peeked out from beneath his upturned collar—as usual. He was magnificent. She couldn't help but smile as she wondered if he sat still for the portrait to be completed. She couldn't picture him sitting still for that long. When they sat for the portrait for The Golden Prophet, his leg tapped in a furious beat and his shadows spun in an agitated pace. Finally, after only about thirty minutes, he asked if they had enough to go from and whisked Evangaline from the room. She giggled to herself at the thought of him sitting long enough for the artist from the book to paint him in all of his glory.

It was through his glittering blue eyes, though, that Evangaline found herself getting lost in. They didn't swirl with their normal shadows lurking in their depths, but the foundation of what made them perfect was there— bright and true. The artist did a wonderful job capturing his likeness. Even the pesky hairs she loved to brush from his brow fell perfectly. He was beautiful and *somehow* fate brought the two of them together. She still would never understand it, but she wasn't one to look a gift horse in the mouth.

Evangaline couldn't help but smile as she looked at him. A small tear slid from her eye.

She only knew the man for a handful of weeks, but somehow, he cast a spell on her heart and soul. She held strong for eighty days, but looking at his bright blue eyes even in two dimensions; she felt seen. She felt safe. So on day eighty-one apart, Evangaline allowed herself to cry for the time they lost due to conflict. On day eighty-one, she made *herself* a promise that she would never let him go no matter how hard he fought her. Where he went, she followed.

"Ma'am?" Wren's small voice whispered behind the settee, making Evangaline jump, slamming the book closed as she whirled around.

Evangaline stood, setting the book on the coffee table, wiping her tears with the back of her hand. "Is it that time?"

Wren nodded.

"Alright. Let's do this!" Evangaline plastered on a smile she was fairly certain Wren could see right through based solely on the handmaiden's pitying stare and wringing hands.

"Your fath—the king sent up a gown for you to wear tonight. He had it specially made for tonight, he said." Wren motioned to a box she set on the dining table when Evangaline was lost in her book.

Evangaline glanced at the green box with a pink bow, the same as the last time she was gifted a special gown. Yet, she ignored it and proceeded into the bedroom, leaving it on the dining table. She would see it soon enough. No need to gawk over it now. If he thought gifts of gowns and jewels would earn her forgiveness and good graces, he was woefully wrong.

"Thank you, Wren. I will see it later, but for now I am excited to see what your artistry has in store for my hair tonight!" Evangaline called over her shoulder, beckoning Wren to follow her.

Chapter Fifty-Five

It took two hours for Wren to curl her hair and do her makeup. Far longer than Evangaline preferred to take getting ready, especially without music to blast at way too high of a decibel. She felt fidgety, wrought with anticipation to talk to Des. As the day progressed, all she wanted to do was beg someone to open a portal and take her to the battlefront. But she stayed still, allowing Wren to flex her affinities for beauty.

Wren meticulously twirled each strand of hair in a slice of material warmed by Evangaline's own flame covered hands. With a delicate and meticulous eye, the handmaiden twirled each strand up and pinned it in place. After Wren swirled a silver shimmer across Evangaline's eyes, she went back to Evangaline's hair. She decorated the soft, glamourous waves with rhinestones and pearls. Each placed with a steady hand one by one.

On the top of Evangaline's head rested Tuatha's glittering flower crown. Its weight was a comfort Evangaline did not expect. An essence of Tuatha herself enveloped Evangaline in a warm, reassuring hug anytime she wore the diadem. The feeling crashed over Evangaline in a blessing like wave. Giving her the strength to get through the night.

Wren finally brought her the box with the gown in it and left it on the bed. Evangaline excused her handmaiden for the evening with a hug and a tear-lined thank you. If Des agreed to Evangaline's plan—which he wouldn't have a choice—she would not see Wren until the war was over. In so many ways, their hug felt like goodbye.

Evangaline dressed in the gown of light blue gossamer. The shift style frock was the opposite of appropriate for a winter ball. Luckily for her, the evening's festivities were to be held inside the warm palace's throne room—far away from the snow and ice.

The gown was virtually see through from mid-thigh down. There were no sleeves, opting instead for strands of diamonds that draped across her upper arms and connected to the back of the bodice in delicate swoops. The entire gown was encrusted with diamonds and glittering pearls from her bust all the way down the hem. Not an inch of her was not sparkling. She was covered in a net of precious jewels.

Around the thin bruise of her throat, she fastened a choker of blue diamonds, ones that reminded her of the color of Ryder's eyes. Deep and sparkling with endless depth.

Between the crown, choker, and gown, there was no way she would be overlooked.

Clattering the small train of the gown out of her bathroom, Evangaline heard the chatter of voices, ones she hadn't heard in her room in such a long time. Jovial, celebratory laughs echoed against the green walls.

Her pace hastened at the sound of laughter and the piercing crack of a bottle popping open. She shuffled as fast as she could. Being that the gown weighed nearly a ton, her pace was slower than normal. With each step, Evangaline jingled and chaffed on the floor.

"Hey! Don't start partying till I'm there!" Evangaline shouted, rushing into the living room.

"Well, then get your ass in here, Lady E! Champagnes already been popped!" Shaw shouted back.

Evangaline rounded the corner, a smile tugging on her lips for the first time since their snowball fight.

"With you lot, the whole fucking bottle will be—" As she cleared the corner, her eyes went wide, and her words stopped flowing from her rosy lips.

Her breath caught at the sight before her, and tears pricked her eyes.

"Hi, my curious little creature." Ryder murmured as he took in every inch of her. He stared at her as though she were the stars and moon personified. He breathed her in as though she was a breath of fresh air after being caught within a cloud of smoke.

"It's been—" Evangaline muttered under her breath. Her tears springing from her lash line in soft, cascading waterfalls.

"Eighty-one days," he finished for her. A small, sad smile pulled at the corners of his mouth.

The cadre fell silent. The only sound filling the room was that of Evangaline's ragged breath and the crackling fire at Ryder's back.

He can't be here.

She spun to look behind her to see if the phantom with the hot breath and jagged fingers was there playing some messed-up trick. Did she doze off and imagine getting ready? Is this all a joke?

But there was no gray fog surrounding her, there was no black abyss at her feet, no phantom taunting her. Just her friends. Just Ryder.

Ryder, with his graceful long strides, slowly approached Evangaline, his hands fisted deep in his pocket, wriggled with each anxious step. His black and silver jacket was wonderfully unbuttoned enough to see his shadows peeking out from their confinement. They stammered slightly but remained, for the most part, still.

He drank in every bit of her, his breathing just as heavy as hers. There was no doubt he felt their separation as viscerally as she did. It was an unexplainable ache deep inside her soul to be parted from him.

His sapphire eyes started at her feet and with a dark sparkle traveled up her body, settling on her eyes that were watering quietly.

"Hi," she managed to squeak out.

He rubbed away the stream of tears from her cheeks, "Hi." Ryder answered as a chuckle tugged up his lips further. "I told you I would come back."

She smiled up at him, stroking those two wayward hairs from his forehead. "I know. Next time, though, we will have to set a time frame." her words were hushed so only Ryder could hear them.

"No." His tone was deep and velvety and finite. Oh, how she missed his voice.

"No?"

He shook his head, "No, next time … I listen to you … next time … you come with me."

She nodded, another tear breaking free. "Where you go, I go. Always?"

He leaned his forehead against hers and closed his eyes, taking a deep, grounding breath.

His hand nestled under her hair to rest on the nape of her neck, the other grasped her hand with a squeeze. Their fate marks practically purred, their souls stopped searching, and their hearts flowed into their harmonious beat as they clung to each other.

"Where you go, I go. Always. Forever." He whispered.

"Is it over?" She whispered.

"Not quite. But they can handle it without me." His eyelashes fluttered against hers softly as he spoke.

She looked up at him, finally smiling at her prince. "Ry?"

"Yes, Eva?"

Evangaline swallowed, "Kiss me. *Please.*"

A smile filled his face, exposing the adorable dimple on his left cheek, "Gladly."

Without missing another beat, his mouth crashed into hers. Every day of longing and yearning soaked through every second of his passionate embrace. His tongue gently swiped Evangaline's lips and she happily opened for him. Letting him show her just how much he missed her. Letting him possess her body and soul.

Evangaline's salty tears mingled perfectly with the smoky and salty taste that was Ryder. He tasted like an ocean breeze on a warm day, exactly how she imagined. His heat enveloped her with the passion of the kiss. He was gentle, but possessive in the best possible ways.

Finally, he pulled back, leaving Evangaline's lips cold and lonely. "I missed you so much, Eva."

"I missed you too."

Then his lips found hers again, this time with a frenzied force. His arms wrapped around her waist, swallowing her in his comfortable, warm embrace, pinning her to his muscular chest. Her hands fisted the back of his head tangling in the silkiness of his hair. A sense of fulfillment filled her as they kissed, like a cog clicked into place and made the clock of her mind chime it's mirthful tune.

"Gods, Get a room!" Des scoffed despite the cheeky smile gracing his now fully bearded face.

It was Evangaline's turn to drop the kiss and pull away. Her face was flushed with a fire that heated not just her now blushing cheeks but her whole body. If she didn't need to make an appearance at the ball, the cadre would be kicked out and her and Ryder would not be leaving her room for a few days at the least.

A sense of contentment flashed through her as Ryder chuckled.

It was just a kiss, but she had never, in that moment, felt closer with anybody.

She waited a beat, soaking in the feel of Ryder's body against hers before she responded to her friend.

"This *is* my room! Go get drunk in your own room," she shouted at Des, never taking her eyes off the two irises full of the depths of the sparkling oceans that shined down at her.

Shaw sauntered over with two champagne flutes in his hands, "*Or* we can all get drunk here, now, and then you two can … you know … later." He winked, "Like the rest of us … hopefully," he finished with a cheeky grin.

Evangaline laughed and rested her head on Ryders' chest, grabbing one of the champagne glasses. "Please don't ever, in this life or the next, Shaw, tell me about your sex life."

Ryder and Shaw bellowed deep, joyous laughs. The former's chest rattling on Eva's forehead.

"Come." Ryder purred, dropping a kiss to her forehead before taking the champagne from Shaw.

Shaw laughed, "That's exactly what I am trying to do tonight too,

Prince!"

Evangaline's face scrunched in thought until the perverted quip of her friend resonated. Disgust marred her face as she shouted, "Shaw! Gross!" She lunged, punching the guard in the arm before clasping her hand firmly around Ryder's copper tattooed hand once more.

As she stood in Ryder's arms drinking her champagne, hearing the cadre laugh and tell stories from their past, it felt just like the good old days. Before their world erupted into battles and death. Occasionally, Ryder would entertain the group with a story of war or mischief. Each velvety timber of his voice finally allowed Evangaline to feel that puzzle piece of her heart settle back in its place. She would never let go of this. Of him. Of her friends. This was what she always yearned for.

This was home, where she belonged, wrapped up in Ryder's arms, surrounded by laughter and warmth. Surrounded by love.

No matter what it will take, she will protect her new family with every ounce of power in her blood. No one will ever make her feel powerless again. Not even herself.

Chapter Fifty-Six

The sweat glistened on Evangaline's brow as Ryder twirled her energetically around the ballroom. Her giggles filled the air while her dress swished with soft snickts and clunks behind her in a weightless grace.

The prince's eyes went wide as a mischievous smile tugged across his face, baring his teeth and the dimple she loved so much. She wanted to kiss it … so she did.

Evangaline gasped as he dipped her down low enough for her hair to graze the polished marble floor beneath her feet. With a light tug on her arm, he hauled her up, flush against his chest just as the crescendo of the music died out. Evangaline laughed right into Ryder's pectorals as they both tried to regain their ragged breaths against one another. They stared into the solace of the others' eyes, as though there was not a single other person in the room.

Many watched them from the moment they entered the ballroom, but Evangaline didn't care. The gawking didn't make her nervous or feel any sense of unease. She wasn't searching for her place in the world anymore. She found it. Right here in this room, with the Prince of Shadows on her arm, Tuatha's crown on her head, and her friends at her back. She felt strong and bold, just like both Chloe and Wren wanted her to feel. Her courage was just another sparkle lining her blue-green eyes. Even the writhing of her magic quieted as though it, too, was content.

There were still many problems that she had sitting on her plate, but currently, just for tonight, she wouldn't think about any of them. Finally, after eighty-one days, Evangaline allowed her brain to quiet and her smile to be genuine. It felt great. She would figure out the war tomorrow. With Ryder back, her hurry to rush off into battle ebbed and her fated heart thrived in his presence, begging for his touch and kiss. She had no plans to deny her fated senses any longer, so she gave into them. Kissing him whenever she felt compelled, holding him close, and letting him twirl her around the empty dance floor as though they were floating on a cloud in the heavens.

"Uh-Hem." Darrin cleared his throat dramatically behind Ryder, ripping them from their trances.

Ryder dipped his head in courtesy to the king, but his eyes spoke differently. There was a war raging within them, one spurned by the king at his front. Evangaline decided before entering the ballroom that the customary bow to the king was unnecessary and instead, upon arrival, escorted her boys to the tables of food and wine. "Your Majesty." Ryder bit out in an uneven breath.

"I require a dance with the princess." Darrin's face was stoic, harsh even and his words were spoken as though he was asking Ryder to do a task like taking out the garbage or folding the laundry. He didn't wish to dance with his daughter, no he *required* a dance with the *princess*. The formality of his statement grated her nerves. She clenched her jaw closed before she said something that got her yelled at or worse. Darrin was too quick to anger as of late. She did not wish to push the matter. After their show of power months ago, she was careful to not draw his power from the shell of the man she once knew. Not because she feared it, but rather Evangaline knew herself better. She felt the power stirring within her own body daily to know that if he lashed out, she would strike to kill, not put in his place.

On days that Evangaline trained where her anger or anxiety sat on the forefront of her being, her power was stronger, more deadly, and far harder to control.

Darrin's stare locked into Evangaline's, causing a tremor to course down her spine. It felt wrong; he felt wrong. For the first time in weeks, she didn't glare at him or refuse to lock eyes with the man, instead she looked deep into his eyes and felt a resentment radiating out at her. She felt a horrid sense of wrongness. Yet she could not place what exactly was wrong. Perhaps he was just a skilled actor before her debut ball and his kindness was only a tool used to gain her trust and complacency.

If The Heretics want me as a weapon, does the king want the same? Her brain whirled different variations of the same question. Why? She should have thought of his disposition sooner instead of being angry at him. But of course, her anxiety and guilt clouded her ability to open her own eyes to the situations around her. She was too consumed with herself, with Ryder, and her boys. She never once took a step back to ponder *why* Darrin was so adamant about not getting involved with the war.

Dread licked down her spine at the same moment she reached for her thread of magic. She always held it at arm's length, but it was weak. Shaking off her thoughts for Darrin, Evangaline held onto the only small thread of power that needled her sternum, trusting the thrashing of distrust in her gut.

"Of course, I shall go get some refreshments." Ryder turned to Evangaline and dropped a kiss on her cheek, hovering by her ear for a moment. "Something is off with him. I will be watching you, alright?" And then he dropped her hand into the king's and strode off before she could answer. He felt the same dark aura she felt around the king.

Darrin grabbed her hand with a bit too much pressure and began to lead her in a slow waltz as the music picked up again.

"You seem happy tonight," Darrin murmured in a clipped tone.

Someone is in a bad mood. Again.

Evangaline wasn't much shorter than Darrin, especially in her heels, so she did not have to look up to regard the man who looked so similar to her. "I have much to celebrate tonight," she replied as her lips fell into a tight line.

"The return of your consort, I suppose," Darrin responded with disdain.

Consort? Ryder was certainly not her consort, she hadn't a clue what they were, but calling someone as powerful and regal as Ryder a consort felt wrong. He was her equal in every way. And he was her fated. If she became queen, he would be king. End of story. Not consort.

Evangaline's brow knitted as she tried to understand where all the king's hostility was coming from. "He's not my consort, and if you have a problem with him, go ahead and get it off your chest. I'm *thrilled* to hear your opinion." She bit off harshly, but she couldn't help it. Her protective nature, thanks to being fated, beat a sturdy drum within her heart. It wouldn't matter if Darrin said he disliked the color of Ryder's coat. She was going to defend him—even if it was the color of a cow pie.

"He will never be king, if that is what you think. He is a problem that will be tolerated." His words had a bite that made Evangaline jerk back in disgust. There was a threat laced into his icy words, but Evangaline, being twirled around the dance floor, could not take it upon herself to fight back in the manner she wished to. More couples joined the floor, waltzing alongside them. To knee the king square in the balls seemed a bit brash, even for her. So she held her tongue.

Evangaline knew very little of Ryder's past, only knowing bits and pieces that he had told her. His relationship with her birth father was fractured well before she was even half her current age. But the hostility of the king toward him was incredibly unnecessary, especially knowing he was fated to her. Ryder never once showed the king that he would not take care of Evangaline. If anything, he proved he was one of a few people that would stop at nothing to make sure she was safe and happy. Wasn't that what fathers wanted for their daughters?

Evangaline stopped her twirling, halting the dance around her. "What is that supposed to mean?"

Darrin rolled his eyes and hauled her back into the motions of the dance.

As he spun her around the dance floor, she caught the gaze of Ryder, his stoic face gave away nothing as he raised a flute of champagne to his lips.

But Evangaline knew his tells well enough, the shadows swirling angrily around his chest being the main one. He appeared calm, but he was a maelstrom contained in a pretty shell. The deep navy hue of his irises was his other tell—his eyes darkened and lightened like a mood ring. Surely those who just glanced at him would not notice, but she loved his eyes and the way they conveyed his emotions with a simple change. He was agitated, on edge. He watched Evangaline with the tenacity of a soldier waiting for battle. A countenance she saw on his stunning face in the nightmare she had where he rode the dapple steed into enemy territory. No doubt his own fate provoked protective nature was warring within him as he watched her dance with Darrin.

Studying Ryder, she knew something bad was coming. She tugged harder on her magic, but this time it hurt something fierce, a vice around her torso.

"Did Atlas explain to you, *Princess*, the price you and the prince pay for that band on your arm? A price the fates don't consult you on prior to enrapturing you in their bidding."

His hand tightened onto her back so hard his fingers dug into her spine with a pinch. Her magic practically begged her to let it out. Evangaline found it always thrashed about in warning in times of danger. At present, the pain intensified in her chest with each unsteady breath she took. Something was wrong with her.

"No, he did not, *my king*." He never called her princess.

Her bones practically screamed that something was malfunctioning within her body. Her pixies fluttered, but not in happiness, in warning.

"What did the old man tell you?"

Evangaline stood taller. "That fate bound us and our souls together. That was the most we could learn."

The king tsked, a smugness settling on his face as he peered down at their moving feet. As he looked back down at her, his eyes weren't the same blue-green as Evangaline's anymore, they were a vibrant forest green. Evangaline stumbled as her ears began ringing. She knew those eyes. The man she thought was the king leaned into her ear, his grip tightening on her back to almost bone crushing levels holding her to his chest.

"Your souls are indeed together, now one, destined to do the bidding of the fates. But you should know if one of you dies, so does the other. Quite the price to pay, huh, Princess?"

Evangaline steeled herself, readying her magic through the pain in her chest, "Or a mercy. The true price would be to live without the person you love by your side. Wouldn't you say, *Bash?*"

The false king stopped his dancing and clasped his hands together in a slow clap as a wicked smile stretched his face to an unnatural angle. "You finally figured it out! Little slower than I hoped, but you got there in your own time! I can't tell you how exhausting this has been."

Noticing the interaction, Ryder was at Evangaline's side in an instant, his arm wrapped around her waist in a bid to hold her close to him. He didn't know the difference between the king and the bastard general—not in the intimate way Evangaline did. She looked into those eyes many nights as he spoke of her beauty and quieted her with ecstasy. "Your Majesty, I shall require Eva for a moment, if you will excuse us." Ryder pulled her away from Darrin. But Evangaline dragged her heels, pushing off Ryder's chest to face what looked like to everyone in the room, the Supreme King of Celadonia. She knew the truth, though.

"Get. Out," she spoke with ice coating her muscles and fire in her veins. "Before I kill you with my own two hands."

"Go ahead, Princess … I know you want to. Try. Blow me out of here. Incinerate me. Freeze me. *Try.*" Bastian said, glancing down at her chest as though he too could feel her magic writhing and coiling inside of her. Her heart began a thunderous thrashing in her chest.

Evangaline raised her hand, willing a ferocious wind to unravel from her fingertips. As soon as the small gust left her hand, it slammed right back into her chest, bringing her to her knees. The force of the blow knocked the breath from her lungs.

The magic writhing inside her body ached to get out, but now seemed afraid to try. Its vibration in her chest almost felt like it was shaking just as hard as she was, cowering in fear deep behind her ribs.

Ryder wrapped her in his arms and threw his jacket around her shaking body. "What did you do?" He shouted at the king, silencing the crowd.

The entire room was fixed on the false king and the princess lying motionless on her knees, trying to regain her breaths.

From an outside perspective, it must have appeared that Darrin wounded the princess. But Evangaline knew it wasn't the king at all, it was the former general coming for his revenge. She felt so stupid. How could she not have known? And where was her father? She never once asked Bastian what magic he possessed, making his shapeshifting abilities all but foreign to her. Magic was unique. Atlas told her once it was, "altered to the individual it belongs to, it fits the wielder like a well-tailored glove."

The room was silent, the music stopped, the talking all but halted into a stunned silence, every eye watching the scene unfold.

The cadre was quickly behind Ryder and Evangaline with their ruby hilted swords drawn.

"Where is he?" Evangaline finally got the pain to subside enough in her chest to speak. Her rage was a fire within her bones. Slowly, with Ryder's help, she rose to her feet.

Bastian laughed; his head tipped back, nearly toppling the golden crown off.

"Tell me!" She shouted. Tears began to seep toward the edges of her eyes. "How did you do it? What did you do to him?"

"That is what you wonder? You don't question why your own magic didn't work? Your priorities are very twisted, Princess," he replied in a condescending tone. "Always worrying about others before yourself. *So noble of you!*" He spat at her feet, but she didn't flinch.

Ryder stood motioning to Des to come to Evangaline's side before looking down upon the man he thought was king, "I am so tired of your bullshit, Darrin—" Her fated's voice was a deadly calm.

"It's the crystals on the dress." Bash said, silencing Ryder, "You're fated is so new here and you're too dull to notice. I had it specially made just for our powerful girl. They look like normal diamonds, don't they, Princess? In fact, you look radiant in all those—"

It was Ryder's turn to interject, "Herkimer diamonds." His voice was distant and trembled a little.

Des looked up at the cadre, "Get everyone out of here. Now!" He shouted.

The cadre made to move before Bastian threw out his hands and spoke to the crowd of onlookers. Ryder stayed right where he was, staring down at the man he thought was king, shielding Evangaline with his body. She was so confused. What are Herkimer diamonds? Why did they affect her magic? She was in a near panic, but as she watched the bastard she once shared a bed with twirl around the room with a sanguine smile on his stolen lips. But with each forest-hued glance the false king gave her, the panic attack morphed into a rage filled explosion.

"People of The Capital. Do you see how your princess and her *friends* treat your king? I—"

"Am nothing but an imposter!" Evangaline shouted, lunging around Ryder toward Bastian in his king skin suit. "Now, where is the king?"

Ryder twisted to Evangaline, confusion riding his eyes.

"Patience love." The poser responded.

Evangaline threaded her arms through Ryder's jacket, so it did not fall from her shoulders. She swam in it, but the ice that coursed through her veins made her unable to get warm. It mingled with the wind and water in her muscles, refracting off the fire in her blood. Cold sweat dripped down her back in beads. Her body ached with all of her own power in a way that felt as though it was tearing her open from the inside out. But she did not cave to the pain. That was what Bastian wanted. For her to get riled up, to become volatile and then tear herself apart with her own magic. She wouldn't allow it. She took calming breaths and regarded the man peacocking to the crowd.

Ryder leaned into her. "Eva, are you okay? What is going on?"

She never took her eyes off of the prick as she nodded to him. "Bastian."

Ryder followed her gaze to Bastian, the false king, and the darkness that he had been holding in settled on the room. His little shadow swung onto Evangaline's shoulders, but through her tremors, she could barely feel the tingling sensation as it snaked around her collarbone and nestled into its place.

Bastian then turned to Ryder slowly, "You are lucky I can't kill you. Trust me, it was a disappointing fact to learn," he jeered with a smile. "Alright enough of the charades. Bring in the king, his daughter requests him."

After a beat of silence, echoes of thunderous footsteps beat down the hall. One after another in a synchronized march.

At the chilling sound, the courtiers parted, securing themselves alongside the hewed walls of the room. The cadre, aside from Des, ran to shield them all. Evangaline studied the room and for the first time that night realized, aside from her friends, no other Royal Guard was present. No wonder the false king before her was so dedicated to planning the Winter Solstice Ball. It was always a trap, one she played into perfectly.

Gasps and cries broke out as two lines of soldiers clad in red leather armor, with crystal swords at their hips, entered the ballroom. Heretics.

Ryder's darkness and shadows swarmed the approaching army but halted as he saw in the same moment what Evangaline did.

Her father. The Supreme King.

Iolite shackles bound his wrists and ankles to his throat with a cord of Herkimer diamonds—the same diamonds that clung to the diaphanous material of her gown. The blue-purple glow from his crystal shackles washed over his skin, but not enough to deter from the gauntness of his face. His ribs were clearly visible through the rags that were draped around him in the form of clothes. Bruises laid a map around his face and body, showing the torture he had endured.

How long had Bastian tortured him?

As the crowd gasped at the king being nearly dragged into the room, Bastian morphed in a flash of green light. His chestnut hair grew darker and longer beneath the gold crown on his head, and his tanned skin stretched and grew along with his limbs and bulbous muscles.

Clad in his red armor, the former general was imposing and terrifying.

With heavy, graceful steps, Bastian strode over to Ryder and Evangaline. The former securing his arm across fated's front. Des was at their side, bearing his weapons with a vengeful tenacity.

"Did you really think I escaped? Ran off to hide? You never once asked what my powers were, Princess." Oh, Evangaline didn't need him to remind her of her naivety. She was kicking herself for it mentally. "You were too enthralled with this bastard's shadows. You never wondered why I earned my position. *Or how.*" Bastian gazed at them, all too happy with the sound of his own voice. "I can take the form of another. If that isn't evident. A skill many didn't know. Bet shadow boy over here didn't even know." Bastian laughed. The hard set of Ryder's molars grinding told Evangaline that Ryder didn't know of Bastian's abilities, either. "I've snuck into your kingdom countless times after you banished me. Long before Darrin gave me my positions. It's how I became hand and general to the crown." Ryder's face contorted around a growl of irritation.

Bastian kept going along, enjoying his moment in the spotlight. "I was a spy and scout long before I was a soldier. Your dear old dad, Evangaline, didn't seem to remember my skill set as he hauled me to the dungeon after your little power trip. But another did and by his good graces, promised me what I wanted and got me out of that hellhole before supper was delivered that very day. All I had to do was trade places with your dear old dad. I glamoured him to look like me and I became him. It was that easy." His hand rested on the hilt of his sword. "See, I always knew I wanted power. I wanted the throne, more specifically. So I had two options. Marry and inherit the throne. Getting rid of you after you popped out a few heirs would have been easy. But this one had to go fuck that plan up—" Bastian pointed at Ryder with his crystal sword.

Ryder tensed, allowing his shadows to circle Bastian's feet.

Des looked to Shaw, who was sheltering courtiers against the wall. The action drew Bastian's attention.

"That will be of no use, *General.* I sent the royal guards away. No one else, besides those in this room, are in the palace tonight. You two did have a nice plan though to go behind my … well, 'the king's' back and deploy the army." Bastian's eyes grew wide with amusement. "I told you, Princess, you would regret threatening me. If only you would have been a good girl and put that ring on your finger, none of this would have happened. I mean, The Heretics were going to take over whether you and I married or not. But all you had to do was call me your husband, spread those pretty legs of yours, and put a crown on my head, and I would have helped you defeat them. Go against them. I knew their plans. But since you said no and threw me in jail, well, I had to make another plan. So with some help, and a well-placed bomb, they were able to kidnap Darrin and I was able to take his place all the while allowing The Heretics to march where they so pleased. Win, win if you ask me. Unfortunate though, I got the crown and had to sacrifice you."

Red with anger and an ache to unleash her magic, Evangaline nearly stripped naked right then and there just to be rid of the jewels that inhibited her power. Yet she froze when Bastian made a move toward the real King Darrin.

Bastian hauled the waif like King to his feet and sneered in his face. Bastian's long chestnut hair trailed like a curtain, blocking his grinning face as he whispered something in Darrin's ear.

"No. *Please*," was all the king muttered. His voice was so horse and full of weakness, "*Please*." Darrin's eyes met hers and all she saw was how truly sorry he was. The same eyes that she bore looked back to her in a way that only spoke of witnessing horrors and doom.

Bastian shook his head, crinkling his face like he was thinking. "Well, now that you say please ..."

Evangaline didn't even think as she shot forward past Ryder and Des just as Bastian released the king. Darrin fell to his knees with a heavy thud. His cry of agony swept through the room like a call from a banshee. It pierced Evangaline right in her heart, bottoming it out in her fear filled stomach.

How did she not see it? The entire time, Bastian was pulling the strings. All the hostility and fighting was never her fae father. Her guilt propelled her forward. She had been blind to the truth, but if she got to him, she could save him. She needed to apologize, needed to hug him.

Bastian grabbed her by the arm before she could make her way to Darrin. With a hand in the air, he halted Ryder and Des by motioning to the army at his back to draw their weapons and turn them on the courtiers and cadre.

"I'm to deliver you to someone very special, Evangaline. He's been eager to formally meet you. He will be here shortly. Between you and I, he's a bit eccentric. Loves a grand entrance." He chortled. "But before then, I think we should have a little fun. I don't want to let you go for good, but a promise is a promise, and I am a man of my word. What do you think Ryder, should we have a little fun? Eh, no need to answer Prince of Shadows. I'll show you what she likes." Bastian said, running his grimy deceitful hands along Evangaline's jaw, winking at Ryder. She forced her eyes shut at the touch. His breath was a steaming inferno that reminded Evangaline of the heat that radiated from the subways in New York during the summertime. Putrid and nauseating.

Evangaline finally opened her eyes and held her chin high. "Why are you doing this, Bash? All of this because I wouldn't let you rape me?"

He tsked, "Oh don't be dramatic, I was simply trying to show you a good time … it's your problem if you wouldn't play along."

Evangaline's mouth flew open, "Is that what this is? A game to you? You could have had the throne well before I came here!"

Bastian snarled in her face, "You will learn to play the game soon enough, Princess."

"I will never play your games," she spit back at his ignorant face, wiping the grin clean off of it.

Bastian straightened and released Evangaline. In the same breath, in one fluid motion, unsheathed the curved blade at his hip once more and lifted it into the air.

Evangaline closed her eyes; the sound of Ryder's hurried footsteps rang in her ears as he let out a desperate cry of her name that would haunt her for eternity. His hand barely gripped the oversized jacket's collar he draped around her as he hauled her against his chest, her back to his front. The way he curled around her spoke of his mental state. Ryder wrapped his body around Evangaline's in a protective shield with his head nuzzled into her neck. She clenched her eyes shut and winced inward, prepared for Bastian's fatal blow to the two of them. At least they would depart the world together.

The cries and gasps of the courtiers forced her eyes open as a spray of wetness splashed across her face.

She looked down to her feet as something rolled and bumped her foot. Vomit threatened to spew from her throat.

"Oh, my god!" She cried as her fear paralyzed her to her prince sized cocoon. She clawed at his arm and thigh, anything to assure her that this wasn't all just a nightmare or hallucination. She had some sparkling wine, but not enough to conjure delusions of such grandeur.

In her next blink, Ryder had a sword drawn and arm wrapped firmly around her waist and still she could not get close enough to him. She wished to burrow under his skin and never come out. Her fear was paralyzing.

A head. His head. The king's head. Her biological father's head lay at her feet.

His face permanently drawn in an expression of fear and anguish. His sallow eyes, the eyes she inherited, were bloodshot and stuck opened. Rimmed in purple bags, he stared right up at the domed ceiling of the room, unseeing, unfeeling, unknowing. Evangaline stared down at what was left of Darrin. Icy cold tears dripped down her cheek. As the fire of her power lit her core in a blazing inferno, the likes only Satan himself would only know of. Wind tickled her throat, drying it out. And the sharp planes of the earth sliced open her heart, till all that remained was a hollow, vengeful creature that craved blood.

"Des." Ryder said in his velvety deep tone as he slowly backed up with Evangaline in his arms. Des inched forward, meeting them halfway.

Evangaline's state of shock was over taking her entire body. All she could hear was the gasps and cries from the court against a backdrop of white noise. She did not hear the whispers of the conversation the two men had at her back. She could only feel the tremble in Ryder's hand on her stomach as he whispered to Des conspiratorially.

She could not peel her eyes from the head of her father on the floor, letting it fuel the rage in her blood. Her eyes were on like a faucet. Her body trembled. Luckily, Ryder's grip on her held her to him and upright.

Slowly, Evangaline glanced up at Bastian's smiling face. His teeth sat exposed in an opportunistic grin as blood dripped from his deranged brow. "I get the throne, he gets you. That's the deal we made. Not my favorite. You did feel so nice in my bed ..."

"No one gets me. I am not a trinket to pass around." Evangaline revolted. Her throat constricted with anger.

"That is where you are wrong, little liar."

It was him. She wouldn't recognize the angular face with high cheekbones. Or the frosty white blonde hair. His lean body was clad in an all black suit with black tie and black dress shirt, all of which made him stand out among the sea of sparkling nobles and crimson soldiers. But that voice. She would know that voice anywhere. It haunted her sleep.

His lithe physique sauntered up to Bastian. His pale hands rested snuggly in his pockets, but as soon as he lifted one, the onyx talons showed on his hands. The very ones that tormented her more nights than she cared to remember. His eyes lifted to finally meet her own.

Blood red irises bore into hers. He was ethereal and ghastly all at the same time. Beautiful and horrifying.

"I see a lesson has been made." The mystery man said in a jovial tone, matching Bastian's. As he spoke, she could see the forked tongue that caressed her skin.

Evangaline's tremors grew worse despite Ryder's warmth surrounding her. Though for once she did not shake with anxiety or nerves, her body shook with vibrations of fury and vengeance. Everything she blamed herself over, all the guilt that gave her unquelled anxiety the past few months, was due to the two men standing before her. She no longer cared that her father's head lay at her feet, for she saw red and craved the blood of the two beings that marked themselves with crimson *A's* before her. They spawned her guilt and shame, and they would pay for her losses in their blood.

"Who are you?" Ryder seethed at the newcomer in the room.

The man looked at Ryder, eyebrows raised. "Oh come now, Prince, are you telling me your fated hasn't mentioned me? We're such good friends! Aren't we darling?" He purred tauntingly.

Evangaline snarled. She didn't know him, not really. She thought he was a figment of her nightmares, or maybe she was just pretending he did not exist. Either way, they did not know one another. "Fuck you! I don't know you!"

The man walked closer to Evangaline, taking his time as though he owned the world. "How is your throat healing darling, I hope our time together last night didn't hurt you too bad? You barely put up a fight this time. A shame. I like my women with a bit of feist." He winked at Ryder. Mind games, that was what this prick loved. He was a sadistic and cruel and heartless being. She didn't need to know him to know those to be his defining traits.

Once he was close enough, Ryder pressed his sword against the man's chest. "*Leave.*" Ryder growled.

"Much better with a clean shave, wouldn't you agree, dove?" The man confidently quizzed Evangaline as he allowed Ryder's sword to poke a hole into his silken black tie. "It was easiest to subdue her when she saw you sleeping or when she thought you might die," he said to Ryder.

Evangaline shook her head. "That wasn't real," she said softly, denying the truth of his words.

"Denial doesn't suit you, my pet."

"On behalf of the crown, we ask you to call your army back. If it is a negotiation you want, we shall have it, civilly not like blood thirsty animals." Des spoke from their side.

Bastian across the room chuckled, "Look at you, Des, putting on your big boy pants."

The unknown man never moved, never swatted away Ryder's sword, never dropped his blood chilling smile. And never dropped his deathly gaze from Evangaline's. "Let me guess. You picked that necklace because it reminded you of his eyes. I see it. I do. Cute notion. Now, *take it off.*" His tone grew sharp on the last words.

"No."

Be strong, Evangaline. She told herself. There was a room full of people that needed their princess. She wasn't going to consider the fact that the second her father's head left his shoulders; she was now queen. No—worry about that after these bastards die.

So, she steeled her spine and rose her chin, and kept the gaze of the frightening man before her.

"What is your name? You want me to play your games? Fine, let's play one. Truth or dare. You already dared me to take off the choker, and I ask for a truth in return. Who are you?" Evangaline tried to sound as authoritative as she could as her tears dried against her cheeks.

The man smiled so wide his teeth showed, white and sparkling. "Ok, darling. Let her go, Prince. This is a game of kings and queens now."

Evangaline swallowed hard and peeked up at Ryder, "It's ok."

Once his arm dropped from her waist and his sword dropped to his side, his shadows surrounded her in a small cyclone by her feet. She glanced over her shoulder at him, but he just shrugged. "Precautions," he whispered to her. They were still flush against one another. He did not back up or move an inch, just dropped his arms.

"Take off her necklace, Prince. Make yourself useful." The man drawled.

Ryder swallowed hard, but obeyed. He put his sword in Evangaline's hand and gripped the necklace.

For a fleeting moment, as Ryder's hands unclasped the link to the choker around her neck, she closed her eyes. She imagined this evening going differently. The moment Evangaline laid her eyes on the Prince of Shadows in her living room, she longed for him to touch her in this manner—reverently, carefully. She yearned for him to take off more than just her necklace. She wanted his hands on her skin. Holding her. Loving her.

It was Ryder's deep growl that spurred her back to reality. The finger sized band of mottled blues and greens and purples that lined her throat had her fated's breath coming out in quick aggravated pants.

"What did you do to her?" Ryder bellowed.

The man didn't answer, just smiled and bowed at the hip. "Dorcha, but you may call me by my title. The Supreme Leader of Munbra, at your service."

Evangaline's breath caught. It was him. Here? The Supreme Leader of Munbra? The man no one had ever seen except for behind a shrouded veil of obscurity? How?

He was everything people spoke of. Beautiful and terrifying. *Honed from poisoned marble*, one article read in Vitalis, and it was entirely true.

How was he the man haunting her nightmares?

Evangaline shook her head. "How? How have you been in my nightmares?"

He paced the floor. The entire cadre pivoted to follow him, their weapons drawn and glistening in the low light of the room, still half darkened by Ryder's shadows. Everyone stood in a shocked silence watching the Supreme Leader of the land no one had ever seen or come back from parade around the palace of the fae.

"I was once born from a highborn fae, once lived right alongside your ancestors but was banished. Cast out and forced to live my life in servitude. Without love or hope. But I clawed my way to power and that, my sweet, is all you need to know." He turned back to face her head on, "As for me popping into your dreams … well, my powers allow me to sleepwalk. Allow me to enter dreams. I am a creature of the night, a servant of death. So are my demons, as you like to call them. Speaking of, I don't take lightly to one of my best being killed." He leveled a look at Evangaline, raising a scathing brow.

Chloe. Chloe killed the demon, the very one who killed her in return. "Neither do I." She breathed through her teeth, flashbacks of that night happening in a blur of emotions.

He shrugged, "Eh, a life for a life, I guess."

As she stared into the eyes of the monster who haunted her dreams, she knew, deep within her heart, that all of those years of distant visions of being something more than a meek, scared little introvert were over. If the Supreme Leader, if Bastian, if *anyone*, felt it was their right to make her feel weak, she would become their greatest villain and make them regret that choice.

Vengeance wasn't a word she used often, but seeing her birth father's head at her feet, mixed with hearing the lackadaisical way the Supreme Leader spoke of the death of her best friend, it was a word that felt good on her tongue. Warm even. It filled her with the strength she needed to grip the sword in her hand tighter.

"My pain is my power," she whispered as she looked back up into Dorcha's crimson eyes after spearing a glance at Darrin's blood across her gown. "If it's a war you want, a war you shall have," Evangaline hissed as she swung Ryder's blade in her hand. An arc of steel crossed through the air in a manner that would have made Chloe proud. She brought it down with as much force as her pained body could muster, aiming for Dorcha's head. A grunt escaped her lips with the effort.

Dorcha lunged to the side at the last minute, barely missing the blow that would have split him straight down the center. A sharp cry bellowed from the Supreme Leader as his talon tipped hand grabbed hold of his eye. Burgundy red blood flowed from the wound that sliced down the center of his left eye.

Blood dripped from his face, through his fingers, in dark rivulets. Painting the floor in splotches of her fury.

Ryder tensed behind her, his hand grabbing her hip. "That's my warrior," he proudly whispered in her ear.

Evangaline held the sword in her grip under Dorcha's chin. The sharp edge of the blade barely scraped the pasty skin above the bump in his throat. The Heretic soldiers and Bastian all had their weapons drawn. Bastian's pointed at Ryder, and the soldiers held theirs aloft to the innocent crowds behind her friends.

"Get out of my realm." Evangaline gritted. "The next blow of my blade will not miss."

It took Dorcha a moment to gather himself, but as he stood straight, the wound that she inflicted to his face drew gasps from the crowds. Flesh parted at a grotesque angle. His eye was untouched, the white of it flashed through the dark blood coating his skin. He looked between Ryder and Evangaline, then to Des and then around the room at all the terrified courtiers still plastered against the wall. A smile etched across his face. "I technically offered you two truths. Does that mean I get an extra dare?"

Her breathing was heavy, and she needed to get out of her dress so she could unleash her powers. She glanced up at Ryder from the corner of her eye, his deep sapphire ocean eyes were locked on Dorcha, but Ryder noticed her. Dorcha was regarding the people around the room and his soldiers, so Evangaline took her opportunity. "Ryder, take off my dress, please," she whispered as calmly as she could while Dorcha was turned away from them.

"Eva?"

She smiled weakly, "I know … wish it was for a different reason, too."

His dimple came out for a split second as Ryder's lips tipped to the side. Before his hand reached for the buttons of her dress under his jacket, Dorcha turned back around in a haste.

"I wouldn't do that, Prince!" Dorcha warned, their gazes snapped back to the Supreme Leader of Munbra. "Bastian wasn't wrong. I would be greatly pleased to see your pretty head on a spike, but I can't afford to lose my darling Evangaline, here. The fates, really did screw us all over on that one, but I will find a way around it."

"They screwed you. They certainly didn't screw me," Ryder said, flashing a smile down to Evangaline, "You will not have her, nor is she yours. Ever. I believe she has made that more than clear."

Dorcha pouted his lips mockingly. "How cute! Time for your dare Evangaline, darling. Remember what happened before when you didn't play along?" He flicked his ruby eyes to Darrin's body.

Dorcha then waved his hands in the air and four guards alongside Bastian made their way over to Ryder, Evangaline, and Des, all carrying iolite shackles.

"Put them on your men. Then kneel before me." He motioned to Evangaline.

A random chuckle found its way up Evangaline's throat. "Fuck that," she quipped, using her free hand to grab Ryders. "I will kneel to no man."

"You will obey me, as my betrothed—"

"There's that fucking word again. First it came from that asshole," She pointed Ryder's sword at Bastian, stopping him in his tracks as he strode to Ryder, "and now from you. You see, when it comes to winning a woman's heart, slaughtering her family, and imprisoning her friends isn't really the best mode of transportation, *Supreme Leader.*"

"Winning your heart is the last thing I want to do. You see, I just can't take any risks. They will be left under Bastian's care, as will Celadonia when we return to Munbra. And believe me dear, you aren't my first choice, but

I have little options left. You, pet, are the closest I will get to salvation, the one I need to break the curse on my bonds. I wrote to your father some time ago asking for aid, but the stubborn ass freaked out. I knew I needed to escalate my efforts. Once I found you, I knew I had little choice. I just needed you outside of Vitalis. I had hoped you'd come to the Shadows to save the day, but that couldn't even draw you out of the palace. So here I am. And here you are. So, if you want your friends to live, I suggest you follow through on your dare."

She ground her teeth, then winced sarcastically. Evangaline snarled, "Yeah, that's gonna be another fuck that."

"What a mouth my queen has. I can't wait to put it to good use. Bastian did rave about it." Dorcha chuckled.

Ryder's heart thundered in his chest as he growled deeply, his warming, "You heard her, fuck off."

Dorcha pointed at Ryder, laughing as his blood flowed from the gash in his face. He turned slowly to the crowd of soldiers and courtiers with the look of male satisfaction leaching across his monstrous face, "That, my friends, is the look of a man who hasn't gotten his dick wet in some time. Tell me, Prince, have you even *tried* to bed her?" Dorcha asked, wiggling his eyebrows at Evangaline in a taunting manner that made her feel dirty and nothing more than a piece of meat.

Ryder snarled before Evangaline cut him off, "Who I have in my bed is no one's business … certainly not yours."

Dorcha stepped up to her. His scent hit her like a bullet from a gun. He smelled of sulfur and belladonna. He was death incarnate. Bringing his voice low so only she could hear, he spoke with an amusing grit, "Maybe when I take you the first time, we will make your prince watch. I can't kill his body, but I can kill his mind. Make him go crazy as he watches me use your body in a way he never did. Is that what you want?" After a deep breath and a moment of maddening silence between Evangaline and Dorcha, he spoke again. "So keen to speak up, but not ready for the punishment. I need you complacent. And I *will* get what I want."

Just as soon as he finished his sentence, he flung his hand out, knocking it into Evangaline's cheek. The impact rattled her mind; the pain tingled and blossomed in the physical manifestation of a red-lined bruise on her cheek. She fell right into Des's arms from the sheer power of the hit. A drop of her blood leaked down her cheek bone streaking through the blood transferred from Dorcha's hand. "It's okay. It's okay!" Des reassured her as he stood her back up. Fury lined her vision.

She raised her sword once more with a cry as the courtiers around the room began shouting over one another, louder than when Bastian killed the king.

"Don't touch her!"

"Let the princess go, you swine!"

"Fuck off back to Munbra, you fucker!"

"Go rot, Bastian!"

But before she could bring the blade down onto Dorcha's grinning face again, she heard a noise through the shouts. A wince of pain and click of shackles. A ping of desperation ricocheted through her body.

Then the room got brighter.

She spun on her heels to see Ryder cuffed in iolite falling to his knees. His pain echoed through her senses, rattling her bones. The lack of his power made her stumble. His shadows no longer swirled around his chest; in fact, they were gone altogether. Only a few remained motionless on his skin.

In the commotion of the hit, she failed to notice Bastian and the guards get closer. In her fit of rage, she allowed the enemy to tear down her awareness of her surroundings and, in the process, allowed Ryder to become vulnerable.

"Ryder!"

She tried to fling herself at Ryder before Des caught her around the waist, hauling her back to his armor-clad chest.

"Des. Now!" Ryder shouted. Then he looked at Evangaline, his eyes lightening slightly. A tear beaded on his lash line as his eyes sparkled at her the way they usually did when he was happy or amused. But this was neither amusing nor happy, so what could make him happy?

"Ryder! Let him go! Let him go and I will go with you!" She pleaded to

Bastian and Dorcha, who were more than amused to have Ryder defenseless before them. If only because it made them feel more powerful. Neither had the strength or magic that coursed through Ryder's veins. He was the most powerful and deadly fae in Celadonia. Plenty of times did Atlas regale her with stories of the Prince of Shadows' power when she felt homesick for the man bound to her by fate. "*Ry* ..." she pleaded through the tears cascading down her cheeks.

"Eva. Be strong, baby."

"What?"

His smile was weak as he muttered, "Come back to me."

"Where you go. I go. *Always.*" It was nothing more than a plead flowing from her lips.

I won't leave you again. Her eyes promised.

Ryder's smiled grew. *"Forever."*

And then she fell.

Chapter Fifty-Seven

The bitter cold bit into Evangaline's skin like one thousand needles. The wind howling in her chest no longer banged against the cage of her ribs, and the fire ceased to course through her veins. There was no more warmth at her back, and the air was strangely quiet.

Her glittering hair fanned around her has she laid face down on the snowy ground. Lights flashed to her right. Each blink gleamed off Tuatha's crown that still sat firmly atop her head.

Her eyes were hazy as she opened them, but she could see the silhouette of a person lying beside her.

Des.

The realization sent her into a scrambling fit despite the hollowness in her muscles. Her breathing was erratic, her hands began to go numb—but that might have been because of the snow and the lack of warm clothing around her. She pushed herself to her knees and rushed to his side the best she could. She dropped her grip on Ryder's sword and allowed it to sink into the snow.

"Des!" Evangaline yelled, shaking him frantically. "Des wake up! Des!" She began to beg, "I can't lose you too Des, please, wake up!"

Des grumbled a moan of pain and pushed himself up. The snow clung to his beard and armor. A breath escaped her in a cloud of white as she grabbed her friend and pulled him into a fierce hug.

"Bug?"

Evangaline stilled.

"Dad?" she whispered.

Evangaline turned slowly to face where the voice came from. Pulling away from Des with a squinted brow.

"Oh, Bug! Felicity!" Stephen charged for her straight out of the cover of the porch where he stood.

Someone ran behind him through the door, but Evangaline didn't see who as her focus was solely on Stephen in his orange snow jacket and untied snow boots. A cup of coffee crashed to the snow-covered pavement as he charged for her.

Des was quick to throw his body before Evangaline, but it was useless with Evangaline holding so tightly onto his arms. She tried to plant her sandal heeled feet in the thick snow, but it stung her toes and allowed little grip. Finally, she pressed up, using Des as a crutch. "Des … what did you do?" Realization smacked her in the face.

Her lack of power should have been the first sign as to where Des brought her. Even with the Herkimer diamonds on her person, she felt the pain of her power. It should have hummed within her skin and yet it was silent.

"Des …" she whimpered helplessly.

Stephen made his way to Evangaline, stopping a couple feet away. His tear-lined cheeks went red from the cold as her nose ran and her throat dried up. Behind her step-father came her family, one by one, filing out of the door and onto the porch.

She knew this place. It was more familiar to her than the Capital Palace had become.

Flashing Christmas lights blinked in succession to illuminate the cursed crystals on her gown and the blood on her face.

She stood as she watched in disbelief. The cold frost of the earth sank into her toes as a helpless fear pierced her soul. She watched her whole family—Miles, James, her mom, Stephen, and finally Katherine, with a small baby in her arms—rush forward onto the porch and stare at her in a stunned silence.

Her whole family was right there in front of her. And yet she felt empty once again. She was in Vitalis, at her sister's house in the suburbs, clearly just in time to celebrate Christmas. And yet she wasn't home at all. Ryder was shackled, powerless, at the hands of monsters, with her friends and the court cowering in fear. Her home was in danger and Des dropped them into a realm where neither of them could use their magic.

"What did you do?" Evangaline whispered to Des again. This time, his face contorted into one of sadness and regret as he was unable to meet her gaze.

Her bones crumbled as she sank to her knees and sobbed into the snow. Evangaline's hands flew up, cupping her face, giving her a full view of the metallic fating mark glistening on her skin. It sparkled as a reminder in the multicolor Christmas lights overhead, of the realm she needed to get back to, because war was upon them, and death was only the beginning.

Epilogue

Only darkness and pain surrounded Ryder.

His head hung heavily as the iolite chains strung him up in the center of the cell beneath the Capital Palace. His eyes struggled to open. The swelling around them went down a little, however the bruises that clung to the sockets were still present and pulsed any time he breathed.

Days, maybe even weeks, passed since he forced Des to get Evangaline out of the palace. And every second she was gone, his heart beat slower and slower. It never ceased to amaze him how he could go from one moment of his life where all that consumed him was work and his royal duties to her— his entire world was her. She gave him something to look forward to. Where his life was once dull and boring, she brought life. And he betrayed her. The sting of guilt battered him at times more than the strike of Bastian's whip, or the curve of his blade.

"You don't get to give instructions for me to be whisked away … Don't do that. Ever again."

I'm sorry, Eva. He prayed within his mind over and over again. It had been months since she wept in his arms, making him promise to not dictate her actions or walk willingly into death's reach. And he had done both, sort of. Knowing Bastian could not kill him was a relief. If he slipped his blade a bit too far and it grazed Ryder's heart, Evangaline would fall. Dorcha would no doubt have Bastian's skull broken before the blade slipped from Ryder's flesh if that happened. However, the second things looked scary and bleak, the moment Ryder saw the threat against Evangaline's life, he acted out. He forced Des to open a portal on his call and take her far from the Capital Palace.

For eighty-one days, Ryder saw the brutal way The Heretic's fought. With death walking beside them as an ally, they feared nothing and no one. Annihilation and suffering were their goals at the behest of Dorcha.

Peace talks were attempted at the start of the Shadow battles. Messengers were sent to The Heretic camp. A small pixie and a young soldier, new to Ryder's regime. They were nothing but carriers of word and peace and yet the head of the boy was sent back in a silver box alongside the mangled body of the pixie. It was horrific. The image of their deaths made Ryder revisit his breakfast behind his tent, away from prying eyes. It was cruel and brutal. Their blood stained his hands.

Ryder vowed he would not allow Evangaline to see those horrors. He would not allow her to step into harm's way and become a bargaining chip, or worse—a weapon. She would make herself a martyr and sacrifice her life if that meant saving everyone else. Fating bond or not, he would not lose her, even if that meant to become a sacrifice himself. He had family with power, had allies and friends, who eventually would come for him once they heard of his predicament. She had only the people in that room. He could not take that risk or let Dorcha take her away to Munbra. The cursed land was too unknown. He had never heard of a man or woman crossing The Mist and returning.

As he hung within his cell, Ryder often dreamed of everything he longed to do with Evangaline. Simple dreams that brought him a sense of comfort. Taking her to his mother's cottage along the southwest coast of Pax. Asking her to marry him one day. Starting a family. His father, at times—especially after his mother had passed—had been cruel. His loyalty to being the Prince of Shadows outweighed his loyalty to his family and in return, Ryder and his siblings were held to high, often unachievable, standards. Since he was a young man, Ryder envisioned a life where he had a family of his own. A family he could raise and love where power wasn't the end all be all. When Evangaline entered his life, she fit into that dream perfectly. He could almost envision her chasing their children across the sandy beaches of Pax with a smile on her face and the wind whisp billowing through her hair.

He never wanted to see her anyway except for smiling.

The look on her face when Darrin's head rolled to her feet frightened even the Prince of Shadows. Behind her fear lurked a fearsome creature. She may be a descendant of the elemental goddess, but as she fought against the power of the Herkimer diamonds and swung his blade, she could have been deemed a goddess of vengeance.

Gods, Ryder's pride swelled just the same way it did when she wrote to him about their forest. Divine power flows through her veins. If those godsdamn diamonds didn't lay upon her skin, her power would have flowed through the room with the twitch of her pinky fingers. But he was too enchanted with her beauty, with the caress of her lips, he failed to feel the pull of the stones around her.

Nasty gems, Herkimer diamonds. Found in a valley between The Kingdom of Fire and The Kingdom of Shadows. In a crevasse where a waterfall of lava meets a waterfall of blessed water from the lake of eternal starlight. The power from the lake mixed with the heat of the lava breeds the imitation diamond, Herkimer. A diamond that locks power within the host and uses it against the wielder was born in that valley the night of the Convergence. Typically, one diamond could render a fae powerless. However, Bastian knew damn well Evangaline was stronger than everyone in that room and bestowed upon her a net of the stones. He captured her fragile heart through more deceit and lies. Ryder felt so stupid he didn't see it sooner. The first beating he took was penance for his stupidity. Or so he told himself.

Every day came with some form of torture and beating. If Ryder's belief was right, he had been held prisoner somewhere around twelve days. There was a small crack in the stones of his cell where the sun shined through and brought light to the darkness. Where the dark was usually his ally, being trapped within it without any form of light was starting to play tricks on his head.

When he did happen to sleep, it was never for long. A Heretic would wake him by a bucket of ice water to the face or a simple punch to the gut. Both *great* ways to greet a new day.

He was not positive, but he felt as though many of his ribs were broken. His entire body had been brutalized, but he was determined to stay strong. Evangaline's life was at stake, and he would not give up where Des took her. He would protect her in any way he could, even if that meant his suffering.

Death came close a few times, but each time Bastian ordered to bring him back to the land of the living without fully healing all of his wounds. However, even with his fae nature of healing ailments quicker, he was stunted. The shackles that bound him stripped the power from his veins and left him practically human.

Whenever Bastian decided he was due to release some pent-up rage against Ryder's body, the Prince of Shadows closed his eyes and pictured his love, his family, his friends. It was the reciting of memories behind his eyelids that he found the strength in his body to carry on.

Earlier, he envisioned the look on Eva's face as she entered the room and saw him standing there with her friends, returned from war—whole and alive. The relief in her eyes broke his heart. He had ached for her from the day he met her. He wanted to hold her and kiss her. Touch her. Love her. But Ryder knew she needed time. So when she asked him to kiss her, he practically leapt through the roof in pure excitement. It took all of his willpower not to order her friends from the room and wrap himself in her essence until they were both breathless and dripping in the sweat of their desire.

Niall practically pissed himself laughing when Ryder told him how he didn't immediately take Eva to his bed when their bond was revealed. It was a shock to Ryder too, if he was honest. The urges the bond amplified made him want to take her and solidify their fating right then and there on that terrace. His urges that night were unbelievable. But between the fating and the bastard that abused her, she deserved better than some lustful animal who craved her every touch and breath. So, he put his urges aside and gave her the space she needed.

An ache prodded the space between his eyebrows as he squeezed his eyes tighter. The visions that swam beneath his lids were far better than the horrors of his lucid state. Ryder tried to keep his eyes closed as often as possible, only lucky if sleep pulled him under. He squeezed with all his power, as images of how beautiful Eva looked that fateful night passed through his mind. Her laugh chimed like the sweet ding of a bell as he twirled her around and forgot every bad thing he had witnessed in the previous months. She kissed his cheek right on his dimple as she laughed. Her hands ran through his hair. His heart had never felt so full. But then it all fell to shit. One second, she was laughing in his arms and the next she was falling wrapped in Des's, tears streaking her gorgeous face.

Why the fuck did he open a portal at their feet?

The shock that rippled along her face when Des opened the portal—

No, Ryder don't remember the fear in her eyes. Breathe.

A nudge against his blood-stained knee had his eyes jolting open. The slight movement sent a wave of pain through his skull, but he fixed his eyes on the shadow that woke him.

The shadows never left him, they were always closely lurking.

Before the shackles went on, many of them got away—they saw Bastian before Ryder even did. But some weren't fast enough. Those ones were frozen to his chest and shoulders. They endure his pain right beside him.

The ones that got away stick close at all times. Without his powers, their whispers were so faint he could barely hear them. But it is a comfort knowing they are there, regardless.

Evangaline's little shadow thrashed against his knee repeatedly, forcing the prince's focus on it. He could not hear what it was saying as it prodded him. Often, little shadow nudged him just to tell him to stay strong. It clung to Eva until she fell with Des. It spoke softly of how it could hear her burgeoning heartbeat and it could feel her anger and fear mix, but even then she was so strong, so fierce, so regal. Often, when it lingered by Ryder, it was encouraging him to adopt the same fearless nature.

She faced the Supreme Leader like the warrior queen the realm deserves.

And Ryder had Des drop her to Vitalis through a fucking portal because he was scared. *Gods Ryder, what did you do?*

The rules they broke to even open the portal were monumental. *Hopefully, the Supreme President will take it easy on her.* Yet again, his fated was now the goddam Supreme Queen of Celadonia, being that her father's head was no longer attached to his body. The crown of Tuatha De sat atop her head as she fell into Vitalis, for fuck's sake. What further proof does anyone need of her right to the throne? That is, if they even understand the importance of the crown on her head. Probably not. Ryder didn't until she told him about it the night of their fating before he bid her goodnight.

Little shadow prodded his leg again, ripping Ryder from his wandering thoughts. His exhaustion clung to his broken mind like a leech, making his focus stray easily.

"What is it?" He gritted out through his bruised jaw.

The shadow wriggled in a way that made Ryder smile before it rose off the ground and hovered before his face. The shadow, unable to stick to his skin thanks to the iolite, hovered above the tanned and bloodied flesh of his neck before twirling around the mark the fates bestowed upon his arm.

The only part of his body not left bloody and bruised was his left arm and hand. For some reason, the fates protected their mark ferociously. Bastian tried repeatedly, and failed every time, to break the finger that bound his fate to Eva. He tried to see it from Ryder's body, tried to rip the skin from his muscles, but nothing. No matter how gruesomely he tried, Ryder's fate marks remained. The pain never once even coursed through the entirety of his appendage. Of course, that made Ryder laugh, earning him a knife between his ribs, but it was worth it to see the anger swell on the bastard's face.

"You took her from me!" Bastian screamed once he realized the fates somehow wouldn't allow their mark to be removed.

The man was delusional with his lust for Evangaline. Obsession edged his lust in an unhealthy way. Though that never stopped Bastian from spreading his seed to any woman who showed a hint of interest. Ryder was gifted that awful visual one fine evening after being brought back from the brink of the afterlife, what felt like eons ago. Bastian grunted his fated's name as he plowed into the woman he bent over the throne. He forced Ryder to watch, taunting him with vulgar comments about Evangaline's body and virtue. It was worse than a knife in the lung.

Bastian, despite his methods of torture, was quite useful at times. In his fits of rage and lust, would let slip his willingness to cross Dorcha if that meant he got Eva. However, Ryder often thought it was more talk than anything. Bastian always enjoyed spewing hot air. Dorcha made him Supreme King of Celadonia and spared him from a life of suffering in the very cells Ryder hung in. Bastian's debts to the vile urchin of a man were so high, Ryder did not even think his lust would allow him to cross the man who saved his hide—and if it did, Bastian was a bigger fool than Ryder thought. Which was saying something.

Both men's plans were still a mystery, but Bastian spoke briefly about Dorcha's curse from a goddess. Ryder filed the information away, curious to know more, but the second Bastian's fist connected with his skull, he suddenly didn't care at all about Dorcha's life.

Ryder hadn't seen Evangaline's friends since that fateful evening. Bastian's soldiers ripped him from the room so quickly that the prince never saw what became of the boys or the civilians at the ball. Occasionally, a fae would be thrown in the cells near him, but they never stayed long, nor did they return. He feared what became of them. Never once had he seen any of Eva's boys, and that scared him more than anything. If she lost them, her suffering would be so intense he feared the woman who laughed in his arms would never return. The last image of any of them he had in his mind was of Shaw the night he was hauled out of the room, Shaw mouthed a grateful, "Thank you." What for, Ryder wouldn't know, but that was the last he saw of them. *Hopefully, they got away.*

Ryder didn't realize he closed his eyes again until the frantic banging of little shadow met his head before it stopped abruptly. Before his eyes could even open, Bastian's fist slammed into the side of his face. Pain seared across his cheekbone and ebbed into his head, which was already throbbing.

Bastian's arrogant laugh filled the stagnant air of the cell.

Ryder spat the blood that filled his mouth onto Bastian's boots with a sneer. The bastard just laughed harder and looked down at Ryder with threats hanging from his tongue.

"Let the games begin."

Author's Note & Acknowledgements

So … How are we feeling? Sorry, readers, I couldn't help but write a good old fashion cliffhanger. That aside, I hope you liked the first book within The Convergence Series and my first book ever! Holy shit! This whole process has been both intoxicating in its stress and excitement. I've had my fair share of ideas to write, but no one's story stuck in my head quite like Evangaline and Ryder's.

Evangaline has many characteristics that I see in myself but so many more that I wish I could be. Writing about her solitary nature and anxiety has been a sort of therapy for me. I struggled for the vast majority of my life with anxiety and depression—still do sometimes. It was always when my own personal rain cloud hung over my head that I never thought I would amount to anything or achieve any of my goals. It always felt like a predator stalking me in the night. A lot of the time I clung to the darkness and allowed it to sweep over me.

Mental health and the way it consumes each and every one of us is different from person to person, and even fictitious characters are no different. I've had plenty of times where I have shut myself away in my closet with the lights off, quietly crying into my knees with my breath sweeping over me in short gasping pants. Obviously, I am not a fae princess (a girl can wish), but at the end of the day pointed ears or not we all have hearts beating in our chests and blood that runs red, and emotions that are sometimes too strong to bear. If you are someone who has struggled or are struggling, I see you; I feel you, and I will always be here to hold your hand in one way or another. Be it to transport you for a short time to a far-off world with dreamy men, fancy clothes, and scenes that have you fanning yourself or just by offering my quiet support. I will always try my hardest to be the reason you forgot for just even a second that the world is not just what ails you. Always remember, you are beautiful and perfect, just as you are.

Both Evangaline and I have let fear dictate our lives sometimes, but like Eva, I have some incredible friends and family. Each and every one back me in the pursuit of stepping out of my comfort zone and achieving my dreams and goals. Sometimes our greatest risks come with our greatest rewards.

Therefore, I want to thank my family for supporting me. Kitty, Matt, Mol, I love you all so much and despite us being on opposite coasts for the duration of me writing this book, your love and support has never once left my side. I am so grateful to call you my siblings. Mama, Papa—I love you guys and I know that my quiet reclusiveness at times is frustrating for you, but thank you for accepting me as I am and letting me get lost in my little fantasy worlds. Also, I need to shout out and give all my love to my Aunt Dawn, who has battled and overcome so much pain and still has the courage to keep plowing forward with grace. Your strength, Aunt Dawn, has been something we all can look up to and learn from—you are a badass.

To Emma Jane at EJL Editing, thank you for helping me become a better writer and helping to flush this story out to make it its best possible version. I am so lucky to have found you and I know that I have said it five hundred times, but thank you for being so amazing.

To the team at Books and Moods, thank you for giving this book the beautification that it needed. You took some words on my computer screen and made it something tangible. Your designs and creativity helped bring this dream into reality, and I am so grateful for your artistic prowess. Also, Julie … sorry for all the emails … you've been a saint.

I want to thank all of the bookish community for making me feel safe and seen as I descended on my journey to being a full-on obsessed book whore. All of your insight, recommendations, artwork, memes, merch, and videos help fuel my desire to become the greatest writer and world builder I can possibly be, and I hope that I have made you proud. I am proud to be a part of this community.

I dedicated this book to *all* female writers out there for a good reason. Every ounce of courage I have is because of you. No one can truly describe the emotions that go into writing fiction. One moment you feel like what you have written is the greatest thing known to humankind, and the very next you see it as a steaming pile of garbage. The tenacity and courage that it takes to write something—to write anything— is an introspective look into one's own self. It is inevitable that little bits and pieces of who we are influence our characters and worlds. The things we have experienced in life inspire us every day to tell our stories, be it through fiction, non-fiction, screenwriting, etc. The courage it takes to bear a piece of your soul through words is immeasurable and something only writers will fully understand. So, to all of the women who have paved my path and given me the courage to dream and share my crazy make-believe worlds, thank you!

Finally, to all of you wonderful, spectacular, superb, gorgeous readers that have read this book. I really hope you all have fallen in love with Eva, Ryder, Des, and the gang as much as I have. I have some seriously fun plans and cannot wait to see where this all goes. This book was truly just the tip of the iceberg and I promise, I will try not to let you down. You just might have to suffer a little first. I have some ultimate book boyfriend goals for our Prince of Shadows, and I would never disappoint you all (*wink, wink*). But that is all I can say on the matter!

All I ever wanted was to provide a sense of escapism for whoever needed it, and I hope with all my heart that you have found that in this series.

See you all in book two!

With all of my love,
Danielle.

About the Author

Danielle D'Arrigo is an *aspiring* best-selling author, with dreams bigger than her pocketbook and a head full of more stories than her iPhone notes app will allow. She graduated with a BA in Digital Film with an emphasis in production and a passion in her heart for storytelling. Aside from writing, her hobbies include cuddling her dogs, art, reading, bingeing tv shows, watching hockey (go Knights go!), and fantasizing about lying on a tropical beach.

Danielle loves getting to hear from her readers! You can find her on Instagram @danielle_darrigo where you will be able to find a link to her website and everything to stay informed about upcoming releases and news regarding her works.

9 798987 760109